D1724656

Praise for *The Quiet Violence of Dreams*

". . . one of the pioneers of what we lazily refer to as post-apartheid literature."  FRED KHUMALO, *Sunday Times*

"In its characters I recognised a new national hybrid – part of the complex fabric that constitutes the 'new South Africa'. I recognised the kwaito/hip-hop generation, the model-C youth. I saw characters grappling with identities . . ."  MCQUEEN MOTUBA, *Mail&Guardian*

"A rising star, a chronicler of our complex world."  DR PALLO JORDAN

"A tour de force."  FRED DE VRIES, *Cape Librarian*

". . . widely regarded as one of the most promising and accomplished literary talents of his generation in South Africa."  *The Star*

". . . an enriching learning curve . . . If you want to know more about South Africa, the dreams and ideals of people, especially the young, this is a great starting point . . . Read it."  DIANE DE BEER, *Pretoria News*

"Duiker is an inspiring writer."  HOPEWELL RADEBE, *The Citizen*

"The language is beautiful and poetic . . ."  AURELIA DYANTYI, *True Love*

". . . taut, abrasive and uncompromisingly, albeit uncomfortably, graphic in detail . . . this is a brave, ambitious book. K. Sello Duiker's voice is loud and clear and needs to be heard."  DALENE DICKSON, *The Natal Witness*

". . . one of the most promising post-apartheid writers, representing the frontier generation who attempt to transcend race in their exploration of South Africa . . . His passing robs South Africa of a talented, perceptive chronicler of its complex evolution."  LIZ MCGREGOR, *The Guardian*

K. SELLO DUIKER

# The Quiet Violence
# of Dreams

Kwela Books

Copyright © 2001 K. Sello Duiker
Published by Kwela Books,
a division of NB Publishers (Pty) Limited,
40 Heerengracht, Cape Town, South Africa
PO Box 6525, Roggebaai, 8012, South Africa
http://www.kwela.com

All rights reserved.
No part of this book may be reproduced or transmitted
in any form or by any electronic or mechanical means, including photocopying
and recording, or by any other information storage or retrieval system,
without written permission from the publisher.

Cover design by Louw Venter
Set in 10 on 12pt Plantin
Printed and bound by Paarl Print
Oosterland Street, Paarl, South Africa
First edition, first impression 2001
Second impression 2004
Third impression 2006

ISBN-10: 0-7957-0120-9
ISBN-13: 978-0-7957-0120-7

FOR DANIELLE LAVAL

## TSHEPO

There's no one to blame. It's about me. It's always been about me. I accept that now. But I still find it hard to explain what really happened, what was really going on in my life. There's a part of me that will never be the same again. I feel like I've lost something or got lost in something too big to describe with easy words. So much happened in a short space of time. I don't know where to begin to look for the answers so for now I live with questions. Every day I ask new questions and every day the answer seems more elusive. It is not easy living with questions, there is enough uncertainty in life as it is.

The truth is I only want to fly, to spread my wings a little and feel warm air form curlicues under my arms as I glide. I want to close my eyes forever and let forever embrace me secretly. I want to be the beloved for a change and not know love as an unreliable friend always making promises. Is that so much to ask for?

Look, these are not excuses. I'm trying my best to say what happened. I was desperately alone. I was running, barely holding onto my life with my teeth. Life was vicious, it left me no options. Things were ugly. I was drowning in my own life, my own events. I had spells. I lost time. Things just happened. Really. I couldn't control anything. It's as if I killed someone, and then ran away from myself. And I've been running away ever since. I've searched my mind for a word to describe the terrible feeling left inside. This hollow ugliness that is always with me when I close my eyes. It's too vile.

So I tell a friend in the tradition that people tell their loved ones Things. Important Things. And friends like apples are sometimes sour. But like apples we remember them for the days when they were sweet and full of sun.

I remember the rain mostly and the disheartening feeling that it would never end, I say to her. That it would rain with so much volition, so much conviction that it would drown out the memories and cries that are haunting me. She doesn't say anything, she just listens, her head slightly bent forward as if in deep thought. I look at her eyes. They are dark and hold secrets. I go on.

I don't sleep well. I eat too little and I smoke too much. I wish for death constantly and sometimes at night when I sleep I catch myself falling, dying but I always wake up. And I feel depressed. And that feeling is there. I cannot escape it. I cannot describe it. It's just too ugly. I have seen too much ugliness and it has made me painfully awkward.

I was going mad because I got a little curious. I flew too close to the sun in my fascination with it and fell very hard.

"Uhuh," she says and licks her lips.

"Is that all you're going to say?"

"Is that it because if it is, it's a bullshit story, Tshepo? Hawu, you can't expect me to go on that stuff, come on."

"Sometimes wena you can be so selfish so heartless," I say a little angry.

"O batlang? You're not helping."

"You're like my fucking therapist. You're giving me an inch of sympathy and I'm pouring out my life to you."

"Oh God here we go again. You're such a drama queen. You're just looking for excuses to justify what you did. Bona, you can't carry on like this. "

I can't think of an immediate response so I brood in silence.

The air is still and is affected by the luscious smell of a nearby lake. It is hot, the heat stifling thought. My face burns slightly. Mmabatho doesn't seem affected by the heat. My head starts to itch so I scratch violently. Perhaps I want a little attention.

"Why don't you just take it off," she remarks, pointing to the cap I wear.

I take it off and keep scratching.

"Tshepo please," she says, putting her hand on mine.

8

"Don't give up on me. I know that you're disappointed," I admit.

She is taken aback a little but remains attentive. Mmabatho is one of those people that never gush forward with emotion. It's too messy, I imagine her saying. She hardly ever spills out her feelings unless they are indignation or disapproval. I suppose she saves it for her acting classes.

"Okay, but you can't do that," she comes back.

"What scratching my head?"

"Not that and you know what I mean. Why are you making me say it? I'm trying to understand. Look, you can't smoke four hundred zols a day because ..."

"Because because. I know I know," I cut her off. You don't understand, I say to myself. Excess is a seductive god. She will let you into her secrets if you follow her way a little. Mmabatho looks at me with incomprehension, with the discouraged look of a teacher who can't get through to a student

"I don't understand you. Are you trying to throw away your life or something? Do you think this is a joke? The fact remains cannabis induced psychosis. Isn't that what your psychiatrist said? So?"

"Okay, fine," I say irritated, "I get the point."

"Tshepo, you're making this hard and it doesn't have to be."

"Don't patronise me. It's easy for you to say that. You're not in my position."

"That's right. I'd never allow myself. I only said it because ..."

"Because because. I know what I said. But I thought I was invincible then. I thought I could do anything but what I didn't realise was that I have to want to do it. You know what I mean? I need to want it bad enough so that I don't have to smoke zol before I get off my arse. But I do. For now I do."

"That's weak. O batla ho re kereng? You know what they're calling you," she says a defeated look about her face.

I look at her.

"Mad cow disease. Is that how you want to be known? I mean for fuck's sakes just wake up. This thing is destroying you."

"But you're also smoking it."

"That's not the point. You're changing the subject," she gets irritated.

We sit together in silence. The sun beats. Words have made us strangers temporarily. I feel angry with the world, with life and its fastidious order of things. There is so much that I don't understand and the riddles seem to be getting more obscure. Too much has been said about my condition, my illness, whatever it is. I don't know what to call it, this thing that happened to me because because. I'm sick of the endless explanations that come with it, the lies and cover-ups, the injustice and humiliation of it all. The indifferent nurses and psychiatrists who only communicate through prescriptions. Heavy prescriptions that dull your senses and seem to drain life force out of you. I'm sick of this familiar feeling of indignation. It's too tiring, too overwhelming to be always angry with life, always questioning. Why me? Why this? And this drug, what does it do? Will it take away this ugly feeling? Will I be able to sleep? Will I have my life back? It's too much. It makes my hands go cold and ties my stomach in knots. After a while anger just takes over your life and comes out in cynical bites when you speak.

My protests seem like insignificant drivel in the greater scheme of things anyway – whatever that means. I'm tired of therapy. I'm sick of trying to get to the root of things. All roots just seem to lead to more roots and more roots. Creation is a mad affair after all. It has no end. And that's what I need, an end. If not at least an answer or some semblance of conclusion. What does "cannabis induced psychosis" mean? There is more to it than that. This is what the medical profession will never understand. I'm looking for a deeper understanding of what happened to me, not an easy answer like cannabis induced psychosis. And why don't they just say it if they truly don't understand what happened? Why blame it on cannabis?

It's too exhausting to be like this all the time. I'm tired, hungry. Washed-up at twenty three, I keep thinking and try to force myself to do something. But I can't. Time is against me. I feel seconds ticking in my veins as I breathe. Minutes are outnumbering the hairs on my body. Hours are disappearing with each nail that grows. Forever. And ever. It's frightening. Time is frightening. It's like dominoes endlessly falling into oblivion.

And forever itself, it's too daunting. There's no way back, no back door to sneak through. I can't undo the mistakes I tripped over. Everything counts and very little is remembered. Forever. It's the only answer life gives us. And we are expected to fit it into some neat equation with death and a blissful after-life. It's too much of a task. It's all too mad.

I begin to feel anxious again and calm myself by scraping off flaking paint from the bench. Mmabatho blocks off the sun's rays from her eyes and looks ahead in the distance. There isn't much to see, just more buildings and faint suggestions of trees. Her bleached crop of untamed hair glistens in the sun. And her mahogany complexion seems to shine. In my dreams Mmabatho is the woman who ran away with the sun and had an affair. It seems like a strange way of thinking about someone but I often think of her as a sun child because I know how much she likes being out in the sun soaking up its sensuous rays.

I like her most when she's quiet. There is something regal about the way she holds herself. An ability to gather strength, summon courage as if calculating the storm ahead. She sits with her legs crossed, a bright sarong with a wild flower print falling to her thick ankles, her feet clad in heavy Doc Martens. She has an imposing presence about her, hard to ignore. There is nothing delicate about her looks except for her long eyelashes but there is something attractive about her strong Amazon-like features. When I first saw her I remember thinking she could give birth to a whole rugby team and she would still have energy and grace. There was just something indomitable about her, a spirit that reminded me of rural women toiling in the fields, a sense of coarse feminine strength. One could never guess where she grew up from the way she dressed. Her wardrobe gave too many conflicting clues. She's the only person I ever saw who wore jeans and a Xhosa head wrap and pulled it off stylishly. The first thing she ever said to me when I first met her was that my eyes were big and something about them revealing too much. I was struck by her boldness and didn't like her immediately. Capetonians take themselves too seriously, I remember thinking after she said that. I was annoyed. She seemed to have an opinion about everything and there was something about her that I couldn't trust, a worldly air about her that always made her the centre of attention. For a while we kept on running into each other at parties and bars and invariably I would end up with her on some couch in the corner talking about something neither of us really cared about. It was more about sussing each other out, trying to measure the depth of each other's character. If experience meant having traveled a lot and leaving behind a trail of jilted lovers then she was more experienced than I. She went so far as to tell me that she'd slept with a woman. She thought I would be shocked but I wasn't. I was indifferent. Besides I'd grown up in Jo'burg. In time she wore down my defenses with charm but not the syrupy kind that oozes with the need to please. I found her charming to watch. I liked the way people responded to her. Maybe that has something to do with the fact that she's a drama student.

We sit like that for a while, each of us quiet in our thoughts. She's an artist, a thought comes to me. A great silence artist. She's mastered silence. I watch her, the sun seducing her soft skin. "We should go inside," I finally say. She nods, a shadow of distress on her face. "Look, there's nothing to worry about," I offer, "I'm gonna get through this."

"Wena," she says and points her finger at me in a concerned mother-ly tone. I say nothing. We get up and go inside.

## MMABATHO

I feel partly responsible for Tshepo. The truth is I introduced him to dagga. Most students in Cape Town do it; at least the circles I move in. Okay, so I was a little shallow to have given in to peer pressure. I can live with that. But the truth is it never ends, it just becomes more subtle the older one gets. I've seen advertising executives in their for-ties "living it up" on coke and zol at parties. And they always have a standard look on their face when they offer someone their first line of schnarf; a misleading look of self-possession and sophistication as they snort the white powder, masquerading the decay and desperation un-der the smart clothes and behind the glazed eyes. I suppose it's the same look I gave Tshepo when I passed him the joint at Anthony's party. The only difference was that I wasn't trying to mislead him, nor was I hiding any skeletons. I consider dube harmless, a relaxant, some-what in the same fashion as coffee or chocolate. I've been smoking zol for three years now and sometimes I forget that it is considered a drug. But that has more to do with the large number of people in Cape Town who use it and how open they are about it. In Observatory where I live talking about dube is like asking for a Kleenex or bumming a cigarette, people have no hang-ups about it. And even if people do consider it a drug, so what? We're chemical creatures anyway. We need vitamins, minerals, calcium, irons and other nutrients. But for a little chemical distraction to offset our bodily functions we take something a little more unorthodox and risky. If it's not drink, it's food, cigarettes, slim-ming tablets or sex to release hormones. The distinctions between hard and soft drugs are irrelevant. It's like saying a little guilty or very guilty. The bottom line is everyone is guilty of a little self-indulgence. It's just a matter of perception.

I don't drink alcohol and I don't do hard drugs. I smoke zol because I enjoy it. It makes me think differently about an otherwise mundane life. And it's never gotten in the way of things. I would never let it hap-pen. I'm too proud to ever let myself be in Tshepo's position. I know my limits. It irritates me a little that he couldn't handle it. It shows poor character on his part. The thing about zol is that it opens you up and if you crack during that process I believe it has more to do with your character than the drug. So I don't buy it that Tshepo has cannabis induced psychosis but I'll go along with it for his sake.

Anway it's not like I forced him. He was eager to try it. He pulled a few drags and said something about it being good weed. It was an obvious giveaway that he'd never tried it before. I didn't offer him after that because I knew he was going to be intensely stoned, a feeling that he might not be used to. I was right.

I sat with him as my high began to sink in, all the while aware of a silly grin growing on his face. We talked some more, this time his guard was down. He was more eager to come forward with his feelings and ideas and less concerned with saying the right thing and being cool. I sensed some uneasiness about him every time we talked about sex, but it wasn't anything I could put my finger on. He talked with feverish energy about the afterlife and kept on making references to different religions and how they viewed existence. I'd read a lot on the subject but I still listened, impressed by his attention to detail. Zol has a habit of doing that. It unleashes the mind like a running zipper, exposing the jagged intricacies of thought. With zol an ordinary thought expressed with zeal becomes an epiphany. Conversation becomes illuminating. I could see him grinning at his own ingenuity as he went on at length to tell me about the Egyptian Book of the Dead. He carried on for what seemed like hours but his enthusiasm kept me interested. I listened and did what I liked doing best – I watched. I analysed every gesture he made, the slightest inflection in his voice, the way he strung ideas together, how he was dressed. People have called me cold, critical, a social predator. If that means choosing carefully whom I associate with, then I'm guilty.

It is Saturday morning. The police find Tshepo roaming around Main road in Woodstock. He is naked except for an old sheepskin seat cover that is precariously wrapped round his waist. He speaks fast, raving at us as David and I approach him. It is hard to keep him calm. I give him my sweater and plead with him to get in the car with us but he refuses. The police are relieved to have us take him home. Sergeant Andrews tells us about how he found him parading naked in front of a busy butchery in Salt River.

It is a windy day. A breeze goes by and makes him shiver, momentarily making him seem sane. After a while I convince him to get in the car with us. A crazed look in his eyes he sits in the back with me. "I've seen Mam'lambo," he keeps saying and whispers to himself. We drive him to Observatory. At the door one of his housemates lets us in.

"Tshepo where have you been for the last three days?" Alice asks.

"Walking," he simply says and walks past her.

"Walking where?" I ask.

"Look, I'm feeling a little cold," he says impatiently.

"Serves you right," Alice says.

David and I look at her harshly.

"Honestly. Strutting about naked like that, what was he thinking? I know you two have more sense than that," she continues.

"Fuck off, Alice," Tshepo says and walks off to his room.

"That's just great, Tshepo," she says after he leaves. "What's he bloody on?"

David and I ignore her and walk towards the kitchen where the others are eating breakfast.

"He's obviously not well," Alex the landlord begins. "I think we should let him see someone."

"You mean a psychiatrist? 'Cause I think he's, you know, gone," Alice says and makes a crude gesture to her head. I can see why Tshepo doesn't like her. She is irritatingly blunt.

The four housemates look at each other and agree.

"Shouldn't you ask him what he thinks should be done?" I ask. No one answers. They look at me with smug irritation as if to say I don't live here, how dare I raise a point.

"Can you take him to hospital?" Alex asks David as if washing his hands of any further responsibility for Tshepo. David agrees.

I don't like the idea but I feel outvoted. Besides, I'm not his mother, I remind myself. After a while I go to his room.

"Tshepo, can I come in?" I knock on his door.

He doesn't answer but his radio is on. I find him huddled in the corner on his mattress. A duvet is wrapped around him.

"Aish. You're not dressed," I say a little annoyed.

"I have nothing clean to wear," he says pathetically in a faraway voice.

"Your digs mates, are they always like this?"

He says nothing and looks confused. The music crescendos into arresting congas beating over strings.

"Café del Mar?" I ask.

"It's the only thing I can listen to."

Hardly appropriate, I think to myself.

"Pretty heavy stuff though don't you think?"

He stares at me blankly as if contemplating my response. I study his face for any clues of well-being and find nothing. He's lost that cotton soft charm in his big eyes. He scratches his head violently, distractedly. Traces of madness begin to creep into his gestures. Absent-mindedly he scratches his balls.

"Tshepo, don't you think?" I ask again.

He doesn't reply. He starts crying.

I go to his tape deck and change the cassette. On a better day Café del Mar can be quite relaxing but not today. I put on Kenny G and rummage through his cupboard. Surprisingly his room is neat. I have known it to be usually as messy as mine. Everything has been meticulously placed. I notice that he has a small shrine near the window. He's put some dried acacia leaves, herbs and various objects on a little table. In the centre there's a wooden box with a delicate branch on top. It sits ominously like Pandora's box. Looking at it sends shivers up my spine.

"And this, what's it about?" I ask, trying to subdue his tears.

"Nothing."

"Is it a shrine?"

"No it's my altar," he corrects me.

"Altar. Any sacrifices, dead babies I should know about?" I say making light of the serious matter. For a moment he looks like he is about to smile but tears sabotage his mood again. His sadness is oppressive and begins to bring down my mood.

I manage to find a tracksuit tucked away behind some towels and a pair of shorts that will have to do for underwear. For socks I scratch in his laundry bag. There are worse things than wearing dirty socks, I reason.

He starts getting dressed in front of me. I don't look the other way. I confront his nakedness. He looks at me and manages a smile, more to suggest that he is comfortable with his own body than to say that his mood has changed. Men can be obsessive about their penises, I'm glad he isn't. A warm feeling settles at the pit of my stomach. I smile back. I'm not his mother, I remind myself and begin to wonder what I'm doing here. I don't like playing nursemaid to anyone, especially friends. But I realise that he is in better hands with me than with his callous housemates. Besides, as a black person I always feel it incumbent upon me to help another black person in need, especially in the company of whites. Growing up in a prestigious boarding school in Swaziland as the only person of colour in my class I was always happy to see black faces trickling through the school's lower standards as the years passed. But I noticed how eager some people were to set us against each other for the sheer sport of confirming the worst suspicions people have about black people. I never gave them that pleasure because I always got on well with the few other black students. Sometimes they were lacking in charm or wit or they didn't have an entirely welcoming presence, but I learned to deceive in order to counter the false impression of black people always fighting and sabotaging each other.

"You're tying my laces," he says.

I catch myself in the act and carry on.

"I'm just helping," I return, a little embarrassed.

"I know," he says, momentarily lucid.

"Right. All set," I look at him.

"I know we have to go now," he says. "They want me to go to Valkenberg, don't they?"

"Tshepo, it's for the best. Le wena, you know it."

"I know, because because," he says and I don't know what it means.

After a routine psychiatric examination at Groote Schuur they send us to Valkenberg. Tshepo is quiet and sulking but he seems resigned. I feel guilty but I know that he needs medical attention. Besides, he knows what's going on, I reassure myself. David and I take him to ward 15. It is a closely monitored ward. The nurses seem aloof and aggressive.

"Tshepo, we have to go," I say to him once he has signed in.

"See you later," he says a little confused. I can't stop worrying about him.

"Maybe we can stay a little longer," I say to David because I can't leave him. He doesn't mind.

A hulking male nurse gives Tshepo a bevy of tablets. The other nurse gets annoyed when Tshepo asks for more water.

"What are you giving him?" David inquires.

"Are you a doctor?" the nurse who gave Tshepo the tablets asks contemptuously.

"No."

"Then just let me get on with my job."

"I'm just concerned. What are you giving him?"

"Haloperidol 10 mg and Orphenadrine 50 mg, are you happy?"

"And what are they supposed to do?"

"I don't have time for this."

"David, let's go," I interrupt.

"I think that's a good idea," the nurse says.

"Tshepo, we're going now," I say and squeeze his hand. He has a puzzled look on his face.

"Hei, vasbyt," David adds. We don't look back when we go out the door. But the sadness of the occasion follows us.

In the car we say nothing to each other for a while.

"I don't know what I'm going to do," I open up to David.

"About what? What do you mean?"

"I mean Tshepo has no family in Cape Town."

"Right, so."

"So I'm not sure if I can fill the role of nursemaid."

"He doesn't need a nursemaid. Valkenberg is taking care of that. He just needs a friend," he says and looks at me accusingly.

"Don't look at me like that. You weren't exactly coming forth with promises of seeing him again," I reply.

"This conversation is stupid," he lets out.

"You're full of crap," I retort.

I stare out the window, brooding in silence.

"Why are you so hard? Really, why are you so hard?" he asks, sounding earnest as usual.

"It takes practice," I say to irritate him. "And why is it okay for a man to be a hard bastard but not for a woman?"

"What are you talking about? You know, sometimes you can be such a bitch," he goes on.

"You're not the first to say it, asshole," I say and remember what it is that I find so infuriating yet attractive about David. Besides the obvious good looks he is painfully honest. David is the kind of person who always tells the truth even if it means he will look bad. I don't believe people are very honest. In fact too much honesty can almost be a weapon. It's disarming to hear too much truth. I remember how defenseless I felt when I first met him. I remember thinking he's too intense. He said he didn't believe much in chit-chat and he always spoke with a gravity that made you feel like you were being attacked. Of course he wasn't attacking you, he was just being himself, always blunt. He told me that most men probably found me threatening. I agreed with him but asked him why he thought so. He said that it mostly had to do with my physique. You're in shape for serious reproduction, he said. I slapped him, I was drunk but he didn't mind. It wasn't news to hear that I wasn't the petite maiden next door. I know I'm big-boned.

I enjoy wearing clothes that reveal my ample bust and suggestive hips. I walk with a gait that some women whisper about in toilets. And I always wear my hair stringently short, in defiance. The lengths that some women will go to just to maintain long hair is enough effort to lead a double life.

"I don't like fighting, you know." I say to him after sulking for a while.

"Well, neither do I. I just can't believe you said that," he says, concentrating on the road.

"Are we ever going to be okay again?" I put my hand on his lap. He looks at it as if to remind me that he's going out with someone else now. I take it away, a pang of humiliation darting through my heart.

"We went out for three years. You can't expect things to be normal overnight," he says but I'm not listening. I feel humiliated.

"You know there's something that I've always wanted to ask you even when we were going out," I say.

"And that is?" he looks at me, his mousy blond hair falling in his face. This is where his little girlfriend sweeps it away from his face. I saw her doing that once, it was nauseating to watch.

"What's your fascination with black women?" I ask with the intention of wounding him.

"Why do you assume that I'm fascinated with black women just because I went out with you and my present girlfriend is black?" he says a little flustered.

"Girlfriend? She has a name," I taunt him.

"Okay, Mmabatho, what is this about? You're being a bitch for no reason," he tells me.

"That's the second time you're calling me a bitch."

He doesn't respond. We drive home in silence.

I was being a little bitchy. I had a lot on my mind. I wanted to talk about us. I wanted to find out how he was doing. I wasn't coming on to him. But it all came out twisted. David has a way of making everything I say or do boomerang back to me. I always end up feeling bad. Why is it so easy for him to move on? Where's the agony, the sense of grief? I always think it's an insult if someone gets over you too quickly. I cried for days after I broke up with him. And I know it seems a little unrealistic to expect the same thing from him but I do. I want to be missed. I want to be thought of as the great catch that he let slip away. It doesn't matter any more who pulled the plug first. I'm not childish. But I care that he should be so casual about our break-up. I keep thinking about what Ntabiseng says: Women want drama and all that stuff so that they can feel like they are the centre of the universe. If that's true, it's perverse. But in some strange way I think I want all the drama so that I can feel good about myself. So that there can be an element of fairness about it. I mean why should I be the only one to suffer?

TSHEPO

Under the doctor's gaze I become a child again. I listen meekly as they plot their strategies against my mind. I don't make a fuss when they medicate me even though I know it is going to assault my system. After medication I find myself oscillating somewhere between sleep and calm. Everything seems to slow down. Without a watch I feel lost, hours disappear. Boredom affects us all. There is nothing to do during occupational therapy, or OT as we call it, except to read a few old magazines, play some board games or just doze off. Even sleep becomes a kind of drug. After a few days I develop a nervous tic. My left eye blinks involuntarily. When I tell the nurses about it they plot further strategies against me by increasing my dosage, something about adjusting the anti-side effect drug Orphenadrine. I take the tablets blindly and swallow. Some days all I want to do is sleep and forget about the life I once led. And since they lock the rooms after breakfast I end up dozing in chairs or on the floor. Sometimes they give me a white tablet, a powerful anti-psychotic drug which everyone seems to take reluctantly. I always feel drowsy after taking it and this lasts for at least three days. The lethargy that follows is unbearable. But when I close my eyes I don't dream.

It's easy to forget that I'm supposed to be ill. Most of the other patients, all older than me, walk around like zombies as if their minds are bent beyond repair. Conversation with them is fractured, if not impossible. Some grunt or bump me when they have anything to say to me. They are lethargic and they stink. They look like they're just getting by, like people who have given up living. And their posture betrays this, it's all wrong. They're slumped forward and their backs are arched as if beckoning the earth, beckoning death. They carry depression and solitude with them wherever they go. I feel imprisoned by their lack of hospitality and their lousy company.

I don't have friends here and it doesn't really bother me. I spend my time thinking about my life, going in endless circles of introspection. There's nothing else to do. I replay events that led me here and keep thinking about how it happened and when it all went wrong. The truth is I still don't know how it happened. Things just got out of hand and I landed in a mental institution. It's hard to accept that. I feel angry with myself.

It doesn't take long to know all the rules; where to sit, when to go to the toilet, which nurse you can trust. They always assign someone to tell you what's going on, a kind of welcoming committee, except that this isn't camp and there's nothing jovial about the occasion. Inappropriate laughter is tacitly discouraged. What does that mean? Humour is such a personal thing. Does it mean you can't giggle, sneer or guffaw? What if I break into laughter recalling an anecdote? Would that be considered inappropriate laughter? I watch the nurses looking at us, recording things. Are they watching who is laughing? I've become afraid to smile. I don't trust my emotions anymore. I don't know what I feel half the time. The drugs do all the work. Are we just supposed to bite the insides of our mouths and sit on uncomfortable chairs the whole afternoon? What are we supposed to do if we cannot laugh at the inappropriateness of being locked up like criminals?

One of the other patients keeps eyeing me. His name is Zebron, if you can believe that is actually someone's name, and he makes me anxious with his dark torturer's eyes. He has a habit of staring at me and then when I look back he gives me these aggressive grimaces. And he usually wears a sadistic look as if he's always contemplating nasty things like how to torture us. Like me, he hardly speaks to anyone. But what is strangest about him is that he doesn't really have a face. He's got these nondescript features that remind me of a police identikit. An identikit never looks like anyone one would meet in real life. Apart from a low brow with deepset eyes, Zebron has a forgettable face. His face would make him the perfect criminal. And when you look at him you have to think a while to gauge his age. For a small man he has a dark presence about him. I avoid being near him as much as I can.

"Staff. Staff my legs are paining, Staff," Salman suddenly screams and throws himself on the ground. We watch him writhe on the floor, his legs caught in a peculiar spasm.

"Staff, please! Staff, my legs!" he yells.

Zebron sulks in a corner alone. Among the other patients he commands the kind of respect reserved for gang leaders in prison. It makes me wonder who he was before he came in here. Everyone has a history in Valkenberg. Doctors, lawyers, accountants, artists, forgotten politicians – they all live anonymously in Valkenberg but you seldom hear the history from the patient. It's usually a source of gossip or intrigue for nosy nurses, especially the female nurses. Zebron gets up and sits next to me. I avoid his eyes and notice that his shadow has fallen over my thighs. He pokes me for a cigarette. I don't have one and let him know that for the umpteenth time. He knows I don't smoke but he always pesters me.

"I don't like you," he says to me one day when I tell him that I don't have a cigarette.

"You're not the first," I say calmly.

"You think you're special? You're just another sick patient," he tells me.

I'm in a mental hospital, I remind myself.

But it doesn't stop there. Routinely he harasses me for cigarettes and I never have any for him. He usually does this when the staff is not watching or if they do then they are turning a blind eye. In a mental hospital you can never be too paranoid about the staff plotting against you. It's kind of an unwritten law that exists between them and the patients. It kind of sets the scene for what to expect – we distrust them and they torture us. Some patients are convinced that the staff is skilfully manipulating them. I have my own theories about people that work in mental hospitals. Working there seems to say as much about their mental health as that of the patients. Some of the most sinister, megalomaniac people I have ever met work in mental hospitals, somehow managing to conceal their weaknesses.

"Give us an entjie," Zebron harasses me again. His breath stinks oppressively.

I shrug my shoulders at him. He goes on asking me for a while but I look the other way. He stares at me again, a furrow forming between his eyebrows. It occurs to me that he is sowing evil thoughts, but I convince myself to ignore him to remain calm. I didn't come here to be driven crazy by anyone.

Salman's shrieking gets louder. "Staff, my legs are paining, Staff! My legs, Staff!"

His crying starts upsetting some of the other patients. Unathi pulls at his grizzled beard and starts rocking incessantly. Sitting next to me, Zebron crosses his legs tightly, crushing his balls. Bruce starts yelling with Salman.

"Alright, shut up or you're all going to the kulukutz," Sipho, the day nurse, says.

He pulls down Salman's pants, swabs him with some cotton and stabs him with a long syringe. Watching it turns my stomach. Surprisingly Salman seems relieved and doesn't scream at the violence of it all. I watch Sipho withdraw the long needle and bite the insides of my mouth till I taste blood. I don't like needles or blades.

Zebron leaves my side. I grab an old magazine from the table. I try to read it but I can't concentrate on the words. I read them apishly, forgetting the previous sentence I read. It's enough to depress me. My head feels heavy and my senses are dull but I still try. It's the drugs, I keep saying to myself as I skip over words. Zebron returns and drops a raw shaving blade on the magazine with crazed glee.


### ZEBRON

Three nurses have to pin him down. They give him a sedative that subdues him in a couple of minutes. Then they drag him off to seclusion.

I feel no remorse for what I did to Tshepo. I'm simply making sure that we are all equally disadvantaged. A few hypochondriacs have come through this ward and my experience with them has always been unpleasant. Their eagerness to show everyone how sick they are crawls under my skin. It is an irritating type of attention seeking, even arse-licking.

Tshepo walked as though he was in a trance and said little to anyone when he first arrived. I would watch him closely. New patients always go through me. Sipho learned early on about my screening tactics. They all know but seem to condone it.

"So have you got an entjie for me?" I'd harass him at breakfast.

He continues staring at his bowl and slurps his porridge. I fill my spoon and flick it at him. The porridge messes his face. He takes a while to respond but when he does he laughs, inappropriately.

"Okay, settle down," Sipho, sitting at the other end of the table, tells him.

"More white pills for you," I taunt him.

Those who are listening, laugh.

"Settle down. Zebron, that's enough," Sipho warns me.

When I collect Tshepo's bowl he tells me to fuck off and stabs me on the side of the abdomen with his spoon. I don't strike back. Sipho grabs him by the scruff and bundles him off to the kulukutz again. He stays there for five nights. On the second day we hear him screaming something awful. It lasts for a while before they sedate him.

Seclusion can do that to a person. It chokes you. Once the screaming starts I know that the spirit has been forcibly evacuated. The drugs fill the screaming with an anxious silence. You feel constantly vulnerable as if you're about to break into tears, only you're too drugged to cry. And the nights are always long and cold, regardless of the warm weather, because there is no window to look through. It stinks in there because the last guy was too broken to piss in the bowl and his shit skids off the walls as if in protest. There is nothing spiritual or healing about the kulukutz. The door is heavy and they bolt it as though you are a dangerous beast that no one should see. During the day fluorescent light flickers and dulls your vision. You feel colour draining from your face. The walls are impenetrable. The room oppresses you with frustration. There is a feeling of interminable doom about it. It is hellishly lonely in there. And the blankets and mattress always stink of urine and crawl with fleas.

He had to break down. There is no other way for them to advance his recovery. Before they mend you they have to break you. I know this because I have been in and out of hospitals for years. I should have never let my brother cajole me into going in the first time nearly ten years ago. I feel more broken now than when I first came in. And Stelazine makes me cranky. It makes me look at the wrong side of people, the side they spend their lives hiding. I notice inconsistencies like the white lies people tell and forget about later. The things people say inadvertently, I always remember them, unforgivingly.

I don't like people. I suppose I never have. I've given up on them. It's easy, you decide one day that people are full of shit and from then on you dismiss them like flies. I don't like the way they try to be likeable or good-natured. Some of us are just born with a streak of badness, even a grudge against the living. It's nothing personal. For every clean public toilet there has to be someone willing to spoil it, to soil it. It's the way people are. We're not all God's children. In here God doesn't exist. I am the forgotten who lies rotting in a barrel of fermenting apples. God never heard my cries. I never saw the light or touched on something sacred inside myself. We're not all mystics who can extract beauty from our pain. Some of us are just born with too much corruption to ever survive it.

When I speak I speak of wounds and pain and anger. They are real to me. I don't know anything about remorse and looking inside myself for beauty. There's nothing worth looking at. There's too much decay. I can't work with that but I can live with it. And having a father who beat me up for sport never helped.

I'm very aware of how twisted my thinking can be. I mean sometimes I catch myself fantasizing about bludgeoning the female nurses – the stupid ones always gossiping about someone's indaba. I wonder what I would use. A spade or a golf club? How loud would they scream? These are things that fill my thoughts sometimes and I accept it. It's the way I am. People always imagine that being a mental patient is a lot about fighting your inner demons. It isn't for me. It's about relenting and learning to live with them. It's a constant struggle. That's why I keep going in and out of institutions.

Sometimes I just refuse to communicate for days on end. It's the last act of protest I can still control. I think the doctors see it as a sign of deterioration and just cause for increasing my dosage. The arseholes – if only they knew what arrogant pompous shits they seem like from my side. They sit there in their immaculately white coats taking apart aspects of my life and then reconstructing them in a form they call therapy. And when I don't respond to their therapy they never stop and question if their methods are effective. Instead they punish me by making my stay longer or increasing the medicine. It's always about me and never about them.

At the last ward round I swore at my psychologist when he asked me how I felt about leaving Valkenberg. I got two days in the kulukutz. I swore at him because I knew they were planning to keep me longer. I'm always difficult with them because they are so convinced that I am sick and only they can help me. Sometimes, not often, the grip of depression gets so tight that you feel you must tell these arseholes something because the pain is too unbearable. I've told my psychologist that I killed someone. I don't think he believes me because they say I suffer from schizophrenia.

"This woman. Tell me more about this woman you say you killed," he says to me in a clinical tone. I tell him but he doesn't really listen. He wants to know if my thoughts are disconnected, if my feelings change. I can see. I'm not stupid. To him I become just another lab experiment. He takes notes furiously.

"There were a few of us. We raped her," I say just to elicit a response from him. But he disappoints me. "How does that make you feel?" he asks. What kind of a question is that? Just once can't they step away from themselves and say something different? In real life no one has conversations like that.

Other times I walk away from the ward rounds with a deeper hatred for people. It becomes easy to picture murdering someone once you've been in a mental hospital. The thing is, they test you, they prod you and ask you a million questions. And at the end of it all you sort of realise that you're the same person you were yesterday before you got sick and you'll be the same person tomorrow when they say you can go home. People don't really change, circumstances change. Even when they say you're psychotic, it's still you but in an intense state. When you start seeing things like that, you become more open to the nastier side of life. Your mind starts having these thoughts that either scare you or thrill you because they are so wicked. I have my stories to tell. But they won't be heard by some God-fearing psychologist who thinks he's my saviour.

Tshepo refuses to speak to anyone when they let him out. In bed one night he attacks me. I wake up to him standing over me, throwing wild punches. I cover my face and lie there while he exercises his anger on me. He beats me till he starts sobbing.

"Shut up now, Sipho's on duty," I tell him. "He's just waiting for you to fuck up again."

"Fuck you," he mumbles, his punches becoming more pathetic with each stroke.

Unathi gets up irritated and switches on the light. He comes straight for Tshepo and wallops him across the face. He falls and his eye hits the corner of the opposite bed.

"Voerstek, thula man! We want to sleep," Unathi says and other voices agree and swear at Tshepo. I warn them to be quiet. "It's straight to the kulukutz if Sipho finds you walking around," I say.

Unathi switches off the light and goes back to bed. Tshepo gets up and also goes to bed.

I don't hear from him for the rest of the night.


TSHEPO

I'm bleeding in the dark. This is what my life has come to. Every night for the last three nights I wake up when they are all sleeping and I attack Zebron. And then Unathi beats me up. And then we go to sleep before the night nurse on duty hears. It seems to be happening all over again, I'm being sucked into events. I'm losing control. You're supposed to be getting better, you're going to get through this, I keep telling myself. But it doesn't help. When I see Zebron I hear chainsaws and I'm reminded of how violent I can be. Couldn't he see my eyes sending out signals? Stop, you are pushing me! I'm going crazy! I'm barely holding on to what's left of my sanity. Why are you sending me over the cliff? Couldn't he see the desperation in my eyes? The kulukutz kills you. I feel my sanity slipping away.

My psychologist asked me why I acted out. It's questions like this that confuse me and make me feel even more desperate. On the outside it would be considered normal to react the way I did after being provoked, at least by some people I know. But in here every gesture is amplified under the psychologist's gaze. I feel hopeless, like I have no control over anything. They are making it seem like I have a problem with Zebron and that he is innocent. Nothing was mentioned about the blade he used to provoke me. I'm drowning in my own events again. I keep reminding myself that he provoked me because it doesn't seem to matter to the staff. You acted out, they keep saying. There's a deep cut under my left eye. I don't think it will heal soon. I still have too much anger to work out. Besides, I can't sleep. The medication makes me restless. And I have scabies. They give me a harsh ointment that I apply when I remember.

The routines are strict. We are woken up at seven o'clock. I'm usually up by then because I'm always hungry and can't wait for breakfast. Then we have to wash. They call it personal hygiene time. There's a name for everything here, even the most banal thing. They march us off to the bathroom where we queue like cattle before the dip. We all have to get naked while the nurses supervise our entry and exit from the showers. Wearing their white coats and shouting orders over the splashing water they look like animal trainers rather than nurses. There's aggression and impatience in their voices, especially Sipho. Three of us go in at a time. Soon the room is steamy and smells of sweat. It smells of balls and fart, of men tired of protest as we go in and go out and others itching with frustration.

"Sepo, hurry up," Sipho shouts. I have hardly been five minutes in the grimy shower.

"It's Tshepo. Tshepo," I correct him.

"I don't give a fuck. Phuma, man," he says and pulls me out. There are no towels left so I shiver in a corner and wait for one of the others to offer me their used towel.

"Here," Zebron says and offers me his damp towel.

I look at him with contempt.

"Just take it man," he snaps at me.

26

It is too early to question his motives. It's only a towel, I tell myself and take it.

After drying ourselves we go to the cupboards where we get clean clothes and gowns. Unathi is still showering but Sipho doesn't bother him.

"He's a timer," Zebron says catching me watching him. "And he pays the staff for a few favours. That's why you always see him eating biscuits."

I say nothing, holding contempt under my breath.

"You have no reason to hate me," he says with a stony face. He brushes his hand against my arm. "Valkenberg can get very lonely, you know," he whispers in my ear tauntingly, his voice thick and layered like that of someone used to excessive drink and smoke. I walk away to avoid another confrontation.

"Zebron's got the box," Sipho says giving him a box filled with shaving sticks, blunt blades and toothbrushes with tired bristles.

I hate blades. I avoid looking at them and grab the first toothbrush I see. Zebron grins at me. We have to stand in a queue while Sipho squirts out a worm of toothpaste for us. When it is my turn Sipho hardly looks at me and makes a little scribble on my toothbrush. I won't be reduced to complaining about toothpaste, I tell myself and do my best to brush my teeth with the little paste. I scrub my teeth till my gums bleed.

"Are you guys done? We must go eat now. Come, come," Sipho says and claps his hands as if speaking to children. I keep brushing my teeth.

"Come, guys," he says again. The others put back their shaving sticks and brushes. I'm the last one to replace my brush. And I don't bother to rinse it. Sipho looks at me and grunts as though to say don't test me. Then he hands out combs.

By the time we are finished the floors are wet. Byron and another guy have bathroom duty. They wipe the floor with the damp towels and rinse out the sinks. They put away the bricks of Lifebouy soap in the cupboard. This is all done while we stand on the opposite side of the room.

When Sipho is satisfied with the state of the bathroom we proceed to the dining room. We all smell of Lifebouy. Lifebouy, ironic isn't it? I think to myself. I repeat Lifebouy over and over till it becomes a silly jumble of letters that don't make sense. We walk past the kulukutz. My heart sinks a little. I take a peek in at one of the doors and the smell of urine assails my nose.

"What do you want in there?" Sipho yells at me. I don't say anything.

We wait restlessly for breakfast in the dining room. My eyes stray across the room. On the other side is a board with miscellaneous notices. On one corner "Get Well Soon" is scribbled. It doesn't seem to be addressed to anyone in particular. Then there is a chart about mental health. Honesty, confidence, self-respect and trust are listed as being amongst the most important qualities of sound mental health. Below the diagram is the reverse diagram for mental illness. What strikes me most about the diagram is that mistrust is the central quality that branches out into other bad qualities. But given the circumstances I find it perfectly reasonable to be mistrustful of people at ward 15. Just the other day someone ratted on Byron for smoking dope in the toilets. He was given four days in the kulukutz. Even minor, petty incidents have been reported. There is no sense of solidarity. Everyone seems to be out to cover his own back. I can't understand how anyone can rat on another person because there is nothing to gain except childish satisfaction for seeing someone getting punished. One doesn't gain any favours from the staff, so why do it? And it seems the staff has nothing to lose by encouraging us to spy on each other.

I'm famished when breakfast finally arrives: porridge and two slices of bread with faint traces of butter and jam. Fortunately, they always cook the porridge to my satisfaction. It is a consolation for the weak tea they serve. I always take Matthew's bowl because he doesn't enjoy porridge.

After breakfast we can walk around the fenced yard till tea time at ten. That is followed by OT which is in the lounge. And that is followed by lunch at twelve. Supper is at five. We are medicated immediately after every meal. The doors to the dormitories are opened between seven and a quarter to eight, depending on how many staff members are on duty.

Routines are followed closely. There is nothing to do but spend time looking forward to the next meal. It keeps my mind off the empty hours that seem to drag.

It is warm outside. I sit on the concrete stoep as the grass is still wet with dew. The others line up for their tobacco ration. Private tuck is also handed out. Zebron walks up to me and starts rolling a smoke.

"You're standing in my sun," I say to him politely.

"Excuse me," he says and moves aside but he remains next to me.

Even though he says nothing, his looming presence makes me feel irritable.

"Don't think so much," he says after a while.

People have said that to me all my life. But coming from Zebron it makes my blood curdle.

"You're just full of kak. I'm not going to fuck up again because of you," I tell him.

"Relax," he taunts me. "Look, you're not the only one. I do it to all new-comers."

I give him a dirty look. He clenches his jaw as if flexing his muscles.

"Don't fuck with me and I won't fuck with you. That's all I was saying," he says.

Unimpressed, I say nothing.

"Friends," he grins and reveals teeth etched with dark nicotine near the gums, betraying neglect. I hide my disgust at the level of decay his teeth are suffering. He's the kind of person who would deliberately neglect his teeth just so that he could have that effect on people when he smiled.

"So you say I think too much," I say, to change the subject and save myself from any unnecessary, binding friendships.

"Ja, I can tell you use your pip too much," he says in his phlegmy voice.

"What else is there to do? You might as well run away in your mind."

"Observe," he says mysteriously, flashing his teeth again.

Byron calls him. He walks away. What a creep, I think to myself after he's left.

"How's it for a entjie there, bra?" Byron begins.

For someone who looks like a thug Zebron is a neat smoker. He always rolls the perfect smoke and is ever careful not to ash on his clothes like the other moegoes, he says. He smokes it meticulously, wetting it on the side when it burns too quickly. And he never has black marks on his fingers like the other addicts. You can't really call them smokers because they only seem to be interested in a nicotine fix, even if it means collecting discarded threads of tobacco on the floor and using old stompies in their desperation. I don't blame them really, there's nothing else to do.

I notice that Byron is the only one that Zebron gives his entjie to – he has no patience for the others. I watch him speaking to Byron. He emits sprays of spit and gesticulates. I think he takes himself too seriously. And I don't think Byron really likes him. I watch them secretly because I don't want Zebron thinking that I find him remotely interesting. After a while he comes back to me.

29

"Don't be so caught up in your own thing," he says to me. Who does he think he is?

"And who are you? The resident psychologist?" I say sarcastically.

"Just listen a little and don't be such a windgat. If you open your eyes a little you'll get out here sooner."

"What do you mean?" I say irritable.

"I'm talking about the ward round. They want to see that you're interacting and talking. I mean you do want to get out of here, don't you?" He looks at me.

"Ja, sure, doesn't everyone here?"

"You're still a lighty; I could tell. Take a look around you. Look at Unathi there. He's got fuck all going for him. You think he's got something waiting for him when he gets out? And Jeremy that irritating prick … Nurse, my medication, nurse, my medication, I'm dying. Nurse, nurse. This is the only place that could tolerate a moegoe like him and he knows it," he says, his tone cold.

He sits next to me and spits out a splotch of saliva, subtly trying to intimidate me with his tsotsi stance. But I'm not impressed. His big gestures and crudeness seem silly and a little overgrown for this grown man trying to come across as a thug.

"Me and you, we're the same," he says, and I nearly laugh.

"I don't think so."

"You don't like people much," he says and looks me straight in the eye. "But in fact, you feel a little betrayed that no one has come to see you. I've been watching you."

"What makes you think you know everything?"

"You can be difficult. I can see. Mother's boy. Your mother let you suck her titties longer than she should have," he says, revealing his ugly teeth.

"You're full of shit."

"Why do you take everything so personal? You make an easy target," he smiles.

I'm temporarily lost for words. I want to get up and leave but that would be admitting defeat too easily.

"How long have you been here?" I ask him.

He studies me, a condescending look on his face.

"Did you hear me?"

"Ja. I'm just thinking you're actually quite boring. Couldn't you come up with a more interesting question?" he says, taunting me, and I fall into his trap.

"I don't have to take this. Fuck off," I say hurt and make a move to get up. He pulls me down swiftly.

"I'm sorry. I don't really communicate that much. My social skills are a bit off," he says with a surprisingly humble look on his face. I'm in a mental hospital, I remind myself.

"Don't talk shit to me then," I say firmly, sitting down reluctantly.

"The thing is, I get bored."

"So you insult people?" I raise my voice a little.

"Don't tell me about people. They're just objects that breathe," he says impassively.

"You're fucked up," I tell him.

"Aren't we all?" he says and manages a smile. "You believe too much in people, that's why you get hurt so easily."

"And you think you're Dr Bauermann. This is fun for you, isn't it? I bet that's what you do. You harass people and talk all this shit just to amuse yourself," I accuse him.

"I had a life outside. You're still a lighty you can't understand," he says, his stony face betraying a little sadness which he soon covers up by spitting again.

"And you think you know everything. No wonder you're here. There's nothing likeable about you," I say.

"Eina. That was a brave remark, even for you," he says. It's hard to tell if he looks hurt, there's a permanent sarcastic look on his face. He's one of those people I'd avoid simply on first impressions. There's something disturbing about him, an unwelcoming air as though a dark cloud is hanging over him. But this same quality also makes him curiously interesting.

"What were you talking about with Byron?" I pry just to irritate him.

"Life," he simply says.

"What do you mean life? That's a little vague."

"That's how life is. You're supposed to fill in the blank spaces yourself," he says trying to sound clever.

"Whatever," I say, tired of his quips.

I look at the mountain top and say nothing. He becomes a little restless. He opens his mouth to say something but I shush him gently and point to the clouds cascading down the mountain like a cloth. I admire the scene. But I notice that he's sulking beside me, annoyed that I shushed him. That's it, I say to myself. He's an egomaniac. A little silence is all I need to shut him up.

"What's the time?" I ask him after he has looked at his wrist watch.

"Who cares?" he says moodily and gets up to leave.

"Look who's being difficult now," I say to taunt him.

Soon after Mmabatho comes to visit. Her smile lifts my spirit. We are allowed to walk around the grounds. The other patients watch with demented envy as they let me out the gates. We walk towards a small park, an awkward moment of silence between us.

"So how is this place treating you?" she finally asks. I hate that question. Some questions are best answered by saying as little as possible.

I look at her face and she seems distracted. "It isn't anything that will kill me," I say and suddenly become aware of how uneasy she seems. She nods her head pensively.

"Is everything alright? You seem ..."

"Everything's fine. It's just that ... uh."

"What?"

"Are you the same?" she says and looks at me. "I know it's a stupid thing to ask but I've never been in this position."

I'm surprised to say the least. I didn't expect that from her.

"What kind of a question is that? Okay so I went off my head a little. But I'm fine now," I say, a little insulted.

"This isn't easy," she says, hardly looking at me. "What happened to you? You really flipped out. I've never seen anyone like that. I don't know what to say."

"Are you trying to tell me something?"

"I feel like I'm walking on egg shells and I hate that."

"Don't be silly. I'm not about to fall apart any minute, okay. You can trust me on that. I know things got out of hand but I feel better now," I say but inside I don't believe it.

"Okay," she says without feeling.

We walk further. I don't believe she thinks I'm well. I think wanted to say something else. She wouldn't be the first friend I've lost since this whole thing happened to me. I've learned the hard way how fickle people can be, how quickly their loyalties change. Today you're their friend, their confidant, but God help you tomorrow when your world crashes. No one calls, no ones asks after you. And you only hear what people say through gossip. I wonder if I should expect the same from Mmabatho. I never know where I stand with her. She keeps an impenetrable wall of caution around her that makes me feel a little anxious and unsure. I feel insecure about our friendship. Nothing she says is ever taken for granted.

"How's David?" I ask, more to find out if he's still friends with me.

"You don't have to worry about David. He's been busy with his thesis," she says.

I say nothing.

"Anyway I'd rather not see him much. We've been fighting lately."

"I thought you were over him."

"I'd rather not talk about him," she says and rolls her eyes.

We sit on a bench with a view of Table Mountain. Mmabatho is wearing her army fatigue pants with a dark T-shirt. She's dyed her hair a stubborn platinum blond colour and wears purple nail varnish. Her Adidas tackies have red laces. I don't know what look she's going for but it makes her interesting to look at.

"Tshepo, you're staring," she says after a while.

"Nice hair."

"There's this new club in town. Utopian Nights. I went with some friends from the drama department on Friday night. I think you'd like it," she says.

"How was it?" I ask.

"Quite cool actually. The crowd gets nice really late. They played drum & bass, hip hop, kwaito and a little r & b, mostly phat sounds. Ja, you'd definitely like it," she adds.

"So bo darkie bateng?"

"Ja, but you know what it's like in Cape Town. If you're black and you don't do the darkie thing then they say you're trying to be white and all that crap. I just don't go for that blacker than thou thing, so I don't pay much attention to where I go," she says dismissing my point. I thought it was valid. Sometimes I think Mmabatho says things just to provoke me.

"I wasn't saying anything like that," I say defensively.

"I know but I'm just tired of that whole argument. There's just so much more to see than being with bo darkie all the time. I mean I was with Felix and these two other white guys and we had a great time. Maybe I like being a little controversial and so what if the last two guys I went out with were white," she says, sounding defensive.

"You don't have to explain yourself to me. I'm on your side."

"Ja, but it's tiring, Tshepo. You know what I mean. I think I came to Cape Town so that I could run away from that whole race thing."

"But it's here, even in Cape Town. You can't really avoid it."

"I know, I'm not kidding myself. I realise that now but at least you can get away with being yourself more in Cape Town. It's more usual to hear of a white guy who likes kwaito and hangs around with bo darkie in Cape Town than in Jo'burg," she says but I'm only vaguely interested in what she says.

"There's that red-haired guy with dreads on TV in Jo'burg," I say tritely. "What's his name, Tim or something?"

"Ja, but who else can you think of? Doesn't it bug you though, that people are so narrow-minded? If you're black you can't listen to rock or go surfing or wear anything you like. You have to fit into this and that." She is preaching. I've heard it all before.

"I know what you mean. So did you meet anyone nice at this club?" I say to change the subject.

"Kind of," she says and smiles to herself.

We sit in silence, the way I like, and admire the view. The sun licks clouds, for a while it hides behind them.

I fantasise about taking a walk in Sea Point and think about what Mmabatho said about the whole colour thing. When you go out in some places in Cape Town no one really cares that you're black and that your mother sent you to a private school so that you could speak well. No one cares that you're white and that your father abuses his colleagues at work and calls them kaffirs at home. On the dance floor it doesn't matter which party you voted for in the last election or whether you know how many provinces make up the country. People only care that you can dance and that you look good. They care that you are wearing Soviet jeans with an expensive Gucci shirt and that you have a cute ass. They care that your girlfriend has a pierced tongue and that sometimes on a Saturday night she goes to bed with another woman and likes you to watch them. They want to see you wearing Diesel jeans with a retro shirt and Nike tackies. They want to see how creatively you can fuse mall shopping with flea market crawling and still remain stylish. Designer labels are the new Esperanto. Dolce e Gabbana kicks more ass than any bill of rights. In some clubs a person will chat you up because you know what drum & bass is and can dance to it while appearing sexy, not because you match the same race group like some arbitrary prerequisite. They want to hear you talking about what half a cap of acid does to you on a Saturday night after taking tequila or which is the best site to get into if you want to know more about Jamiroquai. They want to live out their Trainspotting odyssey of excess in a culture rapidly blurring the borders between the township and the northern suburbs. The people I know never forget that in essence the difference between kwaito and rave is down to a difference in beats per minute and that the margin is becoming narrower. It's not that it's fashionable to be seen going out with a person of a different colour. For Mmabatho it seems to be about exploring another culture. Some people are just sick of the expected. Me Tarzan, you Jane has become monotonous. People want to make their own references about who they are and where they fit in or not. It's not enough to simply offer them certain variables, hoping that they'll fit in there somewhere. And Cape Town is not what it used to be. Foreigners have left their imprint on our culture.

Like every growing metropolis Cape Town aspires to be the next best thing. And why shouldn't it? It has a lot going for it. The burgeoning modelling agencies, the politicians who act like celebrities, the scandals, the crude flaunting of money – they all point to a city that wants to be New York, London or Paris. People want to be seen eating croissants at a chic coffee shop at the Table View, rollerblading in Clifton or going for aromatherapy in bohemian Observatory. People want to see you drinking Valpré while working out at the Health & Racquet, with a personal trainer fashionably at your disposal. You must drive an Audi A4 and watch what you eat if you're going to wear your Speedo. You should rather wear Ray Bans than some cheap flea market knock off so that when people see you they must have something that they can relate to past the obvious. Isn't this the fodder advertisers feed us? You must smoke Peter Stuyvesant cigarettes and live out the fantasy of the fun-filled adverts. You must wear a Swatch so that a swarthy-looking blond can have a pick-up line. So that colour becomes secondary to the person you present. They want to say ah you're cool and not ah you're black or white. You must be into drumming, support world debt relief and have your chart done. You must know what heita means, what magents are and how to shake hands the African way. You must know what a barmitzvah is, in which direction Mecca faces and who charros are. And which Thai foods go best with soya sauce. You must know all these things and more in a culture pushing to be hybrid and past gender and racial lines. You must aspire for the universality of CK One and still you must be willing to absorb more. Until all you can see on the dance floor are people packaged in a way that brings fire to your loins. Until the music becomes the only thing that is important and dancing becomes the only thing separating you from another person. And if you're lucky you get to go home with the girl. These are things that define the club culture in Cape Town, not racial politics.

We relax on the bench and watch swallows going in and out of a tall palm tree. Tshepo does his best to hide his sadness but I can see it spilling out from the corner of his eye and can hear it in his sigh. It unnerves me to see him like this because I don't know what to say. And that isn't like me, or rather, I don't like being in that position.

"Rehearsal's going well," I say after a while, "I'm playing this American blues singer. I'm enjoying the character."

"What's the play called?" he says, a bit unenthusiastically.

"'Millie's piano'. It's a period piece. 1940s, anyway." I trail off into silence again.

"Sorry, I just feel quiet," he says.

"Do you want to go back inside?" I ask him, hoping a little that he'll say yes.

"No, it's nice to be outside. I don't get to be outside much."

"I think I finally met someone I like," I say to change the subject.

"You're not comfortable about me talking about this," he replies.

"Are you asking me or telling me?" I respond.

He laughs a little, the way people do when they try to disguise their real emotion.

"Mmabatho, if I can't talk to you about it – then ..." he says and chooses his words carefully, "then who can I talk to? I mean, I consider you my friend."

I look at him with the guilt I've been avoiding.

"I just don't want to upset you," I say pathetically. It's the best I can do.

"You can't upset me. Don't you understand if you're going to be walking on egg shells around me I'm going to pick it up? I think I know what your problem is."

"What is it?"

"We talk about things we have in common. Let's face it, right down to the kind of schools we went to. We know everything about each other. There's a lot that's shared and unsaid. But now here's something you have no experience of. You can't really relate to this. This is my experience," he says earnestly.

I suck my teeth at him and say, "I've known plenty of crazy people."

"Ja, but you've never been crazy yourself," he simply says and looks at me with a wounded expression. Sometimes I don't think when I speak.

A pang of guilt attacks me again. "Sorry, I didn't mean it like that."

"That's just my point. You don't know what it's like. You and everyone outside this place," he tells me.

"Fine, I admit it. But I mean is this all we're going to be talking about?"

"No," he says, hurt, "but I hope I can open up to you when I need to."

"Of course," I say.

"Don't be so casual about it."

"Let's not start patronising each other."

We sit again in silence, the birds chirping in the tree. Two patients walk past us. I watch them carefully and try to notice anything weird about their gestures. But there's nothing unusual about them. They both look ordinary like people I might pass in Obs although they could use a comb and they look scruffy. The fact that they look untidy doesn't offend me. I mention it because it's the only thing I can pick up which seems different about them.

As much as I hate to admit it, perhaps Tshepo is right. Perhaps I feel a little threatened that he knows more about some things than me. I don't know what to say, my tongue is all tied up. It's not an entirely comfortable feeling, not knowing what to say to a close friend.

"What's the food like?" I venture.

"Mostly boiled. It's crap," he says easily.

"And the people?"

"You don't want to know," he says. I take it as a sign that he doesn't want to talk about it and don't press him.

"So do you still think it's the zol?" I ask.

"I used to. I'm not sure any more," he says and lets out a heavy sigh.

" Zol is not for everyone."

"Ja, but you see, no one told me that. I din't realise that. There are a lot of weird people in Obs and Cape Town. People I don't think I'd like to know too well. And I smoked with them. You know what I'm driving at?" he says, an intense look on his face.

"So you think ba ho loyile?" I say.

"I know it sounds strange, but."

"It doesn't," I reassure him, "There are a lot of people into weird shit, people who wouldn't mind fucking with a person."

"So anyway that's what I'm beginning to think. I never thought I'd say I believe in witchcraft but there you have it."

"In Cape Town you'd be surprised. People are into Wicca and all sorts of things. And of course le dingaka diteng."

"Don't tell me about masangoma. I have my suspicions about certain people already. But I'm still willing to try zol," he says stubbornly.

"After everything you went through. I think you're foolish," I say even though I wanted to say crazy. "I would never repeat something if I knew that it would destroy me like that."

"Destroy. I wouldn't put it like that."

"Then how would you say it?"

"It's not something I'd like to repeat but there were a lot of things that I'm trying to makes sense of that happened to me. It's hard to explain. How can I say? You know like the idea of synchronicity?"

"Ja."

"I experienced it with frightening intensity. There was a period during one of the days when I was just walking around Cape Town when everything made sense and everyone seemed to be communicating with me," he says looking at me.

"Isn't that being delusional?"

"I knew you'd say that. That's why I never bothered saying it before. The thing is there are certain things that just aren't worth telling you or anyone who hasn't been here. You just wouldn't understand," he says, sounding a little bitter.

He breaks into far off silence again, solitude about him.

"How long have we known each other?" I ask him after a while.

"Just under a year."

"I don't think I've ever seen you depressed until now."

"You sound a little disappointed," he says, his expression impassive.

"No, I was just saying it. I suppose you've never seen me."

"Oh, but I have. After you broke up with David. Remember? You were a mess," he reminds me.

"A mess I'd rather forget," I say quickly.

"You said you'd met someone," he begins, perhaps tired of talking about himself.

"Ja," I smile.

"Well, this person must have a name," he teases me, his mood becoming sunnier.

"His name is Arne."

One of the male nurses calls us back. Tshepo gets annoyed, a brooding solitude returning.

"We better go," he says and gets up.

We hug and look at each other as though to say things will work out.

"I don't know when I can come again but I will," I say to him – I know how seriously he takes his promises. We go our separate ways. I walk home briskly.

I run a long bath, burn plenty of oriental incense and cook myself pasta with a spicy Mexican sauce. Later Arne calls. I'm happy to hear from him and enjoy the vertigo of the early days in a new relationship. He tells me that he misses me but with a tenderness that is believable. We go out for a drink in town at the Piano Lounge and meet his friends, two rowdy and slightly irritating South African guys from Pretoria. We drink lots, play pool and smoke a joint between us. He keeps asking me if I'm alright the way men do when you become a little quiet. I think about Tshepo and wonder what he is doing. Arne's friends eventually pick up two Australian girls looking for a taste of "something indigenous and smelling of Castle lager". Odd as that sounds, they appear to be sincere about looking for two blokes to do unspeakable things with. I have little expectations from men but at least I can pick out the boys from the men, I say to myself watching the two girls flirt with them. I suppose that's why women don't like me and why most of my friends are men; I'm quick to criticise. Other women hate me for it. My mother is like that and so is my grandmother. And they also claim women don't like them.

We leave when it starts getting crowded and go in his tired second hand XR3. He likes to have my hand on his thigh when he drives. I don't mind really as long as it stays there. There are certain things I won't do for men.

He takes me to his little flat in Rondebosch. We go up an old elevator and walk down a noisy corridor brimming with students. We pass some Indian students that stare at us accusingly as we walk by as if we're about to do something wrong. The girls say something treacherous under their breath. I ignore them. I'm used to it. Coconut, trash, confused, needy, cheap, desperate, pathetic, tiekieline – I've heard it all before from the same kind of people as them. It used to upset me till I realised that it's them with the problem, not me.

Arne wears a lecherous look on his face and brushes my bum with a large hand. I think he works out.

"You hardly said anything the whole evening," he says and kisses me behind the ear the way I like, once we're inside.

"It was loud in there," I make up an excuse.

"Good, because I was beginning to think you were bored with me," he says and continues kissing me. That's what I like about zero men, they're so insecure. It's easy to keep them guessing.

We kiss till we land up on his large bed, the only real furniture in his room. His table is a wooden box covered with a Hawaii print sarong and two empty crates make chairs. I excuse my self and go to his bathroom. And then I do what sensible women my age do. I scratch in my little Tibetan pouch and take out condoms and a diaphragm. A woman can never be too prepared for sex.

When I return the light is dimmer. He's put a scarf over his lamp. I smile at him and watch him undress. "Come here you," he says and presses me against his large bare torso. I run my hand over his finely sculpted torso. He nibbles my earlobes and fondles my breasts. I squeeze his tight bum. He begins to take off his pants. That's what I like about foreign men; they know how to get a woman in bed. There's no pussy footing when it comes to sex, no silly games or awkwardness that eventually comes out in a clumsy and off-putting blunt request for sex. Some of the things men have said in their desperation to bed me have been less than charming or tolerable.

His pants slide off his legs but I feel a sudden coldness on my leg as we stand naked, our bodies pressing against each other. I look down and realise that he's wearing a prosthesis on his lower leg. I gasp and nearly fall but he holds me.

"Do you mind?" he asks nonplussed.

"No, but you should have told me," I say getting out of his arms to regain my footing.

"What's there to tell? So my leg is like this," he says with unexpected ease.

He walks to me again and kisses me.

"I don't like surprises," I say as he caresses the small of my back.

"I'll remember that," he promises, the faint smell of men's deodorant intoxicating me.


ZEBRON

Once a week on Thursdays I see my psychologist. They are difficult sessions because I make things hard for him by refusing to communicate much. He's younger than me, probably in his early thirties and with that optimistic look of a person who has his whole life ahead of him. Perhaps I'm difficult because things are so easy for him. You can tell he's happy, that he thinks much of life. It's shows in the way he dresses, in the things he says to encourage me to speak. He's always sunny with the persistence of a tenacious Chihuahua. I don't blame him for my problems but he makes an easy target for dislike.

"I want to talk more about this woman you say you killed," he says after asking me a set of routine questions. "And don't look so negative, you might just find this useful."

I ignore him. Maybe five minutes will pass.

"Zebron, I thought we decided that it would be best if you told me when you don't want to talk about something," he says in a parental tone.

"Have you ever raped anyone?" I ask him and look into his eyes. "Have you ever been a little rough with a woman. Ever felt her strength giving in under you?"

"No, but tell me more," he says leaning into me.

"I don't think you have the balls to understand what I'm talking about," I say and sink back into reticence. A few minutes go by.

"I had a girlfriend once who liked me to tie her up," he ventures.

"You're lying," I tell him, "you couldn't even tie up a little dog if you had to. But at least you're trying."

He says nothing and makes notes.

"It irritates me when you do that," I tell him.

"Is that why you won't speak?"

"Maybe."

He puts down his pen and looks at me. I look at the clock and look at him.

"They paid me to do it," I begin, "We were only supposed to shoot her. But I got turned on by her fear. She looked so scared, so innocent. I liked that. I had to have her. We all had her. I don't like flies. Why can't you people do something about them? In my room, there are so many of them."

"You were talking about this woman," he reminds me.

"I'm not stupid." I raise my voice a little. "Don't you think I know what I was talking about? You're asking me these questions that are taking me to places I don't think you want to hear about. You've never had to kill anyone. Never had to wash your hands and clothes because they were stained with somebody's blood."

"You're right, I've never had to do those things," he admits. "Does it bother you that you did them?"

"Don't ask me stupid questions. That's too easy," I tell him.

"Okay, then what do you think I should be asking you?" he offers, his patience running thin.

"I'm not the psychologist," I tell him.

We remain quiet for a while, a little tense. He shuffles his feet and crosses his legs.

"I think you're evil," he finally says, "not because I think you killed someone but because you have no feeling, no compassion. What do you think?"

He looks at me with the intensity of someone who genuinely doesn't like me. He's never done that before – opening up like that.

Perhaps he's trying to provoke me, I say to myself, a little excited by the idea.

"You're being honest. I like that," I say, feeling calm. "You think I care that you think I'm evil. You think I never thought about that. When I was growing up my father used to beat me up and sometimes he didn't need a reason. I would take it out on my little sister. When no one was at home I would force her to have sex with me. It was nice. It made it easier to live when I heard her cry. Can you understand that? I was broken a long time ago. Don't tell me about evil. Once a year during Christmas my father, he was a tsosti, he would clean up. We would sit like a family, drink and eat and look happy even though we were not happy. And he would get poep drunk till he passed out. And just for that couple of days when he was passed out after drinking, my mother, my sister and me, we would all moer him. Bliksem him while he was out. And that poephol didn't bruise easily. You had to work at it. And in the morning when he woke up with bruises we told him he fell or that after drinking he went out with his chommies. It was Christmas, lots of hip hip hooray and all that happy stuff, the idiot always believed us. He never suspected. Those few days are what I remember about my childhood. So don't tell me about evil, it's always been there. I never invited it."

"Do you still see your father?" he asks in that clinical, detached tone of his.

"How can I still see him when I'm in here?" I shout at him.

"I mean when you're out there … I meant to say when you're out there," he says a little irritated with me.

"I left home when I was eighteen. Aren't we supposed to be talking about me?" I say getting annoyed.

"Why are you getting so agitated?" he asks flexing and relaxing his fingers to remain calm.

"Because you're making me mal. We're supposed to be talking about me not my fucking father."

"Okay, let's talk about you, Zebron. Is that what you want?" I can hear the condescending tone in his voice.

"I was telling you about the flies," I say distractedly. I get worked up easily and I hate the way my thoughts get scattered when I'm angry.

"Actually, you were telling me about this woman you raped," he says.

"I was. Anyway, it doesn't matter. She was a silly bitch. I enjoyed shooting her. She didn't stop crying, couldn't shut up."

"Like your sister," he says, "when you raped her."

"My sister? She's also a bitch. She poisoned my mother against me. Sies, my sister. She's Rattex. I hate her."

"Is that why you raped her?"

"Didn't you listen? Didn't you hear what I said? Why do you want me to repeat myself?" I say raising my voice, foaming at the corners of my mouth.

"Zebron, you're getting agitated, calm down. We're only talking," he says.

"Yes, but you must bloody listen," I reprimand him.

His head bent forward as if concealing his feelings, he curls his fingers into a fist but then he relaxes and opens his palm only to brush away a fly on his neck.

"The flies they're everywhere?" I tell him, "they're little messengers, little spies. People are always listening always watching."

"Which people?" he asks almost bored.

"Them down there," I say and point to the ground.

"What do you mean down there?" Some people shouldn't be allowed to open their mouths.

"Don't you know anything? They're listening, you know? They want to hear what we're talking about. And then later when you're not here they're going to ask me to do bad things," I say and laugh. "I'm used to them."

"Are they the same people who asked you to rape your sister?" he asks.

"Why are you going on about that? So what if I raped my sister. I told you she's a silly bitch. She deserved it. These flies are everywhere," I say and swat away two flies with my hand.

"What else do these people tell you to do?" he says.

"You ask too many questions. I don't like you when you do that. Why are you looking at me like that?"

"How am I looking at you?" he stares.

"Like you're looking at a dog, man. I'm not stupid!" I yell and slam my hand on the table.

"I don't like you but this is my job," he tells me finally, battling to restrain his irritation with me. "You are too cold even to be called mentally sick."

"I like you better when you're honest," I say unaffected.

"No, you don't, you thrive on conflict."

I suck my teeth at him.

"You're just annoyed that I didn't get angry with you when you said that." He reaches for his annoying notepad again.

"You people don't realise what it means to be here. You're still a lighty," I say and look into his eyes aggressively. "You think just because I know how to talk properly you can do something with my mind. I know how you guys work. Why isn't anyone helping Unathi?"

"Because we don't have a psychologist who can speak Xhosa for the moment," he explains.

"Kak. Because you think he's too lost. You people choose who you want to help. You don't fool me. You check me, I can speak properly when I have to because I know how you moegoes think. You and all the other whites I stole from. I know what the baas wants to hear. Me, I'm from the township you check. My father, hy was 'n kleurling, you check. But my mother uyathetha ngumxhosa, you check. My father used to beat her because he looked like her. He wasn't coloured enough, Masbieker, and he hated that. So I finished school because I was clever and went to Fort Hare, so what? I know I'm not stupid. I don't need to hear that from anyone. You mustn't think just because I go off on my own things in my head I'm stupid, you check. I'm a chameleon, I can be anyone. Jy's mos 'n lighty. Ek is nege en dertig jaar oud you see my friend. Thirty nine years old. Ja, me, I'm old. I'm not a child. You're still coming into your thirties. I've done things and seen things that would give your mother a heart attack. So just be careful how you speak to me nè?"

"You're not intimidating me," he says, anger in his voice, "I know how you operate. You intimidate everyone until you get your way. That's why you refuse to speak sometimes."

"You haven't been inside yourself deep enough to start telling me what you think I am. You haven't confronted the worst about your-

44

self, my friend. You don't know what really lies in your heart. You don't. You think life is nice that's why you wear powder blue shirts and smile like that. Huh … You don't know what real fear can make you do. What it's like to be called mad. But you dare tell me who you think I am," I let him know.

"So then tell me what it's like to be mad," he says scribbling in his insufferable notepad.

"There isn't enough paper to go around," I say and switch off. I look at the clock above his head and see that only ten minutes remain. Time best spent being quiet, I say to myself and stare at the wall blankly. After a while he gives up and lets me go.

In the afternoon I see my psychiatrist and he gives me my weekly injection. It calms me down and makes the voices stay away but my arse always hurts for two days afterwards. And when I'm alone with my thoughts I can see who I am and not feel scared. I can look around me and not feel persecuted all the time, always wondering who is watching me.

When I start hearing voices, the world becomes darker. Shadows seem to have a sinister life of their own. It's like someone has just broken into my house and won't leave. It's like living with an intruder and being scared of moving around. You have no privacy, no sense of security and you're always scared because all your thoughts are not private. When you can't run away in your mind, it's like being banished into nothingness. There's nowhere else to run to, no shelter to take refuge in. When you don't have the privacy of your thoughts you stop respecting life, you begin to see that you are just a scribble of flesh and breath, someone else's toy and amusement. You're just a joke and people are laughing at you. They're thinking he's a joke. Look at him he's a joke. That's why you look at people suspiciously. Because you know that everyone knows your thoughts. They know what you're thinking and they think you're a joke, a moegoe. And the voices, the terrible voices that come from darkness, make you do terrible things to make them go away, to keep everyone out. So that no one must know how much ugliness there is inside you. It's enough to know that I'm rotten, I don't need everyone else to know by hearing my thoughts.

That stupid psychologist was trying to get to me by insulting me. Insult? I've gone beyond the pain of hearing terrible things. There are infinitely worse things than hearing a few nasty words being directed at me. Life is too creative, too abstract, it finds more sinister ways to torture some of us, the rotten ones lying at the bottom of the barrel.

No, for us it is not enough to simply scratch the surface by hearing a few ugly things or getting a regular beating which you soon feel you deserve. For some of us, it is not enough that we are already broken, fallen angels falling further. Life pulverizes our faith by corrupting everything about us, our feelings and our minds. When the decay begins, it doesn't stop before it becomes the only thing left. For some of us it is not enough that we suffer, we must become suffering so that there should be religion and prayers and clergymen bent to the insular will of God. So that doctors and psychologists and silly people who think they're doing us a favour can congratulate themselves tirelessly, their deeds religious instalments for the next paradise. So that people can sleep safe at night when they rest because the really sick people are locked away while they snore peacefully. So that people can feel better about themselves because somebody else has it worse off.

Some of us have had to learn quickly in order to survive. I've had to be inventive, headstrong, self-centred, cruel. It takes strength to be cruel. I know how to shut off music, let alone people. I know where to go when I want to be alone. When I want to feel my destruction in private, in silence. I know what I need even at times when I'm too stubborn to take it. This is life. I'm not sure if it's mine for the claiming. But I'm always making a plan for myself. I've stepped on others, crushed the infirm, robbed the innocent and violated the little good that came my way. I don't fear hell. I know it. I live it. I've already fallen far enough. There's nowhere else left to go. Things couldn't get any worse. I've had the worst. What remains is for me to be destroyed forever. Annihilated. To cease to exist. And that in itself would be a relief, a strange blessing. I've thought about suicide but the truth is I'm too vain and stubborn to do it. It would be like accepting defeat, admitting the ugly truth about myself, exposing my cards to whatever's out there. There are better ways, not beautiful, just better ways of getting through. This is how things have been. I have no reason to think otherwise.

I don't speak to anyone here except Tshepo. I don't think he likes me but that doesn't bother me. It's not important to me. People put too much faith and importance in each other. I'm not looking for a best friend or a soul mate, just someone to help pass the time. I think he could also use the company because he also keeps to himself.

"When was the last time you had a real hard-on? When was the last time you felt like skommeling?" I ask him. We are sitting in the lounge during OT and the TV doesn't work.

"Come to think of it, I can't remember," Tshepo says, a coy look on his face.

"That's what I thought," I say satisfied.

"And you?"

"The same, can't remember. They medicate the food, you know."

"You think?" he says and pulls a face, the naïve expression of somebody finding his way in life. It makes me want to squash him, to harm him the way children and animals instinctively target the weaker ones. It's his eyes, they give away too much. It's not easy understanding where these impulses fighting inside myself come from but it's enough that at least I can control them, sometimes.

"Think about it. How else can they get us to be so passive? I mean we're all healthy, all full of hormones like other guys."

"But isn't it in our medication?"

"Nonsense. It's in the food," I tell him.

He thinks about it and makes up his own mind. For a while we are quiet but my eyes roam. When he's not looking I stare at him. He can be so serious for his age.

"Andile is about to lose it," I say and pat him on the shoulder.

"Isn't he the one who killed his wife?" he asks.

"Look," I tell him and point to Andile taking off his shirt and pants. We watch intently.

"Rebecca Malope," he starts shouting, "Rebecca Malope, she's the best."

The others ignore him while he stands there naked.

"Rebecca. Rebecca Malope! Rebecca Malope, she's the best!" he carries on.

Sipho comes and bundles him off to the kulukutz.

"There's nothing they can do for him once he starts. He's better off on his own," I say and Tshepo looks shocked.

"How can you say that? It's hell in the kulukutz," he says. "I wouldn't wish it on my worst enemy."

We hear Andile shouting about Rebecca. His voice trails off in the recesses of the ward.

"Did he really kill his wife?" he asks.

"It's not such a long story. He told me about it. But his wife was a silly cow. What happened is that they went out drinking in Langa one night and went home drunk. I could never do that with a woman. So they go home and he goes outside for a while, you know, for a 69. But he was drunk, so the poor fool was probably trying to find his zip and everything. I think he said he passed out for a while.

"Anyway, he comes back only to find his wife with another man in the kitchen. The silly bitch had a boyfriend, you know how women get when you let them drink a little. So this woman tells him to fuck off in front of her boyfriend. She says voertsek wena and starts performing, talking shit. She was a phuza face with a dirty mouth, you know the kind that get ugly after a dop. Eventually this other fool says why can't you get it, she doesn't want you, or something like that. Well that was it. That's when he says he lost it. He grabbed a knife from the drawer and went straight for him. And you know what happened?"

"What?" he says his eyes wide with curiosity.

"The coward pushes the wife in front before the knife gets to him. So he ends up stabbing her by accident. Got her in this part here," I say and point to my neck, "what do they call it?"

"The jugular," he says.

"Ja, that's where they got her. It was a messy death. The cops got him and managed to certify him. One time. He says he never bothered to tell them his story because he knew he was drunk. And who would believe a drunk?"

"What a coward that guy was," he says to me.

"What a bitch she was," I say to him. "She deserved to die. The silly bitch. I would have killed them both if it was my wife. But she would never do that to me."

"You're married," he says surprised.

"Why are you so shocked?"

"It's just that uh ... well, you don't seem like the type to get married," he says carefully.

"Why?"

"Because you don't like people," he says. Sometimes too much honesty irritates me even though I'm the first to tell my psychologist otherwise.

"You're full of shit. I don't like your face when you say stupid things like that," I say just to ruffle his feathers. He mustn't get too comfortable with me, I remind myself.

He tells me to piss off, a wounded look on his face. A violent image of me shooting him with a 9 mm dashes through my head, momentarily making my head spin. It's as if I'm temporarily possessed when that happens.

He sulks at me and moves to the other side of the room, but I know he'll snap out of it. He has that ability. It's great and it's annoying to watch. I'm not used to seeing people getting over things, especially here. I've seen too many glum faces succumb to their trials, to drugs, to Valkenberg. Once people go through ward 12, 13, 14 or 15 there isn't much hope of full recovery and integration into society. I've seen it happen too often. It's too big an adjustment for them. They always come back sooner or later the same way. What haunted them and brought them to Valkenberg in the first place returns as soon as they get home. They end up bouncing between the outside and Valkenberg. Two months at home, three months at Valkenberg, four months at home, two months at Valkenberg and so on. Till they eventually get certified. Once that happens they can't drive, they can't vote, they can't open a bank account, they might as well be called children. The drugs take over and fill the vacuum. The drugs suck all initiative from their veins till what you have are grown men taking four naps a day, usually passed out on the floor or on the lawn outside. And the families stop calling or they start making excuses every time they have to see them. Eventually they lose interest in life, they give up even to the point of not washing properly. Okay, so the nurses are partly to blame for that because they are so impatient with us, but come on, they are grown men.

But I don't see that with Tshepo. He still has too much fight in him, too much voertsek like Unathi says. But he hasn't learned the rules. I don't think anyone bothered to teach him. You can see it in his behaviour. It's his way to be alone. He's used to doing things by himself. And I think he has had his share of bad friendships. I can see it clearly. They are all smoking his Swazi in his flat. Probably eating his food while one of them is screwing his girlfriend in his bed. And they do this often without him ever waking up to this. And he considers them good friends. But I wouldn't blame them, I'd do the same myself. He has that irresistible quality about him that just makes you want to abuse him.

He is plotting to escape. That is how much he wants to leave. That is how desperate he is, how committed to freedom he is. His freedom means the world to him. It's sickening, the way he speaks about wanting to leave. You'd think he was always in solitary confinement. Most days I'm just content that in here at least I have three regular meals and a place to put my head at night. Ja, it's lousy in here but it's worse out there if anyone asks me. I feel pathetic when I consider that I squandered away my freedom during my youth. I was too restless, drifting for much of my twenties. My early years were a series of mistakes and why-nots that eventually led me to marry Kena and father a girl whom I rarely see. Education is not for everyone. It made me a pompous criminal. I was clueless and headstrong, the man, indoda. It was always this way. I was always right. Screw the woman.

Tshepo is not like that. He is the type of guy who probably navigates all his relationships carefully, always with the kind of effusive optimism that makes me sick. There are no five minute quickies without a condom or needles crawling up his arm for a shot of heroin's multiple orgasm. He fears Aids. They all do nowadays. He fears death. In a way he respects life because he fears death. He fears not being able to do the many things going through his mind. I can see his mind going a thousand miles ahead with all the millions of things he is going to do once he gets discharged. That kind of optimism is nauseating because it must consume so much energy to be always looking ahead, to be always concentrating on the race and not the moment. We're different in that respect. I'm too caught up in the moment, in what was said to me yesterday and how I will get my revenge. These are things that I think about.

I wonder why people like him always get their parts caught in the grinder. It's plain to see that he's a decent chap, a nice guy, someone my daughter would be interested in. Why does life always give him a raw deal? I think it's because life is mischievous. It is trouble, it's messy. Life can't resist getting him mixed up and watching him untangle himself and getting out of the mess. Life knows that people will always be watching him. His persistence and bookish smile, they're things that people remember about him.

People like Tshepo make perfect targets for sarcasm or butts of jokes but at least they grow up to be men unlike the rest of us who grow up fearing our kids so much that we end up beating them. And life beats us back and we take it out on our wives. That's why I can never truly like someone like him. He reminds me too much of the distance between us, the gulf that seems to stretch forever. Tshepo will always do right. He has that stubborn streak in him, that nauseating capacity that we all think is for sissies and moffies. He's the kind of person likely to believe that kingdoms are won on dreams, that behind every opportunity lies a diamond of knowledge. You hear this kind of crap everywhere. It never moves me beyond mild irritation. My anger and pain are too real, when I take my medicine the side effects of constipation are too real. No bumper sticker philosophies help me through difficult moments. It makes my life easier to know who my enemies are, who

will betray me, he says. But the truth is he doesn't know who his enemies are. They're almost always a step ahead of him because he's so
trusting. No real good ever comes of anyone foolishly trusting. Life is
too stingy. It makes you work. He will be shocked if I tell him that I
ratted out Byron. I'm helping the poor bastard. I want him to get out.
There is a life to live out there, even if it means getting into deeper shit
but at least he should go out there. Smoking ganja in the toilets is
only going to keep him here longer.

I want Byron to leave but he's thick. He's bloody lazy. He has sharp
eyes, he can see something immediately and understand it but he
doesn't use his mind like Tshepo. He is the other child every mother
always worries about in every family. Byron, die stout een, people will
say when they refer to him. He is the one who learns the rules too
early and gets them all mixed up. The one who cheats his way through
school till he gets expelled in Standard Eight. He is the one with
friends, the one who always gets invited to parties and gets all the popular girls, the ones who paint their faces with cheap make-up and regularly run to abortion clinics, tiekielines. And he lives for the good times.
He doesn't really care about anybody but himself. What is true friendship anyway, he thinks? For hopeless romantics and Care-Bears like
his big brother Tshepo. Ag, he sees through that sentimental crap.
Hy's mos 'n windgat, 'n slim ou, Byron. He is the middle child. He
has his own grudges with life. He goes through life like a soldier, taking hostages when he can and usually getting away with murder.

At Valkenberg he thinks he can see it all – the score, the ward system and the corrupt staff. It's all bullshit to him. He is meant for better places, the high road, not a fucking institution with losers. I'll be
out soon, I've got friends in high places he tells himself. And one of
his shady friends will rescue him only to trap him in his own web of
trickery. For Byron it's all about now, this minute. It's all about money,
about looking good in a pair of Soviets and white Converse tackies.
It's about being a Jita, posing with thug life, listening to Tupac and
taking lots of drugs. What will Magents say if they see him now? Nothing. Or if they have anything to say they'll say he was a barie, a stupid
moegoe, mpintshi. They won't say anything about the good times or
how they value his friendship. It's all about convenience and some
people are convenient to know. Byron doesn't value anything or anyone. Everything has a price in his eyes, why not people? He's a real
houtkop but mother loves him anyway.

"Byron, when are you going to straighten out like your brother

Tshepo?" mother always says. And he shrugs his shoulders at her. She says it for his own good but he never sees it that way. Instead he grows up resenting his own brother Tshepo, the one who went to UCT and college but ended up a malkop from smoking too much ganja. Fuck, he's useless in Byron's eyes. Ganja? How can anyone go to a madhouse for ganja? Byron's been smoking it since he was twelve. Ag, his brother is pathetic. Nyani, what's his problem? He probably can't hold his drink either. The two never go out together. Byron is too ashamed. This is my brother Tshepo, he says and scratches the back of his head with embarrassment. It always makes Tshepo feel like shit but he takes it because Byron is family. And family is family, you can't divorce it.

Your brother … what's wrong with him? He doesn't drink, doesn't roll with Magents and he's too nice to his cherries. Is he a faggot, a fruit? the Jitas will tease him. And that always makes Byron feel awkward, ashamed. Tshepo knows what they think about him. But what hurts him most is his brother never defending him and always running back to the same idiot friends who stab him behind the back as soon as he turns. Byron will steal Tshepo's jackets for these idiots. He'll steal money and get into arguments with everyone at home on their account. It's not fair that I have him for a brother, he will say of Tshepo. Why does he always have to be so sensible? Fuck, he can loosen up a little. And that walk of his, can't he put a little spring and walk like a Jita or at least pretend when they are around? Like so, just bounce a little, don't be in such a hurry to walk. Fuck, why can't he at least pretend, is that so much to ask for? Why is he my brother?

This is what Byron's like, the naughty child who was too eager to be born. And he doesn't understand what women see in his brother. He doesn't understand why they love him so much, all his girlfriends. I could put your looks to better use, he says when he looks at his quiet brother. But he doesn't know the depth of Tshepo's soul, how far he's gone looking for himself. He doesn't know what a lover his brother is, how he makes women swoon. No, for Byron Tshepo is just someone he sees at meal times. Their lives run parallel but their paths never cross. Blood has brought them together. It makes mother sad at times when she looks at them, the one distant in his thoughts, the other aloof and always sure of himself.

At five o'clock they ring the bell for supper. We file towards the dining room, Sipho counting us as we walk past. Tshepo avoids me and sits at the other end of the table. He can be childish. I ignore him and focus on the nurse serving our food. She has a pudgy, forgettable face but her breasts are large and want to spill out of her tight uniform. And her waist is full and curvaceous. I haven't had a woman in a while, I ponder and lick my dry lips. Sipho helps her. They serve us beans, a boiled egg, two slices of bread and lettuce saturated with vinegar. The tea is weak and tepid. We eat slowly, listlessly. When she is not looking, I stare at her voluptuous breasts, stealing perverted moments of pleasure. The things I could do with those jugs. In a shebeen in Langa perhaps I could have had my way with her. She looks like the type who's not too fussy about men, as long as he's clean and pays for my drink, I imagine her saying. Ja, I might even take her to a movie before going home with her. She catches me staring at her and looks the other way. And then she looks back quickly to see if I'm still staring at her. I eat with my face looking at the food. She knew what I was thinking, I say to myself, a little ashamed and annoyed. It is during moments like these when I most despise being a mental patient and when I feel civility ebbing from me. I feel weak and emasculated. Any female nurse becomes cruel simply because she is a woman. And women have breasts, legs and parts that torture me with lust. Like a twisted master dangling a jug of water to a thirsty slave, the nurse seems like a temptress taunting me with her body. I fill my head with violence and the shrill of a woman being raped. It is music in my head and is enough to calm me down, to make the shadows of introspection go away. Perhaps it's not such a bad idea that they medicate the food or whatever they do to make us forget that we are men. But it is cruel that they only make us forget and that like children we are brought back to the harsh reality of being under supervision every time we get an erection.

TSHEPO

I'm tired of this place. During the ward rounds they ask me a lot of questions and I never know how to answer them. My psychologist is a divorced widow, sympathetic and strangely kind. You don't find many kind people in a mental institution. It's the sort of place that doesn't encourage that. It breeds nastiness and ill feelings. There are no unexpected smiles that can lift the veil of depression from you, no spontaneous acts of kindness from other patients or even the staff. Everyone is too consumed by what has brought them here. Sometimes it is hard to appreciate the days that are sunny because there is so much darkness about this place, so much secrecy about the work of the doctors and the staff, so much secrecy even about the way people look at each other. I'm afraid to ask too many questions for fear of the nasty answers that lurk behind closed doors. There is a spirit of evil about this place, it runs through the creaking beds and the cracked walls gathering damp. There is an odious smell devoid of the sterile and comforting cleanliness of a normal hospital. It's hard to ignore this hypnotizing smell that keeps us in perpetual limbo, drifting through the days like exiled zombies.

And this place is not clean. During OT I pace up and down in cramped circles all the time itching from flea bites. We do everything together here, eating, washing, lazing, fading. I have been denied my privacy for so long that I seem to have forgotten what it's like to shit without someone opening the broken door of the toilet. I'm only alone when I go to my bed at night, my mind always restless.

I have a friend here and that is enough for me. His name is Matthew and he's full of sun in his heart, the kind of person who reminds me of the childhood friends I never had and always longed for. We call each other Maestro because we both like the quiet sadness of Cesaria Evora's songs. She sings about lost love with such beauty and clarity of spirit you almost think her sadness is sweet. My story is his story. The world is cruel. It cheated us out of our sanity. Our feet are sore from having walked into all the wrong places and having spoken to all the wrong people. Mental patients with cannabis induced psychosis – that's how they refer to us here. Not Tshepo or Matthew just mental patients. So we call each other Maestro to cheat them, to beat them at their own game and talk about our beloved Cesaria and Sao Tomé. We don't speak much because it takes too much effort just to get through the day. But at night in our beds, when the lights are off and the room settles into snoring we whisper about places we went to and people we met and the music we remember of those occasions. It's always about the music. And then somewhere along the way, when the night grows deeper, we may even give a little detail about what brought us here.

Only God knows what we are doing here. No one else does. The psychiatrists think they do. We are searching, asking, pleading, praying. Love us, we are not mad. Make sure we are alright because sometimes we break easily, that is our unspoken message because we have broken past speech. We always need best friends because they give the best love. And that's what we need, the best love. Our reputations have been ruined by labels and gossip. Who really knows why we are here? Perhaps we are also doing secret work like the doctors – equally important because we don't understand it ourselves. Perhaps we are learning how to see again while straining at the music of the sane. Perhaps our madness is a kind of language, a playful trick that our naughty subconscious is playing on us. And if it is a language it might be called the language of the unspoken or of the deaf and blind because it is so personal. It is a strange blessing to walk around in a room filled with people who spend so much time together, yet who don't know each other and to know that your pain is the only thing you can truly claim as your own. In an institution you are reminded of your difference, of the strange, unique colouring that makes you who you are when you see others succumb to infinite tortures. There is an infinity of stories in each of us. I have spoken about my childhood enough to fill both the Micro and Macro Encyclopedia. I've had enough. Some things are best left unsaid. In silence maybe they will get resolved.

When I ask them why they are still keeping me here they tell me that it is for observation. Observation my foot, most of the time I walk around purposelessly while the staff idle away their time talking about the previous night's jol.

So I have made up my mind, I'm going to break out of here before it destroys what's left of my sanity. I must leave. My spirit is shrinking. I'm fading with depression as each day passes. I have to do something. There's a small broken window at the back of the toilets. I'm sure I can climb though it. Byron says once you abscond from here they don't bother to come running after you. I plan to escape with him. Zebron knows but says nothing. I know he disapproves, I just hope he won't rat us out.

I sleep little and think a lot about escaping. I even dream about it. They are lucid, intense dreams that always leave me confused because they make so much sense. In them I see myself climbing through the window and running away with Byron. But what strikes me about these dreams is that I am always running, yet there doesn't seem to be anyone chasing me. When I wake up in the morning I'm filled with desperation as if the phantom I was running away from in my dreams is slowly closing in on me.

Mmabatho comes to visit on the day of our escape. It is an unusually cold day and she wears her heavy angora coat which falls to her ankles. She wears it with the collar up, concealing part of her face as though she has something to hide. And a beanie covers the rest of her head. I'm always awed at how different she seems to appear by just playing with her clothes. You can divine what her mood is just from the way she's dressed. Today she looks difficult and moody. On me clothes seem to merely hang and not make much of a statement. I'm too practical when it comes to clothes and don't give them much attention. But Mmabatho's clothes are lived in, they're comfortable and fit like a second skin. There's something undeniably personal about them, something that would make them awkward if somebody else tried to wear them. Every item seems to have a story about it, secretly divulging something about her personality. A penchant for eastern things, a prejudice for the Xhosa culture. Her clothes are so much a part of her that it's impossible for me to imagine her naked. The truth about what she looks like underneath would be unsettling. It would be like seeing an ostrich but with all its feathers plucked.

We go for a casual walk around the grounds. The idea of escaping comes to me. I could just not return, I ponder to myself, and just leave. And I said I'd meet Byron at the back anyway. I don't see why I have to go through that window, I say to myself, suddenly feeling uneasy about escaping through a window. I tell Mmabatho about my plan. She berates me and tells me that I'm being stupid and crazy. That's exactly what will keep you in this place forever, she says. She goes on for a while, telling me all the reasons why I should stay. Crushed by her lack of support I respond with anger. It's hell in here, I tell her. You wouldn't survive half a day. We wrestle with words while we walk. I'm going to do it anyway, I finally tell her. She says nothing, upset in her silence. We continue walking and meet Byron near the administration building. We take a stroll to the back of the hospital where there is large hole in the fence. I walk nervously, my heart thumping in my inner ear.

When we get to the hole, Byron goes through first. I look at Mmabatho and see that she is hesitant.

"Tshepo, I'm not doing this," she tells me. "This is wrong. I should be taking you back."

"It's not a crime," I tell her, "We're just walking out and they're not going to come looking for me."

"Are you coming or not?" Byron yells agitated. He starts walking towards the highway. Cars mill past dangerously fast.

"Mmabatho ke eng ya nong? Let's go," I say and take her wrist but she pulls away.

"Tshepo, I'm not going," she tells me stubbornly.

"Fine, then I'm leaving you here," I tell her and turn towards the fence. Byron is safely on the other side. He walks briskly and doesn't turn back.

"Tshepo, wait," she suddenly says. I turn back and watch her, impatient and nervous that someone will spot me.

"I'll meet you at the station," she says quickly and goes the other way.

I go through the hole. I hear her cursing herself as she stomps through the tall wet grass. I hurry to the other side of the highway.

## MMABATHO

I've been seeing a lot of Arne and I don't like it. I don't like it because I like him too much. And it scares me because he could derail my plans. I'm not ready for it, the big one, the final blow, the equaliser which means that sometimes he gets to sleep on the wet spot. It can wait. It doesn't have to come so soon, so unexpectantly. I've still got to finish my studies, work abroad, make some money and perhaps have a few dangerous affairs with married men and write a steamy novel about it.

He comes for me after classes. We always go somewhere – the park, explore the wine route or just laze around naked in his bed in between sessions of aerobic sex. Or sometimes I sit in the other room in his flat and do my work while he reads a book in bed. Or sometimes we just vegetate in front of the TV on Sunday while the Sunday Times lays sprawled in dissected sections across the room.

It's not as if he doesn't have friends, because he does. We're always going out with them and they seem interesting, the sort of people I'd imagine he'd want to see every now and then just to get away from the girlfriend. But we're always together. It's inexplicable, really, because I thrive on being alone. I don't know how I let this one get to my soft spot without seeing the signs, the irrepressible signs of meeting a potential partner. I'm not ready for it because I bargained for a zero guy, a type, not a partner. I know zero guys well, they're easy to figure out. So I don't understand why I like Arne so much, because he fits the profile.

And when we are together we don't fight. It's not that I like fighting but I don't know what to make of this. There's no tension in the relationship, just two people who get along and that makes me edgy because I always expect the crunch to be just around the corner. Sooner or later he will disappoint you, I hear myself thinking. My friend Ntabiseng keeps telling me that I look happy. In some circles when a woman says that to another woman that's a nice way of telling her that she's being colonised by her boyfriend, that she's become one of those women whose lives revolve around their men. They know their schedules, their favourite beer, sporting dates, the things that turn them off and everything else that goes with being with a dominant can-you-scratch-my-back guy. So naturally I felt a little insulted when I heard that I looked happy. I'm the sort of person who takes being a woman seriously, perhaps a little too seriously. Perhaps I'm being too sensitive.

And it's not that we talk much. In fact a lot of the time when we're together we're quiet, but it's a comfortable silence of two people who don't need to impress each other. And he doesn't nag me for sex like most zero men, although he does take his exercise seriously. He goes to the gym religiously five times a week and during weekdays he'll catch a few rugby and football games and talk obsessively about it with his friends. If anyone had to see us together in his flat they'd say we'd settled into marital bliss. I can't help it, I like him. I wake up in the morning and I want to feel his rough stubble against my skin. But I'm always cautious and I think he can sense it. I don't let myself be swept away by impulsive emotions and resort to sickening mollycoddling and baby talk that some couples indulge in when they bond. We don't do that ooh baby and honey stuff. And I like it that way. It cuts through the need to please and appear loving. We're just natural with each other. When he's angry, I know it and leave him. And when I'm moody and can't fully realise a character I'm doing in class, he cooks for me and plays a Django Rheinhardt CD.

So I've been feeling a little edgy over the last few days. I keep wondering where this little fairytale is heading, when will the monster emerge. I've been restless and irritable. I didn't see him yesterday. That was the first time in three weeks. I'm scared but I hope I'm not going to sabotage this relationship. I've done it before and I'm sure I can do it again. But I won't this time. I keep telling myself to be a little adventurous, a little dangerous and bet on a zero guy.

It is a relief to see Tshepo, to have someone to speak with intimately. I haven't seen him for a while and I want to tell him so much about Arne. There is much to be said about me liking a man so much. And

I'm sure my excitement will be met with skepticism from him. Maybe his perspective will be just what I need to hear to come down to reality. I admit I've been in a cocoon, that things have been good. Perhaps too good. I don't want to wake up to another shattering realisation. I've had too many disappointments from men.

I'm disappointed when I hear that Tshepo wants to run away and let him know that. I suppose I'm being selfish because I want to talk about Arne and not hear him proposing to run off. There is a desperate look on his face which is hard to ignore as I watch him crawl through a hole in the fence at the back of Valkenberg. Reluctantly I go out the other way and meet him at the station. But I don't like it. I have a bad feeling about him coming out when he should still be inside. Call it women's intuition. You're heading for trouble, I tell him but he ignores me.

### TSHEPO

Time moves slowly in a mental hospital. It forces you to think about things, to scrutinise the events that make up your life. I have been so alone in my thoughts, so isolated in my pain, I have forgotten what it's like to be with people, to be looked at and not look the other way. Often deep into the night I lie awake alone, listening to the gentle scraping of branches against my window. It is so lonely, so silent I can hear the quiet work of trees growing, their branches stretching towards the sky like dancers.

And in the morning when I wake up I search for a blue sky and a golden sun, they are my prayers. I search for the boy I lost along the way and the stranger who looks back at me in the mirror. I miss that boy terribly. I search for the silence that will bring balance again, that gentle happiness that comes with just being alive. I live with too many questions, crying dreams, I mourn too many missed opportunities and failed relationships. I have my ghosts and they always haunt me here. Sometimes depression becomes a companion, an uninvited friend, a guest overstaying his welcome, a bully. And the air becomes thin with hope as I breathe in hard to fight the demons. Sometimes the tight grip of madness closes in on my senses till I feel my wounded spirit cowering, yelping in a dark corner like an injured dog, help me somebody help me, but no one hears. Sometimes the darkness at night is too real and something to fear, lurking with forgotten monsters which memory mysteriously conjures. Sometimes I just pray for the light of day when I will be able to breathe again instead of holding my breath with fear. Sometimes I live for the sun.

There is never enough food to go around here. They keep us on the edge of hunger from one meal to the next. I wonder if it is a kind of therapy. And in our desperation we have become greedy bargaining cigarettes for food, the chance to wear someone's cap for two slices of bread. Yes, I've known hunger and it doesn't go very well with madness. It brings out the worst in you, the beast prepared to steal a scrap of food. I was sick once lying in bed with agonising stomach cramps. Matthew gave me water and it was a great gift because I was thirsty. I woke up the following day feeling even more thirsty. I drank till I was satisfied. It is like that here. You do anything till you feel better even if it means discovering the magic of water.

Every day is hard. And every day is different because moods change. Faces become masks and your silence becomes the cross you bear. You learn to live with pain when you are in here. People imagine that the medicine does it all for you. It doesn't. It may help but it doesn't make things easier. There is still the load to carry, the work to be done.

They are all sleeping, I am the mad one, I sometimes say to myself as I lie awake at night, unable to sleep. The medication keeps me awake. But the silence inside me grows deeper, religious even, as the days go by. In each of us, everyone, there is a seed that was planted deeper than memory, a light that God only lit. Even when we are called insane and commit suicide no one can turn off that light but God. I have seen the centre of my own troubles. It's my little universe and I guard it with my silence. I can hear God calling me inside this place.

Maybe I have seen God and don't know it. Maybe madness is a way of seeing the divine in our small lives. Maybe the one who made the sun out of a piece of fluff is nearer than we think, more playful than we imagine. Maybe God is an old man who lost his children when he turned his back for a while. Sometimes I feel so bad I can feel the earth. I ache for it and play with suicidal thoughts. I keep wondering why must it be so hard. Why must the suffering drag out and suck out the marrow out of my will? And always when I look at myself and attempt to answer this I find more questions with different tempos. Is God listening? Did somebody call my name? Did I see weakness on another's face and still remain in my place? There is an eternity of questions once you begin.

So in my mind just to make things more bearable I think of God as having many children. And some of us are naughty. But some of us are good. And we play in a large playground. And what has happened is that I went strolling out the playground. I went for a walk and told no one. But God knows. Or sometimes I think of myself as the one who sneaked out the back door to go playing. Or that I got sent on an errand but got distracted because I saw things along the way. The thing is, I'm so easily seduced. I know that. I'm always looking, ever conscious that I don't miss out anything. Perhaps I'm not looking where I should be. Perhaps I was looking too hard and fell because I didn't see the trap set for me. There is much to be said about being here, about being a mental patient. But what does it mean to be crazy, to be off your rocker as they say? It means to play with the Big Ones, the Quiet Ones, the Subtle Ones, to play hide and seek. It means not to rely on any devices, any tricks of the intellect; it is only a tool. It is pointless to rely on your own abilities too much. They were given to you, therefore they can be taken away. There are far more interesting ways of getting acquainted with life than through the mind. The mind can trick, she is a false and fickle god who will deceive and disown you at the drop of a hat. All mental patients know that. We once had lives. We were once respected professors, esteemed teachers and students, inspired architects, skilful accountants, vigilant policemen, hard-working labourers, married husbands and contributing citizens. Knowing things isn't as important as doing things. But where did we go wrong, people wonder. That is the question we spend our lives trying to answer.

Every once in a while, a long while, I feel the real warmth of the sun when I go outside. And suddenly the sky is not so far from me. And there is music in the way people walk, in the whisper between plants. In the air that carries so many secrets, so many conversations and messages. Is anyone listening? Does anyone feel the frenetic pace we're going at? Does anyone hear the music of madness? It is a frequency above the humdrum of living and above the conspiracy of satellites and clandestine societies. People are doing secret things while we lie awake at night. They are plotting to take over the world. They are stealing our dreams, preying on our hopes and doing terrible things in the name God.

I've become deeply suspicious of life. Matthew jokes and says that is the occupational hazard of being a mental patient. Sometimes his humour is my only solace. A flitting glance can open another universe. Details fascinate me. Numbers are magic or secret prayers. I mean a seed can grow into an impressive mustard tree or a majestic sequoia. Maybe life is an equation; a swirling, gyrating, impulsive but simple equation. Maybe long ago before sand became land we were just clouds and gas. And simple forms that floated in a soup called space.

I like thinking like this because it takes away the monotony, it affirms my belief that nothing is more abstract than God. It fills me with a little magic. In here you have to improvise, even if it means you have to run away. But I have run away in my mind as far as I can go. It's easy for Mmabatho to say I should stay here. She doesn't know the madness of tolerating a stay in an institution. It can kill you. It can maim your outlook on life. It can make you a stranger even to yourself. There are worse things than losing yourself. There is the nightmare of being found by darkness, demons and things that lurk in places we think are safe. There is the possibility of never being found or of never finding yourself, forever lost in dementia, a tight space smaller than the distance between two letters.

I'm running away to save myself. Staying means putting up with sickness and not allowing myself to heal. It means watching Zebron plant his darkness in the weaker ones for his amusement. It means living like a shadow and fading away with each day. I'm running because it is the best I can do, the only thing that seems possible. Everything else seems dark. I don't know what will happen. I don't know if I will feel better. I don't know anything anymore. Tomorrow the sun will rise, the stars will shine and maybe something will happen.


MMABATHO

**I** meet him at the station. We take a train to town. For a while we say nothing to each other, each in our own thoughts. I feel like a truant schoolkid, uncomfortable that I let him abscond. Tshepo's expression is pensive and distant, perhaps a little sad.

"Aren't you happy to be out of there?" I ask him.

He tries to smile but it comes out as a difficult vulnerable expression, the look of someone trying to hide his pain behind stoicism. He looks out the window as we pass children playing in a quad at a nearby school.

"It's just that I haven't been outside for a while," he says.

I sink back into my seat and catch a glimpse of his profile. His cheekbones stick out obscenely and his cheeks look gaunt. It is a sudden discovery and it shocks me a little. I also stare out the window.

It is a long ride before we get to Cape Town station. Much of the journey we say nothing to each other. Different people sit next to us and get off as the train stops and starts up again. I have always liked train rides. Apart from being the safest way to travel they fill me with a sense of longing for my childhood. I used to travel to Jo'burg by train during the June and December school holidays to meet my excited and waiting father. My parents are divorced. I especially relished the moments when he recognised me in a crowd of people struggling with their baggage. And the way he would run to me and hug and kiss me joyously, profusely in front of strangers. This always embarrassed the older people. I imagined them thinking that this outward show of emotion was a white thing, something we picked up from watching too much television. They would stare at us painfully, disapprovingly. It always irritated me because I couldn't, I refused to blame history. It was too convenient to blame it on apartheid. Their prurient staring revealed just how uncharitable people had become. And how sad it was that their wounds had taught them to look inside too much. "It comes from too much pain, Mamsi, we have gone through a lot as a people," Papa said one year when I told him how much this disturbed me. "The oppressed spend so much of their time looking at themselves that they sometimes forget to look beyond. It is a mental effort just to keep up with the injustices life is throwing at them," he consoled me.

In the seat in front of me a guy looks at me and when I catch his eyes he winks. Unimpressed I look away.

"I'm hungry," Tshepo finally says to me.

"We can get a chip roll," I suggest as the train pulls into the station. We all get up and leave. Tshepo walks ahead, hardly looking to see if I'm keeping up with him. People push and brush past me impatiently. Annoyed I make my way through the milling crowd.

We get to a chip shop and I buy two chip rolls.

"I'll pay you back," he says by way of thanking me.

"Don't be ridiculous, it's nothing," I tell him.

He insists on eating outside. There is a wonderful garden outside the station. It is well kept. We sit near a pond. In front of us is the towering Cape Sun and towards the left is the Sanlam building. And looming in the background like some friendly phantom is the mountain. He lets out a long sigh and eats in silence.

"What happened to your friend, the other guy?"

"Byron ... phuphh ... who knows where he is now? He could be on his way to Jo'burg, he could be anywhere," he says as if he doesn't really care. He soon finishes his chip roll.

"Do you want another one?" I ask him.

"I'm alright, thanks," he says even though I sense that he is still hungry. His manners are a little bourgeois.

He walks around the lawn while I finish my meal. There are trees and flowers that catch his attention. He disappears down a little path covered with shrubs and trees. When he comes back there is an easier, less troubled look on his face. Perhaps he is just happy to be back after the nightmare of that place, I say to myself. It can't have been easy. We buy two cans of Coke and lounge in the sun for a while.

"We better get back," I say, " I've missed rehearsal today and they'll be worried."

"Sorry I didn't realise ..."

"It's okay. Don't worry about it. I don't mind," I reassure him.

At home I find several messages from the Drama department, each sounding more urgent than the previous one. Tshepo hangs around the house, looking a bit lost.

"Tshepo, I have to go," I say to him.

"Fine, I'll just stay here for a while."

"And do what? No, you better go home. Didn't you say you want to leave that place?" I say a bit irritated.

"Ja, okay .... Aish, wena! It's just that I don't know what to say to my digsmates," he says and sighs.

I'm not equipped to deal with this now, I say to myself. I imagine the director cursing the cast and calling for my name in vain each time my cues appear on his script.

"Tshepo, we'll have to finish this conversation later," I say to him as nicely as possible. I take my bag and walk out with him.

"You'll be fine," I say in a rush and walk briskly towards the station.

After rehearsal Arne picks me up. He kisses me eagerly, fondling the small of my back the way I like. I push him away gently. "I had a long day," I say subdued and he understands. I like that about him, I can be open and direct.

We drive to a small, intimate Mexican restaurant in Obs where the waiters know most of the clients by name. The hostess, Madame Spiers, an oldish charming Frenchwoman who conceals her age behind skilful make-up, kisses us on the cheek before she shows us to a table by the window. Arne orders two tequilas and the waiter lets us look at the menu. Arne talks about his day which he spent in some small town, not far from Cape Town. He's doing his research for his thesis, something about economic constraints in rural areas. I listen absent-mindedly, nodding and aahing in appropriate places but hardly absorbing anything he says. After a while he looks at me and says, "Are you listening to anything I'm saying?"

"Sorry, it's just that Tshepo came out today," I tell him and caress his hand, my thoughts returning to him. His face tenses a little. I don't think he likes Tshepo, he goes quiet every time I talk about him.

The waiter returns with our drinks and takes our order of two chilli con carnes. I ask for a glass of water which he soon brings. Arne drains his drink and orders an Amstel from a passing waiter, his mood changing because I mentioned Tshepo.

"So are you coming back with me tonight?" he asks.

"Actually I was hoping to see Tshepo after this. I'm worried about him."

"Come on. He's not a child," he blurts out.

"That's not fair. You've never been to a mental hospital."

"You're always going on about him," he says. Our waiter returns with his beer and sets our cutlery.

"You're being silly." I've never found jealousy charming in a man.

"I don't like this guy. I mean we made plans and everything. Can't you see him tomorrow?" he whines.

"Arne," I say and look at him, "just listen to yourself. You're being childish. He's my friend, okay? I'm not sleeping with him."

He takes a long slug from his drink and burps.

"Don't be boorish just because you're angry."

"What does that mean, my dear?" he says sarcastically and mumbles something in German under his breath.

"Right, if you're gonna act like a prick all night, I'm leaving."

He gets up and makes his way to the pool table on the other side of the room. Madame Spiers comes over when she sees that I'm alone.

"Alors, what's wrong with les amoureux ce soir?" she smiles.

"The usual, men are pigs," I say and flick my hand at Arne suddenly engrossed in a game of pool two guys are playing. Our first fight over something so stupid. It had to happen sooner or later, I say to myself. Madame Spiers signals to one of the waiters and sits down next to me.

"You are very fiery when you get upset, I think that's why men find you très charmante, chérie," she says and lights up a cigarette. She offers me one.

"He's angry with me because I'm going to see a friend of mine. A guy," I complain.

"Mais bien sûr. He's jealous."

"But it irritates me because there's nothing to be jealous about."

"T'inquite pas, he'll get over it, cherie," she smiles, her eyes twinkling with charm. She looks at Arne and tells me to be patient with him. He's insecure, she says, they all are.

"And I'm supposed to play the little girlfriend who understands everything. Even when he's being silly."

She chuckles a little.

"Things are different today. Quand j'étais jeune when a man met a woman it was a long affair. Even if things didn't work out, it took a long while before people broke up. People had time then. We could afford to be in love and play it out," she says nostalgically. "Mais aujourd'hui, things are not like that. Everything is quick. You meet and soon you leave. I don't understand it. Young women ... My daughter is working in Hout Bay. She's staying with her lover and she tells me that sometimes she tells him that she won't be back until the following day and that he mustn't wait up for her. Tu te rends compte? It was unheard of in my days. Perhaps I'm old-fashioned, chérie."

We smile at each other knowingly – if only men knew how well we know them. She takes a drag from her long, thin cigarette, exposing her delicate wrist. The subtle smell of perfume enhances her beauty. It's not the sort of beauty that shouts at you from across the street but I imagine that she can mesmerise a man. She sweeps back her carefully trimmed, not too long hair discreetly, with finesse; unlike the obvious way in which some women do to bring attention upon themselves. A tired pick-up trick, the hair flick always looks ridiculous as if a woman is trying to incur a whiplash injury in her desperation to attract a man. Madame Spiers is a lady, of the type of European breeding from a forgotten era, polite and with the sort of manners that make anyone feel welcome, comfortable. She's a woman who likes the nicer things in life and surrounds herself with amicable people. But as much as she is charming I'm sure she can be equally shrewd and business-like in the way she deals with people. You can see it in the way she runs her business. Her staff is always impeccably neat and the restaurant never gets overcrowded. And even though the clientele is unpretentious, they are of a certain milieu. For people like her money isn't everything. You can see that in the way she dresses, in the things she says. The restaurant is just something to keep her busy, when she's not going on exotic holidays and shopping for exquisite antiques and paintings to furnish her stylish restaurant. C'est mignon non, she often says when she finds something she likes.

"I better be off, chérie," she says when the waiter brings our meal. She gets up and fixes her long skirt. Courage, she whispers as she walks off. I walk to the pool table and find Arne still watching the game. I lean into his shoulder and put my arm around his waist. He puts his arm around me, a tender schoolboy look on his face.

"That was our first fight," I say to him.

"At least we got the pressure out of the way now."

We walk back to our table and mention nothing of Tshepo. The food is deliciously hot, encouraging thirst. We drink a lot and talk about a movie we saw yesterday.

## TSHEPO

Dear Mama, I've been thinking about you a lot lately. The nights of insomnia spent staring out the window were really spent thinking of you, wherever you are. I miss you and ache for the days when you were around to look after me. I miss silly things about you. The way you said uhm when you wanted to say no but didn't know how to. I miss the way you berated me for drinking water from the tap without using a glass. And the way you liked to be alone with your thoughts at sunset, tossing up something in the kitchen, your type of meditation. And how you liked red peppers and broiled fish. I think about you because I know those were the happiest days in my life.

I ran away from hospital today. It was easy. I knew I had to go and so I left. I took a small walk in Obs and saw my life in the expressions of strangers, in the things people were doing. It was strange. One minute I was walking, the next minute, I saw myself in the little boy sulking because his mother refused to buy him ice cream. In the bergie with eloquent eyes who stood outside the Spar singing and crying, but no one seemed to notice. Or the shop assistant hurrying back to work from her lunch break. I suddenly felt uncomfortable and mad. I wanted to run away. But there was nowhere left to run. I felt cornered. I felt lost and empty like I'd used up all my feelings. Or perhaps I was so depressed I couldn't recognise emotions. The pain was too deep, people almost winced when they looked at me.

So I went to a friend of mine, a guy that used to go to college with me. And he was awkward with me, Ma. He made me feel my scars, how deep the cuts ran. He made me feel embarrassed to admit that I've been away. I desperately craved his friendship and felt pathetic, abandoned. He told me that people were saying things about me, that he was concerned. But I saw him secretly look at his watch. He didn't even offer me a drink, Ma. After a mere ten minutes he made excuses, saying that he was going to see the same vultures who were supposedly saying things about me. The world has left me behind. It moved away and didn't leave a forwarding address. People are cold. They wear so many masks, I've lost count.

I think about you, Ma. I miss your strength, the way you stood by me, even when the storm came. I feel broken. I feel the emptiness of the sky, the coldness of night, the muted silence of the ocean and the suicidal nature of waves crashing in on themselves repeatedly, obsessively. The violence of it all, I understand it. I am not the first person to feel like this nor am I the last. There are legions of other people like me out there, slowly getting on with the quietness of their lives. And when they crumble, our paths cross at places like Valkenberg. I also bump into them in Obs, silent and almost invisible in their struggle with the business of living. Mysteries are welling up inside me. Life is conspiring to teach me it's harshest lessons.

I used to have big dreams, big ideas about a world that was mine for the taking. I was foolishly younger, my youth an excuse to go blindly through life. But with my wounds I realise how delicate the world really is, how preciously everything hangs in the balance. Nowadays I aspire for smaller, better dreams, things I can conceive of – a simple place I can call my own, a car, maybe a string of friends to enjoy a beer with on hot days when I like to be outside. And maybe a walk on the beaches of the Brazil I dream of. These are things that sustain me. The smallness of my life has forced my eyes open to a far greater diversity in people. How different and mysterious people really are, Ma. I'm not sure if I like them.

Every day I get closer to the person I really am and away from the one people want to see. I walk alone unfashionably and know how long my stride is. I don't bother guessing how far I can go. It is enough that I am moving. Some days I don't see colour, I don't hear birds and people seem to eat me with their eyes. Strangely it is on those days when I almost accept my solitude and feel the subtlety of my own breath, how naked I really am.

But there are better days when the sun doesn't feel as harsh, when smiling isn't such an effort. On those days it is enough just to remember the things I like, the people I love, like you. I remember the things I forget in my weaker moments when life seems stronger. But I see now she has been strong all along. It is I who has had to learn about my strength, to have life's rivers test me.

I seem to be spiralling Ma, falling into darkness. I wish you could catch me and save me from the stinging pain of hard lessons. I wish the warmth of the sun was all I needed to get through. I envy the devotion of plants, how little they need to get through – just the sun and water. I wish better days for myself because I feel like I am my only friend. I wish for the courage of street children and try not to feel sorry for myself.

But I mostly wish that the little things I'm beginning to see will make room for a bigger heart, so that tomorrow I may see a little more of the bigger picture.


## MMABATHO

**I** find Tshepo later at Wrensch Road. Alice opens the door and looks relieved to see me. It isn't a good sign.

"I think you better see him. He's been in his room all evening. He hasn't had anything to eat," she says, a furrow between her brows.

I walk to his room and find his door ajar. He lies on his mattress, looking morose and hungry. A large candle burns while ghoulish sounding Ambient music echoes throughout the room. I light a cigarette and switch off the music.

"I'd rather you didn't," he says lounging on his mattress.

"Tshepo, this music is depressing. It's not helping," I say and open a window because the air is stale.

"And you are?"

"Ke eng ka wena? My God, you were perfect this afternoon. What happened?"

"Just say it, Mmabatho," he snaps.

"Say what?" I say impatiently and draw from my cigarette.

"Say it. You were perfect and now you're crazy again."

"Don't do this," I tell him and stub out my cigarette even though it is still long.

"Say it. I know that's what you're thinking."

I take a deep breath and let out a heavy sigh. Tshepo remains on his mattress. I light another cigarette and sit at his desk. He switches on the radio while I gather my thoughts.

"They've asked me to leave," he says after a while.

I listen while blowing out frustrated circles of smoke.

"Alex asked me to leave. Said the others had complained. Bo Alice, ke moloi. She can't stand me but she pretends to like me. She's evil, you know," he says bitterly.

"Tshepo, don't say that about her even if she is evil."

I'm shocked and surprised that the others – whoever they are – think it best to kick out Tshepo in his hour of need. Alex, Paul, Julia and even Alice, can they be that callous?

"I've got a week to find a new place," he says and sinks into himself. I finish my cigarette and get up.

"Let's get something to eat," I say just to get his mind off things.

"I don't feel like going out. Besides I'm broke," he tells me.

"Okay, so let's whip up something. I'll get pasta and tomatoes from the Spar. You can organise onions and the cheese sauce."

"I've got that," he says, getting up.

I want to say I'm sorry, Tshepo, but it isn't appropriate. Besides, I'm a little weary of letting him become too dependent on my sympathy. I'm glad to help him but I hope that eventually he will help himself. That is all I want for him. I don't want him to end up like some of the doomed patients I've seen at Valkenberg. The ones who've given up on living and spend their lives sleeping on the grass, waiting for the next tea break and ask the staff permission for everything, even to use the toilet. I want the old Tshepo back, the one who doesn't have to study his feet before he looks at anyone.

We make a delightful meal and share it with Paul and Julia. Alex is out for supper with another intriguing date I'm told. He likes the weirdos, Paul says. Alice says she isn't hungry but hovers about the kitchen. She has an irritating habit of peeping into pots and commenting about this herb and that spice. She seems fastidious, the sort of bore who probably complains if the rice is a little overcooked. One can see that in her demeanour. When she doesn't like something she pulls a petulant face. I start to get a gist of Tshepo's contempt of her. When we have all eaten she decides to snack on our green salad.

"I thought you weren't hungry, Alice," Tshepo says irritated.

She ignores him.

At that point Paul makes some excuse about an assignment he has to finish. Julia puts her plate in the sink and goes to her room. Tshepo and I wash the dishes while Alice continues hovering round the kitchen, shuffling around in her Oriental slippers. She fidgets with some tapes before she decides that her time will be better spent writing a letter.

Tshepo sits outside while I pack away the last of the dishes. I join him only to discover that he is rolling a joint. I decide not to say anything. Let him think for himself, I tell myself. If he wants to play with fire there's nothing I can do.

"I know what you're thinking," he says before he lights it, "but everything is under control."

"Whatever, it's your life."

"I think we should go to Ganesh after this," he changes the subject.

We smoke a small joint together. Tshepo's eyes dilate and settle into a sleepy gaze, the "stoned immaculate" Jim Morrison sings about. I watch him closely, my mind racing with a thousand different things that can go wrong with him. I go inside and calm myself with a refreshing glass of cold water. Tshepo comes in, a ridiculous grin on his face. We grab our jackets and leave.

Ganesh is an idiosyncratic café-cum-bar tucked away in the heart of Obs, the kind of hang out that plays subliminal, unobtrusive music that grows on you furtively. It's a little hideaway, a find, really, that you always hear stories about but never see advertised anywhere. They are always outlandish stories about lovers' quarrels resembling soap operas or tales about certain regulars who feel the need to belly dance ineptly at night in front of everyone. It's a charming spot because it's small and familiar, you soon get to know everyone and if everyone likes you they get to know you. Tshepo likes it because he likes to think that he blends in well with everyone else. The truth of the matter is that he is always too stoned to have a sensible impression about Ganesh. I think the crowd is a bit too sophisticated for him. They have that all-or-nothing right stuff attitude, they like to think they know everything or that they are interesting people. He laughs politely at their jokes because he thinks people are friendly. I suspect he finds their humour cold, their jokes intellectual. All the same, he hangs on because they are the sort of people who hang around together always like a contagion and who always seem to be having the time of their lives, guffawing and shrieking at the top of their voices for everyone to hear. And if you don't catch their jokes you don't roll with them. That's why he is always with them. He wants to be one of them, to fit in, to be liked, to be asked "what are you doing this weekend" but they never do. They tolerate him like some younger brother who has tagged along. You always find him sitting at the end of the long table, leaning in and always asking what did he say. Perhaps that's why he's always stoned when we go there.

The thing about Ganesh is that it is so small, everyone stands out. When I'm in Ganesh I become aware of how fragile Tshepo is and it annoys me sometimes to see him in this light because the others look at me strangely. They don't understand our friendship, they don't see what I see in him.

We greet Anthony, the owner, and Karuna the deliciously beautiful Indian woman who works behind the bar. I had an affair with her. It didn't last long. I think I was more attracted to the idea of being with a woman than liking a woman. But we remain friends, soulful, whenever we see each other we kiss on the cheek and gossip. And sometimes she teases me with her long curls and soft butterfly eyelashes. But I know I'm not a lesbian. I like men too much. Women's bodies make fragile landscapes.

We sit at the couch table. It is a small crowd for a Tuesday night but I look at my watch and see that it is still early, only half past eight. At another table two French women are trying to have a conversation with a coloured guy who hangs around Ruby in The Dust a lot. I watch them stumbling over words, the guy desperately guessing at what they're trying to say. But I know that before the evening is over they'll be laughing or dancing, making sense whichever way things turn out. Ganesh has that charm, it brings out the person behind the face. I order a Black Label for Tshepo and a Savannah for myself. Tshepo will buy the next round. Karuna brings it and she can see that Tshepo is stoned.

"Hawu, Tshepo, so early, chief, it's not even ten," she says.

"What about Mmabatho?" he defends himself.

I roll my eyes at him.

Arne saunters in with his friends.

"I thought I'd find you here," he says and kisses me. He gives Tshepo a curt "hi" even though they've never met.

"You're checking up on me now," I say in his ear and he pulls me away to the bar. Karuna soon comes and takes Arne's order of drinks.

"So this is who you've been running away with when I'm not looking," he says holding me around the waist.

"There's no need to be like that," I tell him and pull away. "Tshepo knows we're going out, so just relax. And don't be a prick to him." I walk back to the table. Arne comes after me with four drinks and hands them out to his friends.

"I'm sorry, did you want one?" he says when he looks at Tshepo.

"I'm fine thanks," Tshepo says guzzling down the last of his beer before going to the bar to speak to a woman there.

"I asked," he says to me but I give him fierce eyes.

My friend Ntabiseng walks in. She scans the room and when our eyes meet she lights up.

"What's up with you girl? O ipatile kae?" she says, coming over and hugging me. She greets Arne and his friends and sits down with us. The other guys look at her closely, assuming that she's available.

"So what are you guys up to tonight?" she says.

"Nothing much," Arne answers. "Is anything happening?"

"The Piano Lounge is quite nice on a Tuesday," she says, sounding like her regular self. I like Ntabiseng a lot but it annoys me how she's always full of suggestions about things to do while being one of those people who never have any money or transport and always rely on guys or anyone at hand for lifts and hand-outs.

"I'm quite tired actually," I say avoiding an unnecessary expense.

"We can just hang out here," she says and makes herself comfortable, waiting for someone to offer to buy her a drink. I know her routine. One of Arne's tall rugby-types obliges. He speaks English with an awkward German accent.

"He just arrived a week ago," Arne explains after he has gone to the bar to get her drink.

Anthony as usual is closely observing everything going on in the bar. It is his little universe. He created it with his own hands, even the fixtures. Everything on the walls, in secret nooks and shelves, reveals something about his travels and his eclectic sense of culture. He changes the music to lighten up the mood. Boom Shaka belts out "Thobela". Tshepo gets up and dances with the woman he has been talking to. Arne loosens up and asks me to go upstairs to the terrace with him.

We sit against a wall. He lights a small joint and passes it to me. It is a warm evening and the sky is unfathomably dark. The Milky Way runs diagonally over us.

"I don't like it when you play the jealous boyfriend," I tell him, "it's a turn-off."

"Well, I hate the way you go on about this guy."

"He's just a friend. What's the big deal?"

He doesn't answer me. We finish the rest of the joint and go back inside. Arne calls his friends to leave. I kiss him on the cheek but he is distant. Ntabiseng follows them as they leave. Tshepo comes back to the table when he sees me sitting alone.

"You look at bit sour, let's go next door," he suggests.

I kiss Karuna good-bye and we leave. We go to A Touch of Madness next door.

We are greeted at the door by a tall, slender host with a charming effeminate way about him. He shows us to a table but we ask to go upstairs. We go up a steep narrow staircase and come into a small room with a low ceiling. The décor is Baroque with rich, lush maroon velvet hanging from curtain rails. The floor is wooden and squeaks as if it has stories to tell. There is a curious atmosphere. I have a feeling that people are talking about us. I feel eyes crawling on us. Everyone seems to whisper when they speak because sound travels so easily. We sit near the window where we have a good view of the tiny room. Tshepo orders chocolate cake and tea. I settle for a stiff cappucino.

"So that was Arne," he says after a while.

"So what do you think?" I ask him.

"What's there to think about? He's your boyfriend," he says and doesn't seem intent on talking any further about him. I don't blame him. Arne was rude.

A waiter brings our order. I spoon out some of the creamy froth from my cappucino and it is delicious. Tshepo gives me a taste of his delectable chocolate cake.

"You know that woman you were speaking to tonight?" I begin.

"Ja."

"Do you know she's a lesbian?" I ask.

"I know ... So? ... I wasn't hitting on her if that's what you're saying. We were just talking and having a good time," he says.

"How come you never tell me about anyone you like?" I probe.

"I wasn't aware that I had to," he replies, his eyes avoiding me.

"No, it's just that I never hear you talk about anyone, I never see any silly pictures in your room of anyone you like," I persist.

"Ja, well, ha re tshwane kaofela. I don't like talking about things like that," he says and drinks his tea.

I talk about my new play and the character I'm playing. She's a 1940s blues singer in love with a useless guy that she can't get away from. I've been talking to women about some of their lousy relationships, trying to get a feel for the kind of things that their two-timing, heartbreaking men do and say to keep them coming back. A little research always helps me understand the character I'm playing.

74

He drifts between listening and enjoying his own reverie. I don't mind because I've exhausted the subject talking about it. I talked to Karuna about useless men and she didn't have anything uplifting to say. "Not that I'd sleep with a guy but I don't trust charm in a man," she said. "Charm and dicks, they look like a deadly combination."

"It's good to be out," he says and sighs.

"It must have been really shit in there," I sympathise but he doesn't say anything.

He finishes the last of his tea and looks around the room.

"I'm dying to ask you something."

"You're full of questions tonight," he says lightly. "What is it?"

"Why do you never speak about your mother or father?"

"Phuphh, you know how to ask them don't you? Why does anyone never talk about their parents? I don't know. It's difficult."

He rubs his forehead and plays with his hair. When the waiter walks by I ask him to get Tshepo another cup of tea which he soon does. I drink my cappucino slowly while he slurps his tea. A couple across the room keep staring at us and then jab each other, whispering. I try to ignore them.

"I loved my mother," he begins, "maybe too much. There's nothing like having a mother. A mother's love can save you when you're about to jump, before you pull the trigger. It's difficult to ever say how much she meant to me."

"And your father?" I say carefully.

He sighs again.

"It's hard to describe our relationship. We got along but he also worked on my nerves a lot. I don't think I'm the kind of son he wanted. You know how you can love someone, a family member, but not like them. I think it was like that with my father. He didn't like me," he says quietly, almost to himself, deep in thought.

He remains quiet like that, thinking.

"I feel like shit," he says after a while.

"I'm sorry. I didn't mean to upset you," I say.

"No, it's fine. The thing is, I'm beginning to feel like there's nowhere left to run. You know what I mean? Of course you don't. I've got a lot of stuff to deal with. My life is catching up with me."

He becomes quiet again, retreating into the person I saw at Valkenberg. I listen.

"We were all sleeping when they came in," he begins abruptly, holding his cup with both hands as if to absorb its warmth, its comfort.

He hardly looks at me. His eyes stray around the edges of my face and at the table behind me as he speaks gently as if undressing a wound. "It must have been around three in the morning. I can't remember. Anyway, I was seventeen. I remember Mama waking me up. My dad was already awake. Someone's in the house, she said. Papa said he had phoned the police."

The waiter comes and asks if everything is alright. I smile at him and he walks off.

"We locked ourselves in my parents' bedroom. The three of us, we were terrified. After a while we heard footsteps coming down the passage. There were a few of them. They started putting an axe to the door, breaking it down. You'd think we would scream but we didn't. We couldn't. We were paralyzed with fear and sat on the bed. I remember holding Mama's hand and squeezing it."

He is silent for a while, his eyes soft and vulnerable. He holds his head at an angle the way he does when he is thinking about something.

"Did I ever tell you about my crazy extended family?" he suddenly changes the subject. I look at him with surprise but he doesn't seem to notice, so I don't say anything.

"I've got dozens of cousins, especially on my father's side. But my mother never got on with my father's mother. She's a difficult woman, my grandmother. Very demanding and hard to please. I don't think she's a happy person. Hard people often aren't happy. It's hard to talk about her. She put Mama through hell. I don't know if I love her. She never really loved me because she couldn't stand my mother. I suppose she saw me as an extension of my mother. And my aunts too, they were nice to me but distant to my mother. I never got birthday gifts from them when I was growing up. I don't remember them saying well done or congrats or anything aunty like that. You know, it was strange growing up, not really having a family, because that is how it felt. It was always like that with my dad's family. A little fucked up, you never really felt like you were part of them. My grandmother ran the household with an iron fist. She was a bulldozer. My grandfather was just a figure, he was just there. She totally emasculated him."

He gets up and says he has to go to the loo. The sour couple across the room are still watching us. "Is there a problem?" I eventually ask them after Tshepo has left. They are a young couple, early thirties, I guess. The people at the other tables watch us. "What? I don't know what you're talking about," the woman says and tells her partner that they are leaving. She mumbles something about "them taking over everything" as she leaves her table. "What are you looking at?" she attacks me when she walks by. "Oh please, just go," I tell them. "Weeds," a woman sitting by herself at the table closest to me says, "just have to nip them before they get out of hand."

"I know," I say, still feeling tense.

Tshepo soon returns looking depressed. He plays with his tea before he continues.

"They broke down the door. There were five of them. What do you want? Take our money, take our cars, Papa pleaded. I was sitting next to Mama and held on to her hand. They didn't wear balaclavas or try to hide their faces. They started waving their guns everywhere. They tied Papa to a chair with duck tape and put him in the bathroom next door. It was one of those open bathrooms without a door. They wanted to gag him but the leader decided against it. I haven't spoken about this to anyone other than my psychologist," he says with an agonized look.

"You don't have to go on."

"And then they pulled my mother. You don't have to be rough, she said to them calmly. I know what you want. Tshepo, she said and looked at me. I began to cry. They let her undress. I went into the bathroom with Papa. They each took their turns with her – all five of them. They did that to my beautiful mother. She cried but didn't scream. Papa said nothing throughout this. Nothing.

"Then one of them came and got me from the bathroom. I closed my eyes because it would have killed me to see what they'd done to Mama. Mama, I said, Mama, my eyes still shut. She didn't respond but I heard her moaning softly. I heard them bundling her off and cried out Mama, Mama. Tshepo, she barely whispered as they took her away. Then the other two threw me on the bed and tore off my pyjama pants. I opened my eyes and screamed no. A deformed penis with traces of blood was staring at me."

Engrossed I listen. There is a curious stillness in his eyes. It's the look of someone who has stood in the eye of a tornado and survived. He goes on.

"The one took me from behind while the other almost choked me with his dick. They laughed. And you'd think they seemed crazy but they didn't. They looked like they were having a good time. Then in all the madness I heard two gunshots from outside. I yelled. I cried because I knew they were for Mama. When I wet myself they let me go."

"But your father ..." I say and feel weighed down by the thought of it all.

"He never called the cops. The first thing I saw when I got dressed was a stain of blood on the carpet where my mother had been. Then I went to the bathroom and looked at my father. He couldn't look at me. He started crying. I reached for his phone and called 10111. They found me sitting on the bed. They untied my father first and then he told them about my mother. We found her with two bullets to her head in the front seat of the BMW. I didn't say anything.

"He made the funeral arrangements quickly. She was buried two days later, which was unusual. You know bo darkie ba jwang ka kepelo. Anyway, I couldn't look at him during the funeral. When they committed the coffin to the ground I cried. He tried to console me but I pushed him away. Then I lost it.

"I was admitted to Sterkfontein and then Tara. I was supposed to stay there. That was the plan. He thought I would never recover, that I would always be psychotic. He wanted a clean break, to start a new life. But I recovered and remembered everything. I got discharged."

"I'm sorry for asking, but ... why did he do it?" I say replaying the shocking events in my mind.

"Money. Power. It's always the same things that drive scandals. I later found out that my father had connections with the mafia, they recruited him. And my mother began to suspect. She never approved and he knew how she felt. I found this out in her journals. She agonized about his activities. To cut a long story short, she was in a position to incriminate him if she ever felt the need to tell anyone. So he killed her. He was involved in a lot of funny business, she could have put him away for life. I also found out that he made a bit of money out of the whole thing, it turns out that he claimed a nice sum of money from her life insurance. He took out two on her. My father's a shrewd businessman. I spent my late teens and early twenties searching for the truth. It nearly killed me. It was hell but I'm glad I know what happened."

"So where is your father now?" I say, shocked that anyone real could have such a father.

"Fuck knows. I haven't seen him in years. I hear from him every once in a while, you know, for the usual things. Have you got enough money and everything? Other than that we don't speak. But I know he's a big mafia boss now, stinking rich. I don't like to speak about him, that's why I tell people he died in a car accident with my mother. I suppose I felt like an orphan the night she died."

He sips his tea. It must be cold. It's difficult for me to understand how he must feel.

"I don't know what to say to you," I attempt, feeling inept and bereaved myself.

"Don't say sorry. It happened, okay?" he says to me bravely but there is more than just bravery in his voice. "It's just the way it is."

I follow his cue and nod slightly, apologetically.

"After I got discharged I found out that he'd left me some money. So I stayed with an aunt on my mother's side. She put me through school. On my father's side I never heard from them. In fact I found out more disturbing things about them.

"My father has four sisters and three brothers, two of them died, one sister one brother. He is the eldest and they knew that. He bullied them when they were younger. I told you a little about my grandmother. She's a bit of a tyrant. Well, my father is a little like her. My father's family are crazy. You know what she did? You'll never guess. She made my father impregnate her eldest daughter."

"What do you mean, she made your father impregnate his sister? That's disgusting."

"I mean just that. My grandmother, she's evil you know … Huh … You don't know her. She forced them. She was their mother and they listened."

"I have a cousin called Mpho. He was born a few months before me. If you look at him you can see the resemblance, where my father's blood runs. The nose, the encroaching hairline. All the relatives always joked that he looked like his uncle, my father. If only they knew. Or maybe they know, who knows? That family has too many dark secrets. I can't even trace my family beyond my father's parents. It's like a dead-end. The whole thing is shrouded in mystery."

"But why would your grandmother do that?"

"I've thought about it a lot over the years and, I don't know, it's just too obscure to understand. Maybe it was some ritual thing. Maybe it was pure and simply evil."

"And your mother, did she know this bit about your father and his family?"

"I don't think so. So now my half brother, I call him the Anti-Christ, is living in Jo'burg in some mansion. Running a car theft syndicate along with other operations. Of course my father is pulling the strings. That's why I avoid going to Jo'burg. Too much to deal with," he says and drinks his cold tea.

"What about your other uncles and aunts on your father's side?"

"What about them?"

"And your mother's side?"

"I hear from my aunt a lot. But I don't like to bother her. She's struggling herself," he says.

"And money?"

"I have an arrangement with the bank. I have to be careful with the money he left me." He looks tired.

"You look exhausted."

"It's been a long day," he says and stretches out his arms. "I think we better go."

I look at my watch. There's only one other table left with people.

We get up and take our jackets. I put mine on slowly, still recovering from the shock. I feel lethargic and yawn even though my mind is still alert. He is quiet when we walk out. Outside it is a little windy, but the air is still warm.

"I'll see you around, maybe tomorrow," he says and walks in the opposite direction. I wave at him. He walks away with his hands in his pockets but strangely looking alright and not weighed down by what he has told me.

I walk towards Milne road, looking for a little company, someone to take my mind off the sadness. I pass Ntabiseng's house and see that her light is still on. Her fast mouth and empty conversation is just the sort of light-heartedness I need, I say to myself. At the door I catch one of her digsmates on her way out. She tells me that Ntabiseng is in and rushes off with her boyfriend. I close the door quietly. Toni Braxton broods about lost love down the corridor. I follow the music to Ntabiseng's room. I knock twice and turn the knob. She starts in bed and someone gasps, ruffling covers and hiding under them. She looks at me with her big eyes as I stand there feeling like a fool. The first thing I notice is a prosthesis carelessly lying on the floor with Arne's shoe.

"So how long has this been going on?" I look at her. "Arne, you can come out now."

He reveals his head, his hair in all directions. He doesn't say anything like: I can explain. It's not what you think. Don't get the wrong impression, or any of the stupid and insulting clichés men use. He just looks at me. The cheap smell of flea-market perfume is about the room.

"You can get your stuff from my place tomorrow afternoon. Bring my stuff while you're at it. And wena, sies, I don't ever want to see you again," I say to them and walk out with as much dignity as I can muster. My throat is sore, blood spilling everywhere inside me. Let me just make it to the door, I say holding back tears.

I walk out quickly.

I walk home, a few tears finding their way down my face. I should have known better than to gamble on a zero guy, I say to myself. I should have seen it coming. You have a penchant for men who can't keep their pants on, I can hear Tshepo saying on his more lucid days. Men, we're arseholes, baby. We play your strings like marionettes. We fake emotions only to get you in bed. And you guys fake orgasms to keep us. We even fake fights. And when we've had enough we make excuses and run. It's me, we say. I'm the idiot. I'm fucked up. It's not you. I need time. We need to be apart, we say but still expect you to sleep with us. And you do because you believe us and want to make things work. So we run to the next bed and play out another story.

But sometimes you get us back. We end up actually loving you, caring. That just makes things worse because we become jealous, we do anything to keep you for ourselves, even if it means beating you. We're keeping her in line, we say after we've bruised half her face with a fist just because she looked at another guy.

But it's not the same with white boys, hey Mmabatho, I can hear him say. These guys ha batswe kasi. They don't know location love. Ja, white boys go for that truth and honesty stuff. They say, let's talk about it. I can see Tshepo clearly, teasing me. Ja, white boys, I know you like him, he said of David when I used to go out with him. But don't be fooled, he's still a guy. You know, with a penis. That thing, it always betrays us, he laughs.

I wish I could laugh this off or be casual about it. I mean, he's only a zero guy. I wish things like this only happened to the characters I play. Perhaps this whole zero guy thing is just a self-fulfilling prophecy.

I light up a cigarette and walk home, my cheeks damp. Fortunately I don't wear mascara.


TSHEPO

It is a while before I decide to go to the college. You have to go there sooner or later, Mmabatho advises me. Assignments that were due a month ago loom in my thoughts as I summon the courage to go there. I have never been good at facing disappointment, worse facing disappointing others. I take a taxi to town one morning.

When I get there I avoid the gaze of everyone else. The vultures always gossiping about me, piecing together mostly false facts about what happened to me, whisper and poke each other as I walk by. He was on acid. He took ecstasy. He smoked Malawi Gold. He's been a druggy since the beginning of the year, Mmabatho tells me people have said. They'll say anything just to avoid looking at themselves, the ones I used to smoke with during lunch breaks. Vultures, they are all just vultures waiting for our demise. Tomorrow it will be someone else.

Sometimes I wonder why Mmabatho bothers telling me. I don't care what people say. In my mind I don't. I suspect she does it so that I shouldn't do it again. So that the idea of smoking another joint should be repulsive, so that I should always remember that people are fickle and cruel and will disown your friendship if you push them. I suspect that she thinks they are doing me a favour by treating me like a social outcast. He is getting a lesson the likes of which he has never had, I imagine her saying.

Passing the lay-abouts who hang around the cafeteria incessantly smoking and chatting about things no one really cares about, I go to the student advisor's office. The secretary, a genial woman with a face that could tame anyone, asks me to take a seat while she calls Mr Andrews.

"Please come in," he says when he sees me. He smiles broadly and extends an arm, revealing lots of hair where his shirt sleeve is rolled. His hand is large and heavy as I shake it.

"Mr Andrews," I begin as I take a seat in his roomy office.

"Please, it's Mark."

"I haven't been to college for about a month and a half now and I think I've missed too much. So I'm dropping out. I'll start again next year," I say in a rushed breath, a little nervous at the prospect of explaining myself.

He takes a while before he answers.

"Why were you away for so long?" The question I've been dreading, but his eyes are non-threatening.

"Uhmm … I, I phuphh …" He remains patient, quiet, curious. "I was at Valkenberg."

I expect him to look shocked but he remains the same. There is kindness about his face.

"So you feel you've missed too much," he repeats the way people do when they're trying to understand something.

"Yes," I say a little annoyed, not really keen to explain further.

"And what will you do after this?"

"I thought I'd waiter or work in a bookshop, I dunno, something like that."

"I ask because you say you want to come back next year. It makes it easier to get back to academic work if you've been doing something to keep your mind going, like working in a bookshop for instance."

"Look, things have been difficult. It's not easy going to an institution and everyone finding out about it."

"I'm sure it's not easy."

"The thing is I don't think I can go back to my class. I just can't. I can't face them. So I want to deregister."

After that he doesn't ask me any more questions. He wishes me the best and tells me to go to the registration office. A short efficient woman helps me to deregister. And then it is over. I walk out the building into a busy street, the sky brooding with clouds.

For three days I search through the classifieds for a new place to stay. Eventually on the Spar's notice board I see a flat going in Wynberg. I take a train to check it out one afternoon.

I get off at Wynberg station, a crowded place with many itinerant hawkers, always eager to sell their wares. It is a short walk before I arrive at the flat: No. 17 Ergham Court. At the door a beautiful woman with a coffee complexion greets me. "Come in. Come in." She has a rich exotic accent from way up there in Africa. A tall dark man is standing behind her. He looks more indigo than dark brown, his skin glowing in the light. We go through to the lounge and make introductions.

"This is my wife Akousia," he says politely with an equally interesting and layered accent. She holds my hand with both hands when I shake it.

"And I'm Patrick," he says, gripping my hand firmly. I smile dumbly and stare at their foreign features. They are beautiful to look at and their eyes sparkle. They sparkle with hope, I guess. We are going to make it in South Africa, their eyes seem to say.

"Please sit down. I'll make some tea," Akousia says.

I sit on a modest couch in the lounge. A menacing mask with deep incisions on the cheeks and lots of straw hair hangs on the wall, dominating the room. The face of a harsh god.

"That mask is beautiful. From the Congo?" I guess and take a biscuit offered me by Akousia. I take a bite and it tastes stale. I take a large sip of tea and swallow hastily.

"No, it's from Ghana, but I'm from the DRC. My wife's from Nigeria."

There is a defensive tone to his voice. Even Akousia is solemn-faced. I can only guess how many times they have had to say that.

"So, this is the flat."

"You probably want to look around," Patrick says, his face lightening up.

"I'd like that."

It is a two-bedroomed flat with a lounge, a kitchen and a small bare passage. The bathroom is small but manageable.

"You can take this room," he says showing me the smaller of the two bedrooms. Light pours through a large window and there is a generous view of the sleeping mountain. He unlocks a door that leads to a small balcony. There is a small washing line.

"I hope you won't mind us coming in and out to use the line," he says and smiles. I notice that she is always slightly behind him.

There is nothing to consider. It's clean and looks new. Besides, they are black. I don't have to defend my culture all the time. I'm tired of the whole race thing, having to speak on behalf of my blood and brethren, arguing against this and defending that. There have been too many cultural misunderstandings at Wrensch where I used to live. I grew up in a household where I ate well. And eating well means eating a large meal for supper. Most times they just prepare something light for supper like a sandwich or a salad. Or they go out. And I'm left alone at the stove, a costly experience when you're cooking for one. I don't particularly like the fend-for-yourself system where everybody buys their own food and keeps it stashed away in their own cupboard. It's a recipe for pettiness and doesn't encourage a communal spirit.

When I was younger food was always associated with people, laughter and sharing. Mama would be in the kitchen with her red apron frying and tossing this and that with a light spirit while entertaining someone. At Wrensch food is either something that takes up space in a cupboard or something regarded with the same aesthetic rigour as a work of art. They are always going on about this cheese and that spice or that olive oil from some obscure Italian vineyard. Our tastes differ. I put more emphasis on sharing food while they concentrate on the preparation of the food. There is nothing floral to be said about pap except that cooked properly it is tasty and filling. Basic, earthy things like that they would never understand.

"I really like the place."

"Let's sit in there," Patrick says pointing to the lounge. I'm struck by his sense of ceremony, as we are about to talk about money. With him I sense that there is a right way and a wrong way. Akousia leaves to make herself busy in the kitchen. Patrick sits on the edge of his seat and joins his hands together.

As soon as we've agreed on the rent, the door bell rings.

"That must be the landlady," Patrick says and gets up.

The woman greets Akousia as they make their way to the lounge.

"This is your landlady?" I am surprised. I know her. "Sister Hendriks, how are you?"

She smiles awkwardly. I advance to hug her but she puts out her hand to shake mine.

"Tshepo! Fine. What a coincidence," she says and manages a chuckle.

"Ah, so you know each other?" Akousia asks.

"Yes," I say uncomfortably.

"Yes, I know his parents," she lies.

We sit in the lounge now looking a little smaller because all the seats are occupied. Akousia serves more tea and biscuits. Again the tea is tepid and the biscuits crumbly. Sister Hendriks seems unaffected. She drinks and eats with a pleasant face.

She tells me that I can move in the following day. After a while she disappears into the kitchen with Patrick and they talk with low voices. Akousia tells me a little more about the mask on the wall. Then Sister Hendriks says goodbye and leaves. Patrick and I talk about the taxi violence and violence in general in Cape Town. For every gruesome tale I tell him he tells me something worse about Lagos and other exotic parts of Africa. When I look at him closer I see two long scars on his face, one running down the side of his left cheek and the other on his high forehead. But they are hard to spot and easily disguised by his beautiful dark skin. And his teeth are white like ivory. When I ask him if Wynberg is safe, he says elusively, "But is it safe anywhere?"

I nod and consider this: life is dangerous. The more we speak the more I begin to feel how earnest he is. Even his humour is light and laced with irony. He laughs when I tell him what I paid at Wrensch to share a house. "For that price I could get my own flat," he says.

I begin to drown in a surreal world. I start reading too much in every-thing he says and strangely find everything he says profound. "Every-thing is hard," he says with a calm face but the expression of his eyes says more. We talk about the poverty in townships. He speaks with prophetic authority and gestures the way a skilled conductor might. We talk about many things, most of which seem to be of my interest. I start feeling uncomfortable and the more I ask myself why I feel like this, the more I begin to realise that Patrick disturbs me. I feel disturbed by the moments of silence in conversation by the questions these pointed silences seem to pose. He seems to be saying more by saying nothing, by answering some of my questions with an elusive grin, a knowing smile. His face alone communicates his universe. I begin to understand why Akousia is always slightly behind this impressive man, so subtle in his ways. I feel anxious and quickly make an excuse to leave.

Outside, once I regain my strength I tell myself never to mess with Patrick. There are too many layers to him, a sinister darkness comes across in the moments of silence in conversation, in intelligent but shy Akousia's reserve and humility. Even though he has a polite manliness about him I sense cruelty, a sense of someone who's been broken in fragile places. Some wounds are hard to heal.

### DAVID

**N**tombi and I are happy to see Tshepo back on his feet. We invite him for supper one night. It isn't a big deal; I cook rice with a vegetable stew and some meat. Litha the woman we share the house with is there. Elizabeth and Sam, our close friends, also. Tshepo eats well and even has seconds. Yet I notice that he looks thinner. And a certain lightness about his eyes has been extinguished by dark insomniac rings. I suggest that we finish the meal with a spliff. Elizabeth, Sam and Tshepo are keen.

I have some potent Swazi that a Danish friend left for me. I take it out from the vase on the fireplace mantle and start cleaning the large heads carefully, marveling at the big, dark seeds. It is fresh, I can smell faint traces of a wild valley perhaps somewhere near Port St John's. I end up rolling two long cone-shaped joints. I never like to pass around several joints at once, so I only light one.

"So what are you up to now?" I ask him.

"I'm trying to find a job. I don't know, maybe I can get a job waitering at the Spur or something like that," he says.

"Waitering? In Cape Town?" Elizabeth says alarmed.

"Ja, aish, it's a shit job in Cape Town," Ntombi adds.

"It doesn't pay. The Germans are tight-fisted. Everyone knows they don't tip," Elizabeth points out.

"What about the French?" Tshepo asks.

"Oh, they are overrated," she replies, "just a lot of hot air. After fussing around them all night they manage to come up with a complaint so that they don't have to tip you. Arseholes, really. Strangely, South Africans are more generous when it comes to tipping."

"Well, it was a thought," he says disappointed.

"You have a degree in journalism, don't you?" I ask.

"Yes," he sighs and rolls his eyes.

"You could try the Argus. I heard they are always looking," I say passing him the joint for the second time.

"I'm not a journalist."

"Maybe something in radio."

"What is this? Enough, guys. I'll find something," he says and finishes the last of the joint.

We drop the subject and watch television. It is a National Geographic special about killer waves. We watch Nature's might and whimsical destruction with awe. A seaside town in Japan is destroyed in a matter of minutes when a devastating tsunami washes over it.

"I think I need to see a sangoma," Tshepo suddenly says out of the blue.

He gets up and goes to the bathroom and stays in there for a long time, perhaps ten minutes. I begin to worry and call for him, but he doesn't answer. I knock on the door a few times before I turn the knob.

I find him sitting on the toilet seat with the lid down. His face is buried in his hands.

"What's up, chief?" I begin.

He shakes his head and snivels.

"Hey, come on now, it can't be that bad," I say awkwardly. Ntombi is better at this.

"You don't know what it's like," he says and lifts his head. His eyes are red and wet with tears.

He just cries. After a while he looks at himself in the mirror and manages to laugh a little, I think for my benefit.

"I look terrible," he says solemnly.

His cheekbones stick out and his face looks gaunt, like someone carved out his features with a fine sharp instrument.

"Not really."

"You're a good friend, but lying to me won't help. I know that I look like hell."

"You forget that I saw you when you were doing your Full Monty number in Salt River," I joke trying to bring up his spirits.

I leave him and he comes out a few minutes later. He looks less troubled but his eyes are puffy. The others are glad to see him but they don't make a fuss. I burn some Mpepho and light another spliff. We smoke it slowly, allowing the purifying scent of Mpepho to chase away the demons that are after Tshepo.

"Listen, bra, you're going to be fine," Sam says with confidence after a while, but Tshepo doesn't respond, he is distant, drifting somewhere in the recesses of his imagination. He becomes quiet, lonely. Ntombi pokes me again.

"Guys, I have to go," he suddenly says and gets up.

"Alright." I'm not going to argue with him even though I don't think he should be on his own. "But since you have nothing to do and my thesis is going nowhere for now, I was wondering if you'd be interested in going to the nature reserve tomorrow. We always say we'll go. So are you up to it?"

"Sure."

I know he isn't going home. He is going to roam the streets like a vagrant. Mmabatho says he often walks the streets till the early hours of the morning searching for God only knows. Once she bumped into him on Long Street in town and he didn't recognise her. He just walked past like a zombie.

He comes for me early just before Ntombi goes to work. He helps himself to some food while I get dressed. We pack a small lunch, two avocados and some cheese sandwiches. And of course our survival kit of rolled joints and Mpepho. It is a pleasant drive to the nature reserve. He is reticent but I don't mind as I'm also quiet in the morning. We get there after ten and park the car some distance from the entrance.

It is a hot day and I'm already sweating. I have a pair of shorts in the back of the bakkie. I change into them quickly while Tshepo takes off his shoes. We start on a path that leads up a small incline before the land becomes flat again. I walk in front while Tshepo follows. We walk for an hour through fynbos following a narrow path that is supposed to lead to a small lake. Tshepo is unusually quiet.

"Maybe we should have a joint, eh?"

"Ja, fine," he says.

We find a large rock to sit on and light a spliff.

"Have you ever felt that you've seen too much?" he asks, his head slightly tilted and looking away.

"Kind of." He senses that I don't know what he is talking about.

"I feel like time is converging," he says, "I feel like everything is try-

88

ing to fit together, but there's resistance, friction, anger. It's hard to explain. I'm scared because it makes sense, this turbulence. I know where it's coming from and where it's going. It's crazy. There are so many strange things out there." He sucks hard on the joint and looks away again.

"What do you mean, strange things?" I light a sprig of Mpepho.

"Do you believe in angels?"

"I don't know. I've never thought about them."

"Well, I keep seeing them."

"And ..." I say encouragingly.

"They follow me everywhere. On trains, taxis, in the street. Everywhere. I think they are trying to tell me something but I can't hear. There's too much music, too much going on. The music of madness is hard to ignore. It's driving me crazy." He uses that word again, and I flinch.

"Do they have wings?" I ask and hold the burning scent of Mpepho above him.

"No, they're like you and me."

"But how do you know they're angels?"

"Because I do, just trust me."

"Because you do."

"You think I'm crazy. I can see it in your eyes. I've spoken to them, you know, the angels. But not using my voice. Telepathy," he says and points to his temple.

He's hearing voices, I say to myself.

"They're everywhere. In supermarkets, parks, in town. I've seen them in Obs."

"And what do they do to you?"

"Nothing. They just watch me. They are always quiet but sometimes they say something. A word or two. They don't waste words, so I'm always concentrating, always listening. I've seen demons too."

I pass him the spliff.

"Demons?"

"Yes, demons, and they are also people like you and me."

He finishes the last of the spliff and continues.

"Sometimes at night when I try to sleep I hear this terrible screaming. It's so piercing I can hardly think. This animal shriek that comes from somewhere, I don't know where. It's like a dragon is raging, screaming. Sometimes it keeps me awake and I search for it, walking the night. "

"We better get going," I say and get up.

We continue on our path. He becomes uncommunicative and difficult. He insists on walking in front and goes off the path a lot. When I suggest that we stay on the path for the sake of preserving the vegetation he argues. He also becomes tearful and speaks to himself. I don't understand his mood swings. For a while I become convinced that he's possessed, as he speaks to himself incessantly. But I notice that every time I burn some Mpepho he calms down.

We nearly step onto a puffadder near a bush. It has a magnificent ochre and a brick red colour. Tshepo stands in front of it barefoot and oblivious to it. When the snake coils itself ready to attack I pull him away. I hear it slithering away when we cut across the bush in the opposite direction.

We eventually get to the lake. It has dried up a lot. The banks are dry and the earth has cracks like chapped lips. We stop for lunch. I cut the avocados into strips and put them on the cheese sandwiches. We eat in silence. Afterwards he ventures to the water. He stays there a while looking into the dark murky water. He comes back crying, inconsolable.

"You need to see a sangoma," I tell him.

"Credo Mutwa's been walking around here," he says.

"What about him?"

"He frightens me," he says and shivers a little.

"Don't think about him, just enjoy the view," I say but he walks back to the water again and sits down there.

Small waves ripple across the lake, a gentle light shimmering as they travel. The sun scorches. I put some sun block on my face and back and go to offer him some. He squirts out some and rubs it on his nose and forehead.

"Can we go?" he says. "I've seen enough."


TSHEPO


**I** walk around the city aimlessly like unclaimed baggage drifting on an airport conveyor belt. My heart is like an open book because that is the only way to understand, to articulate this thing happening to me. My mind feels disjointed, breaking into a kaleidoscope's fractured colours, disappearing into a larger light, or is it darkness? It's hard to tell how things are. Everything I look at haunts me because it seems to have a life of its own. Trees move and rocks whisper. And sometimes when I look down my own shadow is observing things, observing me and making its own conclusions about my life. Everything seems to be speaking to me. The undead and unseen have voices. And the air is as much alive as I am, breeding stories and messages, populating the earth with ideas about things to come. I keep moving to get away from the noise.

The indifference of people keeps me awake at night. I hear it scratching and grating against a metallic surface. I must keep moving, the noise is driving me crazy. When they look at me they see someone to loathe. And this is not enough, for I must also loathe myself. I must understand the humility of shit. All the ugly things people have said to me. I think of my father. I think about you, Mama. And the whole thing doesn't make sense: you, me and him. Perhaps he is the reason why I am running away. I am running away from loathing him. For loathing myself is really about loathing him.

I don't want to push hate too far. It is too destructive. I could spend eternity with my own wishes for things my father could have been to me. Rather, I must make my own opportunities. I must invoke my own ideas about Father. I must decode the logic of my own madness. Life is telling me something. I am listening. I am trying to see beyond my father. I must look for him in vagrants that plague the streets of Cape Town and horny teenagers screwing in dirty public toilets when they are not injecting themselves with heroin or smoking crack. I must explore the seedy back streets of Sea Point and the hellish nightmare of the Cape Flats, the underbelly of human misery. I must confront the worst in myself, the things I loathe about myself like my small shy penis and my debilitating fear of men. I must wonder why I always surround myself with women, why I can never look another man in the eye, why I won't allow my own masculinity to blossom. For surely just like a flower a man can blossom. I must sleep under a tree, masturbate in public places, get high on acid and feel defeated by a harsh beating sun. I must know the cold, understand the wetness of rain and the thing the wind complains about when it blows through streets. I must feel depression and rejection. I must experience violence and cry for blood. I must see other mad men and people with wizened faces like they have been living in secret in hiding. I must walk as though I'm amputated at the knees, as though there are too many streets to walk, too many routes to attempt, too many interests along the way, too much to see. I must feel overwhelmed by the expanse and intelligence of life and all the varying degrees of living. I must look at cock-roaches and wonder at crawling through a crevice, being that flat, that small. I must become a world to myself, an encyclopaedia unfolding, a garden that needs to be tended.

I must feel that I have won myself, like a bird that remembers that it was taught to fly and succeeded. I must walk till there is nothing left till I have no energy left to expand on ideas of a father. I must walk till I only feel the fatigue, till I drop on my bed when I go to sleep and wake up with the sun shining in my eyes. I must feel my throat tighten and ache when I eat because I earned it. I must remember that every-thing is earned, even self-love. Because to know yourself is to love yourself. I must be obsessed by this walking because no one is going to teach me how to be a man. No one is going to show me how to get across a broken bridge. I must fall a few times trying, sink to the depths of depression. I must learn to crawl again, my face in the dirt. I must become a light unto myself. I must trust no one. No one is the per-son I must trust. Hello, no one. Can you hear me? I must not stop to think too much because I trust nothing anymore. The only thing I know is you, Mama.

A dark cloud is hovering over my head, Mama. The air is pregnant with doom. There are evil forces at work. I see it wherever I go, in the street in town, in my neighbourhood and in the block of flats where I stay. There are eyes following me with sinister intent. Evil cannot hide, Mama, it is too proud and wants to be seen. It comes with different faces: itinerant hawkers, salesmen, beauticians, housewives, fruit sell-ers, students, children. They have all looked at me with a hunger for destruction, taunting me with the music of dementia. They keep me awake at night and chase me in my dreams riding goats and yelling obscenities. I have seen people with a piercing look that only want to crush and annihilate. They try to draw me into their web with their spells and incantations. They chew gum, irritate pigeons so that they fly too close to me, carry large suspicious bags and tie up their hair tightly, concealing their evil. And sometimes the women wear black and blood red robes and when you look at them you know that they are capable of killing their own children. They never smile when they pass me but hiss esoteric curses. Or they try to intimidate me with scents and smells that give me sharp headaches.

I've walked the city drugged into somnambulism. I've walked till my feet have ached with blisters, till I've yearned for sleep as though it were my best friend, my only friend. Sometimes I walk into the city's bowels where they plant their evil; unspeakable evil that keeps us gleefully oppressed. It is under bridges, near the Good Hope Centre, at the Khayelitsha train stop, in town and in libraries. That is where some of their evil lies in the form of rotting filth and pollution. They use darkness and shadows the way an artist understands his palette and the effects of light. And some of the homeless, Mama, they've been trained into the ways of evil much against their will. Street children have run away from me because I saw demons in their eyes. Rats scurry, pigeons flutter.

I lost my bags at the train station in town. I'm convinced that evil has something to do with it. When my stomach troubles me or a disorientating headache attacks me I imagine them cutting up my clothes and using them for occult practices. And when I walk the streets there are always people following me, Mama. Witches, wizards, old men with bent backs, layabouts with dark rings under their eyes because they don't sleep and insidious-looking viragos with long hair wearing ancient pagan symbols. The things they do to their bodies and what they eat – they are darkness itself. Some of the women limp when they walk as though their wombs are shriveling up inside them, as though they are mutilating and torturing themselves in humble places. When I look at them I see decapitated babies and demons with deformed features. I have met an obese woman with so much evil under her wig that her eyes couldn't blink. Evil is paranoid, it wants to see everything. I have heard prayers spoken out in a twisted sequence by someone trying to divine their power and use it for harm. I have been trapped in mid-sleep when the voice of a primeval force whispered a death trance to me. I have been dogged by the idea of a number growing so big in my mind that it takes over my thoughts.

I think about you a lot, Mama, because you are the only beacon of light and love in a moribund landscape where deranged people high on their own ego dance at Death's altar. They are all death-worshipping, these people that are never too far behind me. I know their persistence, the stench of their decay. They fill the air with foreboding wherever they go. It is against them that my instincts protect me. I have seen the darkest angel gloating at his legion of acolytes. I have watched this dark one who walks in the middle of the road, tempting the weak and soulless. Waiting is his game.

And so I walk around the city in cramped circles searching for a little respite while my body succumbs to fatigue. But always my thoughts are with you, Mama. You are my centre even though I feel lost and without form, a leaf drifting on the vagaries of life. You are like a cool river flowing with clear water, the sacred Nile, the mother of all people. You are like the tiger that rides the night in my dreams roaring in a dance to something as old as life. I've known your sweet milk in a time I forgot at birth. When I weep and think of you, it is for Africa that I purge myself so that I may see you clearly. You were only a shadow in life, in death I've grown to know you in spirit. Sleeping Isis, I look for you in troubled places, in neglected gardens, in dark alleys and dingy shebeens with belligerent clients, courting danger and death even though that is not my way. I look for you in my dreams, along the shores of my memories of childhood, they will always be enigmas to me. I will scale indomitable mountains, roam endless cities and subject myself to the worst the world has to offer if only I can feel your soft embrace, a warm sun, a gentle breeze, a pensive sunset that makes me yearn for a place I knew before time. I have sung all my tears away thinking about you as the streets continue to swallow me up and as the shamans of darkness dance around a cauldron of madness.

So I went away to a nature reserve with David, my friend, Mama. David who sees with his heart and not the shallowness of eyes. I had to get away. I was looking for you, waiting for you to call out my name, and you did. You remember my name. You remember how I like to feel warm under my skin, how I appreciate the comfort of shoes but prefer the earth as it is. You remember my song, the music of a gentle stream and the rustling of pebbles. And how playful you are in trying to open my eyes. Look closer, you are always saying, just a little closer. And so I peer into the dark lake whose waters are impenetrable like the Congo River.

And in the lake I see terrible things, Mama; poverty and children with kwashiorkor playing with guns. I see screaming women running with their arms open to the sky because they were sleeping while life snatched away their emaciated children. I see hardship and strife and politicians fattening up on the hopes of people. I see people rising from the putrid smells of oppression. But I also see their wounds, Mama. And they are deep raw gashes. Maggots are never far away. I see industrialists drinking the blood of rivers and defecating on our fears. I see old men tired of protest leading us further into darkness laughing and joking the way they did in the sixties while the world was getting drunk on free love. I see suicidal children who don't know what it means to scratch around in your pockets for coins that are not there, to scratch around till you make holes at the bottom of your pockets.

And people who are indifferent to the greed of banks and the humiliation of an empty stomach always grumbling. The mighty will fall under their own weight, monarchies will collapse. I see the corruption of politicians and cabinet ministers fraternising in parks in broad daylight with gangsters and drug lords. Perhaps we do not fear the scrutiny of daylight enough. I walk because of them and all the ugliness they have left us. But the ugliness from which we are trying to run is us. And always there is this terrifying screaming that comes from the deepest places within me. And it fills my lungs with air when I listen to that primeval scream of a thousand eons. It makes me remember that the story is still unfolding, that there is more to come. A storm is rising, a monster we created in our nightmares is hungry, it is stalking us. The serpent is writhing in fury. Great trees will topple, mountains will come crashing down. The world will be in uproar, people devouring each other while terrible cold and intolerable heat persist. When I listen to the beast's slicing screams I know that a stifled will is longing to break free. A feral creature is out there, every day I feel it advancing.


## PATRICK

**I** don't know much about him but I like him immediately. He seems uncomplicated but he isn't simple. I can tell he has learning, his eyes are always roaming, looking for new things to catch his attention. Details fascinate him the way some people are fussy about their appearance. He has many books and spends hours poring over them like a child playing with a favourite toy. He has a lot of time and patience for those tiny scribbles. I was never like that as a young man. I was too eager to finish school and start out in life. Youth burned me with energy. After I left home I ran out madly to live and got into trouble with everything a young man with hormones encounters. Now the older I get, the less I seem to know, the slower, more cautiously I seem to go. The only thing a man can rely on when he wakes up is that he is breathing and that means something.

Akousia likes him too. He's neat and he's always ready to help around the flat, she says. And I think he likes her too. He has a way with women because she is always fussing over him. And he likes to walk. Sometimes he comes back late at night and when I ask him where he has been he just mumbles. And I can smell that thing on his breath. But I say nothing because he takes his learning seriously.

Smoking ganja is a way of seeing things when you're young. Sometimes it can open your eyes to a world that was dormant before. I understand that, that's why I leave him. He must learn his own lessons.

He can be moody and quiet. I guess that he is an only child. Aloneness is like a blanket to him. It wasn't like that when I was growing up. A man alone is always in bad company, my father used to say. But they are all like that today. A man cannot rely on the friendship of his peers for help. Everyone seems to be getting on with the business of living alone, getting by.

The world is uncaring, he says. He speaks with solemnity that belongs to someone older than him. Sometimes it irritates me. Sometimes I cringe when I listen to him speak. It sounds almost blasphemous to hear him cry about his disillusionment with life. He is too young, I feel. I haven't seen any old scars. Youth blinds one with energetic hope, why has it missed him?

He is serious. Everything affects him: whites, their whining about post-apartheid South Africa, the new government and its corruption, fat politicians, drug lords, the police and the opportunistic heists, pollution, nuclear testing, the price of food, the cost of living, the poor, the rich, the disabled, the aged, the mountain, stars and moon – on and on he goes. I listen because I suspect he doesn't have anyone else to listen to him, to hear his words. He is angry. It is normal, I reassure him. Every black man gets to know anger intimately sooner or later. But control it, mould it, I warn him. It can either be a useful tool or the cause of your ruin.

"You think life is bad. In Zaire Mobuthu used up all the country's wealth. People starved while his children were running to Europe for shopping sprees. Can you imagine that? This man was in charge of a nation. He left us nothing. At least your economy is intact," I tell him.

"But we also have poverty, people on the breadline and most people kid themselves when they call this a First World country. The whites have been evil to us. South Africa during the eighties was a war zone. It was horrible. I don't know if you know about Soweto," he says, his eyes earnest. He speaks about evil a lot.

"Ah, oui, Soweto, I think I've heard about it," I say dumbly even though I know enough about it. I say this to encourage him to speak. He needs to paint a picture of the world with things he can see and understand, with words as his toys. And when he isn't speaking he walks. He's like that, he doesn't give life too many options to deal with him. But I suspect that one day he will see through words, he will outgrow them. When the ideas have been grasped and the howling inside of him stops, he will begin to see and not rely so much on his feelings.

"Yes necklacing and petrol bombs," Akousia says with a disgusted look.

"But what about the security police and their brutality? People vanished. I know people who disappeared overnight because the police came knocking on their door," he says, his breath hot with ardour.

"But it's the same in the DRC and all over the world."

"Yes, but this is different. White people did this to us. The security police, they were evil," he says with a tormented look.

"It's like that in South America too," I put in, "what the Spanish did to the native people and eventually to the African slaves ... That's history, life, you can't change it, you can't control it. Get on with living, leave life alone."

"It's still fresh to me. Can't you understand that? It was like yesterday, the curfews, the running around the township with nothing to do but toyi-toyi, the detentions ... And the vicious lies that come with horrible deaths, I can't forget them. I won't forget them," he says painfully.

Sometimes all a person can do is listen.

After a while he gets up abruptly and says he is going to do some work. But we can see that he is upset.


TSHEPO

**H**e died.

He committed suicide by jumping off John Vorster Square, they will say. Or is it that he died from hitting his head several times against his cell wall? Perhaps he died hanging himself with a rope from nowhere, his hands handcuffed. Maybe he choked himself to death. How about he accidentally slipped on something in an empty cell and injured his brain with one fatal fall? Or was it John Vorster that fell on him? They could say his hands slammed his head and he slipped off the cell walls and fell out of John Vorster. But what about the marks on his neck? And the incisions on his groin? And his mutilated penis? Even when the life in question is only eleven years old?

And the mother? What will they say to the boy's mother?

Nothing.

They won't say anything to her, at least for a while. Perhaps until worry has wrecked her nerves and weeks of waiting, always hungry for news about her child has made her thin and the couple drift apart to find their strengths in private. Perhaps they might even wait a week when the child's body lies cold with others in John Vorster and starts to smell. But definitely they will keep her waiting.

Ja, baas. Ja, waiting will take the kaffir bitch apart bit by bit. Silly bitch, serves her right. Making blerry smear rags to throw petrol bombs at us. Ja, make her wait. Who does she blerry think she is? You're right, baas, kaffirs are getting too clever.

And if her ancestors are with her they might give her the child and not bury him in some mass anonymous grave or leave him for the neighbours to find too early in the morning at some rubbish dump.

And the funeral? They might disrupt it because there are too many people with too many ideas and energy.

And justice for the boy? Fuck justice! Justice se moer! Masepa! This is war and the regime is in power but shhh, no one must know or say this. They will sanitise it, they will call it "unrest", a "disturbance" while the bloody townships go up in flames. Who the fuck cares about the townships anyway, these cageships?

And the neighbours? What about them? What can they do? Their son reported the dead boy in the first place.

But surely comfort … Comfort? What about it? Who will comfort the mother? Who will listen to her cries when the father walks Jo'burg in search of work, secretly crying over his crumbling pride because he cannot afford a loaf of bread for supper? Who will comfort her?

No one!

And she will survive as many have.

And when the yearning to call out for her son at street games fades, she might still have her sanity and a husband beside her in bed. And on days when she feels the sun is warm and the air pleasant, she might smile.

### AKOUSIA

He has hardly been living with us a week when we had to send him away. It's sad but we had to do it. He left us no option.

One night we wake up to policemen banging on our door. One of our neighbours has complained that Tshepo is throwing stuff over the balcony. We open his door and find him on the balcony, throwing papers and clothes away. He doesn't seem surprised to see the cops. He almost snarls at them and continues tearing up papers and throwing them away.

"Tshepo, what are you doing?" Patrick begins.

He doesn't answer.

"Meneer, wat gaan aan hier?" one of the cops says and I tell him that we don't speak the language.

We move to the balcony and look down at the mess he has made.

"I must get on with my work." He pushes us aside and goes into his room to sort out more things to throw out.

"Listen here, you can't just do that here. This is not Gugulethu. The neighbours have complained," the policeman says.

"I guess I've been a bad boy," he mocks them.

"Hey this is serious, man," one of them says.

Patrick slaps him hard to get the point across. He looks at him with all the anger he can muster and then his face becomes calm again. That is when I realise that something is wrong with him.

"What I'm doing is also serious," he smirks. "I'm ridding the world of evil."

"Tshepo, just listen to the policemen," Patrick says annoyed.

"So what are you going to do about it?" the one says and looks at him.

"I suppose I better clean up this mess," he says, not the least bit concerned.

He takes some plastic bags from the kitchen and goes downstairs.

"Listen, folks, the neighbours have complained. This is a quiet block. I've never had trouble. What's wrong with your friend?" the officer asks.

"I don't know. He's been with us a few days," Patrick says.

"He's got a little attitude problem. I can see," the other says crunching his knuckles and making popping sounds.

"I think he's not well in the head," the one says, "is he gerook?"

"What does that mean?" Patrick says a little impatiently as I told them we don't speak the language.

"Does he smoke dagga?" he repeats.

"We don't really know anything about him," Patrick says and looks at me to validate his lie. I shrug and give them a blank expression even though I know that he has been smoking the stuff, excessively. Patrick and him thought it was their little secret. But I know he never encouraged him. He wouldn't do that. Anyway, he's in enough trouble without cops searching for evidence in his room.

I want to say that perhaps Sister Hendriks will be able to tell us more about Tshepo but I decide against this. There was something awkward about the way they greeted each other. I'm not convinced that Sister Hendriks is a family friend.

I take a look around Tshepo's room while they talk on the balcony. I've never really done it because he's so private and spends so much time alone in here; I hate to disturb him. Sometimes when I bring in his washing I'll have a look at what he's reading on his desk. They're mostly obscure books for a person with too much learning and not enough sense. But when I'm alone with him, we talk. He tells me a little about what he does when he's not in his room. I get confused between thinking that he is working or looking for a job. He doesn't say much. What he likes talking about is the places that Patrick and I have been to in Africa. And the masks, how they interest him.

"Your mother must have loved you," I say to him one day as we delight in talking about the Dogon.

"Why do you say that?" His expression suddenly changes, sadness almost clouding his face.

"Because you are so easy around me. You must have many girlfriends," I tease him but the damage is done. He looks hurt and makes an excuse to go somewhere.

That incident always stays with me. It stays with me because it sums up Tshepo. His big overgrown eyes that appear childlike are not what they seem. His face begs many questions. I can't but wonder who his parents are. He has that sort of effect on people. Even though he seems oblivious to anyone who looks at him because he is so caught up in his own thoughts, you can't help feeling like protecting him because he is so adventurous, so foolishly bold in what he thinks, in how he expresses it, and in his lack of concern for what people will think. His idealism intrigues me, that's why I always wonder about his parents. I wonder about the kind of people who brought up such a sad boy. For he is a boy. His moodiness disguised as intellectual posturing is overgrown. He was probably the same with his parents, he didn't say much. And his mother probably went through his things to try to get an idea about what he was thinking about, what was going on in that head of his always in the clouds. She did it because he left her feeling confused, a little inadequate, she probably never knew anything about him and when she discovered something it shocked her because she felt so unprepared. Some children are like that, they are too self-sufficient and leave you anxious about your role as a woman. He probably never said anything to her, never said anything that really mattered like how he felt or what was troubling him. They probably talked about the news or the things that fascinate him from his books. She must have worried, probably spoiled him a little and started confiding in him till he grew up too fast. That's why he has that look, his eyes big and his face awkward with facial hair. Life goes on, people grow up. He doesn't realise that. Or rather he refuses. Everything must be about him and how he views the world, his suffering must come first. It doesn't matter to him how the world views him. It probably never struck him that his mother worried about him and spent sleepless nights. It doesn't matter to him that he will always be a child in her eyes and as such she will never cease to want to know things about him. I think it is a male thing.

There is a postcard by Salvador Dali of Christ on the cross on his wardrobe. He has surrounded it with photos of his few friends. There is a picture of a woman placed below Christ. She is sitting on a bench in some exotic surrounding. She is smiling radiantly while the wind blows her Afro to one side. And she is beautiful. There is something familiar about her. He has her eyes. Past the smile I can see his serious demeanour in her. His mother, I guess. There is another photograph with "Leaver's Dinner" written at the bottom. Tshepo is in the middle, flanked by his friends. He is laughing and wears a suit. It is strange to see him like that. The other photos are of him on Table Mountain. His chest is bare and the photographer catches him just as he turns back, a dreamy romantic look in his eyes. Ahead of him is a panoramic view of the sprawling city. On the wardrobe handle there is a luminous rosary, the kind that absorbs light and glows in the dark. He is a love child, conceived in a moment of intense passion; all his belongings betray this secret.

Tshepo returns after a while with six bags filled with the stuff he threw over the balcony. The police officers give him a stern warning but he is aloof with them and walks to his room while they are still talking. Patrick apologises and sees them to the door. Then he locks the balcony door and keeps the key. He looks at Tshepo angrily.

"What is the meaning of this business?" he shouts.

"I was getting rid of evil," Tshepo says plainly.

"Enough now. You can't do that here. Do you understand?"

"There are people plotting evil things against me. That neighbour across the other side, she's the mother of evil. She and her minions chase me round the city," he says.

"Alright, just stop there, Tshepo. Enough!"

I hold his arm to calm him. He doesn't like to be told he's shouting.

"Enough? I've just begun. You think I'm going to let them get away with it? You think I'm just going to sit back and watch?" Tshepo says incredulously.

"We've been here for a month and we like it here. If you think we are going to watch you mess things up for us, you better think again parce que moi j'en ai marre," he says and points at him.

"Patrick." I press his arm.

He storms off to the bedroom. I try to talk to Tshepo but he is distracted and otherworldly. He keeps telling me that evil is out to get him and starts fiddling with his papers again.

We spend a restless night. Tshepo keeps us awake with his activities. We hear furniture moving, music playing and him talking to himself till the early hours of the morning. Patrick is furious but I convince him to ignore Tshepo. We'll deal with him in the morning, I plead.

We phone Sister Hendriks first thing in the morning and she tells us that Tshepo has been in Valkenberg. Patrick is furious. She should have told us he was a mental patient, he shouts. We manage to convince Tshepo that Sister Hendriks wants to see him. Patrick grudgingly agrees to go with him. A police van is waiting for him outside. "You betrayed me, Patrick," is all he says as he gets in the back of the van. Patrick gets in front. They escort him to Valkenberg. I start to pack his belongings.

TSHEPO

They drive me away. It is a quiet, cloudless day. I can see the back of their heads. They are taking me back to the madhouse, where everyone knows the Truth. They are going to inject me with their poison and brain soups that only nourish amnesia. He is better off, they will justify the stupor that will soon affect me. At least he can rest and be of no danger to himself, they will add while side effects blunt my concentration and I start to develop a nervous tic. He's doing much better, they will say, while healthy natural aggression seeps out of my eyes and soulless defeat becomes my mask.

I won't resist. The truth is I'm tired of fighting. There's nowhere left to run. I will play along. I will swallow their brain soups and I will sleep on their flea-infested beds and watch my skin grow irritable with scabies. I will listen to the dull staff who treat us like imbeciles. I will get up when they tell me, shit when they tell me, wash when they tell me, eat when they tell me and sleep when they tell me. I will suspend all dreams while I'm here because their brain soups are too powerful. I will wear decrepit clothing, the mismatched socks, the oversized underwear, the undersized three-quarter trousers and the stained shirts. I will idle away my time by pacing and napping, napping and pacing. I will watch others succumb to real madness and listen to them scream obscenities. I will listen to my heart when it remembers a walk outside in the sun, a swim in the sea. I will follow all the stupid rules because I know I'm not mad. I know why water tastes so good when I'm thirsty.

When we get to the ward one of the policemen wearing dark glasses opens the back of the van for me. Patrick remains in the front. He says nothing and hardly looks at me as one of the officers escort me in.

It is the usual. They take down my details and I soon change into the hospital fatigues. And then they give me a bevy of tablets. The first course is always the worst. It is like a heavy dose of reality that makes you weak at the knees. After a while I slump into a chair and become part of the furniture. The others walk past me, drooling, farting, saying a thing or two and then walk off again.

Everything becomes slower. It fades. My eyes become heavy with fatigue. I want to sleep. I want to become sleep. Somewhere in the room Zebron has been watching me. I'm too tired to think about him. I must rest. I must let real madness heal me.


## MMABATHO

**A**rne has called a few times, begging and pleading and going on about how sorry he is and how much he misses me. I've heard it all before and it doesn't impress me. I don't have much to say to him, not after what he did to me. And Nthabiseng, I never see her. Just as well that she's slithered out of sight. He says that they are not together, that it was a bad idea, a mistake, something he regrets doing because he was drunk. But men are so stupid, do they really think using alcohol exonerates them? If anything it makes it worse. I mean what other things should I know of that he is capable of doing when he is drunk? It's a pathetic excuse.

"But were you ever going to tell me about it?" I ask him. There is a moment of silence and then he says, "Of course," with a tone of false confidence. So I hang up the phone on him. But he is persistent. He calls at least three times a week and he's always frantic with my digsmates that they take down the messages he leaves.

I've been spending a lot of time at Ganesh when I'm not hanging out with David and Ntombi. Karuna keeps tempting me back to her warm bed when I see her at Ganesh. But I never do it. It would be a mistake. Besides, I don't want to rush into another relationship, not so soon. I don't know how men do it.

"I just feel so disappointed, you know? I was really beginning to like him," I say to Karuna towards the end of her shift at Ganesh. We're both drinking a Savannah and we've already had a few. David, Ntombi and Anthony are on the terrace smoking spliff. The lights are out except for a candle that burns at the couch table where I sit with Karuna, both of us drunk. The hypnotic crooning of Massive Attack fills the room. Anthony is about to close.

"How can you be serious about a penis?" she says and her body jerks a little as she lets out a hiccup.

"Don't start. You know I like men," I say and take a swig from the bottle. "I just feel so stupid because I wasn't supposed to like him, you know how I feel about zero men. He was just another guy. Ag, anyway, I don't want to talk about him."

Karuna puts her hand on my thigh.

"Don't do this, you're drunk." I take her hand away.

"You're such a fuckin' tease," she suddenly explodes, slurring.

"What? You're drunk," I say trying to remain calm.

"I'm not drunk, I'm lonely, but that's beside the point. You're a fuckin' tease." She points at me and gets up to get herself another drink.

"I think you've had enough," I say convincing myself to sober up as I watch her stumble to the bar and come back with another drink.

"Don't you like me?" she goes on.

"This is pathetic. You know if you were a guy you would be considered a snake, a real dickhead. I mean here I am pouring out my heart to you 'cause I consider you a friend and what are you doing? You're trying to take advantage of me."

She says nothing. We drink in silence while I light a cigarette.

"Do you want another one?" she asks once I finish my drink.

"No thanks." I reach for a pitcher of water and a glass.

"I think I love you," she says after a while.

"You're full of shit, Karuna, you're just drunk."

"Do you know the last time anyone touched me?"

I roll my eyes and look at her.

"Six months ago."

"There are worse things," I tell her and begin to drink several glasses of water.

Anthony, Ntombi and David come back. They look suitably stoned and talk in gestures.

"Have you guys seen the moon?" Ntombi says as they sit down at our table. "It's so yellow, it's so fuckin' yellow tonight."

"Maybe that's why Karuna is so horny," I say and they laugh but Karuna doesn't hear or she pretends she doesn't hear. She stumbles to the toilet.

"We should be going," David finally says and invites us to his place. But Anthony says he is too tired and Karuna says she is too drunk. I kiss them both on the cheek and we leave for David's place just up the road. He has been living with Ntombi for about eight months. They seem to be getting on – actually they seem close. I expected them to break up because I thought David was too complex to ever settle down with anyone. He never wanted to move in with me. When we were going out I thought I knew him as well as a person could get to know someone else. I was intensely in love with him, foolishly trusting. How wrong I was about him. But it doesn't irk me anymore to see them together. I'm just upset by the fact that I'm not with anyone. And seeing them together makes me a little sad.

We walk to their place on Dove Street.

"You seem very quiet tonight," David says.

"No, I'm just drunk," I lie but they know the reason for my reticence.

"Ukaruna can be a handful when she's drunk, nè?" Ntombi says and we both smile. "This one time before I went out with David she tried to get me drunk so that I would ask her to go home with me. Shoo, and she can drink! So there we were and all of a sudden she puts her hand on my breast." She smiles and her eyes are red and dilated.

"Ja, she gets out of hand when she's drunk."

"Hey and aganxili Ukaruna. That thing she was doing in there. It's all an act. We once went drinking with her. Do you remember?" Ntombi says and turns to David, who nods, "And she was with this other woman that she wanted. And they had been drinking all night. Anyway, she was going to drive us home and we were worried that she might be drunk. As soon as we got into the car the other woman passed out but Karuna was up and she drove us home safely. Yo haai Ukaruna ..."

"She's very lonely, though," I tell them, "I mean, underneath all that bullshit and toughness, she's very lonely and fragile. Her family hasn't taken to her being gay. It's hard, you know. The things she tells me about her family, they can be so cruel."

David gets to the door and lets us in. Litha, their housemate, isn't in. Ntombi switches on the radio and opens a bottle of white wine. I lounge on the couch with David while she gets glasses in the kitchen. Momentarily alone with him I suddenly feel awkward. It's hard to explain, sometimes I think I'm completely over him and convince myself that I don't find him attractive. Other times, like now, I find myself looking at his neck and other parts of his body that I once knew intimately. Perhaps that is just the effect of the dim, suggestive light in the lounge. Perhaps I'm just lonely tonight. He fiddles with his lighter while I try to convince myself that I don't really like him.

"So how is Tshepo?" Ntombi returns with three glasses.

"Not well. They took him in this morning," I say and sigh.

"You mean he's back in Valkenberg?"

"Ja, I was supposed to see him today but I just couldn't."

"He's really fucked up," Ntombi says. "I could see this coming. Didn't you? I'm not surprised." She gets comfortable on the couch with David.

"What do you mean?"

"I mean he's fucked up. A friend of mine who went to Rhodes with him says he comes from a rich family and went to private schools and all that jazz."

"So?" I say. "I went to private schools. What has that got to do with anything?"

"Well, apparently he didn't mingle much with black people on campus. He was always at those awful rugby and cricket parties, balls and ntoni ntoni. You know how Rhodes can be, very colonial."

"So does that mean he's a perfect candidate for a mental institution?" I say annoyed.

"Well, he was confused, hanging out with white people all the time," she says and David doesn't flinch.

"You know that whole blacker than thou thing just bores me, Ntombi. You assume because he spent time with these guys that he was confused. How do you know that? Maybe he knew what he was doing. Maybe his going mad has nothing to do with that?" I say and look at David for a response but he says nothing.

"Don't get me wrong or anything. When I say white I'm talking about a culture, not a race. The same with private schools. I've met tons of people both black and white who've gone there and they haven't picked up all of the private school ways."

"Like what?" I say irritated.

"You know. Some of these kids are snobbish and they think that they're better off and what have you," she says with a silly look on her face.

"God, you sound like you have an inferiority complex."

"You know what she's trying to say," David comes to her rescue, cuddling her, fondling her hair.

"Anyway, I thought you liked Tshepo," I say.

"We do," Ntombi says but it doesn't sound convincing. They probably tolerate him or find him mildy interesting.

I decide to say nothing further. I know that Ntombi doesn't have the fortune of having gone to a private school but I refuse to be apologetic.

For a while we do nothing but drink and listen to the radio, Mary J Blige belting out one of her anthems to women. Metro is good on a Friday night when you're feeling down and useless.

"Are you going to Fiona's wedding next week?" Ntombi asks.

"Yes." I dread her next question.

"So are you going with that guy, what's his name?"

"Arne. No, I'm not going with him. We broke up," I say. They've been dying to hear me admit that. It's been hovering in the air for a while. Obs is small. Word gets around quickly. People know things that have nothing to do with them. That's what you get living in a place that small where relationships always risk becoming incestuous.

"Oh," she says, "maybe you can bring Tshepo."

"I don't think he'll be out by then. Besides, a day visit out to Fiona's won't do him any good. You know how her friends get with drugs and everything."

When I'm not at Drama class I go out because I don't want to sit at home and start itching to phone Arne and find out how he is doing. And then he'll be nice to me and I'll be polite to him and soon we'll be making arrangements for a little get-together, which is a pathetic name for a date. But saying date would be too presumptuous and impulsive, would be like diving into the sea while recovering from frostbite.

So I wait. I'm waiting for the need to think about Arne to fade. Ntombi has been telling her friends that I'm available again. She's irritating like that. I think she pities me because I'm on my own and she has David, as if it's a disability to be single as a woman. But I think she does it because she feels a little threatened by the fact that I'm single again. I'm not so sure he's all that faithful to her. I see it in his eyes the way he looks at other women, the way he's quiet sometimes while he's making up his mind about someone. It's with that guy expression like I'll fuck you but I'm going out with someone. And he probably does it when she's away at work, doing whatever she does. There are women like that, who don't mind having regular casual sex with guys in a relationship, people like Nthabiseng. No strings attached. I suppose the sex and company are what I want in all these zero guys I keep going out with. The problem with them is that I don't like sharing them with other women. Why couldn't Arne get that? Why did he have to go and spoil a perfectly agreeable situation? He never complained about sex; I have an active libido which complemented our needs.

It's irritating how men are. I'd hate to think that it was a biological prerequisite for them to want to have as many women as they can in a short space of time.

Yesterday I bumped into an old childhood boyfriend, Lukhanyo. He said he'd just moved to Cape Town and was working for some merchant bank. It was nice to get excited about someone I hadn't seen in a long time. We went to dinner.

"I didn't expect you to recognise me," he says while we wait for our food at La Perla in Sea Point.

"Don't be silly, I've known you forever," I say flirting a little.

"No, it's just that the last time I saw you, you were taller than me and my face was plastered with that Clearasil stuff."

"I knew you'd turn out fine in the end," I tease him.

The evening goes like that. We spend much of it reminiscing about growing up and all the people we fancied and the things we did for them. But by the end of our supper it is getting clear that he is trying to rekindle the old flame.

"We were quite cute together, you and me. Do you remember?" he says and plays with my hand casually.

I don't say anything. I always leave things until the last possible moment when it comes to guys. We go Dutch for supper and it annoys him when I insist on this.

"But you're still a student," he reasons as though I'm attacking his masculinity.

"Whatever," I say and watch the waiter take the bill away.

Afterwards he invites me to his bachelor flat in Greenpoint. He puts on Brazilian jazz with a gentle samba rhythm, his dark eyes studying my body. And soon one gesture leads to another and we are kissing on his plush divan. It is strange to feel the weight of a man again. I begin to feel awkward, a little out of step as our noses bump and we twist and turn. I feel his eagerness pressing against my thigh, his breath becoming heavier, wetter.

"I can't do this," I suddenly say and get up, feeling a little silly because this is the sort of thing men hate and use to accuse women for being cockteasers. But he understands and doesn't ask me any questions. It helps that he is a childhood friend. I go to the bathroom to gather my thoughts.

It is too late to drive to Obs so I stay the night at his place. He offers me his bedroom while he sleeps on the divan. Finally when he gives me a T-shirt to sleep in he asks, "So what's his name?"

"It's a long story," I say embarrassed and not eager to get into that.

He looks at me and smiles. I hug him. That look stays with me as I lie in his bed.


TSHEPO

I wake up somewhere between a throbbing headache and swirling reds, blues and yellows. Someone opens the door and says rise and shine in a mocking, dead tone. It hurts to open my eyes as the light comes rushing through the door. Sipho stands over me.

"You thought you were smart, nè, running away like that," he sniggers. I'm still lying on the sponge and rub my eyes.

"Ja, we'll see how you like the kulukutz," he says and leaves, locking the door. He switches on the light. A vapid fluorescent light flickers above me. My eyes ache. I sit on the sponge and peer at my breakfast. Fast colours flash before my eyes again in a fantastic sequence that leaves me dizzy.

I reach for the porridge. The bastard hasn't put in any sugar. I eat slowly. My body feels heavy, like a lump of lead beaten to a flat disc. I try to move my neck but it is stiff. I drink some coffee and spill some. It is excessively sweet. I eventually pour some of the coffee in the porridge just to get a little sweetness. My headache is determined. A tornado is wrecking my brain. Their brain soups are working, they are dissolving my brain. I try to think which day of the week it is but my thoughts are fuzzy. I blink a lot, trying to steady my head from its swaying. It feels so heavy.

Sipho comes back later. "Hini, a'funi ukudla? You didn't eat your bread." I can tell he is thinking of ways to torment me. He gives me my medication and watches me while I swallow three tablets. And then he leaves. I go back to bed and wrap myself with the coarse, fetid blankets. They are cold and uncaring like hospital linen. I lie on my back and watch the fluorescent light flicker. Insects dance wildly round the light.

The smell of tea wakes me from the quiet violence of a dream. It is lunch time. I hear the shuffling of feet and plates scraping against the floor. And then the door is locked again. I get up and reluctantly eat the spaghetti with sparse cheese. The jelly adds sweetness to my mouth. I eat it gladly and think of nothing but sleep. It is cold in my cell and I don't have shoes. My headache returns. I don't wait for it to split my head. I go back to bed.

When the door opens for supper I ask Themba to go to the toilet. I've been suppressing my bowels for two hours. I don't like to shit in the piss pot. Besides, there isn't any toilet paper. He lets me go but waits impatiently.

"Are you finished?" he keeps saying. At first I ignore him. "Jesus, are you finished in there? You're not giving birth, for God's sake."

"Fuck off," I tell him.

Afterwards he grabs be by the arm and doesn't give me a chance to wash my hands.

Supper is minced meat, beans and three slices of bread. I'm famished. The medication keeps me hungry. I eat quickly even though I'm drowsy. Later Sipho comes to give me more brain soup. I swallow the other two tablets and look at the white one suspiciously, the one that makes me drowsy and weak. "Swallow," he orders me. I swallow and go back to bed. The door slams and I hear it click as he locks it. The clicking sound is like a death sentence. It feels as if no one will ever open the door again.

I spend the next day reading the graffiti on the walls and floor. I read everything carefully and try to imagine the people writing it and what frame of mind they were in. Then I pick the best line and think about why I like it. I think about this line a lot: THEYS GOING TO

BE TELING. After lunch, four slices of bread, lettuce and cucumbers dripping with vinegar and two boiled eggs, I reread all the graffiti again but this time backwards. I laugh when I have to say "RADEBE AND HIS BIG COCK WERE HERE".

A cockroach crawls under the door. They are incredibly flat creatures. I jump at the opportunity to amuse myself with it.

### MMABATHO

**I** hate weddings. They are an excuse for some women to band together and gloat that they are successful because they are married while the rest of us clutch onto irritable dates we just met, nervous about the introspection that weddings stir. But since it is my friend Fiona, I don't mind. It isn't a regular wedding anyway. She hand-posted all the invitations and it specifically said that this was to be a dress-up wedding. I'm not surprised. That sort of unusualness is just up her street. Once a month she and her boyfriend hold full moon parties. She's a third year painting student at the Michaelis, brooding and quiet with a face that reminds me of Anna Paquin, the child star of *The Piano*. Her complexion is just as pale as little Anna's, quintessentially English. I've seen Fiona's boyfriend a few times. When they're together they're irritating, the kind of couple who finish each other's sentences and live a breath away from each other when they are not torn apart by work. He's big and intimidating if you don't know him. His name is Jay and he works in a butchery. That's where she gets all the bones and skeletons of cows she paints obsessively. I don't know her well enough to tell her that I think she is making a big mistake; they barely know each other, I feel. But I know enough to see that he makes her happy, and I suppose that's enough for some people.

I met Fiona at Ganesh one night. She bought me a drink because I had beautiful skin she said and then she stuck out her hand to introduce herself. I liked her immediately. And we both learned that we had a passion for Frida Kahlo and her strikingly androgynous unibrow. She asked me to pose nude for her once. It was for part of a triptych involving multiple bodies in a bathroom. But in the end her bold harsh brush strokes, brutal with the rich application of paint somewhat reminiscent of Lucien Freud, made the skin of the bodies look like raw flesh, hardly different from the carcasses of cows she painted. When I told her how repulsed I felt by the image, she said that was the intention. After that I didn't think she was as naïve as she seemed.

I show up at Fiona's house with Lukhanyo. The other guests are also dressed up. We go as Ashford and Simpson. I raided the Drama department and found some fabulous wigs in the style of the two singers. And then I got a pink boa and a low cut, roaring twenties style sequined dress exposing most of my ample bosom while Lukhanyo got a pink V-neck cashmere jersey with flashy MC Hammer type pants and a conspicuous gold chain. I think we make a convincing imitation.

I've been seeing him for a few days. But I haven't slept with him. I'm still playing with the idea. The thing is he is so nice and polite, someone my mother would like and approve of. I fear his intentions are too good, too earnest. He's not playful enough. I don't want to rush into another relationship. I just want to be distracted for a while. When we pet he never tries to take advantage of me or suggest something daring. And he doesn't strike me as being particularly passionate. There's something clinical and rehearsed about his embrace. When he touches my neck I want to cringe because it is so obvious that he is trying to be sensual, sensitive. I prefer men to be themselves, uncoached and awkward, even if it means stumbling through sex. At least there is something honest about sex with a guy who doesn't really know what he's doing and doesn't pretend.

Karuna, Anthony and his girlfriend come as the three musketeers. Ntombi and David show up wearing clogs and costumes faintly Scandinavian. When I ask them who they are supposed to be, they tell me, Hansel and Gretel. They look displeased with their costumes as everyone keeps asking them. After a while a man dressed as a goblin asks the few guests to take their places as the ceremony is about to begin.

We sit in the small back garden, the lawn immaculately short. There must be about twelve couples. A woman dressed as Cruella De Vil keeps eyeing Lukhanyo. I say nothing. Jay, dressed as a Voortrekker complete with veldskoene, and a minister looking somewhat nervous and confused, stand in front. When the music comes on, "Dead Can Dance", Fiona, looking like Marie-Antoinette, walks through without any bridesmaids. She holds a small bouquet of wild orchids, a sad ironic look on her face as though she is about to be guillotined. It is a quick ceremony. The others cheer when the two kiss. Fiona manages to smile but keeps her bouquet and doesn't throw it to all the spinsters. And they don't bother to do the garter thing.

The reception is at Jay's house, a few houses away from Fiona's.

There is plenty of booze and spliff and a plump pig on the spit. Jay lights an enormous bong and passes it around. When he's not deejaying, religiously subjecting us to his collection of Bob Marley albums, he plays the effusive host walking around and asking everyone if they've had enough to drink. After a while someone takes over the music and the sound of Massive Attack comes as a relief to my ears. Reggae can be monotonous. In the kitchen I see two guys dressed as the Devil and the Grim Reaper pop some ecstacy and Fiona offers me half a cap of acid but I decline. Lukhanyo and I settle for light beer. Karuna keeps winking at me every time I meet her eye. We go outside for a while and join the small coterie smoking spliff. Karuna tells me that she met someone and that she thinks this is it for her. I tell her that I'm happy for her, even though I find her excitement and eagerness about such a new relationship juvenile. She always gives away too much too soon and ends up getting hurt. You must always leave something for yourself, I always tell her but I don't think she ever takes heed. I don't smoke much because it is potent Durban Poison and soon go back inside to be with Lukhanyo. I find him speaking to Anthony, mingling with my other friends. It is nice that I don't have to baby-sit him. My eyes must be a little sleepy and red because he brings his head to my ear and says, "You've been smoking that stuff haven't you?" He says it with harmless intent but I pick up the mild disapproval in his voice.

"I forget that you're from Jo'burg," I say to him unapologetically. "It's a lot more open in Cape Town. Everyone does it."

"And you're everyone?" he says and looks at me with his impenetrably dark eyes. I make an excuse to go to the loo.

I bump into Ntombi in the bathroom, fixing her make-up. She looks rather bored with her costume and fusses with her red cheeks in the mirror. Inevitably she asks me about Lukhanyo.

"I've known him since I was small," I tell her.

"He seems like a nice guy," she says, mildly condescending as if I need her approval.

"Ja, he works for some merchant bank in town. I don't know which," I say to show he's not a fool.

"Nice job."

"Listen, I really need the loo," I tell her and she leaves. That's why I don't like women. They are too competitive. Why couldn't she just say I'm happy for you, or at least pretend?

I avoid David and Ntombi for the rest of the day. Lukhanyo and I talk to two gay friends of mine dressed in drag, one as Diana Ross and the other as Mariah Carey. They sit on the couch with their legs entwined, discussing the fate of drag queens in inner cities. I expect Lukhanyo to be uncomfortable but he isn't. I know what the gay scene in Jo'burg is like. People don't have to confront gay people as much as one does in Cape Town. And anyway I have so many gay friends it would make things difficult if Lukhanyo was homophobic. We chat to the two when Arne suddenly walks in.

"Fuck," I let out and look the other way.

"What's wrong?" Lukhanyo asks while I try to hide my face. But soon Arne is standing beside me.

"I didn't think you'd come," I say to him, a little embarrassed.

"Just because we broke up doesn't mean we can't see each other," he says boldly and smiles, wearing a tight floral shirt and fawn corduroy pants.

"It's a dress up wedding, you could have made the effort," I say just to annoy him.

"Everyone's too stoned to notice," he says, his eyes perusing the smoky room.

Lukhanyo studies him and there's a brief moment of silence before I realise that I haven't introduced them. The two on the couch say nothing, they know the story and sit by with lascivious looks on their faces as though a soap opera is about to unfold.

"Arne, this is Lukhanyo and of course you know Ashley and Steven." Arne extends his arm to shake Lukhanyo's hand. They grin at each other with mild hostility. He says hi to Steven and Ashley.

"So why didn't you show up at the ceremony?"

"Ja, I wasn't sure I was going to come and then about an hour ago I just decided what the hell ... Anyway weddings are an excuse to get drunk, ja," he says in his gentle German accent. He has been in the country for three years, his accent is beginning to fade. Lukhanyo quizzes him about his studies and they exchange perfunctory information about where they studied.

"Sorry, are you guys going out?" Arne asks us both. I grind my jaws and give him a quick dirty look before I look at Lukhanyo.

"Well, are we?" he says and looks at me arrogantly.

Ashley and Steven look at us with amused faces, waiting for my response.

"I have to go to the bathroom," I say and get up suddenly leaving Lukhanyo with a disappointed and humiliated look on his face. I don't play along when boys compete like that.

"Women, can't live with them, can't live with them," Ashley says to console Lukhanyo.

At the bathroom Arne walks in behind me and locks the door. He doesn't give me a chance to say anything but lunges towards me and kisses me hard. I don't protest, I kiss him back and think nothing of the consequences. I take off my wig and grab his toned bum. He groans and thrusts his groin against my pelvis. His large hands grab my breast and he breathes hot air past my ear. It makes me wet with desire. My hand moves past his groin and I begin to unbutton his pants. He scrambles in the back pocket for a condom but I tell him to forget about it. I'm fixed, I tell him. We grope till we both trip and fall on the tiled floor. He empties out the laundry basket and we lie on the clothes. I lick his neck teasingly and he moves my short dress to my waist. The last thing I think about as we start rocking against each other is his prosthesis. He didn't bother to take it off.


ZEBRON

I've been in the kulukutz for the last three days. I swore at my psychologist during the previous ward round. He nearly attacked me because I humiliated him in front of his colleagues. So they've assigned a new psychologist to me. A grumpy old woman who looks like she's just hanging on till retirement, her delicate bony hands politely folded whenever she listens to me. She wears small spectacles with long arms that usually sit low on her nose and make her look pretentious when she looks at me by lowering her head slightly. And her hair with streaks of silver is always in a tight bun, it makes her look perpetually constipated because she can't smile. Her bun looks tied too tightly, with almost ascetic aggression and if it were to come loose I fear the pressure released would ravage the room. But I actually like her. She doesn't have any agendas. She doesn't scribble down anything I say and most of the time it doesn't bother her when I refuse to speak. Once or twice when I'm being a little difficult she'll raise her eyebrows and for a brief moment I'll get a glimpse of the fierce woman she used to be. I call her Ma Brooks even though she insists that I either call her Ellen, her first name, or Mrs Brooks. I think she doesn't pay attention to the other doctors because she never forces any ideas on me.

"When I look at the nurses sometimes I want to rape them," I say to her, just to ruffle her feathers.

"Do you really think I'm that old?" she says, her expression the same, always a little sour and bored.

"You never smile, do you know that?"

"You should be more concerned that you're still here than about me smiling."

"My brother hasn't come to see me."

"Your brother? I thought you only had a sister," the old fox answers. "Don't play with me, young man. If you've got nothing to say, just shut up. I'm quite happy to get on with my own things." Her mouth twitches a little.

The sessions usually go like that. I think I like her because she doesn't really care. I don't have to be difficult with her. She doesn't speak to me as a psychologist. But sometimes she does get irritated with me when I don't say much.

"If you were wise you'd be more forthcoming with what you're feeling," she says in her flawless British accent.

"Did you grow up in Zimbabwe? White South Africans don't talk like you. You must be a when-we," I say.

"You need a good clout, you do," she says and raises one of her eyebrows slightly. "If I had the energy I'd clobber you over the head with this desk."

"Aren't you threatened by being near a black man? I'm mean for an old white woman."

She doesn't say anything. She lowers her head and just looks at me from the top of her spectacles always resting studiously on the bridge of her nose. And the silence that follows says more about what she doesn't fear.

"I'm not sleeping well," I finally say.

She listens.

"I've been dreaming about that woman I killed."

"Nightmares?"

"No, just dreams. And then I'll chase her through a forest till she falls off a cliff. I always wake up at the part where I'm also falling. And I feel terrible. When I was at Fort Hare I used to have the same dreams before exams."

"So what's the problem?"

"I can't sleep."

"So why don't you tell your doctor? It's Nikolov, isn't it? I'm sure he can give you something."

"It's not that easy," I say annoyed.

"Balderdash. You think you're the only one who has ever gone through this. Listen, dearie, I had a breakdown twenty years ago and I spent three years in similar circumstance to your own. The problem with some of you is that you make a career out of being a mental patient."

I don't doubt her.

"So what helped you?"

"It was simple. I decided to get better," she says and raises one of her eyebrows.

"Anyway, I think this dream has something to do with being horny," I say after a while.

"You need to grow up before you get better. You've been using your bad manners as a shield all your life," she tells me.

I remain quiet and an image of an axe splitting her head in two flashes in my thoughts. She stares into me, as if penetrating my thoughts, an indomitable look on her face that says: I won't keel over and die.

"So is that all you have to say about that dream?"

I feel inadequate and say nothing. She sinks back into her chair and looks at the clock on the wall, her bony hands slightly fidgety.

"I never had anyone to tell me anything. I just grew up."

"And you did a bad job of it," she says.

"My father was an alcoholic and my mother was happiest when she was fuckin'g other men."

"You don't have to be vulgar about your mother."

"I'm trying. It's not easy. These other idiots made me turn on myself." I wipe the spit gathering at the corners of my mouth and think with hatred of my last psychologist.

"Well, the first step to recovery is speaking properly. You're not an animal, for God's sake."

I begin to see the mother in her.

"Did your husband leave you for another woman?"

She says nothing and adjusts her spectacles.

"I'm only asking because you seem so angry," I say.

"You're the patient, not me. I've done my time," she says, pursing her small lips carefully laced with pink lipstick.

I'm suddenly assailed by a terrible feeling of guilt for having hurt her feelings. I want to apologise but I don't know how. I don't have the words, the humility, the necessary spine to put myself in such a position. So I sit in silence with this terrible feeling ruminating inside me like always when I've done wrong but desire to do right. We sit in silence for the remainder of the session. As I go out I look at her shamefully and hope that she will see how sorry I am. But she devours my pathetic apology by looking at me with her usual grumpy face.

During OT I find Tshepo sitting by himself near the locked piano. I was angry with him when he ran away because I knew that he'd soon be back. Things just work out that way. I walk towards him and realise that it is pointless to be angry with him.

"They're going to keep you here longer," I say and sit down next to him.

"I know," he says depressed, "how long do you think?"

"Maybe three months," I guess.

He doesn't say anything. He looks at the floor and his shoes.

"Three months, that's a lifetime," he says after a while.

"That's if you're lucky, if they think you're getting better. They could keep you longer."

"Three months," he sighs and looks at the floor again.

"Don't think about it. You're here now, you check."

"At least I'm out of the kulukutz."

"But you mustn't slize again. I knew you'd be back."

"I wonder what happened to Byron," he says as though that would give him comfort.

"Ja, Byron. I heard that his drug-dealing chommies got him caught up with the Nigerians in Jo'burg. They say he came back to Cape Town in a body bag." I sit back and shrug my shoulders. I couldn't give a shit about Byron.

"I can't believe it. Byron said things were looking up. He said he was going places," he says gravely.

"Byron said a lot of things. But he was just another outie like you and me. He was just a windgat, you check?"

The bell for mid-morning tea rings but he doesn't bother to go to the line.

"I signed you up for kitchen duty. You know, mopping up and washing dishes. It earns you points with your doctor. Which one is it?" I ask.

"Nikolov."

"Ja, Nikolov."

"What does that mean?"

"Nothing. He's also my doctor. Look, don't piss me off by reading too much into things I say. I hate that shit. I'm very straightforward. If I want to tell you something, I'll tell you," I say annoyed.

"Fine. Why are you helping me?"

"And don't piss me off with questions like that. If you don't need my help then just voertsek. I don't have time for this shit."

He stays and sulks.

After supper they hand out private tuck. I roll a joint and ask him to come with me to the toilets. No one is in there. I close the door and stand against it.

"Here, take it."

"What's this?"

"You and your fucking questions. I know you don't smoke BB."

He lights it and takes a long slow drag.

"Ganja," he breathes out.

"Just hear me now. You're only going to get it from me. I don't want you going to these other clowns. They'll get you back in the kulukutz. And you'll only smoke once a week. Don't ask me when and how. I'll give it to you when I'm ready. Do you understand?"

"Ja, whatever," he says and smokes. It is a small joint and soon expires.

We go to bed at eight-thirty, half an hour earlier because Themba is in a foul mood. Tshepo sleeps on the bed next to mine. I hear him mumble something to himself in the dark.

"Who'you chaffing to?"

"I'm praying," he says and turns over to sleep.

After breakfast Tshepo and I go to kitchen duty. Sipho hovers round us to check on Tshepo. "Clean out that pot properly," he tells him. "That's what I'm doing." Sipho is just passing time. They all have their moods. I wink at Tshepo to ignore him. He soon gets bored and leaves. I mop the floor while he dries the dishes.

"You mustn't let people get to you like that."

"I can't help it, he's a bastard, everyone knows that."

"Ja, but you're an inmate now. You must learn how to be strong."

"Whatever."

We go outside with the others. The sun is hiding behind clouds. We both sit on the floor and wait for it to come out.

"You see that ou over there?" I say pointing at someone.

"The Indian guy?"

"No, the white ou, near the bench."

"What about him?"

"He was on his way to becoming a doctor. He's a slim ou. He lost it in his last year. They found the insides of chickens all over his room when they took him away. And his cherrie was yelling out her eyes. He's been here for three years. They just keep shifting him between the wards. He's alright, on a good day anyway. Pity that his parents have given up on him. They hardly come to see him. You know how white people are when it comes to family scandals."

He nods his head sympathetically.

"And the Indian guy?"

"You mean Salman?"

"No, the other one. The light-skinned one with long hair."

"Zahid. He's convinced that they got someone to work on him. Muslims are like us darkies. They also believe in amaqgwira." He looks at me amazed.

The sun comes out for a while and we soak up its heat.

"Tell me about your parents," I say.

"Why are you always asking me that? I told you they died in a car accident. I don't like talking about it, okay? What's there to say? They died a violent death. I mean, fuck."

We watch the others walking around aimlessly. I tell Tshepo everyone's history. I tell him about the ones who experimented with drugs and the occult. And the alcoholics who abused their families and the perverts who raped children. I tell him about the ones I believe were born with a streak of darkness, looking backwards at life.

"You mean people like you," he says and I smile because he knows so little about me.


TSHEPO

For me the hardest thing to do is to grow up. Animals do it so gracefully. I had an incomplete childhood. The serious stuff of playing and running around carelessly I never really knew. I spent too much time with my mother in my formative years because I was a sickly child with precocious asthma attacks that were closely monitored. Perhaps I resent her a little for that even though it isn't her fault. But the reality is I feel I have become a stranger to people, even to myself. Perhaps it is childish to be adult. There's hardly anything graceful or encouraging about adults. When I look around me, in the nurses and the male staff, I see people who never really got over growing up. There is still the adolescent insecurity which breeds petulance and spite. The snide remarks, bad tempers, insensitivity and cruelty surely cannot be characteristics of fully matured people, fully realised and prospering. And when I think about the people I know they hardly seem complete either. Mmabatho's ferocious wit and her complicated sense of style seem to be consequences of a child who suffered a messy divorce and never got over it. Her flawed relationships with men are an eternal saga. And the way David always goes for black women, it is as if he is trying to reconcile something. Except for Mmabatho, like a serial killer all the black women David goes for seem to be of a certain background, usually under-privileged or from the homelands but strikingly intelligent. The kind of women who are ignored by some men because they are not necessarily attractive but they blossom when given the chance. And Ntombi herself, she has this hungry look on her face like someone who never had enough of anything when she was growing up and now she is going to make up for it. And the way she is clinging on to David, I only hope David is clinging on with as much tenacity. I don't think any of them like me anyway. Even Mmabatho, I wonder how deep the roots of our friendship are.

The sun doesn't shine for three days. Dark clouds like scoops of mulberry ice cream gather but it never rains. The sky is just sour with bad weather. I've been spending a lot of time with Zebron when I'm not with Matthew, mainly because he provides me with marijuana. I need it for now, screw the doctors. And he can be quite interesting when he doesn't intimidate people. I can afford to be less judgmental about whom I speak with here because there's hardly anyone to speak to. Zebron knows a lot about the other patients. But that has more to do with the fact that he's always harassing them, asking them questions that make them crumble. He has a mind that works like a filing cabinet. Everyone has a profile and is categorised. He remembers everything, when people come in and when they leave. There's nothing to do here, he says. You might as well create your own world by observing others. Like a vulture he watches, ready to prey on our weakness when no one is watching.

I try to watch people closely but sometimes it proves to be a boring exercise. I usually end up dozing off or chatting to Matthew. I find his anger with life refreshing because at least he isn't complacent like the others. I like his energy and his willingness to admit that he is miserable and that he misses his freedom and music and women. He is angry about the way the system has treated him. He is bitter about the way his doctor turned his family against him.

"They're convinced I'm a looney," he says, "and there's nothing I can do to change their minds as long as Habib is around."

He talks of wanting to form a Patients' Forum.

"The purpose of this Forum," he says, "is for old patients to induct new patients and tell them about the ins and outs of Valkenberg. Like electrotherapy, people should know what they're getting themselves into. Old patients should tell the new ones about its horrors and that it doesn't work and about the mental scars it leaves."

He starts a petition against electrotherapy. A lot of the patients sign because there is a piece of paper and a pen in front of them. But Matthew isn't discouraged. "We will win."

He gives the petition to his doctor Habib, who is supposed to hand it to the hospital superintendent. I wonder if it will ever reach her.

"They can't ignore me forever, maestro."

"You don't know these arseholes."

"I'll go to the press if I have to. I'll start a media event."

"But, maestro, how?"

"I'll burn up this place if I have to. People must know what goes on in here, that we're treated like monkeys in a cage. They must know that half the food is pilfered before it hits the shelves. And what about the shortage of towels, linen and blankets? Somebody's got to answer for that. I'm tired of this shit. They can't treat us like idiots and get away with it."

"I know, but ..."

"No, really," he fuels himself, "enough of this. Why must they treat us like idiots? Why can't we decide which therapy works and which doesn't? Why don't we have a say in what they're doing to us? There's fuck-all to do during OT. OT is just a few scrappy magazines and newspapers and board games with missing pieces. But it doesn't matter, we're only mental patients. Who gives a fuck that we play chess with half the pieces missing? And the TV? Fuck, that's more for the staff than us. We only see what they like. And I can't see why we can't socialise with the women patients."

"That one you'll never win. Patients getting together, I don't think so. The only thing they'll be thinking is that we want punani," I tell him.

"Why not? We can all have group sex. We'll call it sex therapy. I'm not getting better staying here, that's for sure."

"You're not serious."

"Just think of all that tension we'll be releasing." His mouth goes into a teasing lecherous pout.

"Tension. But maestro, what about pleasure?"

"And pleasure too, of course. We can take pictures and send photos to Hustler. You know that kinky bit in the back where bored house-wives send in pictures of themselves? We can send one of us having group sex. Can you imagine mental patients in Hustler? That's just the sort of media attention we need," he says and scratches his balls.

"I suppose it would be fun," I say and let my imagination wander a little.

"And why won't they let me organise art classes? I know someone who's prepared to come in here once a week. For free, maestro. No charge and she'll provide us with the art materials. Just imagine it. We can have the whole place running with Van Goghs. And we can all slice off our ears to make a point." I don't know what to make of his last remark.

"It's always the same thing. We have to sing their tune," I tell him.

"Ag kak, man. I'm not sure I can do this much longer. This place is killing me."

"How's your medication going?"

"Don't even ask. I mean for fuck's sake, I've been here for three months and all they tell me is that I'm under observation. And you know what a lot of twak that is because most of the time we're mission-ing around with fuck-all to do while Sipho and the boys are in that room talking shit, talking about things we want to do. What does ob-servation mean anyway?" he says and throws his arm out carelessly.

"You should ask Zebron," I say but he misses the joke.

"I'm sick of this shit, maestro," he says and forces his fingers through his hair." If I don't get a reply soon from the superintendent or Habib about having my status reviewed I'm fucking off."

"I don't need this hassle, this aggro. I mean, when was the last time you had a boner? When was the last time you wanked and enjoyed it?"

"I hear you," I say cringing.

"It's in the food, you know. But no one is going to admit it. They don't even have the decency to warn us that they've got stuff in our grub."

"Why are you fighting this so hard? Just go with it, play along ... They'll eventually let you go."

"That's what Basil thought. That poor guy's been playing along for three years. He's been waiting to get out since, when? ... Fuck, that's cruel, to do that to a man, make him wait like that, giving him false hope. I know all about it. If you talk to Basil now and ask him when he's getting out he'll tell you that his wife's coming for him at seven o'clock tomorrow morning. He's been saying that for the last year. You think that's fair?"

"No, but Basil's fucked, maestro." I look at Basil sitting on a chair, swatting flies that are not there.

"Ja, but it doesn't mean we have to write him off. Who's anyone to do that? He's good with his hands. Those little sculptures and flutes he's always making from used toothpaste tubes, that's clever. He could do something with his hands on the outside. Maybe work in some art workshop weaving baskets or do beading. I'm telling you, given the chance he can do it. Okay, so he goes off his head with lies and stuff but he's not hurting anyone. We both know he's not violent. But guys like Andile belong in here."

"Matt, the other thing is that Basil's certified," I say to remind him.

"So? I'm also certified,"

"I didn't know," I say surprised.

"That's why I'm doing everything I can to get my status reviewed and convince them that I'm still useful, that I can do stuff, you know. Because you're fucked once you're certified. I'm fucked. I can't get into any trouble with the law any more, not with this hanging over my head. They'll send me away for life," he says and his eyes are filled with the fear he expresses.

As much as I hate to admit it I feel fortunate that I'm not certified. It seems like a spurious process anyway to declare someone insane. What makes them so certain of a person's state of mind? Sure, there are people who are without doubt insane, especially those inclined to violence; the ones with compulsive and deviant behaviour, the Jeffrey Dahmers of this world who prowled the nights in secrecy, spreading evil while we slept. On the outside I know a guy who works as a manager in a supermarket and he always counts the till money thirteen times when he closes up. And he says he licks his wife seven times under the left armpit before he goes to bed. He says it keeps him virile. In here everyone knows that there are more crazy people out there, and that most of them are politicians, lawyers, judges, accountants and bankers. It seems only a matter of chance that we are in here and they are out there.

"Did I tell you about my court case?" Matthew asks me.

"Ja, you said the farmers dropped the charges against you."

"Not that one. The one about my money and everything. My parents are trying to take away all my signing powers. My grandfather died recently and left me a big inheritance. My parents are trying to get a court interdict that will basically allow them control of my finances and everything I own."

"Can they do that?"

"They're doing it. Anyway, I'm trying to revoke it. There should be a hearing in about a week's time." He crunches his knuckles.

"So if they win they control everything and you're like a six year-old again?"

He nods his head solemnly.

The bell for supper rings. We file into the dining room. Zebron doesn't say much. He trudges into the room with his old stinking shoes with holes in them like eyes. I smile to say hi but he doesn't see me. I stay away from him and sit with Matthew. We finish supper in ten minutes. It is always like that, there is nothing cordial about our meals. Zebron and I gather the dishes and pack them on a trolley. I wheel it to the kitchen.

"I don't like Matthew," he says when we get to the kitchen.

I say nothing and start putting the dishes into the sink.

"Did you hear me? I said I don't like your friend."

"What does that mean? He's my friend."

"He's trying to fill your head with stupid ideas about bringing down this place – as if that's possible. I've heard it all before. He won't succeed, you know. That talk of his will only lead to the kulukutz."

"He's just letting off some steam. Give him a break."

"You're so fucking naïve," he tells me, anger foaming in white spit that gathers at the corners of his mouth.

"You're just in a bad mood and I think you don't like him because he's white." I turn my back on him and start washing the dishes.

He leaps at me and grabs me by the chest. A plate shatters on the floor.

"It's true I don't like him or his kind. It's hard to like them. They're full of shit and they've been fucking me around my whole life. Why won't you listen to me? He's bad news," he says saliva flying out his mouth.

"Let go of me."

He lets me go and wanders off to the other side of the room. I clean the mess on the floor, my thoughts fast and furious.

"You're not my fucking father, okay? I like Matthew, just get over it. What's wrong with you today anyway?"

His face is riddled with thought and he is restless, his gestures erratic. I can see him spinning with anger and other dark emotions, a crazed, deranged look on his face. It is unsettling to see him like this. Sometimes it is like that here. You just have bad days and even the medication can't help.

"I'm wrestling with my demons. I'm wrestling with everyone's demons today. You're all driving me crazy. Just wash the dishes and stay out of my face."

We work on in a strained silence. He is agitated and works furiously, throwing cutlery into the box and banging doors as he closes cupboards. Sipho comes to see what the noise is all about but soon walks out when he sees that Zebron is responsible. I've never seen him like this. He is cantankerous. After we clean up the kitchen he nearly beats up Matthew because he says Matthew eyed him suspiciously. In here tempers flare easily.

The other day Salman had a fight with Zahid over the comfortable armchair. The next day I see them sharing an entjie together. It is like that at ward 15. You can't afford to make enemies, there isn't room for that. Even if you intensely dislike someone you have to speak to them. It isn't like the outside where you display your ego and pride with machismo, indifferent to the number of enemies you're acquiring. In here you have to swallow your pride quickly because your enemy sleeps and eats next to you. And sooner or later you will need his match stick, the time, or another favour.

Doing someone a favour is considered a matter of honour. You have to return a favour, everyone accepts that. When Andile didn't give Matthew one of his last two cigarettes after Matthew had given him a cigarette earlier on in the day, no one gave him a cigarette or shared an entjie with him for two weeks. They spoke to him but they wouldn't give him anything to smoke. And he had to bear it like a man. If he had bummed cigarettes from the staff any chance of him ever redeeming himself in our eyes would have gone up in smoke.

It's interesting how the rule with favours is only applied to cigarettes and tobacco. In my culture traditionally tobacco is a male preserve and even the name for it, motsoko, also means penis. It's a good thing that I'm not a serious smoker. I find nothing appealing about waking up with a grinding cough. Or having perpetually dark stains on my fingertips as a result of the resinous tobacco. It irritates me that some patients squander their time smoking incessantly, the chronic smoking type who beg each other for the last drag. The ones who are generally thin and scruffy and whose fingertips are perennially black. One old bag called Harry is a constant source of irritation to me and I find him nauseating to watch. He is always short of breath and suffers from some malady that leaves him frail and shaking but he insists on smoking a thousand cigarettes a day. And he usually ends up coughing and launching himself into these wrenching paroxysms that have him bent double and his sickly saliva torpedoing around the room. But he won't resign. Twenty minutes later he can be seen lighting another cigarette and soon after coughing up his entrails. I find him crude and revolting and avoid his presence with much vigilance.

"He's trying to kill himself before this place destroys what's left of him," Matthew says.

Even so, he still irritates me.

## MMABATHO

I admit that in the arms of a man sometimes I lose all judgment.

Arne is coming to see me. After our little scene at Fiona's wedding I ran off. For a change I was the one who came up with quick excuses before making my escape. And as for Lukhanyo, I haven't seen him since. I don't think he'd want to see me anyway.

I've been pacing my room all morning. I don't know what to say to him. I don't have a strategy, a game plan. I'm just a mess of emotions. Even though all evidence says I should stay away from this guy I keep hearing myself making excuses for letting him back in my life.

There is a knock at the door. In the mirror I tell myself to be calm and not look so womanly and vulnerable, so tortured by what I feel.

"Hi," he says. Immediately he steps to kiss me on the cheek. I let him in and he strolls to the kitchen at the far end of the house. He sits at the table while I stand.

"Do you want something to drink?" I ask him, my voice a little shaky and unsure.

"No, I'm fine," he smiles, eating a banana. His confidence makes me edgy.

"What we did … It was a mistake. I just wanted to clear that up," I tell him.

He doesn't say anything, so I continue talking.

"I don't know what happened. Maybe I was a little drunk. I just don't want you getting the wrong idea about me. I mean we just had sex right? And it doesn't mean anything." But he doesn't respond. He keeps nibbling at his banana.

"And don't make me do all the work, say something, you prick."

"What do you want me to say? I fucked up, I know that, ja. But would you believe me if I said I haven't been with anyone since that night? Would you believe me if I said I still want to go out and for things to work out between us?"

It pricks my heart to hear him say that. It lights a glimmer of hope and sends a little jolt of excitement through me. But I conceal them as always with men. I've been hurt too many times. I must learn something from all this.

"But how do I know that you won't do it again?"

"Because I was miserable after doing it and missed you when you left," he says immediately. So I'm not the only one who's been doing some thinking. But I'm not going to let him off that easily. There must be some loop-holes.

"Ja, but still you never really told me why you did it in the first place. Why were you so eager to throw it away if it was that good?"

My question throws him a little. A sense of doubt and a little panic cover his face. He starts running his fingers through his hair.

"What do you want me to say? Okay, I miss you. I really miss you. I fucked up. I'm sorry. I don't know how else to say it. I was jealous of Tshepo. I was insecure. I thought maybe you and him … Ag, it's stupid I know. Don't you see it had nothing to do with you? I was being stupid. I wasn't man enough to deal with it," he says and gets up. He throws his banana peel in the bin and pours himself a glass of water. He drinks in huge gulps as though that would absolve him. It is an uncharacteristic admission for a guy to say that he is insecure and jealous. But to admit that he "wasn't man enough to deal with it" – I have never heard that. It counts for something, I smile inside.

"Well, what do you think we should do?" I offer, my suspicions quelled by his confession.

He gets up and takes a step towards me. I don't know whether to run or stay. He holds me around the waist and kisses me. He tastes of banana. "I think I've said enough. You know how bad I feel. Let's just go back to the way things were," he says.

"But I don't want to go back to the way things were. Not if that means you're going to be running around again."

"You know what I mean. Let's start again. I know things can be good again," he pleads, a serious look on his face.

It's in his eyes. We wouldn't be just going out again. And he wouldn't be just another zero guy.

"But how do I know that this isn't just charm?"

"Shhh," he whispers and puts his finger on my mouth and then he kisses me again. I kiss him back and feel as though I've given my heart to him for safe-keeping. Please be gentle with me, my heart breaks easily, I say in my thoughts as we kiss. Eventually it all comes down to that. You must be willing to give up something. There is a place where the fear must go. There is a place where the hope must go and all the beautiful things you aspire to. So I give myself to him. I'll stop divining wisdom out of what happened and follow my foolish heart.

"Don't play with me, Arne, I couldn't handle it again," I warn him as we go to my room.

For the next week Arne spends all his time with me when he's not doing his studies. I think he knows how afraid I still am. And the gossip-mongers are still talking. I don't really follow their idle talk but the word is that he begged me to take him back after he saw me with Lukhanyo. I know it's silly but it makes a difference. It gives me some confidence that they think I have the upper hand.

One night I go to Madame Spiers' restaurant in Obs. Arne is supposed to meet me there.

"Chérie, ça fait longtemps que je t'ai pas vue. How have you been?" She kisses me on the cheeks. She's wearing an elegant navy blue cashmere polo neck and a simple black skirt that falls to her knees and a slit on the side exposes part of her thigh. She stands delicately on flat shoes with a strong Italian design.

"I like your bracelet," I tell her.

"Quoi, this little trinket, a holiday in Brazil with a charming Dutch man that I should have never entertained," she smiles and we make our way to a table.

"Alors, where is Arne ce soir?"

"He's coming. He had some work to do," I say but I don't feel confident saying it, and she notices.

"Mais bien sûr he has work to do, why would he leave such a delicate flower on her own?" she says and manages to put a smile on my face. I might have turned out differently if I had a figure like her in the shadows of adolescence. I might have been more friendly with other women, less aggressive with men and more sure about myself.

"Do you ever doubt anything?" I ask her.

"But what is ever certain about life, chérie? At my age, when people start describing you as a woman of a certain age, you can't but doubt that the world will ever see you the way you see yourself again. It's better to just build on what you have. Nobody builds anything aujourd'hui everything is about fixing or destroying."

A waiter brings the menu and I order sparkling mineral water. Soon after Arne comes, a little bedraggled and tired. He kisses Madame Spiers and they laugh about a joke they share. She leaves as other guests arrive.

"A plus tard, chérie."

"You won't believe the day I've had," he says putting his shoulder bag and file on the floor. "Anyway it doesn't matter. Have you ordered?"

"No," I tell him. He lets out a sigh and looks around for a waiter.

And then without warning I start crying. Tears fall from my eyes plentifully. Arne, stunned and awkward, tries to say something but it doesn't come out.

"I feel as if I'm losing myself," I cry.

The waiter comes and leaves the menus on the table without telling us about the specials when he sees me wiping my eyes with the serviette.

"You wouldn't understand anyway." I cry as though I'm grieving, gentle sobbing that fills me with longing for my father and the comforting embrace of his big arms.

"It's just too much mental effort," I tell him, "trying to keep up. If you're going to break my heart again, do it now."

He just looks at me stunned.

"I don't want to worry about who you're with every time you leave," I tell him. "I'm tired of doing that."

For a while I say nothing. I just cry. And he just sits opposite me and watches me.

I used to think I could control love. I want it to be gentle, I would tell myself. I want to mould it like a piece of sculpture, square within my reach. I've been carrying residual depression from failed relationships for too long. I've been walking around with too many regrets and hurts, things I should have said but didn't. I've been kidding myself that I could tame love, that I could meet a man on my terms when it suits me. I've been reading too many magazines listening to too much pop psychology and experts who only seem to have succeeded in leading me further into confusion: the anatomy of relationships, the feminine ego, the female eunuch, the politics of sex, the road to recovery, the joys of toy boys, sexual personae, a question of immunity, why we love them, when we were just women, when they were just men ... on and on it goes. And the sad thing is he will never know. He will never know the amount of preparation it takes to be a woman, the degree of caution. He will never know how I struggle with myself, with other women. To him I will be just another woman balling her eyes out because women do that. They just cry for no reason. They upset things. They make scenes.

"Do you want to go home?" I finally say when the crying abates.

"No. I want to understand ... I want to know what to do. I thought things were okay. I don't know what to say," he says helplessly.

But can't you see the marathons I've run, the arseholes who've left me scrounging around for my dignity after they disrespected me? My father loves me. He did not pick me from a fruit tree so that men could devour me. I am not an amusement for men. I'm not a man. When I cry it is because I have something to say. When I cry it is because I have nothing to hide. These tears they are not in vain. They are not a weapon. I'm struggling to unburden my heart. Can't you see that? Can't you hear me?

"I think you're not telling me something," he says sympathetically.

"I'm not hiding anything. It's just that I'm tired of games. I don't want to figure you out. I just want to get to know you," I say, "And if you don't want to be with me I want you to tell me. I don't want to walk into a mess again. I don't want to hate you. I just want to know you."

"But you do know me. You do," he insists and stretches out his hand to meet mine.

"I hear you. I also just want something real, no games. Okay?"

I nod my head and wipe my tears. And I don't feel shy or embarrassed, the bumbling female always with a handkerchief. I want him to see me as I am, snot en trane. I want him to know where I'm going, where I'm heading. I'm tired of just catching a ride with men, gambling on a destination called bliss. I want him to know what he's getting himself into.

The waiter comes and hardly looks at me. We order something light, a salad and some tortillas with cheese. And we don't say much. But in his eyes I can see many questions searching for answers. I watch him. We drink a lot of wine.

A woman has to go far to look for herself. She has to go beyond the security of her village, past the men lingering at the gates. She has to go inside herself and get to know the little girl that everyone protected with lies. Rejection, this is not serious, I was told. Men, you must never trust them. Sing, now, alone, like the unsung heroine you must become, for love is unrequited. Sing, for tomorrow may never hear your songs. Sing, always alone because you are destined for your mother's fate – unsung and unloved. Sing because you don't know your mother. Sing always for yourself, because you can't trust men, can't depend on their love. The only real love from a man a woman gets to know is from her father. Sing, Sing.

"If anything I want us always to be friends," I say to him after a while and he nods solemnly. "This ugliness. This crying and everything, sometimes it is necessary."

"I know."

The following morning I wake up with a burning desire to see Tshepo. Perhaps it is guilt because I haven't seen him since he went back. I show up at his ward one afternoon during visiting hours. He is surprised to see me.

"What are you doing here?" he says as we sit in the corridor. After our stunt they will never allow us to walk the grounds again.

"Don't be silly. I wanted to see you," I say feeling guilty.

"Oh," he says with a stone cold look.

"Things have been difficult. I would have come earlier ..."

"Excuses are pathetic, you know, it's better to just say nothing."

I deserved that, I tell myself.

"Arne says hi, by the way," I say.

"Please. Do I look like some charity case? Since when does your boyfriend think about me?"

"Why are you being so difficult?" I say and light a cigarette.

"You're full of shit," he says hardly looking at me. "Can we talk about something else? I'm about to have my weekly joint. I'm not going to spoil it by fucking up my mood."

He looks the other way

"How's therapy going?" I say.

He looks back and scowls at me.

"I don't know, I always thought it would be nice to have someone listen to me bitch about everything for an hour," I venture. God, I should have come earlier.

"What's there to say? I've been through it before. It's the same questions. You talk about your childhood and all that crap," he says, irritating a sore on his hand.

"Listen, I'm sorry, okay? I was going through my own shit."

"Whatever," he says and waves at a tall man walking by. The man sticks out his tongue lecherously at me and clutches his crotch.

"Relax," Tshepo smiles, "Sipho is on duty, he won't do anything."

I watch him walk off to the toilets, probably to do nasty things to himself.

"This place gives me the creeps."

"Trust you to say that," he says coldly. There is something different about him, a detached regard that wasn't there before. I feel stupid, sitting next to him, like meeting someone you haven't seen in a while and realising that perhaps the friendship isn't there anymore.

"I don't blame you for not wanting to come, really. I would probably do the same," he says and his face manages to be friendly. He doesn't quite smile, but a little of the Tshepo I know returns.

"So did you tell your therapist what happened to your folks? I mean the real story, not the accident bit you tell everyone?"

"Ja, I had to. She found my records from Sterkfontein," he says irritably. I'm getting too personal, so I drop the subject and finish my cigarette.

"How's Ganesh?" he asks.

"The same. Karuna's with this new woman from the Philippines. They seem to be getting on. I broke up with Arne for a while but things are okay again."

"Yeah?"

"It was rough, but I think we're getting it together."

"That's good," he says in a flat tone. His disinterested mood returns.

"You seem different," I finally say.

"No, I'm just thinner. But I'm getting better, if that's what you're saying."

I'm not sure what he means but I let it go.

Another guy with a dark coat walks up to us and says nothing. Tshepo tells him to piss off and nearly pushes him. I've never seen him being aggressive.

"A place like this can change a person," he says, looking at the floor. "It's hell. I spend my time looking at that stupid clock in the lounge. There's fuck all to do. I've lost all motivation even to read. Actually that has more to do with the medication. I'm always restless."

"But that guy, what's his name, Zeffron?" I say.

"Zebron," he corrects me.

"He's alright, isn't he?"

"As alright as can be in a place like this. I hang around with him but

I don't pay too much attention to what he says. He's a bit too fucked in the head for me," he says and part of his face twitches involuntarily.

"And the others?"

"They're just like part of the furniture. They hardly say anything, except for Matthew. But he pissed off. Two days ago he found out that he'd lost a court case which gave his parents signing powers over his inheritance and all his money," he says, his eyes skirting around the room.

He hardly looks at me. I don't know if he's pissed off with me or if that is just the effect of this ruinous place.

"Can they do that?" I say.

"That's what I said. Scary, but they can, they did. He said he was going up to Pretoria. But he set fire to his bed before he left. He said it was symbolic, don't ask me. It doesn't help that Matthew is a bit of a free spirit who likes to play with fire. If you provoke him, he's going to react, and worse, he's going to want you to pay for it. He believes in justice and retribution to death. I suppose we all do to some extent, but Matthew was quite hectic about it. Just before he left he was saying to me that some of these people who mistreated him were going to pay. He was really bitter."

"And how was he going to make them pay?" I say, lighting another cigarette.

"He never said. Ja, this place really broke him. They put him in the kulukutz for six weeks after he beat up one of the male nurses. He doesn't know when to quit even if it means he's going down in the end," he says and peels away the scab on his hand.

"But what made his parents do that?" I ask.

"Apparently he's quite well off. He got an inheritance from his grandfather. But he got a little generous with it a while back. Threw a braai for the ward and bought some of the guys shoes and decent winter jackets."

"So his parents flipped out and took him to court?"

He nods and looks at my face briefly. I feel conscious because I have pierced my nose and he hasn't said anything. But I won't mention it.

"How did he get in here in the first place?"

"Long story."

"I'm not in a rush. I've got the afternoon off."

He sniggers.

"Gosh, don't know where to begin," he says sarcastically.

"You've made your point okay," I say a little exasperated.

He growls a little under his breath. "It's quite obscure. He said he got into some shit with farmers in the Cape. Apparently they were using mechanical harvesters and these machines were killing off small animals like chameleons. And you know how important they are in our culture," he says and looks at me.

"I know."

"Anyway, Matthew organised a protest up there, wherever there is. I think it was in Stellenbosch. The press were there. He even torched his own van to make a point. But don't ask me what burning your car does for anything. The whole thing was in the Mail & Guardian. I don't remember seeing it. Ja, so anyway, he really got worked up over this thing. Went on a rampage saying that these farmers should destroy the wine because it's got chameleon blood and that terrible things would happen because it was bad muti. Ntho tsa boloyi," he says and laughs a little.

"This is him telling you this?" I say.

"You know the thing about being here is that you remember everything. Even when you were being irrational. It's not like you get amnesia or anything," he says to me.

"Right," I say.

"So he managed to cause a lot of shit in some wining town in the Cape. The cops arrested him for sabotaging some mechanical harvesters or something like that. It really got nasty. Eventually a friend of his bailed him out and he came home. He says he went off his head when he got home. He became paranoid that someone was after him. He was convinced that the farmers were out to kill him. So he slept in different places. He started hearing voices. He says he lost some of his friends in the process. So after a while he went on the road, running away from these farmers who wanted to kill him. He went to his parents' place in Kokstad, and there his folks convinced him to turn himself in to a hospital. He didn't want to but he eventually did. Went to Townhill in Maritzburg. He says it was the biggest mistake he ever made because they certified him. And you know what that means, don't you?"

I shake my head.

"I wouldn't wish it on my worst enemy. It means you can't vote, can't drive, can't open a bank account, basically you don't exist. You can forget about being treated like an adult. Before the whole chameleon thing he was working in the Transkei with Amaqgira. I remember him saying that for some reason things went sour between them and they fell out and it nearly turned violent. They were accusing him of being a mlungu. Ena he says o bone boloi."

"That's what you think happened to you too, isn't it?"

"It's not out of the question," he says casually even though I know how seriously he believes that notion. "People are capable of a lot of things."

He looks at me and points to his nose.

"I had it done a week ago. What do you think?" I say enthusiastically.

"Whatever," he says, "I can't keep up with you. So anyway, I'm still here. Every day I'm confronted by eight walls, three meals, six tablets and funny men."

"Oh, before I forget, I have to tell you something. I've been dying to talk to someone about this," I say.

He looks at me with a bored expression.

"Try to look interested."

"What?"

"Last Wednesday was the last performance of Macbeth. Our director, Tony, quite a nice guy actually, always throws a party for us. So we had a party after the performance.

It was quite a hectic week so Tony couldn't get around to shopping for stuff for the party. The department always pays for it so we go wild on expensive cheese and wine. Anyway he asked me to do it for him. So I went to Pick 'n Pay at the Waterfront. Tony let me use his car. So I buy the stuff: wine, champagne, cheese, crisps, sweets, you name it I bought it. Now I'm at the check-out. There's this black woman in the next check-out. Stunning woman, Tshepo, she was beautiful. You know, well dressed and sophisticated. You could see that she was a professional. Anyway she's got her trolley full."

"Where is this going?" he says and rolls his eyes.

"Just be patient. So now this black woman who must be about 35 is standing there waiting for her turn. Behind her there are these two white women, also dressed to kill. You know the type, my-husband-owns-a-shopping-complex-kugels from Clifton. They're skinnering about this woman. I can just about hear them but I don't know if this black woman has picked it up and ignores them. So eventually one of them moves closer and taps the black woman on the shoulder. And you know what she says? I couldn't believe it. She says, 'So did the madam send you shopping?' Like that, with this stuck-up look."

Tshepo looks mildly entertained.

"So this black woman turns around with this o 'ntlwayela-ga-mpe look and says, 'No, I'm the madam. Did your husband send you shopping, since you're probably just a silly housewife with nothing to do but say stupid things in supermarkets.'"

"Can you believe that sort of thing still happens? And at the V & A nogal," I say and look at him.

"Nothing surprises me anymore. People, you never really know them," he says with luke-warm conviction.

"I mean I deal with the same shit as well but like on a different level. Like you know how condescending white people can be if you speak good English – and we all know that has more to do with speaking it with a flawless accent. Oh, you speak so well, where did you go to school? Wada wada crap like that.

"I get that a lot because I have to work with kids and I sometimes think I'm the first black person they've ever really sat down and spoken with. The questions they ask! But the worst is the hair thing. A friend of mine, Khanyisa, has dreadlocks. But they'll never ask her about them, they'll ask me because I speak like them in a non-threatening accent, not like Khanyisa who went to school in Mdantsane. Is it held together with cow dung? I heard that they use egg yolk. Is it true that you can't wash it? Is it true that Bob Marley had 42 species of lice in his hair when he died? What kind of crap is that? When they talk shit like that about Bob I tell them to fuck off. It just gets to me."

"I know what you mean," he says looking a bit more interested. "We should write a book for them. We'll call it 'Everything you've ever wanted to know about black people – the truth!'"

"It'll be a runaway best-seller."

"A lot has changed since high school, nè?" he says.

"Wena. At school we were all just kids. The colour thing was there, but also it wasn't there."

"We were all still too horny and thinking about our pimples to realise what was out there," he says.

"And now people I went to school with, people I considered my friends, are turning out to be bigots. Of course darkie will give you crap because you're doing okay. You think you're white. O e ketsa lekgowa. Bana ba di-private school wada wada," I say.

"That's why I don't care any more. What people say. It's deceiving. Everyone's got their own agenda. So I've given up. I know who I am," he says resolutely.

"But why do people do it?" I whine a little.

"Because this is South Africa and don't fool yourself thinking that Cape Town is liberal. Some of the worst bigots and hypocrits come from Cape Town. Old money, Mmabatho, they don't want us, they never have and they never will. Do you know how hard it was for them to watch apartheid and all their privileges go? So they lock themselves behind high walls in Constantia. Wherever you get lots of rich people, you can be sure that they will be as conservative as hell.

"My theory of Cape Town is that you get a lot of rich people, Germans, French, Jewish, Muslim, Italians and of course a few of the nouveau riche ba bo darkie. And then the majority of the population is working class. Perhaps there isn't a strong middle class in Cape Town like you get in Jo'burg. I mean I don't believe that everything that the middle class espouses is good but at least they have the effect of balancing out things. Now in Cape Town you don't get that. I mean there are all these obscenely rich people who don't even know what to do with their money and then you have Gugulethu and the Cape Flats on the other side. Of course there's going to be tension. As a result the rich own everything, the courts, the cops, the politicians, the works. But their biggest mistake is to think they still own people and that they can say whatever they like, like those Pick 'n Pay bitches. Baasskap is dead. They have to face that," he says wiping his mouth.

TSHEPO

I cannot sleep, dear Mama. The medicine keeps me awake. It keeps me restless, pacing up and down in my thoughts around the singular idea of leaving this place. I cannot escape; I must walk out a free man. That is all that I concentrate on. It is like my mantra. I take my tablets, tell them what they want to hear and I make an effort to be sociable. It's humiliating sometimes, to smile at the doctors who come and see me during the ward rounds. Once I caught one of them saying, "Be careful, some of them have fleas." They look at us with a mixture of disgust and pity, as though they don't really know what to do with us, for us. But I force myself to swallow their shit. I must think of nothing but leaving if I'm ever going to get out of this baleful place. Even the cockroaches are malignant, they eat anything even when there's nothing to eat. Zebron claims they once bit him.

And Zebron himself, I am beginning to come round to his way of thinking. His music isn't that strange. This concerns me because I am becoming a little like him. Sometimes after they hand out tobacco, I harass the more psychotic ones and steal their share, only to bargain it for food or chewing gum. And sometimes in the shower when the male nurses are not watching I hog the hot water and push them aside. This place is eating me, its decay is pervasive. That is why I must leave, before the worst happens. And I don't want to find out what the worst version of myself is. I walk around this place with Zebron, both of us like predators, stealthy cats waiting for a chance to be freed. It is a long wait till the morning. My nights are filled with deep silences since Matthew has gone and left me with the rustling trees outside while the others sleep.

I'm changing, I'm evolving. I'm being forced to give up my centre, to surrender my identity because that is what you have to do to survive this place. They are swallowing me up whole with therapy and medicine. At night when I'm alone I try to remember what it is like to be me. I can't remember clearly. I'm becoming something else. And the dreams I have they are like revelations. I wake up with feelings, complicated feelings that are like a set of codes. And then during the day slowly I try to decipher these complicated moods, which are messages really. It's hard to explain. But the essence of the dreams is that things are happening in the air. It is like I have been shut away from the music of living and now all I hear is the music of the dying and the dead.

I have become sensitive to the presence of women. I know I have always been close to women but something has changed. They have infected me with a virus I don't understand. When the nurses stand near me and talk idly it is as though I understand their banter, their complaints. And this goes further. My body is changing, in very subtle ways, Mama. I have been holding a secret for a while now but I feel I must say it, Mama. It hurts me to keep it inside. My body is changing. It is embarrassing to even contemplate this but I must release this thought. No one hears me here. No one listens to me. No one listens to my body giving me messages about women, about understanding them.

It is like this, I have started bleeding, like a woman. But not at the obvious place, at the other place. I know people call this piles but this is different. I know it is different because it comes and goes like a cycle, a strange mutated cycle. Perhaps what I'm proposing is blasphemous. Perhaps it is an insult to women. But my body holds this pain sacred. It forces me to think inwardly. Perhaps the distance between a man and a woman is not that far. I know this sounds strange but this is the only logical explanation I have to acknowledge what is happening to me. How else can I explain this acute sensitivity? And I can smell everything too. Perhaps I'm taking this too far.

This is what happens when you stop sleeping well. Your mind finds excuses to keep you awake. It finds a way to kill the time before it kills you. Perhaps my deviant thoughts are a survival mechanism. Perhaps I'm decoding my own psychosis. But I crave sleep, Mama. I long for the oblivion of dreams. I sleep little but when I do sleep I dream a lot. I dreamt I died and transcended. I dreamt I died and survived the dream. I became suffused with violent gases and dust. A determined star is rising in my horizon. I'm ruled by its violence. It is like a beast which thrills me everytime it growls. I can feel its hunger. It is like a famished tiger stalking its prey. Its unfathomable energy and restlessness keeps me awake at night. I can hear its powerful paws gently patting the earth as it moves. Sometimes I'm not so sure that the medicines are keeping me awake. This violent female energy like a creature of darkness from the depths of human fear has become my moon. It keeps me wondering at night and feeds me with images of destruction. I have rediscovered my childhood fascination with fire.

The day Matthew burned his bed I was there. I did nothing. I watched the flames consume the bed, rising in a dance to something as old as death. I watched curiously, like a child engrossed in watching others play rough and tumble. I watched flaming dragons and Medusa's wild snakes screeching, moaning in slicing screams that pierced me like a ray of light. A serpent was twisting and writhing in fury in the flames. For a brief moment I heard the world collapsing. Trees toppled and mountains came crushing down. There was uproar everywhere, people devouring each other while a terrible cold and intolerable fire persisted. It was the Ragnarok, the battle of the gods, the destruction to end all destruction. It was exhilarating. It was breath-taking to be that near to destruction, that close to fire. It was Zebron who finally called someone and by the time Sipho came, the fire had left its mark, ashes.

Perhaps I'm secretly aching to destroy myself. I have come to understand my urges, how deep and primal they really are. I know I have dark moods, they are like commas that punctuate moments of hope. I don't ignore them, I don't question them. I just feel them. When I step over the weaker ones it is because I must survive, I must do what I can to stay on top of the situation. It is like being in a slave ship. And we are like slaves living on top of each other. And when the food is rationed everyone grabs as much as they can. They do anything to stay alive. Well I must do anything I can to keep my mind alive, to hold onto the last thread of sanity, no matter how little there is left. I'm being forced to learn the language of efficient self-effacement. I give the doctors what they want to see: the recovering patient with cannabis induced psychosis.

When they look at me I know that they don't see a person. They see a case, something that they must work out, decode, diagnose. My mind is merely a jigsaw puzzle to them. They are fascinated by its fragments. They marvel at the broken pieces and swap stories with each other about what they see and hear. They listen to what they want to hear and write down what they understand. Everything else, the gestures, the pauses, the looks of despair and desperation disappear in a vacuum called therapy. We are nothing but question marks and full-stops to them, that is why they will never understand us. Our pain has become a tattoo. No one can erase it, not even their medicines and shock therapies. The silence with which they have forced us to live is feeding us in places we didn't know we had. We have become answers to ourselves, full-stops erasing their question marks. Perhaps that is why our curses are so much more profound. Perhaps that is why they lock us away when we abuse them or swear them. Perhaps they fear the sting of our psychosis, because everything we say is layered with realities which they will never know. What keeps them guessing, what keeps them extending our stay instead of releasing us, is exactly what is strengthening us and teaching us ways of seeing. We are becoming the monsters they fear we are. I am becoming the paranoid schizophrenic they initially told me I was but I'm hiding it. I have to conceal the truth about myself. It is only for me, for my eyes. They have seen my nakedness, my naked thoughts. They have seen everything. They have seen enough. What else is there for them to see except the truth about myself? They have stripped me of everything, this is the last detail I can still claim as my own. And I won't let them see it.

I know who I am. At night my thoughts prowl. And I don't have comforting thoughts.


ZEBRON


**M**a Brooks has brought some paper and a pen for me. She's been asking me to draw things. "It is an exercise to release your subconscious," she says, in her usual impartial tone. It excites me to be near her because she isn't threatened by me. I suppose she is my only ally in this godforsaken place. I never thought I would ever call an old white raisin my ally, but it is true.

"Childhood, draw anything that comes to mind when you think about your childhood," she says.

I draw a stick figure playing alone on a swing. It is a very small image. She looks at the drawing and doesn't comment. She moves on.

"The bedroom," she says and nods her head.

"The bedroom? Which bedroom?" I say.

"Any one, remember whatever comes to mind," she says and looks away.

I start to draw a bed and it soon takes up most of the page. On the bed I draw several stick figures and they are doing something to one of the figures. And I draw many lines and squiggles. The figures end up being mashed into each other as the squiggles and lines go everywhere.

"Tell me about your drawing," she says when I have finished.

"Well there is a woman and five men. And we are doing things to her. You check the way there are all these marks, that is her blood."

She looks at me with unexpected pity, a little compassion sneaks through in her eyes but she controls it. She is a controlled woman, Ma Brooks. Even when she's angry she controls it.

"I have been dreaming about her, a lot," I say and press my temples with both hands. "She won't leave me alone. She is always there."

It feels like a confession to say this.

"What you have done to your sister and to other women is haunting you," she says. "You must face this demon, Zebron."

That is the first time I hear her say out my name.

"I want to be forgiven but I don't know how," I say and my throat aches but I don't cry. I never cry. It scares me to think about the last time I cried. It could have been in childhood.

"There are worse things than not facing up to your feelings," she encourages me, her hands folded, her spectacles fixed on me.

"I want to but I don't know how," I say, meaning that I don't know how to cry. Perhaps that is the strangest thing I have ever said to anyone. I don't know how to cry.

"You must go back to those women, to your sister. You must hear their cries, the terrible things you did to them. You must feel a little bit of their pain, their fear. You must see the man who did this," she says with clear precision, her eyes sharp like a hawk.

"I'm trying," I attempt but only feel tortured by my throat. I feel her eyes on me and they are not judgmental. They are just watching me, perhaps even holding me.

"It takes courage to be weak," she says, and something falls into place inside me. A terrible wound that I had forgotten suddenly opens up again. I begin to feel its pain. I start moaning, terrible low groaning like a wounded boar. But the tears still don't come. My body shrinks into itself as I moan. It is the closest I have come to crying in years.

She watches me, this strange spectacle of a grown man making awful howling noises like a terrifying creature of the night, my mouth drooling with saliva. It hurts. My whole body hurts. It is like a wound, a suppurating wound that has festered over years. I hold myself and moan. And my throat is on fire. "Hurgggh, hurggh."

"You must ask forgiveness," she says, rising a little from her stooped posture. She says it with such authority, it is as though she is giving me a remedy, a magic cure.

"What you have done to these women, it will always haunt you if you don't ask for forgiveness. Only you can do the work."

I sit on the chair, holding myself, rocking a little. Perhaps rocking the pain away, the pain I inflicted on the two women. Perhaps they are rocking me to forgiveness.

"This is what has been holding me back," I finally say.

"No. You have been holding yourself back," she says. It is uncharacteristic of her to correct me, to put forward her opinion. But something has changed. She is no longer just my psychologist. And I am no longer just a patient.

After a moment of silence she takes out a pack of cigarettes. She offers me one and gives me matches to light it up for myself. It is little things like that that warm me up inside. Most people have forgotten that I'm not a child. "Thank you," I say without hesitation and hand back the box of matches. We smoke for the remainder of the session.

At the end of the session I tell her that I will see her next week. "You're not such a bad person," she says as I leave and she smiles with her eyes. But her face remains impartial. It is as though she is saving up her expressions for something else, a better day. At her age, one probably cultivates economy, I say to myself as I go to the lounge.

After two months of monotonous routine they transfer Tshepo to Ward 2, an open ward close to a restive lake. It is a predischarge ward which means that Tshepo will probably get out sooner than he expects. In their eyes he has done well. He has taken the medication and interacted with everyone appropriately. He beams with excitement when he tells me the news.

"This is your chance to leave this place. Don't fuck it up," I tell him. We are sitting on the bench outside. It is a little chilly.

"I'm nervous," he confesses. "I've been here for so long, I've forgotten what it's like to choose anything. At Ward 2 I'll be able to get a pass to go to Obs if I want. I'll be able to walk the grounds. There's so much I can do."

I look at him with a little envy. I know how great these little pleasures can be.

"I have to tell you something," I begin, feeling a little irritable. "I'm not good at this sort of thing. And you're probably going to hate me after this."

"What is it?" he looks at me.

"I'm not sure where to begin. It has been on my mind for a while," I say and look at the ground.

"You're making me nervous," he says and prods me. "Just say it."

I'm about to open up to him when I notice a man standing at the gate, wearing a suit. It is after ten. He's punctual, I say to myself and sit up properly. Themba lets him in and he walks up to us. Tshepo looks at him once and gets up to go inside.

"This is how you greet you father?" the man says after him.

TSHEPO

I have not seen my father for a while. And I'm not prepared to see him. I don't know what to say to him. I feel too many things when I'm around him. I remember things I would rather forget.

He is speaking to Zebron outside. I can see them through the window. I wonder what they are talking about. I wonder if what Zebron wanted to tell me has anything to do with my father. What does he want here? What does he want with me, after all this time? I begin to feel nauseous, my stomach doing somersaults. They speak for a while before he comes in.

He finds me sitting in the lounge. There is nowhere to run, I have to confront him. "Your father is here," Themba says. "You guys look alike." It is a painful truth. For a while I wore dreadlocks to disguise the similarities, to erase his face, my face.

"What do you want?" Why is this happening on my last day here?

"Hawu, you're my son," he says and sits down next to me.

"I haven't seen you for four years," I say contemptuously, "and quite frankly, I'd gotten used to not having you around."

"Don't be so dramatic, you're just like your mother."

"How dare you talk about her?"

I get up and pull my chair so that I sit facing him.

"You're grown up. You're almost a man," he says in a proprietary tone.

"Almost uh ... What's this about?"

"I hear that you're leaving," he says.

"I'm just moving to Ward 2. Are you keeping tabs on me? Who've you been talking to? Zebron?"

"I'm your father," he repeats, "of course I have a right to know. I've been speaking to your doctors. But Zebron has also been helpful. He didn't have a choice."

He looks around the room and pulls a disdainful face.

"What do you mean he didn't have a choice? Did you threaten him? You're still full of shit. I hate your guts. I spent years in therapy just to be able to say that to you, arsehole," I yell and move to leave but he grabs me by the wrist and makes me sit down.

"Did you ever stop to wonder why your little friend is here?"

"I suppose you know."

"That night when your mother died, he was there, you just don't remember." He sits back to wait for the impact of his words.

My heart sinks. I feel blood draining from my face and coagulate in my stomach. My throat is sore with grief. What is he saying? My father seldom lies. He's a bad liar. It's the only redeeming quality of his character.

"Why are you doing this?" I say fighting back tears.

"Because I'm trying to protect you," he says but the words are meaningless, they go like the wind. His eyes are still, colder and darker than I remember. He has become a little heavy around the waist. His face hasn't changed but it has gained an impassive, stony quality. He is aging well. But in his eyes I see a man who regularly fraternises with evil.

"Fuck you." I begin to weep.

"Listen to me. Just grow up for a minute," he shouts at me, "Some very important clients are in town. Things have been difficult. They are not happy with me. You must make yourself scarce, do you understand?"

My face is buried in my hands. He shakes me a little.

"You make me sick," I say and push him away.

"You're the last bargaining piece, a liability. They'll hurt you if they think they can get something out of me," he says.

Exhausted, I look at him with hatred.

"I'm trying to help you, in case things get out of hand. They'll do anything to get to me," he says and takes out a handkerchief to wipe his brow.

"You're sick. You're evil. My own father. I can't even look at you."

"It's hot in here," he says irritably. "You're my son. Whether you like it or not you're my son. I still care about you, that's why I'm telling you this. So do yourself a favour and stay in here. I hear that it's quite nice in Ward 2. You can get a little fresh air, even go to town once in a while, although I wouldn't advise that."

"I don't have to listen to you. Where've you been?"

"Calm down. You're emotional, just like your mother."

"Don't mention her! You have no right to mention her!"

Themba comes to check if everything is alright. My father gestures to him before he leaves.

"Okay, Jesus Christ, you've made your point, but you know that I'm right. I left you some money. I have to go. Think about what I said. This is your life I'm talking about."

He gets up and makes an attempt to shake my hand. I ignore him.

"Why are you making this so difficult?" he says grinding his jaws.

"You killed my mother."

He wipes his face with his handkerchief and leaves.

They move me to Ward 2 that afternoon. I don't say anything to Zebron again and at least he has the decency to leave me alone. Sister Hendriks is in charge of Ward 2. She shows me to my room. I share it with a coloured guy called Freddie. He's friendly and always has something to say but he knows when to leave me alone.

The first couple of weeks in Ward 2 are difficult. I walk around in a depressed mood. I keep thinking about Zebron and what my father said. I feel betrayed.

For a while they step up my medication. They put me on Haloperidol 15 mg and Orphenadrine 50 mg. The side-effects become noticeable. I develop a stiff neck and my jaws are always tight.

Life is different in Ward 2. I get up at seven. Then I make my way leisurely to the bathrooms. No one supervises us. No one watches. And there aren't that many of us so there is always enough hot water. I have breakfast at eight. After breakfast I can wander round the hospital grounds and on the days when I want to buy something, I get permission to go to nearby Obs. Sometimes I visit Mmabatho on my way from the Spar. She doesn't know what to say when I tell her about my father.

"I don't have a father," I tell her. "He died with my mother that night."

## MMABATHO

Tshepo is inconsolable after having found out how Zebron had been deceiving him.

"They'll keep you here longer." I'm concerned by his prolonged depression. Weeks go by and still he hardly smiles, hardly speaks to anyone. In the ward Sister Hendriks tells me that his conversations with other patients are perfunctory, that he only speaks to people when he has to. And his appetite isn't encouraging. He asks for a leave of absence one weekend and spends the time with me at my place.

"I'm sure your mother wouldn't have liked to see you like this. She'd have told you to get on with your life."

He says nothing. He looks at me and goes to the other room. I sigh with frustration. He has retreated into himself, there's nothing you can do, I tell myself. Much of the weekend is spent trying to encourage him to speak. The little that he says makes me sad. He keeps reliving his mother's death.

He soon goes back to the ward and for a while I don't see him.

Arne and I are finding our way in the relationship. It's a relationship, I can't hide from that anymore. I can't call it seeing each other, or any other of the euphemisms used to soften the blow of committing to someone. I expected him to get fed up with me in the first week but he didn't. Perhaps I was secretly hoping that he would leave so that I could eternally have a grudge against men. It has become habit to expect the worst from men, a very difficult habit to break. I keep wondering what women complained about before they decided men were bastards.

But nothing's changed really except that we are more aware of what we mean to each other. Silence between us isn't what it used to be. It holds many secrets. Sometimes when I look at him when he's working at the desk, I find myself praying that things should always be like this. That he should be mine and I should be his.

But the fear never goes away. It has nothing to do with him because he is attentive and faithful. And most of the time when I'm with him I don't feel insecure. I don't feel I have to be someone else.

I'm his girlfriend. I help him out with his laundry, especially on the days when he goes to the gym. He's fastidious when it comes to clean towels and cleanliness in general, which is okay because I like my men clean. But sometimes I take it too far. When I see a nice shirt at a store window, I find myself salivating after it, wondering if it will fit him. Or when I stumble upon an article about his favourite football team, Man. United, I'll pass it to him. Or when I find him dozing on the couch I'll put a blanket on him. It's annoying, this maternal instinct or whatever it is. I liked things the way they were before. He looked after himself and I looked after myself. But now we're both looking after each other. I've resigned something, you have to.

He's just as guilty. He's started cooking for me regularly and the sex is not as spontaneous as it used to be. It's still good but we're becoming a couple. I can't see you on Thursday, wink wink, I've got drama practice. How about Friday during lunch, squeeze my bum? I suppose I could fit you in after the meeting, excuse the pun. That is how it is – we plan everything together. It's silly of me to complain because things are working out this way. Some women complain that they don't get enough of this. And I wouldn't have him doing things behind my back again.

The other day we were bathing together.

"I wonder what Stephen is up to. I haven't seen him in a while," he says.

"What does that mean?" I say defensively. "I'm not stopping you. You can see your friends if you want to."

He looks at me briefly as if to say is this one of your moments again.

"I just meant I haven't seen him in a while. Stop being so defensive," he says calmly.

"I'm sorry. I just don't want you thinking that you have to spend all your time with me now because ..."

He cuts me off.

"I want to spend my time with you. Maybe not all my time; I mean we're not Siamese twins."

"You must get tired of me sometimes. I have so much baggage."

"Ja well, I knew you weren't like the others," he says. "It's not every man who wants a woman who thinks for herself."

148

I look at him and nod.

"But sometimes I think you think about yourself too much," he says honestly. "And I know I can be distant, it's my moods."

"I don't want to be someone you think of as a burden. I have this thing in my mind that men are only free to be themselves when they are with other men. When they are with women they are something else."

"Maybe that's true. But I feel completely comfortable with you," he says and farts. Bubbles emerge from the water.

"Not that comfortable," I say and squirt water in his face. "But tell me the truth, do you ever think of going with another woman?"

"Why do you ask these difficult questions?" He looks at me tenderly. "It's hard to say. I mean yes, I only want to be with you. And yes, I would never pull another stunt like that thing I did with Thabi again, ja. But sometimes on the street I see a beautiful woman, I have a silly thought. It's a guy thing. It's harmless, I would never act on it."

"You could have lied to me you know," I say, a little irritated with his honesty.

"You would have persisted. I like to think I know you," he says and reaches over to kiss me. He has the gentlest way of kissing.

"Oh, and one last thing," I interrupt him, "is the sex ..."

"Don't worry about that. It couldn't get any better," he says and then he becomes serious and alert all at once. "You're not faking, are you?"

There's mild fear on his face.

"Don't be silly," I lie, laughing a little.

I know men too well. It irks them when they find out that they aren't the most proficient and sensitive lovers. It is like an attack on their genes as though a weakness has been detected.

So there have been a couple of times when I faked an orgasm or two. But the thing is he was trying to impress me with his endurance and skill. Where did they hear that if you go at it for hours, it's good? Is it something they pick up in the change rooms at school or in the locker room in a gym.

"But sometimes you could hold me a little more," I tell him.

He thinks about it.

"But sometimes I just like to watch you. It's not that I don't want to hold you. It's just that, uh ..."

There's a concerned look on his face. This is what men hate, I say to myself. They hate to feel cornered by what women perceive as flaws.

"This is not serious," I tell him. "I'm sure there are things that you'd also like me to do."

I cringe having said that.

"Not really," he says in a far-off voice, and it makes me feel guilty.

"I never grew up hugging my parents, ja. It was never done in our house. We never said we loved each other except once a year when you're drunk at Christmas or New Year's."

"You don't have to explain."

"The water is getting cold," he says.


### TSHEPO

I wake up one day and find that the sun fills my room with unusually bright light. It has a strange soothing quality. Where light and shadow meet dust particles flicker and float like shimmering diamonds on ethereal beams. There is magic in the way light feels warm on my face as I stand at the window. I wake up with the anticipation of falling in love. A strange quiet excitement fills me. It is as though I have been sleeping and now have just awoken from deceitful sleep.

I become anxious to leave. I yearn to laugh with insouciance again. I yearn for music and dancing and gentle walks on the beach with soft sand under my feet. I ache for the mountain, for Saturday morning excursions that have me working up a generous sweat.

It comes over me quite suddenly, this wave of euphoria and I ride it gently. I plant a silent promise in my heart that things will work out, that the sun will shine over my horizon. And every day I look to the rising sun for guidance and remind myself of this promise. It becomes my mantra.

And in believing, in thinking about other people, doing other things, happiness sneaks up on me. It comes at me like a fever, sometimes suffusing me with childlike joy. They are golden moments, like prayer itself. Happiness is after all the reward for the work we do in private. It seeks no recognition. It is God smiling at us in hiding, humility always by our side.

Four weeks later they discharge me. It is June and it rains relentlessly. I have a melancholy longing for a clear, open sky that will bath everything in golden sunshine. Mmabatho helps me get a cheap flat in Sea Point. I share it with a coloured guy called Chris Swart.

He is quiet and moody and has the sort of gait that betrays that he was once in prison. It is a terrible thing to say about someone but I know it's true. Behind Valkenberg there is a prison for mental patients. And occasionally I would get to see the ones who got released. They walk with a polite reverence for the earth because they know what it is like to be restricted to a few concrete square metres. There is something measured, unsure and a little clumsy in their step. They never forget how soft the earth is, how tenderly their feet sink into it when they walk and how grass tickles the soles of their feet.

Chris and I share a two-bedroomed flat with a bathroom and a kitchen so small one may be forgiven for thinking it is a pantry. The flat is carpeted except for the kitchen and bathroom. The previous owner left us a bread bin and a hot plate. We don't have a fridge. There is an old broom and dustpan tucked away in the corner where spiders run amok. We buy a set of cutlery, four plates, four cups and four saucers. It is enough for now. I have pots from Wynberg. As for the rest of the things that we need for the kitchen we improvise. For instance we notice that Lifebouy soap is just as good for washing clothes and dishes as it is for personal hygiene. In fact we use it to scrub the kitchen and bathroom floors.

Chris is meticulously clean, something that he learned in prison, he tells me. Prisons like hospitals are supposed to be run on cleanliness. Warders pride themselves in keeping their sections spotless. Chris takes the bigger room without a door while I settle for the smaller one leading into the bathroom. I soon get used to interruptions as he makes his way in and out of the bathroom.

After searching for two weeks we both find jobs at the Waterfront. I get a job as a waiter because they tell me I speak well. Chris is shy and awkward but they give him a job in the kitchen, washing dishes. He is bitter that he didn't get a job as a waiter but he is grateful that at least he got a job. We work crazy shifts, split shifts and are always eager to fill in for anybody not able to make a shift. The tips are lousy initially but I persist and eventually get better at offering customers smiling service. Sometimes Chris asks me how much money I'm making. I always find a way not to answer him. He stops asking after a while.

I use my father's money as little as possible. I consider it blood money and use it only when I'm pressed for cash or when we don't have enough to make rent for the month.

When we aren't working we are stuck in front of my black and white TV. The world has caught World Cup fever. Chris religiously follows every football game better than me and is devastated when Bafana Bafana are knocked out in the first round. But it is a comment by a callous and brutish German coach that really upsets him.

"How can he say African players disgraced themselves at the World Cup and that they shouldn't have been there? What the fuck does he know about Africa and what it means just to qualify for the World Cup?" he says working himself up. He has a fantastic temper and knows every possible swear word. "This is the first time we made the fokken World Cup. You know what a fucking achievement that is? And now that fokken rubbish has to say something so fucking stupit."

He is incensed, outraged. I sympathise as best I can. It isn't just football to Chris. It's a religion and the German coach's remark is sacrilegious. "Wit mense," he says with contempt.

We are eating Nando's and watching TV one night after a gruelling twelve hour shift when I ask him about his past.

"So where were you before Sea Point?"

"Why are you fucking asking me that?" he says suddenly. Does he always have to swear? I think to myself.

"We live together, don't we?" I say and look at him.

"Ja, but I've got my privit life mos," he says and continues watching TV.

"Fine."

But later of his own accord he comes back to me.

"I was in Pollsmoor. Jy weet mos waar Pollsmoor is?" he says with a condescending grin.

"Not really," I say just to irritate him.

"And you?" he asks me.

"Valkenberg."

"Hoarrr, Valkenberg is vir mal mense. Ek ken daai plek," he says and laughs. He can be insensitive.

"I wasn't crazy. I had an episode," I tell him.

"And I was innocent," he sniggers. "It's the same thing. Why else would they send you there? Why do you think they sent me to Pollsmoor if I wasn't guilty? It's because I was guilty. You must just say it, I was crazy. Anyway, it doesn't matter. You were there."

"What were you in for?"

"I stabbed someone and he died. But really he stabbed me first so I was protecting myself. We were fighting over this stupit cherrie, Nadine. And what about you?"

"I was smoking a lot of dope," I say a little embarrassed.

"Ja, zol," he says and smiles, "I've been doing zol for years, even in Pollsmoor. Ganja is spiritual, jy weet mos? That's why it makes people crazy."

"They never said anything about it being spiritual to me," I tell him.

"So what's it like to be with mal mense?" he asks, a curious look on his face.

"Nothing different to being with prisoners, I'm sure," I say confidently.

"I bet you people got hot water in the morning, to wash," he says. "Ja, so?"

"Well, we didn't."

I say nothing.

"We washed kaalgat with cold water. So don't tell me that it was the same," he says, suddenly erupting. His temper comes and goes like a fever.

"There's no need to get that tone with me," I say, controlling my irritation.

"You're full of kak, you know that?"

"Agh, you're just moody," I say and get up.

"Ja, fuck off," he shouts as I go to my room.

"Piss off too," I yell back.


CHRIS

The day I get out of Pollsmoor my mother phones to tell me that I mustn't come home. It is the first time I've heard from her in eight years. She used to come faithfully for the first year of my ten-year sentence. And then one day she stops coming and soon a letter arrives, a long letter full of reasons. Ek het nie meer krag nie Chris, vergewe my, she writes. After that I never hear from her again. And my four gangster brothers, I don't hear from them either. The funny thing is I never cry about this. I kind of accept it as part of my punishment. God is punishing me. I know this.

But I'm not sorry that I stabbed André. I'm sorry that he died. He provoked me. I tried to reason with him that night. I tried to tell him to put the knife away. But he was drunk and showing off in front of Nadine. So he stabbed me. I grab the knife from him and stab him too. He falls down. If I could change things I would have stabbed him in the shoulder or the leg but not the heart. I wasn't aiming for it. It just happened. I got the knife and lunged forward. Ag, who cares anyway? No one believes me. You're a trouble maker, a skollie, gam, they say. They cane me. After that they lock me up.

I was never good at school so I didn't bother going there often. School was just something I had to do. And sometimes it was a pain to do it because it meant I lost out on gambling at the corner shop. I hated school. The teachers were corrupt and only wanted to seduce as many girls as they could. My friends Kleintjie and Zakes never really knew what the inside of a textbook looked like. I saw them the other day and they both have dead-end jobs in some funny looking garage, smoking zol when the manager's not looking. Nothing's changed for them. They still go out for pussy. They still drink till they drop. And I don't think they know what it means to grow up.

I know I'm a fuck up. I was bred in the Cape Flats. They have their own story to tell in a growing ghetto. Slums, broken toilets with shit flies everywhere, tall riot lamps that pour so much orange light you'd think you were at a street disco at night. Two families squatting in three rooms. Ja, ghetto life, cheap bunny chows for breakfast, lunch and supper. Xavier playing Public Enemy till early hours of the morning when he's not beating up senseless his sixteen year-old girlfriend and mother of his child. Tupac, hip hop, break-dancing with a bushy twist, jy verstaan, vir Kleurlings. Ja, die Kaap is duidelik. That is what we sing, even when we go to funerals every weekend. It is like a ritual, everyone expects it. Maybe tomorrow it will be my funeral. And the funerals themselves, they have become a social occasion, a chance to show off your crocodile skin shoes and fake Armani suit. It is a chance to wear that double-breasted jacket you stole. And the girlfriend mourning her dead drive-by killed boyfriend, it is a chance to check her out, to see how many tears she sheds respectfully before she jumps on to the next guy. It is a chance to see whose going up the ranks, who's been made boss, who's running the streets, whose mother sells buttons and rocks. It is a chance to look your best and maybe even get your picture taken while you wear stylish dark glasses by Police.

Ja, the Cape Flats. They are like a complicated underground sewage system. Everyone I know there would like to live somewhere else but they pretend they are having the time of their life. That's why people make so much noise, why they laugh so hard and shriek. They do it because in their private moments they are holding back tears that are choking what's left of them. They are being eaten by jealousy and envy and anger for what so and so did to them. You stop being a person if you spend your whole life in the Cape Flats, if you don't go out for a while, even for a day. The deaths, the rapes, the break-ins, the break-downs, they become a way of life, stupid numbers which amount to nothing and that people soon forget. No one remembers that Mrs Paulse was actually a decent lady before they killed her son. No one re-members that before she became cold and stopped greeting people and started pouring hot water on neighbourhood children who played out-side her door noisily, that she used to smile. No one remembers how pretty she used to be before she became a skinny hag with too much hatred. People take you at face value because they have nothing to of-fer. They have so little themselves, so little pride, so little respect and a sense of worthiness. They have their own story to tell and it is seldom about school or good manners or family values. It is more about thug life, Friday night at Bennie's tavern where you can get bootleg liquor for nothing, doing buttons with zol or getting your piel sucked off by some cheap, HIV positive prostitute that you paid for to do you and your friends. It is about klapping Rochelle because "sy het 'n groot bek en ek likes dit nie". It is about walking the streets wondering where your next meal is coming from, who you have to rob to get it, where you can go to buy a gun for cheap. It is about drug lords running the streets and the streets running them into jail and more trouble. Till the Twenty-Eights don't like the Twenty-Sixes and your connection becomes your enemy. It is the home of misery, of take, take and take till it bleeds. Take till there's nothing left, till there's a hole in the ground.

By the time I was fourteen I was accustomed to magistrate courts. I knew the drill. For delinquency my bum was tanned from the numer-ous canings I got. Maybe André died to save me. My life was going nowhere. I could have been just another gangster wearing Levis and cheap jewellery. I went to prison at sixteen and served nine years of my ten year sentence.

Nine years is a long time to think about your life. You begin to see that you cannot just keep doing things without thinking. Jy moet dink, man, jou houtkop, my mother used to say every time I got in trouble. And then she would bliksem me with the same large wooden spoon she used to dish food. Be careful of the hand that feeds you, I read in prison in some book years later, it can also destroy you. But it's true, I learned to think. I had to. Some of us are not that fast. It took me nine years to learn to think for myself. I grew up watching other people, my brothers. I wanted to be a Gent, respected in my street because I fucked up so and so and could drink a lot. Everyone knew that I had a short temper and that I could dance. It was like that. I thought you lived your life through other people. I thought a life well lived was always spoken about. It mattered what people said because it meant they were looking, they were noticing, they knew who you were. Okay, I was stupid, but that was then. I know what I'm doing now. But it is too late for people like me. All that Mandela and all of them are talking about now is the new syllabus and new school-goers. No one is interested in where I'm going. I'm just Chris who just got out of Pollsmoor. I'm just an outie.

"Why do you give me so much shit about this?" Tshepo says when I tell him to tidy up the kitchen table. "You're not my mother and I pay half the rent," he says and walks off. He's a little spoiled, one of those darkies who went to larney schools and learned to talk like them. He also dresses a bit like them. Doesn't wear All Star tackies like the others, never eats white bread – you know how they are about health – and sometimes listens to 5fm. But I know he hasn't got airs, otherwise he wouldn't have considered living with me.

"It's easy for you to say that," I say walking towards him, "I never had a place of my own, even if I share half of it with you. Do you understand?"

He gives me a complicated look. I want to klap him but I can't, this is what I spent nine years thinking about. I'm not sure if he's listening or if he's dying to leave the room. It's easy for him not to care. He can find another place. I know he's making enough money. I know I get paid peanuts compared to what he's making. But this place means a lot to me. The cleanliness, it's my B.A. Mastership or whatever bloody degree he's got. It's what I learned after nine stubborn years at Pollsmoor. It's what I have to show if someone has to ask me if I have changed. So that if someone walks in they must see that I know how to eat because my kitchen is clean, how to live because my bed is neat and the bathroom smells clean. A person must come here and feel comfortable, they must feel like this is home, not just a place where I put my head down at night. Sometimes I think about my warder and how he made us scrub the floor till he said he could see his reflection smiling back. I think about that and how stupid I felt for putting myself in that situation, to be ridiculed by someone like that and for such a stupid thing like cleaning floors. I think about that and how envious that bastard would be if he saw my little castle now. But Tshepo will never see it like that. He will never see how far some of us have to go looking for self-respect. He will never know how small and insignificant pride can be, it doesn't need big gestures. You don't have to do big things to feel proud of yourself, to feel like a person. Not everyone can speak well and say the right things and go to school as far as it is possible. I am just happy that I'm clean, my home is clean and that I'm working. I'm paying for this place myself, me, with my own sweat. I didn't have to rob anyone or sell buttons.

I don't care that the stupid larney waiters at work only see me as a dustbin because they dump all their dishes on me and then run off to smile at customers who are full of shit from what I hear. I know they see me as just another Kleurling getting by, probably drinking away his money at a tavern, happy to be earning peanuts since he's basically happy when he's drunk. I can hear how the managers speak to us in the kitchen, us who are not light enough or not educated enough to work as waiters, since that is what we all initially wanted. We know where the money is. It's not in the kitchen. But not everyone who goes looking for a job is like Tshepo. They look at your name. If it's Klippie, Kleintjie or something funny like that, they pass off your application form to the kitchen or night staff working security. Then they listen to how you speak and pick up your accent. And of course you must smile, be polite and look at them in the eye. The same bastards who were telling you to scrub floors and fucked you up if you spoke out of line a while ago. Now suddenly you must speak to them like everything is alright, as if alles is kwaai. None of that baas bullshit.

It's difficult to suddenly act like you have always known these people and are comfortable with them because that's what they want. You must be confident and smile. But I can't smile. Naai, there's too much to remember. Smile se poes.


TSHEPO

Chris and I go out a lot. We often go to Long Street where there is a bar Chris likes, called Mash. There we can shoot pool, sip beers and smoke zol leisurely on the balcony. Sometimes we go to the Lounge further up the street, although Chris doesn't like it so much. "Too much tooth-paste in there," he says, which means it has too many white people. But I like the music they play there. The detached, almost aloof atmosphere of white suburbia fascinates me. This is where children of the rich come to spend their obscenely generous spending monies. The kind of brats whose wealthy parents double-park in front of the school drop-off zone so that Junior and Missy won't have to walk too far. The kind of kids who have the luxury of choosing extramural activities like tennis and ballet and quitting them because they interrupt their hectic social calendars. I tolerate the Lounge because I usually get some condescending teenager from Clifton wearing too much base to buy me and Chris drinks all night in exchange for vacuous conversation about Kwaito or Tricky's latest release or Cape Town's newest fad.

It seems fashionable for these pubescent prima donnas to be seen with a person of colour. It has something to do with authentic street culture, being real, suffering, blah, blah, blah – it's all bullshit of course. They are rich and bored, dying for a slice of real living, of a life outside their "Bold and Beautiful" existence. How they crave to suffer and have something genuine to lament about. These are the sort of people who talk about the Himba and the San with highfaluting reverence and go on about spiritual purity and innocence. The same people who'll tell you that black culture is so forgiving and embracing unlike their sterile culture, yet they are the first to call their maids "lazy kaffirs" when they forget to do something. They are fascinated with primitive cultures and search for God in obscure places when He is under their noses all along. He is in the Dubes, the neighbours they so readily dismiss as part of South Africa's gravy train and nouveau riche. Sometimes I think they want us to be poor and backward just so that they can ogle obscenely at our primitiveness. For if I look at my culture and tradition and the rich values ingrained in them I am sure that my people are not primitive. Is that what they find fascinating, our capacity to suffer and survive under the most trying circumstances?

How they love to glorify suffering. Oh my gosh, your father whipped you. You were poor. You bought your first pair of shoes at four. You had what without meat? You father beat your mother. The stories go on. I create them because I'm bored with their fake concern and lousy indifference. They don't really want to know about my life, where I've been, where I'm going. They're only interested in sopping up details about people so that they can swap stories with their friends to make interesting conversation.

One consolation about them is that they usually have the best quality zol that money can buy and they smoke impressive blunts. Chris and I have sampled Africa's cornucopia, even sinsemilla, a particularly potent form of dope obtained by culling the male plants before pollination occurs. This results in larger flowering heads in the female plant.

But Saturdays Chris goes out on his own and never invites me. It's his little ritual. I usually go out with Mmabatho. He usually wears his rasta beanie and always takes his rucksack. I never ask him where he goes although I'm curious. But one Saturday evening with no plans to go out and nothing to do, he asks me if I want to tag along with him.

"This isn't the Lounge," he says, his tone condescending.

I ignore him.

"And don't wear those funny pants of yours," he orders me. "Something simple."

"Alright, Chris, I get the picture. So where are we going?"

"Khayelitsha," he says with a deadpan face." Do you still want to go?"

"Yes," I bark.

We catch the last ten o'clock train to the township and get off at Nyanga station. Chris is quiet and keeps looking at me with disapproving eyes as I fiddle with my long nasal hairs.

"Are you ashamed to be seen with me?" I ask as we walk through shacks and filthy streets.

A flea-ridden dog barks at us. Chris waves his arm at it and it cowers away. The streets are wet from burst sewerage pipes and the air is fetid with rotting refuse and animal soil.

"I've lived in Soweto, so fuck off," I tell him as he continues giving me disapproving looks.

We begin to hear the sound of music as we walk. Loud thumping bass lines that reverberate in your inner ear. A swarm of people go in our direction, towards the music. They are characterised by tall hats that cover their sacred dreadlocks. Chris greets a lot of people along the way. He begins his salutation with "Selassie I Rastafari" and they in turn say "Hellie I Rastafari." I listen to their lingo as they address each other as "I 'n I" and speak with a dignity and politeness that I find rigid. And the women cover their hair with elaborate wraps and wear long skirts. We arrive at a makeshift hall called Peter Tosh Hall. There are a lot of rasta types outside, most of them locked in what seems to be serious conversation.

Chris engages in more ceremonial salutations with the men standing outside and then we go inside. We stand in a long queue and pay five rand to go in. Chris thinks I will be put off by the shabby hall but I walk through with ease, as though it were my home. It's decent and adorned with pictures of reggae artists and strong black leaders. It is not every day that you see people celebrating blackness so vibrantly. The room is a rainbow of colours and the air is spiced with the rich aromas of ganja and other smells. Chris takes off his beanie and puts it in his rucksack. That is the custom, once inside the men can display their locks, their lion's mane, but the women always keep their hair in wraps. We make our way slowly to the back of the hall as Chris greets more people. Everyone looks at me.

The DJ entertains us with a fusion of roots, ragga and sophisticated reggae with an upbeat jive and dance rhythm. I'm shy at first and watch with curiosity and awe as everybody gyrates to the pulsating music. Men and women caught in sumptuous rhythms sway their hips and prance about delightfully like graceful springbuck. I have never seen people dance like that. They sort of leap into the air continuously with the stamina of an athlete, reminiscent of Masai warriors in Kenya. In one corner a coterie of bare-chested men seem to goad each other to jump higher and to keep up these vigourous bursts of energy for longer. It helps that they land on soft beach soil. Jah guide, they smile at me when I meet them. They are mostly poor and their gaunt features betray that the five rand entrance fee they pay is a meal for some. In another corner a group of barefoot men and women dressed in rags with ceremonial ash on their faces chant and shout as the music plays. They seem to be ascetics and their presence is welcomed by the others. They hardly smile and seem angry, as though the shoes and clothes we wear are an insult to their rags. All I think about when I look at them are fleas and the hardship of living on Table Mountain and other nature reserves around Cape Town. "They can read your mind, you know," Chris warns me as I look at them. "Alone in the forest on a mountain like that you learn a lot of things. Don't fuck with these guys, they can do things." I look away when one of them looks at me with contempt and mouths something.

Chris's friends share their pipe with us several times during the night and offer me ital food. When I'm high and feel at one with the music, I take off my shoes and gently sway side to side on the bare earth. I dance gently but with fire. I dance with an impassioned spirit as though I am praying. I feel happy, elated, or is that the effect of being high? I look at Chris and smile. He isn't much of a dancer but he seems glad that I'm having a good time.

After a while I become so in tune with my own breathing and my heartbeat throbbing to the music that I become aware of everyone. It is a strange thing, to see people as they are and not as you imagine them. I become aware of Chris and how fragile he really is, always hiding his fears and hopes behind a particular look. I become aware of how each dancer has their own story to tell and how dancing itself is an eloquent language. I feel strangely connected to everyone and this isn't just the effect of being high. It is a deep feeling that resonates throughout my body as I dance. We are like amoeba cells that make up a majestic multi-coloured creature, beating the earth rapturously with the grace of a centipede.

Some people stare at me brazenly, others look at me askance. Since I'm the newcomer I accept their scrutiny. I look at Chris intermittently and keep smiling at him. Harmless, happy smiles that are like gifts.

CHRIS

**I** go to Peter Tosh Hall as often as I can. Sometimes I go to Marcus Garvey Square where rastas have their own place and they can do their own things without the interference of the white man's law. But it's still no victory for the rastas, the place is small and when they are outside Garvey Square the police harass them for possession of ganja.

It's usually packed on a Saturday night at Tosh, the sisters and the brothers together, preaching the gospel and talking about the end times. It is all that everyone thinks about nowadays. They talk about Armageddon and the fall of Babylon as though they will happen tomorrow. It is hard not to think about your life when you are in here. Everyone is so serious, the whole place is alive with heavy thoughts about Judgment Day and self-styled ghetto intellectuals reading prophecies about the new age of virtue that will arise. But not everyone here has the same serious respect for Rasta. There are those who have dreadlocks and think that is all it takes to be a rasta. Then there are those who claim to be rasta but really they are just individuals who use rasta as an excuse to smoke a lot of ganja and complain about life and its injustices when it's really about their lives and their failures. They are the worst type because on a Saturday night they hold their head high with long dreadlocks falling to their shoulders, smoking long blunts and speaking about One Love One Destiny as though they were priests. But catch them any other day of the week and you might find them smoking a cigarette. In a place like Tosh it is offensive to bring Babylon into the doors, they consider cigarettes poison. Or on another day you might catch one of them drinking fizzy drinks or worse beer even though they preach ital food on a Saturday night. Then there are those who are simply there for the music, the sheer enjoyment of dancing and socialising. They don't wear dreadlocks and they don't pretend to be rasta but they respect that they are in a place for rastas so they don't smoke or drink. And anyway it is the only place where people can get together and dance. There are no community halls or cultural centres in the vicinity. So the rastas are respected a lot because they are peaceful people trying to bring a different argument into this deurmekaar place called Kaapstad. And me, I'm not really rasta but I'm finding my way.

I become aware of how little I know when I'm here, as I make my way around the hall, greeting the elders, the Mamas and the Umfundisi with his fiery passion for redemption. I become aware of how important rasta can be in helping us lead better lives. There is a lot to be said about Bob Marley and what his music meant. Beyond the obvious joint and reggae colours he was preaching a very serious and sincere message in a very simple way. It irritates me the way larneys have adopted Bob as an idol when they don't understand anything about rasta. It is like saying you like living in Mitchell's Plain when you have never set foot there but have only heard stories about it. You can't pretend with rasta, it is about feeling, about going back to the origin of man, that guy who the white man called a savage. It is about getting in touch with this man's deep knowledge of nature and living in harmony with it.

Sometimes when the music isn't to my ears I go outside and talk with the other rastas and they tell me their views about life and what is going on. They are always eager to share their knowledge and understanding.

It heats up inside. I take off my sweater and put it in my rucksack. Tshepo impresses me. He is a good dancer and knows how to let rip. We dance all night. We leave the hall in time to catch the 6:30 morning train. Tshepo is exhausted but he is glad he came.

At home we each take a bath and change our clothes reeking of ganja. We make a big breakfast with bread, eggs and polony. Tshepo makes a jug of Oros and we put the food on the floor in my room because there is space.

"So, what did you think about the place?" I ask him.

"It was alright," he says in a lukewarm way, "but the music was good."

"Is that all you got to say, the music was good?"

"What do you want me to say, Chris?" he says, taking modest bites and chewing with his mouth closed. His manners are very larney.

"Don't bullshit me. Just tell me what you think about the place," I challenge him.

"Fine, but you're not going to like it."

I look at him as though I have all the answers to whatever he might say.

"Well, I think it's a lot of crap," he begins, "how everyone there is basically starving. I mean, Chris, those people aren't eating meat in the name of religion right? They are already poor as it is, how the hell can they supplement their diet with protein when already they are cutting out such an important part of it? I mean, did you see some of the mothers and their skinny children? It was terrible. What chances do those children have of developing and getting a good start if they are not eating properly? I think it's wrong. I think they should let the children eat meat until they are, like, twelve or whatever and then they can decide if they want to be rasta like their parents. And bringing little children to a place like that, with that much sound, ah, ah, Chris," he says and shakes his head.

"It's easy for you to say that," I say, controlling my anger under my breath. He mustn't think I'm a moegoe, I know how to say what I feel. "These people are doing something for themselves. Do you understand that? They are not asking the white man for anything. That place they fought for it. Even the policemen don't go near Peter Tosh. People are getting themselves organised."

"You're not answering my question, Chris. You're just saying what you want. And another thing, if rastas are so close to nature and everything, how come they don't clean up in there? And I'm not talking about poverty. I know they don't have money to smarten up the place. That doesn't bother me. But jeez, Chris, they were throwing their packets and peels everywhere on the floor. I never saw one dustbin. And outside behind the hall there is a rubbish dump. How do you explain that? How can you say they want to go back to nature when they can't even respect her? I mean, if they were so serious about the whole nature thing they would maybe even start a clean up the township kind of thing, you know, where rastas lead the whole community in keeping the locations clean. What do you have to say for that?"

I want to klap him but resist. My thoughts are fuzzy with anger. Who does he think he is, criticising rastas like that? "Of course they live like that because that is all they know," I say in defense.

"Right, and now you're telling me that the same people who can't rise out of their own misery are to be given the right to smoke ganja like responsible adults? That's another thing, who decides how much is too much? I mean surely there must be moderation, even in things with rasta. I mean people were smoking nonstop all night. And the children too, I saw a girl who must have been about ten sucking ganja from an apple. How do you explain that? And this thing that rastas don't send their children to Babylon schools, what are they doing? How do they hope their children are going to earn money? Do you know how many lives are going to be destroyed because everything today is moving towards going to school and getting an education?" he says, moving his arms like a preacher.

"Okay, enough, Desmond Tutu. Maybe I shouldn't have asked you because all you do is criticise. You haven't said anything good."

"I was getting there," he lies. "No, I think it's good that rastas are educating people about people like Marcus Garvey and other black leaders. We need more of that. Chris, I did say the music was good. I never saw any fighting or bitching, you know how women get. No, the sisters, isn't that how you call them? Anyway, they were good. For that many people, it's quite an achievement, not a single act of violence."

"And Selassie, you've said nothing about him. I know you know something," I say and look at him for the fox he is. He mustn't treat me like a child and hide things from me. I know he has something to say.

"We don't have to do this, you know. You're quite sensitive about the whole thing already," he says apologetically and eats from his plate. He has been doing so much talking, he's hardly eaten while my plate is empty. I drink a lot of Oros.

"No, let's do this. I want to hear what you think," I tell him.

"Look, I'm not even going to say anything about whether Selassie was or wasn't God. That is a question of faith. But I'm sorry, Chris, I have historical backing that I read up and this man was not all the wise words he spoke. I mean, people suffered under him. People lived like dogs, they were hungry, like the rastas I saw in there, gaunt faces and skraal children. He was a cruel tyrant," he says and sucks in his cheeks to make his point. "And you know, if he was so African, so pro-black, why did he bother having such a white European coronation? I mean, have you seen the pictures of his coronation. There was nothing African about it. The man might as well have been King George the Fifth or someone like that. You know, it just doesn't wash with me. I don't buy that whole Selassie thing. But that's just my opinion," he says and still looks like he has more to say on the subject.

But my temper is wearing me out. I can feel it rising to the surface, almost crawling under my skin. I clear the plates when he has finished and wash them at once in the kitchen. After tidying up the crumbs and drying and packing the dishes away, I sit on my bed and light a cigarette. I was going to have a joint, but in the mood I'm in I might just moer the guy after smoking it.

"Chris, you're not angry with me, or are you?" he says standing near me.

"Are you asking me or telling me?" I say hardly looking at him.

He says nothing.

"I'm tired okay, I need to sleep."

After he leaves me alone, I unleash my anger by squashing my half-burned cigarette into an ashtray. He fucking has answers for everything. What does he know about anything? You can't learn stuff from books and think it works out there in life. Naai, just because he went to school now he thinks hy ken alles. But I know rastas differently. I know them as people who are positive. They don't want to kill each other. And so what if everything isn't perfect? What about Christians? At least rastas don't go to church and pray and then go back and kill each other, drink and rape women. At least they love ganja openly. They don't hide it the way Christians justify their use of alcohol. And isn't it just like a darkie to put down his own people? He belongs with Mandela and his cronies. Hulle is net skelms. I mean, rastas are trying to get somewhere. No one stands up for the rights of people in the ghetto. No one cares that they have nothing going for them, no way to earn money. Selling zol is a way they can feed themselves and look after their families, why can't he see that? Why can't he see that people are desperate? And now this poes with all his reading just says things like Selassie was a tyrant. You never hear people criticising Jesus Christ or Mohammed like that. And he's not the first to talk badly about Selassie. Why can't people respect the fact that Selassie means something to a lot of other people? They don't have to talk shit like that. Why is it so easy for people to say things against Selassie? Maybe because they aren't true. Maybe because what Tshepo read was probably lies. I mean, who writes these books? White men. Who controls everything we hear? White men.

I should never have bothered taking him there. Too much, too soon, he's just 'n windgat who thinks he understands everything. I don't need this hassle. That place means a lot to me.

TSHEPO

I didn't mean to upset him.

I should have kept my mouth shut but he insisted. I thought he really wanted to know what I thought, so I told him. And he didn't like it. And I don't think he'll ever take me there again.

Why did he ask me for my opinion if he was going to get so upset? I don't understand him. I don't know what he wants.

It's difficult. The thing is, I like him. It's terrible. I can't face myself in the mirror when I think about this.

It's awkward, liking a person, especially a guy, in that way. It's never happened. I don't know what to do.

I desperately like him. Can't he see that? When he asked me for my opinion I thought it was a chance to reveal something about myself. I wanted to please him. I tried to impress him with wit. I tried to be everything people seem to like me for, my awkwardness and solitary stance always watching life from the outside in the rain, the outsider, the eternal albatross. I know how I romanticise my solitude. But that is all I can do to soothe the longing. Perhaps it is a handicap to think about myself like that. I know I tried too hard because I only succeeded in hurting his fragile pride and driving him away.

It's terrible because he won't talk to me. You know what that's like? It's like a death sentence. It's like being excommunicated by your sect. I can't speak to him. I can't exchange idle words with him. He is so beautiful, so furiously attractive, it breaks my heart that I can't say anything to him. His eyes, they shimmer like jade and his lips are pink and full and long to be looked at and observed closely. His features are clothing for a god.

Sometimes he goes out jogging. He always comes back before sunset when the light is orange and strange. I don't know why he does this. Perhaps it reminds him of Pollsmoor or something equally sad. He's so precise, there's something sad about it, about all of his routines. There isn't the joy of doing things. I often wonder if he does them because it was drilled into him or if he does them because he wants to. He goes to sleep at ten every night, even if it means leaving an intriguing film halfway. He wakes up religiously at six in the morning and never goes anywhere without his slippers. But I don't have to wonder about that. He said walking on cold cement floors barefoot in prison in the morning after showering with icy water left an imprint on his mind, an aversion for the cold.

Sometimes I see him after one of his blistering jogs. I catch a fleeting glance of him by the window where the light pours in. And he stands there gracefully, panting like the athlete he is, sweat glistening from his amber skin, his muscles tight and twitching a little from the exercise. There is a certain look on his face, maybe it is anguish or sadness. I can't tell because he is trying to recover his breath. But that look is hard to ignore. There is determination about his eyes, like someone madly chasing the sun even though it only wants to set peacefully. There is that do-or-die resolve about him. It is devastating to look at him. I just want to run towards him and be swallowed whole by his sensual presence. I want to disappear forever in his eyes.

Even when he's doing the dishes, he is enthralling to watch. His hands work deftly and his legs stand astride in a strong stance. Hard labour and prison discipline have only made him more beautiful, his moodiness and reticence more pronounced, even a little artistic as though he were brooding about a beautiful work of art he was about to make. Only, his works are gestures, smiles, looks and funny things he says. They are like a secret plot to possess me.

It is embarrassing to think about a man like this. I don't know what to do. He is so captivating. His powerful arms and strong but elegant neck keep me guessing about the rest of his landscape. I wonder what lies under the clothes that fit him so well. I wonder how soft or rough his skin is, how gently his breath comes and goes. And his scars and the stories that each scar would have to tell. I have studied his movements, his clumsiness when he reads at the desk, his natural grace and ease when he lies on the floor, the manner in which he clutches his groin every now and then, the way his laugh seems to emanate from his pelvis, from the depths of his humanity, a shy innocent place that I rarely see.

If only he would laugh again and forget this awkward business. I don't like fighting. I don't like arguing. I like to be with people. I like to be with him. Can't he see that? I'm clumsy myself. I stretch too far when someone offers me the hand of friendship. I'm indelicate. I say things when I shouldn't. I'm a hopeless fool. I'm not entirely comfortable in my own skin. I'm always looking behind me to see who's laughing, who's pointing fingers at me. Why can't he see that? Why can't he see that words are my last weapon, the only resort left to me? It is hard to know people. I'm trying. I'm fumbling. Why can't he see that?

Why won't he smile, just a little one, and bathe me in delight?

It happened quite suddenly, this onslaught of his. I was at that hall with all those rastas. I never liked them. That is the truth. They seem hard and pretentious and worse, they don't care for their women and children. Their treatment of them is appalling. It is always about the men, the lion, the rasta, nothing about the woman and child.

That night I was watching him. I don't know what happened. He just bewitched me. I felt myself being sucked in by his charm, his presence. Afterwards I was scared because I thought maybe there was more to it. I thought maybe he had resorted to a form of mind control since I felt so incredibly possessed by him, so infatuated. I have read about an ancient Islamic secret society known as assassins, a corruption of hashishin, meaning users of hashish. Heavily stoned on hash these potential assassins were taken to a beautifully scented garden which they were led to believe was paradise. Under the powerful guise of mind control they were promised a return to heaven if they killed for Allah. Driven by an overwhelming vision of a blissful afterlife they perpetrated the worst acts, killing on command, shifting political powers and even winning wars. I started thinking about Chris in a similar manner as my mind struggled to make sense of the attraction I suddenly felt for him. His beauty compels such deep emotions in me, it makes me feel inadequate, unworthy, undeserving of his friendship.

It seems he could ask anything of me and I would comply. Perhaps he won't ask me to kill anyone. Perhaps he won't lead me to betray anyone or win any political allies. Although if ever sacrifices had to be made for Chris, they would be live doves, spring butterflies, cascades of fruit and oceans of sapphire. There would be fields and hanging gardens dedicated to his worship, temples constructed with the same passion and devotion as the Taj Mahal. A dead sacrifice would be an insult to his beauty. Blood itself would corrupt the charm with which he bewitches me.

It is terrible. It is like watching a beautiful flower and not being able to comment on its luminous beauty. I shudder to think what he would do if he knew what I thought of him.

But I can't help myself. When he looks at me with anger, it feels like he's plucking a delicate flower. It hurts. It makes me swoon. It makes me like him more, dive deeper within myself to find a way to make it up to him, to win him back.

Could anything be worse than liking someone who has no regard for you? I suspect he doesn't think much of me because he never asks me for anything. He never borrows anything the way guys do, even if it is something trivial like toothpaste. Even when he doesn't have toothpaste and I leave it out in the bathroom cabinet on purpose, almost begging him to use it. But he won't use it. His pride, his resolve, they devastate me. His discipline makes him all the more beautiful, unattainable.

I wish I could take back those words but it is pointless to say things like that. It leads me nowhere. It makes me feel stupid, childish. I wish, I wish, what's the point? He's angry with me. I must deal with it.

I desperately want to make things alright again. I want to be friends again. I want to laugh with him again.

But how do you communicate with a person who makes you feel embarrassed because you have a little learning? I must be careful what I say. I must tread cautiously when he is around.

He doesn't even watch TV with me anymore. I came back from work one day and found it in my room. It was standing on my desk, no note, nothing. He simply decided that since we weren't talking anymore there was no point in him using my TV like we used to watch it in his room together. I felt terrible, so rejected and abandoned. I haven't put it on since.

It is like Vietnam. There is a lot of tension, strained silences that stretch out till eventually they erupt when he slams the door to leave because I forgot to clean up the kitchen table or I didn't take out the garbage. I forget easily. I can't do things properly when someone is angry with me. It is intimidating. It makes me think about my father. And how he would be scolding me while instructing me to do something. Sometimes he would just get annoyed and take over what I was doing himself and leave me with tears and feelings of inadequacy. It is hard to outgrow childhood memories. There is still the hurt.

I want him to like me. I don't know why this is so important, so urgent.

But I keep messing up. He likes things to be perfect. I'm trying, Chris. Just give me a chance. I'm trying.

One day I come back from work and find him in the kitchen.

"Do you want some? I'm making briyani," he says. "I'm making a lot so that it will last us a couple of days."

"Yes ... I'd like some," I say pleasantly surprised, glad that I don't have to deal with strained silence.

I go to my room and sigh with relief. I take off my uniform and change into track suit bottoms and a T-shirt.

"It's a little cold. You should actually wear shoes or you'll catch a cold," he says casually.

Normally I would have ignored him or anyone for that matter and I would have come up with some quick defense but since it is Chris ...

"Ja, you're right," I say and go back to put on my tackies.

I feel a little silly but it doesn't matter. At least we are talking.

"Isn't that Pirates and Chiefs game on TV tonight?" he asks, stirring a pot on the hotplate.

"Ja, I think so," I improvise.

I go to my room and place the TV in his room.

"The reception is better here," I make up an excuse.

He dishes out the food and I make a jug of Oros. He eats ravenously as always. Sometimes when I look at him I can see a little of the boy who grew up without much on the kitchen table. He keeps looking at me as I struggle to finish the meal.

"What's the matter, not hungry?" he says and looks at my half empty plate.

"No, it's just a little hot," I say even though my real complaint is that there is enough food on my plate for three. But, I remind myself, we are talking again, humour him.

I take a while but I eventually finish the food. By that time he is already engrossed in the game.

"It's fine, I'll do the dishes," he says and burps as I clear the floor, "I know you hate doing them."

"I don't, actually. I'll do them, Chris," I say and go to the kitchen.

The kitchen sink is impeccably clean. This is how you must leave it, I remind myself as I pack the dishes. The table is also clean. And he wiped the hotplate after cooking. It makes less work if you leave things clean, I imagine him saying. I run hot water in the sink and proceed with the job.

Afterwards I wipe the dishes and put them away. He hates it when I wash anything and leave it to dry. It looks messy, he always says. And how do you know that flies haven't left their shit on them, he says? Darling Chris, he can be so crude. I'm not sure if I find that charming.

I dry the sink and make sure that it is in the condition I found it in. I also wipe the table and sweep out any crumbs on the floor. And he always leaves the dishcloth in a small bowl with some bleach, I tell myself and proceed to do this.

"I'm thirsty," he says as he comes in to the kitchen. It's an excuse to see if everything is up to his standard of hygiene and cleanliness. He pours himself a glass of Oros, his eyes quickly skirting the floor and table.

"You're obsessed with this," I tell him.

"What?" he says, walking back to his game. But I know he heard me.

# CHRIS

**I**'m getting to know him. He isn't that bad really, even though I will never take him back to Tosh Hall again. Anyway, it doesn't matter, we never speak about it. We only go out to Mash together. He doesn't drag me to the Lounge, not unless I fancy smoking some nice zol.

Work is going well. I'm saving as much money as I can. I still don't know what I want to do with it but I know that it is good to save. Tshepo always saves, I watch him closely. You can learn a thing or two from a guy like that but you must never make it obvious. Otherwise they think you're a moegoe who doesn't know anything. For a kid who went to a larney school he is quite careful with money. Like I notice that he never leaves money lying around on his desk or other places and he always has small change in his wallet. You know how it is with some people, they only have notes and maybe a five rand coin. It's a dead give-away that they are loaded or that they have never had to worry about going to bed hungry. It would be a mistake to only carry notes, an opportunity for someone to play drunk one day and take advantage of the situation. The thing is with some people, in some circles it is best that people see you handling coins, never large money. Like if you're going to buy a cool drink at a spaza shop in Mitchell's Plain rather give two two rand coins than a ten rand note. Even a five rand coin is a little boastful in some circles. The thing about coins is it's also nice to have something to jingle in your pocket while you bop and walk like an outie from the ghetto. It intimidates white people and ouens know that you're not a moegoe. But these are things you grow up with living on the streets. And Tshepo knows about them, or at least he gives me that impression.

Sometimes I talk about women and boast a little about some of the ones I've had. He never does this, he never has any interesting stories to tell. It's a way to pass time. It doesn't matter how many cherries you fucked. We all lie. What counts is how you tell it, how you manage to make the others envious and their piels stand up a little.

But Tshepo can never rise to the occasion. He's got a little too much of the town boy in him, you know, too much learning and that larney stuff about privacy. He's too private. And he's so quiet and by himself. I sometimes peep through his key hole in the hope of catching him having a skommel and then walking in and laughing. But I never catch him. When he's there he's either sleeping or reading at his desk. He's a bit too dry for me, you know, lacking some juice and guts. He doesn't have enough adventure in him.

But that's good because I need to stay away from jolling and all the trouble I got into from jolling. I need to be sensible. But sometimes I miss the mischief. I can't help it. I get bored quickly. I need things to do like the time I defrauded Telkom by tapping their phone lines. I once phoned New Zealand and spoke to a man I didn't know for two hours for seventy cents. And the time when I used to do ATM scams with my friends so that we could get money for trips to Jo'burg. When I tell him about this he looks at me and says nothing. He smiles a little but I know behind that smile he's thinking, stupid moegoe when are you going to grow up?

So I don't tell him everything about myself anymore. I also do a little like him. I keep some things to myself.

I've been irritable lately. But that has more to do with the fact that I don't have a girlfriend. It hasn't been easy. I haven't met a woman I like. Sea Point bitches got big mouths. They are used to these bloody foreign tourists spoiling them rotten and going crazy over their darker skins. You must spend money if you want to be with them.

And I only need a woman for one thing. It's not good to skommel too much if you're an outie. Every now and then is okay but if you can you must spill your seed inside a woman. Sometimes it gets so bad that I go to nearby Salt River where you can get a cheaper prostitute who doesn't look that bad for a reasonable price. And you can naai her till your piel is sore. The prices you pay for a prostitute in Sea Point are ridiculous. I could get a nice tackie for the prices they ask. I don't think Tshepo would approve so I never tell him when I do this. He wouldn't understand. He's got too many ideas about how things should be. I don't know how he does it, how he handles the lonely nights without any female company. Me, I like to naai. Sometimes I think he brings someone home when I'm at work. But I don't really think so. There's no reason for him to hide. I mean, he's not that private. Or is he? Or sometimes I imagine him with that wild woman friend of his. What's her name? I forget it. I don't remember African names that well. Ja, she with her short, bleached hair although she is quite pretty for her type. She looks quite tough, like she can fuck till she drops. But I don't think they do anything. I always tease him about her. I don't think he likes it but he never says anything.

"Isn't it strange having a woman friend?" I ask him once.

"Not really," he says like I asked something stupid.

"Ag, you … You're lying. I'm sure you naaied her," I carry on.

"It's not like that, you know. She's actually quite interesting. She's got a lot to say. You can learn things from a woman, you know," he says and looks at me.

"What kind? Learn from a woman. Try telling that to the bitches in Mitchell's Plain. They'll have you washing their panties and polishing floors. You must be crazy."

He looks hurt and looks down a little.

"Chris, not all women are bitches," he says and continues watching TV.

"Now you're talking kak," I say, "A woman, you can't trust her. You must always watch what she's doing."

He says nothing. His expression becomes moody as he changes channels.

"You blind, my friend," I continue. "Ja, that woman friend of yours, she gave you korobela, sy het jou lekker geslaat."

Maybe I'm just looking for an argument. Maybe I don't really believe that all women are useless and good for one thing. Maybe I'm just tired of being wrong in his eyes. He never agrees with anything I say. I'm not stupid. I know I don't have reading but I'm not stupid. Ask any guy from the ghetto if he thinks women should be trusted and you will know the truth. So I'm not stupid. I've got things to say. I also see things out there. Okay, so maybe Pollsmoor made me a better criminal. Maybe I'll always think like a tsotsi, but I'm not dik. I can see things.

And I don't like it when Tshepo makes me feel stupid. He always does it. Everything has to be right and wrong with him. Like the other day he caught me stealing the neighbour's milk. The silly bastard dresses well and naais a different woman every day of the week, I told him. Why should he care about milk when he probably drinks Chivas every night? He made a big thing about it. He almost went to the guy to explain things, that it was a mix-up. What! I wasn't going to let that happen. So I stopped him at the door.

TSHEPO

I'm shocked when it happens. It's a mistake. He didn't mean it, I tell myself. He must have slipped. For a moment I even imagine that I dreamt it.

But the mirror doesn't lie.

There is a bruise under my eye. I can't ignore it and pretend that it isn't there.

I'm at the door and I'm about to leave, to go to Mr Saunders' place. Chris – if only he knew the truth ... The thing, is Mr Saunders knew that Chris was stealing his milk twice a week. He knew this. One day after work I bump into him at the car park and he asks me to help him carry some boxes to his flat. We get chatting but as soon as we are indoors he comes straight with me and tells me the situation. He says Chris is stealing from him. And then he takes out a gun from his waist and puts it on the table as it is getting in the way of a box he is trying to lift. He doesn't say anything else after that. He just says, your flat mate is stealing my milk. And then there is a gun. And then he is moving a box. It is a clear message.

At first I gasp and stare at the gun on the table. I don't know what make it is. Every gun is the same to me, it is designed with the same intention. His expression remains calm as he moves the boxes to his room. He looks at me as though to say what are you going to do? I'm nervous. What can you say after someone shows you their gun? I make excuses for Chris. I make foolish promises. I tell him I will handle it. I say anything. Don't worry, it won't happen again, I plead. I leave and confront Chris at the flat. I want him to stop and think for a minute. I want to save him from Mr Saunders and his gun and his friends that call in at odd hours of the night and day. But he doesn't see this. He hears sirens and sees flash lights.

So I'm at the door. I reach for the handle when a lightning-quick punch strikes me. A few moments later I recover from the floor, stunned, a stinging, throbbing pain to my eye. I look at him. Blood trickles from my nose. This is the sacrifice he's been waiting to impose on me and all the doves and butterflies in my head flutter away.

I hurry to the bathroom and it is he who helps me. He holds my head under the tap and runs cold water. It is icy cold but I say nothing. He says nothing. While the water runs he gets some toilet paper. He hands me a towel first to dry my face and head before he gives me toilet paper to stuff in my nostril.

I become mute, like a child.

He goes to the kitchen and wets a dishcloth.

"Here, hold it," he says covering my eye, "and keep your head up."

I tilt my head up a little, my thoughts ringing with the silent screams of slaughtered doves.

He leaves me sitting on the toilet seat.

I sit there for a long time, perhaps ten minutes, and think of nothing. My throat begins to ache but I'm still too confused to think clearly or feel sad. When the bleeding has stopped I take out the bloody piece of toilet paper and flush it.

And then I look at myself in the mirror. There is bluish purple shading under my eye and it is beginning to swell. I prod it carefully, trying to understand the pain.

I go out and find him in his room, standing by the window wearing the canvas tackies he keeps impeccably white and a jacket whose collar he always turns up. There is something distant about him, something unfriendly, even hostile, about the way he stands, about the way his hands form fists in his pockets and the way he leans into the light. The venetian blinds cut the late afternoon light into sharp blades. I stand there and say nothing. He looks at me briefly but there is such anger and violence, like a star spinning out of control. His eyes are cold in their beauty. They show contempt.

I cannot explain the nausea I feel after he turns away.

"Chris," I begin, my voice a little croaky, perhaps a little scared.

"Wat? You fuckin' pushed me," he says and storms towards me. He comes close up to my face, I think he wants to say something ugly but it doesn't come out. It makes him stammer with anger. He storms out and slams the door.

I stand there for a while, confused. How can beauty be so ugly?

I stagger to my room and collapse on my bed. And it isn't sleep that I wish for. I think of another city with kinder people and friendlier, familiar faces, somewhere foreign and far off. I think of Chris in a different climate, his tan more obvious, his temper more disguised. I think of soft beach sand and waves rocking pebbles and samba and pretty lights that light up the night. Perhaps it is Brazil that I dream of.

He comes back late at night. His collar is down and there is laughter in his eyes. "Where've you been?" he says slowly, his mouth reeking of cheap brandy.

He stumbles towards me and flings his arm around my shoulder.

"Why is it so dark in here? Why didn't you put on the lights?" he says and puts on all the lights in the flat.

I rub my eyes and adjust to the light.

"Why are you wearing your pyjamas?" he asks stupidly, an irritating drunken look on his face.

He stumbles towards me again and laughs. I catch him and nearly fall with him.

"You need to go to bed," I tell him and walk him over to his bed. I help him take off his jacket but he pushes me away. He takes off the rest of his clothes. I go back to bed.

Soon after settling in bed the light in my room comes on again. Chris stands at the door stark naked, a taunting lecherous look on his face. "I need a piss," he mumbles and staggers to the bathroom. As always he urinates into the water, as though the drilling sound like an industrial pump were a test of virility. He stays there for a while. Then I hear him flush the toilet.

"You'll catch a cold," I say just to annoy him as he comes out.

"Never!" he says with invincible conviction and starts posing, flexing his muscles the way body builders do but he is drunk and clumsy about it, his sizeable penis flapping between his thighs unabashedly.

It hurts inside to see him like this.

"Chris, I'm going to bed," I say and turn my head the other way.

"Hei." He pokes me, his groin a few inches from my head.

I try to ignore him but he persists.

"Chris, go to bed." I get up, raising my voice a little.

He holds his cock and balls in his hand and sneers. A little aroused, a little angry but very confused I watch him. He pushes me into bed and gets in with me. It is better to let him do what he wants, I tell myself, my thoughts caught somewhere between lust and fear.

Surprisingly he sleeps.

When he's comfortable and starts snoring I get up, the light still on. I watch him, his expression quiet and peaceful. I switch off the light and go to the kitchen to get something to drink. I drain a quarter of a litre of Oros. I don't feel sleepy so I wander off to his room. Even in his drunken state he managed to put away his clothes as neatly as he could on his chair. For some reason I hold up his pants and study them as though they will reveal something about Chris. I smell them and look at the frayed ends. I do the same with his shirt, T-shirt and socks. But I cannot find his underwear. I look carefully through the clothes. I even search in his carefully packed cupboard but cannot find any underwear. So he goes like a cowboy, I say to myself, perhaps excusing his erratic behaviour a little. I begin to feel guilty about snooping through his things and go back to bed.

In the morning when I get up from my bed he is not there. And in the afternoon when I see him he acts like nothing happened. He doesn't even mention my eye, now fully swollen. It is a good thing that I'm not working for the next few days. We go about as though nothing happened. It is his way. He doesn't mention Mr Saunders nor the milk. I pray that he doesn't steal the milk again and go quietly about my business.

He finds me lying on my bed, rereading a novel by Ayi Kwei Armah, "The Beautiful Ones Are Not Yet Born". It is my favourite novel.

"I was thinking," he begins.

"You were?" I cut him off sarcastically. I have become a little angry as the days go by and my eye remains bad.

"I was thinking maybe we could go out with your friend, Mmm..." he says and stops short of pronouncing Mmabatho's name.

"Mmabatho, yes."

"Maybe the three of us could go out," he suggests.

"That's a good idea. I'm sure we could arrange something," I say, already planning some ridiculously pretentious venue that will make him feel out of place.


MMABATHO

It is always better to be honest with your friends.

"It's not going to end there, you know," I say to Tshepo with regards to Chris. We are sitting outside at Ardi's in Sea Point. He is wearing sunglasses to cover his eye.

"We should go out," he says ignoring me, "I haven't been to Ganesh in ages." He sips his coffee slowly.

"Actually it was Chris's idea to go out," he goes on. I don't like the tone in his voice when he talks about Chris. He doesn't seem angry with him. In fact you'd think the whole thing with his eye was a small accident.

"Ke eng ka wena? What has this guy done to you?" I say a little annoyed with his nonchalance.

"What do you mean?" he says looking at me from behind the safety of his dark glasses.

I take them off his face and look hard at him.

"You didn't just trip, okay? This guy fucked you up and you're acting like nothing happened."

"Don't get maternal on me, it's very unbecoming," he says and puts on his sunglasses again.

We sit in silence for a while, to diffuse the tension. I order another two coffees for us.

"I think this is the first time I've ever seen your natural hair colour," he says to me after a while.

"Oh, that. I'm growing out my hair." My mood is getting better but I'm still irritated with him.

We say nothing to each other. We watch a dealer selling something to a not so innocent looking boy. He must be about thirteen, fourteen, the hormones have just kicked in. You can tell from the pimples that cover his rugged face and his gangly awkward build. Tshepo chuckles.

"Are you still on the medication?" I ask him.

His expression becomes contemptuous.

"What is that supposed to mean? I don't need this shit from you. You know I'm fine," he tells me.

I roll my eyes at him and say nothing. He fiddles with his nasal hairs, a habit which irritates me immensely.

"I've got to get going. I'll see you guys tonight at seven at Ganesh," I say and get up.

"Fine," he says and remains on his seat.

I take a taxi to town to attend a meeting at the Drama department. There have been rumours about cutbacks of government subsidies and laying off of a few staff members. For us students it translates into fewer productions, which usually means doing less experimental work and more Shakespeare and other dead white writers that please the establishment. By the time I get there I find the doors closed. I peep through the keyhole and see a throng of people listening to the lamenting voice of the head of the Drama department, Andrew Schiller. I stand outside the door and hear him go on about other institutions struggling to support their arts departments with inadequate funds. He goes on about the new government policy pushing science and technology ahead of the arts. They need scientists and mathematicians first, Andrew says and a low discordant groaning goes out. How can you build a nation without telling its stories, someone says poignantly? I don't wait for Andrew's response, I leave at once.

At home I find Arne lounging in the kitchen with Nadine, my housemate. I greet them with a mild, unenthusiastic hi. Perhaps sensing my irritable mood Nadine goes to her room.

"We're going out to Ganesh tonight," I tell him, "I met Tshepo today. I hope you haven't made any plans."

He moves over to kiss me while I make a sandwich.

"Somehow you don't look too happy about it," he says, his arms around my waist.

I maneuver my hips gently till he lets go.

"He really pisses me off sometimes. He's living with this guy and fuck, he's such an asshole. He beat up Tshepo – well, punched him in the eye – and Tshepo's acting like nothing happened."

"A little punch-up is not the end of the world for guys, you know. It happens."

"Not you too," I say annoyed, disappointed. "Is this a guy thing or something?"

"No, my dear," he says.

He always says that when he's trying to work with my temper or a bad mood.

"The thing with you is that you're always trying to champion people's rights and not everyone appreciates it," he says.

"That's just a polite way of saying I'm nosy. Anyway, it doesn't matter. You're right, he can look after himself."

We all meet at Ganesh at seven. Tshepo and Chris are already there when Arne and I show up. There is the usual ceremony of greeting and introducing everyone. And there is also the usual mild hostility between Tshepo and Arne who hardly say anything to each other. Other than that Tshepo looks radiant while Chris seems quiet and shy.

"Maybe it is a good thing that we came early, as the bar is empty. Ganesh can get rowdy and a little intimidating if you've never been here," Tshepo says to Chris in a condescending tone.

I smile to myself because he says it with such authority, it is as though he were boasting. Except for another table in the corner there is only us and we sit at the couch table. It's suitably positioned to see everyone coming into the bar.

Karuna is behind the bar. She looks miserable and tired. "Haven't seen you in a while," she says and there is something accusatory in her tone.

"I've been busy," I dismiss her, not really keen to encourage one of her dark moods. She gives me my order of three Castles and a Savannah and soon helps someone else.

"She's in a rotten mood," I say to Tshepo when I return to the table.

"So what do you do?" Arne asks Chris. There is slight panic in Chris's eyes as he looks at Tshepo.

"Uhm, I work at the Waterfront," he says.

"He works in the kitchen, you know a dishwasher," Tshepo adds with relish while Chris squirms.

"I fancy some music tonight," Arne says changing the subject.

"So do I, actually," Tshepo adds exuberantly.

"I was going to suggest later that we go to Angels," I say. "A friend of mine is having a coming out party and I've been invited."

"Well there's nothing going on here. We might as well go now," Tshepo says eagerly.

"Darling, it's only going for seven thirty," I remind him.

We drink slowly and don't really say much. People start milling in.

"So where are you from?" Arne asks Chris.

"This is Cape Town, what do you mean where is he from?" I say in his defense. And anyway, it is a rhetorical question. It's clear that Chris is from here.

"I was only making conversation," Arne says to me and nudges my nose.

Chris smiles politely the way a person does in the company of strangers.

"So what did you tell them at work?" I ask Tshepo and gesture to his eye.

Chris's eyes roam the room.

"I went there and they said I must come back when it looks better, well healed. You know what they're like at the V & A. Can't have one of their waiters looking like they get in a fight every weekend," Tshepo says and looks at Chris.

Arne and I cringe. Okay, you've made your point, I say to Tshepo with my eyes.

We order more drinks and eventually my friends start pouring in. Fiona and Jay walk in and pass my table to say hi. We kiss and fuss. I follow them to their table and she tells me about the government cutbacks that will affect Michaelis. We both lament it but soon change the subject when we notice that Jay is quiet. Every now and then I throw an eye to our table where Arne looks miserable with Tshepo and Chris. He goes to the roof for a joint when one of his friends walks in.

A little drunk, Tshepo acts like he knows everyone and keeps greeting people, even though they vaguely know him, showing off in front of Chris that he knows so many people. And the ones who do know him are awkward with him because so much has happened and because Tshepo doesn't really keep contact with anyone. They all avoid the subject of Valkenberg. They smile politely and ask him a few perfunctory questions about where he is staying now but as soon as he turns his back they sigh with relief and pull complicated faces. Nothing has changed. He still doesn't fit in.

Chris clings to his beer and looks subdued. He sits by himself while Tshepo walks around the room making a fool of himself. At nine I call Tshepo and Arne and suggest that we move to Angels. The truth is I was beginning to feel embarrassed for Tshepo. People were beginning to snigger. Chris is only too eager to leave.

In the car the mood is strange. Tshepo looks drunk. Arne is stoned. And Chris is withdrawn, he even seems depressed. We go to Insomnia first, a small bar near Angels. Tshepo orders four iced coffees. They are delicious and sobering.

"So Fiona's married to Jay now. I always thought she was a lesbian," Tshepo says to me.

"You always think everyone is ambiguous," I tell him and he doesn't argue.

"Well, in Cape Town it's kind of a given, it comes with the territory," he asserts.

"That's such a washed up cliché. Not everyone in Cape Town's gay, you know." We finish our drinks and go across the road to Angels.

I get ticked off the guest list and tell the bouncer that the others are with me. But he refuses to let them in because their names are not on the list. He becomes belligerent and intimidating. Chris gets agitated and is about to do his macho thing when Alex, the guy whose party it is, timeously happens to walk by the door. I call out to him and he sorts out the whole thing by letting them in.

House music pumps through the entrance. The place is teeming with gorgeous men out to have a good time and show off their gym-sculpted bodies by wearing skimpy tank tops. "I feel as if I'm in a Village People video," Arne says to me, a little uncomfortable and self-conscious. He clings to my arm as every second man sizes him up. We lose Tshepo and Chris in the crowd but later find them at the bar. "This can only happen here," I say to Tshepo, watching hordes of sexy men gyrating to disco music.

We order more beers and watch with humour and awe as the place fills with even more amicable faces in a jovial spirit. Wearing an emblematic tiara and a shocking pink boa Alex prances around the room, chatting to various men. They peck each other on the cheek, squeeze butts and whisper lecherously into each other's ears. Some are bare-chested and move their bodies lasciviously like drunken hedonists. "It smells like a locker room," Arne says, "except that it isn't your usual locker room." Even though Arne knows gay men I don't think he's ever been in their space. I kiss him every now and then just to reassure his masculinity as men brush past and flirt with him. We guzzle down another round of drinks before Tshepo gets up and goes to the dance floor. I try to make small talk with Chris but he gives me rigid yes and no responses. I don't think he likes me. Eventually, he also goes to the dance floor.

"I didn't think your friend was that way. Are they lovers?" Arne asks after he leaves.

"No, but something's going on," I say and for the first time I consider whether Tshepo is sexually ambiguous. It's funny, but we've never talked about it. I've just assumed that he's had girlfriends. He can be so private, it's hard to know who was the last person he was seeing, if any.

We watch them as they dance. Chris's face beams with pretty-boy arrogance as he dances and other eyes try to catch his gaze. He enjoys the attention. Tshepo closes his eyes and tilts his head up, oblivious to everyone else. It is a sign that he feels insecure.

I'm also eager to dance but Arne refuses to leave his seat. My feet itch for the dance floor but I stay with him. After midnight Tshepo and Chris come to tell us that they are going. "I'm working a day shift tomorrow," Chris says apologetically.

"Well, it was nice seeing you again," I say even though I don't mean it.

TSHEPO

We are walking home on Main Road when I notice a police van on the other side of the road. His elbow leaning out the window, one of the officers scours the road with menacing eyes. He looks at me briefly and soon the van makes a u-turn and comes our way. I begin to sweat.

"Chris, fuck. Fuck! I've got three Malawi cobs on me," I say and alert him of the police van idling behind us. "I couldn't resist, Karuna was selling them."

"What! I told you not to buy at night, especially from your larney friends. Didn't I say I'd sort it out?" he scolds me and throws a look backwards. "Shit!"

"Maybe they're just passing," I pray, even though I can hear the engine close behind. Soon a siren that every black male fears goes off and they park their van just in front of us along the pavement.

"Evening, boys, just doing routine spot checks," a coloured officer says as he comes closer.

My heart beats fast.

"Sorry, a check-up of what?" Chris asks bravely.

"Hey, don't give us any trouble now. We're just going to search you," the coloured officer says, his eyes fierce-looking. The other officer, a white guy, stands nearby.

"Search us for what?" Chris says defensively.

I'm quiet, my voice paralysed with fear.

"Jy, tsek!" The coloured officer becomes nasty and waves his arm at Chris but doesn't hit him. "Are you hiding something?"

"You can't just stop us for nothing and search us. Ek het niks verkeerd gedoen nie. This is unconstitutional," Chris says testily.

I feel faint with fear.

"Constitution se moer," the coloured officer says and grabs Chris. He pins him against a wall and spreads his legs while holding his arm in a vicious vice. Chris moans. The officer goes through his pockets, manhandling him.

We are on a brightly lit street. Prostitutes ignore the kerfuffle and continue with their trade – tired, drugged expressions of angst on their faces. Cars drive by. A group of youngsters driving a convertible BMW slow down and lean out the window to ogle the spectacle as they drive by.

What is going on? I keep saying to myself, disorientated, numbed with fear. Can they just do that? Is this happening? I keep repeating, a million thoughts racing in my mind. I watch with panic as the coloured guy abuses Chris. This is Cape Town, baby, a sobering thought comes to me.

"Now, we tried to be nice. If you want we can do this at the police station," the white officer says to me. I shake my head.

Chris becomes quiet. He lets the coloured guy search him thoroughly, digging his hand into Chris's privates.

"Constitution. Constitution se moer. Julle daggamannetjies dink julle is slim, nè? Fok julle," the coloured guy says when he finds nothing on Chris.

The other officer searches me and finds the three Malawi cobs.

"And what have we got here?" he smiles. I feel dizzy with panic.

"Da's julle fokken constitution. Dis al wat julle verstaan," the coloured guy says and stirs me with an unexpected klap that has my senses alert.

I hold my cheek and it feels hot with blood. I look at the police van, electric blue light spins furiously. I feel nauseous. The stringent light assails me and fills me with angst. It seems to scream with urgency.

"Vat hom," the coloured guy says to the white guy. "We're taking you downtown."

"It's okay, Chris," I say meekly as I get into the back of the van.

They drive off with me and leave Chris standing with disbelief on the pavement. They take me to the city police station. I hardly look up as they bundle me past reception and into a small room where they take my fingerprints. The man who does it, a black man, is quiet and his expression is rigid like a mask. He grunts to tell me that I must relax my hand. I want to say something to him, perhaps hoping for a little sympathy, but the words fail to come. He gives me a dirty rag to wipe my fingers before he bundles me off again. We walk down a small dark passage before he opens a large heavy door. He locks me in a cell with mostly rastas. It is like being in the kulukutz again, I say to myself as I stand there confused and nervous. It is semi dark. The only light is from a small window above.

There are eight people in the cell. Five are sleeping and are curled up in their flea-infested blankets, the kind of colourless blankets that scratch you because they are coarse. I can tell that they are infested from the way some of the men keep scratching themselves intermittently in their sleep. I sit on a concrete bench, trying to contemplate my fate. On the floor three rastas are sitting, having a close conversation. The eldest with grizzled long dreadlocks calls me. I go to him nervously. There is a silver toilet bowl in a corner. It smells like a sewer.

"How did, man?" he says to me, surprisingly cheerful.

"Excuse me?" I say and kneel down to his level.

"How are you, man?" he repeats.

"Oh. I'm alright."

"Come. Sit closer. We're all brothers here. At least dey didn't lock you up with dem mens next door. Dey be chowing buttocks like a woman's thighs, beasts," he says and a torturous image comes to mind.

They make a space for me on the floor and they offer me a blanket to cover myself to keep warm. I want to protest that the blanket has fleas but it would be an insult to them, my manners tell me.

"I'm Ruben and dis here is Benjamin and over here is Isikare," the elder says. He is old enough to be my grandfather. His pupils are a murky colour with wisps of light blue wisdom.

"Rastafari," the other two salute me and raise their open hands. I follow, feeling a little stupid. Everything is ceremony with them, I remind myself.

"So what happened to de man?" Ruben asks.

"I was caught with three Malawi cobs on Main road," I tell them.

"Does I 'n I control?" Isikare asks.

"Excuse me?" I say feeling ignorant again.

"Lion doesn't speak de ghetto tongue," Benjamin smiles.

"What I mean, Papa, is do you sell de herb? Do you control?" Isikare says again.

"Me? No, no … I use dope for my own personal consumption."
Their expression changes.

"Aha. Dat is why man 'n man is in trouble. You must respek de herb, Papa. We call it ganja, you sight. Because Jah-Jah gave it to I 'n I. It is de all holy herb from de I'mighty," Ruben says with a face that looks offended because I said dope.

"Yes, ganja. I meant to say ganja," I say apologetic, embarrassed.

"Dis word ganja is important for I 'n I, you sight, you overstand?" Benjamin reiterates. I suddenly become aware that I'm in their space, that even though we're all in the same situation I'm still a guest. There is a mild threat of violence in Benjamin's posture, as though he wouldn't hesitate to discipline me if he felt the need. I sit up and listen.

"You sight, Papa, ganja is how Jah-Jah speak tru I 'n I. Derefore we respek dis herb from de I'mighty and never call ganja dope or dagga like de white man and mens from Babylon. When you gwoan and get locked for ganja, it is a righteous ting for I 'n I if his heart is wit Jah-Jah. Because you sight, Papa, I 'n I is always fighting de forces of Babylon dat wants to destroy Jahovia's Kingdom. You sight, man?" Ruben continues.

I nod and listen further.

"Where does de man survive?" Ruben asks.

"Sea Point," I say, catching on to their lingo.

"Salt Point. Babylon. I sight why de man is confused about ganja. Dere by Salt Point man 'n man control ganja wit drugs. De greatest of evils survive dere," Ruben says, his expression contemplative.

"And where do you survive?" I inquire.

"We survive dere by Marcus Garvey Square in Nolingile, de ghetto-ship. I 'n I set up living places for all de childrens of Jah, so dat we can lives as righteous people of de eart. You sight teocracy, man?" Ruben says.

"What does that mean?" I ask.

"It means living wit Jah at de centre of I 'n I life," Ruben says.

"And no one hassles you in this Marcus Garvey Square?" I go on.

"Yes, man. De white mens let I 'n I smoke de holy ganja dere. But me not especially tink much of it becoz de white man give I 'n I little freedom. He tinks he givin I 'n I some recognition but me know he not. I 'n I still be sight a criminal from Babylon. I 'n I be judged by de laws of man. Man 'n man can't judge I 'n I, not wit dem laws of Babylon. De laws of mens who drink from dem grapes of wine and kills us wit tobacco and allows dem womens loose walkin and talkin. How can man 'n man judge us wit laws he does not respek and sight, de laws he does all tings to break?" Ruben says and looks at me earnestly.

"Yes, I," Benjamin punctuates.

"So you sight when I 'n I carries de sacred ganja I 'n I must know dat he is doing de work of Jahovia, spreading de gospel. Ganja is serious, man, you overstand?" Ruben says, his murky eyes full of secrets.

"Yes, I do," I say humbly. "But tell me more about the rasta man. Who is he?"

"Yes, Papa, I sight dat you have de tirst for knowings. I 'n I must always ask. Dat is de only way dat I 'n I knows. Now you sight a rasta man is like onion. A rasta man grows from de eart. Everyting he learns is from de eart. I 'n I learns to love de eart, to respek her. He is de roots of de people, de original man. He knows stories, tings about people, he come long time before anyone. He most alone by himself. A true rasta man live on de inskirts and watches and listens and remember everyting about people. He is de people's eyes, sometimes de tongue of de people. A rasta man knows man 'n man better dan man 'n man tink and he knows man 'n man story, where de peoples come from. He knows de power of dem herbs and evils. I 'n I can also sight evil," Ruben says, reaching further into me. "He go tru life looking into de hearts of mens and helping dem when he can, like we be telling you de trut now. We be telling you tings dat people tolt us along de way.

"But of most a rasta man be a servant, he be a servant of Jahovia. He be always humble. He is dere to help man 'n man becoz you know de tings of Babylon dey blind man 'n man. Even us when we goes to Babylon I 'n I must open eyes becoz dere is temptations in Babylon."

"Yes I," Isikare adds. "And so de rastaman is interested in trut wit all tings."

They talk like that for hours. I'm struck by their rigid sense of duty and how easily they seem to see the truth from lies, evil from good. They speak with pragmatic wisdom, of ghetto experiences that have forced them to look inwardly too much. They seem to have been wounded too much. Their observations are stained with blood and the suppurating beginnings of a world collapsing at the seams. When they look out at life I suspect they only see the jagged knife of repression. Their whole life seems to revolve around suffering and making something sacred of it.

We talk about old Africa and how things were before the white man came, with drills and guns and things that frightened the stillness and made the air aware that change was coming. We talk about the days when Zulu kings terrorised the interior in their voracious bid to expand their kingdom. We talk about the bloody wars with the Matabele and the varying degrees of cruelty and hardship they suffered.

"You sight man, de black mens knew about nature protection long before de white mens come. In dem old times dere was more laws for dem protection of nature dan dem protection of de peoples. De Kruger Nations park be a sacred huntin place for Shangaan Kings before what white mens make wit it. De Shangaan Kings be only huntin at certain times of de moon and stars. It be irie place wit lots of I'mighty power wit lions and elephants and dem sacred creatures of Jahovia. If man 'n man be caught hunting in dis place he be punished by killing in de most painful way because man 'n man be upsetting de eart moder. Yes man dat was old Africa.

"Before de white mens man 'n man did not tink of de hills, de waters and de creatures of Jahovia as de wilderness. Man n' man tink of Indle, de great nourisher as de tameness because he be close to dem, he not see himself as different from dem. Dere is a tribe in de hills of Zululand. Dey be called de peoples of de Dube tribe and deir symbol be de Zebra. Now de zebra and de buffalo what de white mens be calling de wildebeest, live one 'n one, dey always share de same grazing because de zebra sight well when de sun be high but de buffalo not sight well in dem light. But at night de buffalo sight very well and de zebra not sight too well. So you sight whe dem lives one 'n one dey be living better becoz dey be each other eyes for protection. And dere be dem birds dat follows like de egret. Now when de Dube protect deir Zebra dey be considering de buffalo and de birds dat follows dem. So you sight where dem nature protections come from. Man 'n man always knows dis. Dere is a history about de peoples of Africa dat be destroyed in Accra, Timbactu, Yorubaland, but de rasta man he be knowing dis. Even de healers, de sangomas dey be holding powerful symbols and relics from dem times when Indle de great nourisher be de moder of man 'n man, before we became de peoples of Babylon. De rastaman knows de folklore and secret herb of de people. You must remember when you gwoan and smoke to be irie dat you be also using de medicine of de I'mighty."

I'm familiar with the diversity of use of this resilient plant but I don't show effrontery by telling them about my scant knowledge. They tell me about clothes, shoes, furniture, books, oils, ingredients and fuel obtained from this paradoxical plant, easily germinating. I ask them many things and they are enthused by my curiosity.

"Where is lion's fada?" Ruben finally asks.

"It is a long story and I don't have the courage for it tonight, I 'n I. But basically we don't see eye to eye," I offer.

"Dat is a ting of Babylon. Fada and son separated. De I'mighty speak about it in de end times dat fada will be against son, broder against sister. I feels for your sorrow and prays dat Jahovia will guide you along de way," he says and gives me a wise smile.

"Is like de journey of a rasta man," Benjamin speaks, "to be a rasta is a long journey, you sight, I 'n I must earn dem locks. When I 'n I be growing because of dem traditions my tribe say man 'n man must gwoan to dem bush, to be cut like a man. But I 'n I be rasta, so I not gwoan to de bush. I not gwoan because I 'n I give up all dem tings to be rasta. Is like a special call from Jahovia. I 'n I is chosen. So because I 'n I not gwoan to de bush I 'n I be laughed at by dem people and loose womens. Dat is why I left dem tribal tings. Because when you rasta every man is I 'n I broder, even de white mens. We all be gwoan for one destiny one love wit Jahovia and de Spirit.

"So you sight, for I 'n I becoming a man is not about dat skin man 'n man cut and trow aways. It be opening dem eyes because Jesus de son of de I'mighty be saying, "No man cometh to de Fada but by my word." Yes, man. Dis mean no man find de way except tru de eyes of Jahovia. Jesus also say, 'Tru my message I brings you de possibility of resurrection from de world of matter and wit it life.'"

"Yes I, Rastafari," Isikare says.

I notice that they all sit with their hands in a strange embrace, forming a triangle.

"And dat is how I 'n I lives. We always looks above for Jah-Jah guidance. Dat be why I 'n I always be saying guidance when I 'n I meet and part. We be saying it because we lives it. His guidance is supreme. We knows dat de spirit of Jahovia be living in all man 'n man and if you listens or not only you and Jah-Jah will knows. You sight man, thina siluke ngengqondo," he says uncharacteristically in Xhosa.

A strange thing happens. When I look at their faces in the dim light I begin to see glimpses of a forgotten people. It is as though they are ancient remnants of old Africa who defied time and refused to die, warriors who outwitted their arch rival, Death. There is age about their faces, about their greying hair and tough skin like old leather, something old and venerable about the way they peer out at the world with gentle breath. But in their shadows I can see the tenacity of a lion's might. Their eloquent expressions allude to experiences gathered over years, wars, kingdoms. We have seen it all, they seem to say, and it is always the same thing. In their eyes there is something unyielding, perhaps a stubbornness that has seen them live for centuries. Perhaps it is also in their large ears bent forward a little and their pugilistic jaws with stained teeth worn down at the edges. They become quiet and brooding as though becoming aware that they have revealed too much about themselves. I lie down to sleep. They remain sitting but say nothing to each other, sleeping or meditating like misplaced Buddhists, I cannot tell. They remain fixed in a triangular form while drowsiness lulls my eyes.

I don't sleep much that night. Besides being bitten by vicious fleas, my mind keeps wandering in and out of dreams about strange ancestral places. A stubborn aged lion follows me through these dreams and when I throw a stone at it, it laughs and says, "I told you Jah guide." It follows me through a confusion of city lights and people wearing lamps on their heads.

We are woken up at seven and served polony sandwiches with weak coffee. When the rastas complain about the meat because they are vegetarians, the attendant in charge tells them to separate the polony from the bread. He walks off. "You sight, dis is how man 'n man treat de rasta man," Benjamin says fresh with irritation. I wonder if they eventually lay their heads to rest or whether they remained sitting all night. Ruben, Isikare and Benjamin refuse to eat the blighted sandwiches. The other rastas and people in the cell eat. I'm hesitant because I don't want to offend the three rastas. "You be hungry. You must eat," Ruben tells me. I eat the sandwich slowly.

At around ten I get called. I expect to be taken to a holding cell like the others but I'm surprised to be led to the reception area. I'm disappointed to meet my father. He is talking to the police officer when I walk in.

"What the hell is wrong with you?" he starts. "Didn't I tell you to stay put?" I walk out the building, sour with disappointment. I should have guessed.

"Don't walk away from me when I'm talking to you. I'm still your father," he shouts and comes after me.

"Unfortunately. But let me put you at ease. You're not really my father. Your contribution was a sperm."

He slaps me hard across the face. I almost fall.

"You're the perpetual thorn in my side," I go on.

He grabs me by the scruff and forces me to listen to him.

"And what is this business that I hear that you go to faggot nightclubs? I didn't bring you up to be a stabane. Are you a faggot?"


MMABATHO

I am growing my hair.

Every day I wash it with tender cucumber shampoo and oil it with lavender scent and herbs to encourage growth. Every day I comb my afro gently and plait it and try new, interesting patterns. I oil my skin and lie in the sun. I look less in the mirror and more into my man's eyes and whisper sweet things to myself. I welcome the woman I will become, I am becoming. I sit by myself at his desk and write my journal. I record the moods that leave me wondering, a little scared, hiding my fears that he will leave. I feel my waist yielding to the charm of his arms, his open hands – too many women know the clenched fist of their lover. I feel myself striding with added rhythm when we walk to the shop together. I memorise the landscape of his body, the gestures of his moods. I revel in being a woman, I light up when he returns gleefully into my arms after an arduous day of research work. I become closer to the woman we all fear and criticise. I become closer to my mother and seek her advice when I find strange messages and telephone numbers in tattered, crumpled bits on the desk. We lie in bed together, our bodies like an artist's image on the large canvas of our bedroom.

We have moved in together.

It seems like a rash decision when I think that we have been together for less than a year. I will not count the months, it is too discouraging.

"It's a waste of money. Me living at your place half the time and you at my place half the time. And the food that wastes and rots because we're never really there," he says.

He can be so practical.

"But are we ready?"

"You mean a lot to me," he says peeling dried skin from his lips with his teeth. "I'd hate to think that I don't mean as much to you."

"Don't be silly," I say and move to kiss him, even though my stomach is doing somersaults.

We get a place together in Mowbray.

It is strange living with your lover, at least for me. I cannot hide any more. I cannot postpone my moods till he's left. I cannot hide the fact that I can also be indelicate like a man, my bodily functions going about their own things just as crudely. I cannot pretend that I am charming and always in a good mood. My little idiosyncrasies have become more obvious, like my aversion of dirty dishes, sticky floors. It is terrible, I have become my mother, nagging him to do his share of the work. But sometimes it is futile to argue. The rosters, the arrangements all done in good faith do not translate into oiling a healthy relationship. I find myself doing his laundry more than I would like to. But then again I rely on him so much for transport. He's always dropping me off and picking me up from the Drama department. And he never complains. That counts for something. And he usually does the cooking because I always come back later than him.

So I do the laundry, the dishes and the cleaning. He tidies up after himself when I'm around. When he's alone he's like a child alone in a toyshop. He can't resist using something and then not returning it to where it belongs. And then I spend frantic moments looking for a stapler for my essay before leaving for lectures because he was the last person to use it. And he's never around when I want to yell at him.

But he knows how to apologise, how to say I'm sorry sweetie and not sound false or restrained. He knows how to be kind with words on the days when I don't feel beautiful. And on the days when I'm just frustrated with a character whose obscure core I'm trying to penetrate, he knows how to encourage me.

I'm beginning to think that it's a good thing that men and women are different. I never thought it was possible to be in a relationship with a man and not lose myself. I have my own skeletons.

Arne is a strange blessing which I didn't expect. I was only looking for a convenience, a tolerable boyfriend who could take me out to interesting places and occasionally I would oblige him with sex. I didn't go out looking for a partner, a person I could grow with. And in the end that is what counts. Beyond looks, aesthetics, culture and lifestyle differences, I want someone to grow with, otherwise the nights alone in bed while he's out with his friends become torturous. I become overwhelmed with fear but I have to trust him. And that means being vulnerable, being always a little insecure. In some respects I must have more faith in him than myself. I have to put him ahead of my weaknesses, my insecurities. It is a walk to my true nature, a test of character. I have been many things to many men but now I must be myself with Arne, I often hear myself saying. The closer we become the more I believe in him. I am finding myself in his moods, his gestures and the things he never says. Isn't it strange how more poignant they are than the things he does say?

We listen to each other. Sometimes it is so subtle, we communicate with gestures, creating moods and giving away something about ourselves by the way we dress, the things we eat, the tempo of our walk. Men don't like to be reminded too much that they are nomads by nature. I have to give him his space. So there are moments, even a string of days, when I will feel his distance, when he seems to sail the seven seas. On those days he becomes quiet, coming in and out of the bedroom with serious activity, restlessly rummaging through his drawers for something only he knows and his questions about its whereabouts sounding like minor accusations. I'm convinced there is a part of human nature that seeks to disrupt, no matter how steady the foundations, there is always the threat of a minor upset. I remember the virtue of silence on those days and don't encourage an argument even though he is asking me for the tenth time where he left the hooks for his fishing rod or whatever he calls them or whether I saw his gardening manual. He is always busy with things to do, fixing this or constructing that with his friends. On those days he comes back late, always exhausted, his clothes smelling as obscure as his moods. And even though I have been lying awake for hours waiting for him, I pretend to be asleep and sigh to myself that he is finally home, that he did not meet a terrible fate in some lonely street. I worry a lot. I know that. I'm working on it. Like I said, I have become my mother.

Then there are the other days when I feel his warmth, when he takes refuge in the security of our relationship. On those days he is everywhere, like a child around its mother's skirts. Him and his hormones cannot get enough of me. So we usually stay indoors, sometimes bunking Monday after a languorous weekend. And he tells me countless times what I mean to him. He even opens up about his childhood, what it meant to him. And so we spend hours talking about things that mean a lot to us. We open up and risk the other drawing too hasty conclusions or failing to understand the importance of an event, the gravity of a remark made in childhood. They are heavy days filled with solitude and closeness. We become our only friends, the world a hostile environment. Everything we talk about is serious. Idle things cease to matter. We may even spend two days in bed, getting out only to eat and use the bathroom. He becomes a galaxy to me. I spend hours asking and telling. The thing about shallow waters is that they are not safe, he once says, especially when you're trying to get to know someone. And then he laughs. But I like it that he is not arrogant enough to scorn at shallow talk. It is those silly conversations that remind me not to take myself too seriously. There is much to laugh at.

But the fear is inescapable. I cannot tame it. Perhaps it will fade with time.

We are lying in bed when he becomes serious and says, "I want to tell you a story."

He has an inventive mind, I find that attractive.

"A young man lived in a small village where everyone knew each other well like brother and sister. One day, one of the neighbours' children, a three week old baby, was stolen outside in the sun while the mother had gone indoors momentarily to attend to the stove. The thieves left a ransom note in the baby's crib. The parents were distraught and did everything to get the money. They borrowed money from friends and family, they even sold some of their meagre possessions. But after the thieves got their money, the parents didn't get their child back. Weeks filled with grief passed for the parents and still they heard nothing of their child, their little one, they hadn't even given him a name.

One day the young man was riding on his bicycle in town when he heard crying. It was sad and piercing, the young man wasn't sure if it was the sound of a child or a baby crying. He had never heard anything as sad as that wailing. He followed the sound and it led him to a house of worship. He walked through the door and saw a group of men dressed in habit. 'Father,' he said to the eldest of the men praying,' Where is that terrible crying coming from?' But the elder with an impressive beard was deep in prayer and couldn't be roused by the young man disturbing such an important activity.

"He walked further through the house, still hearing the crying. He came across a cleaning woman sweeping the floor. 'Excuse me,' he began. But the other, hurriedly sweeping, looked up at him and said, 'Do you know what the time is? I have to be somewhere and it's getting late.' When the young man said he did not have a watch, the woman carried on sweeping past him.

"So the young man walked further into the house because he could still hear the crying. He came across a woman with a baby strapped to her back. She was the laundry woman and worked in a small room in the back with an open window looking out to town. The young man walked up to her and said, 'That baby has been crying a long time. I could hear it from the street on my bicycle.'

"She turned round and handed him the baby because she was still busy doing the washing.

"As soon as the young man had the baby in his arms it stopped crying. There was a strange moment of recognition between the two and when the young man asked the cleaning lady whose baby it was, she said it was lost, she'd found it at the church door a few weeks ago. 'I know this baby's parents,' said the young man. 'It's a miracle,' the woman suddenly said. The young man looked at her suspiciously and said nothing. He took the baby home to its parents."

I look at him, expecting him to say more but he says nothing.

"Is that it?" I finally say, feeling cheated of a better ending. "What was the purpose of that?"

"Does there always have to be a purpose? I read it in a magazine article at the dentist this morning."

"The crux of the story?"

"It was a nice story," he says, more to himself, "I liked the bit about hearing the crying child."

"I wasn't going to tell you but I've been late for three days now," I tell him.

"Late for what?"

"You know, my period."

"Three days, that's nothing, right? We should start worrying after a week, right?"

"A week? By that time a fetus might have started forming."

He looks at me for a while, puzzled.

"But I thought you were taking care of that?" he says.

"I was. I mean I am … Look, this isn't just about me taking care of everything. You're just as responsible," I tell him.

"Don't be ridiculous. We talked about this. You said you were on the pill and you know I'm not fucking around so what's the point of wearing a condom?" he lashes out.

"The point is I have to walk around as this biological time bomb waiting to happen while you just park in and out whenever you want. You don't have to worry about this," I say feeling angry and tearful because he is being so insensitive.

"But what do you want me to do?"

"I want you to be understanding. I want you to consider the options. I mean, what would we do?"

"Hang on. Just hang on a minute," he says and gets out of bed. "Once you start saying what would we do, you're tempting fate, ja. What is this about? Is this about the story? Because it was just a silly story that caught my attention. I don't want to have babies with you now."

There is a little anger in his voice. It hurts to hear him say that. He becomes aware of it. He also becomes aware that I'm crying.

"I'm not ready to be anyone's father," he says and comes to me on my side of the bed.

"I wasn't saying that, I was only saying I'm late and now you're making a big deal out of it," I say wiping my eyes with my sleeve.

"No, but what if you are … you know, pregnant … then what?"

"You expect me to answer that now?" I say irritated.

"We might as well talk about it now."

He climbs back into bed, his mood distant.

"I don't know what I'm capable of doing," I confess. "I honestly don't know if I can kill my own baby…"

"It would be a fetus, not a baby."

"Ja, but still. I don't know if I could do it or even give it up for adoption."

"Then what are you saying?" he says, his eyes crying out with panic.

"I'm saying just that. I don't know. What do you want me to say? I have to wait and see what will happen. It's pointless speculating. I could be wrong."

"You're right. It's probably best to wait and see."

We turn off the lights and sleep far apart on the bed. I feel nauseous at the thought that he would jilt me if I ever got pregnant.

In the morning when I get up he is gone. At Drama I'm restless and moody. The others complain when I miss my cues and the director nearly sends me home for the day.

I come back home and find him at the desk, busy on his computer. We greet each other like strangers and go about our own business. There is tension in the air. I know he is dying to find out if I've had my period but I decide not to tell him. It would be bad news and it would only stir more tension. I take a long bath pleading with my body to bleed but it doesn't. I know I'm not my body because it does things without me instructing it. How does it remember to keep my heart pumping and me breathing, even when I sleep? If the whole thing had been left to me, I would have died a long time ago.

I go to bed early and dream of a million things that can go wrong. I dream of the fear of loneliness that haunts me. In the morning I wake up searching for Arne and again he is not there.


## TSHEPO

I come back exhausted. Irritable. I find Chris lying on the bed in his room. He greets me and asks a few perfunctory questions about what happened. But he isn't really interested because he hardly looks at me when I speak. His eyes are on the TV. I expect him to be more concerned, perhaps more worried. Was it okay? Did anything go wrong? Did they beat you up? Any question would have made me feel better, a little closer to him, I dare say even to feel missed – but he seems indifferent.

"So did you eat this morning?" he says to me while watching the TV comfortably, my TV.

"Yeah, I'm fine. They gave us really crappy polony sandwiches but …" I say and trail off into silence as he screams with excitement at the top of his voice because someone scored a goal on TV.

I go to my room, feeling itchy, dirty, depression rapidly weighing over my mood. I start undressing. He comes in suddenly just before I'm about to take off my underwear. I'm very self-conscious around other men, especially Chris. For a brief moment I torment myself whether I should continue getting undressed or whether I should wait. No, it'll look obvious, like you're a faggot or something, I flagellate myself. I take off my underwear and bite the insides of my mouth. He hardly looks at me and says, "Before I forget, Ross, I think he's the waiters' manager, ja anyway, he said he wanted to see you tomorrow."

"About what?" I ask, naked and feeling awkward but he walks off as though he didn't hear me.

I put my clothes into the laundry basket. There is a stale smell about them. I close the door to the bathroom and lock it. Alone, I examine the welts on my body. Those fucking fleas. In the mirror I look at my eye and there is still purple colouring under my eye, although the swelling is gone. I prod it gently and resolve to wear some base when I go to see my manager tomorrow.

I get into the water and it is just right, hot enough but not scalding. I wash my hair with Lifebouy soap. Its stringent hospital smell is enough to console me that whatever fleas are in my hair will not survive. I lather the soap well and leave it in my hair. I lie back and let the foam soak into my hair and roots.

Inevitably, it is almost a curse, I think about Chris but not with the usual joyful excitement that comes with being infatuated with someone. I'm just depressed and mope to myself. I feel inadequate and loneliness is like a stretch of silence on a desert plain that I must confront. I wash the rest of my body and rinse my hair last. I clean the bath carefully and wipe it as best I can.

Chris walks in again. I'm already dressed, feeling clean. He walks past and goes into the bathroom. He soon comes out again and walks straight towards me. Without any warning he grabs me by the scruff of my neck and drags me to the bathroom.

"I'm sick of this shit," he begins. "You always leave the floors fucking wet. What's wrong with you?"

I'm too shocked to respond immediately. He flounces me towards the other end of the bathroom and orders me to come out when it's dry. For a while I just sit on the toilet seat with the lid down and feel numb. I even shake a little, my throat is sore but I resolve not to cry. Chris, why are you doing this? Why are you being like this? My heart seems to bleed. I take my damp towel and wipe the floor thoroughly. I try to open the door but it is locked.

Chris, Chris, open up, I plead. Chris, please, the floors are clean and dry. Chris. Chris, I go on but he says nothing. I hear the distant whisper of the TV. My heart is heavy and sore. I'm hungry and don't even have the energy to yell, to scream and protest. Chris, why are you doing this? I repeat in my head.

The light coming through the window becomes dimmer as the sun goes down. It eventually grows dark. I can still hear the murmur of my TV and occasionally Chris's footsteps going down the short passage to the kitchen. Chris, I keep saying, even banging on the door. I bang for five minutes but he still doesn't respond. Several hours go by. It is late, probably going for nine. I resign myself to the fate of spending the night in the bathroom. I take out some clothes from the laundry basket and throw them into the bath. And then I put on a dirty sweater and tracksuit pants over my T-shirt and shorts. My stomach still groaning, I climb into the bath and beg sleep to come.

In the morning when I wake up I find the door open. I walk out carefully, expecting Chris around the corner but he is not there. And he isn't in his room. As always his bed is immaculately done, military style but with prison vengeance. The pillow sits with authority on the bed and there is nothing lying over the desk and chair. His other pair of tackies sits neatly in one corner. Everything is where it should be, standing in the pristine order, stuffy with draconian discipline. It sends a shiver down my spine, as though I might disturb the air and Chris would find out that I was snooping in his room.

I get changed and eat. Then I comb my hair and fix my eye with some base at the mirror. I take a walk to the Waterfront and find my manager Ross at the back where the canteen is. There is no one else in his small, insignificant office. He stands there, clicking a Bic pen.

"Ja, listen, glad to see that your eye is alright and everything but things have been quite hectic and stressful around here, you know how it gets. So we had to get someone to replace you. Permanently."

"Oh I see," is all that I say at first. He shuffles some papers on his desk, to create something to do so that I must feel like I'm intruding because he needs to work. But I stand there for a moment and feel weak.

"So what, I don't have a job here any more?" I say even though I know the answer.

"Basically, yes. But we still have your details and everything. If a spot opens up, we'll contact you or we'll just tell Chris to tell you," he says.

"Chris, how did you know I was staying with him? I didn't tell anyone."

"Oh, ja, well, we found out," he says with a suspicious tone as if he's hiding something.

"What, Chris told you guys that I was staying with him?"

"Ja, well. Look, this is not really my place. I mean I don't get involved in the waitrons' personal lives and everything but Chris told us what happened to your eye. Actually he told one of the other waitrons but word got round and ..."

"What did he say?"

"Well, I mean look, I'm not going to lie, he said you had a problem with drugs and that you'd even gone to Valkenberg and everything for it. He said you guys went out after a shift one night and you got completely stoned and then you had a bad trip or whatever and started being difficult and picked a fight with someone. But they fucked you up," he says and I realise the shuffling of papers and the expression on his face isn't one of embarrassment at the prospect of dismissing a worker, it is the look of contempt, of someone who just sees me as a pathetic druggy.

"Look, I really need to get back to work. If you'll just sign here, I'll release your last pay," he says and hands me a sheet that I've signed a dozen times to collect my pay.

He opens a safe and hands me a small brown envelope with my name on it. It is like being given a criminal certificate.

"Did he say anything else?" I ask.

"He said you had a dope record," he says and that look in his eyes squashes my self-esteem.

I don't bother to count the money. I put it in my pocket and turn to leave.

"Sorry, just one last thing. So who's actually filled my position?" I say.

"Look, I don't want to be in the middle of things," he says irritably, "Chris has got your job, okay? He's been working his arse off in the kitchen and uhh ... What do you want me to say? I've got work to do. You know the way out."

He walks past me and goes towards the kitchen.

I want to yell wait! I want to ask him if he knows that Chris went to Pollsmoor. I want to ask him if he knows that Chris went in for murder. But he is gone and leaves me alone, standing like a fool.

I walk out the back and leave the Waterfront. I walk out slowly, almost trudging, sore with disbelief, betrayal. How could he do that to me? I thought we were friends. Why is this happening? I walk towards town, my stomach twisted in knots. I buy a chip roll at a café and eat it outside the square opposite the Standard Bank building.

People walk by, everyone looking like they have something to do, a boss to report to, an essay to type or an appointment to meet. I eat the chip roll slowly, my throat dry. In one part of the square some kids are skateboarding. Two coloured guys who look like ruffians are sitting not far from me. One of them wears a sleeveless T-shirt and his arms are covered in coarse self-made tattoos, thug-life style. At the base of his right hand where the thumb meets the forefinger, is the notorious number twenty eight with two stripes underneath, his rank. The other also has crude tattoos on his forehead and a few on his legs. They scour the square like hawks looking for a quick and easy meal. I watch them but I don't make it obvious. Every once in a while I throw an eye to the skateboarders. Eventually they both get up at once when a tourist clumsily holding a map, flapping in a brief wind, walks by.

It is easy to spot a tourist. They go about with a wide-eyed sense of adventure, a dangerous curiosity that might be encouraged in the colder climes from which they come but isn't really suitable in Cape Town. If only they knew how silly they look with their moon-bags, Nikons and wide eyes ready to devour everything. If only they knew how vulnerable they really were, walking moegoes waiting to be exploited. If only they realised that sometimes you have to leave some of yourself behind and learn something about someone else in the places you go. If they stopped being tourists and became travellers maybe they wouldn't get mugged all the time.

I mean Africa is not backward that we do not know what a traveller is, someone from a different place but with familiar ways. The problem with tourists is that they are their worst enemy because they insist on bringing everything about themselves wherever they go. They seem blind to the subleties of a place that doesn't really have that many sights to see, at least like other faraway places. They seem deaf to the signals a place is always giving them: watch out, be sensible, be careful with your moneybag, people are always hungry here, did you notice that suspicious man standing on the corner with a cap over his eye, that quiet street that seems to be busy, those innocent looking children pretending to play, that thing you read in the paper the other day, and that necklace around your neck, please be careful people are so desperate, so poor that they have nothing to lose even their lives, even yours. Don't take unnecessary risks and throw caution to the wind because you're on holiday. Mind the things you say, the questions you ask and whom you approach. If they were chameleons, they would try to blend. See how many colours Africa has. They should use them, wear them and they will protect them.

They don't seem to heed advice. They forget how dangerous life really is, how quickly opportunities can arise and be exploited. They are numb to the real stories around them, the woman carrying a heavy load with a child strapped to her back, the men who walk in front, ahead and the children who are always going about idly, hungry for attention, love, food, health, parents, sustenance. They miss out on opportunities to understand people because they are always looking for the next exhibition or museum.

The tourist stands around and looks about, oblivious to the vulnerable prey he's become to the two coloured guys. They make themselves busy in the crowd but watch the tourist. He's tall with blond hair and a charming gentleness about his blue eyes, probably German. How they love to holiday in sunny South Africa with their friendly, accommodating Deutschmarks. I follow the tourist with my eyes till he disappears down a small street leading towards the centre of town. The two coloured guys are not far behind. Another one bites the dust.

It is with sadness that I watch them go after their prey. I cannot ignore the fact that the prey was white and the predators coloured. I cannot ignore that they looked dubious. I cannot ignore that a lot of tourists and people in general in Cape Town get mugged and abused and sometimes murdered by people that fit the description of those two guys. I cannot ignore that trouble follows that unsuspecting tourist. And I cannot ignore that I did nothing.

I feel depressed and ineffectual, defeated by circumstances.

I finish my chip roll and my mouth feels dry. I walk towards the train station. At the public toilets I drink lots of water. I splash my face and wash off traces of the farcical base. Why did I bother? I say with sour anger. I walk out into the milling crowds, not really sure what to do. It is a familiar feeling, in itself dizzying, enough to induce vertigo until I throw up. But I tame my stomach to remain calm. I go outside to the fruit sellers. The coloured fruit sellers. How hard they work. How clean and quick they are, a smile there, a remark here, they'll give you ten cents short if you're not careful, if you're too entranced by their charm. Fruit is plentiful and cheap in Cape Town. It is a comforting thought. I buy a lucky packet from a well-dressed coloured guy whose complexion and the texture of his hair is similar to Chris's. I always reference people. I always buy from him. He winks at me – I'm sure he does it to all his regular customers. But it has a noted effect, it always makes me feel noticed, a little special. I bop my head to him and walk towards the park with my lucky packet. I like lucky packets, you get a little bit of everything: bananas, apricots, peaches, plums, apples, grapes and maybe a lychee or two.

I walk up Adderly Street, munching a banana and go through the gates and up the path leading into the gardens. Street kids laugh and run down the path, tameness in their natural unkempt hair. They annoy some of the pedestrians as they brush past them leaving them with their offensive scent of poverty and neglect. I walk towards the gallery and sit down outside on the lawn. It is a little cloudy but the sun looks promising.

Well, I can't move out. I hardly have any money, I say to myself. Dad doesn't regularly leave money in my account. After our last encounter, I doubt if I will receive another cent from him. I think about all the people I know and the ones who owe me favours, the ones who might help me find a job. They are few, three to be precise, and one of them is in Jo'burg. The other two are just students. I don't know anyone, I don't have connections. I can't get things the way Mmabatho can. And I couldn't impose and ask her to ask one of her friends. So I tell myself to look for another job. Fortunately it is Thursday and the Cape Ads is out on Thursdays. It's still early, I can still try. I only sit in the sun for another ten minutes before getting off my arse and going to the nearest café.

I buy a copy and go back to the gardens. I look but I cannot find anything suitable for someone with no experience, buckets of enthusiasm and a little naïveté. Everything either requires too much effort, like working as a gardener or a labourer – frankly I have no experience, and I'm a little clumsy – or there is a prerequisite which I cannot meet: a car, a driver's licence for trucks, experience, a portfolio, a CV, references, a suitable personality (for telesales) or patience. After a while I feel inadequate and skip over to the personals. They are my favourite.

SWM 40, work for myself and looking for someone to share lots of nights by the fireplace, preferably blonde with no kids.

GWM 30, very hot, looking for someone to hold when I wake up. No femmes.

SWF 19, just finished school and ready for anything. Looking for a bi guy or girl.

GCM 22 , looks to die for, looking for a white guy to explore the Cape with.

GWM 28, 8 inches, straight-acting, loves rugby and sports, seeking a clean white guy.

GBM 29, alone but not discouraged, Adonis waiting to be discovered by sugar daddy.

I think about the entry with Adonis. Alone but not discouraged. I like that, I say to myself and decide to go home. I think of going past the Drama department and perhaps finding Mmabatho but I decide against it. I feel too tired and lazy. I go to the station and catch a taxi to Sea Point from the rank. The driver drops me off not far from my place. I unlock the door and pray that Chris is not in. I can't face him. I wouldn't know what to say. It's strange that I should feel uncomfortable and nervous when he's the one who betrayed me.

As usual my room is a little untidy. Untidy is solace for me, it says life doesn't always look perfect, there is always chaos but there is also order. I always find my way in my mess. I think of reading but my mood is sour. I wouldn't really concentrate on what I read.

I decide to take a nap and let the mood and pain be driven away by dreams. I sleep fitfully meandering through Cape Town like a dolphin at sea. I wake up feeling dazed and even more tired than before. I have a slight headache and my lips feel dry and cracked. I lick them and go to the bathroom. I put some Vaseline on my lips and go to Chris's room to watch TV.

He comes in at night. I didn't leave any supper for him. I sit at the desk and don't look at him, my mind is just racing with things I could say, accuse him off. But there is too much to say, I can't open my mouth. And there is still the business of yesterday when he locked me up.

"I need the chair," he says, standing with bare legs, a long T-shirt covering his privates. He holds his pants on his arm like a waiter.

I move to the floor and still I say nothing. The pain of yesterday and the pain of today's news returns. My throat tightens. I want to ask him so many things, say so many things, but I decide against it. He might just moer you, I tell myself. We look at each other briefly and I catch him scratching his balls, his eyes still beautiful, his physique still devastating. I watch him from the corner of one eye as he changes into his tight, lascivious jeans, catching a glimpse of his bare muscled bum. He hums something from the radio to himself, a trivial song that amounts to repeating a sequence of beats.

"I'm going out," he says as he takes his jacket and keys. He walks out the door before I have an opportunity to say anything. I feel helpless and alone.

For the next few days I don't see much of Chris. When he's not at work, he's out doing something or seeing people I never hear about. His moods become darker, colder, he becomes more distant. He hardly says anything to me when I see him. With all the money he's making he becomes stingier. He stops buying bread because he's hardly at home and gets fed at work. And at night I assume he always eats out because he never stays in, at least when I'm home. In the cupboards he starts labeling his food. He never did that before.

And his room starts becoming a little smaller as he accumulates things. He buys himself a second-hand mountain bike and a small stereo. One day I come back to find that my TV is in my room again. On the desk in his room I find a small fish tank with two goldfish, at home in clear water.

I cannot say I'm happy for him but I also cannot say that I wish him ill. For two weeks I walk up and down Cape Town's restaurants looking for a job as a waiter. It's the only thing I feel qualified to do: to serve people so that they can be rude and impossible and stingy when they leave me a meagre tip. They tell me either that there are no posts or that they are looking for a woman, or is that someone white? Some of them just look irritated when I ask them if there are any vacancies. I even tell them that I'll work in the kitchen or scrub floors. I swallow my pride and force myself to walk the merciless streets up and down Tamboerskloof, Clifton, Gardens, Obs, Green Point, Sea Point, Mowbray, Claremont and Rondebosch. I go to every restaurant, bar, bistro and eaterie in Long Street with the persistence of a street merchant. I even contemplate offering my services to a hawker. But it is an ad in the Cape Ads which catches my attention and gets me excited. It claims instant money and flexible working hours. When I pitch at the premises I hear that first I have to buy the goods that I will sell: toys, duvets, pillows and other dubious looking merchandise. After the sprightly "manager" entices us with promises about all the money we can make once we've established ourselves, he offers us tea and biscuits.

I walk out while the others try their luck. I have only twenty rand in my pocket and ten rand left in my savings account. I walk home because I cannot afford taxis anymore. In Green Point I walk past Biloxi, a gay bar and it is closed. On the door there is a poster of two barechested men in a suggestive embrace. It is then that an idea comes to me. It seems the only possible thing left. It seems a last solution, the last chance after the others seem squandered.

I contemplate working for a massage parlour.

I go to the nearest phone and insert some coins eagerly. The operator gives me the number for Steamy Windows, they often advertise in the Cape Ads. The guy at the other end of the line intoduces himself as Shaun in a familiar manly voice. He sounds straight and surprisingly young. He can hear the nervousness in my voice and casually asks me a few "basic" questions. I tell him that I'm black with a swimmer's build and an average height. He tells me that they only have one black "stallion" and that they are always in demand. He tells me about the curious Germans always looking for an authentic African man. "In this business you can make a lot of money," he keeps telling me. I think about hefty Deutschmarks waiting to be exploited under African skies and smile. But you're risking your life, a thought comes to me.

We make an appointment for two. I go to the premises on Waterkant Street. At the door, Shaun, a shortish guy with dark hair and a ready smile meets me. He opens the electric gate and I walk into a plush entrance hall with a garish Rococo finish. We go up a winding staircase to the "lounge" where two other guys sit around. They are both white, well dressed and good looking. I smile nervously and say hi. Shaun offers me a seat. "You're a cutie," the older of the two guys says. Stupidly I say thanks. "I'm Storm," he says and extends a hand. But he is not firm at the wrist and there is a smile growing at the corner of his mouth. The other guy introduces himself as West. "West?" I repeat, to make sure that I heard correctly. "Yes, West," he says confidently in a heavy, hypnotic Afrikaans accent. He smiles, revealing a sexy gap between his front teeth. His hair is dark and short and his complexion is olive. He has the build of an athlete, of someone who constantly needs to work out to look good. They both look well groomed but not good enough to make the grade as models. It is a vicious and competitive industry, I'm told.

"So have you done this sort of thing before?" Shaun asks me, all the time appraising me with his eyes.

"No," I say nervously.

"But you know what kind of services we offer here?" he says and looks into me. He must have seen that terrified, I don't know what I'm doing look, a thousand times.

"Perhaps you should explain, just to be sure," I say.

"If you don't mind me saying so, you're well spoken," he says carefully. "It counts. In this industry everything counts, anything you have can work to your advantage. Now, we are licensed as a massage parlour. That means a client can come in here and expect to get a full, professional body massage for an hour, no extras. But most of our business depends on extras. That means you might offer the client, if he asks, the full body massage with a happy ending."

"What does that mean?" I say with a croaky voice and cough, embarrassed that I sound nervous.

"Don't look so terrified. They've all been there. Storm, make yourself busy and get our friend a drink," Shaun says. Storm gets up with a sulk and traipses out the door. West wears a huge, friendly grin on his face.

"A happy ending just means you get the guy to come," he says and does the appropriate gesture with his hand. "Or you can offer the client a blowjob, a rosie – don't worry, you'll pick up all the slang – or a full house, that means full-on sex, usually involving penetration. But it's all up to you. We have stallions that only work as masseurs, no extras. You can make from R180 to R500 from the simple basic massage to the extras. I take R90 for studio fees and your AR fees are deducted weekly. That means you pay me R60 a week, it's nothing really, for advertising in the paper and other coverage on the Net. And then obviously there are travels and that means you go to the client's place. We have a driver who takes you there and picks you up when you're finished. It's R220 for a travel and I take half, obviously to cover the costs for the driver."

I take in all this information quickly.

"So do you think you have what it takes for this job?" he says and looks at me again with those eyes that have seen it all.

Storm comes back with a glass of Coke and offers it to me with a smile.

"Are you gay? Because it helps," he says.

"Don't worry about him, he's just a slut," West says and smiles at me.

"Jou hol, West," Storm says and sits down to read Femina.

"Ja, I'm keen. I can do this," I say, excitement welling up at the prospect of all the money I can make.

"Well, listen, you can start whenever you want. You can start tonight if you like. Just one thing, what kind of a name were you thinking of?" he says.

"Excuse me?"

"West, Storm, Shaun, they're not our real names. They are our working names. It helps in this industry. It also keeps things professional. So think about a name," he says and gets up to shake my hand.

"Ja, sure. Anyway, I'm keen. I don't think I can start tonight. I've still got a few things to sort out but I'll be here tomorrow night. What time should I be here?"

"Five. All the guys have to be here at five. So shit, shower and shave and do everything you need to look good. And wear formal casual, if you know what I mean. We're working on a skeleton staff at the moment because we've just moved to new premises and everything. Don't even ask where we were before but uhh ... Ja, I'll see you tomorrow at five. And there's a fine of ten rand for every half an hour you're late. It's like that. We're a business, not a pick-up joint," he says and leads me out the door.

I say 'bye to the other two and walk out the room. I feel shabbily dressed as I make my way down the staircase, looking at the large imposing chandelier. At the door Shaun shakes my hand and tells me that he is looking forward to seeing me tomorrow. I walk out with a smile on my face and promising ideas on my mind.

## MMABATHO

It's official, I'm pregnant. After five days I couldn't bear the suspense any more so I went to a doctor. I paid cash. He did the necessary tests, asked me questions and examined me.

I'm still numb, confused. I don't know what to make of it. A baby?

That evening after having seen the doctor I wait up for Arne. He has being coming back late for the last few days. He is also tense.

At around eleven he walks in through the door. He finds me watching TV, my legs crumpled underneath me on the couch, the lights dim.

"Why are you sitting in this darkness?" he says irritably and puts on all the lights.

"Where've you been?"

"Out, work and then I went to Ganesh for a drink." I don't know if he wants to hurt my feelings because we always go out together or at least he always asks me if I want to go with him. He goes to the bedroom to put away his jacket and returns to the other side of the room where the kitchen is.

"Are we breaking up?" I say, terrified.

"What? "

"You heard me. Are we breaking up?"

"No. You're being silly. I don't want to break with you," he says and walks towards me holding a glass of water. "I just don't know what to do. I've being doing a lot of thinking. That thing you told me the other day threw me, ja."

"I know," I sympathise, my stomach in knots. You must tell him the truth. He must know, I tell myself.

"Really, you threw me," he says and sits next to me on the couch. "I just don't have any head space for a baby. I don't. I'm not ready."

"Well," I begin, my heart pounding, "I went to the doctor today and I'm pregnant."

I say it with a clear voice so that he shouldn't ask me to repeat it again. He doesn't say anything, he sighs mutely. If truth has a face, it would be the silence that falls on us.

"I'm not surprised. I kind of guessed that things would work out like this. It was too good to be true, things were going too well."

He drains the rest of his drink and then plays with the remote control, his toy, going through the channels. Normally I would be irritated. But I understand, that is his way of coping.

After a while he says, "You've already made up your mind, haven't you? You're going to have the baby, aren't you?"

"Yes ... yes," I say confidently but softly. "You have no obligation to me. I'll understand if you want to leave and make a clean break."

I say this even though my heart is spilling gallons of blood in my chest.

"How can you say that? I mean, I love you, I can't just walk away. That's the whole point. That's why I haven't been able to think straight for the last few days. Don't you see, I'm in too deep, we're in to deep? I can't just walk away," he says. He drags his fingers through his hair and sighs and plays with the remote control.

I'm speechless. I have never heard him say that he loves me. I have never said it to him either. But it is obvious that this is how we feel about each other. Love found a way, it hatched a plan while we were getting to know each other, while we were sleeping. And now we cannot turn away from it.

I put my hand on his thigh and my head on his shoulder.

"What are we going to do?" he whispers. "I'm only going to fininsh my thesis next year. Okay, so you're going to finish your degree this year, but still. How will we cope? We barely manage as students."

"We'll manage," I tell him. "We'll make a plan. It'll work out. I'll get a job."

"God, I can't believe I'm going to be someone's father," he says with more fear than awe.

"It … I mean the baby, should be due in June."

"I'm going to bath," he says and gets up.

He goes to the bathroom and leaves me alone watching a documentary about tattooing on TV.

Well, he said he'll stay, I say to myself, not really sure if I should be happy or sad. I switch off the TV and go to bed.

For the next few days he goes about with a sort of melancholy concern in his eyes. I become aware of him pulling chairs for me, opening doors and helping me carry things, fussing with things we usually take for granted. I'm an independnt woman and I have always looked after myself. But this is beyond that. It is not just about me and him any more. I am going to be someone's mother. That is why he keeps opening doors for me, helping me.

He spends a lot of time with me and hardly goes out with his friends anymore, even though I keep telling him to go out. And it is quiet time together, time spent sitting together watching TV or reading or him at the desk figuring out something. I can hear him thinking, his pen scribbling furiously, his mind calculating, juggling, constructing bridges across difficult terrains. He is making a plan. He is finding a way for us, to make it work, to make it through the difficult, stormy days ahead. Every day he sits at the desk and scribbles down numbers, how much we have, how much we spend, how much we save, how much we can afford to spend on this and that, how much we can sacrifice. We have even drawn up a budget. We don't shop at the Spar anymore. We go to Checkers and once a week we buy fresh produce at a cheap price from the patients at Valkenberg. We must start thinking about prenatal care, he says. And you must tell me what you need, he tells me, the earnest concern of a man about his eyes. I want my child to have the best start he says, with mild excitement. But he is being very careful. I hardly know whether he is looking forward to this or whether he is making all these plans with dread hanging over his meticulous planning. I suspect that is his way of dealing with a huge responsibility. He is being cautious for a reason. Perhaps zeal is not suitable for all occasions. Perhaps parenthood is not something to celebrate but a chance to reflect.

Every day he thinks about the arrangements that he will have to make, the decisions that will have to be taken. And he always asks me. Could you, do you think, must I, should we? And every day I tell him what I have been thinking should be done. But the dreaded question about what to do when the baby is born hangs in the air. He has not spoken about marriage. He has not spoken about his beloved Germany and whether he could face living away from it. He has not suggested that I consider emigrating with him. But it is always on my mind; and I'm sure on his, too.

"I could finish my thesis by January," he says. "You know, work through December and not go home."

He looks at me with slight panic in his eyes. I feel guilty as though I'm forcing him to make decisions he might not want to make. But I don't know what to say. It is just as much a journey of decision-making for me.

"You know I'm supposed to go home at the end of the term?" he says. "My sister's wedding."

"You mentioned it," I say vaguely.

"Well, I think I should go. The distance will clear my head. It will make it easier to see," he says and I don't know what to make of that. Does he mean I'm confusing him? What does he mean by that?

"Do you ever feel like you're rushing through life?" he asks me.

"Sometimes," I say. "Mostly when I'm feeling helpless like now."

"Me too," he says and sinks back on the couch with me.

My stomach is still flat. When I stare at it I wonder about the life growing inside, feeding off me, finding its own way. It is difficult to imagine how I will feel, how I will walk once my pregnancy protrudes in front. I cannot imagine what this will do for my self-esteem. I don't even know if Arne will be around by then. I don't know how it will be. I don't know if I will ignore the stretch marks. And what about the mood swings, the cravings and everything else that goes with being pregnant? I will become that woman, in the eyes of other people. You know, that one with a coloured baby, shame, she had plans to be an actress, they will say. And she used to be so energetic, they will go. This is how people are.

So every day when I oil my skin I look at my stomach in the mirror and rub Coco butter lotion on it. I comb my Afro and plait my hair into roots. I wish beautiful things for my baby. And I carry his father in my thoughts wherever I go and I always remember that love found me in Arne.

## CHRIS

He doesn't think he's better anymore, not since he lost his job. That smile on his face, it's gone. I took it away. And you know something? I don't feel bad. Why should I? I didn't kill anyone. I did what I had to. No one is looking out for me. Why must people like him always have the best, always have everything? I also want a little bit of sunshine. I don't want to struggle all the time. I'm tired of being poor and needy. And I'm not a moegoe. I can think for myself. I can do things for myself. So I made a plan.

I fixed him good. He doesn't bother me anymore. And he keeps the house clean, like I want. He can leave if he wants, it doesn't matter anymore. I'm making better money, more money. I can get another flat or another housemate. But I know he won't go. He doesn't have money. He doesn't have anyone. No one can help him. Even with all his reading I'm beating him. I'm doing better. What good are his books to him now? They won't feed his stomach. He can't even afford to buy toothpaste.

But I'm sick of him. I don't want to see him any more. He makes me angry. He makes me remember that I had to go through the back door to get to where I am. He's so nice, so fucking nice it makes me sick. It makes me angry. It makes me want to moer him. I mean who does he think he is? Here he is struggling and only living on bread and fried potatoes but he still keeps his manners even when I treat him like a moegoe. He won't break. It makes me naar. Who does he think he is? Everyone gets a little angry, swears a little, fights a little, steals a little.

What's wrong with him? Maybe I'm pushing him into a corner because I want to see what he's going to do. I want to see if he's going to make a plan or if he's going to keep struggling. Maybe I want to see that he's not as strong as he thinks he is, not as good as he pretends.

"Hei, tsek jou naai, I need the toilet," I say and bully him out of the bathroom. Like a fool he doesn't say anything. He stands outside with his washing rag, soap on his face while I take a dump. Afterwards I wash my hands and spray Adrenalin Ego on myself. I spray so that the whole room smells good.

"If I catch you using my things, I'll fuck you up, gemors," I say and push past him.

He still says nothing.

He goes back to the bathroom that smells nice and rinses his face with the water I used to wash my hands. The water he was washing with.

I put on my stereo and listen to Ou da Meesta. I put it on loud and feed my goldfish. He knows he's not allowed in my room anymore. I don't need his fucking TV. When I want to watch football and rugby I go to the Sports Café at the Waterfront. Who needs his fucking TV? It's black and white anyway. And I know the desk and chair are his but fuck him, I'm not giving them up. He can make a plan.

"Hei, gemors, did anyone call for me today?" I ask him.

He is lying on his bed, reading some stupid book he always reads. But I can see he is hungry. He never eats when I'm around. He always waits till I leave and then I'll smell oil and fried chips when I come back later but the dishes won't be there. He will have cleaned up the place, tidied up and everything, like I want.

The rent is due in two weeks time. What is he going to do? How is he going to pay? Does he think I'm stupid or something? I'm not going to pay the whole thing alone. And I know he has no one to help him. That woman friend of his, I don't think she will lend him money. She looks like a tight bitch, clever with money.

But I'm going to fix him.

One day he comes back from wherever he goes looking for a job and finds me at home. Brendan and Virgil are also there. He walks in looking excited but says nothing. He says nothing to me anymore. The three of us, we go to his room and close the door. He stands there looking scared.

"Hei, gemors, how are you going to pay the rent this month?" I begin.

"I got a job. I start tomorrow. I'll get your money," he tells me.

"Where did you get a job? Where you going to work?" I ask him.

"Uhm, I can't really tell you."

"You can't really tell me. What kind of an answer is that, gemors?" I say and give him a warm klap. He falls on his bed, that stupid scared shitless look on his face.

"You ouens check what a moegoe this ou takes me for," I say rolling my shoulders.

"Tsek, sonnie. Salute! Salute! Fuck him up ek sê," Virgil tells me.

"Gemors, do you know who I am?" I ask him.

"No," he says his voice shaking like a woman's voice.

"This is who I am, gemors," I say and show him my twenty eights number on my left hand. I don't think he ever noticed it. "Do you know why it's on my left hand, gemors?" I ask him.

He shakes his head.

"Wait here. I'll tell you. I'll show you," I say and go to the bathroom. I return with a tub of Vaseline.

"Hei jou, naai. Take off your clothes." Brendan says and klaps him.

"No, no," he begins to say but Virgil grabs him rough and tears off his T-shirt.

"You check, these are also my brothers," I say and they show him their twenty eights numbers. But it is on their right hands. And Virgil has three lines under his number. Every time he opens his mouth to scream they klap him or punch him in the stomach. "Don't moer him in the face. I don't want him getting funny ideas about calling the cops," I tell them. Eventually they strip off all his clothes and he lies there on his bed, covering his small piel with his hand while the other hand covers his face.

Virgil stands back and gives me the signal. I take off my pants. Virgil and Brendan pin him down and spread his legs. They bring his chops towards me. I get an erection and put lots of vaseline on my piel. I try to force my way in but he is too tense.

"Hei, jou naai, tsek, tsek!" Virgil says and starts punching him hard on his back. "Relax, jou naai."

He opens up and I thrust my way into him. I hear him grunting, moaning, gurgling.

"You like this, don't you, huh? You like it, don't you? Now you know what I had to do all those years in Pollsmoor, you check, jou naai, gemors," I say while I pump into him and slap his chops. I go for a long time, taking nice long strokes.

"Ek gaan water breek!" I yell and soon spill my come all over his back.

212

"Okay, Brendan," Virgil says and I swop places with him.

"Please use a condom," he says, his mouth bloody.

"Tsek, jou poes, man!" Virgil punches him again and pushes his head into a pillow to muffle his cries, his moaning.

Brendan also doesn't waste time. He pumps into him like he hasn't had a woman in a long time. He makes strange faces as he pumps.

"Ja, you made him nice and wet," Brendan says, meaning the blood and sweat dripping down his chops and thighs.

He goes on for a long time, maybe fifteen minutes. Virgil even starts getting impatient with him and hurries him on to breek water. He pulls out just before he's about to come and makes us turn Tshepo, then he shoots his load all over Tshepo's chest.

I put on my pants and then I grab him by the neck and throw him into the bathroom.

"Get cleaned up, gemors," I say and lock him up inside. "Don't worry, he knows what to do. He won't fuck with me."

But he is quiet in there.

"Hei, gemors, must we come in there and help you?" I say and bang on the door.

Not long after I hear the water for the bath running.

While he does that we go through his things and clothes.

"He's got no money. I have to see how I will make for the month. So we must take anything that we can get money for," I say as we ransack his room.

I take his collection of nine CDs. No, his books are useless, leave them, I tell the others. We take some nice tops, two Levi jeans, a Soviet jacket, Chinos, a pair of Nike tackies, Crockett and Jones formal shoes, two white formal shirts, those things you wear on your wrists with shirts, a Swatch watch, a Gameboy and three cartridges, a silver necklace, two Bermuda shorts, three nice boxer shorts, two leather belts, a blazer and a scarf, a bedside clock-radio buzzer, a Casio type-writer, a Fubu cap, three videos by Spike Lee, two Speedo trunks and a top, a box of condoms, a Malcom X hat, a leather jacket, a suede jacket, a Dolce e Gabanna bag, another Benetton bag, and all his handkerchiefs. "En daai TV, vat dit," I tell them. We pack them into one of those cheap large canvas bags that hawkers, especially Makwere-kwere use. We take the stuff into the car but leave him some clothes.

Virgil starts up his white Granada and we go to Woodstock where a connection of mine can set me up. He knows people who'll buy the stuff, usually second-hand shops in town, but sometimes he gets people himself. We find him at home, alone with his girlfriend. We bring in the bag and open it in the lounge. He tells me that he can make a plan for us. But I'm not stupid, I don't trust this ou. So I sit there and make a list of all the things. I write a long list till I'm done.

He tells me to come back tomorrow. He says he'll have my money by then but he takes a ten percent cut. I ask him how much he can get for the CDs, all nine of them. "They are all imports," I say. "This ou has expensive taste." He looks at me and he can see that prison hasn't changed me, that I'm still the same, still stubborn and tight with money.

"Okay, you can get at least get R700 for the CDs," he says.

"Good, that will cover half the rent," I say relieved. "And the other stuff?"

"Chris you want my help or not?"

"What kind, bra, he's just looking out not to get robbed," Virgil says, a line forming between his eyes. He can be intimidating. We were in Pollsmoor together. I know how he gets.

"Okay, fine, I'll check you tomorrow at around twelve," I say to him.


TSHEPO

**I** feel as though my mother died again.

When Chris comes back he finds me packing what's left of my stuff into my suitcase. Fortunately he did not think of looking in the laundry basket. At least I have a decent pair of black Diesel jeans and one nice casual shirt. I'm already thinking about work. They expect me to look good, I say to myself as I rummage through the laundry bin, relieved when I notice something smart that I can wear to work.

I'm wearing tracksuit bottoms and an old top. I don't even look at him as he walks past and goes into the bathroom. In the door I can see his shadow, examining the cleanliness. He comes out and says nothing because I left it impeccably clean.

I go to the kitchen and take my pots.

"Tsek jou poes, where you think you're taking them?" he says and grabs them from me. He pushes me and lifts his hand as though he would strike me. But he doesn't. I go back to my room. The last thing left to pack is my bedding. I strip the duvet cover and the wrap-around sheet from the mattress. Even though they are a purple colour I can see blood on them and the coarse smell of sex and violence lingers. I fold them and spread them over my clothes and books. I even manage to pack the pillow. But I cannot take the duvet with me.

After packing I go towards the door with the suitcase. There are hooks on the wall where we keep all the keys. I hang my keys on a hook. Chris looks at me from his room, his eyes fiery. In the brief moment that I look at him I feel nauseous.

"Don't ever come back here, jou poes!" he says walking towards me.

I close the door behind me, carrying my suitcase. It isn't heavy at all. But inside I feel heavy with shock. I walk to Main Road and wait for a taxi, my insides on fire. A car hoots and it takes me a short while to figure out that it is Mr Saunders in his Golf GTI. The window slips down as though by magic.

"Can I give you a lift, you look like you've got a handful," he says and smiles.

"I'm going to Obs," I say to him.

"Hop in," he says and presses a button to open the boot. I put my bag in the boot. There are two small boxes in there.

He opens the door for me. I grit my teeth and step in slowly. I take a breath and sit down carefully. It hurts when I meet the seat. I grit my teeth not to wince.

He puts on the radio softly. The car purrs as it moves into the road again.

"So it looks like you're leaving us," he says, "Venus" by Franky Avalon on the radio. I love that song. I think it was in The Graduate.

"Ja, Sea Point is a little too expensive for me," I say.

We drive past Green Point and head into town. That song is so gentle, it is like a lullaby. I just enjoy it and try not to think about the pain tearing at me inside.

"You know, things have a very strange way of working out," he says to me mysteriously. I look at him and he smiles magnanimously. I don't say anything. I listen to my song fading.

We pass Woodstock and head towards Obs.

"You can drop me off at the garage," I say as we approach a Shell service station in Obs.

"No, I insist, I'll drop you off wherever you need to go," he says.

We go to 5 Milne Road. But Mmabatho does not live there anymore, I'm told by Nadine, the French girl. She has always been friendly. She gives me the new address in Mowbray.

Mr Saunders waits patiently while I take down the details. We drive to Mowbray to the new address. He gets out the car and takes out my bag.

"Thanks," I begin.

"Just see first if she's in," he says. He says it as though he would take it upon himself to look after me. His eyes are soft, gentle, friendly and almost maternal in a way that I have come not to expect from men.

I walk with my suitcase to the door and knock. After a while I hear someone slapping their slippers on the floor as they walk. Fortunately it is Mmabatho who stands at the door. "Hi," I say quickly, "just wait a minute." I leave the suitcase at the door and go back to Mr Saunders. The passanger window opens.

"Thanks, she's in."

"Good. Look after yourself," he winks and there is a quick flash in his eyes of recognition. I watch the car drive away and try not to think about Sea Point.

At the door Mmabatho waits. She stands there wearing her gown and slippers, her hair in plaited roots.

"Tshepo, what's this about?" she says and I can see her trying to ignore that there is a suitcase on the floor.

"I ran into some trouble. The guy I was staying with picked up and left without saying anything so I got evicted because I couldn't make rent. I just need a few days. I'm sorting out something," I plead, embarrassed, humiliated that I have to meet her like this. I hate to be a burden.

She unfolds her arms and walks in front of me into the house. I follow her to a small kitchen.

"We don't have much room," she says, and sounds like she's complaining. "You'll have to sleep on the couch or floor, whichever – but put your bags in our bedroom."

I follow her nervously, uncomfortable. I feel like I'm intruding. A bowl of cereal is standing on the table. I leave the suitcase next to the door but not in the way.

"I told you that guy was good for nothing," she says like her usual self, always full of opinions. We go back to the lounge-kitchen.

"I was just eating breakfast, well, late breakfast, I know it's after four in the afternoon but you won't believe the kind of week I've had. Anyway, do you want some?" she offers me. "And please sit down, make yourself comfortable."

I look around a little panic stricken. She is sprawled out on the sofa while she eats the cereal so I can't sit next to her. There are only two other chairs and they are wooden chairs. I won't survive, it will be too painful, I tell myself as I look at the hard surfaces.

"Actually, I just wanted to go out quickly and get today's paper, if you don't mind," I make an excuse.

"No, not at all. It's just down the road. About fifteen minutes there and back. It'll give me time to freshen up," she says.

"Fifteen minutes, is that all you need, I mean for a woman?" I tease her.

She grins and tells me to lock the door when I go out. Just release the latch, she says. I watch her disappear into the furthest room in the small house. It's hard with Mmabatho. I never know if I'm welcome. I always feel like I'm testing our friendship. There is never the ease of just assuming that "ag, she won't mind".

I walk down the road, my insides still on fire. I feel numb and dizzy with hunger. I haven't eaten anything since this morning. I resolve to only eat liquids for the next few days, my body just couldn't cope with a bowel movement. I find the shop, a small grocer. I buy the paper even though I have only fifteen rand left. My stomach groans, saliva floods my mouth. When I breathe I exhale through my mouth so that my ruptured anus can relax. By the time I get back to her place there is a car outside the house. Arne is home.

I knock on the door and it is he who answers. He gives me a rigid, formal hello and closes the door behind me. Mmabatho is already dressed, sitting in front of the TV. Arne goes to the bedroom, his mood sour. He has never liked me.

"Can I use the bathroom?" I say to her.

"Sure, just down there."

I put the paper on the table in the lounge and walk to the bathroom. Once inside I unbutton my pants and sigh with relief. Then I pull down my underpants and take out the swab of toilet paper between my legs. It is drenched with blood and I'm still bleeding. I throw the toilet paper into the toilet bowl and stretch out to reach for more toilet paper when I notice a sanitary pad wrapper on the floor. I pick it up and throw it in the bin it was intended for. And then the idea comes to me. I go through the medicine cabinet. On top I find a pack of Freedom sanitary pads, the ones with wings, the ones guys always laugh at when the ad plays on TV. But I know they will do the job and give me the comfort and confidence I need. I steal a pad from the pack and put it at the appropriate place. It fits snuggly and it is soft. Then I flush the toilet and wash my hands thoroughly as though they have touched evil. I've lived through this violence once. I can survive again, I tell myself, my throat aching. Chris, how could you do that to me?

When I get back, Arne is still in the bedroom. I sit next to Mmabatho on the sofa, carefully. She has started reading part of the paper.

"You don't think he'll mind, do you?" I whisper to her. "I mean, I should only be here four days at the most."

"Don't worry about him," she says, but that is not what I want to hear.

So I sit there feeling awkward and watch TV.

"Actually we're going out for supper. You don't mind if we leave you behind, do you? We're going to meet the head of the Drama department. It's a really formal dinner thing and ..."

"No, please, I don't mind."

"I might be getting a job in the department at the end of the year. It's a long story, I'll tell you about it later," she says and goes back to reading the paper.

Arne comes back and kneels down next to Mmabatho and they fondle each other and kiss.

"I'm going to the gym," he says to her, "What time do we have to be there?"

"I want to be there by ten to eight," she says.

They smooch quickly and he makes a signal to me. I don't know why he doesn't bother to just say 'bye.

"So, tell me, don't keep me in suspense," I say to her once the sound of his car fades. We haven't really opened up to each other in a while.

"Firstly things are going great with us," she says.

"I was surprised when Nadine told me that you'd moved in with him. You and a guy living together? Ke mohlolo. O jele eng?" I tease her.

"It's been good for me. But now I'm pregnant," she sighs.

"Really?"

"Really, ha ke bapale," she says with a serious face.

"And this is a problem?"

"Well, ja. We didn't really plan for it. But I'm going to have it, despite my pro-choice beliefs and everything. I'm keeping my baby."

"So that's what this Drama department thing is about?"

"Ja, but it's not certain. I just told Andrew, the head, that I'd be interested in teaching and working there. I didn't say anything about being pregnant. So he said I must come for supper and discuss it. He said I had a good chance even though some people have been laid off because of cutbacks in government subsidies. But with the Equity Bill coming up he said I stood a good chance of getting a job there, next year. So I'm going to try my luck."

I want to ask what about her dreams of becoming an actress and doing her own stuff, but it would sound juvenile, immature.

"That's great," I say.

"It's not really. I still don't know where I stand with him. We haven't talked about marriage or no marriage, is he going to stay here or are we going over to Germany? But I know that he wants to be with me. He's made so many plans for the baby. He hopes to finish his thesis earlier than expected and just in general we are planning everything. So we've kind of become grown-up, a regular couple. I know it sounds boring but it isn't actually. It's quite nice," she says with soft, nostalgic eyes.

"Security, friendship, they don't sound boring to me," I say to her.

"And you, what's up? Or what's down?" she says loosening up and smiling.

"Nothing much. I'm still waitering at the Waterfront and it's going well. I'm off for the next four days while I sort out a place to stay but otherwise everything's going well. I mean besides being evicted," I say and manage a casual smile just to show her how much this business won't be a problem.

"So where are you thinking of staying?" she asks.

"I was thinking of Woodstock. It's close to town and I don't have a car. Sometimes I work nights. It's a real pain to depend on others and meter taxis – they're too expensive. But I can't stay in Sea Point anymore. It's too expensive."

"You should actually try in town itself, you know the City Bowl, or places like Tamboerskloof, okay Gardens is out, it's too expensive, but try town," she encourages me.

"So you been going out a lot?" I ask her.

"Not really, so much on my mind. In fact this dinner tonight, it's the first time we've gone out together in about two weeks."

"You love him, don't you?"

"Is it that obvious?" she says a little defensively.

"No, but I know you'd have to love the guy to tolerate moving in with him."

"Well, I better fix you something to eat," she says getting up.

"No, really, I'm fine, don't bother. I had a late lunch. I should be fine," I say.

"Well, there's bread and butter. I don't think we've got any jam or Marmite left. But you can check."

"Really, I'm fine, but thanks anyway."

"Are you alright?"

"Of course I'm fine." I say with too much ardour. "Why?"

"I don't know. You seem a little skittish and irritable. You keep moving around," she says.

"You know me. I can't sit still for too long. But the truth is I hurt my back at work, so I'm a little stiff," I say, not sure if my act is convincing. Don't forget she's an actress, I remind myself.

"Anyway," she says. I don't think she's convinced, but she won't persist. "I'll take out some blankets and a pillow for you."

"Don't worry about the pillow. I packed it with my stuff," I say, "Just the blankets, please."

She returns with two sleeping bags that I can lay out to make a thin mattress. There is a duvet and a brown blanket. She puts them out of the way near the desk and chair where the computer is.

We sit around and watch TV till Arne comes back. His face looks friendlier. He even smiles at me and asks me if I am sorted out for food. He goes to the bathroom. I sit alone in the lounge and hear them talking. I hear the toilet flush, I hear the buzzing of an electric shaver, I hear coughing and chattering and smooching. I listen to their accents, their voices mingling with each other like a salad, their lives intricately embroided into each other. I hear the staccato tapping of Mmabatho's shoes as she walks on the wooden floors. When I look behind me I catch a glimpse of her going into the bathroom, fussing with an earing she can't put on.

"Here, let me help you," I hear him say and soon I hear them making kissing and sucking sounds. He goes back into the bedroom and gets dressed. Steam comes out the bathroom and the pleasant smell of aftershave. I love the smell of aftershave. I think he uses Kouros, it has a fresh scent that always makes me think of the sea, especially clear azure water. They laugh and giggle but I can't hear what they are saying because the door is closed. It relaxes me to notice the ease with which they seem to live.

But I still feel like I'm intruding, a little lonely and pathetic.

They come out after a while. He is wearing nice khaki trousers with a powder blue pinstripe shirt and a dark blue casual blazer. Mmabatho looks stunning with a skirt that falls to her knees. It has a long, enticing slit that exposes part of her well-toned thigh. She also wears an elegant shirt and her hair is in a regal head wrap. The material is generous with texture and colour. Her shoes make her seem taller. They look expensive but nice.

"Don't worry, I can't afford Socrati shoes. My dad got them for me on my birthday," she says to me. They have been standing in front of me, I think, half-aware that they have been modelling for me. Arne combs back his hair and goes back to the bathroom.

"Ready?" he says as he comes out.

"Ja, I'm ready," she says holding a small bag.

Arne reaches for the keys.

"Don't wait up for us," she says in jest, as if I'm their son.

"Don't worry," I assure them.

"We'll try and be quiet," Arne says, surprisingly considerate.

"Ag, please. I can sleep through an earthquake."

"Just help yourself in the kitchen if you get hungry," she goes on.

"I'm fine. Please, you guys go, you're going to be late."

Alone I resolve either to sleep or watch TV but I'm not going to think about Sea Point. Sea Point has become Chris, Ross, work and everything bad that went on there. I'm not going to think about it, I tell myself. Perhaps the pain is real enough to keep me concentrated on trying to make myself comfortable. I move around on the sofa to find a comfortable position. Fortunately, I don't need the loo. My stomach moans and groans but I ignore it. I can't risk putting anything solid down my throat. I go to the fridge and find some Oros. I'm thirsty but I refuse to drink it. It reminds me too much of Sea Point, Salt Point like the rastas say.

I crave apple juice but they don't have any. So I boil a pot of water and make some tea. I drink two cups and feel better. In one cupboard I find half a bottle of whisky. My face lights up because now I know what I will do for the pain. Earlier on in the bathroom I searched for Panados or anything to ease the pain but there was nothing. And I'm not prepared to go snooping in their bedroom.

I watch TV until about eleven. Then I get bored and go to the kitchen. I pour myself a quarter of a glass of whisky. And then I pour water half way and drop in some ice cubes. To get drunk quickly, you must drink quickly, I tell myself. I remember something that Oscar Wilde said about alcohol. I find that alcohol taken in sufficient quantities brings about all the effects of drunkenness, he said – or something like that. I drain the drink in about five minutes. And soon enough I begin to feel the effects. A smile grows on my face and I begin to feel my shoulders drop, my lower back yielding. I have been tense all evening. A thought of that terrible night when my mother left me flashes in my mind. And then Chris. I suppress them at once. I will survive. I'm not going back to a mental hospital.

I move the table in the lounge and lay out the sleeping bags. They are cold and slippery. I take out my pillow and lay out the blankets. I stumble a little because I'm drunk but I manage to find the light switch and turn off the lights. I stumble back to my bed. Once inside the covers I sigh and tell myself I never have to see Chris again.

Sleep comes at once, it possesses me like a drug.


## MMABATHO

Tshepo is quiet and hardly eats anything. When I ask him why he tells me that he is not well. I don't persist because I have my own worries. But on the third day I catch him sitting by himself one morning in front of the TV. It is still early, hardly seven. I get out of bed and leave Arne snoring softly.

"Sorry, I thought the volume was low," he apologises when he sees me.

"It was low. I couldn't sleep myself," I lie even though it was the TV that woke me. He turns it down anyway.

I sit down next to him on the couch.

"So what's up? I know something's the matter. You love your sleep as much as me."

"It's nothing," he says.

"You haven't eaten a thing since you got here. Look at you, your face is all drawn. What's wrong? You're looking terrible."

"Nothing. I'm fine," he says and puts on a fake smile.

"You know, I never told you this but you make a lousy actor. Now tell me, what's wrong?"

"Okay, fine. I was a little careless a while back. So I went for an Aids test yesterday. I'll find out the results in one week," he says all in one breath.

"How could you be so stupid?"

He gives me a stern look.

"I'm sorry, it just came out. But what happened?" I try again.

"I met this woman," he begins.

"This woman. You? … Well, actually we, Arne and I, were beginning to think that you and Chris were lovers. I thought you were gay," I say and laugh a little, perhaps hoping that he will tell me straight out once and for all whether he is gay or not.

"Ja, anyway," he says, avoiding my remark, "I met this woman and we got on really well."

"What's her name?"

"Uhm … It doesn't matter."

"You never know, I might just know her."

"Okay, fine, it's Lerato," he says, but it doesn't sound convincing.

"Don't bullshit me," I tell him.

"Her name is Lerato. Do you have a problem with that?"

"Sorry. I'm just being me. Carry on."

"So anyway we had a fling if you can call five nights together that. And I never used a condom. I don't know why, don't ask me. So then she disappeared and I found out that she went back to Jo'burg. I just got nervous and thought it best that I should check and make sure. You never know," he says, his eyes red and looking darker than usual.

"But what if you're positive?" I blurt out.

He sighs and fiddles with his nasal hairs. Does he know how irritating that is?

"I'm going to get you clippers for that." He stops doing it.

"I don't know what I'll do. I'm hoping that the results will be negative. All I can do is wait."

"I know what that feels like." I hug him a little but he feels distant. He is not the same person I first met and neither am I the same. Growing up is a treacherous activity. You never see it coming.

"So are you going to eat for a change? Your cheeks are collapsing," I say and prod his cheek.

"Depends what we're eating," he says.

"I'm making omelets with cheese and spinach," I say enticingly.

He nods gently. "Ja, that would be nice," he says.

We sit around and drink tea together. At eight I start chopping up and frying. When breakfast is ready Arne is already up. We eat together. Tshepo only manages to eat the omelet. He doesn't bother with toast or fruit. Arne keeps eyeing him as he goes through the meal with gusto. I can see his eyes forming questions about Tshepo's puny appetite. But something is wrong. I know that. And perhaps there is more to it than just waiting for the results of his Aids test. In fact I'm not sure if I buy that. He's so careful, his attention to detail so meticulous. Frankly I can't see him just being so impetuous that he forgets the condom, risking his own life. He takes his life seriously, perhaps too seriously. But I don't know what it is. I don't know anyone in Sea Point who could indulge me with gossip about him. He is too private.

After breakfast Arne hurries me along. I've been off for the last three days because I needed time to rest. I needed to think. "I'm going to lectures today," I tell Tshepo, "so you'll be on your own today."

"By the way, I'm leaving tomorrow," he says, "I found a place in

Woodstock. Don't ask me the address, but it's near that small police station on the main road."

TSHEPO

**A**fter they leave I go to the bathroom. I lock the door and start running a bath. And before too much steam condenses on the long mirror, I get undressed and examine myself. My legs, my ribs and my chest are covered in bruises but they are fading quickly. I heal fast. I'll go to work tomorrow, I say to myself, touching the various bruises and not feeling the pain as I used to. I also examine the sanitary pad and there are only two specs of blood. I wrap it with toilet paper and put it in the waste bin. I start pouring cold water into the bath. When the temperature is right I get in.

I don't stay long in the bath. There is something about bathing and relaxing that makes me think a lot. I avoid that. I wash quickly and soon dry myself with a towel. I get changed and sit on the sofa, my hair wrapped in a towel because it is wet and the weather outside is chilly.

In a couple of months time I will have to go for an Aids test. But you mustn't think about that, I tell myself.

And then there is the question about where I will go tomorrow. I promised them that I would only stay for four days. I don't know anyone else in Cape Town who would be prepared to put me up for a few days. I think of all the people I know and realise that they are just faces I greet and make idle chat with.

What to do? The question nags me. I don't even have money to stay a night in a backpacker's lodge. The streets seem like my only option. Think, think, I force myself, pacing around the small lounge. I don't know where the shelters are but I could ask someone. All I know is that you have to be out of there by six in the morning. I could live with that. But where would I put my suitcase? I can't even take the clothes I need for the day because the thugs took all my bags. And anyway, what would I tell Mmabatho? No, you can't leave your suitcase with her, I tell myself.

I consider all the places I could go with my suitcase. I even fantasize about one of those cheap lockers that I always see in American movies. The ones you always see in public places like bus stations or airports. Like the one in Desperately seeking Susan where Madonna puts her round suitcase in or the one in Get Shorty where cops are staking it out, as the Americans say. They seem like such a convenience. I would even guess that they are probably used more by people in ambiguous situations like the characters I always see using them. People like me, always between things, neither here nor there, but always hoping and striving, making a plan to get somewhere by hook or by crook. I get irritated with myself because all this fantasizing is useless. It won't help me.

I spend the day worrying about what I will do and I don't really eat. I still haven't used the loo. It has been three days now.

In the late afternoon Arne finds me by myself in front of the TV. He greets me and disappears into the bedroom. I feel awkward so I tell him that I'm going to make a phone call outside as they don't have a phone line.

I just roam around the neighbourhood. The houses are small and the people are not as friendly as in Obs. But it doesn't matter since you won't be living here, I tell myself. I see someone I know coming from the opposite direction. I turn down another street. I just couldn't handle seeing anyone right now. I walk around for an hour till I get to the lake outside Valkenberg. I stand there watching Egyptian geese gracefully stretching out their wings, but they don't take off for the sky. I begin to feel sad, really sad. But it is residual depression. It comes about because I have always had something to be sad about, my whole life. Being outside Valkenberg makes me sad. I sit on the grass under a weeping willow and let my sadness fill me. Chris you bastard, I loved you.

It is like in the beginning. Before there was God and light, there was Nothing. Just Nothing. And Nothing went on forever. It was always there. It was always alone. And it knew nothing else. And because it was always alone it was very sad. It was always, always depressed. It was always cold. It lived in complete abstraction.

But one day the pain of loneliness got so bad that Nothing began to bleed. The pain just took over Nothing. Nothing became pain. And then a strange thing happened. Nothing made a leap of faith. It believed that it was bleeding for a reason. And so it made love to itself.

And that is how it began, where God comes from, how life evolved. Nothing believed in something more than its pain. It looked inside itself deeply enough till it found love, till it made love to itself. That is why they always say Love has no parents. It went out in the cold and found itself.

And because everything comes from Nothing, that is why sometimes we become a little sad. We become sad and quiet because we also come from Nothing. An inquisitive sperm and a patient egg are remnants of Nothing. It is from that torturous loneliness that everything begins. The tears and frustrations that keeps us awake at night come from a well older and deeper than Time. When we allow ourselves to get sad we honour the courage of Nothing that spent eternity alone, unloved, unknown, unsung, undiscovered. It was a terrible pain to carry for so long, so alone. Forever is a long time to wait to be loved.

I think about Nothing. And I think about Chris. I think about how lucky I really I am. I mean I'm still alive and have my wits. My health is coming on and I have a chance to make something of myself.

I go back to the house, to the quietness of Mowbray. Mmabatho is in when I get there. She looks sullen on the sofa. I greet her but she looks at me moodily. Arne is in the bedroom, doing something. I can hear him moving around a lot. I sit next to Mmabatho on the couch and say nothing. I feel awkward. I don't like her when she is moody. She can be a witch. We watch in silence a documentary on homeless children in Brazil.

After a while she looks at me and grins.

"He's leaving for Germany tomorrow," she says and sounds as if she's angry with him.

"Oh," I say, not sure how to respond.

"Actually he was going to leave anyway, you know, it being the end of term. But just for two weeks before coming back for the last semester," she says looking morose.

"But you're upset," I say.

"Of course I'm upset. Wouldn't you be? The truth is I don't know if he's coming back."

I look behind us because I hate gossiping about someone who is not far away.

"I don't care if he hears me," she says callously.

We sit in silence again.

She gets up and makes supper, something quick and simple but edible: macaroni and cheese. We eat quietly, morbidly.

"Are you taking me to the airport tomorrow or must I ask Andile?" he says and looks at her.

"Better ask Andile. I've got a hectic day."

After supper he goes out alone. She retires to the bedroom where I suspect she is crying her eyes out. That is how she is, Mmabatho is a little too proud. She would never shed her tears for anyone to see.

I sit by myself again and wonder about tomorrow. I don't really have a plan. I'm hoping that a bolt of inspiration will strike me and that I will think of something to save myself. But I mustn't think about it too much.

Arne comes back late. He collapses on the couch next to me. He sighs heavily. I feel a little nervous. We've never been alone together to have a conversation. He sits there and plays with the remote control. I watch passively.

"So you must be looking forward to seeing your family," I say just to break the tension. He is also beginning to annoy me with the remote control. I hate it when someone plays with it and doesn't excuse himself.

"Ja," he says, not particularly enthusiastic, and scratches his neck.

I want to speak on behalf of Mmabatho but decide against it. I don't need to be thrown out tonight.

We sit there in silence for a long time, it feels like an hour. It is agonising for me. I don't feel comfortable around him. I don't feel comfortable around anyone I don't know too well. But he doesn't seem bothered. I don't even think he's thinking about me. He's probably floating in another time zone in faraway Germany, thinking about all the people he will see again, the kisses, the hugs and the inevitable questions he will attempt to answer. I can't even go to another room or make an excuse about going to bed.

After midnight he hands me the remote and tells me that he's off to bed. He opens the door to the bedroom and the light is still on. Soon I hear Mmabatho crying and him saying, "What do you want me to do?" She cries for a long time, the way women can. He closes the door and all I hear after that are muffled sounds. They talk long into the night and intermittently Mmabatho cries. I hear her blowing her nose several times.

I wake up early in the morning. The first thing my body needs is the toilet. I go there and get it over and done with quickly. It hardly hurts. I will be alright in another two days.

Arne leaves for class without breakfast. Mmabatho remains. She tells me that she's bunking again. It's the last Thursday of term, she says and shrugs her shoulders. We eat cereal and watch the morning news. The silence is oppressive. I wish I could be elsewhere.

"I know this is going to sound stupid but can you stay till the weekend's over? I just ... Can you?" she says and looks desperate. I have never seen her like that. I have never felt needed by anyone, especially her.

"Sure," I say, smiling inside.

"But I have to go to work tonight," I tell her, "and the next three nights."

"Couldn't you just stay for a few days longer? I mean I'm sure your landlord … Where was it again that you'll be staying?" she asks.

"Uhm, Woodstock," I throw a name.

"Just tell him that you're still interested. I mean you've paid the deposit and the rent for the month, right?"

"Ja, ja," I lie eagerly.

"So please, could you?"

I take my time to answer. Mmabatho always wants things her way. And she wants them now and she knows how to get them. I'm not going to be her puppet. I don't care how desperate I am.

"I'll stay till Monday," I say. "I really want to get organised."

"Fine." She sulks, a spoiled, petulant look on her face.

We watch the remainder of the news.

She spends the morning moping around. Just before lunch when Arne's due back she suddenly washes, gets changed and leaves without telling me where she's going. I don't bother to ask. At around one Arne comes back with a guy called Andile. He introduces us to each other and we smile with mild recognition. I have seen him a few times at Ganesh, one of Mmabatho's shark friends. Arne asks me where Mmabatho is but I shrug my shoulders. I don't know where she went, I explain. He clicks his tongue and curses womankind as he goes to the bedroom. Andile and I, even though we have just met, secretly laugh together because the gesture was so South African, so black, he could have been just another guy from the township. He comes back with a jacket and a small pouch. I have heard it loosely being called a man's handbag, it's European.

"What's this?" Andile teases him.

"It's where I keep my stuff. You know wallet, passport, documents and my air ticket," he says, unashamed to be carrying a thing which Andile considers feminine.

"Anyway, let's go. I have a plane to catch."

"Nice to meet you," Andile says politely, perhaps mocking me.

I nod my head and watch him help Arne lug a large suitcase and two bags into the car. When everything's loaded Arne comes back to me and hands me the keys.

"Tell her I came and she wasn't here for me," is all he says, his expression unhappy.

"Sure." I say. "Anyway, have a good flight and see you soon."

He looks at me as though I uttered an obscenity. Then he looks at me and smirks and grunts a little.

"Ja, so see you, nè," he says, again sounding very South African.

He will miss this place, I tell myself as I close the door. I hear the car driving away.

In the afternoon I start thinking of work. I go to the bathroom and shower quickly. Shit, shower and shave, I remember Shaun's words. As I stand in front of the mirror and use my electric shaver, I go to great lengths to make sure that I have no hair around my cheeks, chin and neck. I use plenty of aftershave and cologne. In the medicine cabinet I see some dye, Mmabatho's platinum blond dye from the days before Arne. Remember, anything you can use to your advantage helps in this industry, I recall Shaun's words. Why not? I say as I read the instructions, my mind racing ahead with the exotic look I'm hoping to achieve. It takes me about half an hour to dye my hair, but the colour I get is hardly platinum blond. I get a copper colour but it is also charming. I comb my hair and smile and try to think of a name for the face staring back at me. I have always liked the name Michelangelo, and of course the artist's work. I settle for the last part of his name, Angelo. I say it over and over in the mirror till I begin to feel comfortable with it, till I begin to believe it.

I go to the lounge beaming with excitement. I take out my black jeans and a black Guess shirt. I go to the kitchen where the iron is and using the small kitchen table as an ironing board I proceed to get rid of all the wrinkles. When I'm done I put away the iron. I don't have a belt but it does not matter because the jeans fit me perfectly. The only problem is what to do with my feet. I have a pair of Nike tackies but they are tired, old. They are the ones I use for running or walking or anything involving something sporty. I washed them yesterday. They look a little better. I put on the outfit and feel good about myself. In one pocket of my jeans I find a beaded necklace. It is black and white. I wear it eagerly as I know it is the last dash of style to finish the look I'm going for. I go back to the bathroom and stand in front of the long mirror. I comb my hair again and fix it perfectly. And then I fix my collar and brush off some loose threads on my jeans.

Mmabatho comes in. She finds me packing away my other clothes into the suitcase.

"I hope you don't mind, but I figured you wouldn't since you're going au natural."

"Not at all, you look good actually," she says smiling a little as she looks at my hair. "So I guess you're going to work?"

"Ja, I have to be there by about ten to five," I say.

"You better get going."

I take my wallet and my last ten rand and some change.

"Don't wait up for me," I say. It's my turn to tease her.

"Don't worry, I won't," she says, suddenly looking sullen.

"I should be in by about two."

"Did he say anything before he left?"

"He said to say he came but you weren't in. And then he left. Andile took him to the airport."

"Anyway. Here, you can use his keys," she says and hands me the bunch of keys on the table.

I catch a taxi to town. At the station I get another taxi to Sea Point but I get off in Green Point. It is about a quarter to five and the sun is still up, smiling to itself. I walk to Steamy Windows nervously but still excited. At the door I ring the intercom.

"Who is it?" I hear Shaun's voice.

"It's Angelo ... from the other day," I say.

"I'll be down in a sec," he says and opens the gate for me.

At the door I'm met by someone, the host, I presume. He smiles at me, wearing an immaculate tuxedo. "Shaun said he's coming down," I explain. He smiles to himself. It makes me feel embarrassed to be there.

"Oh," he says and goes back to his desk where there's a computer and a TV. I didn't notice them the first time. I stand there patiently looking around the entrance hall, a chandelier floating with regal appeal like a diadem of light above my head. The lights are bright. I try to hide my nervousness. A mirror with a gold frame takes up a large part of the wall. There is also a plush chaise longue of delicate light brown crushed velvet. The room is highly ornamented. I cannot tell whether the floors are genuinely marbled or whether it is a painted effect.

Shaun comes down the stairs, looking comfortable in casual wear. He wears an unmistakable Versace silk shirt with a rich print that has been all the rage this spring. I saw it on TV once.

"Hi, sorry I didn't catch your name," he says and shakes my hand.

"It's Angelo."

"Angelo. I like it," he says and bops his head.

"Ja, sorry I couldn't come earlier, I had some things to sort out."

"Glad to see you again," he says and throws me a quick look from head to toe. When he gets to my shoes he smiles.

"I'm working on it. They broke into our place and cleaned us out," I explain.

"You look great. The others are already in. I'm glad to see that you're good with time. It just makes it easier for everyone," he says.

I smile to hide my nerves.

"This is Francois, the host. And no, he doesn't do what you guys do," Shaun says with a naughty smile.

I shake hands with Francois. He has a permanent smile on his face. I suppose that's why he's the host.

"Ja, all the bookings we get come through Francois, any cancellations and basically any calls we get come through Francois. The intercom is upstairs, so I can tell you guys when a client comes in. Sometimes you guys get a bit noisy and it makes a bad impression, I think, when a client comes in and all he hears is noise. Sometimes you'll also have to answer the intercom, nothing difficult," he says with a winning smile.

He leads me up the stairs. I follow him nervously. Francois watches me. In the lounge there are five other guys. I recognise two of them, Storm and West. "Howzit man?" West says, smoking a cigarette. He's also wearing black jeans. He moves to shake my hand again. He smells good and his white short sleeve shirt looks delicate and expensive. His hair is wavey and immaculately in place.

"West, just introduce Angelo to the other guys and show him what we talked about earlier," Shaun says.

West introduces me to Cole, a tall, handsome black guy. He looks as if he's from Nigeria or somewhere way up there. He shakes my hand and smiles broadly.

"And then, of course, you know this slut," West says and indicates Storm.

"You look gorgeous. I like your beads," Storm says and fiddles with my beads.

He introduces me to another guy called Carrington, who doesn't so much smile as grin. He's good-looking in a boyish sort of way.

"Howzit, bru," he says and does something with his delicate blue eyes.

The last guy is called Sebastian. He's got long black hair and I immediately see that he's effeminate. He wears a T-shirt that looks intended for women but with fashion being so unisexual nowadays it's hard to say. He stretches out his hand as if I'm expected to kiss it. But I shake it.

"Angelo, cool name," he smiles and crosses his legs. There is something charming about the way he is so comfortable with himself. Momentarily I'm mesmerised by him filing his nails.

"Okay, you guys, listen out for the intercom. I'm just going to show Angelo around," West says.

I follow him nervously but he stops at the door.

"You see that mirror there?" he says and points to a large mirror on the side of the wall.

"I've got a secret for you," he says and gestures me to follow him by gesturing. We go to a door next to the lounge. It leads to a small room with dim lights. On the wall is a slightly tinted glass pane through which I can see the others chatting and watching TV. He closes the door and looks at me, expecting me to look surprised or thrilled as though he showed me a great magic trick. There is a big smile on his face.

"Ja it's quite clever," I feign enthusiasm.

"You mustn't worry. This work is easy," he says as he swaggers down the corridor. Does he always walk like that? I ask myself, watching him saunter with the ease and confidence of a cat. We go into the first room.

"Studio one," he says. It is a bedroom with dim lights. There is a grand double bed with a highly decorated headboard, a small couch, a wardrobe, two bedside tables and a long narrow bed for massaging.

"This is my studio. If you look into the wardrobe," he says and opens it, "you'll find my clothes. I have my own studio because I have been working here a long time. Me and Storm, we are here the longest. He also has his own studio next door, number two. We stay here, we sleep here. There are three other studios down the hall. You guys will share them. But don't worry if, say, the other studios are booked and you get a client. You can use my studio or Storm's, he won't mind."

"Okay."

"Right, now Shaun said I must tell you about the business. Did you say you've never done this sort of work before?"

"Ja, never," I say.

"It's easy, man," he smiles. He waves his muscular arm rather effeminately – or am I looking too hard? I imagine the queen in him coming out after a few glasses of wine.

We move to the massage bed but it looks more like a long, narrow, padded table. There is a basket on the table.

"When you get a client, first check that you have everything in the studio. Sometimes you will have to come in ealier to help us fix the place. Now you must make sure that you have condoms," he says and takes out a string of condoms from the basket, "and then you must check if there is enough oil in this bottle. You can get more from the store room. I will show it to you later. You must have enough cream because sometimes the clients don't like to be massaged with oil, they prefer aqueous cream. And then you must check that you have three sheets of this paper."

He unfolds three large sheets of sanitary roll that looks like over-sized toilet paper.

"You know so you can wipe the guy's come," he says. "The magazine the client can keep it if he wants. We get it for free from Gay SA because we always advertise in there. And then you must also have two towels. Right here."

He unwraps one of the towels and there is a small bar of soap inside. "For the client, sometimes they like to take a bath or a shower after this," he says and wraps the towel with the bar of soap skilfully placed inside again. He places the basket at one end of the massage table with the Gay SA magazine underneath. On the other end of the table he places the two blue towels.

"First I will show you everything and then we can talk about massaging and sex," he says without flinching. He opens up the duvet on one side of the bed.

"Now you must always check that the sheets are clean because sometimes they have come stains because the last poephol was too lazy to change them, so you must always check. Remember you must always be professional, that is how you make your money," he says and closes the duvet neatly.

There is a TV next to the bed.

"Now this is for you because sometimes the client is not so nice to look at in the face. You know sometimes he's old or fat or looks funny like he's got too many pimples. That TV is for you. You just put on a video and it helps, you know so that you must get a hard-on because they always expect you to get a hard-on and come no matter how ugly they are." He says it with a straight face, but I want to laugh. I look at some of the videos. Boys from Brazil, California beef, Hungry in Seattle, Before the morning, and so on, the crude, senseless titles go. They are a mixture of straight, gay, lesbian and bisexual pornographic tapes.

"Right, I've shown you the studio. They are all basically the same," he says and we step out into the corridor again. We walk past other

233

doors. I take a peek as we pass the various rooms with varying decorative styles. Storm's studio has a strong Japanese finish. There are two bathrooms. We go inside one.

"Also check that both bathrooms are clean for your client because you never know which one is going to be available. I mean we have Samuel who comes in at three every day to clean so you don't have to worry too much, but make sure that you have toilet paper, that the sink and bath are dry and that there is soap here. "And this Aramis stuff here is only for clients. Shaun will bliksem you if he catches you using it."

His eyes grow big and serious.

"I'm just joking, man. He would never hit you but you mustn't use it," he says and smiles. That gap in his teeth …

I look around the pink bathroom with golden taps and a bidet.

"You know what that is, don't you? It's to wash your hol if you're in a rush because you have another client. It happens, you know. Yesterday I had four clients in three hours. After that I was tired of seeing cocks."

I smile but cringe inside at his candour.

"The other bathroom is the same, it's just that it's blue," he says.

We walk to the furthest room down the corridor.

"Now this is the store room," he says and shows me the various shelves and places where I can get condoms, clean sheets, oil, aqueous cream, sanitary roll, soap and towels. "Sometimes we have to take them to the laundrette," he says. "Oh, and when you've finished with the client, you throw the bar of soap in here," he says and shows me a box where used soaps lie in a pile. "Always, always use new or fresh things. The client must never see you use dirty towels or used soap, you know what I mean? You must always be professional."

I nod my head.

"Now let's go back to my studio," he says. "We can talk about your job and how you do it."

Storm catches us just before we go into studio one.

"West, ons het 'n client," he says and looks at me. "Francois is just bringing him up."

"The others can use studio three, four and five, they are ready," he says.

"Ja, so just keep it down with Angelo cause I'm next door. I hope I get him. I haven't worked all morning," he says and hurries back to the lounge for the "line up".

234

We close the door.

"So what happens?" I say nervously.

"Just relax it's easy, you'll see. First thing is that the client will pick you from the lounge and then Francois will take the client through to the studio. He always talks it over with Shaun before he takes the client so you never worry about which studio to go to, you just follow Francois when he calls you. On the way there Francois will give you a few details about the client, you know, so that you won't be shocked. Sometimes the client has one leg or is deaf or sometimes he is there with his lover but he only wants to watch. Or sometimes he is nervous, like you can see that this is his first time. Or sometimes it's a woman, it doesn't happen often but it does. It just depends. It's just so that you mustn't go in there and look verbaas like an idiot. You understand?" he says.

I nod my head.

"So Francois takes you in there, right? So then he leaves. You close the door. Usually the client will shake your hand or say hi. It's best to wait and see. Sometimes they don't want to shake your hand because then they have to say 'I'm Gary' or whatever and they don't want to give their name. You see? So now you greet each other whatever way. And then you start undressing. It's that easy. You just take off your clothes," he says.

He reaches under the pillow on the bed and takes out a g-string with "Steamy Windows" written on the crotch.

"Now when you take off your clothes just quickly ask the client if he wants you to wear this g-string or be naked. Most of the time they will say you must be naked. But sometimes you get someone who just wants a massage and they want you to keep your clothes on or at least wear this g-string. But you won't get them because you are still new. Shaun usually takes them. He also massages, you know. He's very good, but he doesn't do any extras. He's got a wife and child. Anyway what was I saying? Ja, so now you are both naked. Now this is when you have to think for the client. Sometimes they want a massage to relax a little, so they go on the bed. But sometimes they are just too horny, you can see that they want to come. So you just go to the bed and they will follow and if you're wrong it's not a big thing. You just go to the table and massage them first. Easy, right?" he says and waits for my response.

I'm beginning to doubt whether I can do this. Do I have what it takes to show my rump to a stranger and still be expected to massage him, be courteous and maintain an erection? Performance anxiety lingers at the back of my mind.

"Don't worry, I'll show you how to massage, I'm just talking you through it first. Then after you massage, maybe for fifteen minutes, the client will start touching you and your piel. Then you go to the bed. But now you must take a towel and lay it out like this," he says and opens one of the large bath towels. "So that the client can come on the towel. Now you do whatever you like," he says and smiles.

I look at him with a blank expression, quietly terrified.

"No, you must also have fun, man," he says lightheartedly. "Now when you get on the bed that is when the client will tell you what he wants and he will ask you what you are prepared to do. Like say maybe he will ask you if he can fuck you or if you can suck his piel, you know, anything. I charge R450 for full house, that means fucking. Everyone has their own price. Storm charges R500. But don't get greedy, huh? You can mess things up for yourself. Usually the client does the fucking but sometimes he will pay me to fuck him, easy work. And then if the client asks me to suck his piel I just throw in another seventy to my basic, that makes it R250, you see. But now if I give the client a hand job, I don't charge him extra because that is a happy ending, that is part of the basic. The only extras you charge is when there is real active sex involved, you know what I mean. If the client wants to rub himself all over you until he comes you can't charge him. And you never kiss them and they never kiss you. It just keeps things professional. Believe me, and always use a condom you hear. You mustn't play with your life."

I listen closely, my heart thumping, my mind wondering, furiously searching inside for the courage I will need.

"Now, okay, you have made the client come on your chest. You wipe with the towel but sometimes I take the toilet roll from the basket and use it. And then you get dressed or the client says he wants to bath. You take a clean towel and you both go to the bathroom. You must never leave the client alone by himself. And this is also where you can make some money. Oh, and remember, always always lock the door. Clients don't like accidents. So then you pour nice water. If you want to make real money you bath the client yourself, you know, treat him really nice, talk to him, make him feel special, and I'm telling you man you will make a lot more money. After washing you take the client back to the room. He gets dressed and you get dressed. But before the client leaves the room you must close the deal. You must get your money before he leaves, otherwise problems, you understand? But he won't hassle you. And you mustn't be shy. It's your money. You earned it.

"So say maybe you gave him a blow job, and remember always use a condom, even if it's just a blow job. So now the client owes you R250 but he might give you a fifty rand tip, so you get R300 for an hour's work. And sometimes it's ten minutes. It's crazy. You can make a lot of money. I made R12 000 last month, peanuts. It was a slow month, but I blew it on stupid things," he says and I believe him because his shirt looks intimidatingly expensive.

"So afterwards you clean up the room, change everything like I showed you and you also clean up the bathroom and change everything. And wipe the table properly because if you use it for massaging that oil gets in everywhere. When you are finished you go to Shaun's office. You pay ninety rand for studio fees and the rest is yours. You go back to the lounge and wait for the next client. That simple."

Panic is beginning to eclipse my initial excitement.

"Don't worry, now I'll show you how to massage. It's easy, it's like making bread, you know when you mix the dough," he says and makes a kneading motion with his hands on the bed but his fingers work in a way I have never seen. His movements are deft and I can see that his fingers and wrists are strong from hours of practice. He shows me another technique where I move the palms of my open hands in circles and another one, still using circular motion, but with fists. And another one where I basically roll the flesh but in small delicate movements.

"And you must ask the guy if it's too hard or soft because they are all different. Some of them like it hard and some of them like it soft. So always ask them as you go. You must have a good time huh, you can chat with them. I mean sometimes they are quiet and shy and don't want to say anything, that's alright you just give them what they want. The quicker the better. It means you can get another client sooner. Just remember, go gently. Work the whole body. Start from the neck and shoulders and work your way to the lower back. And start from the feet and work to the bum. Have you ever had a foot massage? Clients go wild for it. Anyway always work towards the back and bum. All that energy and horniness, we want it there. So that when you touch the guy he must just come. I'll show you the hot spots later," he says and I mimick him rolling his wrists gently on the duvet.

I ask him questions about when to put on the oil and when not to put it on. And what about the aqueous cream, and which is better. I ask him about a frontal massage and he smiles but he is helpful, always giving me the facts straight.

"When they are lying on their stomach, you can touch their balls just between the legs very gently, it makes them really horny, jis they go wild for it. And if you really want to make them go you must play with their fingers and toes like this," he says and massages my index finger suggestively. The connection is immediate. I begin to feel aroused and pull back. He smiles with delight.

"So what else do you want to know? Ag, you mustn't think too much, man. It's easy. You'll see once you start you won't want to stop," he says getting up. He puts his arm around my shoulder. He smells divine.

He opens the door carefully and checks to see if anyone is on the corridor. Then he motions to me and quietly we tiptoe back to the lounge. He points out Shaun's office on the other side near the staircase. The others are watching a porno, a bisexual feast that has Sebastian pulling disgruntled faces every time a close-up of the woman's vagina comes on the screen. This is how they get ready for the job, I say to myself, the nerves and madness running in my head, temporarily distracted by the movie.

We watch for about half an hour. Cole is not in the room. He must be in one of the studios. The others comment and criticise the actors as they swap partners and get into awkward positions. "You need to be a contortionist to do that. I refuse to watch that," Sebastian says disgusted and looks away as the woman engages the two men. They poke fun and come up with suggestions, arguing about whether this is effective or whether that really arouses someone. I watch and listen, absorbing everything.

Shaun comes back with two large plastic bags of towels.

"Angelo, are you ready?" he smiles, "Francois just told me that a client phoned about a black stallion. The client's on his way."

I gasp and my throat feels dry.

"Relax, man. You'll be fine. I'm sure West showed you everything. I've got a book on massaging in my office. I'll give it to you later and you can have a look. There's nothing to it."

He sits with us in the lounge till Cole comes back and the client leaves. Shaun gets up to go with Cole to his office.

"Angelo, you can come," he says. I follow them.

Shaun takes out a book, writes in the times when Cole went in and when he left, the client's name or pseudonym and the studio fees.

"So did you make some nice money?" Shaun asks Cole.

"Ja, the guy was French Canadian. We were rapping in French. He tipped me R200 and I didn't even have to suck his dick," he says pleased. Shaun nods his head, pleased for Cole.

After Cole leaves Shaun looks through the drawers of one of his filing cabinets. He finds a book on massaging and hands it to me.

"Have a look at it. It'll give you some ideas. But don't worry too much. You'll be learning along the way as you go," he says confidently. I'm glad someone has confidence in me, I say to myself skeptically.

"Great, so let's get back to the lounge, the client is on his way," he says with large, hopeful eyes and claps his hands. But first he goes to the store room to put away the consignment of new towels.

We hear the intercom. Shaun answers it and tells us to keep it down because a client is on the way. Shaun leaves the room and closes the door to the lounge. After a few nervous minutes he returns and signals to me. "You must go, the client picked you," West says. The others watch me and start singing the famous tune from Jaws when one sees a shark fin and the victim is about to be eaten.

I take a deep breath and go out the door. "I'll see you afterwards, just relax," Shaun tells me. Francois walks me down the passage. He tells me that it is a middle-aged man, South African and slightly chubby. He looks harmless. He opens the door to studio three and leaves. The client is sitting on the bed. I stand there, remembering what West said about shaking hands.

"Hi, I'm Bill," he says but I suspect that is not his real name.

"And I'm Angelo," I say in my best voice.

"Great," he smiles and starts unbuttoning his shirt.

He looks more rotund than "slightly chubby" but he has a warm face and gentle light brown eyes. His hair is greying quickly for his age but it is still plentiful on his head. I also get undressed. I watch him carefully hanging his clothes on the chair.

"Would you like me to wear a g-string?" I say hoping that he will say yes.

"No, that's fine. I want to enjoy all of you," he says politely. My heart beats at a furious speed. I can hear drums beating, mountains tumbling and torrents of water bursting through walls.

"What a day, I'm exhausted beyond … Phew, let me not even start …" he sighs.

He looks educated, something about his neatness as he undresses and his measured movements.

He stands there naked, his modest penis flaccid. I also stand there naked. He moves to the massaging table. I remove the basket and put it near me on the bed.

"Ja, I just got off work," he says and lies on the table exposing his flat bum with many cellulite dimples. His skin is pale. He doesn't even have an underwear tan around his waist. I look at the large mass of flesh and skin with terror. For a moment I just stare and wonder if I'm really doing this. His face is half buried in the towels. But he smells good, clean.

"So, what do you do?" I say beginning to sweat, trying to work out what to do next.

The oil or the cream, make up your fucking mind, dammit, I scold myself. I go for the oil.

"I'm an investment banker," he says and I half listen to what he says while trying to concentrate on the job. He says something about working with a lot of foreigners and something about repo rates and the new governor at the Reserve Bank. It doesn't help that his head is slumped on the towels so I can't properly hear what he's saying.

"My hands are a little cold," I say apologetically as I pour some oil into my palms and gently touch his neck.

"Would you be a darling and please start with my legs? I've been on my feet all day," he says kindly.

"Not a problem," I say at once and move to his legs.

My hands are oily enough, I start working on one foot, kneading into his podgy sole with my thumb. He moans and groans with relief. I work each toe.

"So you must work really long hours," I say trying to get a conversation going. It will make it easier to get through this, I say to myself and observe the clock in the room. Five minutes have gone by.

"I haven't even had time to register. I won't be voting the way things are going. I've got a business to run," he says with a touch of arrogance.

I massage the other foot.

"I asked my partner to do it for me but they wouldn't have it. Apparently you have to be there yourself in person. I can't do it. I've just got too much work," he complains.

I start working up his calf, finding a rhythm and a technique that feels right.

"Am I going too hard?" I ask.

"Just fine, darling."

"So what do you do when you are not working?" I ask him.

I start working on the other leg. I hope I'm going slow enough. I don't want to rush, I still have a long time, I say to myself, glancing at the clock. But he doesn't complain.

"We try to go to our villa in Palermo at least twice a year, once in June and a few days in December," he says but he doesn't sound as if he's boasting. He just says it. I suppose when you have real money there's no need to boast.

"Italy, that must be nice," I say as I brush past his testicles like West said. I brush them a few times, very teasingly, very gently. He lets out a chuckle.

"Very naughty," he says. I start working on his lower back.

"Come here, darling," he says and sits up. His limp penis is beginning to awaken. He moves to the bed. I take a towel and spread it on the bed.

We lie next to each other and start feeling each other up. He gets an erection but I battle to get mine.

"What's wrong, a little stage fright?"

"Actually, it's my first day on the job," I confess, a little sweaty too.

"Well, you're doing fine. I should tell your boss."

I tell myself to relax.

"You know, I could show you a thing or two," he says and asks me to lie on my stomach. He takes some oil and rubs it on my feet. But he expertly handles both feet and starts massaging. His chest is big and so are his hands. His fingers slide between my toes with ease. I moan with pleasure as he massages my feet, and I begin to relax.

"I should have guessed you're good at this," I say embarrassed.

"I only know just a bit," he says modestly but he does wonders with my feet and legs. He starts massaging my calves.

"Who's the guest now?" I say carefully. I avoid the word client. It is too impersonal.

"I also like you to have fun. And besides, I'm used to this. I'm kind of a mentor. I'm always initiating younger people," he says and I get a brief image in my mind of him working with an impressive staff. He massages my legs and also plays with my testicles.

I turn around when I get an erection. He smiles with pleasure. "That's what I was hoping for," he says and touches my erection.

We toss and turn, chatting about this and that, moving through waves of arousal. He shows me a few things, like the ease and intimacy of the spoon position. After a while I feel oddly relaxed and we begin to communicate with our bodies. He responds when I touch him or stroke him. His short fat penis slides between my thighs, my legs pressed together. All the time he blows softly into my ear. It is the most erotic thing that anyone has ever done to me.

After about half an hour we both come with pleasure. For a while we sit there and he tells me something about learning to hold back coming for as long as I can. He tells me to use my "seat" muscles. "What are those?" I say confused. "Your anus, clench your anus and relax it, darling, it will do wonders for you." He probably thinks I'm inexperienced, that I have never been with a man.

"Gosh, I've been sweating so much," he says. "Could we take a shower?" I wipe off the come with the sanitary paper and give him the other clean towel on the massage table. He wraps it around the waist. I take the other towel lying under us and we proceed to the shower. The water is cold but he just stands there, sweat dripping down his back. After a while the water gets nice and warm. I lather the soap on his back and scrub him with a clean coarse rag in the shower. He washes his hair with shampoo. I wash quickly while he rinses his hair. After a while we both come out and dry ourselves. I offer him the Aramis pack but he refuses, saying something about his partner.

"What he doesn't know won't hurt him, darling. Besides, I don't do this often."

I nod my head appropriately.

"Angelo, isn't it?" he says as we leave the bathroom.

He watches me. Strangely it feels good to have someone want to be with me, even if he pays me the sort of attention that wouldn't be deemed customary by a lot of people. I feel his eyes on my back and quietly smile inside.

In the bedroom we start dressing.

"I like you," he tells me. "But what do you do? A bright guy like you can't be doing this as a serious career."

His gaze becomes serious as he buttons up his shirt.

"Actually I'm a student. I'm just taking a year out to be a little adventurous."

"That's good. It's always good to have something at the back of your mind," he says with avuncular regard. I get dressed quickly and wait for him.

"So how much do I owe you?" he asks.

"R180," I say remembering not to be greedy like West said.

He gives me five pink notes. "You earned it," he smiles and gently touches my chin. I see him out the door and walk him down the corridor, all the way to the staircase.

"Maybe I'll see you again," he says as he disappears down the staircase, walking confidently erect. I go back to the room holding the pink notes. There is something important about the fact that the money is pink. Pink Power. Gay power, gay energy, men's energy, a jumbled thought comes to me, celebrating the occasion. Pink money is going to look after you, I smile to myself and shove the money in my pocket. I straighten out the room. The sheets are clean so I don't have to change them. I wipe the massage table and take the two towels to the store room. I dump them in a laundry bin and take out two fresh clean towels and three squares of sanitary paper like West said. I dry the floors in the bathroom with a mop which I find in the store room. When everything is clean and spotless – after Chris I know what clean is – I go to the lounge. The others are waiting for my response. I walk in casually. I'm not a moegoe. "So how did it go?" West says. "Ag it was fine," I say rather blasé. Shaun smiles. We go to his office. I pay my studio fee and he writes down the details in his black book.

"So did you make some money?" he says, not lifting his eyes from the book while he writes.

"He tipped me ninety rand," I exaggerate the seventy rand tip he gave me.

"Not bad. Soon you'll be a veteran," he says. "I'll start taking your A&R costs next week. It's only sixty a week."

I walk back to the lounge and go to Cole. "Listen, I didn't know that I had to bring a toiletries bag and everything. Could you help me out with a comb and some roll-on?" I say to his ear.

"Sure, man, any time," he says and takes out a leather pouch with all his toiletries. The letter C is embroided in gold. I go out with it to the bathroom. I lock the door and stare at my face in the mirror. What a fucking rush, I say and laugh, but I control myself. I open Cole's pouch and see an assortment of men's after care. I take out a wooden comb, finely crafted. I comb my crop and fix it nicely. I clean out the hairs before replacing it in the bag. And then I take out some roll-on and apply it under my armpits. I spray on some cologne and zip up the pouch.

And then I just stand there and look at myself. After a while a terrible feeling comes over me. It's official. You're a slut, a filthy whore, a voice inside me shouts. I had no choice, I say to myself, I don't have to feel guilty. The excitement is taken over by the sobering thought of what I did to make money. I even think of my mother and my priest when I was a boy and all the Hail Marys I would have had to do for such a despicable thing.

There is a knock at the door. I unlock it and West is standing there. He comes in and closes the door. And then he does a strange thing. He reaches for my neck and pulls my face close to his. Soon his tongue is in my mouth and I can smell his cologne. I stand there and let him kiss me. Perhaps I was pining for him myself.

"Welcome," he says afterwards. "Don't get me wrong. I don't like men. I prefer women, but omstandighede, you understand?"

He steps back and sits on the edge of the bath. I look at him confused, an erection raging against my tight jeans.

"The thing is, we never kiss the clients. And after a while greeting people and being personal with them becomes nothing. So I kissed you because it is more meaningful, more personal than shaking your hand. I have shaken many hands and piels," he laughs, "but you see I had to let you know that you're one of us now. We're like brothers here. You will see things that not many people get to see in one life. And you will do things that you never thought you would do. It is like that. That is the job. People look at us and think that is all we do – fucking. But I'm telling you with all the things we have done and seen we could do anything. I could be a president one day," he says and suddenly looks serious.

I sit on the toilet seat with the lid down and listen to him. He has a smile that could light up a chandelier.

"This is the last place for men. How can I say? A bastion," he says and looks at me with a little sadness. "Our fathers don't have anywhere left for them, where men can be on their own without women, you know what I mean? This place it's like a club, an exclusive men's club. That client of yours, he was a regular. Shaun knows him. We all know him. We were screening you. You see it isn't so much that we want guys that look good or have nice bodies. Anyone can have that. We were looking for something deeper, something real, someone who wants to do something with his life. And you passed. I have a degree in bio-chemistry from Stellenbosch. I'm not bullshitting, this stuff is for real, genuine."

He stands there with his arms crossed and for a moment I suddenly feel as if I have just gotten myself involved in something I don't fully understand, perhaps arcane like a secret society or something like that.

"What we do, it is very serious, you know. We are not just fucking these men for money. That is what I wanted to tell you. We are doing important work here. You will see that. They are showing us things, telling us things for the times ahead."

His eyes are glinting.

"I think you know that things are never going to be the same again. The world is changing, things are happening. Nature is talking to us but few are listening. Ja, well, we know that here. And I think you also know that. That's why this work is so important, you understand? These guys that come in here, you think it was a coincidence that Bill owns a bank? You're going to see many men from all walks of life. You mustn't get confused about the sex, hey? Sex is always the same whether you do it with a man or a woman, it's just a matter of choosing. How do you say again? Preferences. Maybe you don't even like men. Maybe you think you do but you don't really," he says and looks into the confusion in my eyes.

"What are you saying?" I finally say.

"I'm saying it didn't happen by chance that you are here. I'm saying we are doing important work. Don't sukkel with this too much, you will see for yourself. But you must remember we are all brothers."

I gasp. "You read my mind. How did you do that?" I say amazed, nervous, confused.

"We are all brothers. We all look after each other. We know each other well. You'll see. I know you want to sleep with me. And I will, tonight after the shift you can come back with me to my studio. You will see once you get past sex there isn't much to it. If you get past an orgasm and feeling nice you'll realise that it is a way of communicating, a way of saying things. I know you don't understand, but you will. You'll see things," he says and moves towards me.

I say nothing. He stands close to me but he doesn't kiss me.

"We must go back now. But just one thing. You have a choice, you can go now and never come back. And if you try to tell anyone no one will believe you. Or you can stay. So it's up to you," he says and walks out the door.

I look at myself in the mirror again, my mind racing with a million questions, theories, wondering who's behind this. Is this some elaborate scam? But you must find out, my mind says. I go back to the lounge and find Shaun sitting on the armchair. The others look at me as though they know what West said to me. I sit on the couch next to West and Carrington.

"So you're staying?" Shaun asks me.

"Ja," I say quickly. I don't like to be the centre of attention. Their eyes go back to what they were doing before I walked in.

"Good."

When the others are not looking I steal a look and try to see beyond their facades and the obviously impeccable grooming. I look at Sebastian, groomed from head to toe like a French poodle. He sits alone, engrossed in his earphones. He suddenly doesn't look as superficial as I thought he was. There is dignity about his effeminate mannerisms and the way he sits with his legs seductively crossed. There is an intellect behind his look, his eyes serenely looking around while his head bops. He catches me staring at him and smiles. Embarrassed, I look away. Cole and West are talking about something on TV. Storm and Carrington talk about yesterday's jol. I keep thinking about West who went to Stellenbosch and wonder about the others. Could Carrington be a scientist, Sebastian a political analyst, Storm a clinical psychologist? And what about charming Carrington? Or was West just winding me up?

At around nine I get called out again. This time I feel a little more relaxed as I walk down the corridor with Francois. He tells me that it is an English gentleman who looks in his thirties. I find him sitting on the edge of the bed. He has mousy blond hair and a lecherous grin.

"Hi, Angelo, isn't it?" he says and shakes my hand.

"That's right." He is no longer just a client. My mind races with a thousand possibilities about his true intentions.

"So what do you do? I mean what do you offer?" he says and looks at me judiciously. He has a prep school accent.

"Uhm …" I begin, stumped. "I offer everything except intercourse."

"No need to concern yourself then. I had no intention of taking things that far," he says and starts taking off his ankle length boots. I also begin to undress. I undress quickly, efficiently.

He stands there naked, his body well toned and muscular. There is a scar that runs down the side of his thigh. Strangely, I find it erotic and stare. He walks up to me, an erection already bouncing between his hairy legs. He kisses my neck.

"Sorry, I couldn't resist," he says.

Instictively I grab a towel and move to the bed.

"Yes, let's dispense with the preamble," he says.

He moves to the bed eagerly, his impressive physique slightly tanned. An adventurous Englishman, I sigh to myself.

"Are you here on holiday?" I begin.

But he doesn't answer. He lavishes my body with soft tender kisses. I'm also expected to reciprocate. I don't complain. His skin is rough but mostly because he is so hairy. In his hair I can smell faint traces of sea water as though he had a swim in the sea before he came. But his skin doesn't smell of the sea. It is clean and a little dry. We stroke and kiss each other for about ten minutes before he comes. But I don't manage to come with him.

"Not to worry," he tells me. He gets up and puts on his underpants, tucking his balls and prick into his white Y-front deftly.

He gets dressed quickly and leaves three hundred rand on the dressing table. With a towel still wrapped around my waist I see him out the corridor.

I go back to the room and straighten it out. There isn't much to do because we didn't do much. I get dressed and fix my hair with my fingers. At the office Shaun takes down my details again.

"I told you you were going to be a hit," he says making me feel embarrassed.

"It was the quickest money I ever made. We were hardly in there for fifteen minutes," I say. Did I rob the guy?

"Whether it takes you five minutes or an hour to give the client what he wants is not important. The important thing to remember is that you gave him a professional service. They didn't have to go looking for it in some dark corner somewhere where they might get Aids or an STD.

"This kind of work, you really have to go into yourself. That's why some people crack, they can't handle the pressure or rather they can't handle making money like this. You know what I mean?" he says.

West also says that all the time, you know what I mean?

"I've seen a lot of stallions come and go," he laughs and says, "Excuse the pun. You'll find that you speak like that a lot. Anyway the ones who stay and do good, the ones with staying power are the ones who don't let themselves in too deep. You must still reserve something for yourself. Don't let this bullshit thing about money become everything. Some guys, the ones who don't stay here long, they think money is power. They start connecting money with some of the rich and powerful people they meet here."

"But there are times, days when you won't get a client. It's like that. Everyone hits a slump, even the best. And you mustn't take it personally. Some people get bent out of shape and feel rejected. That's why I said this business is not for everyone. It's not for the faint-hearted. It either brings out the best in you or the worst in you," he says and leans back into his chair.

"Well, I better get going," I say.

As the hours pass everyone gets a turn with a client. But of all of us West brings in the most clients. He gets five clients throughout the evening. "That's why they call me Kalahari West, because I'm the best," he jokes. At around one o'clock in the morning Carrington and Cole leave to go home. Storm is out on a travel-date. Only West, Sebastian and myself remain in the lounge. It is quiet, time moves sluggishly. We lower the volume of the TV. Shaun is in his office. West is dozing in the armchair, his legs resting on a foot stool. Even when he sleeps he is sexy.

I sit next to Sebastian on the two-seater cream leather sofa. I have taken a liking to him.

"So how long have you been doing this?" I probe.

"Not long, about six months on and off."

"I'm still wondering if I have the stomach for this," I say.

"You will in time," he says with a slightly jaded smile. He has seen too much, done too much.

He catches me watching West.

"Ah yes, our dear West. Isn't he charming?" he says, his face a dictionary of expressions. A quick glance raising one eyebrow, a subtle dimple when he smiles, a furrow between his eyes when he listens, dark eyes brooding with stifled intelligence and lips that pout teasingly, seductively. But always there's a veneer of sarcasm about his face.

I feel embarrassed and grin.

"You know one thing about this job is that you get to the root of your weaknesses and ideas about yourself," he says.

He becomes quiet and watches West. His eyes are lustful, they seem possessive. Or is that me being jealous?

"You must be very careful with your emotions. We all sleep with each other here, all the time, except Shaun, he's married. I could even sleep with you," he says daringly.

But he is not my type.

"West said to me that you were all brothers here." I open.

He laughs a little. I can see where his charm comes from. His eyes are always doing something: captivating, enticing, making you forget, making you smile, taking you places you might not go willingly.

"Because we are so clear about what we're doing it is sex in its most liberated form because you're not answering to a wife or husband or partner. What the client does in there, what you do, is fleeting, it has no restrictions, no agendas. It can be called selfish but sometimes when the mood is right and the client is open I think of it as being selfless."

He looks at West again. A dagger of jealousy stabs me.

"Men really haven't been given the chance to explore their sexuality.

248

Men are either married or expected to be. There is no inbetween. So men haven't nearly explored the possibilities of being men. There's no place for them. In so-called primitive societies men are more aware of themselves. I'm not talking about status or power. I'm talking about self awareness. In so-called primitive societies a man, even a boy, knows what he is doing when he puts his penis inside a woman. He knows that she might fall pregnant. There isn't the blind stupid ignorance you get in urbanised places where you get thirteen and fourteen year olds pregnant because they were experimeting with sex. That sort of thing never happens. And the women too, they are aware of themselves, of how weak they are against a man's strength and how to use sex in their favour. I know this sounds controversial, even offensive. Perhaps it is true that so-called primitive people are more sexual. I would be. It sounds more natural. The thing about Western culture is that it sanitises sex and horniness with politeness and manners, but in a rigid form. I'm not saying so-called primitive people..."

"You've been saying so-called primitive people, who are you talking about?" I cut him off.

"Depends who the West considers to be primitive." He blushes, "It could be native Indians from the Amazon jungle or the Xhosa in the Transkei. Basically anyone who doesn't function in the same modes as the West. Anyway they also have their social values. So politeness and manners would come into play. I don't think people would be just having sex blindly wherever or whenever. But it seems to me there is more openness about sex. And you find this a lot in the humour."

"Whose humour?" I am beginning to get uncomfortable. What is he implying?

"Well, I've spent a few holidays in Port St John's in the Transkei," he says. And you think that gives you enough authority to make sweeping remarks like that, I wonder?

"And?" I say, perhaps a little too aggressively.

"And I found the people very warm and open about sex. They could see that I had a preference for men and they didn't make a big deal of it. They kind of laughed about it. It's hard to explain, it wasn't like they were saying 'ahh moffie,' it was like you know he likes men sort of thing," he says creating moods with his gestures, his arms always moving with the grace of a ballet dancer. His hands are very delicate, they can be very subtle when he wants to make a point.

"What does that have to do with anything?"

"What I'm trying to say is that so-called primitive people understand gender roles and the ambiguities of sexuality better than Western people give them credit for," he says.

"Well, that is true," I put in my five cents worth. "I mean, people always say that black culture is rigid and doesn't accept things like homosexuals and lesbians. You know the argument – it's very unafrican. It's a lot of crap. In my experiences that kind of thinking comes from urbanised blacks, people who've watered down the real origins of our culture and mixed it with Anglo-Saxon notions of the Bible. It's stupid to even suggest that homosexuality and lesbianism are foreign to black culture. Long ago, long before whites, people were aware of the blurs. They must have been."

"That's precisely what I meant," he answers, "The ugliest distortion is the black woman always being portrayed as the sexual virago, you know, like Grace Jones in Conan the Barbarian. Or the stupid stereotypes on TV that you see in rap and R&B music videos of black women as always being sexually available, their whole lives revolving around getting men who are always cheating on them," he says. It makes me feel uncomfortable that he is so perceptive. But I listen.

"It's happening more and more with white women too now. You see them being portrayed in the same gangsta type regard. It's really funny. It's like they're aping black culture, the stereotypes, the cool dude, the easy girlfriend. Have you seen all the white boy bands? They all walk around like they grew up in the ghetto. It's funny because they don't quite pull it off. But it also says where youth culture is looking for role models today. Ask any record store owner who buys their expensive hardcore ghetto rap imports and they'll tell you that usually it's rich white kids whose lives are far removed from the realities of ghetto life.

"You know what it's like? It's like when I watch TV and even people in the street I begin to see that we are actually going back to what it means to be a guy or girl. You know what I mean? Sure, a part of the nineties was ambiguity, was being unisexual. His and hers the same, CK One, you know the rest. But fashion seems to be moving towards guys looking like guys and girls like girls. Versace is a classic example. With all the advances that women have made you'd think that high heels would be seen as a sexist fetish but they're not. They're more popular today than ever. Liberated women are wearing them out of choice. You know what I mean?"

"Hmm."

"But so-called primitive cultures are way ahead of Western man in this regard. They understand sexuality and live it in a way we can't understand. Like you know that in a certain tribe somewhere in the South Pacific, I forget which, when men go away for training as warriors before a battle they stay in a compound without any women. In fact, women are prohibited because women represent life force, peace, their hormones are pacifying. Now here's the interesting bit. What they do is, they get young boys to cook for the men and clean and basically service them sexually by fellating them. Now this says a lot to me. This says these people understand the power, and I use that word carefully, of being a man. They understand what semen is, what it does, what it means. Maybe by those young boys ingesting that semen they are ingesting something about the elders, the warriors. Maybe information is being transmitted. It's so ritualistic, kind of like celebrating the phallus. Perhaps the boys are in turn giving the men strength by doing that, honouring the phallus, which is really just a hot energy spot. It just seems to me like a way of activating energy. Oh and that reminds me of a painting I once saw based on a Greek myth. I don't remember the characters but I remember that the father had been captured and his arms were tied. He was in a cave or something with his daughter. And the only way she could save him was to allow him to suckle from her breast. I wish I could remember the painting or the myth. Anyway that suggested to me that people have always been aware of what feeding off each other meant. You know, to put it crudely they understood the power of bodily liquids and secretions. Even cannibalism's an extreme form of appropriating energy." He is erudite, but it irritates me that he is vague about certain details.

"It's kind of the same relationship that existed in ancient Greece between a man and his catamite, usually a younger boy. Zeus turned Ganymede into an eagle so that he could be his catamite, so that he could love him in body and spirit because he was so captivated by his beauty. He fell in love with him, and don't forget Zeus had wives and children, huh? The Greeks, they understood this, it was acceptable. The relationship was always between a boy and an older man. The Greeks explored the dichotomy of old and young. I think perhaps they understood relationships in life a little better because they didn't see everything as black and white. There were a lot of grey areas. And the funny thing, well what we would consider funny, is that these boys grew up to be normal men who eventually got married, but in turn also had sexual relations with younger men later.

"I think men have always been more sexual than women, and women know this. Perhaps that's why the Greeks were so open, so willing to explore sexuality to accommodate the different sexes. We all know that if married men had their way, they would be having a lot more sex with their wives. But women aren't like that. Their sexuality is a lot more introspective. I don't think lesbians are as sexual as gay men, I don't know. It doesn't seem so. There would be more pick up joints, more bars for them, more porno and skin magazines," he says, impressing me with his audacious ideas.

"What if we don't understand what they are really doing? Throughout history and time, semen, the preservation of semen through abstinence, was encouraged by the wise. Goethe is said to have remained celibate while writing and countless other artists shut themselves away to draw on their own strengths, their own semen. And talking of another so-called primitive culture, some people have suggested that perhaps the Vikings were so successful in their expansion because they were a little friendlier with each other than people thought. You know, that away from home, family, wives, kids, and with the sea as a harsh companion they sought comfort and strength in each other by fellating each other. That perhaps to be a man meant looking past the obvious."

"Where do you read all this stuff? It sounds a little spurious," I tell him honestly.

"Spurious, because it's unsettling to think of all those guys who pillaged and were brave, hard warriors as being that intimate, as allowing themselves to be that vulnerable. Look, all I'm saying is that there is more to two men getting together than meets the eye, how ever ugly it may seem to other people. The ancients were not preaching abstinence as a way to wisdom without reason, you know, the preservation of semen as a vehicle to unravel mysteries in life. And neither were the mystics who tried to see beyond it, who saw semen as divinely inspired. You have to believe in the intelligence of life."

"What do you mean?"

"I mean being ambiguous, being attracted to your own sex or to both sexes, maybe understanding it is beyond us. Maybe it is life responding on its own. You know that theory about the frogs that if you have only a set of male frogs and no female ones, somehow nature finds a plan and some of them adapt and change?"

I nod my head.

"Why are we any different? We could also be governed by the same high power," he says.

"But what has that got to do with us, as a species?"

"Well, I'm suggesting that perhaps sexual ambiguity is nature reacting. Maybe being gay or whatever, is nature balancing things out. I mean we are going out of control as a species, we are our own biggest threat. You know. And things can't carry on the way they have been much longer. Perhaps being gay is God-inspired," he says and his face, that moves through many expressions with ease becomes a little pious, his hands displaying humility. He would make an excellent orator.

"I mean, really. Think of all the gay people you have ever known," he says.

I smile to myself.

"See what I mean? I didn't have to say it. It's beyond words. And now think of the ones in Cape Town. I'll tell you about them. Okay, besides being a little superficial and clicky they are also loaded, very qualified, very outgoing, cultured. I'm talking predominatly white here. I can't speak for the township. They have a lot of disposable income. A hell of a lot. The kind of business we do here ..."

"But where are you going with this?" I'm getting a little impatient.

"I'm trying to say that it's as if life is engineering a group of people who've triumphed over the worst, the ugliest prejudice, the worst bigotry, on every level of society. Perhaps it is preparing them for something else, bigger challenges. This is one of the prejudices that cuts across racial, social and cultural boundaries. Some of the top achievers I personally know of are gay, people I admire, people I look up to. Oscar Wilde, James Baldwin, Navratilova, George Michael, he's such a cutie. I mean look at what's his name David Geffen? That media mogul guy who runs that thing with Spielberg and the other guy?"

"Ja what about him?"

"He's a classic example of what a gay man can do when he puts his mind to something. Unfortunately not many people in the upper echelons of society are willing to come out of the closet. Society has always been oppressive to gays. What with all that extra energy, dying for an outlet. I'm thinking of Michelangelo, Alexander the Great, even da Vinci, some have claimed. And of course all the designers, chefs, most of them seem gay. And the arts. A lot of gay people seem to be lured into the arts. It's no coincidence. There seems to be a greater intelligence behind it. Life. God. Call it whatever you like. We're kind of moving to the end of our history, of our lesson. Humanity is an eighteen year-old stepping out into the world. It's going to go either way. Some people will survive and some people will die. You just need to watch the news and the weather to know that. Americans are freaking out. They are killing each other every other day of the week. They're saying fuck the nuclear family. Who gives a shit? Give me an automatic weapon, some speed and lots of people to abuse. It's hectic. Everyone. Everywhere. It's real. The tension, people are irritable. It's like the whole planet is a pimple with puss and its about to erupt. And that puss is just going to spill out everywhere. It's already begun," he says, his gestures becoming bigger.

West mumbles something to himself. We watch him briefly scratch his crotch. But Sebastian doesn't miss a beat.

"I think gay men are going to play a more prominent role in future. You know why? Because they don't have wives. They don't have children, well, theoretically. Straight men are tired, burnt out, raising kids but failing to equip them as best they can. They want to jump ship, they want more sex, they're always looking for better sex, look at Clinton. They are dissatisfied. But gay men have always been liberated sexually because they understand each other's needs better than a woman. Therefore they have the energy, time and resources to plough back a lot into a struggling civilisation. I mean we are on the brink of destruction. Don't you feel it? Gay men are going to take their place in the world arena in the future, and I'm not talking about the gay mafia. I'm talking about something beautiful, pure, something worth celebrating because it's honest," he says with fervour.

"Gay men, gay men. You've said nothing about gay women. In fact any woman listening to you would think you're a misogynist, all this pro-male rhetoric," I reprimand him.

"I was getting to that. Now you see in the new order gay women are going to be the wise women of the community, the wise mothers, the elders. They are going to be the wise people leading the community because they understand women's strength, they understand that there is strength in weakness, strength in being a woman, spiritual, intuitive strength. Women make things work in a way that men can't, even gay men. Women operate on a different level because they're so introspective. Women's role is going to be greater than men's because society will revert to a reverence for the earth mother. It's already happening, that whole thing with Gaia. Men may rule, but women will dominate, if you know what I mean. Women's influence will be felt everywhere, it's already being felt. Women make better bosses in general, at least when they are not trying to be men, because they don't use aggression as a tool. Aggression is what built civilisations and as a result they will crumble because of it. Some companies have caught on that a woman can be an excellent and efficient head.

"Understandably this woman power is a little scary for some people. What do you think genital mutilation is all about? Not all men are going to welcome women taking their true positions. There is a lot of resistance. Women work twice as hard as men in corporate structures. The same is true of gay people. Gay people are constantly having to prove themselves, work harder, achieve, achieve, achieve," he says and pounds one hand into the other.

"I hear you, but why do you seem reluctant to say we? You talk about gay people as though you weren't one of them."

"I'm willing to bet that I might be wrong. Like I said I believe supremely in the intelligence of life. I don't know everything. I'm willing to risk being wrong about prefering men, about who I think I am. What if the information I have about myself is all that life is willing to give me for the moment? What if there's more out there but we haven't crossed that bridge? This whole gay thing, it's us that created it. It's been around forever. I'm not saying it wasn't noticed but people were willing to let it do its own thing. You know like the native Americans and the berdache thing, which was usually a gay man who was honoured with the privilege of being like a village shaman, a person who looked after the children, gave advice, saw things that people didn't because they took them for granted. Now I'm saying we are moving towards that," he says and sighs.

"Shoo, that's quite a theory. I'm not sure many people would agree," I say.

"I'm not sure many people would be willing to be in my shoes or yours for that matter," he says ironically.

Some people are just like that; they have an effect on others. Sebastian was probably a loner at school, a drifter. He was probably one of those children everyone considered weird and eccentric because he always wore his hair a little differently or managed to manipulate his uniform without getting into trouble. He was a little advanced, his essays and compositions were probably obscure. Teachers were always taking him aside so that he could expound on his maverick ideas. The cool girls probably made him an honourary sister who gave them advice about what was in and what wasn't. And boys detested him because he knew so much about women. They also detested him because they thought he was a faggot, even the ones who were macho but were confused because quietly, secretly they found him attractive – they wanted to do unspeakable things with him in the dark. And the principal never liked him because he was always starting trends that threatened to corrupt discipline. He was oblivious to his secret charm and inner intelligence. He always knew what was going on, what was expected, but he always had his own ideas and plans about how things would be. He was always a step ahead. But he was probably also willing to hear other people, other ideas. I like that about him. It makes him approachable.

My mind is spinning with dizzying ideas. I feel wide awake even though it is late. West begins to snore a bit. One arm coursing with veins, lies lamely on the chair.

"So you guys take this brotherhood thing of yours quite seriously?"

"Ja," he says, annoyed, as though I don't appreciate how important it is. "The closeness, the openness, they are our modus operandi."

Does he have to use such floral language? I say to myself.

"I wasn't going to tell you this but I might as well since you're so eager. West was supposed to show you the ropes. The thing is … Maybe I should ask you. Did you notice anything about this place since you've been here? Anything unusual about the décor?"

I ponder for a moment but I can't think of anything unusual. I shake my head.

"Well, that painting over there," he says and points to the wall in front of us.

I walk up to it. It is a copy. A woman wearing classical robes with long wavey hair dominates the foreground. In the background above her head two angels beaming with light seem to be in prayer. Much of the light in the painting emanates from the woman's skin. The rest of the areas on the painting are dark and sombre.

"It's a very moody painting," I say.

"Ja, but what does it say?" he encourages me.

I look closer and read out.

"Astarte Syriaca, oil painting by Dante Gabriel Rosetti, one of the members of the Pre-raphaelite Brotherhood, 1877, in the City of Manchester Art Galleries."

"Does it ring a bell? Does it say anything to you?" he asks.

"Not really," I say pathetically.

"If you'd noticed there are several copies of Pre-Raphaelite Brotherhood paintings all over the premises. We take our inspiration from them," he says and looks at me, waiting for a response. But I know nothing about them. I look back with ignorance plastered on my face.

"Hmm, the Pre-Raphaelites. Where do I begin?" he says condescendingly, "You see, in their day the Pre-Raphaelites were pioneers, they were reacting against the unimaginative painting of the time. They wanted to set new ideas, new standards in their work by expressing genuine ideas and painting directly from nature. There were three guys, Hunt, Millais and Rosetti. All were under twenty-five. They were probably a little horny and a little ambiguous if you ask me. They saw themselves more as artistic revolutionaries, attacked social injustices and celebrated the values and quality of life in the past. They always exhibited with the initials PRB because they stood together and not apart. They believed in their work, in the purity of being free and creative.

"Do you understand where we're coming from when we talk about this brotherhood? Can you appreciate a little why it's so important to us?"

"Somebody gave this a lot of thought," I say tritely. I don't know what else to say. The information overwhelms me.

He becomes momentarily quiet.

"This thing, it's like a huge intellectual exercise," I say exasperated by everything I've heard about Steamy Windows. "I thought I was just going to massage and get my rocks off on the side."

"I know it seems like that now. But you'll understand why things are like this. The inspiration of the Pre-Raphaelites is like our foundation, you know. It's like our motto, our mission statement, it's very important. It gives us a direction, a vision, somewhere to go, something to work towards. Without it we would be just another massage parlour. Sex is so ugly today, so basic, so stripped of anything beautiful, transcendental or aesthetic. I'm not interested in that. We're trying to move beyond that. We're also artistic revolutionaries but of a different sort. That's why we stand out from the other massage parlours. Because we offer a different service. And we don't really advertise that much. Not like other places do. The people that come here get referred by someone, it's more word of mouth because that's how we get our core clientele, the people that really know what we're about." He puts his hand on mine. I feel his warmth.

"Well, I'm pushing off. I don't see myself getting another client tonight. I'll see you tomorrow night," he says and gets up. He packs his earphones into a leather bag.

"Ja, great talking to you. What a night," I say and see him out. Francois has already left. But I hear Shaun in his office. He is on the phone with someone. I go back to the lounge.

Alone with West I watch him sleep. I squat beside him. He opens his eyes as though he senses that I am watching him.

"Where are the others?" he says through bleary eyes and yawns.

"Gone home, and Storm is away on a travel," I tell him.

"You must be tired," he says and gently massages the back of my neck. My shoulders drop. "You want to go to sleep? I don't think any more clients are coming tonight."

"Ja, I'm a bit tired," I say even though I feel wide awake.

"Let me just tell Shaun that we are going to bed," he says and leaves. He soon comes back and finds me sitting on the armchair, my legs spread out on the footstool. "Come, let's go," he says and stretches out his hand.

I go to him.

He puts his arm around my neck casually, as we go to his studio. Around his eyes I see tiny wrinkles like he could be pushing thirty, and his bones creak a bit. We walk like compadres, comrades, our postures saying idle things to each other.

He closes the door and locks it. Above the headboard there is a painting. It is of that woman I saw in the lounge but she is floating in water. She's a red-head with wavy hair. The realism is creepy. There is something religious about her expression as she lies there, clothed in classical robes, her wavy hair wispy and fragile in the water.

West starts getting undressed. I also get undressed. We climb into bed together, both of us naked. He opens his arms and invites me to find warmth in his body.

"I'm so tired," he says and squeezes me a little. It is nice just to lie next to him, to feel warm, to feel wanted. I think about what Sebastian said and try to imagine the Vikings alone and estranged in some inhospitable land, with only themselves as comfort against the Scandinavian cold. I take in his smells, his fatigue, his smooth supple skin, his hairy groin, his muscular neck and the fine veins of his large hands.

We lie like that, gently stirring every once in a while. We lie there not as lovers but as men seeking comfort in each other.


MMABATHO

Tshepo comes back late in the morning. I ask him why he didn't come back last night and he tells me that they went out for a drink after work. We drank ourselves silly, so I just crashed at Simon's place, he says going to the bathroom. He runs a bath and stays in there a long time, maybe an hour.

When he comes out he finds me sitting on the couch, fidgeting with a nail clipper and half watching TV.

"I was worried. Did you have to be so impetuous?" I say moodily, picking my nails.

"I'm sorry. Actually the other reason why I didn't come back last night is that I finished late, you know at around three and taxis are expensive. I never had to worry about that when I was living in Sea Point. So that's why Simon was a relief, otherwise I would be spending half the money I make on taxi fares. In fact Simon offered that I sleep over at his place, you know for this week while I'm working night shifts, so I'll always come back the following day," he says.

"Well I'm not a stop-over or a pit stop, you know," I say, my grumpiness finding expression.

"Do you want me to go?" he says, as though ready to leave any minute.

"I'm just in a bad mood," I mumble.

He opens his suitcase and gets changed.

"So did you make some money last night?" I return.

"Ja, a bit," he says. He'll never tell me how much he made. It's pointless to try asking.

I switch channels on TV.

"So did he phone to say he arrived safely?" he asks.

"No, we don't have a phone," I say, "but he could have phoned someone to come and tell me."

"I'm sure he got there alright. I mean what's there to say?" he says.

There's a lot to say, I answer him in my mind.

"We should get out. It's a nice day outside. I was thinking of going to the station to buy myself a bag or a rucksack and a few other things. Are you interested?" he asks me.

"It would be better than sitting here and moping," I say.

"You could use a bit of sun, you look terrible. O tshwana le Lesilo," he teases me.

We fix something to eat before leaving, a light sandwich. Before we catch a taxi he goes to the local ATM machine and deposits some money. I try not to make it obvious but I watch him deposit a small wad of notes into an envelope before the machine eagerly devours it, softly humming something to himself. Afterwards he hails a taxi and it takes us to town. We get off at the station. I don't like the station. The men there always look at the women as if they possess them. Their eyes are always stripping me, ever rapacious as they wolf-whistle or call me baby, skattie or something stupid like that. Thank God Arne never felt tempted to call me by any other name except my own. I walk close to Tshepo, almost clutching his arm, so that they won't harass me. But inevitably they do. Hey, Big Mama, one of them calls out and kisses the air at me. I give him a dirty look but my second response is to feel self-conscious. Am I showing? Can they already tell that I'm pregnant? Tshepo tells me to ignore the idiot as we walk into the bowels of the station. Going down the stairs it stinks of urine.

As always it is busy, people walking in a cacophony of discordant chattering, someone announcing something over the loudspeaker and music blaring from the video games arcade. I don't like crowds. I don't like people brushing against me. Everyone seems to walk fast and they also seem to be impatient. And the tsotsis are never far behind. But it's a good thing that I never brought my bag.

We go outside where a community of hawkers and informal stall owners display their wares. They are mostly foreigners, dark and tall and with features that don't really blend in with the general population.

"Exactly what are you looking for?" I ask him, getting a little impatient among the people and the stalls. He looks at everything, touches things and asks about prices but he doesn't buy anything.

"I'm looking for a rucksack for work. You know, something that I can put my stuff in," he says to a dark woman with a chador over her head. But he doesn't buy the canvas bag she shows him. We keep walking.

"You must be careful of Makwere-kwere," I warn him. "Dintho tsa bona …"

"Don't be silly, there's nothing wrong with their stuff. They're actually quite friendly if you ask me," he says casually.

"You're so naïve. Of course they're friendly, they want your money so that they can sell you something cheap that will break as soon as you get home," I say to him.

He looks at me incredulously.

"I can't believe you're xenophobic."

"Don't call me that."

"Yes you with a German boyfriend. Oh, but sorry, he's German, not African," he says and walks ahead.

"Are you buying your bag or not?" I say irritably.

"I'm still looking. Do you want to go home?"

I want to tell him to shut up. I want to say, I'm just moody today okay, just bear with me, but he isn't Arne and he won't understand.

"Fine, whatever," I say and follow him.

We spend about fifteen minutes at the station. Tshepo keeps going to them. Them with their funny smells and accents. I don't like them.

A friend of mine who stays in a block of flats dominated by them tells me that they bring strange diseases into the country because they insist on performing their queer rituals even though this isn't really Third World Africa, at least by African standards. I wouldn't mind them so much if they weren't always selling imitation goods, if they weren't always together like a group of thugs hatching a conspiracy.

Tshepo is friendly with them, patient. I think he likes them. He likes anyone who is nice to him, anyone who gives him a little attention, even if it is just for two minutes. He's so naïve. They always go to great lengths to sell anything, showing him this and taking out that. They could sell their mothers if they had to. After a while he sees that I'm getting impatient and we leave the station. He still hasn't bought anything.

"What was the point of that?" I say as we head towards Greenmarket Square.

"They sell nice things," is all he says.

At Greenmarket Square he goes to a stall manned by another one of them. He tells the guy that Philippe from the station sent him, that he said he would find a bag. The guy, a tall, blue-black man, I don't mind the complexion, looks at him through spectacles. He wears their traditional garb, one of those huge flowing caftans that the men wear with a little hat. He also has a small dubious-looking pouch hanging round his neck. It's probably muti, that's how they drug us to buy their wares. My friend also told me that these people were full of muti. I watch the guy reaching into a large multi-coloured canvas bag. He takes out a tan leather bag and gives it to Tshepo. For a while Tshepo looks at it. He opens it up, tries the buckle and zips.

"It's nice, don't you think?" he says to me as he handles it.

"Ja," I say curtly. But it really is a nice bag, finely crafted and with no silly impostor names shouting from it. All their stuff seems to be pathetic imitations of established, popular brands.

"How much?" Tshepo finally asks.

"For you R120," he says, but smiles.

Tshepo also smiles. I get bored and look at the stall next to them. I hear them haggling over a price but Tshepo's manner is always polite. The other guy dances around the price, taking off a rand here and there, but he doesn't seem like a pushover. After a while Tshepo comes to me, proudly holding his tan leather bag.

"Did he rip you off?" I ask him.

"What are you talking about? If I went to a proper shop I would have had to pay at least R250 but I got away with R110. Okay, so it's not that big, but it will suit my purposes," he says and takes out wads of newspaper used to retain the bag's shape.

"Anything else you'll be needing?" I say and it comes out sarcastically.

"Have you got your period or something?"

We go to Clicks where he buys some toiletries. At Edgars he buys a towel and looks at an expensive men's after-shave and cologne pack but he doesn't buy it. I watch him make a mental note of it. Afterwards we go to a coffee shop in Long Street. He is quiet. I think he's irritated with me.

"So what's up?" I probe him.

"Just thinking about work," he answers.

"You work too much," I say.

"I don't have a father or mother to pay for things for me," he says and it stings.

"You've changed," I say sipping my herbal tea.

"And you're still the same."

"You don't understand. My life has been complicated."

"Oh," he says and he sounds a little sarcastic. But I go on anyway.

"Tshepo, I'm pregnant and I don't know if this guy is coming back."

"You'll make a plan," he says coldly.

"What's that supposed to mean. Ke eng ka wena?"

"Mmabatho, the thing about you is that you love drama, even off the stage. You like to create stress and all that worry shit. I don't know if it makes you feel like you're doing something with your life when you have worries or something but the thing is, fuck there's always some-body worse off. I could tell you shit that you'd never believe, but what's the point?"

"When did you become such an arsehole?" I say.

"I mean you're always going on about yourself. Do you know that? I know more about you than you'll ever begin to know about me," he says licking cream from his spoon.

"That's not my problem," I defend.

"Ja, but it's tiresome, e a halefisa, e a ntena this thing. People change. We're not kids anymore. I don't have to pretend to like you because I want to be popular," he goes on.

"So you pretend to like me?" I say.

"Sometimes. Like just back there at the station. You were such a bitch, and for no reason. Makwere-kwere, how could you say that? She was within earshot but you couldn't give a damn. I never thought you were a hypocrite. Maybe it's true what you say. Maybe I am naïve, be-cause I never pegged you as being so narrow," he says.

262

"Me narrow? Just because of Makwere-kwere."

"Ke batho, you know? I work with a guy from Senegal," he says as though to impress me.

"Oh, please, and now I'm supposed to applaud you? Don't lecture me about foreigners. I know all about them."

"The white ones."

"Don't make this ugly," I warn him. "Foreigners are just like everybody else. Good and bad. You get your arseholes."

"And you nominated the black ones to be the arseholes, is that it?"

I smile at him. I can see he is hungry for an argument.

"What pisses me off is that actually you don't know anything about them," he says.

"Fuck off. Nthabiseng says they…"

"Nthabiseng? You are going to tell me about Nthabiseng, after you called her a bitch and a slut because she slept with Arne?" he says raising his voice a little, a mocking smile plastered on his face.

"You don't know everything," is all I can muster.

"Ja, but at least I'm not racist," he says.

"Racist, you're calling me a racist now?" I say, now hurt and wounded.

"Ja. I mean just because the Germans and French and all the other white nationalities that come here blend into the background I don't hear you saying anything about them. There's an influx of people from ex-Eastern Bloc countries to Cape Town. A lot of Russians and Czechs. And I'm sure you meet them or at least you hear them. They're just as full of tricks as the next guy with false certificates and shady operations," he says.

"You're making this black and white and it isn't. All I'm saying is that these guys come into the country and okay I'm not going to say the obvious thing that they are taking jobs away. But they come here with all their strange practices from wherever. I mean the Somalian ones still practice genital mutilation even though it's prohibited. Did you know that?" I ask him.

"Did you know there are certain Ndebele and Nguni tribes that practice it in South Africa?" he retaliates.

"And they're always together. I never see them mingling with other people."

"Maybe because people like you don't want to associate with them," he says.

"I don't have to listen to this. Everyone knows that foreigners are a pain in the arse, and that's got nothing to do with race. You're just being silly. The crime, white collar and street crime, it didn't just come from nowhere. It doesn't take a genuis to figure out that the police are not helping. People will pay anything for a chance to succeed," I say rapidly.

"But how are you personally affected? What have they done to you to deserve that kind of contempt?"

"You think you're clever, don't you? Well this isn't about wit."

"Do you know what it means to be desperate, to be hungry, to be at the mercy of someone else?" he says, his eyes clouded with anger.

"Do you? When did you become the UN?"

"This is pointless. Forget it. It's such a nice day. Let's not waste it arguing about something we're going to regret," he says and finishes his hot chocolate.

"I think you're full of shit. So now we must stop this because you've decided?" I say.

"Well, what do you want to say, Mmabatho?" he says, exasperated.

"Nothing. Let's just go," I say getting up.

We go to the counter and pay the bill.

He goes to Checkers and buys some groceries for supper. Then we catch a taxi back home. We say nothing to each other the whole way. At home I go to the bedroom and stay there. At around half past four he comes to the door and knocks.

"Listen, I'm off. Maybe we can catch a movie tomorrow."

"Ja, that would be nice," I say mildly excited.

I hear him close the front door and lock it.


TSHEPO

**I** get to work on time. Francois opens up for me. In the entrance hall I notice one of the Pre-Raphaelite paintings Sebastian was talking about. It is of a tall man wearing a white robe. He stands in a forest at night holding a lantern. On his head he wears a crown. The foreground of the painting is dominated by him. There is something regal about his humility, about the way he holds the lantern, the way he lights up the night. He is calm, vigilant. There is no fear about his face, just beauty, serene beauty.

I go to the lounge and find the others already there. Some have been there since two o'clock in the afternoon. Shaun asks me to check that each studio has two towels. After doing this he calls me to his office.

"We need to do your profile. That's just like a short description of who you are, so that Francois can sell you when clients ask and make bookings," he says.

"Okay," I say.

"You're lucky that you work for us. At other places, before you get the job, they make you strip and that's how they write up your profile," he says. He takes out a pad and asks me how tall I am and how much I weigh. He studies the colour of my dark brown eyes and writes down all these details.

"So what, a swimmer's build?" he asks me, more to find out if I approve of being described like that. "Now the other business. How many inches erect, and are you cut?"

He says it with a straight face. I suppose this is when the other places would have made me strip.

"I've never thought about it," I say embarrassed.

"Well ten inches is about this long," he says and shows me with his hands. It looks ridiculously long.

"Just tell me when to stop," he says as he shrinks the distance between his forefingers. I stop him before his fingers get too close.

"Okay, that's about six and a half inches. We'll put it down as seven. I always go up half," he says, still not smiling. "So are you cut?"

"If you mean circumcised, yes," I say, very uncomfortable.

"Great. Tell me how this reads. Angelo: Swimmer's build, weighs about 65 kg, height 1,69 m, dark brown eyes, good looking but not effeminate. Sometimes the client specifically doesn't want femmes, no matter how hot you are," he says and carries on, "7 inches and cut. Ja, I think that should do it. Obviously that's just a sketch. When Francois sells you he'll describe you better."

"That sounds alright," I say tritely. Good looking? No one has ever described me like that.

He takes the sketch to Francois. I go back to the lounge. There is another guy that I have never seen. His name is Adrian and he is tall and well built. We shake hands and say howzit to each other the way only South Africans do. At around six I get a client, a French guy on holiday in Cape Town. He is skittish. I don't think he's ever done this before. But as soon as he sees me naked he relaxes. I don't bother massaging him. We go to bed. We spend a titillating hour together but he doesn't come. He pays me R400 even though there wasn't any penetration involved. I don't think I would ever go that far with a client. But you never know, like West always says. Wait till the right one comes along.

At around eight I get another client, a South African guy. He doesn't wear a ring but something about him tells me that he is married. Perhaps it is the way in which he sits on one side of the bed, probably his side of the bed at home, while he takes off his clothes. And the way he opens up the bed, there is the manner of someone accustomed to it. Usually they just stand there and wait for me. I take a towel as I go to him. "How much if I want to kiss you?" he says, his prick rising quickly.

"I don't do kissing," I say firmly.

He looks hurt but he doesn't persist.

"Can you just sit on me then?" he almost begs.

"I don't do penetration either," I say.

"I know but just sit on my crotch," he says.

The room is dimly lit. So I sit on him and try to force myself to have an erection, but I can't. I consider putting on a video, but that would disturb him, so I don't. After a while he gently rolls me over and then without warning he hugs me close to him. It takes me by surprise and for a moment I fear that this is a trick about to go nasty because he holds me very tightly against him.

"I can't breathe," I whisper and he relaxes.

Suddenly my shoulder is wet. I turn round on the bed and see that he is crying. I don't say anything immediately.

"You are so beautiful," he says through tearful eyes. He still has an erection.

"Are you married?"

He wipes his tears.

"I have three children. I don't think I even like men," he says, "but I keep coming here."

I tickle his back as we lie there facing each other. My other hand gently massages his prick.

"You have a nice body," I smile, "Your skin is soft." I'll say anything to be nice to them.

He tightens my grip around his prick.

"When I was your age I thought I would never get married," he says. His eyes are dry now.

"So why did you?" I ask.

"Parents. Respectability. The usual. I know I compromised. A person like me should have never gotten married. I don't even think I make a good father. I'm just a provider." I quicken my wrist. He moans a little.

"But why don't you leave if you're that unhappy?"

"It's not that easy. In reality it's not that easy to leave," he says. "I really want to kiss you."

His eyes are begging again. Is this how he begs his wife too, I wonder?

"Why did you pick me? You could have chosen one of the other white boys," I say just to throw him.

He thinks a bit.

"Because you're anonymous. Your colour makes you anonymous, just another guy. The truth is, except at work I hardly interact with black people. It makes it easier to distance myself from these excursions of mine if I do it with a black guy," he says.

"Do you prefer boys?" I ask.

"No," he says immediately.

"But you want to fuck me. You want to kiss me," I go on.

"When you get to my age you learn to adapt," he says.

"I don't understand. You could have gone for a woman."

"That would feel closer to cheating on my wife."

Married men seem to deal with a lot of sexual guilt, I say to myself as I bring him off to come. He shoots a phenomenal amount of come on me. I find it erotic and mildly get an erection. I wipe myself with sanitary paper.

"I still want to kiss you. I'll pay you well," he says, his eyes servile, pathetic.

"How much?"

"Five hundred. If you let me kiss you for the remainder of the hour."

"Why is it so important to you?"

"Because then it won't feel like cheap sex," he says.

"So will it feel like expensive sex then?"

"I can get anonymous sex anywhere. I want to walk out of here having felt a little warmth," he says.

"Fine."

He puts his fingers on my lips, gently mapping them out. I lie still and watch him. His eyes speak of quiet desperation. Inside there lies a stifled will. He starts kissing my neck, very tenderly. I think of Mmabatho to try and detach myself from the intimacy. He eventually gets to my mouth, licking it at first. It puts me off a little. He soon has his tongue inside my mouth.

Where are his thoughts as he does this, I wonder. With his wife? With his children? Or can he also just detach himself?

He kisses me for about twenty minutes. I feel strange and uncomfortable after we're done. I feel like he was inside me and I was inside

267

him. There is the sudden awareness of being naked. I feel vulnerable, self-conscious, and get dressed. He gets dressed quickly. We sit on the edge of the bed together. He takes out his wallet and hands me five hundred rand in six notes.

"I could be your regular client," he says. "At least once a week you'd have your regular bread and butter."

"What's your name?" I ask him.

He hesitates.

"Your real name."

He looks at me tenderly and puts my hand on his crotch. He still has an erection.

"Peter," he says, "and don't ask me my surname because I won't give it to you, Angelo. What's your real name?"

"Angelo," I lie with a straight face.

I don't know whether he believes me. He gets up and tucks in his shirt. Afterwards I see him out the door and all the way to the stairs. I go back to the room and straighten it out. In the lounge the others are watching another bi porno. Sebastian is reading a comic, listening to his ear phones. At nine Shaun always gives us a break. We take fifteen minute breaks and go out in twos either down the road to buy a drink at a nearby cafe or outside for a quick smoke. I go outside with Sebastian. We stand around the corner where it is dark. Sebastian lights a joint.

"Durban poison, darling, be careful. It's like a pickaxe. It really opens you up. Have you ever done a trick high?" he asks me.

"No, have you?"

"Ja. If you're in the right mood it's divine. But if you're not it's really freaky," he says and in the dim light I can see the whites of his eyes coming out. He flicks back his long dark hair.

"I wish tonight would just happen," he complains," I'm dying for some fun. I haven't been on a travel in ages."

He sucks hard on the joint.

My eyes begin to feel dry. That means I'm stoned. I become quiet and listen to a small wind going past. Sebastian finishes the last of the joint and we go back inside. At the door Francois tells me that I have a travel booking for one o'clock. "Don't let this shark take advantage of you," he warns me of Sebastian. I'm too stoned to work out whether he is joking or being serious. I just smile.

"Jy's gerook, nè?" Francois says and only then do I realise that he might be Afrikaans. Sebastian and I walk upstairs. His platform shoes clank against the wooden blocks of the stairs. West and Cole get up to take their break when we return.

Having sat down the intensity of being stoned increases. I become hypersensitive to everyone. Carrington seems to smile every time I look at him.

"A booking that late," Sebastian says to me, "that's probably from Angels or Biloxi. It either means the guys look like crap or the guy's really old and disgusting and can't get a pick-up so he phones here and makes a booking. But he might get lucky towards the end of the evening and get a guy. That usually means he cancels the booking or if he's a real arsehole he just won't pitch and you'll wait here till four in the morning. Or sometimes he'll come but still expect you to get it off with him and his mate or whatever. And if you're really lucky it might be an overnight. That's a thousand in your pocket. The studio gets two hundred."

I nod my head slowly.

"Drink some water, darling. Your body is dehydrating, that's why your eyes are so red. They probably feel dry as well," he says.

I get up and move to the bathroom. But it feels like I float there. In the mirror I get a shock because my eyes are really red. I splash my face with water and a tingling sensation travels from the nerve endings of my face. I drink lots of water and go back feeling better. But later hunger pangs attack me. My stomach moans. Fortunately I brought something to eat in my bag. I take out a pie. Sebastian looks at my bag and says, "It's quite nice for a flea market knock-off."

They are all like that, very conscious of labels and brands. "Sweety, if there's one thing that gay people have an ESP for it's picking out a real label from a knock-off," he tells me with a sardonic laugh.

"It's only temporary," I excuse myself, embarrassed.

"Of course. You should go to the Waterfront. You can get good quality Gucci bags that will cost you and arm and a leg but they last forever and you never worry about looking good," he says.

I tuck my bag away in a corner.

"Guess how much I paid for these platforms?" he says.

"Six hundred?"

"Try again. R900, darling, Italian shoes. Prada. You can't beat the quality and craftsmanship," he says with fastidious attention to the detail as he shows me the stitching. "Hand-made darling."

I feel awkward wearing my tackies.

"I'll give you a few pointers if you want?"

I have plans for that money, I want to say but don't. I have to save,

269

to keep a nest egg. Next year I want to study. Next year I must become someone. Next year I must think ahead, I want to say. But he won't understand. And it would sound corny, uncool. Besides, I don't want them to know too much.

"That would be nice," I say and study his outfit.

He wears a metallic lycra top that seems to bring out his dark eyes. He probably bought it in the women's department. I've never seen it being advertised anywhere in men's shops. His hair is clean, it always smells nice. A delicate watch by Raymond Weil sits elegantly on his wrist. It also looks intended for women. To cover his legs he wears shiny, silky trousers from Levis and of course his feet are clad in the Prada platforms.

After a while Shaun comes in to tell Sebastian that he must get ready in five minutes. A client booked him for a travel to Llandudno. His face lights up with excitement.

"That's like being asked to trick in Beverly Hillls or Saint Tropez, darling. Lots of dosh and the chance to have some fun on their money," he says gathering his comic and ear phones into a beaded bag by Fendi. He moistens his lips with lip balm and smiles. He takes out a brush and combs his long mane. And then he sprays on some cologne by Jean Paul Gaultier. "I don't really like it," he says after spraying himself and asking me to sniff for approval, "it's a bit aggressive. I only tried it because it was on special." Shaun comes back and tells him that the driver is here. "Kiss kiss," he says and hugs me, "have fun." He gets up elegantly, confidently, slings the bag over one shoulder and disappears leaving his scent behind.

Storm and Carrington are busy with clients in the studios. West and Cole are watching TV while Adrian, the new guy, broods by himself on the armchair. I don't think he's had a client all evening. He looks like a rugby player. He's a bit dressed like one too, ubiquitous blue jeans with tackies and a casual shirt, probably from Mr Price or Jet. Shaun probably gave him the look when he showed up dressed like that, I say to myself, quietly absorbed by him.

I sit around till two o'clock in the morning. I'm just about to leave when Shaun tells me that my booking came through. "The guy is on his way," he says. "It might be an overnight booking. Usually the driver takes you there, but not this time. The client's coming to pick you up. When you get there you call us from the client's place to say that everything is alright. Sometimes it might not be right. Sometimes they pick you up but when you get there you find that there are a few guys waiting. I don't want to scare you but things happen, not here, but things can get nasty."

He says it quickly. I still feel a bit stoned. Like Sebastian I also fix myself up a little and spray on some cologne.

Shaun soon comes back to tell me that the client is waiting for me downstairs. I take my overnight bag.

"Now remember this is your chance to make some money. If you can get an overnight booking go for it," he says.

I go down the stairs nervously. At the large gilded mirror, a medium height middle-aged man with a clean shaven bald head, stands there admiring himself.

"So this is Angelo," he says and quickly appraises me. "Isn't there another black guy?"

My smile shrinks.

"No, I'm afraid Cole, our other black stallion, is busy with a client," Shaun says politely.

"Mmmh," he says and stands there. I could die. I have never felt so humiliated.

Shaun says nothing. He waits for the client's response.

"No, he'll do," he says a little offishly. "You guys do overnights don't you?"

"Yes, that will be a thousand rand for the night."

"A thousand rand, that's a bit steep," he says and looks at me as though to check if I warrant such a high price. He doesn't seem convinced.

"Other places don't charge ..."

"Yes, but we're not other places. We offer a respectable service. Now if you don't mind, Angelo is one of our most sought after stallions. In fact there was another client also interested." Shaun is rescuing my pride.

"You drive a hard bargain," he says and opens the door for me.

"Take care," Shaun says at the door. "Angelo, call tomorrow and we'll have the driver come pick you up."

"So what's your name?" I ask, once outside.

He takes a while to answer. "Alex."

I walk quietly to the car. He presses a button to open his Mercedes SLK. I slip into the front and soon the car purrs as it pulls into the road. He puts on a CD, classical music. A diva reaches high notes. I don't know who it is but it sounds pleasant enough. He doesn't say anything. He doesn't look at me. He just drives and listens to the CD, his head moving in places where the music stirs him. I feel awkward but decide to remain quiet like him. The car still smells of being new. The dashboard is like a mini circus of lights and gadgets. I say nothing as we head towards Sea Point. We pass it and go past Clifton and Camps Bay. He drives for a while before I realise that we are in the quiet suburb of Hout Bay. He drives down a winding road. Trees form a tunnel over the road. We come to a house perched on a cliff. He parks the car in a garage situated underneath the house. Inside the garage we walk upstairs and come out into a lounge. He presses a button on the wall and all the lights in the house seem to come on. There is a large window on the other side of the expansive open room with an impressive view of the sea and part of the beach. "Make yourself comfortable," he says and disappears up some more steps. I hear his footsteps faintly. The floors are of pine, but bare untreated pine, almost cream or pale yellow, so bleached they are. I feel like taking off my shoes as I stand there. The colour scheme of the room is almost monochromatic. Plump white sofas and armchairs feature with scatter cushions so fat they look like small clouds. There is lots of space so the sofas and chairs are not close together. In the centre there is a small wooden coffee table with an ornament on it. A cream vase with dark brown dried reeds that look exotic stands on top of a decorative ceramic plate. At the window there is a powder blue chaise longue with chrome legs. It makes an interesting contrast to the cream colour that dominates. I sit on a diamond buttoned cream ottoman and put my bag beside me. My tan bag goes well with the floor.

"Do you want something to drink?" he says, standing by an art deco lamp behind me. I turn round.

"I wouldn't mind," I say politely, nervously. He stands there barefoot, wearing black trousers and a white shirt I saw somewhere and liked. It is long and has slits on either sides, vaguely Chinese inspired. The material looks like coarse rag but it isn't. It's quite soft.

"I'm making juice," he says and goes back up the stairs. I can't hear him any more because he is barefoot. I admire a simple watercolour painting of a bamboo reed. The whole room is sparsely furnished but I feel comfortable. In front of the fireplace there is a basket with pale, large beach pebbles. I tell myself not to touch even though I'm curious. Cylindrical wicker baskets with stained varnish stand in one corner.

He soon comes back with two glasses of freshly squeezed orange juice. He offers me a glass and asks me to sit with him on the sofa.

"Are you mute?" he says after a long moment of silence.

"Just savouring the juice," I reply.

"Please take off your shoes," he says.

Carefully I undo my laces and take off my takkies. My socks are clean so I don't have to worry.

"Who dresses you?" he says with contempt.

"I do," I say.

He raises his eyebrows and drinks. He watches me, studies me.

"Let me see your feet," he says.

I bring them closer to him.

"Well they make up for other inadequacies," he says.

I feel awkward.

"Are you always this quiet?" he says irritably.

"You're making me nervous," I tell him.

He drinks quickly.

"Do you fancy a swim?" he says but his eyes don't really give me a choice to decline.

"Sure, but isn't it a little cold?" I say as I look out to sea through the window. My heart also beats a bit faster. I have never swum in the sea at night. The sea is a person, my culture says. I wouldn't like to test that person tonight.

"Not there, silly. I have an indoor pool."

"I didn't bring trunks," I say.

"You won't be needing them," he says. We finish our drinks. I follow him as we go upstairs. The house has an open plan. I could see kids running around if he wasn't gay. A man that fastidious, that fussy would have to be gay. We go through a small corridor where a few sparse bleak watercolour paintings hang. There is a guest toilet on the left. We pass a dining room with rustic furniture and a kitchen that looks like a space station for all the chrome and silver. There is also a sitting room with one of those expensive home theatre systems that seem to be in vogue with the rich. The TV screen is massive and I catch a glimpse of a hifi and many speakers. We walk into a room situated at the furthest end of the house. Inside there is a stretch of clear blue water illuminated by several spotlights. The air is thick with the sterile smell of chlorine. I breathe in and smile. I love water. The floors are tiled. On the other side there are sliding doors that lead to a pagoda. There are also three pool chairs with pale blue cushions. At the bottom of the swimming pool is a huge mosaic of a dolphin. He takes off his clothes and places them on the pool chair. I also start undressing and soon we stand there naked.

He goes to one end of the long swimming pool where there is a short diving board. He walks on confidently, takes one spring before he plummets into the water like an arrow. He hardly makes a splash. He stays underwater and holds his breath. I'm amazed and impressed when he emerges on the other side. The pool must be at least twenty five metres long.

"Perfect ten?" he asks, rubbing his eyes. I dive in myself, but not from the diving board. It is a clean enough dive. I swim towards him. When I get there I find that he is on the other side. He does a few laps of butterfly, his tight muscles working deftly. The water splashes onto the tiles. I do a few laps of breast stroke but soon get bored. I mess around underwater. He goes at it as if this is part of his daily routine, except that it is around half past two in the morning. After a while I get out the water. There is a rack of towels on the wall. I take one and wrap its pink sumptuous softness around me. I go to the pool chairs and wipe vigorously till I'm dry. Then I lie back on a chair and watch him. He goes at it for about twenty minutes. He comes out dripping wet, his prick surprisingly alive, gorging blood. It starts to rise as he walks towards me. He takes the towel from my waist and wipes himself, teasing me with his groin. But he is not my type. He is just a client. I watch him and play along.

"Endorphin rush. It always gives me a hard-on," he says as he rubs himself. I get up, also beginning to get an erection.

"Come," he says softly to my ear. He takes my hand. I follow him, watching the blue water make interesting light effects on the white ceiling. I'm a little nervous with this guy. He could be into S&M or something strange like that. He's got just the right temperament to be capable of something bizarre. We go into a Japanese style bedroom. The simplicity of the beechwood headboard and interior calms me. Simple natural objets of wonderful shapes and lines stand against a plain almost white background. Beechwood screens are half open and lead into a wall of beechwood wardrobes. Between the wardrobes I can see another screen. It probably leads to the bathroom. On the floor in one corner there is a bamboo tray with an incense holder. He lights a stick of incense. Besides the long wardrobes peering from behind the screen, another dressing area is created with low deep cupboards acting as the headboard. A line of Japanese script runs down the duvet. He opens the covers.

I wake up at around eight. That's early enough for me. He has been holding me all night. I try to pry his arm away but he wakes up. "Sorry, I need the loo," I say and get up. He turns over and says nothing. Without any clothes on I walk through the screen and slide open another one. The bathroom is covered with green slate on the floor and walls. The ceiling is a chromatic cream colour with sunken spotlights. It is a big room. I walk around curiously. An open shower is lit by a skylight. It has a strange dormitory feel because it is open. But the skylight and green slate make it stylish and appropriate. Two silver basins lie on black polished granite. There's an African teak cabinet and taps with a curved aquiline design. The bath is deep and long, two people could fit in. I study two exquisitely framed graphic prints of kangaroos on the wall. I take a piss into a stylish toilet bowl. I flush and the toilet absorbs the usually loud shushing noise.

I walk out again and find my way to the lounge where my bag is. Light pours gloriously through the large window. I stand there alone, naked. There's no one to see me. There is just lots of water below, waves crashing in on each other, and traces of a beach. I go to the ottoman where my bag is. I take it back to the bathroom and slide the doors closed. Alone inside I take out a washing rag and some soap. But first I brush my teeth at the basin. He comes in when I rinse my mouth.

"I like you. You wake up early. No point in wasting the day," he says and also takes a piss. "Usually I have to drag them away." That is the first nice thing he has said to me.

I stand underneath the skylight and play with a large silver tap that is supposed to operate both hot and cold water.

"You have a lovely home Alex," I say as water begins to pour. "Very eclectic. Each room has its own feel." I find a suitable temperature.

"How very perceptive of you," he says. I can see that he's used to initiating, the one in control, the older of the two. There is something of a teacher in his manner and in the way he talks. I find him a bit condescending. But I don't think he's aware of that. He stands there also brushing his teeth. Soon he joins me in the shower. The shower has a large head which emits a big spray. I let him stand under the water while I soap myself all over. He reaches for soap on a small shelf that juts out of the slate. He also soaps himself all over while I rinse my body.

"You too," he laughs when he notices that I wash my face last, "I thought I was the only one who did that. Here, use this. It's expensive but it's good for your face." He hands me a green bar of soap that smells of something herbal. I use only enough and don't waste it. I give it back to him. We both massage and vigourously lather the soap on our faces and together we rinse off. My face smells clean. I rinse my washing rag and step off the shower, he stays there a minute longer and adjusts the shower head until a powerful back massaging spray is emitted. After a while he also comes out. I take out a comb from my toiletries pouch and comb my slightly flattened hair. I pick it carefully, till there's an even afro. He watches me at the sink while he dries himself. Actually he doesn't dry himself, he kind of delicately pats his fragile skin. His head is still immaculately bald. He probably had it laser treated for a permanent effect.

"So where do you have to be today?" he asks me.

"Nowhere special. It's Sunday. I was going to do some window shopping and maybe catch a movie with a friend before going back to work," I answer. I put some lotion all over my body.

"Why do black people always like that, lots of cream all over the body?" he asks bluntly. "I also watched another guy doing it."

"Because we grey easily," I say and put cream on my back. "And it doesn't look attractive. But makes your skin nice."

He watches me.

"What are you doing today?" I ask.

"Nothing. I was supposed to go somewhere with my boyfriend today. But we broke up last night," he says, still patting his skin.

That explains the mood, I say to myself.

"I can't bear to be alone today," he admits, a towel wrapped around his waist.

"I could stay, no extra charge, at least till I have to go back to work this afternoon," I offer. I have nothing better to do.

He looks surprised.

"That's nice of you," he says.

I shrug it off. "Whatever."

I take my bag and we go back to his bedroom. The bed is already made. I go to the pool room where our clothes are and bring them back. I lay his on the bed. He goes to the long wardrobes and I hear him open them up. He comes back with a pair of CK underpants, cream linen pants and a matching top with a Chinese collar. I get dressed into a clean pair of underpants and slip into my black jeans. I put on a fresh T-shirt and socks. We go out together, the bag over my shoulder. "Let me take it," he says and puts it into a concealed closet near the sitting room. In this house everything is where it should be. Nothing just lingers inappropriately. He'd get on famously with Chris, I say to myself. He puts on the TV and MTV is on. I sit on a black sofa, glued to a fast-paced music video on a massive screen. The sound quality is hyper real.

"Do you eat bran?" he asks.

"I eat anything."

"Pigs eat anything and you hardly qualify. Now seriously, do you eat bran, because I have coco pops and corn flakes," he says, the generous host.

"Bran is fine," I say.

I hear him opening cupboards.

"Come, no eating in the sitting room," he says after a while. I leave the TV on. I wouldn't know where to switch it off.

We sit on high chairs, our bowls of bran on a small table that looks like a counter in a shop. I eat carefully, taking small mouthfuls. I chew with my mouth closed and speak when my mouth is empty.

"What's that?" I say, pointing to an intriguing silver object that looks like a rocket.

"It's a juice extractor," he says as if it's as mundane as a table knife. "You put half of the orange on top and you twist. You see those ridges? That's how you get the juice. It's by Starck."

I eat some more.

"What do you do?"

"I'm an architecht by training but lately I've been branching out into other things like interior decorating and designing furniture. I've got my own business," he says confidently, not arrogantly.

"Wow, no wonder your house is this nice," I say.

"What about you?" he says.

"I did a degree in Journalism at Rhodes but I'm not really a journalist. Then I went to college in town but that didn't work out. So I'm just kind of taking an adventurous year. I hope something will come up. The year is about to run out."

We finish the cereal. Filter coffee drips into a machine. When it's done he pours me a cup and one for himself.

"I still don't know what to do. I'm hoping that one of these days one of you guys will inspire me to do something. So far I've met an investment banker, but that's not me; a web designer but I'm not good with computers; an intrepid Englishman, that's a career in itself, and a few guys with regular nine to five jobs. Of course then there's you. But the idea of studying for seven years just puts me off," I say.

"What about taking this massage thing further? You could eventually open your own studio."

"And battle for customers and put up with shitty twentysomethings? No thanks. This is just a stopover job. Who knows, maybe I will pursue journalism after all."

"I've got a friend working at the Argus. I could pull some strings if you want," he offers.

"No thanks. It would be wasted on me. You know what I really want to do? Maybe it sounds stupid. I want to paint. I don't want to be an artist, that's like being a doctor, it comes with a title. I just want to paint," I tell him. I have never told anyone before. I have been secretly nurturing this fantasy for years.

"You should do it. Can you paint?"

"At Rhodes in my first year I took History of Art and did Art as a credit. I learned to draw. That's all we did the whole year, nothing but charcoal and pencil. It was great. That was my best year at Rhodes. I learned so much from Art. In my second year I had to give up Art because it was clashing with my major, Journalism. The hours were too demanding for Painting I. So I took Journ II and Pysch II. I played it safe. I should have just taken the plunge. Anyway, those three years at Rhodes I painted furiously on the side. Water-colour, although I don't like it too much, and oil, my best medium. You need to be clear with acrylic. It dries too quickly for me, I don't really like it. But since I left I haven't picked up a brush," I say.

"Painting. That's a noble calling to follow, you know. You should do it if that's what you really want," he advises me. "It will always nag you. They say the gods don't smile kindly upon ill spent or wasted talent. Who knows, you could be good at this if you gave it a shot."

"Actually I was thinking of going back to college next year ... But you're right, I should do it. It's the only thing I've ever wanted to do with my heart and soul," I say. I can still feel the burning desire to paint.

"And you're in Cape Town. There are plenty of galleries and people in the know here. I could set you up myself. I've got a few contacts," he says. He's an action man. I can see it, every decision is followed up, he never hesitates. When he wants to do something he just does it. There is no time to idle about and waste. But I don't have a place to stay. I don't have money. I still need to organise myself.

"Perhaps in a few months or maybe a year I'll take you up on that offer. I still need to get sorted out, to start painting," I say.

We finish our coffee. He puts the mugs and bowls into the dishwasher. We go to the sitting room.

"So what do you feel like doing?" he asks.

"We can hang out if you want, or I can go home."

"I'd like you to stay," he says.

"I'm easy," I say, perhaps too eager to please. "I could park here the whole day. You've got books." I point to an impressive wall with many shelves and books.

"I don't really feel like going out," he says, "but we could go down to the beach for a while. It's a nice day. Do you want to swim?"

I shake my head. He takes the keys and leads me to the swimming pool room. He unlocks the sliding doors and we step into a pagoda with polished slates on the floor. The sea is calm, there's hardly any wind. Cane furniture and a rustic trestle table look out to sea. We go towards the balcony. At one end there are stairs. They lead to the beach going down in a gentle but long zig-zag. We reach the beach and the sand is soft and pale. On the one side there are rocks which look like they would make an interesting climb. On the other side the beach just continues. We take a walk towards the open stretch of sand. There are a few people in the distance. "Your neighbours?" I ask him and he nods. He doesn't seem happy to acknowledge them so I don't ask further about them. A big dog barks near them in the distance. It makes a lot of noise.

"We better go back," he suddenly says. "I don't like dogs and that one is full of shit."

"But they won't just let it go …"

"Let's just go back. I've changed my mind, okay?" he says stubbornly.

We turn back even though we've hardly left his property. His mood changes, he becomes sour.

Inside he leaves me in the sitting room with a remote control to operate the entertainment system. He goes to his study where he says he has some sketches to look over and approve. I hear him close a door somewhere in the recesses of the house.

But I don't bother with the TV. I go to the shelves and look at his books. Most of them seem to be about architecture and design. They are large, colourful and probably expensive, and neatly stacked in alphabetical order. I peruse the titles but find nothing that compels my interest. I go through another shelf of art books. There is everything from history of art to biographies of individual artists. He seems to have a particular interest in Picasso's work because there are many books on him. Picasso, I sigh and remember what my Art lecturer used to say about him. She used to castigate him as being a trickster, a shyster who conned the art world and they bought it. She would complain about the way he misappropriated sacred African imagery and reinterpreted it in disguise as his own genius without ever really acknowledging the real artists from whom he stole his "brilliant" images. Cubism wasn't so much an invention, a natural artistic development, but a blatant type of artistic plagiarism, sourcing inspiration from ritual masks and sacrificial fetish sculpture from pre-colonial West Africa, she said. The objects that Picasso studied were circulating in Europe during his time, loosely bandied as Native exotica, as something to be looked at from the safe distance of western culture and civility. They were relics of the savages that Europe was trying to civilise. The result of spoils appropriated by colonial despots during the scramble for Africa, booty that was the right and privilege of any self-respecting conqueror. To say she never liked him is putting it mildly, she frequently got into bitter arguments with certain students who saw Picasso as a kind of artistic Messiah. I look through another shelf and there are many books on mythology. A particular one on South American mythology catches my attention. The other books are mostly novels – with a large contingency of gay literature.

I lie on the angora carpet with simple angular patterns and open the book. It is old and fragile but seems well kept. The pictures of ancient Inca temples and terraces are in black and white, that is how old the book is. I handle it with care as I turn the pages. I find an enchanting story about the jaguar.

After a while I put down the book and fall into a deep sleep.

Alex nudges me out of a long conflicting dream.

"What do you want for lunch? I usually eat out on a Sunday," he says. Still sleepy I look at him with confusion.

"Oh, anything," I say, yawning, getting up. My eyes adjust to the light.

"I was thinking of going to the Waterfront," he says.

I put on my shoes while he fetches the keys. Before we leave I ask for my bag.

"We still haven't discussed the other matter," I hint.

"What other matter?" he says as we go to the car.

"The money. I wouldn't like to wait till the last possible moment. You understand?" Surprisingly I don't feel guilty.

"No, sure," he says a little embarrassed. From the glove compartment of his feline car he takes out a wallet.

"I don't suppose you take cheques," he says testily, perhaps joking. I shake my head and don't smile.

He takes out five crisp two hundred rand notes.

"And this one is for the company when I needed it," he says and takes out a sixth two hundred rand note. He hands them to me. I open the front zipper of my bag and put the money inside.

"Don't you have a wallet?" he asks as the garage door opens up.

"I forgot it at home." The truth is Chris and his thug friends took it.

He doesn't seem to believe me but he leaves it at that. He presses a button and the roof slowly lifts itself up and folds away behind us. With the wind rushing past as he speeds down the road, we don't say anything to each other. I enjoy the views as the winding road finds its way back to Sea Point. We take the turn-off for the Waterfront and soon we are parked in the underground parking lot. It is pleasantly hot.

It isn't till we're heading towards the restaurant that I realise that we are going to the place where I used to work. I say nothing, even though I want to go somewhere else. Besides, it would be rude, he offered to take me out to lunch. A sheepish guy called Andrew, one of the managers, sees us to a table. He doesn't seem to recognise me, or if he does he's made a conscious decision to ignore me. We sit at a table by the wall. There is a pleasant view of the harbour when you look out. I fidget in my bag and look for some lip balm.

"Can I take your drinks order, sir?" a waiter with a coloured accent says to him.

I look up and see Chris.

He looks at me and there is surprise on his face, but he doesn't say anything.

"I'll have an Appletiser and please, no ice, I hate ice," Alex says expressly, "What are you having?"

"Make it two," I say just so that he can leave and I can think.

He tries to signal to me with his eyes but I ignore him. He leaves at once.

"Do you come here often?" I ask, my thoughts reeling ahead with how to handle Chris.

"Sometimes. It's not exactly a first-rate restaurant but they make nice salads and small meals if you're in a hurry. I don't really like fast food but this place makes it edible," he says and puts his keys and wallet on the table against the wall.

I decide against telling him that I used to work here.

Chris returns with a tray and our drinks. He places the tray on the table and hands him his drink without ice. There is an irritating, unnatural smile on his face. It is the servile smile most waiters wear to charm customers to be generous. I watch him closely. His hands are careful, clean.

"And for you sir," he says to me and smiles. He puts my drink next to me. I hardly look at him. I concentrate on the harbour.

"Are you ready to order?" Chris says.

"Ready to order? We haven't seen the bloody menus," I explode from nowhere. Chris steps back a little.

Alex looks at me surprised but he says nothing.

"Sorry, sir," Chris mumbles. "I'll get them at once."

He shuffles to the kitchen. Out of the corner of my eye I catch Andrew, the lazy manager, giving Chris a harsh look. He must have heard what I said. And then a terrible thought comes to me. Quietly I resolve to get my own back. I was so wrong about Chris. He wasn't that beautiful at all.

He comes back with the menus, saying, "I'll come back in about five minutes."

I watch him walk towards the waitron's bay where they are allowed to stand around if their tables are not busy. He mumbles something to Lance, one of the other waiters. I watch them talking and looking my way. A demon creeps inside me.

When Chris returns Alex orders chips, no sauce and a Greek salad with the dressing on the side. Chris writes furiously. I didn't know you could write, I say in my head. I order an impossible meal. I ask for a cheese burger but could they put in a slice of pineapple as the Hawaiian burger has no cheese? I ask for a baked potato instead of chips. And could he bring the garlic butter in a little side bowl? I also ask for extra monkey gland sauce mixed with pepper sauce for my burger. I do this because I'm not convinced that Chris can read or write properly.

He scribbles on his little notepad and nods his head. But he holds the tiny pad close to him so I can't see if he has actually written anything. Amongst other things Chris is a con artist.

"Will that be all?"

"That should do it. What about you?" Alex says to me.

I nod. Chris looks a bit uncertain but he doesn't read out the order to check. He's too proud for that.

"So what are you going to do with all that money?" Alex says sipping his drink through a straw. I don't think he trusts anyone to be as clean as him. I watch him roll the straw wrapper into a ball and look for an ashtray but there isn't one. He puts it delicately in a corner close to the wall.

"I need to get some shoes and a few other things," I say, looking around to see what Chris is doing. I catch him buzzing around another table. He takes down their order.

"Don't blow it all at once."

"I'm not stupid."

There is a large mounted TV screen at the bar. We watch a game of tennis. After about fifteen minutes Chris returns with our order.

I grimace because it is all wrong.

"I didn't ask for chips, he did. The baked potato on his plate should be on mine. And I asked you to put the garlic butter on the side. That looks like sour cream. And where's my monkey gland and pepper sauce mix? That looks like peri-peri. It tastes like it too." Alex looks irritated.

"What kind of service is this? I asked for a slice of pineapple. I didn't ask for half the pineapple."

He looks confused.

Ineffectual Andrew soon comes. He ignores me. I think he knows who I am.

"Is there a problem, sir?" he says to Alex, that irritating sheepish look that only Andrew can do is on his face. He does something with his eyebrows when he speaks. He kind of raises them till they form a triangle. I always found that it made him look stupid like a shy junior school squirt, hardly the stuff required for a respectable manager.

"This meal is all wrong. Weren't you listening?"

"We apologise for that inconvenience. Could I take down the right order?"

"I just wanted a Greek salad and some chips," he says curtly.

"And you, sir?"

"Make that two. He's put me off the burger," I say and push the plate aside.

Andrew writes down the order. Chris apologises profusely but Alex doesn't really want to hear it. When I look at Chris I still feel unwelcome tenderness and it makes me a little nauseous because I was hoping to feel rage. I watch him take away the order, battered from abuse, his tail between his legs. His head bowed a little, his eyes quiet. That shine, that light needed to be a waiter, has been turned off.

I expect to feel vindicated but I don't. Instead, I feel hollow and shallow. I was in fact hurting myself and not Chris. A terrible feeling of guilt and shame assails me. Vengeance is a kind of self-mutilation. It eats into me that I plotted against Chris, that I set him up. I feel no wiser, no better about myself.

Soon our meal comes. I'm not surprised because I know the procedure. When a serious complaint comes through, the kitchen staff is put on alert to deal with the troublesome meal immediately.

We eat in silence but I hardly enjoy it. Andrew comes around to check that everything is okay, but Alex is in a bad mood. He ignores Andrew and I also say nothing to him. I feel awful and begin to feel a little sad when I remember how Chris used to be the apple of my eye. I remember how entranced I was by him. How he made me swoon.

We finish our meal quickly and he pays for both of us.

"Thanks for the meal."

"It was nothing," he says as we go to the car park. "So where do I drop you off?"

"Actually I'm fine here. I'd like to go to the bookshop upstairs," I say even though I really just want to be alone.

"Well. Fine. It was nice to meet you, Angelo," he says and shakes my hand. "I'd like to say that I'll see you again but last night was a once-off. I don't usually do that sort of thing. I was upset. My boyfriend ran off with another prick in a gay stack."

I catch the joke and smile.

He also lights a quick smile and gets in his car. I stand and watch him drive off. My mood is rapidly becoming depressed. Calm down, I tell myself, it was only Chris. I go to the nearest ATM machine. You must always think of the nest egg, I encourage myself as I deposit seven hundred rand into my bank account and keep the other five hundred. I buy myself a stylish Fossil wallet and a beaded bracelet.

It is after three. I catch a taxi to Mowbray. I find no one in the house.

The bathroom is untidy. A towel lies on the floor and the brown inside core of a toilet paper idles near the bath. The floor is wet and some of Mmabatho's hair is in the sink. I close the door and moan to myself about the state of the bathroom. I shit, shower and shave as expected. After half an hour I come out suitably groomed, my hair combed, my teeth clean, my breath fresh and my skin supple and soft after using coco butter lotion. I get dressed, wearing my black jeans again and the last of my decent tops, a cream viscose sleeveless T-shirt that clings to me lecherously and reveals a physique with potential. Tomorrow I will get a better wardrobe, I tell myself as I lace up my tackies. I change the dirty underwear in my overnight bag but I don't have a decent top to take. I just hope I won't get an overnight travel.

I catch a taxi to Green Point.

The first thing I do is to sort out the money with Shaun. I pay him the two hundred studio fee.

"So how was that guy? He seemed like an arsehole," he says, writing down the details.

"Actually, he was alright. His boyfriend broke up with him last night," I explain.

"So that's why he was like that. For a minute I thought he was going to go kaffir on us last night," he says and looks up suddenly. "Sorry I didn't mean it like that."

I'm shocked, offended. That word has always stung, but I smile to dismiss the comment. The bubble had to burst sometime I say to myself, my mind still reeling from that word.

"Angelo, sorry, hey. Genuine. It's just a stupid expression. I wasn't thinking. You know I don't think of you guys like that. Cole has been with me for a year," he says, embarrassed that his tongue betrayed him.

"It's fine, really. I understand."

I don't want to discuss it.

"You know what it means actually. It's not what everybody thinks," he says and looks for something on his desk. "Now if I can find that damn dictionary I'll tell you what it really means."

I begin to feel irritated and really offended.

"Shaun, it doesn't matter," I tell him while he searches on another desk for the book.

"No, I just want to show you something," he says, eager to absolve himself.

"It wouldn't matter anyhow. Most people only use that word with one intention."

"Angelo. You know I didn't mean it like that, bru."

"Of course. Now let's just get back to work. I came early to give you guys a hand."

He tells me that clean towels have just come back from the laundrette.

"They just need folding and packing away. You'll find them in a basket in the storeroom. And remember half of them you pack with a bar of soap. They're also in the storeroom. But don't use the ones in the bucket, they're all used. Thanks, hey," he says as I leave.

Going kaffir? What does that mean? I have never heard that expression before. It was probably meant only for white ears. You never know with white people.

First I go to the lounge where the others are. West is napping in the armchair. He doesn't look showered and dressed. Cole smokes a cigarette while Storm speaks to Sebastian. Carrington and Adrian, the new guy, haven't arrived. I greet them and tell them I'm going to sort out the towels. Sebastian tells me to bring them to the lounge where they will help me fold them. I go to the storeroom and get the towels and the mini bars of soap in a box.

Storm, Sebastian and I sit together on the sofa folding them appropriately, making two piles, one with soap and another without. But I can't stop thinking about the stupid indelicacy that Shaun uttered. I feel shattered, having so readily embraced them as brothers, at least in keeping with the spirit of the Pre-Raphaelites. But Shaun is the boss and invariably, bosses are also idiots, I console myself. Besides, he isn't really part of the brotherhood precisely because he only gives a straight massage with no extras no risks. And the extras, the risks involved, are what define our work. Our commitment to being sexual visionaries with the fervour of artists is the secret badge, the unspoken password that makes us part of something bigger. As I look at the others, I begin to realise that perhaps Shaun might have forgotten the original motivation for Steamy Windows. That perhaps the whole idea of forming a brotherhood might have been a gimmick he thought was clever, or whoever it was who originated the concept. But it doesn't matter because the truth is we, the stallions, have translated it into our work ...

When all the towels are done Sebastian helps me take one of each to every studio. We pack the rest into the storeroom. Afterwards they tell me that there is nothing else to do. West soon comes back showered and shaved.

"Now when do you guys take a day off?" I ask no one in particular.

"You have to arrange that with Shaun, sweety," Storm says. He loves that word, sweety.

"You ask him a week in advance and you usually get the Friday off. Sometimes he'll give you the Saturday off as well," Sebastian adds, "It just depends."

"On what?" I ask, suddenly becoming a little weary of Shaun.

"Depends how hard you've worked. When was the last time you took a day off? That sort of thing," he says.

That's harsh but I don't say anything. One thing about the guys is that they never complain. It's a strength I admire and wish to cultivate.

"Anyway, Sundays are good for business," Storm tells me, "Someone is always alone and probably randy as hell. It's a pity that the weather's nice. That means they'll be out at the beach or something, so the calls will only start coming in after sunset. But on any wet Sunday you'd think this place was a hot number."

At around five Carrington comes in. Sebastian teases him about his tight, lascivious leather pants. "Don't you think they look very S&M?" he says to me and laughs. He has the most infectious laugh.

Clients start coming in after seven and two of them book Carrington, one after the other. He grins more than smiles, pleased with himself. Among the other guys Carrington seems to stand out. He fits in but something about his personality separates him from us. Perhaps it has to do with his aloof manner, even though he manages to pass off his arrogance as charming, I still find something disagreeable about him. It isn't anything I can put my finger on. Perhaps his effusive confidence makes me uneasy. His boyish good looks have helped him get away with murder, I can see. He probably grew up never doubting himself, his seductive appearance a passport to anywhere he wished to go. People like him grow up with the corrupt privilege of being able to choose their friends. If he didn't like you I should imagine he could be unpleasant, even cruel.

Indeed, the longer I look at him the more I begin to see traces of Chris in him. There is the same mercurial temperament, the same intensity of tragedy about his looks, of the misunderstood beautiful boy. It is a good thing that I don't find him attractive but it also makes me wonder what I ever saw in Chris. Why was I so drawn to him, even when he was a voracious black hole that gave nothing in return except filling me with deep silences and longing? And I think it isn't so much the looks that caught my attention. His enchanting appearance was like a signpost that spoke of something deeper, perhaps an older truth. In Chris I thought I saw someone a little broken, a little scared, but willing to go out in the night alone, no matter how cold the air was. I thought I saw someone who understood the beauty and sadness that came with sunset, someone willing to see me as I was. Perhaps it is just a coincidence that he was good-looking, for there were many moments when I caught that beautiful face looking sad, hinting at the ugliness he had seen but never dared speak about – so that in a weird twist life blessed him with unusual, strange beauty. In my eyes he was like a flower that grew stubbornly in a clump of dried thistles. I begin to feel sad when I think in this way about Chris. I listen to West. He talks about a travel to Kuils River which he isn't particularly pleased about.

"It's my regular," he says. "He's going to ask me to fuck him and I'm not in the mood. I'm tired, man. Or worse, he's going to ask me if he can give me a rosie."

"What's that?"

"Rimming, darling, you know what that is, don't you?"

"Oh, that," I say embarrassed.

West takes a smart-looking executive bag with all the massaging para-phernalia neatly packed inside from a pile that stands in a corner. He tells me that I must take an executive bag every time I do a travel, that sometimes we get asked to go to elite, exclusive places like the Mount Nelson hotel. He says that an executive bag makes us look unassuming and professional. But he says it in his charming Afrikaans accent.

For me it is a slow evening. The guys that do come in want a tall black guy without any hair on his chest like Cole. I cannot believe that people can be so finicky about body hair. But Storm tells me that he waxes his chest because clients prefer him that way. In fact very few clients like hairy chests, he says. Well I'm not going to shave my chest for anyone, I tell him. He chuckles as though to say you'll see, give it some time.

At around ten I get a friendly Afrikaans guy. He tells me that he's from Pretoria, but he doesn't say what he does. It's an easy enough hour, mostly spent fooling around, rather than doing anything serious. I think he just wanted to get his rocks off before facing Monday. He gives me a small tip but for him it is big, something about the smile on his face and the confidence with which he gives me two hundred rand for the R180 session tells me. After that I get another client and again I don't make a lot of money. But I'm not fazed. You can't be greedy about this.

At the end of the evening when all the clients have left, I stay behind and sleep with Sebastian in one of the other studios. Even though we sleep naked, we do nothing except masturbate. Alone in the dark he tells me a few tricks to enhance the experience. We postpone coming for a long time and when we do come it is ecstatic. We talk deep into the night about many things. Sebastian has a predilection for anything unusual and esoteric. We talk about secret societies and the strange, advanced gadgets they use to spy on an unsuspecting world. As always his theories are fantastical, outrageous.

"I'm sure they have the technology for shape shifting. I know that is a reality," he says mysteriously.

"What makes you say that?"

"Because sometimes when I look at animals I could swear that they are thinking as they're looking at me. You know what I mean? Analysing, forming opinions. That there isn't just this passivity that people accept."

"It's like they say ... well, I have a friend and he says that apparently there is like this frequency that you can reach, like above radio waves and all the other interfering electronic signals, that if you tap into it you can hear everything. You can hear everyone. It's like a super frequency, the superhighway that everyone talks about but few really know what it is. And like with this super frequency those who have the technology to tap into it, they can sample any information, thought patterns included, that is how fine, how subtle this frequency is. Imagine something like that?" he says amazed by his own ideas.

"Governments would kill for that type of thing," I point out.

"That's why we have all these spy networks everywhere because somebody has to know what's going on. People could be manipulating humanity without us actually knowing it. But sometimes I wonder about things. Like the other day I was just thinking that maybe there was more to colour. I mean if you define it in a scientifc way colour is basically light of a certain frequency. So if it's a frequency, which it is, then people can manipulate it the same way that they manipulate electrical frequencies, if that makes any sense," he says to me, the room sedate in darkness.

"Ja, I'm with you."

"So if that's true, then everything we take for granted could be like a complicated, sophisticated system," he says elusively.

"Like what?"

"Take traffic lines for instance. The actual white and yellow markings on the road," he says.

"What about them?"

"Maybe that's a complicated system, a type of computer. I mean, think about it. All those lines on the road, red, white, yellow, they could be part of a complex circuit so that whoever could tap into the system, the system being the road and of course all the different roads signs, then it means that no one would ever be really alone and hidden. That wherever you were as long as there was a frequency of some sort, people would be able to follow you, to know you, to tap into your thoughts and everything," he says.

"That sounds crazy," I say and realise immediately what an insensitive thing that was to say. He must have given this some thought.

"We wouldn't have the technology in South Africa."

"Who knows, though? Maybe we do. I mean, have you ever wondered why the whole traffic system on the road is the same everywhere, in every country. It's virtually international. One huge universal system, the ultimate internet, the metatext. I think it has something to do with this complicated system, the information superhighway that must operate on a hectic level. But maybe you're right, that kind of technology would be dangerous. I don't think we have it. Maybe the Americans do. Telepathy is a reality, you know. It's just that the world isn't ready for it yet," he says.

I begin to feel drowsy.

"Listen I'm going to nod off."

"Night," he says.

I turn over and beckon sleep. Even though I can't see him I sense that he is still awake, his mind sifting through ideas, theories. I like Sebastian. He is like a complex painting that demands time and space to be appreciated.

### MMABATHO

After Monday Tshepo leaves. He tells me that he got a place in lower Gardens in town, that things didn't work out in Woodstock where he was supposed to stay. There is something strange about the way he says it. But I don't bug him with questions. The day he leaves, Tuesday morning, I go with him to see the place. It's a small two bedroom flat which he shares with a guy called Jacques. I don't like him from the start because he doesn't greet me when we meet. I don't like his manner. Perhaps it has something to do with the way he dresses. We find him wearing white jeans with a black gothic top, his hair dyed an impenetrable black. I also notice a silver pentagram dangling from his pale neck. His face, his hands, they are pale, he avoids the sun. He hovers round the flat while we are both there.

"So what about the rest of your stuff?" I ask Tshepo. There is only an old mattress on the floor and it looks dirty, probably flea-infested.

"Uhm," he begins but Jacques comes in.

"You can use the mattress in the meantime," he says. "The last guy left without paying rent. I don't think he'll be coming back for it. But I will organise you a second-hand bed from the deposit."

There is also a dilapidated chest with one of the four wooden drawers broken. The wooden floors are stained with white paint. From his room there are French doors leading to a small balcony. The modest lounge is sparsely furnished. An old cream sofa is covered with a yellow curtain. A swing chair that can accommodate at least three people is standing inappropriately in the lounge. It belongs outside, on the balcony, but there isn't much space there. There is a single sofa badly frayed in one corner where the cats have their fun. But the room is dark. Thick heavy curtains block out the light and the air is stale, smelling of cats.

In Tshepo's room afternoon light pours through a small window with a charming view of the city below. He puts his suitcase upright in one corner. The floors are still dusty.

"What about your pots and pans, TV and everything else?" I ask him as Jacques hands us a broom.

"Someone's keeping them for me," Tshepo says. He takes the broom and sweeps the floors. A cloud of dust rises. We open the window.

"And you don't have a wardrobe except that thing," I say pointing to a metal rail fitted in a corner. A few hangers dangle from the rail.

"You can just cover it up with some material or a sarong," Jacques says butting into the conversation. "It looks quite nice, actually. I don't have a wardrobe myself."

But Tshepo isn't listening. There is excitement on his face, or is that relief that he has his own place? He would never let up if he hadn't been happy at my place. I go to the kitchen to get a glass of water. In the sink I find a fawning, fat, lazy cat lounging on the cold metallic sink. It is a hot day. It puts me off to see this and I decide not to drink. I don't like cats. I go sit in the lounge while Jacques and Tshepo talk about the rent, R650, which is reasonable around this area. Jacques tells him about the cleaning lady and about the laundry which he will do for a fee of twenty rand a week. But that does not include ironing. He also tells Tshepo that no one except him is to operate the washing machine in the bathroom.

"I bought it for a bit of money and it's lasted me this long because I don't let just anyone fiddle with it."

"And your cats?" Tshepo says carefully, "I'm allergic to them."

"If you want to keep them out, just close your door."

But all over the house the smell of the two felines is inescapable. Their fur is everywhere. I go to the balcony, hoping for some fresh air. But it is a hot, still day without a breeze. In one corner on the floor there is a cardboard box with kitty litter. There are deep cuts down one side of the box where the cats sharpen their claws. I go back inside and find Jacques giving Tshepo his keys and explaining to him how to operate the intercom downstairs. There is something condescending about the way he speaks to him, but I can see that Tshepo doesn't care. He is just happy to have a place of his own. Jacques gives him a duvet to use in the meantime. He tells him that he will look through the Cape Ads for a second hand bed.

We leave after he has explained everything.

"So you think this guy is alright?"

"Ja, why?" he says.

"Nothing. I'm probably reading too much into things but did you notice the chain he was wearing?" I say, perhaps trying to raise alarm on his happy face. Perhaps I can't be happy for him. Perhaps I'm being a little bitchy.

"Why do you have to spoil everything?" he says annoyed.

Perhaps I deserve that.

"It's decent. It's near work and I don't have to pay through my neck," he says.

He walks me to the station where the taxi rank is.

"Thanks for letting me crash at your place," he says, his jovial mood ruined. He hugs me when we get to the bus stop. "Keep well. I don't know when I'll see you. I'll be busy trying to sort out the place for the next few days, and of course I'm always at work."

"It was nice having you. Don't be a stranger now. Anyway, 'bye."

I walk away with dread because I'm going to an empty, lonely house. I catch a taxi to Mowbray. I pick up a bottle of white wine at Checkers. It will see me through the night. I even convince myself that I'm not pregnant so that I can allow myself this little indulgence. Karuna from Ganesh waves to me from another check-out line as I pay for my drink. I wave back but leave as soon as the woman behind the machine hands me my slip. I don't want to see anyone.

The first week seems long, the loneliness excruciating. I can't stop thinking about Arne. I miss him. I miss his breath on my neck when we make love. I miss his temper that flares quickly and the way he says "ja". I miss his energy, the way he does things with meticulous attention. And as much as I fought it in the beginning, I love him. I love him.

I don't know how it happened but I love him. And it is making me miserable that he is away.

WEST

Kalahari West, dark hair, blue eyes, rugged marine looks, 1,75 m, 85 kg, 8 inches uncut – that is how they describe me. I go to the gym at least once a day to maintain those vital statistics. And the people that want me aren't always men. Once or twice a month I get a woman

292

client. They usually want a genuine escort to take them somewhere nice while their rich husbands are overseas on business or they are in desparate need of a fuck. Rich bitch women who are frisky in bed and always know what they want and where they want it. I don't mind because I like women. Unlike the others I prefer them to men. Which is not to say that I'm bisexual, because I'm not. I don't like men like that. But the women that come to me are usually sad, a little bitter. Maybe they married an older man who can't perform any more. Maybe a cruel husband who cheats them and starves them sexually. Maybe they are not happy in the relationship but don't know how to leave. I don't ask them questions. I usually fuck them till sometimes they end up sobbing about the terrible things that the men in their lives do to them. When I'm not being their psychologist it's a chance for me to shine a little and show off my sexual prowess.

It's hard to explain to an ordinary heterosexual guy who would never take the plunge of sleeping with another man why I do this job. But the men I meet are not ordinary men. They are businessmen, lawyers, bankers, stockbrokers, analysts, chartered accountants, pharmacists, engineers, doctors, surgeons, architects, editors, journalists, writers, poets, artists, academics – generally, people with serious education, money and influence. Even sports personalities, certain prominent rugby players, have come my way. Men who've worked hard for the success they enjoy. I think they come here because they know they will be appreciated, held in esteem. At home I imagine they are unhappy with their wives. They don't seem to understand women and what they really want, or if they do it is of no interest to them. This is what I see when I look at these men. They always make an impression on me and my interaction with them is far from only being sexual. The sex is just the beginning. It is like an improbable vehicle that we must take to get to a certain destination. My interaction with them is sometimes akin to a kind teacher and a willing student.

My father walked out on my mother when I was twelve. I was just beginning to skommel. They weren't good for each other in the end, they argued too much. He left for a life of adventure, travelling through Africa and other continents far away. I never heard from him again. I grew up with my mother and her much older blind brother oom Sarel. He got injured in a mining accident when he was a young man. It's funny, because I'm called Karel. During my early school years I was quiet. I did my work. At home I was also quiet. I did my chores. But it was difficult growing up without a father, especially for an Afrikaans boy like me in a small quiet town like Hermanus where everyone knows your besigheid. At school I was bullied and taunted by boys who boasted of having a father to watch them play in rugby matches. I hated those matches because I missed my father the most when I played. I felt his absence. The other boys bragged about going on fishing trips with their fathers, holidays spent in the Transvaal where they saw Naas Botha score excellent drop kicks at Loftus Versfeld and the cheering crowds. They never forgot to remind me that it was a man who was supposed to teach me how to ride a bike, to buy an air pistol for me or to give me a hiding when I got out of hand. But I never bothered my mother and she never hit me. She was always there at my rugby games, quietly rooting for me to score a try and show the others while oom Sarel listened closely. Oom is very bright, he never misses a trick. Towards the end of my school years when I was in standard eight I started getting into fights a lot. I was tired of defending myself for not having a father around. I was tired of the cheap shots, the sniggers. I would come home with cuts, bruises and a blue eye. My mother never said anything. She was also fighting her own battles, the gossip of the scandal that always followed us. Mevrou De Villiers and her poor son.

She's a tigress, my mother. In my first year at Stellenbosch I met an Englishman doing a postgraduate course in something. Every time he talked about his mother there was sadness and longing in his eyes, but still not the affection I felt for my mother. My mother would move mountains for me, she's like all Afrikaans mothers. She would kill for me. When she calls me "seun", even now with all of my twenty eight years, I feel tenderness in my heart. So it was difficult when I started roaming between jobs after finishing my degree in Bio-Chemistry. She couldn't understand why I couldn't settle down with a job like a good seun, why I wasn't happy. They were dark days because we argued a lot, and my mother had always been my ally before that. Oom Sarel never said much, never tried to replace my father.

I knew why I was drifting. I felt incomplete, hardly a man. Some people feel like that if they grow up without the active involvement of a man in their lives. And even a degree from Stellenbosch wasn't going to make that go away. It wasn't going to take away the emptiness and the lack of confidence. I lacked a basic self love that only a man could have shown me. I don't remember how exactly I ended up calling Shaun but it was during an intensely unhappy period in my life. I had just been fired. I was living from one cheque to another, drinking, sleeping around like a rabbit. It's like that Sting song "too proud to beg and too dumb to steal". And I still had a student loan to pay off. That was another reason why this job was so appealing. The money was so good that I knew I could squash my loan in a few months. And I did.

But any ordinary heterosexual guy would wonder: why men? It's simple. I know men. I understand them. I'm one of them. And most important, I know how the kit works, how the parts fit together. I know what gets them off. I find it easier than working with women. I still have too much inside of me to sort out before I can face women, before I can be with women. My mother brought me up to be open and faithful and I wouldn't like to be like the men I meet at Steamy Windows. But I understand them. It's not so much that they suddenly find men attractive but rather that they are looking for a type of tenderness and understanding that women cannot give. It's hard to explain, but when you see a man with a broken look in his eyes, and he asks you to touch him in a certain way, you stop and put away your opinions and ideas about life. You open yourself up. And that is what I like about this job. I'm going deeper inside myself.

The men I've met have taught me a lot of things. They taught me how to shave, how to go with the grain and not against it. I never had a father to show me that, and oom Sarel ... well, he was blind. I don't blame him. I don't hold it against him. I learned to dress properly, to use roll-on instead of tons of cologne and nothing under the armpits. I learned to hold a magnum of champagne properly, to serve wine, to carve a duck, to eat a lobster, to be a considerate guest, to jumpstart a car, to introduce myself with a firm but gentle handshake, little things that my mother never could teach me. Things that you can only learn from another guy. I learned how to use money, to apply for a credit card, to balance a cheque book, to try my luck on the stock market. These are not difficult things when someone takes the time to show you. I learned to organise my time, to honour a commitment, to be professional, to remember to be always courteous, always grateful. So the money is good, I know that. This past March I made R20 000, that was during our peak season. It coincides with the European Spring. And I was sensible with it. I invested it in offshore ventures with a reliable stockbroker and analyst. A few times my clients have been generous and asked me to come with them on holiday. I've been snow-boarding in Switzerland, mountain-climbing in Peru, jet-skiing in Cannes and white water-rafting in Colorado. Where else can a young, inexperienced and hopelessly clueless guy like me get the grooming and skill it takes to be a man today?

And anyway, what are people my age doing? They are rushing into the job market when they should be thinking about what they really want to do with their lives. They complain about affirmative action and dread the Employment Equity Bill, blind to opportunities to be self employed and rely on their own resources instead of a steady but dead-end job where they will be rewarded with a watch after twenty five-years of tireless service. They are having babies when they shouldn't and starting monthly instalments on their mortages. They have children to worry about when they are still children themselves in some respects. They get married young and get divorced in few years later because they didn't really give themselves time to figure out what it means to be a man and what a woman is, what she needs, what she wants, and how you treat her. And I wasn't prepared to be just another casualty of mediocrity. I also have dreams. The money I make, it's not just for enjoyment. I'm buying time, my character ripening for a better season, because I'm convinced that it is character that makes a man, not so much knowledge. How you came out the other side after the long night.

It is not about the sex. It takes a different sort of man to see that. It requires a different, matured level of courage and weakness to put yourself in that position. That is why I don't see other guys. I don't keep contact with anyone I knew before I started working at Steamy Windows because they wouldn't understand. Morals are like stumbling blocks to them. They don't seem to advance their humanity, their cause. What's the point of subscribing to something that isn't going to help you grow or at least to see things from a different perspective?

It's an intense job because it forces you to think about things, to examine your beliefs, to test your tolerance. And it is certainly better than being frustrated and resorting to violence like some guys do when they are cornered. The trick is not to become too comfortable in the passenger seat of the men we meet and the many privileges they afford us, like Storm.

He has been doing this job for years. He could be 33 years old. No one really knows how old he is. But he doesn't seem to think about quitting. And it is sad because soon his looks will fail him. And then what will he do? I don't think he has any ambitions of becoming anything else. I don't think he saves his money either, he's too extravagant. That much I know, because he has a coke habit. Drugs eventually get us if we're not strong enough. And it is an ugly, bitter end when the drugs destroy everything. I have seen too many guys shine for a while before they disappear into the night. Once I recognised a guy I used to know, he was a hobo, pestering people in town for a few lousy cents so that he could probably buy some zol. The fear is always there. No one is invincible. I have had a passing fascination with drugs. But even if you can use the drugs and yet keep your head above water, you are the worst kind of person because you are lying to yourself. If you are coping so well, why use the drugs? Every time I ask Storm this he gets upset. And the other day I caught him covering a suspicious blemish on his chest with base. He closed the door in my face. Aids is real. Twice a year Shaun makes us go for tests. Storm has been clear thus far. But now I wonder ... Ever since that incident he has been aloof with me.

It's difficult because we're so close. Even though there is an unwritten rule that we never ask each other about our pasts, we still share everything. There are times when the job becomes too personal, when we want to ask the client for a little tenderness because everything is so sterile, so raw and fleeting. When that happens I just retreat into myself and become quiet. Sometimes I find comfort in Cole's arms. I suppose Cole is my best friend, even though I don't know anything about him except that he speaks French, studied Medicine in Nigeria and that he wants to be a surgeon one day. I can't explain why I sleep with him sometimes. I don't know everything about life. Perhaps me landing up in Steamy Windows was life saving me from self-destruction. I was going nowhere. I was drinking. I was clueless. I'd like to think that I'm a different person now, that I've grown up a bit. Certainly my world view is wider. Life has many possibilities. We will never run out of options, of different ways of being, living, surviving.

TSHEPO

**I**'m glad to finally have a place to stay. Mmabatho was beginning to annoy me. And I didn't want to overstay my welcome. On the floor in a corner my books have found a safe place. And I have an enchanting view of Cape Town through my small window. Jacques has since bought me a second-hand bed and a small mattress. It is a decent pine bed but I don't see myself with anyone in it. It is too small. As for Jacques himself, I find him a little strange, secretive. The door to his room is always closed. We don't talk much because I don't see him often. He is always busy. He works in a porn shop in town and the hours are long. But he is doing a part-time course in computer studies, he tells me.

With some money to spend I decide to go shopping and ask Sebastian along. He takes me to the Waterfront where we buy black leather shoes, smart casual trousers, and a few shirts. Sebastian is also the master of accessories: chains, scarves, elbow bracelets, earrings, belts, toe rings, sunglasses, wallets, sandals, watches – any detail that creates an aura of uniqueness. He has an eye for style. I trust his taste even though it is a bit too expensive for me. "But that is part of the grooming, trust me, darling," he says. He helps me choose a tan cotton suit to be worn with a white T-shirt and my black shoes. For simple casual wear I buy white Guess jeans, a black knitted top and black sandals held together by elegant thin straps. I don't get much and I spend a lot but I know that the clothes will give me the added confidence I will need to feel the part.

I have also started going to the gym. West says it wouldn't hurt to improve my physique if I can. Besides, you can advertise your rump while you're at it, he says. So I've joined an exclusive gym in Sea Point where the clientele is mostly gay but they act straight. In the showers a few times I have seen men displaying their erections proudly. No one seems to bat an eye. And in the early afternoon sometimes I go for a walk on the Sea Point promenade. There is a hang out spot for gay men, an enclave like a small jetty except that it isn't for boats. Against whitewashed walls beautifully sculpted men lie in the sun and absorb the heat as though in a Turkish bath. Sometimes they don't wear anything. There could be up to ten men, all different creeds and colours, their robust bodies igniting the air with sexual tension. Sometimes, when the weather is not so accommodating, there are only a few people. I like going there anyway. I like to stand at the water's edge and listen to the waves lull themselves. And Sea Point has the most breathtaking sunsets.

At work one Friday Shaun tells us that we can all have the evening off. West tells me that he does this once a month and that we all go out together to let off some steam. We start off the evening at Biloxi. Everyone comes: West, Cole, Storm, Carrington, Sebastian, Adrian and another new guy called Martin. Shaun doesn't come with us. He says it is the only time he gets to spend with his wife and six-month-old baby.

It is a warm evening in late September. I wear my white jeans, black knitted top and my black shoes. My face is clean-shaven, my breath fresh, my skin soft, scented. We get to Biloxi at around nine. It is a decent disco pub in the heart of the gay district. The men are generally a little older and some look tired, jaded. West points out the manager to me. He looks strange with his bleached hair and his funny gait. West says he walks like he's got a carrot stuck up his arse. His clothes scream with too much youthful colour and style, clothes that don't really suit his physique or his maturity. The clothes betray his age, mocking his futile fight as the years advance. The baggy pants exaggerate his awkward gait and it doesn't help that he wears a fairly tight T-shirt that exposes his comical paunch. He chats to someone, briefly throwing an eye to the door. Like all the other men at Biloxi he is a shark. They watch us walk in. It isn't full. We go towards the corner, near a massive rusted anchor with a thick sailor's rope around it. Pictures of handsome, husky men are plastered around the phallic anchor.

"Angelo and I will get the first round," West says. I follow him without protest to the bar. He walks with unbridled arrogance.

"You know, I've had some of these poephols," he whispers to my ear. He smells of Old Spice. They watch us as we get to the bar.

The bar itself is large and a little gaudy. Two highly polished brass pelicans with pointed beaks sit ominously at either side of the long counter. The more I study the myriad lights that illuminate the bar the more I realise that it looks like a strange altar, mesmerising the eyes. Everything leads to the bar. The best-looking guys in the room are draped round the bar where the best lighting is. There is a bell connected to a long rope entwined with lights. Intermittently one of the bartenders rings the bell and it swings with splendour. I don't know what it means when they ring it, whether someone tipped them really well or whether something just happened. But there is always delight on the bartender's face when he does it. Above there is a nude mannequin without arms, also wrapped in lights. Suspended in the air it looks like a space cadet. Three metallic blue helium dolphins float up one corner, near the ceiling. There is a small DJ's booth up there. The heavily made up DJ catches my gaze as I look around with wonder. I have never seen so many lights in a place, yet the room remains strangely dim. West orders exorbitantly flaming Lamborghinis for everyone and takes out a two hundred rand note to pay.

"Don't worry, Angelo. I got this one," he says and squeezes my arse a little. "You must come with me to the gym one day. I'll work you so hard you won't be able to sit." He smiles and a dimple shines from his cheek.

I help him carry the shooters to the others. We make a quick toast and drink with gusto, eager to get drunk. Storm and Carrington ask us what we want for seconds. We settle for beer and cider.

The DJ plays facile pop songs but mixes them with house music. I'm eager to dance but there is no one on the dance floor. I feel excited every time a man looks at me. I'm still new at this thing. I'm intrigued by the way gay men communicate. Across the room, near the cigarette vending machine a medium built blond guy stares at me. He looks at me for a long time but I feel too shy to meet his gaze, his lust. But when I do look at him, a bolt of lightning travels between our eyes as we make contact. Still I don't take it seriously. The night is young and he is probably just flirting, just getting warmed up for the night ahead. He does something with his head, a slight nod. Then he walks past us standing and sitting near a large empty barrel used as a table. I follow him with my eyes. He goes out the back where it is open and the air is cool. I don't know whether he expects me to follow him. But I don't. I'm too nervous. Besides, I'm with the others, this is supposed to be our night out. After a while the guy comes back, a disappointed look on his face. He walks past me again but avoids eye contact. I watch him sitting in another part of the room, fishing for a more eager mate.

Gradually the room fills as throngs of men enter. By eleven the music is pumping and we all feel a little drunk. I stay with Sebastian while the others disperse. We go out the back for a while. The sky is clear with stars.

"I've never seen so many gay men at once," I say, excited, thrilled.

"You mean you've never been to a gay bar?" he says incredulously.

"No," I confess.

"Well, just be careful. My advice is, don't go off with anyone, you're probably going to bump into them at work anyway," he says. "I never do. Not in Cape Town anyway."

A black guy wearing a loose white shirt looks me up and down as he walks by. Sebastian smiles and follows him with his eyes. He stands with a group of men not far from us.

"Do you know who that is?" Sebastian asks.

"Should I?" I say looking at the stranger. His complexion is as dark as the night and he is tall, his body athletic.

"That, darling, is the doyen of our industry. He's the best in the business. They call him Andromeda, or the prince. He's supposed to be a real Nubian prince by birth. But who knows anything ... Anyway, he's kind of a big brother to us all. Everyone talks about his professionalism. He's supposed to be really well-off from all his work and travels. Most of his bookings are from people with serious wealth, foreigners, aristocracy, rich arseholes who wouldn't think twice about spending ten thousand dollars a night. He gets treated almost like royalty. Like if you go inside on one of the walls you'll find his picture there." I have never heard Sebastian talk this reverently about anyone. He's usually very sarcastic about most people.

I watch Andromeda talking to a coterie of men.

"Now here is the interesting part: no one knows how old he is or how he's survived for this long. If you look at him you'd say he was thirty. But it's impossible. He's been doing this for about twenty years," he says.

"That's a long time to be sleeping with men."

"Angelo, I'm surprised. I thought you would have worked it out by now that this kind of work isn't so much about sex," he says, a little disappointed.

"What do you mean?"

"What do you do with your clients after they've come?" he says.

"The usual. We chat a bit and then they go."

He looks at me and smiles.

"You're missing the point, darling. You should chat with them a bit more. Get to know them. You'll be surprised what they tell you. You know they say Andromeda understands his body so well that he can control the amount of come. Can you believe that? I couldn't imagine a more impressive party trick," Sebastian says and laughs.

"He's watching us," I tell him.

"He's watching you, darling. You're the new kid on the block," he teases me.

"What's this big deal about him? This big brother thing?"

"Principles, darling, principles. After a while they're all you have. They are what keeps the brotherhood alive. Andromeda kind of represents the male archetype, the original guy. Adam, if you want to be Biblical about it. His sexual prowess, his blackness, we celebrate them in a very overt way. Now on the outside this might be considered racial stereotyping, you know what I mean?" He looks at me. "I'm talking about the myth about black men and large penises and all the rest. Well, we celebrate him and the phallus openly," he says.

Sometimes Sebastian is too obscure for me.

"So you're saying he's like a role model for you guys."

"Something like that, except there are deeper implications in adopting a black man as a male archetype. We're saying there is something to be said about the experience of masculinity when you have a dark complexion, that because of history and society automatically you become a threat, an outsider. And because you're forced into this position you see things, what other guys cannot. Your experiences as a man are deeper, more masculine-affirming. I mean I'm not being condescending but I'm sure you can confirm for yourself that the black experience is different from mine."

"Sure. But are you saying that Andromeda is just a sex symbol for you guys to ape?"

"I'm saying he is even more than that. He represents to us the best a man can be in being comfortable with himself, knowing himself, understanding what that thing between his legs is. I mean don't forget he doesn't just fuck men. Some of his clients are women, and I'm sure some of yours one day will be too. You must try and see beyond the sex, you know. Otherwise you're missing the subtleties. I mean part of what we're doing is a power play. To be sexual with another man is a pretty brutal rejection of women. I have always had the feeling that in some respects a so-called gay man might be even more masculine, more macho than your typical straight guy. That because his whole world gravitates around men and getting them, it's a more overt celebration of the phallus. The thing about women is that in a way they have kept us in fear, because they can reproduce, they can have babies. They have a receptacle which we don't have, a uterus. In ancient times the elders created many myths around this receptacle. Men were taught to fear it because it could do this incredible thing, bring life. That is why witches were so feared, because they could use their receptacles for evil purposes. This knowledge alone about what women could do emasculated men. That's why I think the rise of patriarchy, subordination of women and things like genital mutilation have been attempts by men to undermine the uterus. But they lost sight of the phallus and its own magic. Okay, so maybe that has something to do with the church. But almost all pre-Christian societies have held the phallus in some esteem. That's where we're coming from. That's what Andromeda represents. He represents that era when the phallus was also celebrated. Married men today can't do it. Only we can. If you look at those guys standing with Andromeda, they're not all necessarily gay. That's why I keep telling you to look beyond the sex."

Must everything with him be an intellectual exercise, I wonder.

"So he's like an elder for you guys?"

"To celebrate ourselves it's important to have appropriate role models, symbols. What good would an academic do us? Or an accomplished artist, or whatever? We're saying don't be apologetic about masculinity. Celebrate it and to do that you need relevant figureheads. And fuck, apparently he's got a big cock, which doesn't hurt our cause. You don't have to be a gun-toting idiot to celebrate masculinity. Violence is not a solution. The brotherhood renounces it because it's regressing. To be a man you must be fully aware and you can't be that when you're being violent. Violence and masculinity – that's just a myth that straight men have stupidly accepted, very Neanderthal. Part of the brotherhood ethos is to reject violence. Who says violence has to be synonymous with men? Who says men can't be tender? Who says men can't look to each other for love and comfort beyond sexual preference? Who says women are the only ones who understand tenderness and what it means to be nurturing? I don't pretend to be a woman. I mean I know I'm a queen and everything. In a lot of ways I celebrate women with the clothes I wear, the things I do. But I still feel masculine. The same impulses that govern the next guy, I feel them. You know, the best way to understand this is to just trust your impulses."

"I'm getting sober," I tell him. Andromeda watches us as we walk back inside. Light seems to shine off his black skin, shimmering like a black pearl. He smiles at me. Inside the room is hot with the lusty breath of horny men.

The DJ is proficient and has the party going. Soon throngs of men are on the small dance floor, gyrating with energy, like small galaxies. A hypnotic mix with a masterful fusion of violins, slide guitars and emotive poetry has some people cheering. The music is bleak yet beautifully structured around deftly spoken lines about "twisted metal" and the nightmare of being "trapped in the belly of a horrible machine and the machine is bleeding to death." The mix blends into an instrumental cut with electro shock sounds. The bass sounds vibrate inside my chest. All the men cheer and dance, drink and laugh, everyone enjoying every moment of the Bacchanalian feast.

The music layered with a dirty hip hop funk loop becomes increasingly atmospheric, mysterious, alluring. It has everyone hypnotised, slaves to the rhythm. In another song slinky piano is blended with Indian flavour bongos with rhythmic brilliance. Lo-fidelity drums amidst the piano score makes for rapt listening. As we cheer with appreciation, sweat glistening off our bodies like mad hedonists, the DJ eggs us on with more phat sounds. Chugging metallic beats and double bass has the ravers swinging their arms in the air with delight as though praising an old god, the god of dance and art. The same god that filled men with fear when they walked into darkness but still gave them

courage to look beyond, to search within. Analogue synths and glock-
enspiels, the DJ creates a cacophony of electronic whirls. The cut-up
beats drop, the smoky horns blow and the double bass plucks out the
most solemn of stringed melodies. The music shifts from recognisable sampled bassline to eerie breakbeat mayhem.

It is not the usual gay repertoire like Gaynor's "I will survive". The
clinically innovative DJ moves us into deeper areas of ourselves. We
become absorbed by the music. A song with the chorus "Music is my
life" has most of us singing along. An infectious bassline manoeuvres
effortlessly beneath the grooves. Rattling drums and high pressure at-
mospherics remind us how soulful the beat is. The music seems to beg
us, to enslave us to its sublime and hypnotic hip hop beats. Wacky reggae riffs come and go. The DJ sends us into higher states of bliss. We
dance and dance. On one of the walls I notice a large photo of Andromeda, bare-chested, a lecherous smile on his face.

When I look around most of the men are bare-chested, light bouncing and shining off them. I feel strangely connected to them, my mood
acutely serene. There is dancing, smiling, laughing. I catch a glimpse
of Andromeda shadow-dancing by himself on a table near the wall.
He is also topless. His beauty could enchant any god. I watch him
dance. I watch the others lusting after him, feeding off his magnificent energy. A strange feeling comes over me when I look at his torso.
Perhaps his chest is the secret face of a god. Perhaps his nipples are eyes,
his belly button a nose and beneath his zip lies a curious mouth with
a moustache. I look at the other men and see this too. The two guys next
to me sniff poppers and soon smile with delight. When I look at them
I see the same face on their chests. It is everywhere around the room
and everywhere it is the same. Perhaps it is the true face of humanity.


MMABATHO

Listening to the wind howling outside my window, I do nothing but
wait. I count the days as they encroach. In three days' time he should
be back. But what if he doesn't come? Where will I be? I fear I'll go mad.
It's stupid. I never thought I would say that over a man. But I have become another neurotic woman obsessing over a man.

Perhaps living is closer to dying than we think. This uncertainty is
hell. I don't eat well and I don't sleep well. I feel like a wreck. All this fussing over a man, Mmabatho, I keep berating myself. Love is making me

ill. I don't know who I am any more. Where is he? Why won't he write? Why won't he tell someone to tell me that everything is fine, that he is coming back soon? Why hasn't he bothered about me? I keep thinking about him and how happy we were. Why did I have to get pregnant? Why is love so difficult, the path so crooked and thorny?

Perhaps love is the light and darkness that found each other. Perhaps it is learning to see beyond the light and darkness. It is like walking a thin, silvery line. Sometimes I become so depressed when I think about him, I can hear light and darkness beckoning me at once. It is violent. Love demands everything that I have held secret in my heart. I grew up hearing that it is not wise to give away too much too soon. But I have surrendered so much already. I couldn't give any more to another person. I couldn't give any more to a man. And I don't know if I could survive another heartbreak.

It is what I cannot understand that keeps me awake at night. It feels like being sane and insane at the same time. There is so much violence about my moods. I have given up everything for him, my desires, my hopes, my fears. My self. And it seems foolish to be like this because I don't know if he thinks as much about me. I keep thinking about before and how he went off with Nthabiseng. I fear that he won't come back, that once in Germany he will find excuses to stay. Holding on to a bad memory is like picking the only rotten apple in an orchard. There are other good memories but they cannot find space in my thoughts. I'm too depressed. I feel so painfully alone. There is no one to hear the echo of my thoughts. For some reason I feel I deserve this. I brought it on myself. Perhaps to love yourself is more difficult than being loved. Everyday I massage my stomach with oils and plait my growing hair. I think about the baby growing inside me. I still wish beautiful things for him, a father, a solid roof over his head. I wish for the sun to be always kind to him. I don't know why but I think my child is a boy.

TSHEPO

There is something dark about Jacques.

In the bathroom there is a large medicine cabinet. It is mostly filled with blades, old rusted blades piled on top of each other in a small box. I don't know why he won't throw them away but I won't ask. There is also an extra door in there, leaning against the wall. I wonder why he won't get rid of it because all the rooms have doors. I found strange inscriptions on this other door, minute markings that are hardly noticeable if you're not scrutinising. And the bath has been scraped with something metallic. There are deep striations along the inside of the tub. Once a week the cleaning lady comes. I contribute something towards her salary. She cleans the flat thoroughly except the bathroom. I don't know why. Perhaps he told her not to go near it. There are always cobwebs and the tiles on the walls are a little grimy and dirty.

Sometimes I feel Jacques and I are playing a strange game of chess. He is always doing things that force me to examine his motives, to challenge him. When I first moved in he was very polite, very friendly. But gradually I began to sense a dark side about him. Like the other day when I went to the bathroom I found that he had not flushed the toilet. Now Jacques is a meticulous man. His trousers and jeans are always impeccably ironed. Such a simple act of decency, how could he forget? Confronted with this move, how was I going to react? Of course I didn't flush. The following day in the morning I caught him before he dashed off to work. I said nothing to him. And he said nothing. When I went to the bathroom I find that the toilet had been flushed.

And he doesn't bother to rinse the tub. At first I used to clean it out before bathing myself because I prefer bathing to showering but then I realised that this was another offensive move by him. So I stopped bathing and I started showering in the tub, also leaving hair in the tub. A few days later I find a small brush and a bottle of Handy Andy in the corner of the bath. But the bath is still not clean. When the cleaning lady comes she doesn't touch the bathroom. I keep showering without cleaning the tub.

Then I get tired of the stalemate and go to spend a few days with West at Steamy Windows. When I come back I find the tub clean. The Handy Andy and the small brush have been strategically placed near my washing rag.

The basin is usually clean because we both shave. We keep our shaving sticks separate. But his are always the cheaper kind, the kind you have to throw away after a while. And he also uses no-name brand aftershave. A guy like him is cheap when it comes to grooming. In the laundry bin a couple of times I noticed that his underwear was frayed, in a bad state. He would rather look good on the outside, buy expensive shoes and clothes than spend some money on the other things which are less obvious.

I make my next offensive move. I had a small bottle of Aramis aftershave that a client gave me after an overnight date. It was almost empty.

I fill the small bottle with paraffin and with a little bit of my own urine to keep the colour yellow. I smile and put my trap in the medicine cabinet. I know he won't resist. As the days go by I notice that he is using it. He probably thinks I won't notice and if I do he probably wants me to confront him. I smile to myself every time I watch him leave to go to work in the morning, a stupid grin on his face.

A few times I find that when he does my laundry my socks come back with holes in them. And for some reason he starts packing in his old clothes with mine. Old slightly torn T-shirts and shirts with paint stains. I never protest but I always leave his clothes on the washing machine. Eventually I tell him that I will be taking care of my own laundry. He doesn't say anything. But I start to notice more strange things.

Once I come back from work exhausted. In my room I start sneezing violently. That can only mean one thing: the cats have been in my room. I inspect the covers but find no fur, the desk that I got myself, even the floor. But there is no fur. Then I look under my bed where my suitcase lies. I pull it out and find fur on top. The following morning half of my Aramis bottle has been emptied. I bump into him on his way to the bathroom. His neck has developed a small rash. I want to laugh but hold myself back. After that I remove the bottle.

It is strange because we never talk. He hardly says anything to me. And I don't say much to him either.

There is a small piece of frozen meat in the fridge which he never eats. It's always there in the freezer. But he won't get rid of it. And in the other compartment there is an old mouldy pie that he won't throw away either. We cook separately, and we have never discussed the option of sharing food. I always buy bread. A few times I have seen one or two slices of my fresh bread in the bin. Perhaps that is the most offensive thing he has ever done, to waste my food. And I can't say anything because he is never there. I try reverse psychology on him.

There are two elephant ear pot plants in the flat, very badly kept and abused. Several sticks of incense jut out from the soil. And he uses the pot plants as an ashtray. I remove the sticks and buy small cheap fertiliser for the plants. I also water them and leave them out on the balcony in the sun with their withered leaves and pale sickly green complexion. But he keeps on using the plants as an ashtray and burning incense from them. At every opportunity I clean them out. For a while I agonise about what to do. We have gone so long without speaking, without protesting about each other's habits, that it would almost be admitting defeat to ask him why he insists on doing this to the plants. But one day, inspiration comes my way.

I place a book near the plant, choosing a very provocative title: House of hunger by Dambudzo Marachera. When I go back to the balcony the following day to water the plants I find the book turned over and the plants clean. The victory is sweet.

Reading the paper there's an article on homeless children. I take out the article and lay it on the inside of the bread bin. The following day I find the plastic wrapper around the bread open even though I sealed it. The article is scrunched into a ball inside the bin. After that I keep the bread in the cupboard with my other food. He never touches my bread again. In fact, he starts buying his own bread. Why couldn't he just ask me to move my bread instead of going through all that shit?

I notice that my books are not stacked in the order I left them in. Also, one of my drawers is not closed properly. A white sock hangs from it. I take out the sock and find that it is his. While he is at work I go to his room. It is perpetually closed but I don't feel guilty as I open the door. One of his cats, the fat fawn one lies regally on the bed. I look at it with contempt. It just stares back aloof. On his desk there are several papers, and a book with the title exposed: To Kill A Mocking Bird. I turn back and realise that he trapped me. On the floor there is a broken string of wool attached to the door. I close the door and admit defeat.

The next day I sweep out my room because fleas bite me during the night. I have heard that they lie between floor boards. I take rough salt and sprinkle it on the floor on my way out to work. But before doing this I leave a book on my desk: No Longer At Ease by Chinua Achebe.

The next day I come back and find a footprint of crushed salt. Immediately I go to the hardware store and buy a new door handle. I get a guy from the hardware store to install it for me for a small fee. I lock my door when I go to work. But the following day I find another print of crushed salt on my floor near the French doors. I sweep out the salt and lie down on my bed to think. I think for a long time but I can't come up with a strategy. I go to his room, but the door is also locked. I go to town, to all the department stores. I get a pile of brochures about clothing: spring and summer collections. I also get brochures about men's underwear, fragrances and aftercare. I clear my desk of everything and strategically arrange the brochures the way people arrange magazines. From work I take one of several signs that says "Please take one". We use the sign on the entrance hall table where a stack of Gay SA magazines are displayed. Near the stack of brochures stylishly arranged like a fan I place the sign.

The following day I find one of my drawers open. There is a stapler on the brochures. After that he doesn't come into my room again but the tension between us still mounts. And yet every time we are together we are always polite, grinning at each other artificially.

## MMABATHO

The night before Arne is due back I have a nightmare.

I dream that I'm alone in the house. It is a rainy day. Outside it is dark. All I hear is the wind howling. The lights are down. Intermittent flashes of lightning illuminate the room. Frantically I search for candles but find none. Instead I find an old paraffin lamp. I take it to the lounge and put it on the TV. The light is bright enough. There is a scratching sound coming from behind me in the kitchen. I turn round and see a shadow doing something behind me. I let out a sharp scream.

"O jele eng?" the shadow says. It comes towards me clutching something in its hand. I stand away from the lamp so that I can see who it is.

"Kere o jele eng?" the voice continues.

In the light I suddenly recognise the shadowy figure. It is my grandmother who died when I was very young. But I still remember her. She still walks with a shuffle to support her large frame. The rain intensifies.

"Ma. You scared me," I say to her, suddenly calm. She is holding a piece of bread in her hand. We sit together on the sofa. She nibbles her bread. We observe the lamp, gnats and midges fly around us.

"So I was hoping that you would know what to do about this," Ma says and points to her head.

"What is it? I can't see properly."

We go towards the TV. She squats under the light while I inspect her scalp. She is almost completely bald. She has several ring worms. Some of them look really bad, oozing a clear liquid, and she has ugly scabs. Towards the back of her neck she has a violent rash and pimples with pussy white heads. Her scalp looks tough and slightly swollen. She moves with a stiff neck to reduce the discomfort.

"Ma, what happened?" I say appalled. I don't touch or prod.

We go back to the sofa. She turns to me, her neck stiff like a robot's.

"I wanted to do something nice with my hair. But it all fell out," she says casually. I expect her to be upset but she isn't.

"Doesn't this bother you, Ma? Who did this to you?"

"It doesn't matter, it will heal," she says stoically.

"It will take a long time, Ma."

She nibbles her dry bread.

"I wanted to tell you something," she says, suddenly sad.

"Yes, Ma, I'm listening," I tell her.

"I wanted to tell you to stop using those chemicals. They are what destroyed my hair," she says and delicately touches a spot on her head where a tuft of thin hair stubbornly grows. It makes me sad to watch her do that.

"But Ma, I don't use chemicals in my hair. Look." I take her hand and put it on my scalp. But when she takes it off there is grease on her hand. I run to the bathroom where there is a small mirror. I come back with it and stand near the paraffin lamp. I gasp with horror, when I realise that my hair has been straightened and curled. I look different. Even the surprise on my face is different.

"But Ma …"

"You must stop putting these poisons into your scalp. You don't know what they are doing to us," she says angrily. "Did you ever wonder why you little whores are always miscarrying and getting cancer down there?" she says and points with her finger.

My throat is sore with guilt. I want to cry.

"Your hair, why do you think it is there?" she asks me and bangs her fist on the table. Her piece of bread flies out her hand. She gets up to pick it up. I sit there, shivering a little with cold and fear.

"So that I can look nice?"

"So that God can see what you're doing with what he gave you," she says with a shrill, hoarse voice.

She takes the lamp from the TV and puts it closer on the table.

"So this is what you're doing with God's garden?" she says with contempt. She inspects my straightened hair.

"His garden?"

"What did you think it was? Don't you see how your hair is like a plant, how it grows like a plant, how it loves the sun?"

I have never seen Ma look angry. I remember her as sweet and kind. But I also remember her with lots of hair on her head. She used to plait my hair when I was a little girl.

"You have taken it upon yourself to inject this garden with poisons that burn at night. Look at me. I look like a bald vulture!"

She swallows the last piece of her dried bread.

"And you wonder why rainforests are disappearing, ghettos sprawling, why rivers are dying and deserts growing," she says and spits out something. Green slime lands on the table. Steam rises as it sizzles, eating into the wood. I watch with horror.

"Children are running hungry in ghettos, sewerage, masepa in the street."

She spits out a gob of saliva again. This time it is yellow. There is something familiar about the smell. It is the toxic smell of a relaxer that I use, a smell that creeps up your nostrils and stings you at the back of your throat. I touch my hair and it is straight and greasy.

"What is wrong with kaffir hair? Are you ashamed? There is power in a spiral. God is planting secrets in your hair and you are destroying them with poison."

She spits red saliva. It is blood. Her scalp is wet with the clear liquid that oozes from her wounds.

"You are killing me!" she yells in a piercing cry.

"Are you jealous of white women? Why won't you let them wear their long hair? Why do you crave that which distorts your beauty? Redemption starts with self."

She touches her head lightly. A wound opens and a scab falls. Sebaceous liquid oozes from it.

"I used to be a queen," she says.

I think about all the women of colour I know, our struggle with hair. It is our struggle, nobody else's. We have been swallowing too many lies about the virtues of long, straight hair. We have enslaved ourselves willingly. We complain about racism yet we are hair fascists. I cannot blame the media or white people or men. It is my own greed that I must confront.

I sit there stupidly while Ma peels off her scabs. Soon there is a pile of scabs on the floor and they begin to scurry like spiders. I jump on the sofa and scream while the spiders multiply. Ma says nothing. She looks serene in her agony, as she peels her wounds.

I wake up when Ma herself becomes a large spider.

I feel my hair. I sigh with relief because it was only a dream. But what did it all mean? My hair is not straight.

Peter has become my regular. He comes at least once a week. And every week he talks me into becoming more intimate with him. And it isn't because of the good money he pays me that I oblige him. I cannot stand to see the desperation in his eyes every time he begs me to kiss him, to touch and stroke him in a certain way.

"You should really leave if you're that unhappy," I say to him.

"You've never been married. You've never had kids. You can't just leave," he says.

I am lying with my head on his chest. He strokes my cheek.

"I just don't see how you can spend the rest of your life this unhappy."

"I could say that I'm staying for the children. But that wouldn't be true. The truth is I have become lazy, complacent. It's an English South African thing," he chuckles.

"What do you mean?"

"Ignore it, it will go away. Back in the old days I learned that hating Afrikaans was a convenient way of suggesting you condemned the government without having to do anything about it. It was a cop-out because while the Boers took the blame we, the English-speaking, generally took advantage. That was how things were. You did as little as possible."

I stroke his stomach. It is hard and has a few ridges. He still looks good for a guy his age.

"But it doesn't mean you have to go on like this."

He turns me over, then lies on top of me and kisses me very gently.

"Are your other clients as nice as I am?" he asks.

"Generally, yes."

At the end of the hour he sits on the edge of the bed as he probably does at home when he puts on his socks.

"This is ridiculous. I feel like your mistress," I tell him.

He pulls me towards him swiftly and hugs me around the waist.

"I don't think you should keep coming. Soon I'll start feeling guilty about all the money you're paying me," I say.

He hands me three hundred rand. He doesn't answer but I know he'll be back next week.

"You're not my mistress. I wanted someone professional. I don't want to deal with someone who wants me to run away with her and leave my wife. I'm a married man. I don't think you understand the implications."

I straighten out the room and have a quick shower before I go back to the lounge. Later in the evening I get another client. As I walk to the studio Francois warns me that it is a couple, that the boyfriend probably wants to watch. If that's the case, charge them double, he advises me. I walk in nervously.

Two white guys sit on the sleeper couch. They both get up and shake my hand. They could be my age, restless and horny.

"So what do you do?" the one with dark hair asks.

"Everything except penetration."

"We were hoping you'd be more versatile," says the blond one.

"Sorry, but that's as far as I'm prepared to go."

"Very well," the blond one says.

They both start getting undressed. I want to say hang on I thought it was just the one, but they seem eager and I've been warned enough about pissing off clients. I also get undressed.

"You realise the fee will be double," I say, trying to sound professional even though I'm nervous as hell. I put on a porn video, knowing that this is going to be a hard trick. I have never done a threesome.

They lure me into the bed immediately. I feel awkward and self-conscious. We kiss and fondle each other in a feast of limbs. Eventually I get an erection. They seem comfortable as if they have done this before. We change roles and take turns to service each other. They moan and groan a lot, saying trite things like yeah baby, give it to me. The same stupid pillow talk one finds in gay porn videos. It puts me off a little to hear them but I manage to maintain a steady erection.

We get done in about half an hour, the bed and sheets with damp islands from our seed. They give me six hundred rand and leave. I straighten out the room but this time I have to change the towels, sheets and duvet cover. I go back to the lounge feeling empty, like a whore. It has never happened. I usually come out feeling like a psychologist, a confidant, more than anything else.

"What's wrong sweety? Had a bad client?" Storm says but there is a sarcastic edge to his voice. He breaks into a cough.

"That sounds serious," I say," Maybe you should get it checked out."

He gives me the evil eye. The others, watching a movie, suddenly look at Storm.

In this industry, coughing or bad health is an ominous sign, I remember Sebastian once saying. Storm gets up and leaves the room, still coughing. We look at each other but say nothing, Aids lurking quietly in our thoughts. I sit down next to Sebastian.

"I still haven't done it, you know," I say to Sebastian, "and I think it's bugging me."

He sits with his legs elegantly crossed as always, fanning himself with a Japanese paper fan. It is a little hot but the air conditioner works. I don't think it calls for a fan as well. Sebastian is just being dramatic.

"Have you never gone all the way?" he says with his big eyes full of expression.

"No. Does it hurt?" But I know what the answer is.

"Depends on your pain-pleasure threshold. It's different for everyone, darling," he says obscurely.

It all comes down to that: penetration. That's what they all want eventually. It's also what they persecute us for, that unspeakable thing that men do together, corrupting nature. That final act. I will have to confront my own prejudices about anal sex. Too much has been said about it. I think of my father and it is enough to make me wish for death.

Shaun comes in to tell me that I have a travel booking and that I should get ready in ten minutes. It is for the Mount Nelson. Storm looks at me enviously. I take an executive bag and my overnight rucksack. The driver soon comes and whisks me off to town.

The hotel lobby is grand and intimidating. An exquisite chandelier hovers above like a galaxy of light. All the employees look suitably groomed and dressed in uniform. A wealthy looking couple walks out the door. The woman wears expensive looking shoes with gold straps and her ankles are small and delicate. I go to the reception desk. A tall woman with her hair in a bun smiles at me. The client asked me to use the name of Mr Daniels. She makes a call to his room to inform him that I'm on my way. I get into a lift and go up several floors. Down the corridor to his room the carpet is thick and clean and looks new. It is dead quiet. I can only hear my black strappy sandals as they gently slap against the soles of my feet. At the door a tall coloured looking man lets me in. He smiles broadly as I step into a plush room with a view.

"Hi, I'm Arthur," he says with an unmistakable American drawl. "Please, come in."

I follow him into a small, luxurious lounge. A large bed, probably queen-sized, stares at us from another room. I think about his name. The only Arthur I ever knew was a black gay monosyllabic character in a novel. He was beautiful the way black men are sometimes expected to be. But he was fated for a tragic life after he killed someone. In the novel he falls for a rich spoiled aristocrat who sees him only as something to amuse himself with.

"Can I get you a drink?" this Arthur says. "Please, put down your bags. Take a seat. We have an hour, don't we?"

I put the bags down and sit down in a grand armchair.

"I'm having a brandy and coke," he says and pours two miniature bottles of brandy into two glasses. He mixes them with two small cans of coke. He hands me my drink. I ask him if I may phone the studio to confirm that everything is alright.

"So, are you here on holiday?" I say when I return.

"Yes and no. I'm sort of here to see if I'd like to stay here. I work in real estate in Washington D.C. It's been good to me but I'm ready for new challenges. I've heard a lot about South Africa, especially Cape Town. So I figured at least I could come down and see how things are for myself, check out the place a bit," he says with a smile.

He sits across me, wearing a T-shirt and boxer shorts. I can see his balls.

"And what do you think of the place so far?"

"Pretty good. I'm impressed. The place has got lots of potential as far as real estate goes."

"So would you like a massage?" I say boldly once I have finished my drink.

He fondles his crotch.

"If I wanted one I wouldn't have bothered calling you up," he says but he doesn't sound offensive.

"Just checking," I say and pull a silly smile.

"I've never had a real African man. So what tribe are you from?" he says, still sipping his drink. I hate that question. It's like asking what's your breed.

"Xhosa." I know he won't be able to pronounce it. Americans and their quaint ideas of Africa, I say to myself, irritated by the condescending tone of his voice.

"So what's it like being gay and black is South Africa?"

"I'm sure nothing different to being gay and black in America."

"Yes, but Africans are so ... How should I put it? You're expected to be manly, aren't you?"

"It sounds to me like you're the one with the problem. No one ever said there was anything unmanly about being with another guy." It comes out a little angry.

"This is interesting," he says sarcastically. "I always imagined that it would be difficult with the whole tribe thing."

He gets up and beckons me with his index finger. I follow him to the bedroom. On a large dressing table is a portable CD player. He gets undressed and asks me to give him a blow-job.

But eventually he asks if he may penetrate me. When I refuse he asks if I would penetrate him. I still refuse. I get a little upset and rush off to the bathroom. He comes after me but I close the door and lock it.

"Are you okay in there? Should I get someone?"

"No, I'm fine. It's my eye. One of my lenses was falling out."

I feel edgy and a little tearful. I splash water on my face and convince myself to calm down. He starts banging on the door impatiently.

"Okay, you can come out now, you're making me nervous," he says.

I open the door and find him standing there, naked.

"I'm sorry," I say and walk past him.

We go back to the bedroom and I get on the bed again.

"Oh, I'm not in the mood now," he says offishly.

"Do you want me to leave? You don't have to pay," I offer.

"Actually I just wanted a little company. You can stay," he says flippantly.

This is what I hate about this job sometimes, I'm always at the mercy of their every whim.

He puts on his boxers again. I also get dressed. He puts on a CD.

"Do you know what Negro Spirituals are?" he goes on.

I shake my head even though I know.

"Well, this here is by Barbara Hendricks. I think you'll like it," he says confidently. We both lie on the large bed while a plaintive piano intro begins.

"Sometimes I feel like a motherless child." Her operatic voice searches deep inside me. He picks up a book he was reading next to his bed, something about Africa. I try to listen to the music but I feel, restless. My stomach moans with hunger. He hears it and looks over. I grin stupidly.

"There's a menu on the table. Order whatever you like," he says and goes back to his book.

"Do you want something?" I ask reaching for a menu near the bedside phone.

"Nah, I'm fine," he says.

Barbara sings.

There are no prices on the meals. I call room service and order a cheese and tomato sandwich.

"Do a lot of African Americans travel to Africa?" I use that term so that he mustn't talk down to me, the poor African. I'm not a moegoe.

"Are you serious? They won't go anywhere where there isn't air conditioning, fast food and easy access. You guys, well maybe South Africa is doing okay, but certainly from what we see on TV about the rest of the continent, you're still way behind. So nah, most people wouldn't dream of going to Africa. Americans in general, black or white."

"But we're not backward. What you guys call progress, those are just things. They don't make your life any better, maybe quicker. But they don't make you better people, inside. That is real progress. Anyone can have things. You can't even take them with you when you die. We know that we don't have everything, smooth economies, working governments. We know that. And we're working on it."

"But at least we're still willing to learn. In Africa we don't pretend to have all the answers. There's a lot of opportunity. You can be anything. And people know this. Unfortunately we attract the wrong sort of people, opportunists who want to make a quick buck and fuck off back to their country with lots of money." I suddenly become aware of the insinuation I'm making and cringe.

He doesn't say anything immediately. He looks a bit stumped. Somebody's at the door.

"That's probably room service," I say, eager to change the subject.

He goes to the door and signs for it. A waiter wheels in a table.

"There's a bar over there if you want a drink," he says as he hands me the plate.

"Would you mind? Can I eat in there? I like the music."

"Don't be silly," he says and I follow him back to the bedroom, already munching my delicious sandwich. He leaves the slip on the dressing table. I take a peek and nearly choke when I see that it is R45 for a cheese and tomato sandwich.

"So you like this music?" He puts on the TV but mutes the sound, wielding a remote control.

"Ja, it's quite nice. I've never heard any of the songs though."

"Well, they go way back. A long time. Back in the days when we were slaves on plantations," he says and his expression becomes very serious.

He tells me a bit about the South and slavery and how the songs evolved from long lost African rhythms. I have never understood that about African Americans, at least the ones that I've seen on TV. Every time they speak about slavery, you'd think that it was only yesterday. There is still the grief and pain. The humiliation that they suffered, it has branded their memory. Perhaps as a free-born African whose ancestors were also free, I don't appreciate enough their experience. I can't even compare it with apartheid. Slavery just conjures up the worst images of human imagination.

Arthur talks about his ancestry with pride but there is still pain in his eyes. It is like a wound that not even we Africans can heal. I listen to the plaintive music. Barbara sings "Nobody knows de trouble I've seen."

"Why do you listen to this music if it makes you sad?"

"Because you can never forget. After a while the pain becomes your companion. You can do things with it, prove the world otherwise," he says with fervour, his eyes almost flaming with passion. "I can't forget where we came from. We had nothing. We were nothing. They owned us. We were like property."

"We're no different, really," I say finishing the last morsel of the sandwich. "We also have our songs. But we celebrate our past."

"It's hard to celebrate a past where women were raped regardless of whether they had husbands or not. Children were sold. And if you tried to run, God help you if they caught you. You were just a dirty nigger to them."

"But you survived. You're here. That's something to celebrate," I say carefully.

"But the pain, can't forget the pain. You know like the Jews have their pain that they can't forget? Well, we have ours," he says.

"But doesn't it weigh you down to be walking around with that much pain?"

"You wouldn't understand."

"I didn't mean to offend you."

"It's not that. We live in different worlds. To be black in America is different than being black in Africa. You guys belong here. You take that for granted. We have to constantly remind them that we didn't ask to be there and now that we're there we're going to make it work. You always stand out because you're a minority. Everything about you was made for a warmer climate, your metabolism, your moods, the way you socialise. We're still guests in our own country even though part of me feels as American as the next white American."

"Yes but the same can be said about the Native Americans and if anyone should lay claim to America it's them. But they are also in the minority. What about their pain?"

"Look, I'm tired. Actually I have to be somewhere," he says and gets up. "I hate to cut this short but I have to be somewhere. How much do I owe you?"

"Three fifty," I say.

He goes to his pants hanging on a chair and takes out a wallet. He checks the notes before he gives me five hundred rand in three notes. I thank him and put on my shoes. When he looks at me there is suspicion in his eyes.

"So can I get you at the same place again?" he asks, politely.

"Ja," I respond, even though I know he won't.

I ask to use the phone to call the driver. I take my bags. The last thing I hear as I leave the posh suite is Barbara singing "Roun' about de mountain". I go out the lobby through the impressive swirling doors. I walk all the way down the long driveway to the gates where there is a security guard dressed in a comical colonial uniform. I smile at him but he remains rigid, vigilant. The driver soon comes and takes me back to Green Point.

Back at Steamy Windows I catch Sebastian also taking an executive bag.

"So, where you off to?"

"Hout Bay. No time to chat, darling. I've just had a client and now I have to rush off again. I had to settle for an Italian shower," he says quickly. He gathers his bags and is off

Carrington is sitting next to me on the sofa.

"What's an Italian shower?"

"You know when you don't have time? So you just spray half a can of deodorant."

Later in the evening West and I get a double booking for a travel in Llandudno. I'm nervous as I have never done a double. The last time West and Carrington had a double booking together West complained that he did all the work while Carrington just lay there with a stupid erection.

We get there and find that in fact there are two guys, both Afrikaans. West phones back to Shaun to confirm the booking. The house is exquisite. The one with dark hair picks me while the other slightly bald one goes for West. They offer us a drink before we disappear into separate bedrooms. I don't bother about massaging. He just climbs into bed with me. He kisses me all over. I reciprocate. After a while we both come. He has a very hairy groin.

"It's a jungle. Someone could get lost in there," I say.

He laughs a little.

"How long have you been doing this?" he asks, our legs entwined.

"Not that long. But long enough to handle anything or anyone," I say.

"But you mustn't do it too long, you know. You should be shacked up with a suitable boyfriend to give you lots of good love," he says kindly.

It stings a little to hear him say that. I feel a little sad and lonely. I tickle his chest. Most guys like that.

At the end of the hour they pay us well and we leave. In the car I think about what that guy said about being with a suitable boyfriend. But you mustn't lose sight of why you're doing this, I remind myself. You need the money.

We go back to Steamy Windows. It is late already. I stay for another hour at Steamy Windows before I call it quits and walk home. It is a long walk and it is dark. Street children huddle together in Buitengracht Street. Some of them have many sores on their bodies, like obscene eyes. I go down Adderley Street and it is quiet, except for a police van on its way towards the police station around the corner.

I get home exhausted, emotionally not physically. I see so many people and I hold on to so little. Perhaps that is what is making me tired. I'm making a lot of money and getting to meet interesting people. So what? After a while the glamour wears off. The bright lights become more intrusive than dazzling. And all the clothes in the world cannot hide, cannot cover the loneliness that haunts me, the feelings of inadequacy. I cannot run away from myself, from who I am. Money hasn't boosted my self esteem. I look good and dress fine. It just means I'm wearing a different mask. Underneath I'm still the same, I still hurt. I still think about my father and wonder why he killed my mother. I still wonder why he has left me with so much confusion, so much self-hatred. There is still the same punishing cycle of introspection. I crave a joint. I crave its instant bliss even though smoking it now would only exacerbate my sour mood. Sebastian always has. I should have asked him before I left.

I sleep with my clothes and the lights on as I did when I was a child.

The following day I go on a small shopping spree to console myself. I buy a Motorola cellphone and expensive cologne by Ralph Lauren.


MMABATHO

It is early Sunday morning. I haven't slept much. My bedroom is a mess. The kitchen looks like a war zone. I take a long bath and clean the bathroom.

I get dressed and begin cleaning the house.

He is supposed to be coming back today. He might not come back at all. I have to be ready for that. That's why I'm cleaning, not for him but for me. A clean house will make it easier to accept the news if it is bad.

I have been thinking about what this is doing to my unborn child, this worrying and fussing. It can't be any good. If I can just get through today. If only I can wake up tomorrow and know how the rest of my days will unfold. I must be strong. I wouldn't be the only woman who raised a child alone but I don't know how others do it. There is so much fear to overcome.

I still have my dreams, my hopes. What am I to do with them? It is hard to become a mother when you still feel like you're on your way to being a woman. I still haven't told my parents. My mother, what will she say? How will I break the news? All her sacrifices, all the hopes she had for me. Were they all in vain, she will wonder.

Why is it always easier for the men? I'm the one who must walk around while people whisper and snigger. I think about Arne and fear what his parents will say. A native girl? African? I often picture him sitting in an ordinary family room, his father irate but quiet, his mother weeping, mourning for the white grandchildren she will never have. And it is unfair of me to think like this because he has never spoken about his parents. I do not know what their relationship is like. But my scared and desperate mind wanders far, creating unhappy scenarios. I don't think I fear being alone so much. I fear that whatever happens Arne and I will be connected in a way he might not accept. I fear that he will loathe me one day, no matter the outcome.

The stubborn, proud, darker side of my personality wishes he would not come back. The side that wishes things had been different. It would have been nicer if he didn't feel obligated to me because I was pregnant, if he had wanted to stay for me and no other reason. If he does come back I wonder if I will ever feel as though he truly wants to be with me. Will I always wonder if he wants to be elsewhere? What about his dreams and ambitions? South Africa was not supposed to be a permanent destination for him. Have I taken him prisoner?

Does he love me? Does he love me enough to want to stay and start a life with me? Do I love him? Do I love myself enough to bring a person into this world? There is so much to consider. This baby growing inside me is already asking questions and it isn't even born yet.

Perhaps I will say, my child when you look at your father and I, that is all you will ever need to know about yourself. That people come from two halves. I will tell him about the days when people would stare and make comments. Is it the maid? Is he a foreigner? He must be. I will tell my child about the lighter side, the embarrassed faces, the comical shock, the heart-stopping disapproval of the old and mean. I will tell him about our first moments together. I have always loved your father, I might even say so that when people ask him questions which he finds difficult to answer he will always have the most important answer to the most important question. And that will be yes, my parents love each other, that is why I'm here.

My child might have Arne's eyes or mine or hair blond and light yet curly. It really doesn't matter because every time I look at my child I will remember that I love a man. And if he isn't there, I will still have the satisfaction of saying I loved a man. I didn't just fall pregnant. Perhaps happiness is selfish and always looks after itself first while we mortals struggle with issues, short-sighted to a future that stretches too far forward. Perhaps there will be great happiness from this union, if he comes, if we give it a try. I just don't want him to feel obligated.

And I wonder if he will expect me to surrender my independence like most white women when they have children. They retreat to being home sitters. It is his culture to be what he is: white. Will he ask me to stay at home and look after our child? Would I allow myself to accept that role? Me the mother and him the provider, the bread winner? My mother started working a mere two months after I was born. That is what women had to do in those days because there wasn't enough to go around on one salary. And that made for stronger, tougher women. Will I be able to fill their shoes?

Perhaps I should consider being a stay-at-home mum and use the opportunity to grow with my child. Perhaps it isn't only about kissing husbands good-bye in the morning and wiping little tears during the day. Women have made so many advances. Surely I can stay at home guilt-free while others toil in the male domain. Perhaps I won't be missing much. My child will be growing. Perhaps one day he will think of those early years with me fondly. Perhaps he will be grateful that he had a mother to stay home with him and help him along. I must think about him first now. The career, the ambition, they are not the most important thing. I must think about this beautiful little life growing inside me. Will my child have Arne's smile, his quick temper? Will he always ask about his colour? Will I struggle to make sense of it for him? Is it important? There are ever so many questions to consider.

I feel like I'm constructing a bridge that will unite two worlds, Arne's and mine. Perhaps the bridge is the little life inside me. Can he feel my anxiety, my tears? Does he know how I worry for him? He must be a boy. Only a boy could put up with me.

Mummy, mama, mum, ma? How will my precious call me? What will he say when he cries?

I'm so scared, little one. Your father hasn't called. Land and sea separate us. I don't know where he is or when he will come back. I feel his distance. It is crushing. I don't know if I have the strength to have you alone. Where is your father, little one? Why didn't he write? How could he be so cruel? Doesn't he know how fragile women are in pregnancy? Doesn't he know that I could miscarry because of all this worry? That's why I'm certain that you're a boy, little one. You are so strong to persist in there, despite the little turmoil in my life.

What excuse will he use for not contacting me? What could possibly be important enough to make him forget us? I'm searching for answers, little one, but all I find are deeper questions. Do I know enough about him to want to spend the rest of my life with him? He is kind and loving, a little impatient sometimes but I can train him. He can learn to be a father. Do I believe that? Men take a while to ripen.

Oh, little one, I'm so scared, so alone. You are so real. But your father is like a dream in the past. I have to remind myself that he was here. The bed is so big and lonely. Sometimes I feel dizzy with fear. But I eat well and I've stopped drinking and smoking completely. I must think of you. No more Graça. It will have to wait for you. And tomorrow I must go to the hospital. Pre-natal care is important, your father said to me before he left. He was very serious about it. If only he was here now. I wake up alone, bilious in the morning. Every morning I throw up. I don't know if that is from fear or from the pregnancy. But I'm glad I was not born during earlier times when women took thalidomide for relief. But you know, little one, if – God forbid – but even if you looked like a fragile thalidomide baby you would still be my little one. I do not pray for how you will turn out. I only pray that life will deliver you to me, to us, safely.

I fear the weight gain and back aches. I fear the moodiness, I am moody enough. I fear the stretch marks and blemishes. I fear that my hormones will bring out the worst in me and chase him away. I fear that I will discover just how unpleasant I can be, how shallow I allow myself to become sometimes. Meeting yourself isn't such a pleasant affair, little one.

The days are getting warmer. Summer is almost upon us. I have to keep track of the seasons because this will be the third summer I will spend at SteamyWindows. I can't go on indefinitely. Shaun always says, don't do it if you've had enough. That's when you get in trouble. You start looking for easy answers, you start looking for reasons to stay. And sometimes you get what you want. It is terrible how true that is of life – in the end you really get what you want. Maybe not in the package you expected but all the evidence of what you wanted will be there. Like Storm, he has been praying for an easy meal, a dream boat.

Last night he tells me that one of his regulars offered to set him up with an apartment and a car in Hermanus. He is excited when he tells me this.

"But then you must stay with him. You can't leave or choose. You are obligated to him," I point out. He looks at me with tired eyes.

"West, don't be such a spoil sport. Alles is altyd moeilikheid vir jou," he complains, his smile shrinking.

I realise that he is only thinking about his next fix, his next stash. That is what keeps him up at night. He doesn't seem to worry about the commitment or rather the false commitment he will be making. If anything he will make things harder for himself because he will be surrendering his freedom. The client will be calling the shots. He will fool around while Storm is expected to wait at home, the faithful boyfriend. And I have seen some of Storm's regulars. They are shady guys who look like drug dealers. People who look as if they wouldn't hesitate to use force if things don't go their way.

It is difficult because Storm is a member of the brotherhood. We cannot throw him out. We accept that part of the experience means going into darker, unorthodox areas of human endeavour. Transgression is part of the journey. We have always had the encouragement to explore, to try things. But we must think about limits. And habits form easily. It is not so easy to break them. But who says Storm doesn't know what he is doing? There comes a point when you must realise your responsibility to yourself as an individual, as a man. That is an important part of the brotherhood. We aspire to refrain from judging each other as much as we can. We respect that we cannot walk in each other's shoes. But it is difficult to be faithful to this ideal when you grow to care and love the people you work with. Emotions can be messy, they breed familiarity and we all know what that breeds.

I never had brothers or sisters growing up. I played alone. I discovered the world alone. The brotherhood is another chance to be a child again and discover the world with fresh eyes and fellow mates, solitary souls also searching for meaning. I think of the others as brothers. When we lie with each other sometimes I forget that those things between our legs are what people say they are. People have said a lot to me. And they have told me many lies. I have had to unlearn much. Like that thing between my legs. There is more to it. In it's own energetic way it is quietly significant, passive even. It is no coincidence that a gun emits fire that maims and kills. Perhaps some people have looked at that thing only with dark eyes. A gun is the ugliest realisation of that thing between my legs. A gun is a man half realised. But that is not how I have learned to communicate, how I have learned to use that thing. There is tenderness between my legs. That thing is not a weapon but a beautiful instrument, a strange melody maker that fills men with passion. There is compassion for the men that seek comfort in my arms. Maybe they are secretly women inside but don't have anyone to share it with. Maybe the road inside is too dark and obscure and they need a guide. Maybe they come to me because that is the only way they can love themselves as men. At work my groin becomes the point at which everything becomes clear and simple. I make them forget a little, laugh a little, enjoy themselves a little. We dispense with calculation. That is what I like about men.

There was something in Storm's voice when he told me about Hermanus. He seemed a little dreamy. He was glad, perhaps he was in love. The worst thing that can happen is to fall in love with a client, a regular. I have seen it a few times and I never heard of a happy ending. A while back there was a black stallion working with us. The European clients were enamoured of him, his energy, especially the German guys. One September he left with his German client who was taking him back home to Munich to start a life with him. They left with much excitement and fanfare. But in a month he was back. He spoke bitterly about how the client changed once in his native Germany. It was cold, and also, he couldn't really cope, and he had underestimated the foreign culture. Love alone does not guarantee a happy ending. But this job is like that. You are always being tempted. There are always opportunities, which one will you take? When do you open yourself and when is enough? That is the driving question. I find I'm always being challenged about limits. Without limits how can you know how far you can go?

Experimenting and failing makes you tougher. You learn to evaluate another person's opinion. How deep was the experience that prompted them to believe something? The first boundary to transcend is within. I'm not impressed by ideas any more, only the depth to which another human being will go to communicate with me. Anything – it doesn't have to be elaborate or eloquent. In fact, I prefer the simpler cruder things that men have said to me. You have a nice cock, cute arse, great smile, small teeth. They ring with inner truth, a charming naïveté that confirms that men are not like women. They are awkward, gangly, even crude. They can never be truly beautiful and graceful like women but remain the clumsy, ugly creatures they are. I don't mind looking like a fool any more. Perhaps it is more sincere than trying to look wise.

Behind the great façades like money, wealth, position, influence and power there are still only people. They still ache for tenderness. I always thought there was something civilising about money, something that made a person see clearer, deeper because the mundane worries were out of the way. But I have come to realise that it never changes, those with money just find bigger, not necessarily better things to worry about. The men I meet aren't different, they are like all people. Some give me advice about the stock market and offshore schemes. And so I gamble and sometimes I lose a lot of money. But I also save, so it makes it easier to handle the losses. That is another thing I have learned: everything is loss and gain, it is like a dance, back and forth. Sometimes four days will go and I won't get a client. I become miserable and feel bad about myself. Nobody likes to feel left out. In my heart I'm a team player. There is much to be said for the camaraderie among men. Once a month we have our ritual on a Friday night. We get drunk and party. It is stupid. It is nothing but men drinking, flirting and having a great time. But that simplicity carries me through the month.

Men are under too much pressure to know things, to lead. For a man to be artless it seems to be an affront. You are looked upon as a weakling for showing a little weakness and ignorance. Perhaps that is why our Friday night ritual once a month is so important. It is the only time we allow ourselves to be artless, to be stupid and silly.

Who knows really what it means to be a man? I'm still learning. My father left me no clues, no answers. His departure was complete. I have had to sukkel by myself, to vasbyt. It was like walking in darkness. Perhaps my father did me a favour because I have learned from other men. I don't have an older father figure in my life. Oom Sarel is more of a friend. Sometimes I curse my father for his wickedness. It is like a spell. Once a month I think about my father. I become angry. Then I find solace in another's arms. The other day Angelo slept over again. He is a quiet guy. He seems to get on well with Sebastian.

"So, Angelo tell me something about women," I ask him.

We are lying in bed together. He is very fragile. I feel it in his breath when we kiss and he touches me. Something about him is careful. His touch is unusually light.

"Women. What's there to say?"

He snuggles up against me. I open my chest for him.

"Well, at Rhodes most of my friends were women. And they weren't all that nice. Like Rachel, a coloured girl. She was a pharmacy student. I liked her a lot. I thought we were friends, really tight. I knew everything about her. I don't think she really ever knew me, and I never fancied her in that way. I just thought she was a good friend. She graduated before me and went to Cape Town. After I graduated I followed. But it wasn't the same. She had changed, even her sense of humour changed. I found her cold and cynical. Then I ran into some trouble and I had to go away for a while. She heard of it and was supportive in the beginning, but soon she withdrew. I never heard from her again. It hurt because I really loved her.

"I had an Indian girlfriend in my second year. Subashnee. She was crazy, but I liked that about her. She was the only woman I ever truly loved. If she asked me to give up all of this and marry her, I might consider it. We had a difficult relationship, though. I didn't enjoy the fighting. I liked the make up sex, but not the fighting. We had lots of sex. I enjoy sex with women. Anyway, we only lasted six months. She had too many issues.

"But I was miserable after she broke up with me. She went off with another guy. It's funny because she used to joke that I was going to leave her for another man. We used to hang around a lot of ambiguous people at the time. It was weird, but I liked it. The other thing about her was it was the first time that people took notice of me. At school I was kind of a shadow, and even at varsity. But this girl was interesting, funny, witty, beautiful. I never understood what she saw in me but I was happy to go along with her and her entourage of friends. They were all black. It was strange because most of the Indian students on campus used to hang around with each other. There wasn't much mixing at Rhodes. She had a flat because she was a senior student and all her friends were popular, you know, the in-crowd. I used to hang with them and we had a great time. Lots of drinking, going out, partying and lots of sex. Subashnee. I wonder where she is now. I miss her laugh, her energy. We would go to a bottle store on a Friday after lectures and buy Russian Bear and Oude Meester because they were cheap. And fuck, we got wasted. There were about nine or ten of us, Sbu, Dante, Nomsa, Nkuli, Sammy, Dudu, Siyanda, I don't remember the other names. One or two of the other guys wanted her. When I wasn't watching they were always trying to get in bed with her.

"I knew they hated my guts. Nothing had changed. At school I was a bit of an outsider. In essence, that didn't change at varsity. They were pretending with me. I knew this. If I broke up with her they would immediately lose interest in me. Anyway, she left. And they all left. All of them, I never heard from them again. When I think about it now it's like a burst of excitement. I know it sounds pathetic but I think of that time fondly because I did so much. I finally got to hang with the in-crowd, people who had always intimidated me at school, people who made me feel inadequate. And there was nothing to them, once I got to know them. It was more of an anti-climax. They were full of shit because they were so empty themselves. Anyway that was Subashnee."

I feel his breath on my shoulder.

"What else?" I am enjoying his openness.

"Where is this all going? I hope you're going to tell me something, buddy."

"Ja, ja. Just get on with the story I'm listening."

The room is sleeping in darkness.

"There was this other girl I knew, Belinda, a white girl. When I was about twelve I got into dancing. I did tap and jazz. It was only a phase. I'm sure you had yours. I got into this dancing troupe and we used to do shows. It was a multi-racial show – very brave for those times, the eighties.

"In the show Belinda and I had a number together from 'Cats' and in the end about six of us form a circle on the floor.

"So this one time we finish the number. The audience loved it. Now we're supposed to crouch in a circle. I was twelve. I'll never forget this. Accidentally my hand goes on her thigh as we crouch there. She doesn't say anything. She just quickly takes it away. After the show I'm in the change rooms, one of the other older boys from the other numbers, a singer, big guy, comes to me. 'I'll break every bone in your legs and you won't ever dance again,' he says. I was confused. I stood there and looked at him stupidly. He was a white guy, tall and hairy. 'What are you talking about?' I ask him. He tells me that Belinda said I felt her up. He didn't hit me but he really scared the shit out of me. After that Belinda never spoke to me again. At the end of the week she left. And for the rest of the season this guy intimidated me, always watching me. Later I heard that Belinda had a crush on him. David, that's his name.

"Years later I realised that in a different time I could have been beaten up for that, even killed. If a black guy happened to look at a white woman in a certain way back in those days he would be fucked up. Clever kaffir.

"I always felt bad that here was this fifteen year old girl who was going to go out in life with the false belief that black men are perverts. I never said anything after she took my hand away, probably because I didn't think much of it. I gave up dancing after that, and I have been careful with white women ever since. They seem very fragile. Are they? Is that how they are brought up? To fear black men and always rely on white men?" he asks.

"Don't ask me, I never had a sister."

"That's an easy answer. You can do better than that."

"You must understand things were different in the past. Vroumense were told a lot of things. It was just propaganda. They wanted everyone to be scared. The blacks were supposed to be scared of the whites and the whites of the blacks. Things were difficult."

"You know, in America it is the same. The preservation of the white woman's dignity fuelled racism, and it continues. People went on lynching sprees because a black man had been clever with a white woman by smiling or looking at her. I will never understand that about men. That is so stupid. It means your women are weak, that is the position you hold them in. Black women are much stronger. If Belinda was black she would have come back to me after the performance and said something. Maybe she would have told me to fuck off or slapped me, but something. This idea that women run to men every time they have a problem, it doesn't exist in my culture, the way it is today. And I find black women more independent in some respects, more resourceful and resilient than white women."

A moment of strained silence follows.

"Anyway, tell me about you and women," he says eventually.

"It's late."

"Don't fuck with me," he says and grabs me by the nuts.

"Okay, fine. Nou waar moet ek begin? Jiss, I lost my virginity when I was thirteen. Everything happened quickly with me. I wasn't a, how do you say, late bloomer? Ja, well, I wasn't that. I grew up in Hermanus. I did it with this girl who was fifteen, not that nice to look at in the face but she had big tits. One day we were alone at my place, watching TV. I asked her if I could fuck her, just like that. She said yes. We went upstairs and did it. She didn't bleed. I don't think she was a virgin. But I wasn't stupid, I used a condom. Oom Sarel was clever. He could sense that I was near that age. I don't know where he got them or how he got them but I used to find them lying around at the bottom of my underpants drawer. My mother never went through my stuff. She always left the clothes on my bed, so I knew that only Oom could have put them there. Anyway, it didn't last more than five minutes. And you know what I did? You'll think this is disgusting."

"Try me."

"I kept the condom for a souvenir."

"That's gross. West, you're a pig."

"No, but I threw it away after a few months."

"That's even worse."

"Then at school I had many girlfriends. The guys didn't like me for that. At Stellenbosch I had a girlfriend but she was cheating on me with another guy I didn't know. I broke up with her and for the rest of my time there I didn't go out with anyone. I wasn't very adventurous. I didn't go for coloured women or anything like that. I didn't know anything. But since working here I've had just about all types," I say.

"Really, even black women?"

"Yes. I'm a professional, mos. Okay, so it only happened once. It was a couple. The guy wanted to watch me fucking his wife. Very nice couple from the Transvaal. They were here on holiday. He was an engineer or something. Are you surprised?"

"No, not really."

"Anyway, that was the only time. It wasn't different to fucking white women. All the same equipment. Ag, what's there to say? After Stellenbosch I went to work. I didn't know anything. I didn't fit in. I couldn't dress. I felt stupid. I didn't have confidence. I was a mess. Changed jobs twice in nine months. I was drinking. I was sleeping around. Not a very nice period in my life. And now I'm here."

"Why were you so unhappy before?"

"Many reasons. I didn't feel like a person, you know, a complete person. I missed something. I know it has something to do with the fact that I never had a father to point out things to me. Life just fell on me. Maybe everyone goes through this."

"It's hard to be a man," he says.

I hold him closer, tighter.

"That feels nice," he sighs.

The next moment he's asleep.

Sleep doesn't come easily to me. I stay awake and think about the day, the money I made and the clients I had. I think about tomorrow and make a mental note to take my suit to the cleaners. One of my clients asked me to go with him to Durban for the weekend. And I mustn't forget to send my mother some money. Every month I send her something. Not much, my mother is not extravagant and she won't tolerate it from me. Buy yourself something nice so that when you go on a date you can make him crazy over you, I tease her. But I know she doesn't go on dates.

Angelo's hair feels like a soft carpet on my chest. It smells of Dimensions shampoo. I think about what he said about men. It's true, it is difficult to be a man. It is even harder to love a man.


ANGELO

**I** wonder why almost all the men that come see me are white. Where are all the black men? I have seen one or two disappear down the corridor with one of the other white guys. Even Cole says this, he never has black clients. Except for Arthur the other day I have never had a black client. Perhaps it has something to do with money. Perhaps the idea of paying for our service is too foreign for black culture. But even so the ones who do come, why don't they come to me?

When I see black men in the street I'm overcome by how much pressure our culture exerts on us. A few times in town I have spotted men that I recognise from Biloxi. But in the humdrum of daily life they walk like rigid, macho men. There isn't the loose charm of being a little camp. And the ones that recognise me look away. Or they give me a dirty look so that I mustn't come by and say hi. I wouldn't anyway. But I'm always struck by how angry they seem to feel about liking men.

It has only left me with deeper questions about myself, this thing with black men. I was hoping to find comfort, perhaps guidance in them. Instead I have only met schizophrenic dancing queens by night who are rigid grey suits by day. Everything about their lives is secretive.

Perhaps one day I will meet a dark prince. Andromeda is too far away.

Yesterday I had a woman client. I was scared that I wouldn't be able to perform. But I managed. Her name was Sophie, a Norwegian girl, here on holiday. She said that she was only here for a few days and didn't believe that she would have enough time to get to meet a South African black man. She was very specific about him being black. She also said that she'd read too much about South African men and rape. So she decided that her safest bet was a massage parlour.

We had an interesting enough time. She spoke a lot. But unlike men who go to bed immediately if sex is all they want from me, Sophie asked for a massage. I had to work a little. My massage technique has gotten better.

So she's lying on the massaging table, her slim figure exposed, a Celtic tattoo on her calf. I feel strangely calm. After massaging her feet, legs and lower back, she asks me to massage her while lying on the bed. We move to the bed. I open the covers and put a towel there. Perhaps ten minutes go by and nothing happens, I just massage her. Then I realise that even though she's paying, she still expects me to make the first move. I touch her breast and press her inner thigh in a sensitive spot. There are seven lethal spots on a woman's body. She moans, and soon we are kissing. That is another thing about women. It is impossible to do a trick with them without kissing them. It's easier with men, it's kind of an unwritten rule that even the clients understand, no kissing. But women are different. Perhaps they associate us with their husbands or boyfriends.

I don't protest when we kiss but I don't enjoy the kissing either. We pet heavily, but for me it is mechanical. After a while she gleefully puts a condom on me.

She is a pretty girl. Any straight guy would die to be in bed with her. I look at her soft blue eyes and feign enthusiasm as I kiss her. Soon I'm inside her and she is wet. I look at the clock and I still have half an hour. Her thighs are firm and smooth, no prickly hairs. We pump and grind against each other. The smell of our sex is unmistakable. The smell of a woman's sex is unmistakable. We try several positions. They all expect it. I'm also expected to moan. I go at it with passion but with the discipline of a professional. Soon the stickiness makes squelching sounds, her body wet and glistening. She comments that I have a nice arse. I tell her that she has shapely boobs and a beautiful mouth.

For a while I don't kiss her, I just pump. She stops half way just so that I must kiss her. You're dealing with a woman, I remind myself. She moans. She presses my bum, encouraging me to go deeper inside her. She says something in Norwegian. She scratches my back. She closes her eyes and drifts off in her own fantasy.

A strange thing happens. I watch her and want to laugh. There is something so comical about watching a woman having sex. They let go so completely. Really, it makes me want to laugh. I have to hold myself back as I watch her face twisted in comical expressions, moaning about things that only she knows about. I thrust quicker and deeper into her. Her expression becomes too much. I have to hide my laugh by pretending to moan harder. I can't help it.

Five minutes before time up I go at it like an industrial pump. She breaks into short frantic breaths as I reach climax, her body vigorously shaking and moving beneath me like a building about to collapse. We both lie back to recover our breaths. Instinctively she puts her head on my chest. It feels awkward but I let her. I give her a towel and we go to the bathroom to shower where she kisses me again. We talk about what she can do in Cape Town with the few days she has left. In the bedroom she dresses slowly, taking her time, like all women when they dress. I'm so used to guys getting it off and on in five minutes. She pays me well, R600, and she goes smiling.

I feel strangely guilty after taking her money. I feel like a whore. I even think about my mother but dismiss this thought quickly and straighten out the room. I pay Shaun the studio cut and my A&R costs for the week. I have my own line in the Cape Ads – Exotic Angelo, and my cellphone number.

My next client is about my age. He is good-looking but in a rugged sort of way. Something about his mouth and his chin with a cleft reminds me of a cowboy. He asks me if I'm versatile. That means, would I go all the way? And for the first time I accept. I don't think about my parents or my culture. I just do it. Perhaps it has something to do with the guilt I feel over Sophie. Perhaps it is just that this guy is good-looking and friendly. We both use condoms.

It feels a little strange because I have had such a bad experience with men. But this cowboy touches me in the right places with the right mixture of tenderness and aggression. I forget everything I mean to anyone, even myself. We burn a lot of energy and use plenty of KY jelly. He is playful and adventurous about it, trying this, laughing about that.

Afterwards he leaves me with R700 and a large hickey on my neck. I go back to the lounge with a smile on my face. The world can send me to hell if it wants. I would go if my cowboy was there.

Quietly I have held my body a prisoner. I put limits on my body, cordoned off a certain part of me. I starved myself of the curiosity of discovery. Every time they asked me if I was versatile I said no. I have done that, no thanks, I cried in my thoughts. Love hurts. The truth is it takes courage to love a man, to sleep with him. That is all there is to it. It has nothing to do with the sordid pictures that people imagine when they think of two men having sex. Gay men are as clean as other people, and anal sex is nothing new. It is not even a gay invention. So why the uproar about it? Why shouldn't two men show each other love, the way they want? Who is anyone to judge the same impulses that govern all of us?

So I'm having this conversation with myself after the cowboy fucked me. We didn't make love. It was wet and slippery, not love. He fucked me and he fucked me real good. I'm thinking why have I held myself in bondage? No one is going to liberate me. Who am I waiting for? What am I waiting for? It's not like anything is going to change. There are always going to be those who disapprove. There will always be bigots, hypocrites, hetero-fascists who only want to further their own prejudices and intolerance of life. What was I waiting for? The earth didn't open up and swallow me. Permission? Whose permission? Who really cares? Who knows anything about me, what I'm capable of? Surely that should be more important than what I do with men in bed. Permission? Fuck permission. I'm doing this for myself, because I want to. Perhaps this is the last rite of passage for me: liberating my body. No one should tell me what I can and can't do with it, when it is I who face loneliness, despair, confusion. No one has all the answers. No one has all the reasons. Life is not built on superiorities.

To love a man? It is like feeling the roaring ocean inside you. It is like knowing the source of the north wind. It is like getting your reward at the top of a mountain, a breathtaking panorama. It is like running with wild horses, panting with excitement. It is like deep sea diving, with the water below being perfectly clear. It is like walking on the beach naked, the sun licking your sweat. It is like falling backwards and laughing after realising there is nothing to fear.

To explore a man's body? It is like getting to know your own shadow intimately. It is like being a child again. It is like playing with fire safely and not getting burned. It is like snowboarding without drugs, with skill as your high. It is like skiing in your own backyard. It is like big wave surfing, decimating waves of any size. It is like making an ollie waist height from flat. It is like rollerblading on the highway. It is like white water rafting down the Zambezi. To love a man is not like loving a woman.

To be with a man, to feel his strength? It is like a road whose twists and bends you know well. It is like knowing all the answers to all the questions in an exam. It is like being passed before being tested. It is like being in a foreign country but speaking their language. It is like being welcomed to the carnival. It is like singing alone and hearing your echo. It is like dancing with the one that has been flirting with you all night

To know a man? It is like serenading yourself and all men. It is like having the choice of all the delicious forbidden fruit in a garden. It is like hearing butterflies sing. It is like hearing the music and understanding it. It is like being the orchestra. It is like being the matador and the bull, the ballerina and the audience, Fred and Ginger. It is like having your cake and eating it, scraping the depths of desire and satisfaction. It is like scaling a sacred sequoia. It is like knowing a secret that everyone is asleep to.

Oh, the infinite beauty of a man and his penis.


### SEBASTIAN

**I** have a ritual. Every day I wank, sometimes for an hour. I think about all the men I lust after when I do this. I think about all the ones I see on TV and the movies. The sometimes stupid ones wielding guns like toys. The ones burning with machismo and who always get the girl, the ones who think with their dicks and joke about it. The classic adventure hero type – if only they knew the sordid things I did with them in my fantasies. I think about them and masturbate. In my mind I do things that bring pleasure to both of us. It is my ritual. It is my magic, my anti-spell for impotent men who are leading us further towards the abyss. It is my small contribution to advancing peace. There are too many idiots wielding guns; I would rather be an insatiable hedonist. So I masturbate instead of joining the ranks and carrying a gun. Every day I do this, faithfully. It is my ritual. Instead of spilling another's blood I spill my own seed, gladly, passionately, wastefully. I am the profligate son. Everyday I have wild sex in my thoughts and bring peace to the questions that haunt me. I also have my ghosts.

I have scars on the insides of my wrists. I wear anything to cover them up, scarves, watches, bracelets. I have since decided that death chooses us, even suicide.

I was fifteen and in love with a boy called Stephen. At school in class he used to sit across from me. He would devastate me with his dimples

335

and dark eyes. I always knew I was different. I figured out early that it was sexual, that all that latent energy inside that made me a stranger and a loner was something that made me who I was. I longed for Stephen, yet I don't think I ever existed in his thoughts.

One day after sport in the afternoon Stephen asks me to meet him in the change rooms. He must have sensed that I like him. So I follow him. No one is there except us. There is the rank smell of sweat. He stands towards the showers with his tog bag in his hand, a mysterious smile on his face. I say nothing. He says nothing. But excitement wells up in my chest. He starts undressing. First he takes off his shoes and then his socks. All the time he watches me, carefully. I stare at him. And then he takes off his T-shirt. I move closer. I want to touch him. I want to say something but I'm nervous. He rubs his chest and his hand moves to his crotch. He grabs it. I stare, lusting after him, a frantic erection growing in my shorts.

"Do you want this?" he teases me.

I say nothing. I just stretch out my hand to touch his.

"Okay guys, you can come out," he suddenly shouts to the back. His expression becomes mocking.

I hear the toilet doors at the back of the change rooms opening. Six guys, all Stephen's friends, come out and walk towards me, swaggering, sniggering.

Blood drains from my face. I want to die, to shrivel up and wither. I have never been so embarrassed, so humiliated.

"So you're a moffie, Bastian," Stephen says.

I look at his beautiful face and imagine daggers flying towards me.

The others grab me from behind.

"Is this what you wanted?" Stephen says and drops his shorts, revealing his cock and balls.

The others laugh. They laugh and hold my arms behind my back. Stephen pulls up his shorts again. They push me towards the toilets into one of the cubicles.

"Do it," I hear Stephen say to them.

They shove my head into a dirty toilet bowl and flush. I struggle and scream but they overpower me.

Perhaps I will never forgive Stephen. But that night at home, humiliated, I steal one of my older brother's hunting knives. I run a hot bath. But as fate would have it, I forget to lock the door. My mother intervenes.

I don't go back to school for the rest of the year.

It was a long and lonely time in my life. But I decided that I was never going to be shy about loving men again. At night when I had fantasies, I stopped feeling guilty. I learned how to arouse myself, how to love my anus. I would spend an hour in bed, wanking to men who always loved me and wanted me. It made it easier to forget Stephen and the humiliation I suffered.

Wanking is my ritual. When I feel terrible and moody, I wank. When I feel lonely and sad I wank. When I'm happy and horny I wank. It is like using my own resources, finding my own strengths, licking my own wounds, nursing my own ego, celebrating my own victories.

At work I find pleasure in men. I don't get women clients because I'm too camp, and effeminate. I'm considered a sissy, a queen, and I revel in the blurry path I travel. The men that come for me are not looking for a woman. Sometimes they are not even looking for a man. Perhaps they want someone who can resolve the differences between the two sexes. Perhaps they want a woman who ejaculates like a man. Or a man who can be penetrated like a woman.

I take pleasure in my work. And like all queens I take pride in how I look. My luxuriant dark hair, my long legs and delicate profile, perhaps they are gifts. Sometimes I dress up. Sometimes during the day I go to town dressed as a woman. It is an art form. It is older than writing. It is an ode to the wise and open, the ancient and initiated. It is an ode to the beautiful enchantress in Japanese Kabuki theatre who is really a man, an ode to the oracle of Delphi whom I imagine as a drag artist, an ode to St Sebastian, my namesake. An ode to Thor in Norse mythology when he dressed up as a woman in order to retrieve Mjollnir, the potent and powerful hammer the giants had stolen from him.

When it was discovered that he was a Christian who converted soldiers, Sebastian was ordered to be killed by arrows. The archers left him for dead but a Christian widow nursed him back to health. Tragically Diocletian condemned him to be beaten to death. His body was thrown into a sewer but found by another pious woman. She dreamed that Sebastian told her to bury him near the catacombs. When I look at paintings and sculptures of him, naked and bound to a tree in an image that courts paganism, I'm reminded of the tragic lives that so many of my sisters have lead. The quiet inner beauty of a drag queen, the sadness behind the mask of make-up, behind the careful gestures and the furious wit and charm. She is like Pierrot, the sad clown of the Italian commedia dell'arte; forever fated as the unsuccessful lover who falls victim to the pranks of his fellow comedians.

We queens have quietly been living in the shadow of women for so long, observing them, scrutinising and refining their gestures, reinterpreting and exaggerating their gait. Being in drag is performing. Perhaps it is the highest compliment a man can pay women. Perhaps it is hinting at what a liberated woman could be like. But other times being in drag is power play. There are those who know who you are and there are those who blindly fall under your spell. The thrill and danger of fooling innocent men is always there. Perhaps we are here to remind the world that life is not innocent, that she is a whore, a nymphomaniac who likes to take chances.

Perhaps it is no coincidence that I have ended up doing this kind of work. Where else can a girl with style and wit go? There are never any vacancies for us. So we create our own world and live in a parallel reality.

My mother doesn't wonder what will become of me. She doesn't ask me what I will do when I grow up. And my father never asks me anything about my life. It is like being consigned to the outskirts of life. I am my own best friend, my only ally. Confidants come and go. Aids has been so brutal, so unforgiving to so many of my sisters.

St Sebastian, sometimes I think of him and fantasize about his manic death, all those phallic arrows ending my life in one orgy of violence, my blood dripping like semen. Sometimes it is easier to confront life when you wish for death. It makes it easier to handle disappointment and the cold heart of life – that bitch, she is too busy having a good time to care about anyone. So I don't waste my breath praying for answers that will bring sense to my questions even though I yearn for the peace and sobriety of married couples, the spirit of children.

I have grown up too quickly and I have grown up in funny places. It doesn't surprise me that I have such a voracious libido. It is my way of longing for love, companionship, trust. The truth is gay men, we can be whores. We sleep around because we are all we have but we don't see that. I have also done my rounds in dark alleys, in shopping centres, public toilets, gyms, parks, unlit roads, dark rooms in seedy night clubs hunting for sex like a shark, craving the smell of another man. I have also cruised beaches. It is not the rough and eager groping of a stranger that keeps me coming back, it is the feeling that I cannot overcome the loneliness inside. Poor Sebastian, they said of me after I slit my wrists. It has always followed me.

Perhaps the best I can be is to do what I do best and that is to entertain men and their fragile egos. To titillate them, to make them come like a flood and celebrate that; to camp it up, live it up with verve and style like a worldly geisha. Queens, we always seem to be having the time of our lives in public. Yes, honey, girlfriend, sugar plum, angel cake. Perhaps that is our understanding of what it means to be a man, to be unsung, censored, banished to the shadows of the night because of that bitch, life. She is too busy sucking cock to care. Where are all the sisters when you need them walking alone through a shopping mall in stilettos? Where is their comfort and support when the shoe attendant refuses to let you try on stunning platform shoes that you fancy because you are a size nine? Or that skirt you couldn't resist? Where are all the men when homophobes beat us senseless, death deep-throating us? Why do policemen snigger when we report rape?

I have tried them all: love, sex and drugs. I hold on to the drugs. Sex is a job. Love is sex inside out, it has the biggest dick because it buggers you inside out.

Every day I perform my ritual.

Every day I wank and I enjoy it.

I feel closer to myself and truer to my instincts as a prowling male when I wank.

I know how my semen tastes. I know how other men taste.


MMABATHO

He hasn't come back.

On the third day I resume going to lectures. We talk about the end of year project and the final performance piece. I listen but I'm not really there. The threat was always there, I say to myself, he might not come back. I go through the day in a doleful mood, haphazardly taking notes. I go home as soon as I can.

I cook supper early, at around four. I make lasagna and a Greek salad but I eat the salad without dressing. There is a knock at the door. In town I bumped into Karuna, she said she would come over to fetch me for a drink. I go to the door, already thinking of some excuse for not going out.

But it is him. Arne. He stands there with his suitcase and a bag over his shoulder, a smile on his face.

"Are you going to let me in?"

I still can't say anything.

"Your hair has grown."

"You could have called," I then manage to say and walk back into the house.

I go back to my meal. He trundles behind with his luggage.

"Nice to see you too," he says sarcastically as he goes to the bedroom. The house is spotless. I even have a vase of fresh carnations on the coffee table. They cheered me up.

He comes back to me in the kitchen.

"Is there some leftovers?" he says up close, but he doesn't touch me.

He pulls out the small tray of lasagna from the oven and dishes out half. He also helps himself to the salad.

We sit on the stools and eat. I feel awkward, but anger takes precedence.

"I know I should have called. I just thought it would be good for us if we didn't hear from each other for two weeks."

I just give him a stern look.

"I wanted to think this out clearly. And I have. I want to be here. I want to be a father. I want us," he goes on.

I take my time chewing, hardly looking at him.

"I didn't want to say something I would later regret. I needed to be sure. Please look at me," he begs and lifts my chin gently. That is the first time he touches me.

"You bastard. I could have miscarried with all the stress you put me through. What if I had lost the baby, you selfish prick?"

"I'm sorry. I thought ..."

"You thought wrong. You weren't thinking about me. You weren't thinking about us. You were thinking about yourself. And if this is the kind of commitment you're showing me, if this is what you think commitment is, then get out. Leave. I don't want to have this baby with you. I can look after myself." I take my plate and clear the remains into the bin. I go to the sink and start washing the dishes.

After a while he comes to me. He puts his hand on my shoulder. I shiver with anger, with fear, with pain and all the loneliness he left me with.

"I'm sorry," he says again.

"This is not a joke. This is for real. I'm pregnant, Arne. I'm going to be a mother," I tell him, my hands wet as the hot water fills the sink.

"I love you," he says.

"Really? Well, that's not enough. That's not going to put clothes on the baby's back. It doesn't pay the rent either."

"What do you want me to say?"

"I want you to be here for me if you care, if you want to be a father. I don't want to wake up in the morning alone, throwing up and looking for you. I don't want to sit in a maternity clinic alone. Do you understand? This is no joke."

"All I've done is think about you and the baby. Don't you know I'm planning my life around you?" he goes on.

"Don't plan it around us. Either you're with us or not." He moves his hand from my shoulder.

"You're just pissed off," he says and goes back to his meal.

"How dare you? Why shouldn't I be angry, after the way you left me?" I shout.

"Me. What about you? Where were you when I left?"

"That's different. I didn't endanger your life."

For a while we keep quiet. When he has finished he places his plate in the sink and his arms around me, his crotch against me, his smell on me.

"I'm sorry. I missed you. All I did was think about you," he says to my ear and kisses me.

I keep washing the dishes. He holds me. For a while I stand there with my hands in the sink, looking out the window, my lover strangely clinging to me. Do I want this? Do I need him?

I feel his erection against me.

"Look, I'm pissed off. I need to be like that for now." He lets go of me and goes to the sofa and switches on the TV. He watches cartoons.

I keep looking at him as I wipe the dishes. I keep wondering about him. Perhaps he was with another woman. Perhaps his mother said go back and be a man. Perhaps his father disowned him.

After I've finished in the kitchen I go to the bathroom. I run a bath and soak my anger. I hear the door handle turn. He gives up after he realises that I've locked it.

I come out after half an hour. I find him in the bedroom, on his side of the bed, sitting there with his head bent low, his elbows on his knees. The light is dim.

"Don't break up with me. Please. Don't leave me. I need you," he says and lifts his head. There are tears in his eyes. He sits there, fidgeting with his hands in his lap.

"I thought I'd lost you," I say and come closer. He gets up and hugs me, tears still in his eyes. I have cried too much over the last two weeks. I hold him, while he cries, my throat aching.

"This child needs a father. I can't tell you how to be a man," I say tenderly and feel his wet cheek.

**B**efore work I go to a posh bar in Green Point's gay district called New Yorkers. It has been a slow week. I have only had one client in the last four days. It happens sometimes, West consoles me.

The entrance is such that anyone who enters immediately becomes the centre of attention. I'm wearing a blue cotton shirt with loose fitting Levi black jeans and black shoes. A Diesel bag is strapped over my shoulder, my hair properly manicured and dyed in a copper colour that brings out my dark eyes. I saunter to the bar confidently.

The are two bartenders, both white. One of them is large and his height makes him look clumsy because he slouches his shoulders and back. He has sideburns styled into curlicues and his black hair is tied back in a greasy tight ponytail. The ponytail makes him look older, a little out of style, very eighties. The other younger guy wears his blond hair in short sharp punk spikes. Four people sit at the bar. And other people occupy the surrounding tables. I wait for about five minutes before the campy blond one serves me. "Can I help you?" he says with a bland voice. I order an Amstel. When I give him the ten rand note, he almost grabs it from my hand while hardly looking at me. I ignore this. Everyone can be a little moody and have a bad day.

I drink leisurely and watch MTV on a mounted TV. The bartender still hasn't given me my change back. Perhaps he's waiting for change. But the cash register opens and closes several times. I watch him dispensing change with ease to the other customers.

I finish my drink and want to order another one. They both seem to ignore me. I watch them serving two white guys who have just come in.

"Excuse me," I finally say to them.

"Billy," the blond one says and rolls his eyes at me.

Billy, the dark-haired oaf with the ponytail, comes over.

"Yes?" he says with decided displeasure.

"I ordered a beer and paid. I still haven't got my change back," I say and point to the blond one.

"You better come here. I don't understand what he's saying. Something about his accent," Billy says with a put-on American drawl. He sounds pathetic, like certain desperate DJ's and TV personalities who twang like Americans even though they have never set foot there.

The blond one comes back, chewing gum. He stands there with his hand on his hip.

"Look, I'm a little busy now. Can I help you?" he says cattily.

"My change?" I say, my eyes furious.

"Your change? What are you talking about? You paid a long time ago, I must have given it back to you."

"You didn't."

"Well, I'm sorry, I can't just open the cash register for no reason."

"I want my money," I say, losing my calm a bit.

"Billy, situation. I'm taking my tea break," he says and disappears. The oaf comes to me.

"Look, we're not looking for trouble. Why don't you just leave before I get security?" he says with a threatening voice. I look around the bar and suddenly realise that I'm the only black person, in fact the only person of colour. A young black boy wearing an apron comes from the kitchen and clears empty bottles on the tables. I watch him carefully making his way between the patrons like an invisible shadow, hardly looking up. I take my bag. The oaf watches me, perhaps a smile on his face. As I go out I catch a glimpse of the blond one smoking towards the back, happily chatting on his cellphone.

I'm shocked and hurt, my insides doing somersaults. I can't believe that gay men can be like that. I can't believe they can be so racist. I feel confused as I wander down a road. It is still early. I walk towards a small park, just a clearing, opposite Buitengracht Street where the advertising school is. I sit under a tree with long branches that cascade to the ground, but it is not a weeping willow.

I feel depressed and disillusioned, naïve for ever fooling myself that gay people are different. They are white people before they are gay, I tell myself bitterly. I start thinking about where my life is. At work I hardly see any black faces. Biloxi is a haven for white people. A few times at the door I have caught sight of the bouncer hassling one of the patrons. Why is it that they were always black or coloured?

I watch cars milling towards town and rushing back towards Green Point. I feel hopeless. Someone just tore up a beautiful image I had in my mind. It is offensive, even ludicrous, to imagine that a gay person can be prejudiced when we live with so much fear and prejudice. It is like a rude awakening. You are black. You will always be black.

It isn't that I have forgotten that but I have become accustomed to the sincerity and openness of the brotherhood. If anything I have gone deeper into my blackness. I have become comfortable with seeing people before naming their colour. West, Cole, Storm, Carrington, Adrian, Martin and the others, I don't think of them in terms of race groups, but that does not mean I'm not aware of their race. Cape Town never ceases to remind us who we are. When we leave the sanctuary of our Utopia at work we become pigments in a whirlpool of colour. In the centre it is lily white. On the edges of the whirlpool the other colours gather like froth and dregs.

I start thinking deeper about the brotherhood itself. Why is it that Cole and I are the only black faces? Where are the coloured or Indian stallions? Surely there are Indian and coloured masseurs out there. Surely they have also applied for a post. My stomach turns as I think deeper about Biloxi, all the black people I have ever seen there. They are not the ones I would meet in the township or in a squatter camp. They were all dressed in a certain way and spoke with a certain accent, sophisticated, with manners that everyone probably found charming, endearing. And because of that they were acceptable. That is why the bouncer didn't hassle them at the door, I begin to see.

I feel cornered. I feel my blackness. I have always felt it.

I get up and make my way to work, heavy with disillusionment.

At work the mood is also tense for some reason. After ten minutes of silence and watching TV I finally say something to Carrington.

"Did somebody die?"

"Didn't you hear? Of course, you weren't here. West has been fired. He's been asked to leave. Got into a fight with one of the clients. So Shaun asked him to leave for bringing the place into disrepute," he says softly, almost whispering.

"What? When did this happen?"

"About an hour ago. You can go see him, he's in his studio packing," he tells me.

It is not yet five when we all have to be in the lounge. I go to West's studio. There is a large suitcase on the floor and his clothes are on the bed. He has arranged the shirts and pants in two piles.

"West, you're not serious, are you?"

"Ag, I knew it was coming soon, Angelo. The party can't go on forever. At least now I can get on with other things. You can't do this for the rest of your life," he says, hardly bitter. He packs his clothes. I collapse on his small couch.

"You can't leave me," I say desperately. I want to say I love him.

"Angelo, you'll be fine. Just don't let this place become everything," he says, his voice serious, older.

"I don't understand. What happened?"

"Omstandighede. It was bound to happen sooner or later. It was stupid. The client leaves six hundred rand on the table for me while I'm dressing. We discussed the price before. But when I take the money he says no. I only said it was four hundred, which is a lie. Angelo, you know me, bra. I'm not greedy. I've got my own fucking investments, I don't need to steal from anyone," he says, a little angry. "So that's what happened. He stormed off to Shaun and said he was going to warn people about this place and that he had power, hanna hanna. Just a lot of kak basically. He said I must apologise and I refused. Shaun said I must do it or I must go, so ek loop."

He packs his expensive underwear.

"I'm sorry," is all I can manage.

"Ag, man, what for? Like I said, I knew I was going to leave sooner or later. This is all the excuse I need," he says, his back to me.

"What are you going to do?"

"For now I'm getting a taxi to the Holiday Inn. I'll stay there tonight, you know, treat myself a bit. Then I'm going back home tomorrow. My mother lives in Somerset West. I'll catch a train and go home. Think a bit, you know? I have a rough idea about what I want to do," he says optimistically.

I feel bereaved. I suddenly realise how easy it is to form a bond and how easy it is to get used to something. What would Steamy Windows be without Kalahari West?

"You can come visit if you like," he says.

"Really?"

"Of course." He crouches beside me. "We'll always be bras. No one can take that away from us."

"I know," I mutter.

He goes back to packing.

"Well, I still haven't taken any time off except for that Friday thing once a month. I think I'll ask Shaun for time off. Can I go with you tomorrow, or is that too soon?" I ask eagerly.

"Ja, come. It will be great. I could use the company. It will be fine with my mother. I'll phone her," he says excitedly, which makes me feel good.

"Have you told her that you got fired."

"She doesn't have to know everything. I just told her that I need to change jobs," he says quickly.

After packing all his stuff into a suitcase and two bags he straightens out the room. I feel sad but I try to act happy for him that he is ready to do the next thing. He calls Bee Line taxis on his cellphone. I help him lug his bags downstairs. He leaves them at the entrance where Francois is, wearing his impeccable tuxedo. We go back upstairs and sit in the lounge with the others. Cole, his best friend, is not there. Storm says he called this morning to say that he was coming in later. "But I have his cell number anyway," West says cheerfully. We're a bit awkward because we've become so close, everyone knowing each other's moods. Francois comes up to say West's taxi is here. The others hug him and wish him well. When West asks where Shaun is, Storm says he went out. But he says it with unease. I walk him down the stairs and help him carry his bags to the taxi. It is a little windy, the sky cloudy and grey.

I smile to hide my sadness. West gets into the car and drives off.

It is another slow evening. But I don't mind because I use the time to think about my life. I have only been at this for a month. I think about New Yorkers and it depresses me all over again. I even consider leaving, but it wouldn't be wise. I'm just starting. I'm just beginning to get my regulars and orientate my world. Besides, this could be a test of strength, of courage. I can't give up now.

At around nine I take my break with Cole. He goes outside for a cigarette. We talk about West.

"Well, life goes on," he says, his tone indifferent as he sucks on his cigarette.

"But I thought West was your best friend."

"He is. But look, grow up. This isn't high school or camp. People move on."

"That's not what I meant. It's just that he didn't leave under pleasant circumstances and you don't seem concerned."

"At least they didn't fuck him up," he says. "Don't get carried away. It's nice that we're all friendly and everything. I mean, I believe in the brotherhood too. But who's pushing all the buttons? Who's got all the power? Who decides who stays or leaves?"

He looks at me under the garish light of a street lamp.

"Shaun. White people," I admit.

"Exactly. Don't lose sight of that. This whole brotherhood thing is a clever gimmick. Very convenient, because it works. People want to believe in that sort of thing. But make no mistake, when Shaun's done with you, you'll know," he says. "You're only useful as long as you bring in money. That's why I say don't get too excited. Shit happens. This thing is about power and about who has it and who doesn't. We don't have it. They come here, they pay. Okay, so we choose what we want to do with them, but we don't really have any power. It's just sex cleaned up, given a better look. You see that, don't you?"

"Ja," I say, my thoughts going at a furious speed.

"This place, it's only a pit stop. Don't lose sight of that. Don't go soft because you think the money will carry you through. You're still black. That is how they see you," he says, but with a tender voice.

"Yesterday everything was fine. Today everything is upside down. Some idiots at New Yorkers were being racist to me this afternoon," I tell him what happened.

"You see what I mean? Money will never rescue you. People don't change overnight, even gay men. Sometimes I think I'm doing this job just so that I can confirm what arseholes white people can be. Really. I've met some real idiots. You know in Senegal and other parts of Africa we don't have this problem with white people because they're hardly there. But because you have them in South Africa some black South Africans have acquired their hang-ups," he says passionately.

"What do you mean?"

"I mean some black people walk around with this superior air as if they are better than us blacks from other parts of Africa. I think you get it from the whites," he says.

Perhaps he has a complex. Still, Cole is very adult about things, he wouldn't just say something without having given it some thought.

"Sometimes I get so pissed off. We don't need this racism shit." He flicks away the cigarette butt and lights up another one.

"But it's making me stronger. You have to wear your colour inside out so that the race shit will not matter. The deeper blackness is more important. It's what makes you an African, not your skin colour, eh? Guys like West, they are really black," he says.

I nod my head.

"You know what Kenyatta said? He said when the whites came to Africa we had the land and they had the Bible. They taught us how to pray with our eyes closed. When we opened them they had the land and we had the bible." He stands there smoking quietly, sadly. We share a moment of silence, as though gathering strength from each other. Francois opens the door to call us. Storm and Adrian go out for their break.

I spend the evening thinking about West, thinking about my life, wondering about all the things that have influenced me. What do they mean? Is it possible to draw sincere meaning from all the things that I have known from black and white culture? Is it possible to feel South African and feel like I can draw inspiration from white South Africa, that I can identify with them? Is it possible to feel South African and not to always source my culture to a particular race group? Can I claim Afrikaans, Coloured tsotsi taal, Indian cuisine or English sensibilities as my own? Must I always be apologetic for wanting more than what my culture offers? Am I a sell-out, an Uncle Tom? Isn't sticking to your own culture ruthlessly a kind of stagnation, a type of incest that animals experience where all the genes remain in the same familial group, eventually becoming the cause of ruin? Isn't that a bigger transgression than going beyond the boundaries? Will whites ever really hear us? And will we blacks always be on the defensive? Is it possible to be comfortable with each other as we are, not wanting to alter each other?

I think about the racist whites I have known and heard of from friends and family. The ones who have humiliated me or someone I knew, and how new racists complain about the new dispensation. Nobody ever expected the changes to go this well. Everyone expected South Africa to erupt in a boil of violence and civil war. How quickly people have forgotten that. They seem to have become uncharitable and stingy with optimism. Perhaps the smaller changes are more meaningful and a clearer sign about the progress we are making. Do whites still call the man who tends their lawn a garden boy? Do they still serve him his lunch with a tin cup and plate? Do the children know how to call an older black man or woman respectfully? Does the baas ride alone in the front seat of the bakkie while the back is loaded with darkies? Little things, these are the signs I look for when I go on travels with my clients because they are more revealing than grand words and gestures. It is the little things that slip out unconsciously that reveal their evolution as people, like Shaun and his expression about "going kaffir". Do they always refer to black men as boys or guys and never as men? Do they take certain things for granted because I'm black, like my preference for wine over beer? Do they always go on with stories about their black employees in their youth and how they got on with simple David or Angelina? Do they patronise me without being aware, blind to their own insensibilities? And the brief times when I catch a glimpse of their maids, I wonder what they pay her. Does she know about her rights? Do they have a pension fund for her?

And us as blacks, do we still look up to them instead of standing as equals? Do we sabotage each other because we are still indoctrinated to think otherwise about our worth? Do we steal and pillage from whites because we are getting revenge or have we become victims of our own bitterness and anger? Do neo-black fascist politicians steal money from everyone because they think they are balancing the scales, returning an equal blow, enjoying the same privileges, or are they dipping into the same cesspool of corruption and greed we fought and rebelled against? The other day someone broke into Shaun's car but found nothing to steal. When they realised that they couldn't take anything they smashed the dashboard. Is it acceptable to imagine immediately that blacks or coloureds probably did it? And when I hear the others complaining about a radio that was swiped from an open window at home or the clothes that disappeared from the washing line, is it fair of them to expect me to feel guilty and cringe because they assume it was someone black? And that I should feel embarrassed if it was a black person and become parsimonious about it? Why can't we just look upon them as criminals, neither black nor white? I only know how to be accountable for myself.

Perhaps we are moving into the territory of the oppressor. Perhaps one day whites will also speak about us with the same despicable nostalgia that we reserve for apartheid and its days. When blacks were in power, they might say.

These thoughts have so depressed me that I decide not to think any more about this. It is enough that I have a job and that I get paid well. I try to concentrate on that but find it hard as I get no clients throughout the evening. Before leaving I go to Shaun's office and ask him for the weekend off. Besides, I can't bear the thought of Jacques. We don't even greet each other any more.

I tell Shaun that I'm stressed out and that I haven't had time to adjust. Everything's kind of happened quickly over the last month, I explain. He understands but says he expects me back on Monday. There is authority in his voice. I suddenly realise what Cole was talking about. When I no longer bring in clients, he'll give me the sack. It is a sobering thought. I must be aware of things. I mustn't take anything for granted. And I must always remember to save, to think about tomorrow, to look after my nest egg. No one else is looking out for me.

WEST

**A**ngelo calls in the morning. We meet at the train station at twelve. It is hot. He wears a traditional Indian cotton shirt with delicate embroidery around the collar with blue jeans and brown sandals. I'm happy to see him. We hug like friends. I get two tickets to Somerset West. He takes out money to pay for his ticket but I refuse. "We'll square it later," I say.

"Aren't we going too far?" he says after I pass first class on the platform.

"No. I got third class tickets. It's more interesting, you see more."

We don't have to wait long. After ten minutes sitting outside on the benches we take our seats in the train near the end of the carriage. It soon fills up, third class always does. An old coloured woman with murky eyes comes in with two young children. There are no seats left. I stand up to offer her my seat. She thanks me, wiping sweat off her face. "Lekker warm, nè?" she says gratefully. I nod my head. The train jerks before it starts moving slowly.

I look at Angelo and feel the strange urge to kiss him in front of all these strangers. I get like that sometimes, strange impulses that would shock people just come over me. I smile to myself.

"Why are you smiling?"

"Nothing, nothing." But he doesn't believe me.

When we get to Salt River the old woman gets off with the two children and I take my seat again. My skin feels damp with sweat. I want to take off my shirt.

"So did you tell your mother I was coming?" he asks, a little concerned.

"Ja, don't worry. I told her you were coming."

I feel horny, I always do when it's hot, something about the heat. I look around the carriage and spot a beautiful coloured girl with honey skin and green eyes. She sits next to another coloured girl. I smile at her. She looks away with an aloof expression. At Wynberg the two girls get off. A lot of people get on again. A tall Indian woman with legs to die for stands near us. I keep looking at her waist and legs. "Is there something wrong?" she says to me after a while, aggression in her voice. I shake my head.

But I get a slight erection in my pants when I think of all the fun things I could do with her legs. She gets off at the next station.

"Don't sleep. Keep an eye on your bags," I whisper to his ear in the kerfuffle when people go in and out.

"Of course," he says at once.

"I feel horny," I tell him and laugh a bit.

"West, already? You just stopped working yesterday," he teases me.

"Ja, but that was work. I'm talking about a woman. I feel for a woman."

He looks at me with surprise, then becomes quiet and a little sad.

He doesn't get it. I don't like men like that, it was only a job to me.

350

I know he likes me a lot, perhaps more than one normally likes someone you consider a close friend, which is what we all were to each other at Steamy Windows.

At Kuils River some of the black people on the train get off and a lot of coloured people get on. A stunning black girl with long dreadlocks sits across from me with her boyfriend, who also wears dreadlocks. They look good together. She is wearing a long sarong, so I can't see her legs properly. But she wears a sexy black sleeveless T-shirt. Her breasts are large but not droopy. My erection starts up again. I'm wearing tight black jeans so it feels a little uncomfortable. I tell myself to ignore her till my erection goes away. She gets off at the next station where the train changes lines. A lot of coloured people get on and off, peppering the air with their jive talk lingo. I think about my childhood, growing up in Hermanus, and how I thought it was funny that some coloured men had no front teeth. I found it ridiculous that for some it was a requirement for entering a particular gang. I couldn't imagine knocking out my own incisors for anyone.

After about an hour and a half we get to Somerset West. There are few people left in our carriage.

"Angelo, this is where we get off, bra."

We take our bags and go. The sun is piercingly hot but there is some wind. Angelo's fragile shirt makes a bubble at the back. Outside the station I spot an old but resilient Toyota Corolla.

"By the way, don't call me West. My name is Karel," I say as my mother approaches.

"Okay, Karel," he says nervously.

"Pampoen," my mother says. We kiss and hug.

I lift her off her feet.

"Hoekom is jy so maer?" she says and studies my biceps.

"Ma, I've been eating well," I say in English for Angelo's sake.

"Moenie hier kom met jou Engels nie," she says and pokes me in the ribs.

She looks at Angelo.

"Mrs ..." he begins but looks stumped. He looks at me with slight panic.

"De Villiers," she smiles and shakes his hand, "but please call me Elanie. What's your name?" He thinks about the question a bit.

"Angelo," he says a little flustered.

"Nice to meet you," she says.

"Waar's Oom?" I ask.

351

"Oom's waiting at home. He didn't fancy coming out in the sun," she says in English.

My mother still looks good, still as slim as the days before she had me. She still wears her dark brown hair long.

"So where's your new kêrel?" I tease her as we go to the car.

"Pampoen, jy's terug," she smiles.

"Is that his nickname?" Angelo asks.

"Ja. He got it as a child," she says fondly. We pack the bags in the boot and the back seat of the car.

"I got it from my father, probably the only thing he left me," I say.

"I hope you're hungry, Angelo," my mother jumps in.

He nods his head eagerly. He smiles a lot when he responds to her questions.

We drive past the small quiet town. I have never really understood why Ma left Hermanus for this back street called Somerset West. Perhaps she got tired of the stigma that always followed us. We have no family in Somerset West.

"Do you want to go for a swim later?" I ask Angelo, thinking of the small reservoir not far from our plot.

But there are no dogs to bark at us in our driveway.

"What happened to Rex and Jaco?"

"Oom will tell you. Angelo, welcome, this is my home," Ma says warmly as we approach the house.

We park the car near the house under a tall shady eucalyptus tree. Angelo helps me take out the bags. On the porch Oom is sitting in his rocking chair, wearing his impenetrable dark glasses and smoking a pipe.

"Karel, wat kyk jy? Kom hierso, man," he says excitedly and takes out his pipe from his mouth. He gets up to hug me.

"En wie's jou vriend?" he says, perceptive as ever.

"This is my friend Angelo, Oom."

Angelo sticks out his hand. Oom sticks out both his hands to feel Angelo's. They shake hands.

"Ek sien 'n bietjie swak," he jokes and Angelo smiles, "Aangename kennis. Ek is Sarel."

We go inside where the house is cool. I take Angelo to my room where he will be staying. Ma still has both beds and all the pictures and posters I had growing up. I feel a little embarrassed as we walk in. A poster of Jason Donovan and Kylie Minogue embracing hangs on one wall.

"My mother, she won't let me grow up."

"It's quite sweet that you once liked them."

He takes the bed on the right. We go downstairs. I'm hungry. In the kitchen Ma has already laid out a spread for us: sosaties, boerewors, potato salad, green salad, coleslaw and for dessert, melktert and koeksisters.

"Go wash your hands," Ma orders us both. I take him to the guest toilet near the lounge where we wash our hands. Before we eat we hold hands and Ma says grace.

We eat in the cool kitchen. Ma offers Angelo everything. And like the polite person he is, he accepts. "Ma, I'm sure he's had enough," I say to her when she insists that he try her melktert after eating koeksisters.

After the meal Angelo and I go out for a walk. We go to the bottom of the garden where there is a fence at the end of our plot. There is a small hole in the barbwire fence where Rex and Jaco, our dogs go through. We climb through and head up a small hill. It is peaceful and quiet. On the other side of the hill at the bottom is the small dam. On the banks there are logs.

I start taking off my clothes and strip naked. I hang my clothes over the logs.

"Just like that?" Angelo says.

I don't answer him. I walk towards the water and it is cool.

"You should come in. No one's watching," I say.

Nervously he takes off his clothes.

I swim towards the deep end of the dam. A log is floating on the water. There are marks on it as if a dog was trying to chew it. Angelo swims up close to me.

"It's nice, huh?" I say, happy to be home.

"It is," he says. "So your uncle is completely blind?"

"Ja, after that mining accident."

"He seems like a nice guy," he says.

We do a few lengths and swim under the brackish water. It is dark like ink. He gets tired quickly and goes out. I soon follow him. We lie on the grass and let the sun dry us.

"Hey, we mustn't stay in the sun too long. We didn't put on any sunblock," I say.

He sighs.

"So what are you going to do?" he asks.

"Why are you so worried?"

"It's not that I'm worried. I just wonder if I'll ever see you again," he says solemnly.

"You can't get rid of me that easily. You're still going to see me."

Soon we start getting dressed and head back home. When we go down the hill on the other side I spot our neighbour, a farmer, on his tractor. He waves to us.

"He's a prick but at least he looks out for my mother," I say to Angelo while I wave back.

We find Ma knitting on the porch while Oom smokes. He asks me to take him for a short walk while Angelo goes to take a nap.

We go down the driveway.

"What happened to Rex and Jaco, Oom?"

He refills his pipe.

"Your mother was very upset. She loved those dogs. It happened about a month ago. Someone tried to break in, so they poisoned the dogs first."

He says it quickly and doesn't indulge me with details.

"We called Kobus, our neighbour, when I realised that there was something wrong, the dogs weren't responding when I called them. I told your mother to call Kobus and he called the cops," he says, holding his pipe delicately. "There were two of them. They found them in the shed, loading tools into the bakkie. It was only a matter of time before they were going to head for the house. Things will never be the same again. You're not safe in your own home."

He says it as though he accepts it. I don't know what to say. My heart beats with fear at the thought that my mother could have been killed.

"And you still stay here? Why don't you go back to Hermanus?"

"Your mother is stubborn."

I breath in his smoke and sigh.


ANGELO

I wake up at around eight and find that West is gone. I still have to remind myself to say Karel every time I want to call him. His bed is already made. I open the curtains and morning light streams through. My eyes are tired but I feel awake. I rub them gently and sit on the bed.

Above the headboard of the bed there is a small hand-written placard. It looks like a fragment of a poem. C. Louis Leipoldt is written at the bottom.

354

Dis vrede, man, die oorlog is verby!
Hoor jy die mense skreeu die strate vol?
Sien jy die hele wêreld is op hol?
Kom, hier 's 'n bottel soetwyn; laat ons drink!
Ons nasie, wat so wild was, is nou mak ...
... Die beste wat ons nasie het – die vrou!

*It's peace now, man, at last the war is over!*
*Why, can't you hear those screeches wild and glad?*
*And can't you see the whole world going mad?*
*Come, here's a jug of wine; let's have a spree!*
*Our nation that was wild and free, is ripe ...*
*... Of all that's best: Woman! Our nation's treasure!*

I think of West and try to imagine him as a student in Stellenbosch, his hair probably long and unkempt. I try to imagine him struggling to find his feet, searching for meaning in words and poetry and unfaithful girlfriends. I look at the books on his shelf. They are mostly volumes of poetry. He seems to have a preference for Breyten Breytenbach.

Before West I never thought of Afrikaans people as being sensitive or as being anything other than oppressors. Too many incidents and memories had bludgeoned any hope of me ever seeing them as people, just as complex and fallible as any other people. It is almost an implicit part of my culture to hate the Afrikaner, to remember how unkind and insular they have been to my people. I think about Arthur the American guy who said every people have their pain. For us it would be what the Afrikaner did, what Verwoerd instituted. And for the Afrikaners it would probably be what the British did to them during the Boer War and how their women and children perished in concentration camps. But what about the British themselves, what would be their pain? I think about my mother and the stories she told me about travelling through Bloemfontein in an earlier, darker time when it was dangerous to be black, educated and with a car. I feel stupid, almost embarrassed when I recall how I despised a people I hardly knew anything about with such patriotic fervour. How little I knew. How small my world was.

It was so subtle, West's charm. I didn't realise that he was opening up his world to me, secretly winning me over, letting me in on his magic, healing wounds that history was too mute to ever confess or plead forgiveness for. There are ever so many questions left unanswered.

Perhaps in the end there is no one to blame. Things just happen because they need to; our lives are too small to understand the bigger scheme of things. When people look at ancient aqueducts, Inca shrines, pyramids, the Great Wall of China, the Parthenon or any other remnant of the old world, I suspect they only see them as structures, buildings, slabs of rock and stone that inspire scientific intrigue. I suspect they don't stop to wonder whether slaves or unionised labourers built them. The human dramas that were involved have ceased to exist. I hope that is how South Africa will be looked upon one day. When people walk through its streets and enjoy its pleasures perhaps they won't think that this land was built on the hardship of blacks and the greed of whites. Perhaps they won't be interested to know who was the oppressor and who was the oppressed.

I begin to think about Afrikaans people in a way I never have before. They also love this land, I admit to myself as I study a small watercolour print on the wall of a berg reminiscent of the Drakensberg. It is also their home, I see as I observe the veldskoene in the corner. I think about the buildings, the bridges, the railway stations, the roads and other marvels of infrastructure that the early pioneers brought to this land, the progress that we have always begrudged them for because it came at such a cost – it undermined the inward progress of African culture. I think of pylons, lighthouses, harbours, airports and the uniqueness of Cape Dutch houses. I think of the early architects, road planners and engineers and the vision they had of building a country from humble beginnings. Perhaps there was fear in their eyes when they saw Africa running bare except for a loincloth around her waist. Perhaps they were too eager to dismiss old African deities that held communities together. The same communities that disintegrated into a fend-for-yourself stupor, wrecked by the disaffection of modernity. I look at West's shelves made of different woods, probably discarded wood. I marvel at the mat beside his bed. It is made of knitted plastic. And his quilted bedspread has its own story. They are very practical people, hardly wasteful, I say to myself, hardly different from us, really. Perhaps we will fully appreciate them one day, in a better season. Perhaps they will only get to know us in a less angry time.

I take my toiletries pouch and go to the bathroom. It is clean and fresh and reminds me of home. I take a quick shower and use one of the towels on the rack. On the door there is another handwritten placard modestly mounted on mauve board. It is by N.P. van Wyk Louw.

O Heer, laat hierdie dae heilig word:
Laat alles val wat pronk en sieraad was
Of enkel jeug, en ver was van die pyn;
Laat ryp word, Heer, laat U wind waai, laat stort
My waan, tot al die hoogheid eindelik vas
En nakend uit my teerder jeug verskyn.

*Dear Lord, may all these days be sanctified:*
*Let all things fall that were showy and vain*
*Or merely young and far removed from tears;*
*Make riper, Lord, let your wind blow; my pride*
*Strip off, till all that's great at last shows plain*
*Naked and firm above my greener years.*

I leave the bathroom as clean as I found it. In the bedroom I find West, wearing his shorts and tackies, his chest bare and wet with sweat.

"Why didn't you wake me? I would have gone with you for a jog," I say.

"You looked tired," he says, wiping his forehead with his T-shirt. He goes to the bathroom to shower.

I get dressed and go outside on the porch. Oom Sarel is alone.

"Morning," I greet him.

"Môre, môre," he returns warmly. "You must forgive me, my Engels is 'n bietjie vrot."

I sit next to him, a little nervous. Perhaps because except for West I have never really known anyone Afrikaans personally. It is strange not to be on the defensive.

"You know, when Karel was a boy, he ran two hours every day. One hour in the morning and one hour in the afternoon. Hy was baie fiks. Does he still run two hours a day?" he asks me. He looks in my direction with his dark glasses. Does he even know that I'm black?

"I think so," I say, careful not to tarnish West's reputation.

"He was very good at rugby," he says proudly. "Not as big as the other seuns, maar hy was vinnig."

West comes out, his hair wet and neatly combed back. He wears shorts, his hairy legs rippling with muscles, and a brown T-shirt and flip-flops. I feel a little overdressed in my jeans and takkies.

"It's a little hot. Didn't you bring any shorts?" he says to me when he sees me.

"No. I didn't think it would be this hot," I say.

"I've got some for you if you want."

"That would be nice," I say and follow him to his room.

He gives me a pair of old rugby shorts but they are comfortable. West's mother calls us to the kitchen for breakfast. We go past the lounge and dinning room. An oxwagon wheel is quaintly used as a light fitting above the dinning room table with several bulbs spaced along the outer rim. On the fireplace mantle there is also a miniature oxwagon with four oxen. Cognac and homemade brews are displayed on the bar. Riempie chairs stand around an old stinkwood table.

We sit in the kitchen and hold hands while West says grace. I feel awkward and self conscious when I hold oom Sarel's hand. I hold it gently while he holds mine firmly. We eat porridge and toast with honey and jam. I don't eat much. I never do in the morning. I settle for a bowl of porridge.

"Is that all you're going to have? How did you manage at Steamy Windows?" West's mother asks. I go blank with surprise and don't know what to say. I didn't know that she knew about what West did.

"Uh, ja, I don't eat much for breakfast," I say with a stupid grin. West does something with his eyes to say don't panic, she knows.

Later West and I go to town on some errands for his mother. We load a lawnmower that needs fixing into a bakkie.

"I didn't know that your mother knew. I almost had a heart attack when she mentioned Steamy Windows," I say.

"Ja, I saw. I nearly laughed. Look, she knows I worked there as a masseur. That's all I told her," he says, driving down a dusty road.

"Your mother's not stupid. I'm sure she figured out what really goes on in there. Anyway, what possessed you to tell her the truth?"

He looks at me with surprise.

"I have no reason to ever lie to my mother. Even when I know it's going to get me into shit."

"You must have a good relationship with your mother," I say, a little envious.

"She's my rock."

"In Xhosa they say you mess with a woman you mess with a rock."

"Same thing with my mother," he says and becomes quiet again, a little uncomfortable. He puts on the radio. The quality of the sound is poor. It makes the music sound tinny.

Why is it that guys are so uncomfortable, so protective and private when it comes to their mothers? I watch him from the corner of my eye as we drive to town in silence. We stop outside a hardware store where they also fix appliances. I follow him inside. He greets a man he seems to know, a tall stocky guy wearing khaki shorts and thick bobby socks up to the knees. I stand back and look around while they talk in rapid Afrikaans. They go outside after a while. West opens the back of the bakkie. I help him unload the lawnmower. The guy looks at me irritably as I advise West to turn this way to take out the mower without damaging it. West pushes it to the back of the shop where a humble black guy receives it. He greets West in Afrikaans and smiles at me. When the stocky guy calls Jacob, the black worker, I'm surprised to hear Jacob say "baas" with a servile look. I go back to the bakkie disappointed. West stays and talks with them.

He comes back and finds me inside the bakkie. The man waves to West as we drive off. We go to a filling station and then to the local grocery shop. I stay in the car. West comes back with some groceries.

In the car he changes the radio station. I had found 5fm. He finds an Afrikaans station that has monotonous stringy music.

"That music is crap," I tell him after a while.

"There's nothing wrong with Boeremusiek," he says defensively.

"Whatever."

"What's wrong? You've been quiet and pulling a face like a vrot appelkoos since we got into town," he complains.

"Since we got back from the hardware store," I correct him. "I found it very charming that Jacob still calls your friend baas."

"Angelo grow up!" he has the gall to say to me, "Not everyone gets it. Not everyone is open-minded. This is not Cape Town. You work with what you have. Magtig, what do you want me to say to him? Sorry, apartheid is finished now, no more baas? What do you want me to say? I mean shit, man, not everyone is like that. You can't turn from your people, even the ones that don't know certain things."

"So ignorance is an excuse?"

"Don't be like that. All I'm saying is that pointing fingers at someone like that and saying I'm not going to talk to you or do business at your place solves nothing. He is still going to think like that. So I must show him. You understand? It's not that I agree with him. You know me. But you cannot just abandon people. I am Afrikaans. I will never abandon my people. Even if they are going to the grave because of their stupidity sometimes. Because if I do, then I'm saying I'm better. I'm saying I'm better than you if I stay away. And I'm not like that," he says and looks at me.

"So in the meantime Jacob gets treated like this is still apartheid ..."

"It is still apartheid for some, for him. Don't you get that? It's painful for some that blacks are in power now. It makes some of them the moer in. That's why they still do things like that, you know, treat Jacob like that," he explains.

"Okay, fine, West, whatever."

We drive back in silence.

At home we help his mother in the garden. She takes us to the shed where there are five bags of manure which we are supposed to spread on the front lawn. We each take a wheelbarrow and work in silence while his mother supervises. Afterwards we help her plant a new bed of plants that she says will do well over the summer and take out some stubborn weeds. West feeds the ducks and chickens at the back. By lunchtime we are dirty and hungry. She orders us to get cleaned up. We wash our hands. On the porch there are elegant plastic garden chairs and a table. She lays out another modest spread for lunch. I eat well. She smiles when I ask for a second helping of dessert.

After lunch we go again for a swim at the dam. But we still don't say much to each other. In the evening West tells me to shower and get changed. He says a friend called and that we have been invited to a party. My face becomes sour. I didn't bargain for a night out in Orania.

"What's wrong? They don't bite. Don't worry, I'm not taking you to the guy at the hardware store. They are friends of mine. We went to Stellenbosch together," he says.

He asks his mother for the car. "Don't come back too late, you two," she says with concern. She kisses West on the cheek. I haven't seen oom Sarel since breakfast. When I ask about him she says he went to visit a friend.

It takes about fifteen minutes to get to the house. It is big. Several cars are parked outside.

"Don't worry, man. His parents went away on holiday. So there are only young people tonight," he says confidently as he gets out of the car. He straightens out his expensive Dolce e Gabbana shirt, his black cotton pants immaculately pressed. I also look good in my Gucci shirt and Guess jeans but I feel nervous, my stomach in knots. It was only yesterday that I went to a fine establishment appropriately dressed, only to be rudely snubbed.

He walks in front. I follow him. At the door we are met by a beautiful woman about West's age. She has long dark hair which she keeps flicking away from her face.

"Karel, lekker om jou te sien man," they hug.

He introduces me as Angelo, his friend from Cape Town. I smile and am pleasantly surprised by her immediate warmth when she hugs me. Behind her West greets a tall guy. They hug and call each other "ouboet" and laugh, something about rugby and a strict rugby coach at Stellenbosch they remind each other. I also shake his hand. In the kitchen they offer me wine. The only white wine they have is a late harvest. It is a little too sweet. We move to the lounge. There are about twelve other people, all eagerly expecting West. I'm nervous but remain calm on the outside. When they see him they almost cheer and call him strange nicknames. The dark-haired girl, Marlene, stays with me, her arm already wrapped around mine, her charm and spontaneous warmth disarming. She introduces me to the others. They smile and ask me basic friendly questions to make small talk, where I'm from, where I studied, why I'm in Cape Town. They seem impressed but don't make too much of it when I tell them that I went to Rhodes. Sting plays in the background. The wine goes to my head. I begin to relax on the couch while André, one of the guys, talks about Jo'burg, the big city. We chat easily. They move effortlessly between Afrikaans amongst themselves and English when they speak to me. After a while I hardly notice they are Afrikaans. Perhaps it is the wine.

We get up to dance to a few numbers when Tina Turner comes on. Marlene dances with me. André cuts in politely to finish the dance. Back on the couch I meet Hannes and we talk about Cape Town. He asks me if I have gone on the wine route. I tell him that I have, even though I can't really remember. I decide to go easy on the wine. You don't want to make a bad impression, they are watching you, I tell myself.

Later in the evening after the snacks and the dancing, the music slows down to Enya. Magnus, the guy West calls Ouboet and whose house it is, starts rolling a joint. I smile inside because I always imagined Afrikaans kids to be as strict as their parents, the lawmakers of the land. He lights some candles and incense sticks and passes two joints around the room. We lounge about on the sofas and the floor, satiated but not offensively stoned and inebriated. For my benefit they all talk in English.

"Genuine, bra," André says, "you can't drink alcohol in Egypt. It is against their religion. I was there these last two months. Even in Cairo there aren't any bars or places like that where you can drink. It's totally Muslim. But they have this herb they chew, they call it qat. It's legal but in large quantities you start feeling stoned."

"But it's quite a difficult country if you're a woman," Mimi, the girl resting between André's legs, says. I think they are going out. "You can't just walk around wearing anything you like. And you know they have female circumcision. The men are a bit creepy if you're alone and a woman. They always harass you. I met this British girl there, but she wasn't complaining with all the attention she was getting."

"But most of Africa is quite conservative," another says. "My uncle and aunt and their two children left two years ago to set up in Zambia. There's lots of opportunity there. And my aunt who's running her own clothing business was complaining that the women get bullied by their men and they accept it. Not like South African women," he says, careful not to say blacks.

I'm struck by how easily and affectionately they talk about Africa, their home. The ones that travelled talk about their experiences with strange African customs. They talk about the poverty and dilapidation openly. But they seem mostly interested in talking about the places in Africa where someone young and with energy and innovation can build a career and make anything of themselves. They talk about their relatives exploring other parts of Africa, trying to find a safer place to raise their children. They talk about an isolated village in the Congo where one Afrikaans man remains yet he still speaks his mother tongue. There is pride in their eyes, but not the colonial arrogant Anglo-Saxon type that presupposes that white people are superior. There is love for the textured language that vigorously sprang up during the early years of the Cape of Good Hope, when other languages were also vying for attention. I listen to them laugh, sometimes forgetting to speak in English, muttering things that sound like they could only be said in Afrikaans. Like Marlene talking about her brother in Zimbabwe, saying "Ek is lief vir hom," a simple thing, I love him, I love my brother. There is poetry in the way the words fall out and how they force the mouth open, unlike English. Ek is lief vir hom, it is like saying I have love for him. It sounds more urgent more daring than the way the English would say it. There is the same depth, the same vivid expressions I find in African languages.

"So have you been anywhere, Angelo?" André asks me. They all look at me with anticipation. I have never been anywhere outside the borders of the country but I cannot disappoint their enthusiasm. I have always loved Brazil and yearn to go there one day. I have travelled to the rainforests of the Amazon, run down the favelas, the slums of Rio de Janeiro, danced to forro music at carnivals and discovered the vibrant metropolis of Sao Paulo between pages and in daydreams. How I long for Brazil.

"I went to Brazil on holiday with my parents once," I lie. I have read a lot about it.

Their eyes light up.

"What was it like?" André, the forthright one, says.

"No different from us in some respects. I mean they have the same kind of history with many people and diverse cultures. But they have a different attitude to life," I say, their eyes silently upon me. "They love to live. You watch them walking down a street and you know that the sun is falling on them with grace. Very friendly people. I went there during the carnival. When I watched them doing the samba, I saw glimpses of Africa, it was fascinating. That's what I liked about Brazil, they are totally into celebrating their different cultures. They have this festival called Kuarup for the native Indians, African-based religions like Candomble, Lucimi, Voodoo and Santeria, and then the Portuguese and Spanish have their influence as well. Even Asian people. So it's like a fruit salad of different cultures, not this terrible melting pot thing with Americans where everyone just gets sucked in and loses their culture to something artificial and shallow. And the people are so beautiful. The most amazing combinations, like a dark skin with blond blond hair, or blue eyes with dark skin, or light skin with a really kinky Afro. Everyone just accepts that somewhere along their family bloodline they are a bit African, Indian or white. Even the ones who really look white know this. They are so cool about it. They love football and partying.

"Oh, and they love the beach. It's like a way of life."

"What about the street children? Don't they have like hit squads or something from the police? I once a read an article about it in Huisgenoot," Liezel, says.

"Ja, it is a problem," I say, recalling an article I also read up. "You have a lot of homeless street kids in Rio. And they all beg. If you look like a tourist you're an easy target. They just zoom in on you and they won't leave until you've given them something. I thought our squatter camps were bad, but you should see Rio. Anyway, there are a lot of NGOs monitoring the whole thing."

"What are the woman like, bra?" Magnus asks eagerly.

"Delicious," I say and everyone laughs. "No, they're very friendly. Perhaps I shouldn't speak any more about that. I don't want to offend the women in the room."

"Ag, man. So you probably slept with a few," Marlene jokes, "We know what you guys get up to when no one is around to watch."

We all laugh.

"I was just a kid then," I protest.

They talk about expatriates and the scores of white South Africans gearing up to leave, selling houses, applying for work permits. They talk about young students hardly out of varsity but already looking to take their skills elsewhere. They talk about Canada and how much easier it is than other countries to emigrate. I listen with sadness when they talk about the ones who are miserable in their new countries. Even Australia with all its good weather is not Africa, Marlene says. There is irony in her voice when she tells us about how some white South Africans go excitedly towards any black South African they come across. This thing with blacks and whites, there are aspects of it that are uniquely South African. I try to imagine these whites belting out "sawubona" or "dumela" to try and get a response. There is more to the relationship between oppressor and the oppressed, between love and hate. The settler and the native are old acquaintances, Franz Fanon once wrote.

They laugh when Magnus says he wants to emigrate to a small island somewhere in the South Pacific. "What about your rugby and Castle beer?" Marlene teases. "I'll start my own team and brew," he laughs back.

But to myself I say he probably would. They are like that, pioneers. Perhaps they are here to show us that anyone can live anywhere. Perhaps their lesson is to learn how to live with other people without interfering with their culture.

We watch a home video of Magnus and his girlfriend in Mauritius. We drink some more and smoke some more. I feel pleasantly high. Valkenberg crosses my mind but I dismiss the thought. It seems like something that happened to someone else in another time. I hardly speak to West all night but I don't feel angry with him.

At around two when the others start leaving West says to me that we should also go. "My mother ..." he says concerned. The others scold him that he should be in contact with them more often. "Nice to meet you," most of them say to me as we hug and say good-bye. I feel different about myself. I feel like I've been let in on a secret that I didn't know.

I drive back because West says he is a little too stoned. At home his mother left the outside light and the kitchen light on. We go in quietly and drink lots of water. "So, you had a nice time?" he says to me.

"Ja. I did, actually."

I take off my shoes and tiptoe to his room.

"Don't worry, my mother could sleep through a storm," he says.

Inside his room it is dark, but the curtains and windows are open. I search for the light switch in the dark. He comes behind me.

"Don't worry about that," he says, his accent sounding more Afrikaans than usual.

"West, put on the lights." I turn around, finding his face against mine. He smells of Kouros, a fresh smell that always reminds me of the sea.

"You know, you're leaving tomorrow," he says, "and I don't know when I'll see you again. I might just take a year to travel."

It makes me a little sad to hear that. Just as well that it is dark.

"I know. I might never see you again," I say.

Very gently he kisses me. I pull back a little.

"West why are you doing this? You like women."

"Angelo, you are my friend."

"You're just horny," I say and begin to walk away.

But he grabs me and pulls me close to him. He kisses me again, his arm supporting my back.

"I don't want to fall in love with you," I protest. "I have a habit of falling for people I can't have. Omstandighede, like you always say."

But he has a way with me. He lavishes my neck with kisses and starts unbuttoning my shirt.

"West, don't do this," I plead. I feel so much for this guy. Can't he see that? Doesn't he know what it is doing to me? I don't want to be always lamenting over people, crying over unrequited love like a hapless Mills & Boon character.

"Maybe this is the only way I can say what you mean to me, what our friendship means to me," he says tenderly and caresses my arse.

What can you say after someone says that? I kiss him back. We kiss for a while, our crotches rubbing against each other.

"Wait," he says after a while. In the dark he finds his casette player and presses a button. Music comes on softly. It is Billy Joel and that song that says something about "don't go changing to try and please me". I will always remember West with that song.

"This is how I want to remember you," he says as we move to his bed. We both sit on the edge kissing and taking off our clothes in our own time. He has the most beautiful torso like the work of a virtuoso artist. I kiss his nipples and he tickles my back.

In bed he is warm and mysterious, I touch him everywhere to discover his pleasures. Skilfully he takes out a condom from the inside of the pillow cover.

No one has ever made love to me. West is the first. He doesn't say anything and neither do I. But we are both aware that it is my first time. The intensity of someone making love to you is enough to bring back happy memories of childhood. There is the dizziness of acute joy, the humility of feeling another person's breath and all the clues it gives about that person. How weak they are, how strong they can be, how selfish or considerate. He nibbles my ears as I discover my own limits of pleasure. I feel warm inside, complete, as though before I was an incomplete jigsaw puzzle. So that's what it feels like to be loved, I buzz inside, moaning, smiling, sweating.

"Angelo," he whispers to my ear. His breath is hot and frantic. We climax together and collapse into each other. It is strange how comfortable we are. Some guys don't want to be touched after sex. They feel too vulnerable, they need to recover. But West stays with me.

"I'm not going to say I'll write or that you should," I say, "It never works out in the end and I don't want to have unrealistic expectations and end up bitter because I don't hear from you."

"But I will see you again," he says with certainty. I sigh. I want to cry, but resist it. I feel confused. I feel too much for him.

"Let's go for a swim," he says in the dark.

"You're crazy," I say as I watch him jump out of bed in the dark.

But I follow him, his schoolboy charm is irresistible. We only wear shoes and wrap towels around our waists. The night is hot and accommodating.

The water looks eerie, like a massive black hole that could swallow us. In the waning moon I make out his body as he moves to the water. He dives into a splash. A bird flutters in a nearby tree, probably an owl. I follow him. He swims to the centre. The water is cool. It feels like being kissed all over. I float beside him. He laughs but doesn't tell me why. I swim to the other side pulling gentle strokes. We don't stay long in the water, maybe fifteen minutes.

But once out of the water we suddenly feel cold and miss the maternal warmth of the sun. I rub myself vigorously with the towel. We sneak back inside and lock the door. I feel like a child, like I got away with doing something naughty that gave me lots of pleasure.

In the room I slip into my own bed. He slips into his own bed. We both sigh simultaneously, satisfied after the swim.

"Angelo."

"Ja?"

"You know the brotherhood?"

"Ja?"

"Don't think too much about what it is and isn't. Like everything it's not perfect, you know."

"Okay."

"Just remember one thing."

"What?"

"I know it sounds corny, but ..."

"Say it anyway."

"Somebody said it to me when I started. It helped," he says and waits to hear if I'm listening.

"Ja, I'm listening."

"You must always go where love leads you, even when you are going towards trouble," he says.

I go to sleep with that thought. A dream entangles me in its web. I find myself walking alone up a steep road in a secluded neighbourhood. It is dawn. The road is quiet. I do not see any people or any cars. I walk up the road a long time till I see a path leading towards the wilderness. I take the path and leave the road. The climb gets steeper. I walk past tall pine trees, the city below as I begin to climb what appears to be Table Mountain.

I meet a robin and it tells me to change my shape. I become a small dassie, scurrying over the rocks, happy to be small and quick. I soon see a group of people but I keep my distance. Tall men with funny hats that look like furry creatures wearing clothes in the colours red, blue and white. They are holding bayonets. They antagonise a group of women and children. The path seems long but it is not too narrow. I watch while these men with bayonets and strange hats bark orders at the helpless women and children. The women wear dresses that cover their ankles, wrists and necks. They also wear large hats that make their heads look like lampshades. The children complain that the path is too steep and that the sharp rocks are cutting their bare feet but the soldiers ignore their pleas to slow down. They taunt them and tell them to move on.

I follow the strange caravan of soldiers, women and children till they reach the mountain. At the top the leader of the soldiers plants a flag between two slabs of rock and proclaims Martial Law. He sings a song which, he boasts to the women and children, is his "national anthem". "God save the Queen," the soldiers all say in unison. A large eagle flies above me. When I see that it is about to swoop down I hide in a prickly bush because I'm small and look tender. But once the eagle has gone I come out again.

To my horror I find the women and children on their knees, licking the rocks around the flag, the leader of the soldiers egging them on with mad glee. "Clean it up!" he shouts dementedly, waving his bayonet near their terrified faces. The other soldiers stand by and threaten the ones who refuse to lick. A woman gets shot. Another suddenly stands up and rushes towards the cliff. She plummets to her death. "This is what will happen to you if you don't clean the rocks," the leader says, his complexion pink and slightly sunburnt.

The women and children moan but they continue licking the rock surfaces. In the distance a canon goes off. A horn blows. The soldiers soon get bored and round up the women and children, their knees cracked and bleeding, their faces dirty with humiliation. I watch the mad soldiers lead them down the path again. The women start singing as they trudge down the steep path. The children join in their dirge. From the mountain top I watch them shrink into a small shadow of sadness. They seem to evaporate as clouds move in and hug the mountain. It begins to rain. Huge, heavy drops that fall to the ground like peas. I take shelter from a small cave in the rocks. I'm startled when I hear a scratching noise beside me. When I look I notice a small boy crouched in the corner, a scared, hungry look on his face. He looks at me tenderly but I sense desperation behind the soft eyes. I need to eat, his eyes seem to say. He grabs me suddenly and takes out a knife.

I wake up in a cold sweat. West sleeps peacefully beside me on his bed. I feel strange, disoriented. I feel as if the room swallowed me and infected me with its stories and histories. I want to get up and drink water but this is not my house. It is still dark outside. Go back to sleep, I tell myself. It is difficult. The image of emaciated women and children with dirty clothes and broken faces sticks to my mind.

### WEST

**I** get up early and leave Angelo still sleeping. It is a little windy outside. I go for a jog, my muscles aching for the discipline of a gym. My chest has lost at least an inch.

After breakfast I take Angelo to the station.

"I don't wait for goodbyes to tell people how I feel," I tell him. "You know how I feel. So I'm not coming in."

He gets out of the car and takes out his bags. He looks sad but I can see him making an effort to be upbeat. I can see through his thin smile.

"Well, it was nice of you to invite me … I guess that's it. Thanks, see you whenever," he says awkwardly and walks away. I know he would have wanted to say goodbye differently, in his own sentimental way, pouring out his heart like a dam overflowing. But I think it's better this way. I never had a crutch. And I won't allow myself to be one for anyone.

I watch him disappear behind the doors before I start the car. I wish him well. Everyone has to try and find their own way.

On the road I think of my mother as I drive back. I know she won't want to move away, that stubborn woman. She won't hear of it. No one is going to drive me from my home, I imagine her saying. It was hard enough leaving Hermanus. I don't think she could do it again.

ANGELO

**A**t work I find two new guys, both white and tall. They look nothing like West. Storm and Carrington are showing them the ropes. But they still need to be screened. Not everyone who applies makes the grade. It's hard not to think about West. I miss him. I miss the way he was comfortable with himself. I miss his charisma, Kalahari West. I miss the Afrikaans accent that peppered everything he said. I miss his "eet jou rape eerste" philosophy which advocates delayed gratification. Hold back, don't give away too much too soon. Wait a bit. Leave something for yourself. Make the client work a little, make him beg a little. Pace yourself. I promise you in the end the sex will be great, he would say. I haven't been in his studio since he left. It would feel strange.

At around nine Francois comes in to tell me that I have an overnight booking. I freshen up and go downstairs. The client soon comes. He picks me up in a black Jaguar, a young guy in his early thirties. His name is Oliver. I feel his eyes on me as I bend over to put my bags in the boot.

"You've got a nice arse," he says with a polished, private school accent with a slight American twang.

"What do you do?" I say, even though I don't really want to know.

"I work in advertising," he says and there is an arrogant look on his face as if he expects me to be thrilled.

"Wow," I feign a response.

"I hope you're hungry," he says as we drive towards Sea Point.

I say nothing. He puts his hand on my thigh while he drives with the other.

"Feel that," he says and puts my hand on his crotch. He has an erec-

369

tion. "That's for you. You make me really horny." People have said cruder things, darling, I imagine Sebastian consoling me.

He's good-looking but there's nothing attractive about his vain manner. He keeps brushing back his hair intermittently as though to check that it isn't falling off. It's irritating to watch. And he keeps looking at himself in the rear view mirror. I think of West. Okay, so he wasn't the best-looking guy I ever saw. But he was charming, interesting, attractive. Perhaps truly attractive people are neither beautiful nor ugly, just plain. With ordinary clothes West would be plain but he would still stand out.

We stop outside a chic nouvelle cuisine restaurant in Camps Bay. I once went there with a former client. The décor is black and white, the patrons smile with impeccable white teeth , their manner artificial, pretentious. We go to a large table where everyone seems to wear the ubiquitous black and white, most dressed in smart casual, a few formal. Oliver introduces me to a group of his friends. I want to run out when I see them. One of the skinny women gets up to kiss Oliver on the cheeks, exposing her carefully starved frame. They all seem to be in their early thirties, rich and spoilt, probably the children of wealthy industrialists and heads of corporations, their arrogance and self-assuredness pervasive in their manner. I sit on a stylish chair made of chrome and crushed velvet, fashionably uncomfortable. Oliver orders for me. We drink lots of champagne. A well-coifed woman sitting next to me wearing a sexy top that looks like lingerie and a Cartier watch gleaming with too many diamonds feels me up under the table. I don't think Oliver sees. She nearly unbuttons my fly. I become uncomfortable and excuse myself to go to the men's room. In the toilet I find a guy alone standing at the basin. The floor is made of marble. He sees me but carries on sniffing a line of coke. I stand at a urinal and take a piss. When I wash my hands he offers me some. I decline politely and head back to the table.

The meals arrive, the portions fashionably small but highly decorative. They eat leisurely, talking about things I cannot relate to, like the jet set, obscure artists in vogue whose works sell for millions, English milords, continental aristocrats, yachting, models, stars, penthouses and tax exiles in Mediterranean havens; their conversations always fleeting. They whip through a bevy of easily recognisable famous names, criticising them for this faux pas when they used a fish knife for a salad or that one when they served salad as a starter instead of at the end of the meal. The buzzwords seem to be très American, retro, bon vivant and pleaz, short for pleasure. They are difficult with waiters as a matter of course, to the point of being childish. I asked for a quarter slice of lemon. You gave me half, one of them whines to the poor waiter. He insists that the waiter take back his sparkling mineral water.

"Isn't he gorgeous?" Oliver keeps saying of me and forces me to blush.

"I could eat him whole," one of the guys says of me.

After the meal the entourage of eight people, five guys and three girls, leaves. They drive fancy cars: Porsche, Ferrari, Bentley, Maserati and a vintage Aston Martin. Alone in the car with Oliver he kisses me. We drive towards Llandudno. We go up a long secluded driveway before we arrive at a mansion. I admire its unusual European façade. It's in Monaco's neo belle époque style Oliver, tells me even though I didn't ask. He must have seen the awe on my face, I say to myself, feeling stupid. I find him rather pedantic. The other cars park in the accommodating parking lot, discreetly away from the front house and its impressive façade. We go up some steps to get to the entrance. At the door a white butler with a haughty look lets us in. Oliver hands him his keys and invites his guests into the billiard room. I walk into an oak-panelled room. He shuts the heavy door and locks it. The ceilings are high and the room is expansive with many paintings adorning the walls. Oliver tells us to help ourselves to everything at the bar. A chandelier hangs above the billiard table with a red cloth covering it. Oliver adjusts the light till it is dimly lit.

"Can you play?" he asks as I stand next to the table.

"No."

"It doesn't matter. We won't be playing," he says lasciviously, like a vulture sizing up its prey.

We move to aristocratic Louise Philippe chairs. A thick Persian rug with an intricate pattern lies on the floor. The others are drinking brandy. Oliver French-kisses me. The woman who was feeling me up starts giving one of the other guys a blow job. It seems nothing unusual to them, just the decadence of the obscenely rich.

The guy receiving the blow job takes off his shirt, revealing a bronzed torso. Another guy kisses him while the woman lavishes his groin. The others nurse their drinks and watch. For a while Oliver and I watch too. The guy has an enormous erection. On the Persian rug Oliver takes off my top and unzips his pants. A hairy male arm reaches between his legs as I kiss him. The same male hand reaches between my legs and massages my balls. We group into two threesomes while the other two look on with lust.

There are moans, soft pleas and whispering, the smell of sweat and bodily fluids gradually filling the air, intoxicating us. Oliver gets up. He takes my hand and we sit down on the sofa while a different coupling is taking place.

At this stage we are all naked. The two women being fucked become the centre of attention. One of them gets taken from the rear on the billiard table. I cannot help but wince at the red cloth. There is something violent about its garish colour. On the sofa a guy is licking the balls of the one doing the fucking, fluids dripping. The other woman bounces up and down his shaft with infectious glee. Oliver massages my cock while we watch. I reciprocate. The third woman joins in and moans with pleasure. She gets fucked on the floor, missionary style. She seems more demure as she doesn't make as much noise as the others. I spot a wedding ring that looks like it cost a small fortune on her finger. Stockings, underwear and clothing line the floor. Condoms slip on and off effortless, plentifully.

The etiquette is easy, a simple nudge or a signal, and you don't have to accept. A blond guy signals to me. I look at Oliver and he signals for me to go. We couple on the floor. The woman begs me to fuck her. While I fuck her the guy begs me to let him fuck me. I let him and get lost in sensuous pleasure. He is skilled and she is wet. The atmosphere is not aggressive or threatening. I moan shamelessly. The wave of a hand discourages another guy from fucking another woman in the arse. Her clean pink anus is exposed as she gets fingered by a guy with long thick fingers and a hairy groin.

We go at it for a while before all the guys eventually come on the three women. They lie on the floor while we wank on them. Afterwards we move to a large indoor pool in another room. We splash about in the water and don't really swim. They soon start their antics again, coupling, licking and fucking. Oliver tells us that he wants to go to bed. "You know where to sleep if you want to stay," he says to Fiona, one of the women. They bid us goodnight as I disappear with Oliver. We go up a flight of stairs and into a large bedroom with a lounge suite and a king-sized bed. I'm tired and want to sleep, but Oliver is still horny. We suck each other off and fuck. He doesn't come easily. I have to use all the tricks in the trade to make him come. And when he does, it is prodigious, like a small flood.

Between slippery silk sheets that strangely make me think of drowning, I sleep exhausted.

I wake up tired in the morning and take a shower in an en suite bathroom. Oliver joins me in the shower when he hears the water spraying. I suddenly discover a morning glory bouncing behind me.

"Don't you ever get enough?" I complain.

"Of you? Who could, darling?" he says and kisses me, stroking me so that I must also get an erection.

I masturbate him in the shower till he comes. We both get out and dry ourselves. I feel hot and don't want to dress immediately. On the phone I hear him calling the butler to bring his breakfast to his room. He lounges in a thick white bath robe. The thought of a stranger walking in on us urges me to get dressed.

"Don't worry about Alfred. He's seen it all," he says as though he reads my mind. I look for my bags but remember that they are in the boot of his car. "You can get them after breakfast."

"What does your father make of your little sessions like last night?" I ask bravely. West told me never to ask extremely rich people personal questions. Something about them being wary of having to justify themselves having so much money and their bizarre, unusual habits. "Darling, the father screws the babysitter while the mother has it off with someone at bridge. Of course, they are into therapy," I remember Sebastian saying once. He was talking about a regular of his.

"He has sessions of his own," Oliver says as though it is an adequate response.

I nod my head.

"Was that your first time?" he asks.

"Of course not," I retort arrogantly, but of course it is.

"It's all the rage in Europe. In Paris there are certain clubs for it. Un club échangiste or une boîte à partouze if you want to be vulgar about it. Last night, quite liberating though, didn't you find? I mean you had sex to your heart's content," he says reverently. "It saved Jonathan and Lorraine's marriage. You know, the guy with the dick and that woman with the fuck-off ring?"

"What about your boyfriend, or should I be saying your girlfriend?" I go on.

"What about them? Screw them. I don't want to settle down anyway. People come, people go. It's the same with relationships," he says callously.

"Let me guess, you're a serial monogamist?"

"Me, a cliché? Please, don't insult me. No thank you. I'm just not interested in doing the couple thing if it means I'm going to end up like Jonathan and Lorraine one day," he says.

"But who do you bond with then?" I say.

"My friends from last night. Don't get me wrong, we're still friends, we still have deep feelings for each other. We just also fuck each other. It's not that complicated. It's quite boring actually, the way people imagine it being complicated. If you can't stand the heat you leave the circle, that simple. We've been friends for years," he says and leans over to kiss me.

"Your appetite is voracious. I should have brought West along with me," I say casually.

"Oh yes, West. I remember him. We had him once. Didn't enjoy his company, though. Found him a bit too sober although he fucks like a stallion," he says while my hand is massaging him between his legs.

There is a knock at the door. He gets up, straightens out his bath robe and goes to the door. Alfred wheels in a tray of food: croissants, yoghurt, fruit salad, juice, coffee and a white carnation for a little homely detail. Alfred gives Oliver his messages, all the time calling him sir. Oliver is polite with Alfred as though that is the protocol.

I start with some fruit salad.

"So, where did you go to school?" I ask curiously.

"Everywhere. It's a long story. I got my international baccalaureate in Monaco. Amongst other places we lived there for a while."

"I ask because of Alfred and that accent of yours. It's not really American, nor is it English."

"Observant, I could become your regular although our policy is to get a new ami each time we have a soirée," he says, eating his croissant with butter and jam. Everything he says sounds insincere, I can't help but notice that.

"So where's Mummy now?" I tease the overgrown brat.

"At home in England with Papa," he says pronouncing it the haughty English way. I wince inside when I hear him say that.

"You mean this isn't your home?"

"It is for me, but it's more of a holiday stop for them. They come here during the summer months. But they won't be here this December. I think they'll be spending Christmas and New Year's in St Moritz."

"What about you?"

"I don't want to be anywhere cold, that's for sure. So I'll probably stay. There's plenty to keep me busy in Cape Town," he says, sounding thoroughly spoilt like he has too many choices, the kind of person who thinks it is reasonable to be difficult, petulant.

He looks at the time. It is going on for eight thirty.

"Listen, darling I need to be at work at nine. We should be pushing off," he says suddenly getting frantic. He gets up and goes to an elaborate wardrobe.

"Fine, just drop me off in Green Point," I say, resigned to the fact that I'm not going to change into fresh clothes.

"I don't suppose you want to give me a blow job quickly," he says while putting on his Versace underwear.

I look at him strangely.

"Just a little humour, darling," he smiles but in his eyes I see that he would have been game had I accepted.

He changes into a casual monochromatic two-piece outfit by Armani, minimalist with simple clean lines that create an aura of calm. We leave the house. The others have already gone. He gets into his feline car.

"Your friends, what do they do? Are they also in advertising?"

"You're big on questions, aren't you, darling? I usually just fuck them and they thank me afterwards for the tip," he says caustically and starts talking on his cellphone.

He talks to someone called Michele as we drive towards town. He reminds her of the meeting, about the Ericsson account and the caterers who are supposed to arrive at ten. "Kiss, kiss," he says and hangs up. He doesn't say anything to me for the rest of the journey. In fact, he becomes a little moody and puts on his Gucci sunglasses. We arrive outside Steamy Windows.

"Uh, my money," I say awkwardly.

"Ah yes, even prostitutes have to eat," he sniggers and takes out a long wallet from the glove compartment.

"That should be enough for you not to worry your pretty little head," he says and gives me two thousand rand in crisp two hundred notes. I want to tell him to fuck off but I can't. You always find your pricks, I remember West saying. I get out unceremoniously and don't thank him as I close the door. I get my bags from the automatically opened boot and he speeds off, burning some tyre on the road as though to make a statement. Arsehole, prick, I curse him once he leaves.

I go inside and pay my studio cut. I also pay my A&R costs for the remainder of the month, instead of paying weekly. I don't really keep track. Sometimes I think Shaun is aware and takes advantage. I have recently started writing everything down, every cent I make and every cent I spend or save. But I know that my nest egg is coming on nicely.

**T**shepo comes to visit us one day out of the blue. I haven't heard from him since he left here. He finds us watching TV. We have become a regular, boring couple watching TV. But regular and boring is okay for me. It means I know where my man is. I don't have to worry.

He sits on the chair next to the sofa. Arne greets him but hardly says anything to him as usual.

"Do you guys want to go for a drink?" he asks.

I smile at Arne and poke him in the ribs.

"A drink? We can't afford to do that anymore," I say, trying to think of the last time I went out. It seems ages ago.

"It's fine, my treat. I insist. I know you have a baby on the way," he says and Arne looks at him defensively at the mention of the word baby.

"I'll drop you guys off but I'm not coming. I've got work to do," he says moodily. It is hard for him to accept that we have no money, that we have to make sacrifices and plan everything. He grew up differently. As for me growing up in the township and in an extended family that was sometimes needy and struggling, I learned that sometimes there wasn't enough to go around. That sometimes you had to hold back and not spend your money as freely as you would like for the sake of others. There were always people watching.

"I was thinking of going to Ganesh," he says.

"Not Ganesh," I insist. " Let's go next door, A Touch of Madness, they serve nice cappucino."

Arne reluctantly drives us to Obs and leaves us outside the coffee salon. I tell him not to worry about picking me up. "I'll find my own way home," I say.

"No ways. Call me," he insists. "I'm not having you taking a taxi if you can't find a lift."

He looks at Tshepo sternly as we get off.

"Sorry about him," I apologise to Tshepo once he leaves. "I think the idea of being a father is freaking him out."

Inside we are met by a woman with long blond hair and a calm face. We opt for a table upstairs and sit in the corner.

"You look good," I offer, looking at his shoes and expensive shirt.

"Thanks, you too. Your hair's really grown."

"How's waitering at the Waterfront going?"

"Fine, making decent money."

"You're full of shit, you know? You told us you were working at the Waterfront. I went there with Arne once to celebrate our anniversary and they told us you'd left. In fact, the guy was very weird about it."

He doesn't answer immediately.

"Don't lie to me," I say.

"I'm working somewhere else," he says vaguely.

"I spotted you outside Blah Bar with a really old guy one night. I was just driving past with Arne. And everyone says they haven't seen you in ages," I go on.

"Who's everyone? Like they ever cared about me anyway," he says defensively.

A skinny waitress comes and takes our order.

"So really, where do you work?"

"What difference does it make?" he says irritably.

"I'm just concerned."

"O maka o rata ditaba," he lashes back. "You just want something to talk about."

I look at him, hurt.

"I just thought you were in trouble, that's all. Someone said you were selling drugs."

He laughs artificially. "That's ridiculous."

"Really? They said with the clothes you wear and the places they've seen you at, you could only be selling drugs."

"Since when do you listen to stupid gossip? You know what Cape Town's like sometimes. People always want something to gossip about," he says unconvincingly.

"But you still haven't told me where you work."

"Fine, I sell drugs. Can we just move on now? I'm getting bored. This isn't my idea of a good time," he says uncharacteristically cold.

The waitress comes with my cappucino, his hot chocolate and two plates of chocolate cake.

We drink and nibble.

"You can't imagine what being pregnant is like." I feel guilty after that outburst.

"Tell me," he says, mildly interested.

"To start with my figure is going. My breasts are growing ..."

"I thought Arne would be happy about that."

"Wait. I'm more moody. I throw up in the morning. Sometimes I don't want sex or a man around me. And then there's my mother. I still haven't told her."

"You are going to have to tell her some time."

"I know. I know. I just can't find the right words."

"There's no way of saying it nicely. If you're pregnant, you're pregnant," he says.

We sip our drinks.

"So why didn't you want to go to Ganesh anymore?" he asks.

"I'm not the same person. I'm about to become a mother."

"I didn't realise what a big deal it was," he says, sounding a little more like his usually naïve self.

"We should do something together over Christmas. I'm not going home," I say.

"Your boyfriend hates my guts."

"No, he doesn't. I think he just feels threatened by you. Don't ask me why."

"Anyway," he says, indifferent.

"Just consider it. It would be nice. I'd hate to think of just Arne and me for Christmas. Things have been a little tense."

"Okay, I'll come."

We finish our drinks and cake but linger on. That's what I like about A Touch of Madness, you can just linger and not feel guilty.

"Why are you not at work now? I thought you worked nights."

"I called in sick," he says. "We better get going before the Terminator comes looking for you." He asks if we have a phone at home now and hands me his minute Motorola cellphone to call Arne.

At the door he pays. He takes out a fifty rand note from a wad in his fancy Fossil wallet and leaves a generous tip for the skinny waitress. I also catch a glimpse of an expensive looking watch on his wrist. I hope he knows what he's doing.

We find Arne waiting outside on the pavement. Tshepo tells us that he will make his own way home, that he still wants to see some people in Obs. We leave him walking towards Obz Café.

ANGELO-TSHEPO

Dear Mother, I have been thinking of you. I have been thinking about you a lot lately.

Sometimes I feel you when I wake up in the morning, still a little disorientated after a dream.

My life with you, it feels like a dream. It feels like it happened to

378

someone else. It feels like I knew you in a different light, in a different time and under a different sky, not this one that always seems to rain with coldness. I miss your warmth, your fierce protection and endless strength.

I still remember your scent. Time stopped in my memories of you when you left. I feel like a child when I think of you and remember that photo of your wedding day. How happy you seemed, father clutching you proudly. What has become of him? Why is he so evil, this lord of the underworld? I caught a glimpse of him in town going in a fancy car, chauffeured by men with brutal facial scars who look like askaris; men who wouldn't hesitate to shoot, to maim, to kill. When I think of him I become depressed, I feel dark. He is like the night that eats the sun.

He is darkness, Mother. I hate him. I hate what he did to you. I hate that I feel like an orphan. Why did he take you away? How could he be so cruel? He is my father I cannot deny that. I cannot divorce myself from him, this lord of the underworld. When I sleep he weaves nightmares for me, visions of walking the city endlessly, always searching for the ray of light that will bring me back to you. And of course if I find you, he finds us. He will never leave us alone.

He has left me to fend for myself in a world of vampires. But I am building a nest. I'm putting away something so that I won't have to sell my flesh to make a living. I have plans and dreams. It is difficult because I cannot say he hates me. He has never expressed any emotion towards me other than indignation, disapproval. That is why I find refuge in the dreams you weave for me, Mother.

The morning belongs to you, it is when I miss you most. It is as though a myth is growing inside me, a story that was written long ago by someone else, perhaps a benign god. This wise god revealed to me that you are Isis, resting in the garden of delights, the mother who never forgot her child, eternally awaiting his return. Perhaps I knew you in a grander, bolder age when it was okay to love your mother and tell the world about it. Perhaps I knew you during kinder days when it was okay to love myself.

That myth, it is growing inside me, nourishing questions that make me wonder and keep me awake at night. I read interesting truths from its narrative. I remember moments of light and intense love, skies with gentle giants and a vigilant sun. I remember a time that stretches back further than memory when I was whole, when I felt complete. I walk around with heavy, painful truths, dark secrets that my mind won't expel.

The first universal human beings were born of three sexes from the Sun, Earth and Moon. There were men, women and hermaphrodites, each of the three sexes doubled over and united as a whole. At some point in the unknowable past they were brutally cleaved in two, doomed to go through history suffering the violence and anguish of separation, constantly longing to be reunited with the lost half of the self, the better self. Being cut in half resulted in the forms of heterosexuality from the hermaphrodites and homosexuality in both female and male forms, the amnesia of the brutal separation mutating into bisexuality in others. And since then we have all suffered the same fate. That is why some of us are what we are. That is why we are called moffies and faggots. Perhaps we took secret oaths with ourselves before we got separated, so that we would stubbornly remember that we were incomplete, the clue being that it is someone of our own sex. Perhaps we are the coarse self searching for the refined self, or vice versa.

I'm becoming aware of myself as different types of people discover oceans of pleasure with me. I sleep with so many people mother, I must be honest. The differences between men and women, it is hard to resolve them. Necessity, survival, progeny has brought us together. Or perhaps a trickster who couldn't resist having fun, an ingenious god who managed to convince us to play together till one day we noticed that her belly was growing. But in our hearts we know that we are different, awkward with each other sometimes. That even when a man and a woman come together in the act of love, their union remains ultimately incomplete, limited by the constraints of the human body. It stops short of a full merging of lovers because we came into this life incomplete and half asleep. The truth about who we really are is only beginning to dawn on us, it is just beginning to haunt us. Sometimes when I'm alone and feel rejected by the world, it is as though I remember the violence of being born and how sorely I cried, mourning the warmth of your womb. Nothing can soothe the loss I feel when I remember that we were once so close.

I think about you, Mother. In some mysterious way my life is connected to you. It is as though we made vows of love to each other in a different life, in preparation for the confusion of this life. My love for you has deepened with death, it has matured. Sleeping Isis, I see you in my dreams pouring wine into a delicate goblet but you are always on your own. Father is never far behind, the angels of death eagerly clinging to his black cloak. I dreamt he killed his child and ate him. It could have been me. I fear that he would do the same with me if given the chance, but love burns him with its wild fires every time the noose tightens around my neck in my dreams.

Perhaps I sense that I will die young, the burden of having such a dark father weighs too much on me. Death is begging at my heels in my dreams. Perhaps I won't reach the nubile age you were when you got married, Mother. I feel like my luck has run out. Mother, you cannot save me from the jaws of destruction that father controls; no one can. I have been quietly living in your shadow, its shade like a safety net for me. It is time that I step out into the light and observe the shadows it conjures. I must be strong. There comes a time when we must face who we are boldly, when we must listen to the music of our dreams and delight ourselves with courage as we grasp our destinies firmly in our hands. I'm only beginning to see beyond the horizon, past the cliff and waterfall. Perhaps we have forgotten how to listen to our own restless instincts and the longing of our hearts. Perhaps we have forgotten how to question, how to stand up and stand alone, unfashionably, even when the storm is raging. It is not enough just to live. We must aspire to the sky, to the freedom of living with truth. Tomorrow waits for no one, it is happening now. Mother, I feel your embrace.

In the morning I wake up glad that I'm another day closer to being with you again. I cannot escape my fate. It is like a spiral, going in only one direction, towards the infinite centre. I have contemplated this fate often enough. I'm going to die young, it is that simple, nothing unusual, we all die. But for me I sense the complexity of travelling through the underworld before being reunited with you. But I feel stronger, Mother. I have been feeding from my own strengths. The chance to love you again is all the faith I need to get through the darkest hour. I would confront the master of darkness himself, if it meant I would see you again. Indeed I need to see you. I need your gaze to fall upon me and bathe me clean of all the ugliness father has left me with, so that I can love myself. I feel doomed because I cannot love him, Mother. And not being able to love your father is akin to not being able to love yourself. Our lives are inextricably connected, the three of us.

Every day when I put away something for my little nest I shake and shiver a little because the intensity of fear is always there. What if I don't succeed? What if I never see you again? It is maddening. To search for peace I had to cultivate silence inside, to sit alone. Sometimes it is like getting a brief glimpse of what you felt when I was born, this sitting alone. It is strange to be a person, so insignificant, so alone and scared in the world. Sometimes I think if the anatomy of a man is a model of the universe, then the smallest possible fragment of the surface area of the tip of his eyelash would be our galaxy. We are so insignificant, our lives so inconsequential it is frightening. It is a miracle that God hasn't forgotten us. We only exist in our minds. In life we are just moving atoms, no different to still rocks savouring eternity, impulsive winds and feverish fires.

How I dream of you, Mother. Where are you? The scent of death is not far behind. I will go wherever you beckon me.


### SEBASTIAN

**A**ngelo and I stay behind one night after a shift. We take refuge in Studio One. It used to be West's studio. I have decided to let him in on one of my rituals. We've become close and I find him receptive to different ideas.

We sit on the large bed. In the middle of the bed, between us, I have assembled my favourite images of naked men, erotica neatly stashed between clear plastic: porn stars like Peter Norton, Rocco and the legendary Jeff Stryker, rock stars, actors, models in stylish and glossy magazines, artists, reproductions of the infamous pictures of Jeff Koons fucking his wife, certain images in art and sculpture, Robert Mapplethorpe and his take on black men, Bruce Weber's male seraphs, cutouts of regular men that bored wives sent pictures of to Hustler for Big Dick competitions, images of naked black men and native people from The National Geographic, copies from straight and gay porn sites on the internet, Pamela Anderson and Tommy Lee, Brad Pitt, Seal, Bobitt, and calendar teases. They are images of naked men, close-ups of big black dicks, white dicks, unusually shaped dicks, ejaculating dicks. Images of men posing, moving, fucking, rimming, sucking, getting sucked, moaning, groaning; men alone, in couples, threesomes, foursomes, orgies. One image consists of a train of fifteen men, their dicks in each other, all different colours, all smiling.

"So this is what we do," I explain to him. "We study them, all of them. Maybe for fifteen minutes. But you're not allowed to touch yourself. The point is to get aroused till you feel like you're going to come in your pants."

He is sitting in his boxer shorts.

"Fifteen minutes. I don't think I can last that long," he says, already lusting.

"Just try, believe me it's worth it. You'll feel a buzz afterwards, rejuvenated."

While he studies the images I burn a stick of incense and light a joint, potent Malawi Gold that can transport you anywhere and give you vivid hallucinations. I take two drags, savouring the sweet scent, smoke moving like a friendly ghost around my face. I offer him some.

"This is part of the experience, it just heightens it," I say. He takes a couple of deep drags before he hands it back. It is a small joint. I already start to feel high, but a clean high that doesn't irritate my eyes or make me clench my jaws like acid does. Fucking on acid is confusing, it pushes you into yourself too deep, you don't really enjoy the sex. It is a reality drug. It brings you back, it doesn't take you out. Having sex on acid is creepy, you feel helpless, alone as if someone's doing something to you. You don't feel like you're engaged in something creative. I once had a bad trip where I started thinking that the guy fucking me was my mother. Acid does that, it drags you into yourself violently. You feel like a hostage, impotent. You may have an erection but you don't enjoy it properly. Emotions get in the way of everything. Ecstasy, I don't trust what has been said and written about MDMA, so I haven't tried it and I wouldn't. The long term lasting effects are not worth the gamble. Cocaine is too expensive and it controls you. You can't control it. Rocks are for scabs. Heroin is overrated. So you have a great orgasmic experience but you look like shit afterwards. I can't afford that in my job. Besides, the come-down is lousy. Speed upsets my metabolism. I don't sniff anything, they say sniffing fucks up your sense of smell as well as your sense of taste, since the two senses are connected. I'm not crazy about hashish. And I have never tried peyote. But marijuana is different. You can travel safely, freely, if you know your boundaries, like your moods. You must cultivate a positive state of mind if you want to move with marijuana. Sex on ganja can be ecstatic, tantric, transcendental. If it's fresh and the plant is matured you will feel a burst of energy expanding inside you till eventually it moves through the energy spots in your body, what they call chakras in the East. But drink lots of water.

He passes back the joint to me, his eyes a little red. I finish off what's left of it and put the ashes in the incense holder. "Fuck," he says, high and horny. I offer him some juice.

We sit among the feast of men. The lights are dim. We are both in our underwear, unthreatened by each other. It doesn't matter who's got the bigger dick. The images begin to move a little because I'm high, the colours and flesh tones becoming real. I get to a favourite image. It is of a handsome enough army officer naked except for his white y-front underpants. And he also wears his army cap. Men in uniform are my best turn-on. It has something to do with authority and my deep-seated desire to play the transgressor. At school I was the outsider, every rugby coach's nightmare. I grew up not fitting in, clashing with teachers and constantly being sent to the principal's office. He was good-looking, my principal, but ruthlessly severe with me. I always thought he had a big bulge in his pants and often fantasised about him coming in my mouth. I suppose that's where my erotic fixation with authority and men in uniform began.

I study the image closer. He's well built with a washboard stomach, his thighs muscular and defined. A tattoo runs down the side of his left shoulder and crawls onto part of his chest. I want to lick him. He's got his hand in his underpants, exposing part of his semi-erect dick. It's especially erotic because you don't see his whole kit and he wears this unusually serious look, like he's dying for a fuck. Then there's another image of two guys wanking, their legs around each other.

We exchange images, sighing and beginning to breathe hard. After fifteen minutes I'm ready to explode. I pack the images in a folder and put them away in my bag. Angelo gets two towels from the massaging table. I switch off the light.

We lie next to each other on the bed but we don't touch each other. My mind swirls with the image of that guy with his hand in his under-pants.

"So now try and keep this up for at least forty five minutes," I say, already stimulating myself.

"That long. How do you do it?" he says.

"Experience, trust me," I reply. "Just follow my lead. When you feel like you're going to come just hold back, visualise a woman, that usually does the trick for me."

"Visualise a woman, huh?" he says, already panting a little. "I can just about visualise anything at the moment." He slurs a little.

"Just think of it as a journey. We're going somewhere. You're going to meet the man of your dreams and you guys are going to have a great time. So start when you meet him in the shower or wherever and he's naked. Play it out. Take your time. See every detail, how he moves what he smells like and how big his dick is. No one likes a small dick, darling." We laugh together.

In the dark we masturbate. A few times I hear him speeding up.

"Steady, hold it back," I rescue him. The point is the longer you go, the deeper you see into your own sexuality. It is like coming face to face with your shame of sex. Everyone has something to be ashamed of, and most of the time it has something to do with sex. That says something about the society we live in.

"How are you doing?" I say, the bed shaking, creaking a little.

"Fine. I'm just enjoying my dream boat," he says. In the dark I hear him panting.

We wank for more than half an hour. I use my anus as a kind of control pad, releasing and intensifying my erection as I mount states of pleasure. I play with my nipples and lick my lips.

"I can't go on much longer, I have to come," he says urgently.

"Okay, just wait a minute. We're at the last stage," I say, feeling my own nuts boiling with spunk. "Here's a little magic about male fertility rites for you. Before you come, picture your most cherished aspiration. Anything beautiful that you would like to have or see. It could be meeting a person or getting something you've always wanted. The point is that it must appeal to the highest self in you, the ideal. So picture it, something ideal, it could be as daring as world peace or as obscure as freeing Tibet. Anything. Now, once you've got that image in mind, just let go, come."

The bed starts shaking vigorously as we both accelerate towards the finish line. We almost come together, ecstatic, releasing a small flood of sperm. We lie still in the aftermath and sigh, satiated, sanguine.

I'm the first to speak.

"Male fertility rites are important, you know."

"I can see why if they are this good," he says and reaches for the towels. He hands me mine. We both wipe ourselves. My chest is wet from sweat. In the dark I look for the fan and switch it on. It comes as a relief.

"So you think this stuff can make a difference?" he says to me.

"It's like anything, if you believe it. If you take an aspirin but you don't believe it will heal your headache, it probably won't," I say.

"I still feel horny though, like I could go for another round," he says eagerly.

"Don't. The point is to go once and do it properly. The horniness you feel now is just potent energy circulating your body. You don't want to get rid of that. Just be still. Feel yourself. After a while the frantic energy that's making you horny will settle. You'll feel rejuvenated. Trust me. Think about something else. What are you doing for Christmas?"

"I haven't really given it much thought. A friend of mine invited me to spend the day with them. I might do that. And you?" he says.

"Nothing special. I'll be at home," I say. We reach for our underwear and put it on.

I switch on the TV and we watch a late night edition of World News on CNN but soon get bored. I change channels and come across Janet Jackson in a slinky green gown, seducing someone. We watch music videos on Channel O.

"I still feel horny," he says.

"Don't waste the energy. Just relax. Think of your father," I offer.

"That doesn't relax me. It agitates me."

"Well, do whatever it takes to get your mind off sex."

He keeps quiet for a while.

"You can do things with true erotic longing, you know. It can be a way to discover yourself, who you really are. Like if you do this often enough, you'll start seeing a pattern in all the things you wish for just before you come. If you ever wondered how fickle you could be, try this often enough and you'll get your answers," I say.

"I feel calmer," he says after a long while.

He is a very earnest person. I find myself free to talk about things that mean a lot to me. Few people have tried to understand me. Sometimes life experiences can only be defined or explained in a language that is easily accessible. I believe sex is one such language.

### ANGELO-TSHEPO

Peter has become my favourite client, my faithful regular. He comes in on a Thursday at around five thirty, usually tired but looking forward to seeing me. He says he tells his wife that he's going to the gym for an hour and a half of weight-lifting followed by a relaxing sauna and shower. I have grown to like him in an impermanent way. Sometimes just to amuse me he'll dazzle me with new, expensive underwear or a nice cologne. Once he bought me a watch. I refused, politely. He understood. It just seemed like a bad idea, like it could lead to a scenario that neither of us could afford.

He is sitting on his side of the bed, taking off his shoes. He likes me to massage his shoulders while he does this. As always his hair smells clean, invigorating to smell. I help him take off his shirt. We kiss for a while. I still haven't become comfortable with that, because I know that he pays me for it afterwards. And that's not what kissing is for me, it's very personal, an intimate expression. But Peter has been good to me, regular, although a little needy.

I have eventually let him fuck me. He has been patiently begging me for so long. I just gave in one day. I don't do penetration often, the fear of Aids always lurks at the back of my mind. I choose my clients carefully. Something has to be in it for me if I'm going to take the risk. Maybe the guy is foreign and seems interesting. Maybe he has a physique to die for. Maybe he is friendly, charming, the kind of person who would rather win me over than offer me more money. Maybe he looks at me in a certain way and I know that it just feels right. Maybe I've heard that he's good in bed or that he comes like the Victoria Falls. Maybe I haven't had a client all night. There are many reasons to sleep with a man.

I take off his pants. He is wearing a pair of bright red Tommy Hilfiger boxer shorts. I am naked.

We move to the bed where he kisses me some more.

"I still don't see why you insist on kissing me, now that you can also fuck me."

"You don't know everything at your age," he smiles.

"And you do?"

He lavishes my neck, the scent of Jako by Lagerfeld drugging me. With all the men I meet, I have become adept at recognising men's fragrances.

I caress his arse. It is firm, tight, toned. His erection lolls in his boxers. I slip them off.

"Do that thing again please," he asks.

I sit on his thighs and slap his arse, making cracking noises. But I mustn't do it too much otherwise he will get marks that his wife might notice.

"Oh, that feels so good," he says, his pelvis digging into the bed.

"I can't do it much longer, you're going red, Peter. The problem with being white," I joke.

"Just a little more," he begs.

I slap him a few more times. He groans. He once told me that at school he used to get in trouble on purpose so that he would be sent to the principal's office to get flogged. He said during one such session he came in his pants but the principal was none the wiser.

He kisses me again, his erect cock sliding between my legs.

"Does you wife ever give you a blow job?" I ask.

"Never. She thinks only desperate ugly girls do that. She thinks it's for sluts," he says grinding his pelvis against mine.

I grab his cock and massage it gently. He moans. He is so sensitive, so hungry for a little abandon like most men his age. Their wives are starving them of wanton sex.

He takes some KY Jelly and starts fingering my anus, but very gently. I'm sensitive to rough hands.

I put a condom on his cock but with my mouth. They all go wild for that. His scrotum holds two large testicles, the skin soft and supple as if it has loosened with time, age, experience. I lick it and suck it gently, stimulating the base of his shaft.

Once inside me it is as if Peter becomes another man. He takes his time, beginning slowly with gentle strokes. I trust him not to be so rough that the condom breaks. His breath is hot, a little frantic but steady. I feel it on my neck.

Over the sessions he has become adventurous. He once gave me a series of photocopies of Kama-Sutra-like pictures of men fucking, eager to try new things with the enthusiasm of an intrepid teenager. I indulge him because he is kind. How many other men live such quiet lives of desperation and forced protocol, longing to roar when they can only purr?

We try several poses. He grunts. I moan. He paces himself, observing the clock when he thinks I'm not watching. But I know his pattern, he likes to go on for as long as possible. Ten minutes before time up I tell him that I'm about to come. He accelerates. I feel his strength, his muscles working like an efficient machine. By that time I'm wet and relaxed. The quick pace and controlled aggression are like punctuation marks after the steady build up. We ejaculate blissfully. I take off his condom carefully, tie it into a knot and wrap it with some sanitary paper.

Afterwards I massage his balls. He is always quiet when I do this after sex. I don't bother him with questions about where his thoughts are.

"You're nice and bronze. Did you go to the beach last weekend?" I ask him after a while.

He takes his time to respond.

"We went to Knysna," he says but without excitement or pleasure.

I keep massaging his balls.

"You know, when I come in you, I know this is how it is supposed to be with my wife."

"Do you want to go for another hour? I won't charge you."

His expression changes as he snaps out of introspection.

"Thanks, but I can't. My daughter's got a performance at school tonight. Don't ask me what," he says, looking at the clock.

We take a shower together. Standing in the water he looks taller. I come up to his neck. He squirts out water from his mouth, comfortable around me. I massage his balls again. His shoulders are broad, athletic, his hands big but not clumsy. I know how subtle he can be when he touches me. A man with so much experience, so much to learn from, what a waste, I say to myself while I scrub his back, perhaps unfairly judging his wife and kids. When he turns around, he has an erection. I wank him, playing with soap. The pleasure on his face gives me pleasure. Sometimes watching a man enjoying sex is like eating with your king at his table. But you are not his subject, you are just another guy, like him, also with needs. There is the comfort and pleasure of standing as equals, as worthy men. The expression on a man's face when he comes, for me it would be the true expression of a patriot when he serenades his land and his people.

I work his shaft nicely, delicately gripping him tighter as he begins to moan. Perhaps this is all he wants every once in a while from his wife, a good wank, just a little naughtiness, the old slap and tickle. Certainly it would make him happier, he wouldn't complain as much about how frigid and puritanical she can be. The church, it hasn't served us all that well, he once said bitterly.

I have come to the conclusion that yes, sex can be one measure of how fulfilled a man is, how close he is to realising his inner ideals of freedom, how deep his knowledge and experience of his body and himself is. It is a measure of how liberated he is, how creative he can be, how easily he confronts issues. I notice whether he improvises, does he read the little messages I'm sending out, can he tell whether I am also enjoying it or does he have to ask me first? I suspect that the men who have lousy, unfulfilling sex at home make tyrannical bosses at work. It would seem to be the only outlet for all that pent-up energy which should naturally be spent through meaningful sex or masturbation.

Peter comes in my hand. He kisses me again. We rinse ourselves and go back to the room to get dressed.

"So will I see you again next week?" I know what the answer is.

"You're my Thursday afternoon after graft," he says zipping up his pants.

"But shouldn't you be wearing the clothes from gym?" I remark.

"I don't have time to get changed after work. I just come straight here. I'm still going to the gym. She thinks I go for about two hours," he says.

He pays me R500.

"So how are my voyager miles coming?"

"Pretty well. You should soon be qualifying for a free trip around the world."

I see him out.

Later I get an unusual client. I walk in and greet him. He shakes my hand firmly. He tells me that he doesn't want a massage. "I want to mess around with you in bed," he says with a stolid voice. We start getting undressed. To my surprise I notice that he has a prosthesis on his left leg. But I say nothing. Perhaps he noticed my surprise but he also says nothing.

He sits on the bed and takes it off. I massage his shoulders while he does this. On the bed he gets an enormous erection.

"So what do you do?" I ask politely, to make conversation. I feel a little tense.

"I used to be a journalist," he says without emotion. "Do you give blow jobs?"

"Yes," I say awkwardly.

He lies back. He smells clean. He spreads his thighs but his left stump stares at me.

"Is there a problem?" he says without emotion again.

"No. I was just wondering if you want to be wanked with cream or oil," I improvise.

"Whichever. You're the expert," he says impartially.

I lick his balls. He hardly moans. He doesn't even touch me on the back of the head like the others whenever I assume this position. He just lies still. But his dick is rock hard. I lick it for a long time, playing with it, teasing it. He still doesn't move, doesn't moan or show pleasure.

"Are you enjoying this?" I finally ask, a little exasperated.

"Ja," he says coldly.

I go back to his groin.

"Do you do dry fucks?" he asks after a while.

"Yes," I say with relief, happy to let him do the work.

I spread my legs and he lies on top of me, his stump digging into the bed. I try to look relaxed, like I'm enjoying it. Concentrate on his big dick, I tell myself as he starts to grind his pelvis against mine. His balls rub against mine. I close my eyes. He starts slowly but builds up his thrust, sweat beginning to drip from his chest. But he still remains

390

quiet. When I open my eyes and briefly gaze into his they look icy, impenetrable. His mouth is closed. His jaws stick out and relax as he grinds them. I have never seen anyone look more angry during sex.

I resolve to close my eyes again. He rubs against me for a long time, eventually he comes, spectacularly, his huge load spilling on my chest. I even stare at it with wonder.

"Can you fuck me?" he says again with an impartial voice.

I hesitate. His eyes draw me in.

"Ja, fine. Let me just get a condom."

I strap it on quickly.

He lies on his side. He has a nice arse. I use KY Jelly and gently finger him. Only then he starts moaning, short little moans that encourage me to tease him some more.

"Please, now," he begs me after a while, his initial coldness melting.

I thrust inside him gently. He moans again. I grab his cock while I do this. He lifts his good leg to let me in.

Soon I'm pumping him. He moans with pathos. I have never heard anyone moan like that, deep wrenching moans that sound like they come from the depths of his reticence. It is like listening to a secret language, a private conversation. Every time I vary my strokes, he responds, moaning in a different way.

I ask him to change positions and take him lying on his back. I wrap his good leg over my shoulder. His stump stares at me. He says nothing. He just looks at me. Eventually I touch it, caressing it gently. He says nothing again. I slip inside him, his large cock rock hard. I start thrusting.

He moans but this time I can see his face. There is so much tenderness about it. He closes his eyes, his mouth open, his throat lustful. I kiss his throat, sucking it. He moans and puts his hands around my arse, encouraging me to go deeper. I give him everything I have. We go for a long time, our sweat and fluids mingling to make an erotic scent.

He reaches between his legs, feeling me as I plunge into him. I start accelerating. He clenches his arse, also grinding against me. Together we work like a piston. When I come he splashes all over his chest. I collapse onto him, momentarily.

He says nothing and soon recovers. I take a towel and wipe off his come. I take off the condom, tie a knot and wrap it with sanitary paper.

"Well, how was that?" I say afterwards.

"You fucked me good," he says with an impassive look.

He puts on his prosthesis. We go to the bathroom. He takes it off before we go into the shower.

"You have a nice cock," I compliment him, intrigued that he doesn't say much.

"Thanks," he says, proudly. I massage his balls. It always relaxes them. But he soon gets another erection. Sometimes after coming and getting another erection soon after, a guy's dick actually becomes bigger. I can't explain it. I only noticed this with guys with really big dicks. I handle it in my hand, blood pumping through its veins.

"Do you want me to wank you?" I ask him. He is slightly taller than me.

"I want to fuck you," he says, soberly.

I hesitate.

"You can get a condom. I'll wait here," he says, but noncommittally.

Do I want to be fucked by this guy? I ask myself, but salivating at his large cock.

I get out the shower, slip into a towel and go to the studio. I return with a condom and some KY. His erection is still waiting. I play with him for a while before I put it on.

He moves his cock between my legs but doesn't slide it in. That sacred place between the balls and anus, what I sometimes call "no man's land", he plays with it. I feel his bulbous head rubbing me there. Like him I keep quiet. I don't respond. Skilfully he massages my arse. I still don't react. Incredibly he balances himself on his one strong leg. He turns off the taps and massages me with KY. His fingers are deft and gentle.

I soon hear myself moaning. He slides in gently, teasing me, giving me a few inches and then pumping. When I moan some more, he gives me more inches till eventually all of him is inside me. I stand with my face against the cool wet tiles of the shower. He lavishes my neck and touches me in places that few people know about. He is an expert, a tourist guide travelling through a foreign country. He touches me everywhere while behind me. My ears, they give me such pleasure, I don't know what he does with them.

I even forget how enormous he is. I just become aware of his energy circulating inside me. We lock. For a while he does very small movements inside me. An image flashes in my mind. I see him walking in a bush. A landmine explodes underneath him. I gasp and open my eyes. He pumps quickly, as though sensing that I've had enough. He soon comes.

I turn around. To my horror the condom still on him is ruptured. I take it off him annoyed.

"Don't worry, I'm negative. I got my results four months ago," he says.

"A lot can happen in four months," I say turning on the water.

I scrub myself. I don't bother with him.

I can't believe the condom broke. What was I thinking? I berate myself.

In the room I say nothing to him.

"How much do I owe you?" he asks.

"R500," I say hardly looking at him.

He moves close to me and looks at me. I want to look away. Without warning he kisses me.

"I haven't come like that all year," he says, still impassive, his voice hoarse.

He hands me R700.

"Don't worry. I'll see myself out," he says and leaves.

I try not to worry that he came in me but I do. The room smells different, the odour of sex unusually strong, intoxicating like a secret potion.

I go home in a foul mood. Jacques is in the lounge with two other people. He has never introduced anyone to me as his friend. They grunt and nod rather than greet me properly.

"Why is it so dark in here?" I say, remarking about the dim light. A large candle burns.

He doesn't say anything.

I go to the kitchen and pour myself some orange juice. On the coffee table I notice a bottle that looks like red wine. But there is something sinister about the subdued atmosphere that tells me it might be blood.

"And what's that funny smell?" I say, annoyed by their reticence.

One of them sniggers. Jacques says nothing and holds a small book. They are all dressed in black.

I go to my room and lock the door. After a while I hear them going to Jacques room. They play discordant esoteric music. And soon I hear strange chanting. After a while the music and chanting stops. And then I hear them leave. I go back to the kitchen and pour myself another glass of juice. The fawn fat cat stares at me. "What do you want fat-mog?" It scurries off to the lounge.

At night I have a dream of the guy with the prosthesis fucking me. He tells that he is the god of fertility, that he is sowing sacred seeds inside me. A falcon flies above us as we fuck, the sun, the large eye in the sky, watching. In the morning I wake up feeling heavy, as if a part of me stayed behind in the dream. I lounge in bed all morning, contemplating the significance or the insignificance of the dream. When it is time to go to work, I put on my favourite powder blue shirt by Ralph Lauren and my black strappy shoes. They always make me feel different, like I belong somewhere else, like this world is just a stopover, a transit lounge where I meet people before proceeding on my journey. Jacques is at work. I search for the mysterious bottle of wine in the fridge and in the bin, but I don't find it. As usual the door to his room is locked. Forget him, I say and leave.

At work everyone raves about my blue shirt. I get two clients and both of them pay me well. At the end of the evening I crash in Studio Four with Cole. We don't do anything. We never do. I think of him as a big brother. But a big brother with a big dick. I always tease him about it. I don't think he likes it.

I sleep quickly, once he puts out the light. The god of fertility comes to me in the night again. We eat peaches together before we fuck, his body a temple of love. The music of the East strangely plays in the background. I travel on the wings of a falcon. The sun falls on my back and burns me a little, leaving behind a delicate image of a dragon. It hardly hurts. When it heals the image looks real.

I meet men with the heads of wolves, foxes and jackals. In the corner of a large room a person trapped in a tree tries to grab me but I burn him with fire. I follow the god of fertility into a strange room, where roses grow on the floor. We lie on this bed of roses without any thorns and fuck to our hearts content. A lion watches us, its eyes glowing with divine solar power. But the god never smiles, he never says anything. He goes about fucking me in a serious manner.

In the morning when I wake up Cole is gone. I feel heavy again, as if I lost something in the previous night's dream. I go home tired, empty, my mind spinning with images of petals falling from the sky. I feel a little high and breathe deeply. For a moment I stand still and close my eyes, trying to centre myself. An impulsive energy force moves through me. I have the distinct image of miniature blazing suns. It moves from my stomach till it reaches my crown, exploding into a thousand-petalled lotus of light. I watch inside myself as the image disappears, the light scattering. When I open them, a strange blinding light rushes towards me. I faint and fall down.

A woman walking by helps me up. I tell her that I'm fine, that I just need to rest. I can see she's in a hurry. "Please, go," I beg her. She insists that I sit on the pavement with my head between my knees. Cars go by, people pass us. She stays with me for a while. When I attempt to stand up she helps me. I feel better, I smile, even though my head is still a little dizzy. "You're sure," she says concerned. I tell her that I'm fine.

She hails a taxi. "Where do you live?" she asks me. "Gardens," I say tired. "Get in," she orders me and takes it upon herself to take me home. I get in the taxi with her. It stops outside the flat. "Really, I'm fine," I tell her as I get out. She wishes me well. The taxi leaves.

As I walk towards the steps I get a view of the infamous three tall circular apartment buildings, their profiles standing out against the mountain. The three graces, I say without thinking. I don't know where the image of three graces comes from.

I get home and find Jacques out. I go into my room and lock it. The bed takes me into a deep hypnotic slumber.

MMABATHO

After my exams I call my mother. We make small talk. How are you, how are things? She tells me about her new job and the lousy pay. I become irritable and come out with it.

"I'm pregnant," I blurt out mid-conversation over the phone, "The baby's due in June."

The line is silent.

"I haven't told Papa," I add.

Then she lashes out. "How could you be so careless? How could you be so stupid when there are so many ways to prevent …?"

"I was using something. Anyway, I don't need a lecture from you," I say defensively.

"Mmabatho, I'm still your mother."

Now I'm sulking.

"Who's the father?" she says after a while. "I can't believe you're going to have a child. You're hardly out of school."

"You don't know him."

"What kind of an answer is that? Who is the father?" she yells.

"I don't need this," I say and hang up the phone.

I have never been able to open up to my mother about anything. We live in two worlds. She wouldn't understand that Arne is more than just being white.

Later in the evening, I call my father.

He is happy to hear from me. Did you get your money last month, he asks? Yes thanks, and the extra something, I say. Since they got divorced he has been looking after my finances. How were the exams? I give him a brief synopsis of how my life at university has been going. I tell him that I called Mama but that we had a fight.

"What happened?"

My heart is beating fast.

"Papa, I have to tell you something. I'm pregnant." I hold my breath.

"I see."

"Are you disappointed?" My father means the world to me, more than my mother. His approval is important.

"Well, I know that you have been on the pill. I get the monthly statements from my medical aid scheme, so I can't blame you for that. You're not a child anymore. I know it happens sometimes. But don't call it bad luck. You are bringing a person into this world. There's enough bad luck going around."

"I'm glad you feel like that, Papa. I didn't go looking for this, honestly. And he's a nice guy. We're in love," I say embarrassed, relieved that he isn't angry.

"Has he asked you to marry him?"

The question takes me by surprise. I hesitate, wincing inside.

"Yes."

"You don't sound too sure."

"I am. He asked me to marry him, Papa."

"And?"

"Of course I said yes."

"My baby is going to have a baby," he says tenderly. Does he look sad as he is saying this?

"Anyway, Papa, I'd better go. I'm actually on my way out. I'll write to you."

"Give me your number," he says. Then, "Look after yourself."

"Don't worry, Papa. He's looking after me."

"What's his name? This he must have a name."

"Arne."

"Who?"

"Arne," I speak up.

"What kind of a name is that?"

"He's German."

"We'd better talk about this another time," he says quickly. "Are you in tomorrow evening? I'll call you."

"Ja, I'll be home," I say nervously. "Bye."

His goodbye is a little curtly.

Arne is at the library, labouring on his thesis. I think it has become a burden to him. Life has become urgent. I sense his panic. In his sleep I often hear him talking, nonsensical things that I don't understand. He doesn't go to the gym as often as he used to and every decision we make is usually based on money. Can we afford it? Is it necessary? It is difficult for him. But he must adjust and learn the humility of counting one's coins gratefully if we are going to make it. I'm getting tired of his moaning about what he misses and how things were before. I need him to be here with me now, body and mind. Every day my baby is growing.

And why hasn't he said anything about marriage? Does he think this thing is going to peter out like a story that comes to a pathetic ending? Why is he sticking around if he thinks he's going to leave later?

He comes back late. I'm irritable and tired. He starts getting changed to go to bed.

"I called my parents today. I told them I was pregnant," I say.

"How did they take it?" he turns round to face me.

I fiddle with a loose string from my night dress.

"My father wants to know if we're going to get married," I say.

"Well, we haven't discussed it." He carries on taking off his clothes.

"I want to discuss it. We can't just leave it hanging in the air."

"What do you want from me?"

"Don't stick around if you think I'm going to have this baby without some commitment," I tell him. "I'm not some wench you picked up and now you have to find a way around her."

"I don't have any headspace for marriage," he says, shaking his arms.

Headspace? I hate it when he uses that as an excuse for anything.

"Fuck headspace. Why don't you be a man and just tell me outright if you don't want to marry me."

He puts on his sleep shorts angrily, almost falling over.

"I don't want to get married. I never intended to get married, to you or anyone."

"So exactly what did you think was going to happen after June?"

"You would have the baby and we would continue living together, see how we like it, if it works."

Are men that stupid?

"If you think we're just going to hang around and see what happens, then I think you should pack your bags and go. I'm not waiting around for you to make up your mind. I'm having this baby. I don't need you and your crap."

"You can't expect me to give up my life."

"You shouldn't have come back. You should have stayed in Germany. If you don't have the balls, just leave me alone."

He rushes towards me. I cover my face thinking he is going to hit me. He grabs me tightly around the shoulders and shakes me.

"Don't talk to me as if I'm a child."

"You're hurting me." I cry.

Then the baby kicks. I gasp and hold my stomach. It kicks again. He lets me go.

"Tomorrow I think you should leave," I say to him tearfully.

"And go where?" He takes a blanket and a pillow and goes to the lounge. I lock the door behind him and have a good cry.

I'm sorry, baby. I'm sorry that men are such idiots. I'm sorry that Mummy is always crying, always worrying about you. Your father only thinks about himself. I'm sorry, my angel, that Mummy gets so upset that you have to kick me to calm me down. I'm sorry that I have such lousy luck with men. Your father thinks that you will evaporate mysteriously. He doesn't talk about things because he thinks that they will sort themselves out. I'm sorry, my baby, that you have to be in the middle.

I have a secret for you. I have been thinking about a name for you. I was going to tell your father, but what's the point? When I think of you I imagine such beautiful things that I have decided that you are a love child. I will name you Venus first, whether you are a boy or a girl, but I know that you are a boy, so tough, you even kick Mummy. And then I will name you Kgotso because you bring peace to me. But definitely I will call you Venus, my shining star, spreading love across the universe.

You mustn't worry. Mummy will take care of you. I know people. I'm resourceful. I don't need to wait for a man to get some headspace. Where did he hear that stupid expression anyway?

I don't know what to do, Venus. I still love your father, but he is pig-headed and selfish. I don't want him if he is going to be a father like that. At the end of the month I will move out and get a place alone, or share with someone like before. I'm not a fool. Perhaps your father doesn't love me. The chance to love is always a chance to grow. Why won't your father see that? It was the blindness of love that brought us together, that created you, Venus. How can he be so shallow and selfish? Love gave us you, can't he see that?

I don't want to mother him. I'm tired of telling him to act like a man but he leaves me no choice. Venus, I will do everything I can for you, my little one. I had one bad parent. I won't subject you to the same. It is hellish, you spend your life in therapy, trying to regurgitate the anger and hatred. It is not worth the risk. Definitely, I will do my best for you, Venus. You are my rock, my centre. Everything I do is for you. I plait my hair, oil my tummy and eat well, so that you can be strong, so that Mummy will be strong for you.

ANGELO-TSHEPO

**I** go to work one day, at the door Francois tells me to go to Shaun's office. He tells me that I have a visitor. I have never had a visitor. Who could it be? I go there nervously, praying that it is not my father.

I knock on the door when I get to Shaun's office. He opens it and half smiles. Someone is sitting behind him. Fortunately it doesn't look like my father.

"What's going on?" I say confused.

"I'll leave you guys alone," Shaun says and leaves, closing the door.

The man stands up. He is tall, hefty and looks Malay.

"I'm Abdul," he says. His incisors are capped with gold and he wears an expensive suit. It looks tailor-made because he is a large man but the suit fits him well.

I shake his hand but I don't introduce myself.

"Your father has been shot. He's in hospital. They didn't think he would live this long. I think you'd better see him," he says.

I sit down, shocked, voiceless. My father has been shot. What?

"Is he dying?" I ask plainly.

"I think you'd better come," he says humbly, his hands folded in front of his groin.

I'm shaking a little.

I go to the lounge where the others are. I don't say anything to Shaun, I just nod. Strangely, as though he understands me, he nods back.

I leave with Abdul. He drives me in a black Z3. We drive to Groote Schuur.

I hate hospitals, after Valkenberg I hate any place with nurses and doctors. We walk down several corridors, wide and long. I feel naked with fear. Abdul walks slightly ahead of me, I suppose to avoid questions. I have so many. What happened? When? Who? A fat woman with thick lenses helps Abdul at the reception desk.

I feel faint and scared but I go on. Abdul signs something. We go into a private room.

The first thing I notice as I walk in is the beeping machine that monitors the heart. There is a drip beside the bed. He is sleeping. But his face is slightly swollen and grazed, with a bump in one corner of his head. I see a lot of bandages on him. It sends a shiver down my spine.

"Where did they shoot him?" I whisper to Abdul.

"In Woodstock," he says.

"I mean where on the body?"

"Oh, sorry. Four bullets on the body. Two in one leg. One in another leg and one in his arm," he says and cracks his knuckles. I notice that part of his little finger on his left hand is missing.

"Tshepo, is that you?" Papa says, a tube protruding from his nose. He startles me. I walk closer.

"I'll be just outside," Abdul says and leaves.

"Come closer," Papa says. I take a chair and move closer nervously.

"You look good. Are you eating well?" he asks.

"Yes, Papa," I say, sounding like a ten year old. He looks at me with his intense eyes. I look at his grazed and swollen face. He looks terrible but he still has that fight in his eyes, that fuck-off arrogance about him.

"Who shot you?"

"It doesn't matter now. I'm on my deathbed. Besides, would you avenge me?" he says cynically. He hasn't changed.

"I came because I was worried," I hear myself say.

"About me? No need to," he says arrogantly. "I know what I'm doing. I'm dying."

It makes me uncomfortable, sad.

"Why did you call me?"

"Because you need to hear certain things before I die," he says, coughing a little.

"Don't be dramatic, you're not dying," I say irritated.

"They think they patched me up but I know I'm bleeding inside. I can feel it. I'm dying," he says unfazed.

"What was it you wanted to tell me?"

"Your mother. You never understood our relationship," he says.

Now I'm angry.

"I understand that you are reaping what you sowed," I tell him.

"Exactly."

"What do you mean exactly?"

400

"Like I said, you never understood our relationship. It was complex. It goes back a long way."

"Where is this going?" I'm sensitive when anyone talks about Mama, especially Papa.

"I'm going to join your mother."

"After what you did to her? Even Satan would expel you."

"She was my wife. Those sacred vows, I took them seriously."

"Yes, but it says till death do us part."

"That's what they said. I had my own ideas about things," he says and coughs a little again.

"I knew you would be alright," he says. As if he did a good job fathering me. It annoys me to hear him say that. Where was he when I was eating bread and fried potatoes for breakfast, lunch and supper for weeks because I couldn't get a job, that stingy bastard Chris torturing me?

I only grind my teeth.

"I'm preparing you for the road ahead. It's a jungle eat jungle world out there." He has never been good with expressions, my father.

"You think I was hard on you. I was doing you a favour. I know you're a moffie. What can I do? I'm dying. You have to be tough today. If you're too hard, things come back to haunt you. If you're too easy, you don't advance them. You can't win. There isn't a science to bringing up kids. I did the best for you, despite what you think."

I listen in a way I have never listened to my father.

"I loved your mother, no matter what you think. She was my wife before she was your mother. Maybe I was a little jealous of you sometimes. I know how you were around her but you were always my son, even if I hated you a little."

"It's good to hear you being honest," I say.

"But there are certain things that you don't know that I have seen, that I have done. I know you think there is nothing to my life, that I'm just a criminal. But I'm more than that. Books can only take you so far, I know how you read. Don't tell me about wisdom. Perhaps my death will be the biggest lesson, the most valuable lesson I could possibly offer you."

"Violence in its purest form – when it is the last resort, when it is the result of deliberation, deep thought, even inspiration – can be an act of love, of kindness."

"What are you talking about?" I say confused. "You sound like those idiots planting pipe bombs all over Cape Town."

"I'm talking about your mother. You don't understand everything. There are forces at work that you couldn't possibly imagine. You still have a lot to learn. Don't judge so quickly, so easily, especially when all the evidence seems to confirm your suspicions. That is when life is being most deceptive. Don't hate me so easily. Think about it a bit more. Defy your instincts. Challenge them. Challenge yourself."

"Are you trying to talk yourself out of guilt?"

"I was paving a road for you. We sacrificed a lot for you. Even our lives."

"We? Is this about guilt? Are you feeling guilty for what you did to Mama and your pathetic life in the Mafia?"

"Just trust me. Everything is at it should be. The process has already started, what is done, is done. The circle completes itself. No one can touch you. Your mother and I opened and sealed the dark face of violence and death. Between us the forces of good and evil have been reconciled," he says, sounding crazy.

"Is it the medicine?" Maybe he's delusional.

"Tshepo. You must go back to Johannesburg. Your work is done here. I know what you do for a living. It's time to go. Go see your cousin," he says.

"You mean my halfbrother? I know what happened. I know that you had a child with your sister."

But he looks weak. I cannot give him too much contempt.

"One day you'll realise that I loved you. We don't really choose what we do, what we become. Life chooses us."

"Oh, God. Should I be calling the priest?"

"I want you to promise me something," he says. His energy is ebbing.

"What?"

"Promise me that you will do something with that anger. I know you're a bright boy." I don't think I have ever heard him say that about me. I am scared. What if he dies? What will I do? How will I feel? Who will be my object of hatred? Hating him has given me strength.

"You gave your mother all the love and me all the hatred. You were right. Men are not like women. We understand each other best when there is some hatred between us."

"So you knew I despised you."

"Absolutely. I encouraged it. I didn't want you to walk around with your eyes closed. You loved your mother too deeply."

"What would you know about love?" I say bitterly.

"I know the love of a woman. Your mother had absolute faith in me.

Do you know what that means? It means you feel so free that you can even gamble with your soul," he says and coughs.

"Do you want some water?"

He shakes his head.

"Your mother loved me and I loved her. Right till the end," he says and breathes in deeply, that tube in his nose bothering me.

"But you killed her."

"Like I said, you don't understand everything. Details."

"You want me to ignore a detail like that?"

"You don't know everything."

"Look, I have to be somewhere. I'll come back tomorrow," I say. The anger is becoming too much for me.

"Don't think like a woman. I know you're a man," he says.

"I'll see you tomorrow," I say at the door. Abdul goes in as I leave.

Once outside the hospital I crave a cigarette even though I'm no regular smoker. I bum one from one of the nurses taking a break outside. It burns my throat but I continue inhaling the smoke. I feel sick and even want to throw up.

He can't die on me. Not now. Not until I have proven myself, proven that I can make it without him. Not until he sees me succeeding, happy, even with a man in my life. He can't die now. Life would be cheating me. Where is justice? I need him around to get through. Knowing he's there makes me strong, it gives me all the reason to think about a better future for myself. He can't die. The doctors must do something, everything. They can't let him die. My life depends on his life. The only thing that's kept me from slashing my wrists is knowing that I am stronger than him, that I can beat the odds, come heaven or hell. He can't go. Not when I still harbour so much anger, so much self-loathing. Not when I can't love myself and feel good about myself.

He can't leave. He hasn't seen me at my best. I have been working so hard towards being a better person, doing something with my life. I want to see the envy on his face when I succeed. I want him to say I was wrong about Tshepo. I didn't know my son. I wronged and failed my son. I hated him. I want him to say that. But I want him to say it with humility.

Why did he have to get shot? That final blow was supposed to be mine. He was supposed to turn pale and feel a heart-attack approaching when he saw me doing well. He should at least have suffered a little on my account. He should at least have felt what it was like to be alone and rejected. No, he can't die.

I catch a taxi to town. At home I find Jacques vegetating in the lounge, his two fat cats lounging on the armrests of the sofa. The floor is lined with their fur. Their smell permeates the flat. I hate that smell.

"This place stinks like a zoo."

He doesn't say anything. I go to the kitchen. The sink is filled with dirty dishes, his dirty dishes. He never cleans up. He leaves everything for the woman who comes in once a week. I feel nauseous when I see big cockroaches scurrying across the sink, their long antennae clashing.

I go to my room and lock the door. Depression comes over me, like a dark cloud. I feel powerful with anger. I could smash something. Why is he doing this to me? He is the only person who can drive me to such extremes.

I get horny when I'm depressed or very angry. I get a violent erection. On the bed I unzip my pants and start masturbating. I imagine that guy with the stump, the god of fertility in my dreams fucking me. After I have come I wipe myself with a dirty T-shirt. Outside it is windy but hot. I open the window. I feel better but still edgy. I decide not to go back to work. I spend the rest of the evening listening to music on my new Sansui stereo. The one I got with my money, not his. I clean my room and neatly stack my shoes in the corner, my books in another corner. The shoes are new and look clean. Ha! I wish he could see that. I wish he could see how well I dress, how well I eat, how I know my wines, my etiquette. I wish he could see how responsible I am. I'm planning to buy myself a laptop, something legitimate. I wish he knew that West and some of the men I've met have taught me a thing or two about the stock market. I wish he knew that I've invested my money in equities, in IPOs. I know he would be impressed. I know he doesn't know anything about equities, that historically this might be the safest strategy to make money if one has patience. Agricultural commodities, All-Share, dividends, Nasdaq, do these mean anything to him? Probably not, but I wish he knew that they meant something to me. I wish he knew that I wasn't stupid and clumsy like he always thought I was.

He doesn't know me but he has the audacity to say that one day I will love him.

The following morning I get up at about eight. I wash and dress myself quickly. My stomach moans but I ignore it and leave without eating. I go to town and catch a taxi to Groote Schuur Hospital. At the reception desk I meet a different woman, small and skinny, her face a little gaunt. I tell her that I'm here to see my father. She checks on the list and then she looks at me strangely.

"Didn't someone notify you? I'm sure we called. Your father died at three o'clock this morning."

Upon hearing the news I feel as if I am containing inside me the impact of an atomic explosion. I feel numb. I stand there and feel like pissing in my pants. "Are you sure?" I say desperately, "I was only here yesterday and he looked fine."

"He just suddenly complicated. We rushed him to surgery. He died on the operating table. I'm very sorry."

How many times has she had to give that kind of news to people?

"Sorry, are you Tshepo?" she asks, reading something from the book.

"Yes."

"There's a message for you here. I almost didn't see it," she says and writes a number on a piece of paper and gives it to me. The number has Abdul's name beside it.

"My God, he's really dead," I say to myself as I take the piece of paper, strangely feeling bereaved. I summon my reserves of anger but they are not there. My throats tightens, it becomes sore, but I refuse to cry. Not for him.

"Can I get you something to drink?" she asks kindly.

"No thank you." I don't know where to go, what to do.

I sit on one of the chairs in the reception area and let the news permeate my being. Bastard, he died on me. I stare at the piece of paper for a long time. Well, it's official now, I'm an orphan. I always felt like an orphan after my mother died, but now it's official.

I take out my cellphone.

"I left a message where you work," Abdul says in a mournful tone.

"I didn't go there," I reply, my voice, low and heavy. It feels as if someone dropped an anvil on my chest.

"So when do we bury him?" I ask.

"Don't worry about that. It's already been taken care of."

"What do you mean it's been taken care of?"

"I'll bury him this afternoon."

"What?" I say astounded.

"Your father was Muslim," he says, "and you know the custom. He has to be buried within twenty four hours."

"Muslim. When did this happen? When did he convert?"

"I have always known him to be Muslim."

"I see. I suppose there's no point in me coming there, then."

"You're not Muslim?"

"No."

"Of course not, not at the place you work." I ignore the comment.

"I wouldn't advise you to come. You wouldn't understand the custom. Besides, I think he would have wanted it that way." What does he know about my father that I don't?

A moment of silence follows.

"He left you something, a letter. I dropped it at work," he says.

"Is that all?" I say but I'm not hoping for more.

"Yes. He was very specific about the other things he had, what was to be done with them. Don't worry, it's all been taken care of," he says, sounding as if he wants to hang up.

But I don't want the conversation to end, because he is the last link I have with my father.

"Abdul, what do I do now? You are going to bury my father and I will never see him again."

My throat aches.

"Get on with life. He is in the merciful hands of Allah now," he says magnanimously, but it doesn't soothe me.

"This is terrible. I can't hang up the phone," I say pathetically.

"It's okay. I'll wait for you to hang up first."

I feel like crying.

"Abdul?"

"Yes."

"Is he really dead?" I ask.

"You must go home and rest."

Silence creeps in, but I can hear him breathing on the other side.

"Abdul?"

"Yes.

"Tell him I love him," I say and hang up the phone.

I feel weak with hunger and grief. I go outside and look for a chip shop on the main road. I buy a chip-roll with lots of chillies, to burn away the grief, the ugliness inside. My mouth is on fire from the fresh chillies. I buy a can of Coke. The combination of the effervescent drink and the chillies creates a small torture chamber in my mouth. I feel like mutilating myself with a knife. I walk to town, passing several street merchants and the dingy side shops of downtown Salt River. I walk till I get to the station but my legs do not feel the distance. I walk to Sea Point. The sky is overcast but the sun can still be seen through a veil of clouds. It creates a sedative, hypnotic effect with its opaque light. I want the earth to swallow me as I walk. I want thunder to splinter me into pieces. I want the wind to carry me away to a desert.

Once in Sea Point I catch a taxi home. I lock myself in my room and sleep oppressively. I wake up at four in the afternoon, tired, hungry and dazed. I should have gone to the gym today, I say to myself, trying to make sense of life. I go there every second day. I get up and change for work. It will keep my mind off things.

SEBASTIAN

It is hot. Hot days mean slow evenings. People are happy to stay at the beach for as long as they can. And afterwards they would rather go out than come here. There are only five of us working tonight, me, Angelo, Storm, Carrington and Adrian. The others are sick or on leave. The excuses are a prelude to their leaving. The staff always changes around Christmas time. Introspection, guilt, the church, Aids – who knows what suddenly makes them jump ship. This is not a job for everyone, Shaun never tires of saying to the new stallions.

Storm and Carrington are out on a travel and an overnight. Adrian is sleeping on the other couch. He was out all night on a multiple. Angelo sits with me on the sofa. We all heard what happened to his father but no one has said anything to him. He sits quietly beside me, watching TV.

"Listen, I heard what happened to your father. I don't know what to say. I'm sorry," I finally open.

"Thanks," is all he says.

Shaun comes in to tell us that four German guys might be coming in later, looking for stallions who fit our profiles.

"You don't have to stay, you know," he says to Angelo.

"I know. I just don't want to be on my own right now," he says, looking sad.

Shaun goes back to his office. I light a cigarette. He asks me for one and I offer him.

"You know what the worst thing is? I secretly wished he would die," he says to me.

"We all wish that one of our parents or both would die at some stage."

"You don't understand, I hated him," he says with difficulty, "but I also loved him. Does that make sense?"

He takes deep drags.

"Where do I go from here, Sebastian? I feel like evil is out to get me. He left me a letter. I couldn't bear to read it so I burned it."

"I'm going to tell you a story, call it a myth if you want. It's not the happiest story but it always gives me strength when I feel down," I say.

He looks at me expectantly. I get an ashtray from the coffee table and put it on my lap.

"They say that somewhere in the world, somewhere secretive and dark, there is a woman who lives in a dungeon that she never leaves. This woman is a prisoner. Now they say this woman is the original mother, the one who gave birth to the first people. She's immortal, the only person like that on the planet. That makes her the most revered person on earth.

"Over the centuries, people learned that she had managed to defy death. But she was humble and secretive. Only awakened souls recognised her. Over the millennia people followed her, trying to learn from her the secret of immortality. However, conspiracies started, cabals were formed. Everyone wanted to get the elixir of youth and they spied on her. But she was careful, self-effacing, she never left any traces wherever she went, roaming the world freely, watching over her children.

"However, when man started writing, a very long time ago as you can imagine, she was taken prisoner. And once they captured her, they abused her to wring from her the secret of life. But she refused. Until this day they continue, torturing her. You see, they knew that she could manipulate things like the weather, plant and animal life, that things responded to her. They knew that her knowledge of the earth was deep and ancient. The civilisation of Atlantis knew this. They had stolen their psychic and astral gifts from this woman, the mother. They used psychic energies for wrong purposes and ultimately they destroyed themselves because nature became imbalanced. A few people survived the cataclysm of Atlantis, and over millennia they left their legacy for modern man. That is why all over the earth many cultures know bits and pieces of the Great Deluge. It is part of the legacy of Atlantis, part of our collective consciousness.

"Even today there are people living amongst us who are not what they seem to be, people who know the secret laws of life and nature and can manipulate them. People who influence weather patterns subtly but ultimately aggressively. These secretive people are present at every level of society. They decide what we eat, where progress is going and where it isn't going. Perhaps you've heard of the Illuminati. Well, they are just a tip of the iceberg. There is a complex society out there that functions at the highest and most elite level. People who are beyond banks and countries, people who literally control certain portions of the globe. They might even have the cure for Aids but are holding it back for political reasons or simply trying to play God. I mean how many billions have been spent on the disease? They can send a spaceship to Mars but they can't get a cure for Aids, something just doesn't add up.

"Now, all this power and information they have depends on this woman. Somewhere between these conflicting cabals and secret societies someone knows where the woman is. In the meantime a kind of war is going on out there between these spy networks. Ordinary people are not even aware of it. But if you watch TV, if you read certain newspapers, magazines, you start to see that there is more to what is going on out there than meets the eye. Smear campaigns, mysterious deaths, people being implicated, exposes of people who claim to have been members of secret societies. You have to plough through a lot of shit but there is some truth out there, if you surf the Net patiently.

"These people who've inherited this ancient knowledge, it is said that they can function at ninety percent of their brain capacity or more, that they have really stretched the boundaries of human ability. Shapeshifting, telepathy, astral travel, being invisible, communicating with dark forces, trapping angels and celestial beings, these are all realities. They are part of a complicated Underworld. It is said that they can relay information with just a look. They are everywhere in society, in different functions and on different levels of ability and knowledge. At the top of the structure are the elite guardians, then the intermediaries, followed by auxiliaries and an army of informants with minions everywhere. They are school teachers, civil servants, flight attendants, bus drivers, paramedics, fathers, housewives, ordinary people you see in the street, people who look unassuming. It is said to be a predominantly male domain. You see the point is to have enough information to be able to be anywhere and penetrate anything. Ultimately this whole thing is about information. It's about who has it and who hasn't. How to get it by any means and how to protect it by any means necessary. The world is becoming more abstract, more virtual and less real. These guys are way ahead of current technology, the things they can do are nothing short of science fiction. That means being divorced from nature. And that can only have one result: doom.

"What I'm telling you is the result of bits of conversations that I overheard secretly, tripping over things on the Net, conversations with clients, putting one and one together. These are things that no one would volunteer to me openly. They say in these societies there is no verbal communication, nor do they write anything down, to avoid information being leaked. So they have to be very careful. You must be aware of your clients, you must notice things, open your eyes. You never know who they are or what they might be trying to tell you."

"These elite people, can they also live forever?" he asks.

"No. That is why the woman is still being held hostage. There is a theory that she is being held by a powerful, dominating church that has so much money it can stand as a country. This church wants to use this information as the ultimate tool, the ultimate opium to drug the masses about the church and eternal life. They want to take out God from the equation. If they know how to live forever, who needs God? The church would become a demi-god, the ultimate authority, telling people how to live their lives, dangling eternal life like a biscuit to a dog in front of them. Can you imagine how the church would manipulate people? We would know darkness. People would control who got to live forever and who didn't. There would be pandemonium. Of course the power would always end up in the hands of the elite, of the few who feel they are chosen, when in fact they have imposed their will, misused sacred information and gone against natural laws of the universe.

"And all the while this woman is locked away in a deep, ugly pit where they torture her regularly. To control nature, they must control her. They have raped her and had children from her but they always died at birth or didn't live long. They have beaten her, made her eat her own foetuses, to force her to give them information. But she refuses. So she has been suffering, unimaginable tortures throughout all these centuries. There is a connection between the rapid progress of humanity since the so-called Age of Enlightenment and the suffering of this woman. The more advanced we get, the more they torture her, the more monstrous they become. She tells them things, but not willingly. They can't kill her because she's immortal, touched by divinity.

"Yet they are trying. It just so happens that unfortunately this woman is black. She's dispensable. It is unfortunate because black people suffer so much as it is. I'm not being condescending or anything but that's the reality. History, who knows? We all have our parts to play. But that is also part of the reason why people are so numbed, so unaffected by Africa and its atrocities. It has to do with this woman being taken hostage. They can watch black children starving in Ethiopia and not bat at eye because they accept it as 'their lot' in life. But what did they do when Bosnia was up in flames?

"Now hear this. This is what inspires me. All living things, plants and animals, know about this woman. They identify her as the universal mother. They respect her because they feel her slavery, her imprisonment. All living creatures were traumatised by what was done to the woman, the guardian of animals and plants. In sympathy, as a salute, plants and animals have remained mute, passive, withholding their secrets. This woman, however could communicate with all living things.

"We are being manipulated by some of these cabals at every step of the way. In some shopping centres oestrogen is secretly being pumped through air vents and air conditioning systems while people carry on with their lives. They do this to pacify us, to keep us in our place, half asleep, happy to follow meaningless routines without thinking much. And certain foods, certain labels that are globally accepted as cultural icons, who knows what they put into them? More and more people are beginning to find out, to question, what is going on. That's why this whole conspiracy is such a hot topic at the moment. There is a collective awakening, they can't control us much longer. They can't control the information much longer. There is too much. They are also beginning to panic. There is too much to hide, too much to protect, it is all bursting at the seams.

"But now the earth out of control, so out of balance after years of abuse that the worst is still to come. The same reason why Atlantis disappeared is going to affect us.

"That is why most governments who know something, are taking measures to prepare themselves. Look at the US. The army has changed its role. Soldiers are not what they used to be. Today they are trained more to work with civilians than anything. Survival training is more important than learning how to use a gun. They are being trained in crisis management and conflict resolution because our future is at stake. The bad guy isn't the Russians or good old Saddam any more. It's us. The Deluge is on the tip of everyone's tongue but no one will mention it.

"Seismologists, vulcanologists, geologists – they are all studying the earth and they know that we are headed for something big and ugly. The big one everyone is waiting for is Tokyo. It will come. And when it does, the Japanese will have to recall all their monetary resources abroad. The GDP of Tokyo is greater than that of the whole Britain. Can you imagine what that will do? It will devastate the world economy, resulting in global economic chaos, the fall of the mythic Babylon that rastas talk about. But it is too abstract to imagine, to put into words. It overwhelms people, so they don't say anything. It's like the matter of natural resources running out. We all know that they are running out, but people are still carrying on as if they will last forever. It's too abstract, too big. It will only hit home when it starts to affect us directly little by little. A natural disaster that will bring humanity to its knees is coming. But governments know this yet they are not telling people because they would panic. People are people. Information is protected at all costs.

"I'm quite psychic. On a scale of one to ten I would say that I'm an eight.

"In the last year I have been having the most violent dreams, and they all have to do with natural disasters, people drowning, people burning, people screaming, stepping over their own children to save themselves. Fire, volcanoes, earthquakes. It used to really freak me out but I've just learned to accept the dreams. I think of them as intuitions. It is inevitable. I have seen it. More than half of humanity will perish in times to come. Can you imagine destruction on that scale?

"People imagine this to be the Armageddon, what God is going to do to us. But we don't realise that we have done it to ourselves. The earth is reacting. We have imbalanced her, she is going to set herself right. And the cleansing will result in massive deaths like we have never seen and ultimately, in the release of the woman, the original mother. What are the elites going to do about the uncontrollable carnage? I mean, there are six billion people on the planet. What do you do with more than three billion corpses? It's creepy, because Auschwitz comes to mind. Is history revisiting us in a twisted, ironic way? Do you remember Rwanda and what happened after that carnage? Dogs just went on the rampage, gorging themselves. It was intolerable to breathe the air because there was so much rotting.

"The elites have always known about this cataclysm. At the end of the seventies they gave us Aids because they thought twenty years would be enough to decimate half the world population, to prepare for end times. What they didn't count on is how resilient people would be. People fought back against Aids. Anyway, I have a strong suspicion there is a cure out there, that the disease was engineered by man. It's all just a matter of time before people start coming out with the truth. Our survival is at stake.

"Violence and destruction the likes of which we have never seen are coming.

"But peace will follow, a new period, a spiritual rebirth is coming. Even the Bible talks about this. But before peace can reign dark days are ahead. Animals are going to turn on us. Pets will attack their owners, viciously, to avenge the woman held captive. The church will suffer the most. We will know what it is like to live like animals. That expression ,'you're an animal', we don't really know what it means. But we will one day. The earth will rule again when instinct will be stronger than intellect. Nature will flex her muscles and dominate. It's going to be about the survival of the fittest. As people, as a species, we have been spoiled, we have never really known strife. We have had easy air, water, resources, land, never having had to really fight for survival. We take it for granted that we will be here forever. But what happened to the dinosaurs?

"We will be forced to bow to Nature again, to feel her womb, to know suffering. There is a revival of earth mother worship. It's a prelude for times to come.

"But out of the confusion a being will arise, a young man, and he will lead us out of the darkness. After the carnage and cleansing, this person, who has been quietly living, will come into full blossom. He will be pure at heart but wise to the world and its wiles. It will be a day of sunshine and light, a day to celebrate, when those who have been virtuous will receive their gifts from the light. After the carnage, the remaining souls on earth will face the last stage, which is the shower of light. Virtuous people will be able to process the light, thereby transmitting its energies to the highest realms. But some people will be unable to process the light, it will scorch them. They will either have to spend their days in darkness or they will burn to death. The soul, after all, is a fallen divinity trapped in material incarnation. It comes from light and thus it will return to the light. And those who perish will simply be recycled into other possibilities. I suppose being burned is a bit like being purified. Nature is economical, it doesn't waste anything. At the same time it is generous. The soul cannot be destroyed. It is immortal. It has no beginning and no end. It's nature is to be in a state of self-movement, whether that means filling one's life with more light or darkness, spiralling out of control or looking for higher possibilities."

"I have been having strange feelings myself about what is going to happen. In fact, I think that we are close to the final days," Angelo says.

"It's something to celebrate though, don't you think?" I say.

"I suppose so," he says unconvincingly, "But the scent of death is everywhere. It is making me ill."

It is late. I am in a meter taxi. The driver, a chubby Indian man, drops me outside the flat and leaves. A white cat walks proudly across the road. I let myself in.

Jacques is in his room. I can hear him snoring even though the door is closed. The cats are in the lounge. They look restless. Outside the moon is full. I sit in the darkness and feel drowsy, but I know that sleeping won't take away the fatigue. Something else has gotten a hold of me and I don't know what to call it. I feel different. Something inside me has resigned, as if I know the fate that awaits me.

This morning I had a strange dream again. I was a falcon flying over rotten meat, dead people. A huge woman who changed into a dinosaur began eating them. I couldn't watch, so I woke up.

The cats brush their tails against my leg. I want to kick them. There is something evil about cats, perhaps it is their arrogance. They want me to brush them, to tickle them but I just ignore them. Eventually one of them jumps onto my lap. I throw it off and it lets out a scream. After a while the door to Jacques' room opens. In his underwear he comes out. He puts on the light and gathers his cats, giving me a dirty look. He smells terrible. "You smell like a pig," I say venomously. He doesn't answer, he just gives me the evil eye and disappears into his room. "Switch off the light, dammit," I yell, but he ignores me.

I get up and switch off the light myself. I'm tired of living with arseholes. I have a knack for picking them. Perhaps I may even be turning into one myself. I go to my room where it is hot. I collapse on the bed and drift into sleep, still wearing my clothes.

In the morning I wake up with an unusually strong feeling to check my finances.

I phone a connection that I met through West, an investment manager at Old Mutual. He has been helping me manage my money for a small fee. I tell him to cash in all my investments. "I have a bad feeling about share prices dropping," I explain.

"Fine. I understand. You'll have your money in your account by tomorrow," he says moodily, but I refuse to feel guilty.

I still feel tired. I force myself to get changed for the gym and catch a taxi to Sea Point. At the gym I do an advanced step-class that has me on my wits trying to figure out the complicated routine. I come out feeling that I have had a good workout. An intensive forty-five minutes doing weights follows. In the change rooms I shower quickly and go into the sauna. There are six of us in there. I only last five minutes before I take a lukewarm shower. In Sea Point I go to Ardi's for lunch. I feel strangely alone, isolated, as if people are watching me. I can't say who, it's just a feeling I get. Then I go to Exclusive Books at the Waterfront. The man behind the till keeps looking at me intermittently as if I might steal a book and shove it in my bag. I disappear to another part of the large book shop. He soon comes by making himself busy with some books he packs in a nearby shelf. I feel uncomfortable and soon leave.

Walking outside to catch a taxi a guy mouths something to me but I can't tell what he is saying. He walks in the opposite direction. What is going on? I feel eyes on me wherever I go and begin to panic a little. I get into a minibus taxi and sit in the back seat where no one can stare at the back of my head. I get off down the road from the flat and walk home briskly. In the next block, sitting on a crate, a dirty homeless-looking guy stares at me as I make my way in. He looks like a human rat.

Jacques isn't home. The smell of cat food permeates the flat. I go into my room and feel relieved to be alone. I lock the door and soon feel drowsy. Sleep comes over me.

I dream of home, Soweto. I haven't dreamt of it in a long time. But in the dream all my friends, all the people I grew up with, have the heads of jackals and wolves. I can recognise them from their bodies, from the way they walk. I dream of Mshenguville and other squatter camps. I see gold in the sky and when someone drinks I observe that it is blood that they are drinking. I feel trapped in the dream, wandering around my neighbourhood in Orlando East. Strangely I hear the muezzin. I meet an old man with skin so loose around his face that his face looks like a mask.

We sit on bar stools in the middle of a traffic island, watching cars drive by with delirious speed. I become dizzy and keep looking at the old man to keep from falling over.

"Your father has opened a long road for you," he says mysteriously, little cockroaches falling out of his mouth as he speaks.

"But what has that got to do with me?" I say confused.

"Your father, he isn't really Muslim. They inherited some of their customs from a great people, an ancient people."

"Who?"

He smiles mysteriously again.

"I have no answers for you," he says.

I watch cars speeding, miraculously managing not to bump into each other. When I turn back the old man has gone.

I walk the city of Soweto. Everywhere I go small children play cowboys and Indians with real guns and little girls and boys play house with condoms and dildos. I run away from them in horror. In Rockville I come to a stadium. Wild horses are running there, their manes magnificently flapping in the wind. In another field I see a group of bare-chested men playing soccer. But as I get closer they metamorphose into graceful centaurs with long untamed tails. I run towards them and they form a circle around me. They are handsome in a rugged way and are of every colour imaginable. I become aroused as I watch this rainbow of muscular torsos. They drink wine and run riot on the field, kicking the ball, sweating, galloping, the earth thudding with their hooves.

I wake up with a pleasant erection and masturbate. But I don't think of anyone in particular. I just masturbate and enjoy it.

At night I decide not to go to work. What's the point? I feel confused, different. Besides, Shaun said I could take a few days off. It is as though each time I sleep and wake up I bring back something from the dream, from another world. At around nine I decide to go for a drink at Biloxi. It is packed as usual on a Saturday night. The men look horny. When I walk among the crowd, someone grabs my arse, another brushes my crotch. The smell of men and their cologne intoxicates me. I begin to feel relaxed, I finally have a perspective on things. Why have I been so edgy, so paranoid? I go to the bar and buy an Amstel from a vain bartender who keeps rubbing his washboard stomach, giving everyone sleepy come-to-bed eyes. Good-looking vain men are a put-off. I have always liked the quiet, unassuming type. Inner strength in men comes in the form of silence. The loquacious, arrogant type who have an answer for everything are only good for that: jabbering.

I stand at the back and watch scores of men dancing, my eyes roaming. But I have given up on searching for a mate. In my line of business sex is not a problem, so I never do pick-ups. I recognise a few men from the crowd and they smile at me, trying to lure me with their loose pelvises and open shirts. But I never meet clients outside of Steamy Windows. I don't even accept a drink from an ex-client. I get bored and go outside. I go on the roof and accidentally walk into a guy giving another guy a blowjob. They don't seem surprised or embarrassed. The one continues sucking while the other moans. It is only then that I realise why I have been feeling edgy. I think it has to do with men. I am attracted to their scent, their hormones keep me balanced. Around women and shopping centres treacherously pumping out oestrogen I become weak, confused, vulnerable. This makes me feel like a bit of a misogynist, but I believe I have a twisted aversion to female hormones, even to women sometimes. It is strange, because I don't have any reason to avoid women. Or do I?

I go inside where a hothouse of testosterone rules, the musky smell of male sweat hovering like a secret scent to be savoured. The bell rings several times. I still don't know what that means. I start dancing when the DJ plays some house music. I look around me and feel my aloneness as one of the few black faces in the room. I am sick of that. With all their moaning, crying and campaigning for equal rights gay men are also just as bigoted. With all the organisations we have and the Aids centres, specifically aimed at addressing the individual needs of gay men, gay friendly places are still a white male preserve. I hate the way some guys think it is easier to pick up a black or a coloured guy than a white guy. I hate the way some black and coloured guys are in awe of white men. As gay men we don't stand as equals.

I become irritable when a tall dark-haired white guy dances close behind me. I go to another part of the dance floor. A blond guy looks me up and down, appraising me, examining my clothes, looking at labels. We are slaves to labels, gay men, even labels that infringe on what we think of ourselves as people, the ones we wear when we look at each other: I'm fussy, I like GWM, I prefer them to have a smooth chest, only the latest in fashion thank you, where did you go to school? Insignificant, vacuous things that are not a measure of a person's worth. Upstairs two queens dance and laugh. They seem to be having a grand time. They are probably the most liberated of all gay men. I watch them tease an older guy, probably in his fifties. They flash their eyes and tease him with their hips.

Later I go to Angels, next door. I go there looking for better music and a more representative crowd. What did Chris use to say? Too much toothpaste, too many white faces. In Angels I find familiar black and coloured faces. The music is also more to my personal taste. I sashay to the dance floor when a groovy R&B number by Janet Jackson comes on. The other thing that I like about a mixed crowd is that the people tend to be friendlier, less snobbish. There is a scourge out there of fastidious, snobbish gay white men who give being gay a bad name because they gossip incessantly and thrive on cutting sarcasms that reveal just how shallow they can be. They also come in black and other colours.

In the middle of the dance floor the guys have formed a small circle while two people dance in the middle. It's a coloured and black thing. White guys in Biloxi like to dance in their own galaxies. I watch a red-haired guy and a black guy dancing, getting down, while the others cheer. Another two come into the middle. At the end of the number I feel thirsty and go for a drink at the bar. The bartender looks miserable and gives me my Southern Comfort and Coke without smiling. I usually tip bartenders, but not this one.

I go upstairs to Detour where the crowd is younger and the music is rave, trance and other fusions of techno. The lights are dazzling, a laser display making the mood different, surreal. Everyone looks smacked on ecstasy. I stand at the railings and watch the others dance, their arms in the air while they dance as if they were high. The next song has everyone cheering a little, everyone pouring onto the dance floor. It is "God is a DJ" by Faithless. The band has a cult following. I don't dance. I watch the others, intrigued at how personal rave music has become. Every second person dances with their eyes closed as though praying. I wonder if they listen to the searching lyrics and the message behind the music. There is something too underground and subliminal about rave music for me to appreciate fully. I don't like the way the music is so layered that sometimes the lyrics are lost in the effects. And why do they always digitally alter the voice of the person belting out the lyrics? It is usually a harsh, pseudo-computerised male voice that sounds like the voice of a megalomaniac fascist. And why do DJs and the musical digirati have such arcane names? Christos, Excel, Da Vinci, Admiral, Flight, Isa, Ope, Flyz – they sound like codes, the names of secret agents. After the song I go back downstairs where the crowd is more casual. At Angels people don't take their music as seriously as the people in Detour do. I lounge in a chair and watch people. Two black guys French kiss next to me. It is a rare sight, but one that is enchanting and liberating to watch. I feel lonely when I watch them caressing each other. They are my age. I could be one of them. I could be kissing my boyfriend.

They go to the dance floor. I watch them dance kwaito style. I can tell that they are from the township that they are accustomed to the rhythms of kwaito. I watch them dance and probably think about home, Soweto. Perhaps my dad is right, my work is done here. I could never see myself doing any other job than working at Steamy Windows. I know Cape Town and its people too well. I'm a little wary of them.

I could live in Yeoville or Berea. People say it's nice there. Rocky Street is an interesting pastiche of different nationalities and drug dealers, I hear. I could finally pursue my dream of being an artist. I could finally give it a go and stop procrastinating. My mother is gone. My father is gone. There is no one to push me. Perhaps this is all the motivation I need, knowing that no one is there to watch over me, to nag me. I skip feeling sad when I think about my father and concentrate on Jo'burg.

I could be happy. The gay life there is better anyway. And the whites are a bit more worldly, not as provincial and conservative as the whites in Cape Town with all their fine breeding and impeccable manners that really amount to their being arseholes who fuck you over with a polite smile. I wouldn't have to feel like the only black face all the time, always carrying this heavy load because whites in Cape Town are so critical, so quick to judge and jump to conclusions. I sink deeper into my own prejudices about people. But we're all the same. We all have something to bitch about in other people. I'm no different and don't feel guilty about making sweeping statements and generalisations about white people.

The fact is I feel as if I have had to be well behaved, to toe the line a bit to make ends meet in Cape Town. I have put up with so much crap, so much compromise. But I feel stronger, better equipped to deal with people, especially whites. The veneer of superiority is only a veil. I have also had to go into myself into my own feelings of inferiority. South Africa doesn't give you a chance to feel good about yourself, if you're not white, at least historically. Having gone to multiracial private schools made a difference, but my journey into myself and the true nature of people has been no different from that of township blacks, trying to find their place, their voice. I am black and I'm proud of it, even if it is a bit silly to remind myself. But it is not the only way to define who I am even if I feel the world looks upon me like that. Labels are easier to identify with. Even when I have looked my best and spoken in my best private school accent, I have confronted the harshest, the crudest prejudice from whites. They probably felt it their duty to remind me that I'm nothing but a kaffir who talks like a larney. That is how it feels when people are rude to you for no reason other than your different complexion. We still have a long way to go.

I watch a group of gay boys, probably just out of high school. Amongst them is a black boy. I remember myself when I look at him. It will not be easy to navigate through life, I say to myself, wincing at the challenges that lay ahead of him. You will probably feel schizophrenic half the time, switching between two cultures and languages that are as different and diverse as flowers and apples. You will probably feel the influence of the one at the expense of the other, I say to him secretly, remembering how conflicted I felt at whether I should concentrate on speaking Sotho or English. But it is impossible to do both equally and feel complete. Each language and its culture dictates different modes, it compels different feelings and responses, each holds its own universe. When I'm with Mmabatho and we talk about growing up in Jo'burg it seems we can only speak in Sotho. Our memories and experiences are too rooted in the township and its language is black. But when we talk about Cape Town or a new bar to go to we find ourselves talking in English more than Sotho. Cape Town is very white, the influence of European traditions like coffee shops and bistros is inescapable. In some places in Cape Town you don't feel like you're in Africa. And this is what they call progress, obliterate any traces of the native cultures. Jo'burg is different, the other cultures more aggressive to the domination of white culture. I think that has something to do with a bigger, more established black middle class than in Cape Town. Going out in Jo'burg is more pleasant, it isn't such a process of elimination to find a suitable place to enjoy yourself. In Cape Town there are certain places where you know you are not welcome and the patrons make you feel like an outcast. The culture of having a good time, of jolling is different in Gauteng. In Jo'burg people hang out. In Cape Town people go out. In Jo'burg people are into dancing, clothes and what's fashionable. In Cape Town people are into drumming, doing their charts and doing drugs. Cape Town tries too hard, it looks too much to the West for inspiration when there is enough inspiration in Africa.

I watch the black boy happily chatting with his friends. A terrible thought comes to me. Will they stand up for him when they are confronted by bigots who want to pick a fight? It happens in Cape Town.

The DJ plays some rave music. The dance floor clears a little. I go to a different bar to get another drink. The bartender is friendlier. I get an Amstel. I don't drink much. At varsity I drank myself to death, and that was enough.

A coloured guy chats me up. He asks me for a lighter and I tell him that I don't have one. He finds someone to light his cigarette but soon comes back to chat me up, something about crap music and being from PE. We strike an easy conversation, talking about where to go out in Cape Town, that has a reasonable crowd. I tell him that I'm from Jo'burg and that I'm going to go back soon. I feel excited to say it, enjoying the reaction on his face. Most people look at people who live in Jo'bug with a bit of awe or horror, it is difficult to tell sometimes. But what is clear is that the idea of living in a city plagued by violence, high murder and rape statistics, house break-ins, hi-jackings, where personal safety is an issue that everyone faces, leaves a dark image in the mind.

We go outside for a while and snog, but he is a lousy kisser, slobbering around my mouth. On the dance floor I ask him to excuse me while I go to the toilet. But I don't go to the toilet I find the furthest exit and leave. I catch a meter taxi home, feeling exhausted.

### MMABATHO

He hasn't tried to call. I left him my new address and telephone number in Rosebank but he hasn't called.

I think it is better this way. I have given him all the "headspace" he needs. I don't know if this means we have broken up. We didn't say anything. I just left.

Maybe it was bound to end like this – with us apart. I don't feel surprised. Men have consistently pulled the rug from under me. He left me when he found out I was pregnant. Packing my bags and moving out was just a formality. He should have told me from the start that he had no intentions with a pregnant woman.

I think about all the plans he was making. They would have been useless anyway. He was planning around me, not with me. What good is planning when the most important aspect about it has been overlooked: commitment? I don't want to have a child with a boyfriend. I want my child to have a father. He wasn't ready for that. And I could never force him. I have my pride. Perhaps another woman might have compromised, might have been patient. Hang in there, you'll change him, win him over with time, she might have thought.

I don't want to change men. Why must it be a pattern that women follow? If he isn't willing to meet me halfway he never will. Me changing him would just be a pleasant way of saying I outwitted him, I forced him.

What will my mother say? Pregnant and alone and black and a woman, are you crazy? Didn't I teach you anything?

But I know that you are my purpose in life, Venus. You came to be loved. You are love. And you will be loved. I don't have answers and excuses for the difficult questions people will ask. Where is the father? Why is your baby coloured? I don't know what to say to myself even when I try to answer a simple question like what will happen to Arne and me. Will I allow him to be part of your life, Venus? Will he want to be part of your life?

My father was right, though. You are not a curse, Venus. You are love and love is impulsive and does what it needs to. It's nature is to be disruptive, to awaken people from their slumber. I was becoming comfortably cynical about relationships until I met your father, Venus. He found the combination number to my heart, the bastard, I still love him. Perhaps you are preparing Mummy to be strong, not to wait for men, to do what I think is right for us, not what will look right for people.

I am young, I still have my energy, my wits. I am in a better position than most women because I am educated. Venus is always reminding me to be brave. Love is the bravest warrior because it does everything it needs to survive, it looks after itself.

Is it really such a bad thing to have a child alone? I would rather give Venus a chance than go for a quicker option that might leave me with a lifetime of guilt. I know it will be tough. I know that I will feel alone, isolated, overwhelmed, but I can raise my child. I can be a good mother. I will do anything for my child. I want to be the kind of person I would have loved to have known growing up.

Venus, each day I feel you growing in my belly. Kicking me, forcing me to open my eyes and see things for what they are. Your father is selfish like most men. Perhaps I should be patient with him. Perhaps he will come around later. But no, you say to me, Venus. Stop wishing and waiting. Make your own plans. Better depend on yourself. You don't know what is waiting around the corner.

I can feel you, Venus, you are such a strong-willed child, so full of initiative and love. I feel you listening to me when I weep alone at night, wondering how I got to this junction in life alone. Everything happened so quickly. Only yesterday I was single, enjoying the arrogance of youth, aloof to a world full of problems and few remedies. You must forgive me when I cry. I do not mean to make you sad. But I feel outwitted by circumstances. I am hardly the girl I used to be. I am more inward looking. My body is telling me that I am a woman.

I got a job waitressing at Obz Café. It will see us through December. Mid January I will go home and confront my parents with the truth. My belly will be obvious by then, perhaps they will be more sympathetic. I fear my mother. She can be so harsh and unforgiving, her tongue as quick as lightning. I fear that she will dismiss me as a slut. A young woman pregnant and alone surely must be a slut. This is what my mother and her spinster sisters would think. I don't know if she would say it. The three of them, they are the reason why dad left, why he wanted a divorce. They have an opinion about everything, nothing just is.

My mother is very controlling, but subtle about it. She hides behind the mask of a helpless victim. I don't think you would like her, Venus, not such a forthright and energetic personality like you. She thinks she is goodness itself, that's what makes her type of venom more poisonous. The marriage was difficult. My in-laws were cold, she always moans, happy to play the victim. Life was unkind to her, everyone took advantage of her. Me, me poor me, this is her song, Venus. I know it too well. I know how she hides behind her faith, what the Bible says and doesn't say. I suspect she struggles with her own inner demons but she will never admit it. Her life is a pattern of light and dark areas. There is no in-between, no grey areas. Where there is conflict or confusion her quick anger and self-righteous Bible bashing rescue her. Is it easier to criticise another person because you feel you know the word of God? Her faith seems to have only sharpened her tongue, to have made it easier to disapprove and be aloof. I'm a woman, I'm a lady, she would often say, oblivious to how arrogant and self-righteous she sounded.

God will punish you, she would threaten me when I was a little girl, naughty and rebellious. I grew to hate the church and fear my mother. She is so convinced of her particular brand of Christianity that nothing can move her. People who praise their own goodness too much are asleep to their own flaws. No one is perfect Venus, especially I.

I don't think you would like her, Venus. She is too oppressive. Her life is governed by following rules and regulations to reserve a seat in Paradise. There is no room for creative thinking in her eyes, other possibilities, other ways of being. I will always be the daughter who was wild and got pregnant young. I didn't live up to her expectations of what a woman is. I wasn't a lady like her. I wasn't dainty. I refused to wear delicate, womanly things. I didn't aspire to be noticed by other women. I didn't buy into that crap. She wanted me to grow up a little snob, a pretty girl who was always innocent and ever wary of boys. She wanted another version of herself and I refused. I know that I harbour a lot of ill feelings towards my mother. Perhaps being a mother myself will help me forgive her.

I will try as hard as I can not to pollute your mind with ideas about how I think the world should be, Venus, how I think you should be. I will try very hard to let you be your own person.

Angelo comes in after a couple of days. There is an absent look on his face and dark rings under his eyes. Quietly while we sit in the lounge I get a sense of something watching him. It is hard to say what it is but I know that it leaves him drained, in a trance state. When it is time to take our break, I go outside with him.

"I feel I have to tell you something," I say lighting a cigarette.

I have always been psychic but it has always been a personal thing that I have kept to myself, hidden from my family, even when I foresaw terrible events like the car accident that killed my grandfather.

He looks at me calmly, also smoking.

"When did you start smoking? I thought you were just fooling around. Anyway, it doesn't matter. I need to tell you something," I continue, struggling to find a pleasant way to say this.

He doesn't say anything, he just looks at me with this vapid expression, his eyes tired.

"When was the last time you slept?"

"What was it you wanted to tell me?" he says, a little impatient, destroying the cigarette with powerful drags.

"I'm not going to see you again," I say and look at him.

"And?"

"I said I'm not going to see you again. Trust me. I have a strong feeling and it isn't good," I say with difficulty. A wind suddenly goes by and stirs rubbish piled in a gutter. He stands there as though nothing happened, pretending to ignore the sudden wind.

"What are you talking about?" he snaps.

It is not an advantage to have this gift, this curse, I still can't reconcile myself with the ability to see into things. "You are my friend. I just feel I have to tell you this. I won't see you again."

"The other day I went shopping at the Waterfront," he suddenly changes the subject. "And I bought this fabulous Ralph Lauren shirt, gorgeous material. You should see it. I got it at a sale."

We finish our cigarettes and head back inside. He doesn't say much. I watch him the whole evening. He gets three clients and tells me that they tipped him nicely. When he looks at me I feel strange, awkward, a little scared of him. There are things that I can see in people's eyes when I look closely enough. Things that reveal their past and where their small lives are going. I see violence in his eyes. God is a mad child who plays with our lives as though we were toys.

After a while I begin to notice that he avoids speaking to me. He chats with Storm about silly, stupid things that I have never heard him talk about.

Later in the evening I try to talk to him again.

"I don't think you are safe where you are staying."

"What are you talking about? You have been talking rubbish all evening." He gets up abruptly and goes to the bathroom. When he returns he sits in another place.

I feel terrible. It is difficult carrying the news about him. I almost feel like Cassandra. He won't listen. Perhaps he doesn't believe me. I would hate to prove him wrong. But it is futile, the wheel has started rolling, I can't stop it. I can only watch the destruction it's going to cause.

At the end of the evening when he leaves he doesn't greet me. He just leaves. Only then do I realise how fundamental the change is. Perhaps he isn't even aware of it. He isn't himself. I shiver with fear when I think about him. I see twisted roads and demons eager to eat when I think of him. It leaves me feeling tired and a little dizzy. Darkness is closing in around him and I don't think he knows it. How do you warn someone that his life is about to change drastically? How do you tell someone that there is another world that watches us while we sleep? How do I explain to him that sometimes realities cross each other's paths like raw electric wires and the short-circuit caused disrupts our lives in sometimes permanent ways?

I feel alone when I sense that something is about to happen. I feel small and powerless. We control so little. The world goes on in spite of us, without us. Its wheels and cogs have been oiled by an old and demented god. I wonder if there is anything to be learned from madness.

ANGELO-TSHEPO

I am walking. I don't know where I am going. The road is itching for my feet, aching to be walked on, lusting to be explored. It keeps me awake. I am having conversations in my head. Someone is watching, listening. I am drifting. My shadow is watching me, making little gestures when it thinks I'm not watching. The sun is made of honey. The air carries too many messages, that is why I have headaches all the time. I am feeling close to madness again, that old suicidal, psychopathic feeling that used to haunt me as a teenager is trying to find a voice. But I won't go back to Valkenberg.

There is a part of me that is dark, that seeks oblivion, another self. It is the part I struggle with on moody days when I want nothing to do with people, the part that remembers everything and holds grudges against people. The part that reminds me how petty and unforgiving I can be. It is the price for being human, material. Didn't Sebastian say that the flesh was fallen divinity? My other self is always watching from the corners of darkness, that is why I get lost all the time. It tempts me, go there, try this, watch that. Sometimes I fantasise about suicide. I fantasise about diving into a volcano alive with fire and molten lava. Sometimes I want to swim out into the ocean till my strength ebbs. Sometimes I wish for death as though it were life. I accept this as part of me like the hair on my scalp, like the skin on my flesh. To trust life I must trust death.

There is a long road in town but it is not Long Street. This road is silently long, its name only known by the madness driving me to walk. I don't know where I am going. I'm just moving. I feel lost. I don't remember where home is. I can't get there. There are too many roads, too many turns, too many forks.

It is late, town deserted like a beach at night, apart from street children roaming. They keep watching me, taunting me, saying things to each other and then saying things to me. But they never harm me. They follow me till they corner me at the station. I don't know how I got there. Under the trees in the garden we smoke zol. Some of them sniff glue. They stink and look dirty but they are warm with kindness, friendliness. They look like small rats, hardly people, they are so comfortable in the dark. I keep straining to look at their faces but they seem to be accustomed to the dark. A security guard comes out and throws a brick at us. It hits me in the thigh. I get up sore and run off with them.

We go into the Company Gardens. The zol has made me see things. Dragons, black spirits that look like stingray fish hover above me. I walk with the children. I am the tallest. They take me to a fountain. The water looks like black ink. I put my hand into it to make sure that it is water, when I take out my hand the children are gone.

Fear grips me. My high intensifies. A dark figure shuffles behind me, hissing something. I start running. Those stingray spirits hover above me again, their tails long and windy. I run till I come out into a small side street with street lamps. But there is no one on the road. It is quiet, the cars look deserted. Where are all the criminals? Shouldn't they be breaking into something?

I walk around in endless circles. I walk till I get to a bridge under which squatters stay. Among the makeshift homes there is a spaza shop. It is a meeting place where everyone sits on crates outside under a spotlight, drinking, dancing and listening to music. I feel overdressed and clean when I look at the people. They all have brutally scarred faces. A woman with thick scars around her eyes asks me for twenty cents. I search my pockets for money and realise that I don't have my wallet. I lost it. No, the children stole it. And my house keys, where are they? The woman asks me to dance with her.

"I like your jersey," she keeps saying.

I get tired of hearing her say that.

"Here, you can have it," I say and take off my comfortable polo neck jersey by Comme des Garçons.

She offers me part of her zol as she puts on my jersey. It is a little chilly but I soon get warm from dancing.

I feel myself drifting again, as if someone took my mind. I can't remember where home is. I don't know how to get home.

A man wearing blue jeans and a hat slanted to one side like a tsotsi comes to me. He tells me to leave his woman alone, the woman I gave my jersey to. He pushes me and drags her off, slapping her as he forces her to take off the jersey. I hear them arguing. They disappear into a shack, swearing at each other obscenely. The spotlight shines in my face. The others look at me from their crates. One of the men gets up and comes to me. He dances near me and points to my shadow. I look on the floor and see him dancing over my head. A headache suddenly attacks me. I move away and sit down where he was sitting. But another man soon pushes me off. They laugh at me.

Confusion is not a feeling. It is a state of mind, when everything doesn't work properly. Your mind holds you prisoner. But somebody controls it all. Who is it? Why are they doing this to me? Who is the prince of darkness?

I dance alone in the spotlight, compelled by the need to keep moving. I mustn't sit or stand still. A woman wearing a turban asks me to kiss her. She smiles and I see her soft gums where there should be teeth. I run away with fear. Someone throws an empty bottle at me. It crashes beside me, drops of wine splashing on my khaki pants. A chained up rottweiler suddenly jumps out of the dark and comes dangerously close to biting me, but is prevented by the chain.

I hear them laughing, listening to TKZee. They are diamond people, they live under constant pressure. Their light shines inwards, for themselves.

427

I run out into a road full of cars. I want to scream but I don't have a voice. The drivers hoot at me as I cross. I keep running, not knowing where I'm going. I run till I get to the station.

Inside the station there is light and safety. Security guards also patrol. I walk up and down the station. A security guard asks me if I'm crazy. I tell him that I need to go home. I need to catch the train home urgently. He tells me that the first train going out leaves at six thirty. It is four o'clock in the morning.

I stand against the wall and watch the clock. My mind is awake, broken but awake. There is lots of activity up there, it's trying to mend itself, repair bridges that have been broken. I go outside for a piss. The darkness is alive. It stares at me. Stingray spirits float as though at sea. I hear children laughing but somewhere far off.

I go back inside where the lights make me safe. I stay up till half past six. I catch the first free train going to Khayelitsha. There aren't that many people in the compartment. I watch them closely. They all look like they know where they are going. The train takes me into the bowels of the township. I get off in Nyanga, a sprawling ghetto of mostly squatters.

The station is small and dirty. I get off and roam the streets, fetid with dog shit and urine. The sun is already rising. In one street corner a group of women with huge enamel dishes that look like small bath tubs are gathered round a horse that must have dropped dead there. They wield long and dangerous looking knives, carving up the horse, passing huge chunks of meat among themselves. I watch them arguing about its entrails. I walk alone, driven by the need to find home. I must get back home, I keep telling myself. They are expecting me. Maybe determination is a type of intelligence.

A gang of dogs patrols a street I walk down. The alpha dog of dubious breed snarls at me. I pick up a rock beside the road. The other dogs also start snarling. "Voertsek!" a woman yells from nearby and throws hot water over them. They run away crying, their flea-infested coats appearing to melt. When I look at the woman she tells me that she will eat me if I don't leave at once. You are disturbing my magic, she tells me, her hair dishevelled and a twisted look in her eyes. I walk briskly down the road.

There is a maze of streets and shacks. More and more people become visible, each one clean and fresh. It amazes me because they come out of such dingy and dilapidated little shacks. They walk with purpose, dignity, but they have no time for me when I ask them where I am.

The sun rises. I see the golden disc and feel powerfully awake. It is as though sleep forgot me. I keep walking deeper into Nyanga. I think about that word. In Xhosa Nyanga means to cure a person, to be healed. But I don't feel healed by the walking. I feel myself drifting into delirium, a world of spirits and whispers. I walk further into confusion, my mind wrapped around finding home. The township is a maze. People tell you things if they think they will get something out of you. No one helps me when I ask them where I am. A confused boy with a question mark expression means nothing to them. They look at me with angry, sad, harsh faces, nothing different to people in town and suburbia. The township is layered, you have to look underneath the surface decay to see anything. I walk freely. It is easier to be weird and be considered eccentric in the township. No one cares. People have so much to worry about, their lives a perpetual struggle against the crush. Life can crush you to death with hardship if you don't fight hard enough. They know this. Ufunani? they snap at me. Go here, down there. But I walk further into madness. There is something calming about the many streets and turns, vibrant with activity and not quiet and sedated like suburbia. In the township you know whether your neighbour is alive or dead. I feel safe, there aren't any policemen to be seen. There is something going down, a different energy circulates the air. And it speaks nothing of happiness or success. Perhaps kwaito and the many things it aspires to express is struggling to define the real message of the ghetto. Good times, nice clothes, going out, getting the girl, getting the boy, fast cars, lots of cheap jewellery and all the other fickle things kwaito celebrates are signposts of lives lived in noisy confusion. Help us, listen to us, they seem to say. There are too many voices to hear, each sounding desperate, hopeless. But on the outside they seem content. Perhaps it is evil to imagine that anyone can be truly happy in poverty. They are used to it – who can be happily accustomed to waking up at four in the morning to prepare for work by fetching water from a tap shared by a hundred other people? I walk further, the messages in the air intoxicating, mesmerising. A barefoot old woman walks in the opposite direction. She is skinny, bent double and looks hungry. She could be my grandmother. But this is normal. In the township even the elders are nothing. Why is it so? Wouldn't it be strange if she was a white woman? Wouldn't it be disturbing – white, barefoot, skinny and old? Where is the dignity of the aged? I walk further, drawn to voices that remind me of my childhood. I was once a child. It seems silly to think this.

"Kwedini," an older man says to me with disrespect. I get irritated and flash my circumcised penis to him. Xhosa men can be full of shit. "Haai!" he shouts because women are watching. He comes after me with a knobkierie. I outrun him and disappear between the shacks. Schools are closed for the December holidays. Children run about idly. There are no parks to go to, no video arcades to explore, just dirty streets and longdrops festering with diseases. A lot of capable looking men hang around corners, their hands idle, frustrated, itchy with desperation. Are they plotting their crimes quietly? There is a goldmine in the suburbs, even the dustbins eat well. Perhaps inside they are bruised, feeling forgotten, progress going at lightning speed while poverty takes them at a snail's pace. No one knows how shattered we are inside, they seem to say with their eyes, how desperate we are. Given a chance we can do anything. We lived through '76, Casspirs, detention, Botha, and now this, everyone grabbing as much as they can for themselves, they seem to say. Perhaps we are not that different from the rest of Africa, our leaders are just better thieves. Too much money and a small ruling elite, are we that far from the rest of Africa? A Coca-Cola sign towers above on a billboard. What does it mean to us, what does it mean to them who have nothing? Buy more even when you have nothing?

A car drives by and splashes my ankles with water from a pothole. There is no point in protesting. Who would listen? Nobody sympathises with us, the men seem to say to me with their eyes always holding anger. I walk past a shebeen. A lot of people are crowded outside, drinking. I heard that you can get at the shebeen a potent alcoholic pineapple mixture which can leave you drunk for days. What is the alternative? I would also do the same, I admit to myself, feeling sad and heavy. But walking is more important. My body concentrates on the journey. I walk into places I don't know and eventually stop asking people for directions. They live with enough questions. Where is the money to buy bread? What will I feed my child? Will I find a job tomorrow? Can I sleep on an empty stomach for the second night in a row? Will they catch me if I steal at night? I don't have to ask anymore, it's clear that there's no one to ask, nowhere to go and nothing to do. After a while even nothing becomes something. I see this when I watch four guys sitting outside their shack, watching neighbourhood girls, their eyes lustful. How many girls will they seduce and impregnate? How many have Aids? How many know anything about sex? Statistics fly in my head and I feel awake. Facts are useless when people have nothing. They need to see through their stomachs first before they can see with their eyes.

A man rides his bicycle. He has adorned it with mirrors like a scooter and a number plate on the back. It is also brightly painted. No matter how meagre they are, possessions are kingdoms within a tight universe. It is this principle of the infinite in so little that built the universe, the belief in humility, in the small and the forgettable.

I can feel my feet beginning to blister but I must walk. Who will help me? This is how they feel all the time. You must help yourself, I answer with my eyes, stubbornly walking even though the township is swallowing me whole.

Three kids are torturing a dog. They have tied some wire around its throat and are poking it with sharp sticks, its shanks bleeding. They laugh hysterically every time it shrieks. Children are cruel because their parents are also probably cruel. I chase them away and go towards the wretched animal. It snarls at me before it runs away. The children swear at me for spoiling their fun. They could be seven or eight years old. I want to catch them and beat them senseless. But this is how grown-ups always speak to them. Beating them will only shut them away further from reason and compassion. Can't they see how ugly they are when they do that? Who do you think you are? a woman standing by seems to say. The township is full of people like her, complacent, mean-spirited. The children tell me to voertsek, that this is their kasi, their neighbourhood. I resolve to ignore them and go down another street. I keep walking, compelled by a demented energy, questions raging in my head. But the silence inside is more important than the jarring questions that keep me awake, that keep me roaming like a zombie. I must find the answers to the questions. Perhaps the real question is the answer. Cogs and wheels are turning in my mind, ticking, winding.

I want to take a piss but there is no where to piss. There are no public toilets, no bushes or trees, only shacks and people. I walk for a while before I find a shack situated in a dead-end street, politely called a cul-de-sac in suburbia. I take a long deserved piss, hiding my prick with one hand. Children play nearby, but what else can I do? Manners amount to nothing if they are not encouraged by appropriate surroundings. I keep walking. In another street a little girl squats and I see a yellow stream pouring down between her legs. She gets up and carries on playing with her friends.

Everywhere I go I look. I feel like I'm decoding the madness, wrapping my brain around it, facing it, making it easier to see, to understand, giving it a name. Maybe it is called capitalism, making money for the sake of making money, not building communities. With capitalism it seems someone has to lose, someone has to be the underdog, someone has to play the poor bastard that holds up the structure, so that the rich can be rich. Maybe the problem isn't capitalism, maybe it is the elites who run the structure. Maybe it is the stifling class system that keeps us all rigid in our places, everyone behaving, everyone going as far as their lives allow them. Maybe the poor are more powerful than they imagine, a whole system, a way of being depends on their wretched lives, their complicity. How did we get here? Who did this? Someone must have been navigating.

The township is alive with noise, gunshots, music, screaming, cars hooting. There is always something going on, someone dying, someone fighting. It never runs out of stories, like the madness. People live on top of each other because they think that this is what they deserve. You take each day as it is given, no questions, because you believe it is your lot. How do you help people when they live in ghettos in their minds? I begin to feel shattered and depressed. The truth is rarely beautiful. A group of people are accusing a woman of poisoning her husband. I don't wait to listen to the gossip. They look ready to beat her. Someone rolls a tire towards her. Someone shakes a box of matches. I take another street.

The air is like a blanket. It has colour, a pale grey colour that makes you cough. I pass a taxi rank. The women inside one taxi look impatient, waiting for it to leave. But the driver will only leave when the taxi is full of passengers. He does this because he needs the money, every cent counts. So they will be late. And at work their bosses won't understand. Lazy nè, always taking chances, that's what you people are like, they will say, while the truth remains in the township. Eventually they might lose their jobs because taxis are unreliable and bosses only make money, they don't build people. Petrol prices go up, fares go up, people squeeze a lot out of little. It is nothing unusual, a mother who earns two hundred rand a month as a domestic worker feeding and clothing her family.

I walk past a narrow street. Even the church is dilapidated. The grass grows wild and long outside. The church hasn't been painted for years. It doesn't matter, they are still heathens, impossible to civilise even with the Bible.

The sun is high in the sky. I get warmer, my skin becoming moist with sweat. I become aware of my own scent. My legs carry me further. I walk down muddy streets with many potholes. Little children run around half naked. Hawkers sell their meagre wares. Taxis own the road, other cars accept this. A man asks me for a lighter. A woman runs to catch a taxi. The sky looks distant. A cat walks by, it looks emaciated, dirty, very uncatlike. Brenda Fassie sings an old favourite from a near-by radio, "Weekend Special". People walk on the pavement, they walk on the road, they walk in my thoughts. How many people live here? Too many numbers, many hells and few heavens. A rasta saunters down the street, his locks patting his back. A gunshot startles me. In the distance I see smoke rising. Nothing to worry about, I tell myself, it could be just a braai. But why is the smoke so black? What are they braaing, the neighbourhood? My throat aches because there is so much to see. How do you take it all in and feel nothing? When do I stop thinking and just see?

A pig digs its snout into a pile of rubbish. Goats nibble a few tufts of grass near one pavement. Animals and people. People and animals. Who are the people and who are the animals?

A dog lies dead on the road, its innards splattered. Cars run over it. It must have been dead for a few days because it stinks. The closer I get the more offensive the smell becomes. Everyone goes about as though it isn't there. I mustn't pull a face or cover my mouth and nose. I am no better. But why won't anyone take it away? Maybe it is there to re-mind us that we live in decay. Maybe we forget sometimes and have to remind each other all the time. In town they have police stations, in the township we have dead dogs.

I pass a small chain of stores. A woman sits outside on the shady ve-randah of one store with a small board advertising prices for braiding and perming. Next to the prices are amateur drawings of hairstyles. She looks bored and watches me looking at her. That is her job, to sit there and hold the board. How much will they pay her for that?

My tackies are stained with dirt. How much further? I must get home. But there is no point rushing, everything does what it needs to do with-out me getting over-anxious. I settle into a comfortable pace, taking in everything as it comes. Every place has its own rhythm. In town you walk briskly because there is stuff to do and little time. The township forces you to slow down because it has too much time and not enough stuff. The filth is inescapable. Every wire mesh fence I see is plastered with plastic bags. Buy and dump, that is the message. After a while the pollution becomes a language, like a strange installation in a gallery that spreads across the township. You can see who is better off by the filth, the endless plastic bags that fly around. A fat woman sells fatcakes in a corner. Flies bother her. She swats them intermittently.

A lorry passes down the road carrying coal and men coated in black. They look faceless like ghosts. A guy on a large tricyle sells ice cream from his mobile fridge. I watch kids buying from him, their faces lighting up as they sink their teeth into the bright colours.

I no longer have parents. Saying it sends an arrow to my heart. The grief is deep and dense, it doesn't allow me to cry, to feel sorry for myself. I must think about it. I must think about my life. Perhaps I'm not really human. Perhaps I am part light, part darkness and part human. I cannot feel that little part aching to be free, screaming for attention. My humanity has been suffocated all my life, it says. I have had to struggle for it, to show people that I am a person. Isn't that madness? It only matters to me. I must deal with the pain, I must resolve the hatred. I must always struggle for love alone. I must live like a dog for love, it breaks me and makes me work for it. Perhaps the madness is love. I do not understand it. I do not understand how I got here. And why am I so fucked up that I can't even see my own grief? Why must I always be distracted by others? You must forget yourself if you want to survive, life is almost saying to me. Look out there, not inside. Struggle, suffer, shit and maybe you'll learn something. It is always about falling. But I am stubborn, I carry on, the hell with courage. It is wanting to go on even though the bridge is broken. It is trying to transcend the edge of the cliff. It is never about how much I know but about how much I'm willing to surrender, gambling everything and winning nothing but myself, my sanity. I have gambled everything and lost it all. I must learn to see beyond the light and darkness. I mustn't judge, I must listen. Maybe life isn't that clever. I can outsmart it, is that the challenge? I have been groomed with hatred. Hide and seek, it is the same with everything in life, just a game, just more serious, but still a game. Who says I must play the willing victim forever? Maybe I can also write my own rules, insist on my own points. The idea is that I have been everyone and now I must become no one, like life, faceless, the perfect weapon. I can also be the perfect weapon.

The perfect weapon is not a computer. It is something closer to home, a person, someone who understands the landscape of the human heart. The perfect weapon doesn't wear a mask, it has nothing to hide because it is like everyone else. It says look at yourself, it says look within where the real war is going on. It is always focused. The perfect weapon knows who the target is and how to destroy it. It knows who the innocent are, the blameless, the unsuspecting civilians. It doesn't destroy blindly, indiscriminately. There are no accidents, no political impasses. Everything is precise, everything is calculated. The perfect weapon gives orders, it doesn't take them. It considers advice, it analyses things, weighs them and takes the most efficient course of destruction. The perfect weapon doesn't waste energy, it does what it needs to, no less, no more. The perfect weapon is sane and insane at the same time, it can exist in multiple realities, it knows the tricks. The perfect weapon would be dangerous because its intentions would be pure.

Violence was once a god. Perhaps I seek to discover that god again. I have too much conflict in me to ever resolve it without breaking something, without spilling blood, even my own. I feel like the earth is begging me for destruction, it wants me to awaken this ancient god that once terrorised us. There is too much going on inside me, too many voices vying for attention. I must eliminate some. I long to destroy that which I cannot tolerate. And that is the madness. I cannot tolerate the cruelty of people, the greed of the rich and the hypocrisy of the church. I have chased all the big demons and they beg me to unleash them into the world of the living. It is as though darkness wants me to open a gate that will allow chaos to reign, when everything will cancel each other out. Perhaps I am a pathfinder, a strange gate opener retracing steps that I once walked in another life when destruction was imminent. Light can exist in darkness but can darkness exist in light? This is what life wants me to prove.

My father wasn't really my father, he was just someone I met along the way. I come from the longest possible journey but the distance is short. I come from a world where love matures and is tested like the seasons test an animal's will to endure and survive. It is a rite of passage. You have to earn life. My season is at hand. I can feel the earth beckoning me with roots that yearn to grow stronger, trees that ache to bear real fruit. The air remembers too much. It longs for someone to listen, to hear the madness we live with. Computers will not kill us, but they will be aiding our demise every step of the way.

They are all watching me, waiting for me. They come from distant places, from the furthest corners of the imagination. And they are not going away. They are ancient warriors whose sole purpose is war and destruction. Other worlds have borrowed their expertise. Now it is our turn. I have seen these Defenders riding in their indestructible chariots that carry them anywhere. An impressive army is assembling. When the oceans touch beaches, their waves secretly send out legions, populating every corner of the earth for the final countdown. Clouds are not the amorphous vagaries they seem to be, some of them are warships in disguise. Strange looking people walk amongst us, making precise calculations for our destruction. Diseases far deadlier than Aids, more insidious, are germinating, waiting for ideal conditions to wreak havoc and death. The ocean and the sky are plotting against us. Whales and other wise creatures of the sea are changing migration patterns, settling in different places and warning other creatures. I feel close to my dark side. The forces of darkness are hungry, famished. I will open the gates of chaos and feed them the madness we have sown. It will be a feast of anarchy.

I seek my oblivion and it will be pure. My eyes have drunk the poisons and the sweet juices. I have had enough to eat. I have walked further than I expected. It is enough. I must go back home. My family left me because I was embarking on a different journey, the return home. Everything has been a preparation for the return journey. I see that. I feel that. The road is long and winding. I have rested enough. I must go back. I will not stop, I will never stop until everything is done so that I can go home.

People are watching me, listening, recording. Spy networks are never far away. Perhaps they think I do not see them but I can smell them. I can smell their fear. They visit me at night. We have done so little with so much. Terrible things wait for us when we sleep. The night is eating us out of futures we believe we deserve. The air is poisoning us with anger. The earth is holding back its secrets, allowing disease to exterminate us. We have become vermin, pests, jeopardising everything that lives. We have squandered away paradise and we have nothing to show for it. The decay is pervasive. The core is corrupted. The roots have been lost. The emptiness leaves us impotent yet we continue worshipping it. Perhaps it is not death that we worship but its ideal, a beautiful, heroic death like mythic Icarus who flew too close to the sun and fell to his death. But he was a fool for daring to imagine himself a god when he was a mere mortal. Nature never fails to remind us who we are, nothing but beings, imperfect beings. Where is the wisdom in flying too close to the sun? Of course it will scorch! We are not different from Icarus, sending men to the moon while some of our children starve. But still we have the audacity to cry that no one is listening to us.

No matter, our luck has run out. The forces of light and darkness have united in an unholy marriage that will cleanse the ugliness that we are left with. For even darkness aspires for better, higher. Didn't Lucifer sing most beautifully of all before his fall? We have offered little and showed nothing. Even darkness is ashamed of us. Our blood is slowly beginning to curdle. I feel the hatred, the bitterness, the anger and confusion transforming itself; a language forming that has nothing to do with reason anymore. It is too late for talk and fancy words. The bell tolls past midnight. Someone is blowing the ancestral horn heralding the end of time, history. The vultures have landed, they have come home to scavenge. We are the scraps of water, fire, air and earth. Our stupidity, our blindness, will be eagerly eaten, the vultures will peck out our eyes so that our children will see better than us. We are not deserving of mercy or pity. Too many children have died unnoticed, unsung, their little voices disappearing into a void. We are all to blame.

I have been sent here by emergency powers. I am just a messenger. Within me are the seeds of our eventual destruction and redemption. These are the final moments, they are divorced of time. There is no turning back, no answers that will spare us. We stand alone, guilty, having learned nothing from hindsight.

I hear the township moaning, dying. My limbs are tired. My feet are blistering, bleeding. I cannot feel my pain. I cannot pretend that this is a dream. The vultures have landed. Maybe death is waking up from a dream. Maybe. I don't know. I don't know anything for certain. I only know that I must face death, my death. I must confront the moment we are all taught to dread. The process has already started. We are all dying yet we appear to be living. I can smell the stench of death. It is in the air, in the food we cook and disguise with herbs and spices. It is in the water we drink and its poisons that are draining our energy, forcing us to become old when we are young. The message is clear, time has run out. We are running out. I feel close to madness because it is the only way of understanding what is happening. There is nothing grand, poetic or tragic about our lives, our failure. The poets have lied to us. The historians soiled honour. We will meet our demise with the smallness of our lives. Our heros have been clowns, charlatans, they have led us further into blindness. I don't believe in anyone anymore.

I can't follow the whites, they are heading for the abyss with stupid pride. The coloureds are waiting for their own coloured messiah. The Indians will only tolerate you if you eat their hot food and laugh at their jokes. And the new blacks are too angry and grab everything for themselves. I don't think they see clearly. So I follow the Africans, the enlightened ones, the elusive ones who see into my being and communicate with subtle hints and gestures. I follow the ones I read about, I sense in the air, the ones time always remembers and never forgets. They are part of the changing African landscape. Sometimes I see them in the street, but this is rare. And they smile, warming my heart in a way I have never known. I have been sad for as long as I can remember.

I don't care for purists. They are dangerous and full of lies, there is a little bit of everything in everything. That is the truth they work hard to hide. I don't care for people who want to prescribe what it means and doesn't mean to be African. People say things just for the hell of it, to hear their own voices blowing out vacuous breath. I know who I am. Why must Africans be quintessentially kind, open and generous when everyone else can be cold, calculating and greedy? I do not suffer fools. I am like the Nile, my roots ancient and dark, reaching into the heart of the Congo, remembering the floods that are coming, that are waiting. We must all wait. The waiting is energy, it is receiving divine instructions. It means everything is being carefully considered.

My stomach moans.

I feel hungry and thirsty. I search my pockets but there are no coins.

I spend the whole day walking, my stomach shrinking from hunger, my throat parched. How do people eat and drink in such squalor and decay? How do they breathe? Everywhere I look there is poverty and people live with it miraculously. Abused and emaciated dogs pick their way through garbage piling up in a dump. My tackies are smeared with mud and water from burst sewerage pipes. I sweat profusely, walking anywhere my feet take me. At a soccer field I see an Indian guy watching people playing. He stands out because you don't see Indians and whites in the township. I stand next to him.

"Who is playing?" I ask him.

"What is your name?" he asks me.

I have to think about it. My first reaction is to say Angelo.

"How can you forget your own name?"

"What is your name?"

"Nasuib," he says and flexes his jaws.

We watch them play but they are lousy. After a while Nasuib tells me that he is leaving.

"Where do you stay? You don't look like you belong here."

"I stay in town." I feel relieved that I remember.

"Come with me," he says with authority, and I follow.

We soon find our way to a train station. He buys me a ticket and I thank him. I look at the sun and think of sweet honey. People look at Nasuib with contempt as we get on the train. Their hatred for him puzzles me. A woman sitting on a seat extends her leg to trip him or to prevent him from going past her, I cannot tell. But he remains calm, chewing something. We remain standing the whole way.

In Cape Town I lose Nasuib in the rush when people get off. I search for him outside but I do not find him. I go back inside and go to the toilets to drink some water. A man is washing his feet at the sink while I drink water. I'm terribly hungry. To suppress the pangs I drink a lot of water. And then I go back outside where people are packing up their stalls. The sun looks unusually beautiful. I stare into it and my eyes don't get scorched. A woman looks at me with mean eyes when she realises that I can stare into the sun and not go blind. It is like staring God in the face, you evil child, she says to me with her hypnotic eyes. I walk away. I walk down several streets feeling dirty, hungry. A crippled boy sits in a corner holding a cardboard sign that is supposed to move people to pity. I pass him without reading his trick. In another street corner a woman sits with a severely crippled child. The child has thin, delicate limbs, fragile like fish bones, and a deformed head. Exhausted I rest a while and look at the two. The child smiles at me, her eyes sparkling. She kisses me with her eyes, inside I experience a moment of bliss. But a hooting car startles me and sends me walking again.

Minibus taxi drivers are rude in Cape Town. They are like most taxi drivers, they think the road is theirs. They stop in inappropriate places while other cars struggle behind them. The attendants brutally scream various destinations. I watch them and begin to notice that the engine of each taxi hums with its own sound. Even the hooter is unique.

Above the humdrum I begin to decipher the different sounds as a series of messages. One taxi driver catches me tapping into his frequency and swears at me. When he opens his mouth a dark force that looks like a shadow emerges and rushes towards me. I fall backwards with fear. The driver shakes his finger at me before driving off.

As I walk to Sea Point I begin to realise that all cars have their own frequencies and that complicated conversations are going on all the time while we get on with our lives obliviously. I feel confused and alone. Darkness gradually fills one part of the sky like spilled ink taking over a clean piece of paper. I walk down the Sea Point promenade where gay men pick each other up but I am not in the mood for sex or men. I just walk there because I have nowhere else to go. I can't remember where I live. But I know that I live with a guy called Jacques. Isn't that strange that I remember him but I cannot remember where I live? A thought comes to me. I imagine Jacques going through my things, stealing some of my clothes and then cutting them up in his room and doing occult things with them. The idiot, he is signing for his own death. I have always been suspicious of him. The idea of having two doors in one room is ominous. What does he use the other door for? Where does he go through it? Or who comes through it?

I think some more about Jacques and begin to wonder if perhaps he has anything to do with my present state of mind. Lately he has been more strange than usual around me. The other day I accidentally walked in on him having a shit. He seemed pleased that I caught him in this position, a puerile smile on his face. Enraged I walked out of the flat. I also have the nasty suspicion that he has a scatological fascination. It is disturbing to think this but everything about that dirty, grimy, dark bathroom points to that. I don't think he changes his underwear regularly. And the fact that he doesn't remove the kitty litter regularly disturbs me. I once caught him sniffing it as though savouring a pleasant smell. I have heard things about what some people do in Cape Town. Bored people with too much time and money on their hands, who desperately search to communicate with dark forces that they know little about. Darkness is very precise, it doesn't suffer fools. These are people who would do anything, including unspeakable things with their bodies. Drinking their own urine because it is said to fortify the body; that is just the first step down a dark and steep slope of malignant decadence.

I do not like Jacques and I do not pretend. His reticence is odious. And his stinginess is repugnant. I once forgot to give him change which amounted to three cents. He hounded me till I gave him each cent. They say with evil every transaction needs to be recorded because unlike heaven the door through which you pass is so narrow, so oppressive, that you have to be on your guard not to get cheated. There is always the fear of being crushed by the slightest error, so there is no room for being careless.

In Regent Road I bump into Nasuib. Stunned, I call out to him.

"Where were you? You just disappeared at the station," he scolds me. He sounds distant.

"I lost you," I try to explain.

"Have you eaten?"

"No."

"Then I must take you home at once," he says.

I notice that he is wearing an ankh around his neck. We walk back to town. Leaving Sea Point, we pass the women prostitutes that parade along Main Road. I will never look at another prostitute and have small thoughts. Our lives are driven by so much more than the disapproval of people. Nasuib looks at them with contempt as we walk past. To work your trade on the streets is tough. The weather is your master and men can be pricks. I feel lucky that I never had to resort to that. We walk past them and go towards Green Point. I ache for the loo because I drank too much water at the station.

"Nasuib, I'm going in there," I say pointing to Biloxi. "I need to piss."

At the door a big white bouncer sits on a stool wearing a bomber jacket that makes him look indestructible. He asks me for an ID as I try to go in. An ID, since when? I say to him, surprised. He refuses to let me in. But behind the door the manager who walks like he's got a carrot stuck up his arse, watches me. That guy knows me, I say and point to the manager. He looks behind and the two exchange looks. Then the manager disappears into the bar. The bouncer refuses to let me in. Insulted I walk back to Nasuib.

"These people will eat you," Nasuib warns me.

"Your manager is a prick!" I yell to the bouncer.

"Don't come cause shit here!" he says and stands up, coming towards me.

Nasuib lifts his shirt, revealing a gun.

"Just fuck off before I call someone," the irate bouncer says.

"I will never set foot here again," I say and spit on the ground.

Nasuib mumbles something in Arabic.

"May you eat your own shit," he says to the bouncer fiercely and we leave.

I feel angry and confused. Just two days ago I was welcome. What happened?

"Nasuib, what is happening? My life is going out of control."

He flexes his jaws and says nothing. We walk in silence for a long time.

"Where do you live?" he asks once we are in town.

"In Gardens, near the three white buildings," I say to him, relieved to remember. It is as though having him around me helps me remember.

We get to the flat and I remember that I do not have my keys or wallet.

"Jacques will be home from work," I say.

Through the intercom I call for him. I call for about ten minutes.

"Jacques. It's me. Please open up. I lost my keys," I say.

I plead for another ten minutes, but the door doesn't click open. The light is on. I know he is there. I know he can hear me but he won't open up.

"Jacques, Jacques," I plead but he ignores me. The bastard says nothing. Why is he doing this to me? It sends me into a state of panic. I go to a nearby tree and take a long piss.

"This boy is not going to open up," Nasuib says to me when I come back. He opens his fly and pisses outside the door.

We walk back to town. I feel depressed, defeated. My life, what is happening? It is as though someone is skilfully taking it apart. I follow Nasuib. We go to a part of town that I have never been to and enter a small humble Ethiopian restaurant that I have heard a lot about. But I have never found it each time I went looking for it. At the door a gaunt-faced man with a disarming smile welcomes us in. He chats with Nasuib in their native tongue, I think it is Ahmaric. The lighting is dim but appropriate. There are a few customers. We go to the back where we wash our hands under a sink. Wash your head and feet, Nasuib tells me sternly, but there is concern too in his voice. I run the water over my hands and run my fingers through my hair. I wash my face and feet with a piece of soap. The man who owns the restaurant hands me a towel and comb. I dry my face and feet. I comb my hair neatly.

"Don't put on your shoes. They have been polluted," Nasuib says and takes them. The other man gives me a pair of rubber flip-flops. We go up a small flight of stairs that leads to a room at the back of the restaurant. Nasuib switches on the light and invites me into a sparsely furnished room. There is a thick Persian rug in the middle of the room with an image of a mosque on it, a wardrobe on one wall and two chairs leaning against another wall. A small table has a stereo on it.

"I'll send your food," the man says and leaves us.

Nasuib and I sit on the floor. He suddenly looks tired.

"I'm sorry to inconvenience you like this," I say.

"I could have ripped out that guy's tongue," he says and wipes sweat from his forehead with a big hand and a powerful wrist.

"Which one?" I say.

"The one who works outside the slaughter-house."

"You mean Biloxi?"

"There are a lot of evil people in that place. They have done all sorts of things to your mind."

"Like what?"

"You are a walking information tank and you don't know it. They are trying to find a back door to your mind."

"What do you mean?" I say, frightened for what he says sounds like the truth. You know the truth when you hear it.

"If people control you they will know certain things, at least that is what they think," he says.

"And you? What do you want with me?"

"Who couldn't get into his flat?" he says sharply.

"This is my father's doing," I say convinced. "My father was evil. He died recently," I say hoping he will say something that will make me feel better.

"You do not know your father," he tells me.

"Believe me, I know what I'm talking about," I say confidently, a little irritated at him for saying this.

"You do not know your father because you would never call him evil if you did. That man who died, he wasn't really your father."

"Then who was he?"

"A convenience. Family relations are not important. There is always a deeper identity to a person, a deeper reality."

He grins. Something travels through his eyes and settles between my loins. I get a slight erection and gasp. He smiles.

"How did you do that?"

The other man returns with a large tray with food. I love exotic food. Nasuib thanks him. There is some couscous and a flat bread that Nasuib tells me is delicious. We eat the bread and couscous with a traditional lamb stew. I feel comfortable eating with my hands.

We eat a lot but don't finish the food. Later a coy Ethiopian woman wearing a chador that only reveals her eyes comes and takes the food away. "You should wash," Nasuib tells me. He opens the wardrobe and takes out a bar of soap, a small towel and a face cloth which he hands to me. He tells me to go downstairs again where there is a shower.

I go into a small, modest shower. I wash leisurely but my mind still feels fragmented. Who is this man? I wonder. In the shower I wash my Diesel shirt because it is unbearable to smell. I finish and dry myself, walking back upstairs wearing my stained khaki pants and flip flops. I thank Nasuib and hang my T-shirt on a chair near the window. It is hot. I hope it will dry. Nasuib goes downstairs and washes himself. He comes back upstairs, closes the door and locks it. He takes out a large sponge mattress lying on top of the wardrobe and rolls it out on the floor. We lay out a blanket and a sheet. He offers me a pillow.

"Are we going to sleep already?"

"We have a long day tomorrow. Besides, I need to tell you some things." I get into bed with him, not really knowing what to expect, but grateful that at least I have eaten and have a roof over my head.

He snuggles close to me, his kit between my legs.

"What do you want to tell me?" I ask, nervously.

He doesn't answer. I feel his erection growing. I lie there and act as if nothing is happening. He wouldn't just expect me to sleep with him like that, I tell myself. Without warning he puts his big hand in my underpants.

"Nasuib," I protest and grab his arm, but he resists. He is tough, but he isn't rough with me. He just keeps his hand there.

And then the strangest thing happens.

"I have been looking for you for a long time," he says. He says it in my thoughts. I am very nervous, but I lie still.

"You have been gone for so long Horus. I thought I would never see you again," he says.

"Is this happening?" I say, also communicating through my thoughts, amazed at this ability.

"Mother is waiting for you. Father is eager to see you again," he says tenderly, "Oh Horus. I have missed you."

He kisses me softly in the nape of my neck. Many images flash in my mind. I remember tall reeds and the smell of moist soil after floods.

"Why are you calling me Horus?"

"We have a lot of work to do. Tomorrow you must leave this place and go back to Johannesburg. It is important that you leave tomorrow. The future depends on it," he says gravely and I feel weighed down by his words.

My erection grows. I feel his between my thighs.

"That man you stay with, he is evil. He stole your keys. You didn't lose them. He is trying to steal your mind, to control you. I dreamt it. But you mustn't worry about him. I dreamt that a demon that he has been abusing ate him," he says.

"I think he eats his own shit," I say to him, still amazed by this strange ability to communicate without a voice. It makes me painfully aware of myself.

"He does more than that, Horus. He eats your thoughts sometimes. That is why you have been walking around the city so lost. That is why you have vicious headaches. They are trying to eat you alive."

"Why is evil out to get me. And who is this Horus?"

"I have a lot to tell you but I can't say it all at once. Your mind is still fragile. Tomorrow," he says, massaging me expertly.

"Are you my brother?" I turn around and face him in the dark.

He kisses me. I feel him between my legs. He is warm.

"I have something important to give you," he says urgently, "It comes from very far and there is only one way that I can give it to you."

"What is it?"

He manoeuvres his hips and his cock teases me.

"Oh," I say, surprised but willing.

We start kissing. There is the smell of olive oil.

"What is it?" I repeat.

"You will know tomorrow. I mustn't tell you too much," he says.

Soon he is inside me. But it is not making love. It is a process of communicating. I read things in his breath, his thrusts, the way he holds me. We go on for a long time. When he comes, he ejaculates for what feels like five minutes.

I don't come, but for me satisfaction is not important. My mind buzzes with questions. What did he just give me? I had so many thoughts as he was coming.

"Horus," he says with his mind again.

"Ja?"

"Your body is a receptacle but not like a woman's. One day you will give birth to your real self. That's why women hate you. You must be very careful around them. They can sense that you are doing things unknowingly with your body."

"But what do you mean?"

"You will meet many men in Johannesburg and they will all have secret gifts for you like I do. Choose wisely."

"Yes but what do you mean about women?"

"Forget about women. The only important one is Mother," he says reverently.

"And who is that?"

"Horus, why are you testing me? We heard you crying for mother. Everyone with ears heard you," he says tenderly and I feel shattered with grief as I recall my mother.

I become quiet and try to sleep. He curls around me. We sleep holding each other.

I dream as I have never dreamt. The sky has never looked brighter, the sun never more golden in my dreams. I roam the skies for a long time, a chariot of fire blazing in my path. There are secret gates and guards that only I know. The guards open other dimensions for me where people exist in supreme states, existing as galaxies. I roam the sky endlessly, happy on my journey, my father watching me, my mother proud of me.

In the morning when I wake up Nasuib is already dressed. I look at him shyly and he says, "What's wrong, the cat got your tongue?" I put on my T-shirt, it is slightly damp. I put on my khaki pants. We pack away the sponge and straighten out the room.

I have the unusual feeling that I know what I'm doing. I tell Nasuib that we must go to the other side of town where Jacques works. We go to the porn shop where he works. When we get there we find him behind the desk, moody as ever. An old man is looking at shrink-wrapped magazines of women with their vaginas exposed, wearing black S&M clothes.

"I need the spare keys. I lost mine," I say to Jacques.

"That's not my problem," he says coldly.

"I know you have spare keys."

"Well, I'm busy. You'll have to wait till I finish," he says, hardly looking at me, punching something on the keyboard.

"Give him the fucking keys," Nasuib says and pulls out his gun.

"Jesus fuck." Jacques fumbles and nearly falls out of his chair.

The man at the S&M section looks our way but can't see what's going on.

"I'll call the cops," Jacuqes says.

"I know where you live, you piece of filth." Nasuib says.

Reluctantly he takes out two keys from his bunch. His hands are pale and pasty.

We walk home briskly. I'm relieved to be inside once I get there.

"Start packing," Nasuib says to me immediately. But the first thing I do is change into clean clothes and a comfortable pair of tackies. I take out my suitcase and start filling it with everything I own. Nasuib inspects the various rooms.

"Is this where he stays?" he says when he gets to a locked door, Jacques' room.

"Yes," I say. He pulls down his zip and urinates on the door, leaving a small puddle. I say nothing. I feel nothing for Jacques. He has never been kind to me, he has never extended the arm of friendship to me. I watch Nasuib go into the bathroom and quickly come out covering his mouth.

"That man is evil," he says, "Don't go in there. Forget your toiletries."

446

"But what if he uses them for his evil purposes?"

"You'll be in Johannesburg, where the sun protects you," he says, recovering from whatever he saw.

I pack all my things into a large suitcase and three bags, including my books. I pack my stereo into its box. I leave the room bare except for the bed, mattress and covers. I can't take them with me. And I can't do anything about the desk and chair I bought or my food in the kitchen. I cannot see the cats. They must be locked in his room. I hear them crying, ripping something.

"Well, that's it," I say.

Nasuib pisses outside my door and outside the other entrance from the balcony. Fortunately I always keep spare cash for emergencies in the house. I call Bee-line taxis on my cellphone.

"Tonight you will stay with me," he instructs me.

We go again to where Nasuib stays. I leave my stuff in his room but take my ID book. I go to my bank and report that my wallet has been stolen. They give me a form to fill out to cancel my credit card and savings account card. There is no point ordering new cards since I'm leaving. I'll do that in Jo'burg. But I withdraw R700 from my savings account. I ask for statements of all my accounts. I'm happy to see that all my money is there, that all my investments have been terminated. R168 000 is a lot of money when you are single, owe nothing and own nothing. I can always start up again in Jo'burg, I say.

At the bus station I buy a one-way Greyhound ticket to Jo'burg for the following morning. I don't feel nostalgic about leaving Cape Town. Some people have eaten my dreams here.

MMABATHO

At the door one evening Tshepo suddenly shows up. I don't have to guess how he found me. Arne probably gave him my address. I still haven't heard from him. He comes in and we sit in my small room which I pay a lot for. But what can I do? Prices for accommodation in Cape Town always go up around December. Everybody wants to make some money during Christmas.

We hug awkwardly, conscious of each other. He is not the same. I am not the same. Things have changed. I hardly see anyone nowadays, but there is life after retreat from life. I am about to become a mother, that is where my focus lies.

447

"I bet women are dying for you," I say looking at him. He is well dressed and looks good.

"Not really," he says coyly. He hasn't changed that much.

He wears a loose silk shirt and cotton pants. I feel embarrassed in my large overweight shirt, trying to hide my stomach. My waist is doing its own thing. I cannot wear what I like anymore.

"Did you come to make plans for Christmas. I can't believe it's only two weeks away. Where has the year gone?" I say.

"Actually I came to tell you that I can't come. I'm leaving tomorrow. I'm going back to Jo'burg," he says calmly.

"You're leaving? When did this happen?" I was hoping that we would rekindle our friendship. We were close once. We used to tell each other everything before Arne came.

"Ja, I've already bought the ticket."

"I can't believe you're leaving." I have lost Arne and now I'm going to lose probably the only friend who understood me.

"Sorry, I didn't even ask you why you are leaving," I say after a while. I feel abandoned.

"It's time to move on. I can't be a student forever."

It makes me feel stuck to hear him say that. I feel trapped by circumstances.

"But I thought you were going back to college next year."

"There are more colleges in Jo'burg," he says optimistically.

I feel shattered. I've been taking him for granted. I thought he was always going to be there. Men are good at disappearing acts.

"Did you meet someone?"

"No. I just can't stay here, that's all. I'm not making progress. It's always the same shit. But life goes on. Besides, the are better jobs in Jo'burg," he says rubbing his hands. His nails are impeccably manicured.

"Wow. Just like that. O a tsamaya," I say.

"There wasn't much of a choice."

"But there's so much crime in Jo'burg."

"As if Cape Town is any better. The only difference is that here there are more white people with money. They can afford to get private security and fortress themselves. But the same shit happens, hijacking, murder, rape. In fact I think it's worse here. And then there are the bombs," he replies calmly.

"We used to be close," I say pathetically.

"We're still close."

"Ja, but I would have been the first person you told when you first thought of leaving. Now it looks like I'm the last person to find out. You're leaving tomorrow."

"You had your own situation with Arne," he says carefully.

"I suppose you heard. Did he tell you anything when he gave you the new address?" I ask, eager to hear his explanation.

"You know what he's like. He can't stand my guts. He just gave me your address and that was it. What happened?"

"I left him. He doesn't want to get married. And I don't want to have this baby with a boyfriend."

"Have you told your parents?"

"They know I'm pregnant."

We become quiet for a while. It seems as if we don't know each other after all. I suspect he is eager to leave. In his eyes I can see he is already gone, already in Rocky Street in Yeoville. When he thinks of me he might say, "We shared a brief history together."

He is staying for my sake because he is polite. It makes me remember what a terrible friend I have been to him. In all honesty I could have been more sensitive.

"Have you got somewhere to stay?"

"Not really, but I'm not worried. I mean if I'm desperate I can always stay with my aunt. Anyway, it's much cheaper to find accommodation in Jo'burg."

"You still never told me what you do for money, how you can afford to dress so well."

"I told you I sell drugs," he says with a straight face and I don't know whether to believe him or not. I really don't know him anymore, but all the gestures are still there.

"At least you're not picking your nasal hairs anymore," I tease him.

"That had to go sometime."

"You seem aloof."

"I think you feel alone," he answers.

"Perhaps." He has become assertive, giving as good as he gets.

"I didn't want to just leave and have you find out from someone else," he says politely after a while. Sometimes manners are a weapon. They can remind you of how crude you have been. I always said I'd come visit him in Gardens but I never did.

"Will you write?"

"Mmmh," he says in his new adult tone. It intrigues me. People grow up quietly. It makes me feel backward, still a child.

"I don't think it's a good idea to promise to write or phone. The one always expects to hear from the other and then it becomes awkward when one forgets and time passes," he says.

"But how will I find you in Jo'burg? I'll be there in January," I tell him.

"Well, you know where my aunt lives. I'll leave all my details with her."

It irritates me a little that he doesn't seem affected.

"You look pleased to leave," I say dryly.

"I'm a little tired."

"Don't let me keep you if you have to go."

"That's not what I meant. I could be out with other friends tonight but I wanted to see you."

I sulk a little. It is as if we have swapped lives. I have become him and he has become me. I used to be the one getting dressed and going out, always picking him up. He was always alone at home, shy and awkward, eager for my company. Now the tables have turned. My belle époque has come and gone.

A pregnant woman is just a pregnant woman to everyone, even an invalid to some. I cannot expect people to look at me the same way again. They see someone's mother when they look at me, youth ripped out of my eyes.

"When was the last time you went to Ganesh?" he asks me.

"The last time we went to A Touch of Madness that day when Arne didn't come is the closest I have been to Ganesh. And you?"

"I don't go there anymore," he says making a face. "Town is nearer. I go to Long Street."

"I hope things work out for you in Jo'burg."

"Thanks. I hope things work out for you and your baby and ..."

"Oh no, we're not getting back together. Even if he came begging at my doorstep. Not this time. I'm having this baby alone."

He seems embarrassed by this little outburst. After a while he says, "I like your hairstyle."

"Thanks. I got it from a book about ancient African hairstyles and their ritual and cultural significance. Apparently women in the Gambia wear their hair like this when they are pregnant. The eight splits in the crown of my head are supposed to symbolise the eight ancestors of health and prosperity." I'm proud to share this information with him. I have quietly gone deeper into myself and discovered a woman.

"Gosh, I have been such a lousy host, can I get you some juice?"

I get up and go to the kitchen. Perhaps he hasn't changed that much.

And why am I so concerned if he has changed? I'm not scared of change, I tell myself, saying it like a mantra.

I return with a glass of orange juice and some biscuits on a saucer.

"I'll miss you," he says, "I don't think I have met a stronger woman than you."

No one has ever said that to me. I allow a little grin to hide the compliment that makes me blush and shine inside.

"You know, I misjudged you," I reply.

"How so?"

"I don't think I ever looked past the obvious. You seemed naïve, if you don't mind me saying so."

"Most people think I'm an idiot. But I know. Appearances are deceptive. That's nothing new," he says nonchalantly.

"But now you seem to be something that you have been hiding all along."

"I wasn't hiding anything. Just waiting for the right time to be me."

I feel confused because I sense more to him, an inner confidence I never saw before. He has been hiding behind naïveté. What has he been protecting, his wisdom? He smiles and looks at me as though he can read my mind. It makes me uncomfortable and I get up to put on some music. I put on Jamiroquai, but softly.

He looks around my room but without a critical eye. Two of my housemates and their noisy friends come in. They go to Alex's room next to mine and play loud music. It's Friday, so I can't complain. We have noise hours in the house rules and Friday after seven till midnight is noise hours. Tshepo makes a disapproving face when he hears them playing Marilyn Manson.

He gets up and straightens out his pants.

"You're not leaving already?" If he leaves me now with this lot next door playing their shit music I will feel depressed.

"I have some packing to do. I was running around the whole day organising everything else."

I get up and hug him.

"Don't be a stranger."

"I won't," he smiles and I walk him to the door.

"So this is it." I force myself to smile. "I hope things go well for you." I feel terrible because I say that with difficulty. "And don't go out in funny places. Hillbrow is full of Nigerians and makwere-kwere. Ba loya, and they sell drugs."

"Don't worry, Mmabatho," he says with a weary face. "Stay well."

I wave to him and watch him go down the short path leading to the gate and disappear down the street.

I close the door. Another chapter in my life has been closed. I feel alone and miserable. I should have been more prudent, I scold myself, thinking how holding back has eventually served Tshepo. People herald being forthright and uncompromising as important, indispensable qualities in a person. The small guy who shuts up in the corner and gets on with his life simply dissolves in the background. Until someday.

I go back to my room in an introspective mood. I cannot change anything. I must work with what I have. I probably won't hear from Tshepo again. And I have the nasty suspicion that things will work out for him, that he will become successful, even famous. Just a feeling I get. My sixth sense has become more proficient since I became pregnant.

I lie back in bed and listen to Jamiroquai chanting ethereal music with a strong Aboriginal flavour, using the didgereedoo. I float away in my own reverie, a healthy bouncing baby boy called Venus laughing with me.

TSHEPO

**In** Jo'burg everyone knows me as Tshepo. I left Angelo behind in Cape Town, still roaming its streets and exploring the underworld. I don't think I will go back there for a while. I have too many wounds that need to heal.

Christmas and New Year came and went with much fanfare. Everyone goes on about the millenium. I went to a party in Rocky Street. It reminds me a little of Cape Town, but the people are different, the mixture is better.

I live in Hillbrow with all its decay. Two weeks after New Year's Day I got a job working in a children's home. There was a little advertisement in the paper that just caught my attention. I called and went there. I think I was the only one to respond. The money is not good, but I get free lodging and food. I have a small room in the back.

The kids are interesting, not great or terrible, just interesting. In the morning I wake up early and help them get dressed and ready for school. I drop them off and pick them up later. In the afternoon I help them with their homework and supervise their duties. Our little home is a model home in the Jo'burg district. All the other kids from different homes want to move here but it is hard to get in. Ma Thembi, the house mother, runs a clean house and doesn't tolerate laziness, even from me. She keeps me on my toes. But we get on fabulously because she doesn't treat me like a child.

Most of the children come from broken homes, parents who drink, fathers who abuse them or families who live in absolute poverty, if there is such a thing. When they first come in they are tough and difficult. A simple chore like asking them to make their beds can become a preamble for an argument or a fight. They still have the street in them. In their eyes I can see their defiance, always fighting anyone bigger than themselves. And then they bully the other smaller children because that is how it works on the street. But I have to be patient with them. For the first week I follow them around closely. I stay on their backs and don't let up the pressure, so that they must know what is means to live by rules. Rules hold the home together, they keep the structure from crumbling . They prevent us from getting sloppy with each other. Even Ma Thembi has rules to follow.

Gradually after two weeks they start loosening up. You might even get a smile from them but it comes out awkward, strangely beautiful. A smile from a child is better than all the apologies and niceties put together. There isn't a more sincere way of saying I'm sorry. And I forgive them when they make mistakes, when they bully other children, when they become careless and selfish. But only if they ask me to forgive them. They must learn to put themselves in that position, too much damage has been done by people who do not know how to ask forgiveness, like my father. We must face our past boldly if we are to progress. To be honest is to allow oneself to be weak. To be weak is a step towards forgiveness. And this much I know, forgiveness is bestowed upon those who ask for it.

They call me uncle because that is part of the protocol. It makes it easier for them to know how to respond to me appropriately. I am not another glue sniffing tsotsi from the street. They have to learn what a responsible adult is like and how you speak to him. Our children are fragile, they inherit everything we leave for them, good and bad. When I read in the papers about people lobbying for ganja to be legalised, I think of our children. They are still too fragile, too important. They need our guidance, our discipline. They need rules so they can see and learn. Ganja has led too many down the wrong path. They are struggling enough at school, distracted by crime that makes easy money and truancy. I battle to get them to stop smoking or sniffing glue. And when I catch them sometimes I have to impose the harshest punishment, which is to move them to another home with different rules and a structure that isn't as homely as ours with a live-in house mother. I do it with difficulty, crying in private sometimes, especially when I see how well they have settled in and how their grades are steadily improving, but I cannot afford to be nice when the future is at stake.

I believe in our children. I believe in people, in humankind, in personhood. In Hillbrow I live with foreigners, illegal and legal immigrants, what black South Africans call makwere-kwere with derogatory and defiant arrogance. I feel at home with them because they are trying to find a home in our country. They are so fragile, so cultured and beautiful, our foreign guests. In their eyes I feel at home, I see Africa. I feel like I live in Africa when I walk out in the street and hear dark-skinned beauties rapping in Lingala or Congo or a French patois that I don't understand. I like the way they dress up and work hard and do jobs that ordinary South Africans consider beneath them, yet we complain about unemployment. I like the way they stick together but don't protect each other when one of them has wronged. I find their honesty and optimism refreshing. And how they love education and learning. "My daughter is ten but she is in grade one," Mrs Jegede, a Senegalese neighbour proudly says. "I know it is difficult for her, but I want her to start at the bottom and reach the top," she says, her husband smiling beside her, wearing a fitting agbada. I like their food and their willingness to try new things, to adapt their cultural practices along the way. I know that some of them are part of the crime problem and that they bring illegal practices into the country, especially the tall and beautiful Nigerians. How I lament for the Nigerians and what they have come to represent. In an earlier time when Olokun was a kind goddess they brought culture and dignity to everyone they met. I find comfort in Soyinka and Okri. But perhaps time is saving the Nigerians for kinder days, perhaps Africa is a late bloomer, not a late starter.

In my room in the back I have an easel. It is my most prized possession, next to my books, and it stands in the middle of the room. I walk around it. I stand near it. I lie underneath it. I still haven't used it. I still haven't drawn anything or attempted a painting. I am waiting. I am absorbing, remembering, deciphering. I am making love with all the images that lie fecund in my mind, waiting to be released into life. I am waiting for the impulse and desire to use my easel to become insurmountable, unbearable. Quietly I am nurturing my talents. I want the hunger to be complete so that when I touch a piece of newsprint

454

with charcoal, images should jump onto the surface without much intellectual intervention.

It is beautiful, my easel. When the children come into my room, they always stare at it with wonder, too awe-struck by this strange contraption to ask me what it is, what I do with it. But it is finding its own life, its own significance, like an ancestral mask. The wood breathes life into my room.

I love my easel. I lie under it and tell it beautiful thoughts, describe beautiful images that I want to share with it. With it I am remembering everything about my life. I tell it about the men I like, the ones I fantasise about it. There is a spiritual dimension to liking men, I tell it.

Jo'burg has given me space, time to think. I was suffocated in Cape Town. I was still looking for myself, searching furiously. I have had to wade through so much. And I met a few nasty surprises along the way, which I don't regret. Bad things lead to good things lead to bad things. It seems the good are always outnumbered. Perhaps the universe is love that went looking for itself.

Sometimes the terror of days to come wells up inside me and leaves me irritable and feeling mute with fear. But that is only because my mind is occupied with the destruction humanity will know. The nature of change is violent. It goes without saying that blood will be spilled. But there is the other side to consider, the sunnier side of fresh beginnings. I'm not permitted to ponder about that yet. It seems that first I must be aware of the difficulties that lie ahead. We are living in days of calm before the storm. And slowly people are listening.

Once a week I go for a night out in town. Sometimes I go to clubs, sometimes bars, sometimes bistros, it depends on my mood. But I always meet special men who come from different places. They have gifts for me like Nasuib delicately alluded. I don't always sleep with them, but intimacy of some sort is a part of our ritual. They offer me blueprints for survival, for building a new civilisation, a new way of life. I have met bankers, architects, poets, builders, miners, diplomats, engineers, labourers, waiters, sailors, firemen, soldiers, farmers, teachers, men worth their salt and men of integrity. They all go about the quiet business of telling me their secrets, sharing their wisdom. We have so much to learn from each other. There are better ways, they keep telling me, capitalism is not the only way. We haven't nearly exhausted all the possibilities, they say. We know that the future depends on everyone working together.

I have developed a few unique abilities that I didn't know were humanly possible. My horizon is broadening. When I am with these men I realise how fragile we are, how complete our destruction will be. The truth will rescue those who need it, those who have earned it. Other people will suddenly find themselves in the wrong place at the wrong time with the wrong crowd. And then it will be too late. But those who know their way around life will survive. Survival of the fittest, it is a test we will all be subjected to.

I have vivid dreams of how we will end. Terrible disasters await us. Maybe God fears his own strength that is why He doesn't lift his hand against us but transforms his wrath in other ways.

When I think about Cape Town and walking along its pristine beaches, I remember how kelp floated in vast quantities in the surf. It looked like the heads of people floating at sea. One night I dreamt it was the heads of rastas that I saw floating. When I think about Cape Town and all the experiences I had with the many coloured faces I met, I become suspicious and curious. Perhaps life was giving me a hint. Perhaps the future of mankind lies in each other, not in separate continents with separate people. We are still evolving as a species, our differences are merging.

When I look at the children I work with, mostly black, with some coloured and white faces, I sense that God can't be one story. He is a series of narratives. And He is watching. We are all being watched.

I am leaving behind life as I know it. Great changes await us. All the hatred and disappointment is falling away. We must think about each other, about how we feel, and what we will do to comfort each other. I am tired of pointing fingers, of assigning blame. Too much is happening. There is too much to organise and think about. I am still nurturing my nest egg. Tomorrow the children need to go to school. I must get up early and help out in the kitchen. I must make sure that the little ones have all their things in order and that all their homework books have been signed. I must do all that I can for them while I still have my strength.

Each day is a blessing. I feel close to whom I am supposed to be, the person behind the smile. I feel mother's eyes upon me, my father guiding me.

I am Horus, the son of the sun.

I am my mother's child, from the curve of my lips to the slight shuffle in my walk.

One day I went for a walk in the tameness, wandering through southern skies, exploring the Lower Kingdom. I went on a journey and found that trees had more stories to tell than animals, that they remembered more. And their pain is deeper, quieter.

I am a dancer, a painter. My gaze is filled with fecund stories that come from my mother's womb. I must create and delight, that is my mother's way. I must keep moving, that is my father's way.

My sister told me a secret once. I was happy that it was sacred enough to be explained in time. She said in letting go, in suffering, we are investing our hearts in love, placing deep treasures in silences that make us weep and remember when we are sad.

In keeping still we hear more.

In choosing less we get more.

And in trusting more, we trust ourselves. We must always trust the process.

I know where my greatest treasures lie. They are within me.